NEW YORK REVIEW BOOKS
CLASSICS

THE BALKAN TRILOGY

OLIVIA MANNING (1908–1980) was born in Portsmouth, England, and spent much of her childhood in Northern Ireland. Her father, Oliver, was a penniless British sailor who rose to become a naval commander, and her mother, Olivia, had a prosperous Anglo-Irish background. Manning trained as a painter at the Portsmouth School of Art, then moved to London and turned to writing. She published her first novel under her own name in 1938 (she had published several potboilers in a local paper under the name Jacob Morrow while a teenager). The next year she married R. D. "Reggie" Smith, and the couple moved to Romania, where Smith was employed by the British Council. During World War II, the couple fled before the Nazi advance, first to Greece and then to Jerusalem, where they lived until the end of the war. Manning wrote several novels during the 1950s, but her first real success as a novelist was *The Great Fortune* (1960), the first of six books concerning Guy and Harriet Pringle, whose wartime experiences and troubled marriage echoed that of the diffident Manning and her gregarious husband. In the 1980s these novels were collected in two volumes, *The Balkan Trilogy* and *The Levant Trilogy*, known collectively as *Fortunes of War*. In addition to her novels, Manning wrote essays and criticism, history, a screenplay, and a book about Burmese and Siamese cats. She was made Commander of the Order of the British Empire in 1976, and died four years later.

RACHEL CUSK is the author of seven novels and two works of non-fiction. She teaches creative writing at Kingston University, London.

Fortunes of War
THE BALKAN TRILOGY

OLIVIA MANNING

Introduction by
RACHEL CUSK

NEW YORK REVIEW BOOKS

New York

THIS IS A NEW YORK REVIEW BOOK
PUBLISHED BY THE NEW YORK REVIEW OF BOOKS
435 Hudson Street, New York, NY 10014
www.nyrb.com

Published here by arrangement with William Heinemann, the Random House
Group, Ltd., London

Library of Congress Cataloging-in-Publication Data
Manning, Olivia.
 [Balkan trilogy]
 Fortunes of war : the Balkan trilogy / by Olivia Manning ; introduction by
Rachel Cusk.
    p. cm. — (New York Review Books classics)
 ISBN 978-1-59017-331-2 (alk. paper)
 1. World War, 1939-1945—Fiction. I. Title.
 PR6063.A384B27 2009
 823'.914—dc22

                          2009021404

ISBN 978-1-59017-331-2

Printed in the United States of America on acid-free paper.
10 9 8 7 6 5

CONTENTS

Introduction

"I HAVEN'T ANY PARENTS," says Harriet Pringle, heroine and presiding spirit of Olivia Manning's *Balkan Trilogy*. "At least, none to speak of. They divorced when I was very small. They both remarried and neither found it convenient to have me. My Aunt Penny brought me up. I was a nuisance to her, too, and when I was naughty she used to say: 'No wonder your mummy and daddy don't love you.'"

If a project as lengthy and diverse as *The Balkan Trilogy* can be represented by a few lines, these words of Harriet's are those lines. Indeed, to be able to discover in a small fragment the structure of the whole is one the hallmarks of a work of art, and in this sense the compendiousness of *The Balkan Trilogy* is somewhat deceiving. Harriet's impoverished heart is the unvarying leitmotif of its thousand-odd densely filled pages; a nondescript twenty-one-year-old English girl's lack of parental love the central metaphor for war, displacement, cataclysm, and the death of the old world in 1940s Europe.

Nevertheless, it is by virtue of this strange and striking parallel that *The Balkan Trilogy* preserves its freshness and makes its claim to greatness. In these novels we are shown wartime Europe as a world of emotionally stunted men and women, of people starved by the reticence and coldness of their upbringing, of people who have lacked attention and acceptance and love, who have lacked it generationally; a lack so deep in the grain of (English) social institutions and attitudes that only total destruction could erase it. Indifference, injustice, cruelty, hatred, neglect: in *The Balkan Trilogy* these are the constituents both of personal memory and of social reality, of private unhappiness and of public violence. In Olivia Manning's analogy, war is the work of unhappy children; but while Harriet embodies the darkness of this perception, she represents too the individual struggle to refute it. Harriet's determination—against every provocation—to preserve her marriage, to stay rather than to abandon, to keep instead of smashing, is the novel's other, private war.

Manning claimed to be at her happiest when writing of her own life, and the events of the Balkan and Levant trilogies correspond closely to those of the years (1938–46) she spent in Romania, Greece, Egypt and later Palestine with her husband, the socialist R.D. "Reggie" Smith, who, barred by poor eyesight from military service, worked as a lecturer for the British Council. Guy and Harriet, newlyweds arriving in Romania on the eve of Britain's declaration of war against Germany, are Olivia and Reggie's undisguised alter egos; and the narrative, so naturalistic, so full of incident and coincidence, so detailed, so densely populated with minor characters, confirms that Manning did indeed have a genius for writing at first hand. But her autobiographical presence in these novels is strikingly magnetized by the world: she is here not to describe herself but to witness. Her eye and ear are a match for the large canvas of war; her Bucharest of 1939–40 is riven with unease and changing political values, filled with sundry foreigners—hacks, hangers-on, diplomats, wanderers, profiteers—uncomfortably exposed by the flash of conflict, and it is brought so brilliantly and meticulously to life that by the end the reader feels she could easily find her own way around its chaotic streets and would recognize half the clientele in the English Bar.

Manning's "people" are more than literary characters: they have the feeling of real beings who happen to find themselves in the narrative frame, like passersby caught on camera. Indeed, *The*

Balkan Trilogy is frequently so faithful to the sense of lived life that it is often difficult to discern the hand that is shaping it. The prolix conversations of men and the pointed conversations of women, the hours Guy likes to spend discussing politics with his British legation cronies, evenings at restaurants that are sometimes interminably boring and sometimes fun, the configuration of a room, a street, a shop front, the slow passage of time and season, most of all the way other people come and go, becoming known or half known, by a process that seems utterly random and yet on which life is dependent at the deepest level for its structure and form: this river of narrative is both the chief beauty and the central mystery of *The Balkan Trilogy*.

The "truth" of a writer's experiences is difficult to unravel, but in these novels the striking impassivity of the point of view is the place to look for it. The shaping hand, we realize, is Harriet's; Harriet's is the recondite soul we are occupying; Harriet who watches, who pays attention, yet so rarely draws the drama to herself. When, as readers, we crave some evidence of sensibility from this fictional world, some attention, some disinterested gift of love, it is Harriet's craving we are experiencing. And as we pass from admiration of Guy, lecturer in English literature and incurably sociable socialist, to a profoundly critical disillusion that nonetheless recognizes the impossibility of ever rejecting or abandoning him, we are reliving every twist and turn of Harriet's lonely journey of marriage.

What Guy represents in *The Balkan Trilogy* is the concept of society as the only possible force for good, and as such he is pitted against the emotional individualism represented by Harriet. Guy would give his last penny to a beggar, his last ounce of strength to a stranger in the street; Harriet, on the other hand, wants exclusivity, attention, possession. "He gave her an illusion of security—for it was, she was coming to believe, an illusion. He was one of those harbours that prove to be too shallow: there was no getting into it. For him, personal relationships were incidental. His fulfilment came from the outside world." This conflict, of course, is not just Guy and Harriet's: it is the dialectic of the twentieth century, the essence of the struggle to create a new social order. What is interesting is that Guy's dedication to "the world," and his concomitant refusal to give Harriet the attention she craves, makes her feel "safe," for it returns her to the original sensation of being unloved. She is constantly being told that Guy is a "great man," a "saint," and in this way we come to understand that it is not only Harriet who feels safe with Guy, who experiences emotional need as a form of shame. Other people—a great number of them—feel it too. What Guy (Guy as socialism) represents for them is a kind of extruded subjectivity, whereby "need" is separated from "self," and Manning cleverly gives us the reason why such a representation appears virtuous. For Harriet, and those like her, it entails a new discipline of self-renunciation that eerily re-echoes the old; it offers security, or perhaps "an illusion of security."

It is in Harriet's relationship with Clarence, a British legation officer in Bucharest and fellow lost soul, that these ideas are explored. When Clarence tries to tell her about his unhappy childhood, Harriet experiences violent feelings of resistance. "Don't think about it: don't talk about it," she silently abjures him. "She knew [Clarence] was one who, given a chance, would shut her off into a private world." And she has sufficient self-knowledge to understand that in this way he is exactly like her. "What was it they both wanted? Exclusive attention, no doubt: the attention each had missed in childhood. Perversely, she did not want it now it was offered. She was drawn to Guy... and the open world about him." Later, in an extraordinary scene, Harriet participates in the "de-bagging" (a public-school prank whereby a person's trousers are forcibly removed) of Clarence at the Pringles' flat, with Guy and Guy's boorish friend David. David, a bully, identifies Clarence as a victim and Harriet finds herself "caught into the same impulse to ill-treat Clarence in some way." After Clarence has left, Harriet wonders:

> "What is the matter with us? Why did we do that?"
> "It was a joke," said Guy, though he did not sound sure of what he said.
> "Really, we behaved like children," Harriet said and it occurred to her that they were not, in fact, grown-up enough for the life they were living.

As this vast narrative progresses it becomes clear that what these people lack, what stunts them and renders them no more than oversized children, is the transformative experience of love. It is here that Manning's subtle control of her characters is most skillfully demonstrated, for this lack can be detected everywhere in these densely peopled novels. The disloyalty of Guy's colleagues Lush and Dubedat, the moral cowardice of petty officials like Dobson, Sophie Oresanu's attention-seeking, the emotionally stilted kindness of Inchcape or Alan Frewen, most of all the hermetic childlike selfishness of Harriet's bête noir (and Manning's masterpiece) Yakimov: again and again Manning elicits from her reader not scorn but pity for this handicapped race, encourages us to see them as more damaged than monstrous. Manning was a talented painter who once thought she would pursue a career as an artist, and it is often her physical portraits of her characters that convey most powerfully their loneliness. In this world of repressed emotion it is the body that speaks, that sculpts itself into pitiful and sometimes grotesque forms.

> Professor Pinkrose was a rounded man, narrow-shouldered and broad-hipped, thickening down from the crown of his hat to the edge of his greatcoat. His nose, blunt and greyish,

poked out between collar and hat-brim. His eyes, grey as rain-water, moved about, alert and suspicious, like the eyes of a chameleon.

Late in the narrative, when Harriet's experience of transformative love finally and briefly comes, she feels it as a demolishing of that formal loneliness, of bodily isolation.

Their [Harriet's and Charles Warden's] sense of likeness astonished them. It resembled magic. They felt themselves held in a spellbound condition which they feared to injure. Although she could not pin down any overt point of resemblance, Harriet at times imagined he was the person most like her in the world, her mirror image.

Modern readers of the *Balkan Trilogy* will certainly marvel at it as a technical accomplishment, as a good read, and perhaps even as a meticulous historical document; but its value as a complete chronicle of an important period in the emotional evolution of Western society is likely to strike today's audience most of all. The relationship between institutional representation and personal experience has been reconfigured in our era; the self is ascendant, the concept of duty remote. But we, too, are part of the eternal flux. The personal and the political, peace and war, the individual and the communal, the need and the obligation, the self and its society: all are in motion, just as they always have been. And if readers conclude that ours at least is a more liberated world than Guy and Harriet's, a more expressive and tolerant world, perhaps even a more loving world, they will also have gained a greater sense of how it came to be so, and of the value of that love, so desperately sought, so bitterly fought for.

—RACHEL CUSK

THE BALKAN TRILOGY

VOLUME ONE

The Great Fortune

To Johnny and Jerry Slattery

PART ONE

The Assassination

1

SOMEWHERE NEAR VENICE, Guy began talking with a heavy, elderly man, a refugee from Germany on his way to Trieste. Guy asked questions. The refugee eagerly replied. Neither seemed aware when the train stopped. In the confusion of a newly created war, the train was stopping every twenty minutes or so. Harriet looked out and saw girders, darker than the twilit darkness, holding an upper rail. Between the girders a couple fumbled and struggled, every now and then thrusting a foot or an elbow out into the light that fell from the carriage windows. Beyond the girders water glinted, reflecting the phosphorescent globes lighting the high rail.

When the train was suddenly shunted into the night, leaving behind the lovers and the glinting water, she thought: 'Anything can happen now.'

Guy and the refugee went on talking across the carriage, their eyes fixed upon each other. Guy's sympathy had drawn the German half out of his seat. He held out his hands, cupped, palms up, side by side, occasionally shaking them for emphasis, while Guy gave him an anxious attention that lightened into excitement as he nodded his head, indicating that all he heard was exactly what he had expected to hear.

"What is he saying?" asked Harriet, who did not speak German.

Guy put a hand on hers to keep her quiet.

A current, like affection, seemed to keep Guy's attention directed on the refugee, but the refugee several times stared about him at the other passengers, with an aggressive confidence, as though to say: 'I am talking? Well what about it? I am a free man.'

The train stopped again: a ticket collector came round. The refugee rose and felt in an inner pocket of his greatcoat that hung beside him. His hand lingered, he caught his breath: he withdrew his hand and looked in an outer pocket. This time he withdrew his hand quickly and looked in another pocket, then another and another. He began pulling things out of the pockets of the jacket he was wearing, then out of his trouser pockets. His breath came and went violently. He returned to the greatcoat and began his search all over again.

Guy and Harriet Pringle, watching him, were dismayed. His face had become ashen, his cheeks fallen like the cheeks of a very old man. As he grew hot with the effort of his search, a sticky dampness spread over his skin and his hands shook. When he started again on his jacket, his head was trembling and his eyes darting about.

"What is it?" Guy asked. "What have you lost?"

"Everything. Everything."

"Your ticket?"

"Yes," the man panted between words. "My pocket-book, my passport, my money, my identity card . . . My visa, my visa!" His voice broke on the last word. He stopped searching and tried to pull himself together. He clenched his hands, then shook one out in disbelief of his loss.

"What about the lining?" said Harriet. "The things may have fallen through into the lining."

Guy did his best to translate this.

The man turned on him, almost sobbing as he was beset by this suggestion. He understood at last and started feeling wildly over the coat lining. He found nothing.

The other passengers had been watching him with detached interest while the collector took their tickets. When everyone else had handed over a ticket, the collector turned to him as though the scene had conveyed nothing at all.

Guy explained to the man that the refugee had lost his ticket. Several other people in the carriage murmured confirmation. The collector looked dumbly back at some officials who stood in the corridor. They took over. One remained at the carriage door while the other went off for reinforcements.

"He's penniless, too," said Guy to his wife. "What can we give him?"

They were on their way to Bucharest. Not being permitted to take money into Rumania, they had very little with them. Harriet brought out a thousand-franc note. Guy had three English pound notes. When offered this money, the refugee could not give it his attention. He was absorbed again in looking through his pockets as though the pocket-book might in the interval have reappeared. He seemed unaware of the group of officials now arrived at the door. When one touched his arm, he turned impatiently. He was required to go with them.

He took down his coat and luggage. His colour was normal now, his face expressionless. When Guy held the money out to him, he accepted it blankly, without a word.

After he had been led away, Guy said: "What will become of him?" He looked worried and helpless, frowning like a good-tempered child whose toy has been stolen out of its hands.

Harriet shook her head. No one could answer him. No one tried.

The day before had been spent on familiar territory, even if the Orient Express had kept to no schedule. Harriet had watched the vineyards pass in the late summer sunlight. Balls of greasy sandwich paper had unscrewed themselves in the heat, empty Vichy bottles rolled about under seats. When the train stopped, there was no sign of a station-master, no porters came to the windows. On the deserted platform, loud-speakers gave out the numbers of reservists being called to their regiments. The monotony of the announcer's voice had the quality of silence. It was possible to hear through it the hum of bees, the chirrupings of birds. The little squeak of the guard's trumpet came from a great distance, like a noise from the waking world intruding upon sleep. The train, gathering itself together, moved on for a few more miles and stopped again to the voice of the same announcer giving the numbers without comment.

In France they were among friends. Italy, which they crossed next day, seemed the end of the known world. When they awoke next morning, they were on the Slovenian plain. All day its monotonous cultivation, its fawn-coloured grainland and fields with hay-cocks, passed under a heavy sky. Every half mile or so there was a peasant hut, the size of a tool shed, with a vegetable garden and beds of great, flat-faced sun-flowers. At each station the peasants stood like the blind. Harriet attempted a smile at one of them: there was no response. The lean face remained as before, weathered and withered into a fixed desolation.

Guy, who was doing this journey for the second time, gave his attention to his books. He was too short-sighted to make much of the passing landscape, and he had to prepare his lectures. He was employed in the English Department of the University of Bucharest, where he had already spent a year. He had met and married Harriet during his summer holiday.

With only enough money left to pay for one meal, Harriet had chosen that the meal should be supper. As the day passed without breakfast, luncheon or tea, hunger lay bleakly over the Slovenian plain. Twilight fell, then darkness, then, at last, the waiter came tinkling his little bell again. The Pringles were first in the dining-car. There everything was normal, the food good, but before the meal ended the head waiter began to behave like a man in a panic. Baskets of fruit had been placed on the tables. He brushed them aside to tot up the bills, for which he demanded immediate payment. The charge, which was high, included coffee. When someone demanded coffee, he said "Later", throwing down change and hurrying on. One diner said he would not pay until coffee was served. The head waiter replied that no coffee would be served until all had paid. He kept an eye on those who had still to pay as though fearing they might make off before he reached them.

In the end, all paid. The train stopped. It had reached the frontier. Coffee was served, too hot to drink, and at the same time an official appeared and ordered everyone out of the car, which was about to be detached from the train. One man gulped at his coffee, gave a howl and threw down his cup. Several wanted to know why the car was being detached. A waiter explained that the car belonged to the Yugoslav railways and no sane country would permit its rolling-stock to cross a frontier in these hazardous times. The passengers were thrust out, all raging together in half-a-dozen languages, the war forgotten.

The frontier officials made a leisurely trip down the corridor. When that was over, the train stood on the small station, where the air, pouring cold and autumnal through open windows, smelt of straw.

Guy, in their compartment, which had now been arranged as a sleeping compartment, was still writing in his notebook. Harriet, at a corridor window, was trying to see something of the frontier village. She could not even be sure there was a village. The darkness seemed as empty as outer space, yet, blazing like a sun in the midst of it, there was a fair-ground. Not a sound came from it. A wheel moved slowly, bearing up into the sky empty carriages shaped like boats.

Immediately outside the window there was a platform lit by three weak, yellow bulbs strung on a wire. Beneath the furthest of these was a group of people – a tall man, unusually thin, with a long coat trailing from one shoulder as from a door-knob, surrounded by five small men in uniform. They were persuading him along. He seemed, in their midst, bewildered like some long, timid animal harried by terriers. Every few yards he paused to remonstrate with them and they, circling about him and gesticulating, edged him on until he reached the carriage from which Harriet was watching. He was carrying in one hand a crocodile dressing-case, in the other a British passport. One of the five men was a porter who carried two large suitcases.

"Yakimov," the tall man kept repeating, "Prince Yakimov. *Gospodin*," he suddenly wailed, "*gospodin*."

At this they gathered round him, reassuring him with "*Da, da*," and "*Dobo, gospodin*". His long, odd face was sad and resigned as he let himself be impelled towards the front of the train. There he was urged into a carriage as though at any moment the express would move.

The uniformed men dispersed. The platform emptied. The train remained where it was another half-an-hour, then slowly puffed its way across the frontier.

When the Rumanian officials came on board there was a change of atmosphere in the corridors. The Rumanian passengers were now in the majority. Stout, little Rumanian women, not noticeable before, pushed their way through the *wagon-lit* chattering in French. There was a general air of congratulation that they were safely within their own country. They gave little squeals of excitement as they chatted to the officials and the officials smiled down on them indulgently. When Guy emerged with the passports, one of the women recognised him as the *professor* who taught her son English. He answered her in Rumanian and the women crowded about him admiring his fluency and his pronunciation.

"But you are perfect," said one woman.

Guy, flushed by the attention he was receiving, made a reply in Rumanian that set them all squealing again.

Harriet, not understanding what he had said, smiled at the fun, pretending to be part of it. She observed how, in his response, Guy looked a little drunk and put out his arms to these unknown women as though he would embrace them all.

The Pringles had been married less than a week. Though she would have claimed to know about him everything there was to be known, she was now beginning to wonder if she really knew anything.

When the train got under way, the women dispersed. Guy returned to his bunk. Harriet remained a while at the window, watching the mountains rise and grow, ebony against the dim and starless sky. A pine forest came down to the edge of the track: the light from the carriages rippled over the bordering trees. As she gazed out into the dark heart of the forest, she began to see small moving lights. For an instant a grey dog-shape skirted the rail, then returned to darkness. The lights, she realised, were the eyes of beasts. She drew her head in and closed the window.

Guy looked up as she joined him and said: "What's the matter?" He took her hands, saw they were shrunken with cold and rubbed them between his hands: "Little monkey's paws," he said. As his warmth passed into her, she said: "I love you," which was something she had not admitted before.

The moment seemed to her one that should expand into rapture, but Guy took it lightly. He said: "I know," and, giving her fingers a parting squeeze, he released them and returned his attention to his book.

2

ON REACHING THE MAIN STATION at Bucharest, Yakimov carried his luggage to the luggage office. He held a suitcase in each hand and his crocodile dressing-case hoisted up under his right elbow. His sable-lined greatcoat hung from his left arm. The porters – there were about a dozen to each passenger – followed him aghast. He might have been mobbed had not his vague, gentle gaze, ranging over their heads from his unusual height, given the impression he was out of reach.

When the dressing-case slipped, one of the porters snatched at it. Yakimov dodged him with a skilled sidestep, then wandered on, his shoulders drooping, his coat sweeping the dirty platform, his check suit and yellow cardigan sagging and fluttering as though carried on a coat-hanger. His shirt, changed on the train, was clean. His other clothes were not. His tie, bought for him years before by Dollie, who had admired its 'angelic blue', was now so blotched and be-yellowed by spilt food. it was no colour at all. His head, with its thin, pale hair, its nose that, long and delicate, widened suddenly at the nostrils, its thin clown's mouth, was remote and mild as the head of a giraffe. On top of it he wore a shabby check cap. His whole sad aspect was made sadder by the fact that he had not eaten for forty-eight hours.

He deposited the two suitcases. The crocodile case, that held, among his unwashed nightwear, a British passport and a receipt for his Hispano-Suiza, he kept with him. When the car had been impounded for debt by the Yugoslav officials at the frontier, he had had on him just enough to buy a third class ticket to Bucharest. This purchase left him with a few pieces of small change.

He emerged from the station into the confusion of a street market where flares were being lit in the first fall of twilight. He had shaken off the porters. Beggars now crowded about him. Feeling in the air the first freshness of autumn, he decided to wear rather than carry his coat. Holding his case out of reach of the ragged children round his knees, he managed to shuffle first one arm and then the other into the coat.

He looked about him. Hounded (his own word) out of one capital after another, he had now reached the edge of Europe, a region in which he already smelt the Orient. Each time he arrived at a new capital, he made for the British Legation, where he usually found some figure from his past. Here, he had heard, the Cultural Attaché was known to him; was, indeed, indebted, having come to one of those opulent parties Dollie and he had given in the old days. It occurred to him that if he drove to the Legation in a taxi, Dobson might pay for it. But if Dobson had been posted and there was no one willing to pay, he would be at the mercy of the taxi-driver. For the first time in his life he hesitated to take a risk. Standing amid the babble of beggars, his coat hanging like a bell-tent from the apex of his neck, he sighed to himself and thought: 'Your poor old Yaki's not the boy he was.'

Seeing him there, one driver threw open the door of his cab. Yakimov shook his head. In Italian, a language he had been told was the same as Rumanian, he asked to be directed to the British Legation. The driver waved him to get in. When Yakimov shook his head a second time, the man gave a snarl of disgust and began to pick his teeth.

Yakimov persisted: "*La legazione britannica, per piacere?*"

To get rid of him, the man flicked a hand over his shoulder.

"*Grazie tanto*, dear boy." Gathering his coat about him, Yakimov turned and followed a street that seemed a tunnel into desolation.

The light was failing. He was beginning to doubt his direction when, at a junction of roads, it seemed confirmed by a statue, in boyar's robes, wearing a turban the size of a pumpkin, that pointed him dramatically to the right.

Here the city had come to life again. The pavements were crowded with small men, all much alike in shabby city clothes, each carrying a brief-case. Yakimov recognised them for what they were; minor government officials and poor clerks, a generation struggling out of the peasantry, at work from eight in the morning until eight at night, now hurrying home to supper. In his hunger, he envied them. A tramway car stopped at the kerb. As the crowd pressed past him, he was buffeted mercilessly from side to side, but maintained his course, his head and shoulders rising above the surge with an appearance of unconcern.

He stopped at a window displaying jars of a jam-like substance that held in suspension transparent peaches and apricots. The light shone through them. This golden, sugared fruit, glowing through the chill blue twilight, brought a tear to his eye. He was pushed on roughly by a woman using a shopping basket as a weapon.

He crossed the road junction. Tramway cars, hung with passengers like swarming bees, clanged and shrilled upon him. He reached the other side. Here as he followed a down-sloping road, the crowd thinned and changed. He passed peasants in their country dress of whitish frieze, thin men, lethargic, down-staring, beneath pointed astrakhan caps, and Orthodox Jews with ringlets hanging on either side of greenish, indoor faces.

A wind, blowing up towards Yakimov, brought a rancid odour that settled in his throat like the first intimations of sea-sickness. He began to feel worried. These small shops did not promise the approach of the British Legation.

The street divided into smaller streets. Keeping to the widest of them, Yakimov saw in every window the minutiae of the tailoring trade – horse-hair, buckram, braid, ready-made pockets, clips, waistcoat buckles, cards of buttons, reels of cotton, rolls of lining. Who on earth wanted all this stuff? In search of even the sight of food, he turned into a passage-way where the stench of the district was muffled for a space by the odour of steam-heated cloth. Here, in gas-lit rooms no bigger than cupboards, moving behind bleared windows like sea creatures in tanks, coatless men thumped their irons and filled the air with hissing fog. The passage ended in a little box of a square so congested with basket-work that the creepers swathed about the balconies seemed to sprout from the wicker jungle below. A man leaning against the single lamp-post straightened himself, threw away his cigarette and began talking to Yakimov, pointing to bassinets, dress-baskets and bird-cages.

Yakimov enquired for the British Legation. For reply the man hauled out a dozen shopping-baskets tied with string and started to untie them. Yakimov slipped away down another passage that brought him, abruptly, to the quayside of a river. This was more hopeful. A river usually indicated a city's centre, but when he went to the single rusted rail that edged the quay, he looked down on a wretched soapy-coloured stream trickling between steep, raw banks of clay. On either bank stood houses of a dilapidated elegance. Here and there he saw windows masked with the harem grilles of the receded Ottoman Empire. A little paint still clung to the plaster, showing, where touched by the street lights, pallid grey or a red the colour of dried blood.

On Yakimov's side of the river, the ground floors had been converted into shops and cafés. China lettering on windows said 'Restaurantul' and 'Cafea'. At the first doorway, where the bead curtain was looped up to invite entry, he endured the sight of a man sucking-in soup from a bowl – onion soup. Strings of melted cheese hung from the spoon, a pollen of cheese and broken toast lay on the soup's surface.

He moved on. The interiors were full of speckled mirrors, rough chairs, and tables with dirty paper covers. An oily smell of cooking came from them. Again he was conscious that he had changed. In the past, often enough, he had eaten his fill, then somehow explained away his inability to pay. In different parts of the town, he might still attempt it: here he was afraid.

As he sidled from doorway to doorway, there suddenly came to him the rich scent of roasting meat. Saliva sprang into his mouth. He was drawn towards the scent, which came from a brazier where a peasant was cooking small pads of meat. The peasant customers, lit by a single flare, stood at a respectful distance, staring at the meat or occasionally turning to look at each other in a nervous, unsmiling intensity of anticipation. The cook seemed conscious of his superior position. He offered the meat with an air of bestowing it. He whose turn it was glanced about uncertainly before taking it and, when he had paid with a small coin, slipped away to eat in the shadows, alone.

After Yakimov had watched this exchange take place half a dozen times, he took the coins from his pocket and spread them on his palm. They comprised of a few *lire*, *filler* and *para*. The cook, to whom he presented them, examined them closely then picked out the largest of the Hungarian coins. He handed Yakimov a piece of meat. Like the others, Yakimov went aside to eat. The savour unbalanced him. He swallowed too quickly. For an ecstatic moment the meat was there, then it was gone. Nothing remained but a taste lingering about his neglected teeth, so honey-sweet it gave him heart to ask his way again.

He returned to the brazier and spoke to a peasant who looked a little more alert than the others. The man did not answer or meet his eyes but, hanging his head, glanced from side to side as though at a loss to account for the noise he heard. A little dark gypsy of a fellow came bustling up and, pushing the peasant contemptuously aside, asked in English: "What is it you are wanting?"

"I am looking for the British Legation."

"Not here. Not anywhere here."

"But where?"

"A long way. It is necessary to find a conveyance."

"Tell me the way. I can walk."

"No, no. Too far. Too difficult." Dropping Yakimov abruptly, the gypsy went across to the other side of the brazier, where he stood looking resentfully across at him.

Yakimov was growing tired. His coat hung hot and heavy on his shoulders. He wondered if he could find some sort of lodging for the night, making his usual promise to pay next day.

As he went on, the quayside widened into an open cobbled space where a gritty wind sprang up and blew feathers into his face. On the further side, near a main road, stood several crates packed with live fowl. This, he realised, was a chicken market, the source of the pervading stench.

He crossed to the crates and took down one so that the others formed a seat. He sat protected by the crates behind him. The hens, stringy Balkan birds, stirred and cackled a while, then slept again. From somewhere in the market a clock struck nine. He had been wandering about for two hours or more. He sighed. His fragile body had become too heavy to move. Wedging his case out of sight between the crates, he drew up his feet, put down his head and slept.

When awakened by the long scream of a braking car, he murmured: "Unholy hour, dear boy", and tried to turn round. His knees struck the wire of the coop behind him. The cramp in his limbs forced him to full consciousness. He scrambled up to see what vehicles could be passing, so erratically and in such profusion when it was barely daylight. He saw a procession of mud-caked lorries swerving and swaying on the crown of the road. One lorry dipped towards the kerb, causing him to jump back in alarm. As it straightened and went on, he gazed after it, shocked, the more so because he himself drove with inspired skill.

Behind the lorries came a string of private cars – a seemingly endless string: all the same mud-grey, all oddly swollen in shape, the result, Yakimov realised, of their being padded top and sides with mattresses. The windscreens were cracked. The bonnets and wings were pockmarked. Inside the cars, the passengers – men, women and children – lay about, abandoned in sleep. The drivers nodded over the steering-wheels.

Who could they be? Where had they come from? Aching, famished, racked by the light of this unfamiliar hour, Yakimov did not try to answer his questions. But the destination of the cars? Looking where they were heading, he saw tall, concrete buildings evolving pearly out of the pinks and blues of dawn. Beacons of civilisation. He followed the road towards them.

After walking a couple of miles, he reached the main square as the sun, rising above the roof-tops, flecked the cobblestones. A statue, heavily planted on a horse too big for it, saluted the long, grey front of what must be the royal palace. At either end of the palace workmen had started screwing pieces of pre-fabricated classical façade on to scaffolding. The rest of the square was, apparently, being demolished. He crossed to the sunlit side where a white, modern building proclaimed itself the Athénée Palace Hotel. Here the leading cars had come to rest. Only a few of the occupants had roused themselves. The rest slept on, their faces ashen and grim. Some of them had roughly bandaged wounds. In one car, Yakimov noticed, the grey upholstery was soaked with blood.

He pushed through the hotel's revolving door into a marble hall lit brilliantly with glass chandeliers. As he entered, his name was called aloud: "*Yakimov!*"

He started back. He had not received this sort of welcome for many a day. He was the more suspicious when he saw it came from a journalist called McCann, who when they met in the bars of Budapest had usually turned his back. McCann was propped up on a long sofa just inside the vestibule, while a man in a black suit was cutting away the blood-soaked shirt-sleeve which stuck to his right arm. Yakimov felt enough concern to approach the sofa and ask: "What has happened, dear boy? Can I do anything to help?"

"You certainly can. For the last half-hour I've been telling these dumb clucks to find me a bloke who can speak English."

Yakimov would have been glad to sink down beside McCann, feeling himself as weak as any wounded man, but the other end of the sofa was occupied by a girl, a dark beauty, haggard and very dirty, who sprawled there asleep.

Leaning forward in an attitude of sympathetic enquiry, he hoped McCann would not want much of him.

"It's this!" McCann's left hand dug clumsily about in the jacket that lay behind him. "Here!" – he produced some sheets torn from a notebook – "Get this out for me. It's the whole story."

"Really, dear boy! What story?"

"Why, the break-up of Poland; surrender of Gdynia; flight of the Government; the German advance on Warsaw; the refugees streaming out, me with them. Cars machine-gunned from the air; men, women and children wounded and killed; the dead buried by the roadside. Magnificent stuff; first hand; must get it out while it's hot. Here, take it."

"But how do I get it out?" Yakimov was almost put to flight by the prospect of such an arduous employment.

"Ring our agency in Geneva, dictate it over the line. A child could do it."

"Impossible, dear boy. Haven't a bean."

"Reverse the charges."

"Oh, they'd never let me" – Yakimov backed away – "I'm not known here. I don't speak the language. I'm a refugee like yourself."

"Where from?"

Before Yakimov had time to answer his question, a man thrust in through the doors, moving all his limbs with the unnatural fervour of exhaustion. He rushed at McCann. "Where, please," he asked, "is the man with red hairs in your car?"

"Dead," said McCann.

"Where, please, then, is the scarf I lent to him? The big, blue scarf?"

"God knows. I'd guess it's underground. We buried him the other side of Lublin, if you want to go back and look."

"You buried the scarf? Are you mad that you buried the scarf?"

"Oh, go away!" shouted McCann, at which the man ran to the wall opposite and beat on it with his fists.

Taking advantage of this diversion, Yakimov began to move off. McCann seized a fold of his coat and gave a howl of rage: "For God's sake! Come back, you bastard. Here I am with this arm gone, a bullet in my ribs, not allowed to move – and here's this story! You've got to send it, d'you hear me? You've got to."

Yakimov moaned: "Haven't had a bite for three days. Your poor old Yaki's faint. His feet are killing him."

"Wait!" Pushing impatiently about in his coat again, McCann brought out his journalist's card. "Take this. You can eat here. Get yourself a drink. Get yourself a bed. Get what you damned well like – but first, 'phone this stuff through."

Taking the card and seeing on it the picture of McCann's lined and crumpled face, Yakimov was slowly revivified by the possibilities of the situation. "You mean they'll give me credit?"

"Infinite credit. The paper says. Work for me, you dopey duck, and you can booze and stuff to your heart's content."

"Dear boy!" breathed Yakimov; he smiled with docile sweetness. "Explain again, *rather* slowly, just what you want poor Yaki to do."

3

THE PRINGLES SETTLED INTO A SMALL HOTEL in the square, on the side opposite the Athénée Palace. Their window looked out on to ruins. That day, the day after their arrival, they had been awakened at sunrise by the fall of masonry. At evening, as Harriet watched for Guy's return, she saw the figures of workmen, black and imp-small in the dusk, carrying flares about the broken buildings.

These buildings had been almost the last of the Biedermeier prettiness bestowed on Bucharest by Austria. The King, who planned a square where, dared he ever venture out so openly, he might review a regiment, had ordered that the demolitions be completed before winter.

Harriet had spent most of her day watching from the window. Though the university term had not started, Guy had set out that morning to see if there were any students in the common-room. He had promised to take Harriet out after luncheon but had returned late, his face aglow, and said he must eat quickly and hurry back. The students had been crowding in all morning eager for news of their English teachers and the term's work.

"But, darling" – Harriet, still filled with the faith and forbearance of the newly married, spoke only with regret – "couldn't you wait until Professor Inchcape arrives?"

"One must never discourage students," said Guy and he hurried off, promising to take her that evening to dine "up the Chaussée".

During the afternoon the receptionist rang through three times to say a lady wished to speak to Domnul Pringle. "The same lady?" Harriet asked the third time. Yes, the same lady.

When, at sunset, Guy's figure appeared in the square, Harriet's forbearance was not what it had been. She watched him emerge out of a blur of dust – a large, untidy man clutching an armful of books and papers with the awkwardness of a bear. A piece of pediment crashed before him. He paused, blinded; peered about through his glasses and started off in the wrong direction. She felt an appalled compassion for him. Where he had been a moment before, a wall came down. Its fall revealed the interior of a vast white room, fretted with baroque scrolls and set with a mirror that glimmered like a lake. Nearby could be seen the red wall-paper of a café – the famous Café Napoleon that had been the meeting-place of artists, musicians, poets and other natural non-conformists. Guy had said that all this destruction had been planned simply to wipe out this one centre of revolt.

Entering the hotel room, Guy threw down his armful of papers. With a casualness that denoted drama, he announced: "The Russians have occupied Vilna." He set about changing his shirt.

"You mean, they're inside Poland?" asked Harriet.

"A good move." Her tone had set him on the defensive. "A move to protect Poland."

"A good excuse, anyway."

The telephone rang and Guy jumped at it before anything more could be said: "Inchcape!" he called delightedly and without consulting Harriet added: "We're dining up the Chaussée. Pavel's. Come and join us." He put down the receiver and, pulling a shirt over his head without undoing the buttons, he said: "You'll like Inchcape. All you need do with him is encourage him to talk."

Harriet, who never believed she would like anyone she did not know, said: "Someone rang you three times this afternoon. A woman."

"Really!" The information did not disconcert him. He merely said: "People here are crazy about the telephone. It hasn't been installed long. Women with nothing better to do ring up complete strangers and say: 'Allo! Who are you? Let us have a nice little flirt.' I'm always getting them."

"I don't think a stranger would ring three times."

"Perhaps not. Whoever it was, she'll ring again."

As they left the room, the telephone did ring again. Guy hurried back to it. Harriet, on the stairs, heard him say: "Why, Sophie!" and she went down. Turning a corner, she saw the hall below crowded with people. All the hotel guests and servants were gathered there, moving about talking excitedly. Behind the reception desk the wireless, like a mechanical bird, was whirring in the persistent, nerve-racking music of the Rumanian *hora*. Harriet came to a stop, feeling in the air the twang of anxiety. When Guy caught her up, she said: "I think something has happened."

Guy went to the manager, who attended him with deference. The English were important in Bucharest. England had guaranteed Rumanian safety. Guy was told that foreign troops were massing on the frontier.

"What part of the frontier?" he asked.

That was not known: nor was it known whether the troops were German or Russian. The King was about to broadcast from his apartments and it was believed that at any moment general mobilisation would be ordered.

Moved by the stress of the occasion, the Pringles waited to hear the King. The mechanical bird stopped. In the abrupt silence, voices that had been bawling to be heard above the din now trickled self-consciously away. The wireless announced that the King would address his subjects in Rumanian.

At that. a man in a cape, too stout to turn only his head, turned his whole body and surveyed the gathering with an air of enquiring innocence. "*Sans doute l'émission est en retard parce que sa Majesté s'instruit dans la langue.*"

There was a laugh, but a brief one, an instant extracted from fear, then the faces were taut again. The group waited; a collection of drawn yellow-skinned men and heavily powdered women with dark eyes fixed on the wireless set, from which the King's voice came suddenly out of long silence. The audience bent expectantly forward, then began shifting and complaining that it could not understand his broken Rumanian. Guy did his best to translate the speech for Harriet:

"If we are attacked; we will defend our country to the last man. We will defend it to the last foot of soil. We have learned from Poland's mistakes. Rumania will never suffer defeat. Her strength will be formidable."

A few people nodded their heads and one repeated: "*Formidabil, eh! Formidabil!*", but several of the others looked furtively about fearing an enemy might mistake these words for provocation. The man in the cape turned again, screwing up his large, flexible, putty-coloured face and spreading his hands as though to say 'And now you know!' but the others were not so responsive. This was no time for humour. Giving Guy the smile of a fellow conspirator he strode away and Guy, flushed like a schoolboy, whispered that that had been an actor from the National Theatre.

The Pringles left by a side door that opened on to the Calea

Victoriei, the main shopping street, where the blocks of flats rose to such a height they caught the last rose-violet glow of the sun. A glimmer of this, reflected down into the dusty valley of the street, lit with violet-grey the crowds that clotted either pavement.

This was the time of the evening promenade. Guy suggested they should walk a little way; but first, they had to pass through the purgatory of the hotel's attendant beggars. These were professional beggars, blinded or maimed by beggar parents in infancy. Guy, during his apprentice year, had grown accustomed, if not inured, to the sight of white eyeballs and running sores, to have stumps and withered arms and the breasts of nursing mothers thrust into his face. The Rumanians accepted all this as part of life and donated coins so small that a beggar might spend his day collecting the price of a meal.

However, when Guy tried to do the same thing, a howl went up. Foreigners were not let off so lightly. All the beggars set upon the Pringles together. One hid half a loaf behind his back to join in the age old cry of: "*Mi-e foame, foame, foame.*" They were hemmed in by a stench of sweat, garlic and putrid wounds. The beggars took what Guy distributed among them, then whined for more. Harriet, looking at a child that trembled violently at her elbow, thought she saw in its face glee at its own persistence. A man on the ground, attempting to bar their way, stretched out a naked leg bone-thin, on which the skin was mottled purple and rosetted with yellow scabs. As she stepped over it, the leg slapped the ground in rage that she should escape it.

"Do they want to annoy one?" she asked, and realised there might be revenge for all this abasement in provoking some stranger like herself to the break-down of pure hatred.

At last they were free to join the promenade. The crowd was a sombre crowd, comprising more men than women. Women of the older generation did not walk abroad alone. There were a few groups of girls, their eyes only for each other, seeming unaware of the savage stares of solitary men. Mostly there were couples; tailored, padded, close-buttoned, self-consciously correct: for this, Guy explained, was an hour when only the employing class was free to walk abroad, Harriet might now observe the new bourgeoisie, risen from the peasantry and pretty pleased with itself for having done so.

Because the peasants themselves were given to holiday colours of great brilliance, their male descendants dressed in grey, the women in Parisian black with such pearls, diamonds and silver fox furs as they could afford.

Harriet, meeting glances that became critical, even slightly derisive, of the fact the Pringles were hatless and rather oddly dressed, became censorious herself. "They have," she said, "the uniformity of their insecurity."

"They're not all Rumanians," said Guy. "There are a great many stateless Jews; and there are, of course, Hungarians, Germans and Slavs. The percentages are . . ." Guy, his head lifted above the trivialities of conduct, brought out statistics, but Harriet was not listening. She was absorbed in warfare with the crowd.

The promenade was for her a trial of physical strength. Though leisurely, the Rumanians were ruthless in their determination to keep on the pavement. Only peasants or servants could be seen walking in the road. The men might, under pressure, yield an inch or two, but the women were as implacable as steam-rollers. Short and strong, they remained bland-faced while wielding buttocks and breasts as heavy as bladders of lard.

The position most fiercely held was the inner pavement beside the shop windows. Guy, too temperate, and Harriet, too light-boned, for the fray, were easily thrust out to the kerb, where Guy gripped Harriet's elbow to keep her from slipping into the gutter. She broke from him, saying: "I'll walk in the road. I'm not a Rumanian. I can do what I like."

Following her, Guy caught her hand and squeezed it, trying to induce in her his own imperturbable good humour. Harriet, looking back at the crowd, more tolerant now she was released from it, realised that behind its apparent complacency there was a nervous air of enquiry, an alert unease. Were someone to shout: 'The invasion has begun,' the whole smug façade would collapse.

This unease unmasked itself at the end of the Calea Victoriei where the road widened in a no-man's-land of public buildings. Here were parked a dozen or so of the Polish refugee cars that were still streaming down from the north. Some of the cars had been abandoned. From the others women and children, left while the men sought shelter, gazed out blankly. The well-dressed Rumanians, out to appreciate and be appreciated, looked affronted by these ruined faces that were too tired to care.

Harriet wondered what would be done with the Poles. Guy said the Rumanians, once stirred, were kindly enough. Some who owned summer villas were offering them to Polish families, but stories were already going round about the refugees; old anti-Polish stories remembered from the last war.

Near the end of the road, near the cross roads where the turbaned boyar, Cantacuzino, pointed the way to the Chicken Market, a row of open *trăsurăs* waited to be hired. Guy suggested they drive up the Chaussée. Harriet peered at the horses, whose true condition was hidden by the failing of the light.

"They look wretchedly thin," she said.

"They're very old."

"I don't think we should employ them."

"If no one employed them, they would starve to death."

Choosing the least decrepit of the horses, the Pringles climbed into the carriage, which was about to start when commanded to a halt. A tall, elderly man was holding out his walking-stick with an imperious air.

Guy recognised the man with surprise. "It's Woolley," he said. "He usually ignores 'the culture boys'." Then his face lit with pleasure: "I expect he wants to meet you." Before Woolley could state his business, Guy introduced him to Harriet: "The leading English businessman, the chairman of the Golf Club", enhancing from sheer liberality of spirit such importance as Woolley had; then, turning with tender pride towards Harriet, he said: "My wife."

Woolley's cold nod indicated that duty not frivolity had caused him to accost them. "The order is," he announced in a nasal twang, "the ladies must return to England."

"But," said Guy, "I called at the Legation this morning. No one said anything about it."

"Well, there it is," said Woolley in a tone that implied he was not arguing, he was telling them.

Harriet, exasperated by the mildness of Guy's protest asked: "Who has given this order? The Minister?"

Woolley started, surprised, it seemed, not only by the edge on her voice but by the fact she had a voice at all. His head, hairless, with toad-mottled skin, jerked round and hung towards her like a lantern tremulous on a bamboo: "No, it's a general order, like. I've sent me lady wife home as an example. That was enough for the other ladies."

"Not for me, I'm afraid. I never follow examples."

Woolley's throat moved several times before he said: "Oh, don't you? Well, young woman, I can tell you this: if trouble starts here, there'll be a proper schemozzle. The cars and petrol will be requisitioned by the army and the trains'll be packed with troops. I doubt if anyone'll get away, but if you do, you'll go empty-handed, and it won't be no Cook's tour. Don't say I haven't warned you. What I say is, it's the duty of the ladies to go back home and not to be a drag on the gents."

"You imagine they'll be safer in England? I can only say, you don't know much about modern warfare. I think, Mr. Woolley, it would be better if you set an example by not getting into a panic."

Harriet poked at the coachman and the *trăsură*, seeming about to break fore from aft, heaved itself to a start. As it went, Harriet looked back to give a regal nod and saw that Woolley's face, under a street lamp, had lost what colour it had. He shouted after them, his voice passing out of control: "You young people these days have no respect for authority. I'd have you know, the Minister described me as the leader of the English colony."

They were under way. Guy, his brows raised, gazed at Harriet, having seen an extra dimension added to the woman he had achieved. "I never dreamt you could be so grand," he said.

Pleased with herself, she said: "He's an impossible old ass. How could you let him bully you?"

Guy laughed. "Darling, he's pathetic."

"Pathetic? With all that self-importance?"

"The self-importance is pathetic. Can't you see?"

For a sudden moment she could see, and her triumph subsided. His hand slipped into hers and she raised to her lips his long, unpractical fingers. "You're right, of course. Still . . ." She gave his little finger a bite that made him yelp. "That," she said, "is in case you get too good to be true."

They had returned down the Calea Victoriei, crossed the square and had reached the broad avenue where the German Embassy stood among the mansions of the very rich. This led to the Chaussée, that stretched, wide and tree-lined, into open country. The trees, a row on either side of the pavements, were almost bare, what leaves that remained so scorched by the summer's heat that they hung like scraps blown from a bonfire.

It was almost dark. The stars grew brilliant in the sky. The

Pringles, sitting hand-in-hand in the old four-wheeler that smelt of horse, were more aware of each other than of anything else. Here they were, a long way from home, alone together in a warring world.

Made a little self-conscious by these thoughts, Guy pointed out an archway at the end of the vista. "The Arc de Triomphe," he said.

"The Paris of the East," Harriet said, somewhat in ridicule, for they had disagreed as to the attractions of Bucharest. Guy, who had spent here his first year of adult freedom, living on the first money earned by his own efforts, saw Bucharest with a pleasure she, a Londoner, rather jealous of his year alone here, was not inclined to share.

"What is it made of, the arch? Marble?" she asked.

"Concrete." It had been built previously by a fraudulent contractor who had used inferior cement. When it fell down, the contractor was put in prison and the arch re-erected to the glory of Greater Rumania – the Rumania that came into existence in 1919 when the Old Kingdom acquired, as a reward for entering the war on the side of the victors, parts of Russia, Austria and Hungary. "And so," said Guy, "like most people who did well out of the war, she is now a nice comfortable shape."

While Guy talked, young men howled past the *trăsură* in racing cars, each with a foot on his accelerator, a hand thumping up and down on the hooter. The horse – revealed by the street lights as a phantom horse, a skeleton in a battered hide – was not disturbed. Equally undisturbed was the coachman, a vast cottage loaf in a velvet robe.

Guy whispered: "A *Skopit*. One of the sights of the city. The *Skopits* belong to a Russian sect. They believe that to find grace we must all be completely flat in front, women as well as men. So, after they've reproduced themselves, the young people hold tremendous orgies, working themselves into frenzies in which they mutilate themselves."

"Oh!" said Harriet. She gazed in wonder at the vast velvet backside of the eunuch before her, then she gazed out at the dark reaches of the Muntenia plain, on which the city stood like a bride-cake on a plate. "A barbarous country," she said.

They had now passed the last of the houses. On either side of the road, adazzle beneath the dark, star-lighted violet of the sky, were the open areas owned by the restaurants that had no gardens in the town. Each spring, when the weather settled, they shut their winter premises and brought their chairs and tables up the Chaussée. Within these enclosures the limes and chestnuts, hose-drenched each morning, spread a ceiling of leaves.

When the *trăsură* stopped at Pavel's, one of the largest of the open-air restaurants, there could be heard above the traffic the shrill squeak of a gypsy violin. Within the shrub hedge of the garden, all was uproar.

The place was crowded. The silver-gilt glow from the globes set in the trees lit in detail the wrinkled tree-trunks, the pebbled ground, and the blanched faces of the diners that, damp with the excitement of food, gazed about them with deranged looks, demanding to be served. Some rapped with knives on wine-glasses, some clapped their hands, some made kissing noises at the waiters, while others clutched at every passing coat-tail, crying: '*Domnule, domnule!*' for in this country even the meanest was addressed as 'lord'.

The waiters, sweating and disarranged, snapped their civilities and made off before orders were complete. The diners shouted to the empty air, sometimes shaking their fists as they seethed in their seats, talking, gesturing, jerking their heads this way and that. It was an uproar in which there was little laughter.

"They all seem very cross," said Harriet, who, caught into the atmosphere, began to feel cross herself.

A waiter, flapping at the Pringles like an angry bird, conveyed to them the fact they were blocking the way to the kitchen building. They stood aside and watched him as he rushed to an open window and bawled into the kitchen's bang and clatter. The cooks, scowling in the heat from the giant grill, ignored him. The waiter brought his fists down on the sill, at which one of the cooks lunged at the window, flinging himself half from it as an enraged dog flings himself the length of his chain. He struck the waiter, who fell gibbering.

"It's all just Rumanian animation," said Guy as he led Harriet to an alcove where the foods were displayed beneath a canopy of vines.

The heart of the display was a rosy bouquet of roasts, chops, steaks and fillets frilled round with a froth of cauliflowers. Heaped extravagantly about the centre were aubergines as big as melons, baskets of artichokes, small coral carrots, mushrooms, mountain raspberries, apricots, peaches, apples and grapes. On one side there were French cheeses; on the other tins of caviare, grey river fish in powdered ice, and lobsters and crayfish groping in dark waters. The poultry and game lay unsorted on the ground.

"Choose," said Guy.

"What can we afford?"

"Oh, anything. The chicken is good here." He pointed in to the grill, where spitted birds were changing from gold to deeper gold.

As he spoke a woman standing nearby turned, looked accusingly at him, and said in English: "You are English, yes? The English *professor*?"

Guy agreed that he was.

"This war," she said, "it is a terrible thing for Rumania." Her husband, who was standing apart, gazed away with an air of non-participation. "England has guaranteed us," said the woman, "England must protect us."

"Of course," said Guy as though offering her his own personal guarantee of protection. He glanced over at the husband, smiling to introduce himself, and at once the man started into ingratiating life, bowing and beaming at the Pringles.

"Even if we are not attacked," said the woman, impatient of this interruption, "there will be many scarcities," she looked down at her high-heeled shoes, shoes that seemed too small for the legs above them, and said: "In the last war there were many scarcities. I remember my father paid for me two thousand *lei* for shoes of felt. I wear them to school the one day only, and when I return, no soles left. And food! How terrible if Rumania were short of food!"

Guy turned, laughing, towards the alcove. "Could Rumania be short of food?"

"No? You think not?" She paused and glanced at her husband. "It is true," she said, "we have much food." The husband shrugged and smiled again.

At last Guy was released. Harriet, who had been watching the activity of the restaurant, said: "There are no free tables."

"Oh yes, there are." Firmly, short-sightedly, Guy led her to a table marked '*Rezervat*'.

"*Nu nu, domnule.*" The head waiter pointed them to a vacant table beside the orchestra.

Harriet shook her head: "The noise would be intolerable." The man grumbled.

"He says," said Guy, "we are fortunate to find any table in a time of war."

"Tell him it's our war, not his. We must have a better table."

The head waiter flung out his hands in a distracted way and called to an assistant to take charge of the Pringles. The assistant, dodging like a rugger player through the hazards of the garden, led them to a platform where half-a-dozen privileged tables were raised above the rest. He whipped a 'reserved' notice from one and presented it like a conjurer completing a trick. Guy handed him a bundle of small notes.

Now, seated as on a headland, the Pringles gazed across the surge at a wrought-iron cage, lighted with 'fairy' lights and hung with green branches and gilded oranges, where the orchestra laboured to be heard above the general din. Squeaking and pom-pomming at an insane pitch, the instruments produced an effect not so much of high spirits as of tearing rage.

Guy tilted forward his glasses and tried to focus the spectacle before him. He was, Harriet knew, happy to be in this advanta-geous position even though he would not have demanded it for himself. In appreciation, he stretched his hand to her across the table. As she touched it, she saw they were being observed from the next table by a man who, meeting her glance, smiled and looked away.

"Who is that?" Harriet whispered. "Does he know us?"

"Everyone knows us. We are the English. We are at war."

"But who is he?"

"Ionescu, the Minister of Information. He's always here."

"How odd to live in such a small capital!"

"There are advantages. Whatever happens here, one is in the midst of it."

Ionescu was not alone at his table. He had with him five women of different ages, all plain, staid and subdued in appearance, from whom he sat apart. He gazed fixedly at the orchestra stand and picked his teeth with a golden pick.

"Who are the women?"

"His wife and her relatives. The wife is the one nearest him."

"She looks down-trodden."

"She probably is. Everyone knows he comes here only to see the singer Florica. He's her latest *affaire*."

Harriet watched a man below, who, newly served, guarded his plate with one hand against the waiters and passers-by while with the other he forked-in his food, eyes oblique, as though fearing to have it snatched from him. She was hungry herself.

"Will they ever bring the menu?" she asked.

Guy said: "Sooner or later someone will remember us. There's Inchcape." He pointed to a man in late middle-age, thickly built and very upright, who had paused with an ironically humorous courtesy while a group pushed fiercely past him searching for a table. As Guy rose and waved, Inchcape nodded up to him, then, when free to move, did so with the same air of amused irony, giving, for all his lack of height, the impression of towering over those about him. He had, Harriet remembered, once been head-master of a minor public school.

As he advanced, she noticed someone was following him – a taller, leaner man, no more than thirty years of age, who came sidling among the tables, effacing himself behind his com-panion.

"Why, Clarence!" Guy called on a rising note of delighted surprise, and the second man, smirking, cast down his eyes. "That," said Guy, "is my colleague Clarence Lawson. So we're all back together again!" He stretched out his hands as the two arrived at the table. They seemed both pleased and embarrassed by his enthusiasm.

Taking Guy's left hand, Inchcape gave it an admonitory tweak. "So you've got yourself married!" he said and turned with a mocking half-smile towards Harriet. She saw that beneath the smile his glance was critical and vulnerable. One of his men had brought back a wife – an unknown quantity, perhaps a threat to his authority. When Guy made the introductions, she greeted Inchcape gravely, making no attempt to charm.

His manner, when responding, admitted her to his grown-up world. It changed as he turned back to Guy. Guy, it seemed, was not a grown-up; he was a boy – a favoured boy, a senior prefect, perhaps, but still a boy.

"Where did you go this summer?" Guy asked Clarence, who was standing, a little aloof, from the table. "Did you do that bus journey from Beirut to Kashmir?"

"Well, no, I didn't." Clarence had an awkward, rather confused smile, that made the more surprising the firm and resonant richness of his voice. Catching Harriet's eyes on him, he looked quickly from her. "Actually, I just stuck in Beirut. I spent the summer bathing and lounging around the beach. Much as you might expect. I did think of flying home to see Brenda, but somehow I never got around to it."

Guy asked Inchcape what he had done.

"I was in Rome," he said, "I spent a lot of time in the Vatican Library." He looked at Harriet. "How was England when you left it?"

"Calm enough. Foreigners were leaving, of course. The official who examined our passports at Dover said: 'The first today'."

Inchcape took a seat. "Well" – he frowned at Clarence – "sit down, sit down," but there was nowhere for Clarence to sit.

A chair was brought from a neighbouring table but Clarence remained standing. "As a matter of fact," he said, "I only came to say 'Hallo'."

"*Sit down.*" Inchcape impatiently slapped the chair seat and Clarence sat. When all the party was settled, Inchcape surveyed it, drawing down the corners of his lips in ridicule of the announcement he had to make. "I've just been put in charge of British propaganda in the Balkans," he said. "An official appointment."

"Why, splendid!" exclaimed Guy.

"Umph! It'll lead to a rearrangement of duties, of course. You," he nodded to Guy, "will take over the English Department – a much reduced department, needless to say. You can get some of the local teachers of English to give you a hand. I'll remain in charge; all you'll have to do my dear fellow is work." He pushed Guy's shoulder in humorous dismissal, then turned to Clarence: "We're opening a propaganda bureau in the Calea Victoriei opposite the rival establishment. You will be required to bring out a news sheet." He smiled at Clarence but did not attempt to touch him. Clarence, tilted back from the table, his hands in his pockets, his chin on his chest, was not responsive. He seemed to be rejecting patronage with an uneasy air of ease. "You'll have plenty of other jobs to do, of course."

Clarence said slowly: "I'm not at all sure I can take on this sort of work. I'm seconded from the British Council. The Council is purely cultural and Lord Lloyd . . ."

"I'll deal with Lloyd." Inchcape jerked upright and looked about him. "Where's the waiter? What about a drink?" He turned his neat Napoleonic face towards a waiter, who, conscious of having neglected the table, now sprang on to the platform with exaggerated alacrity.

When their order had been given, Harriet said to Inchcape: "So you think we shall stay here?"

"Why should we not?"

Guy said: "Woolley stopped us earlier this evening and tried to order Harriet home."

Inchcape, eyes and nostrils distended, looked from Guy to Harriet and back again: "Woolley took it upon himself to give you orders?"

Enjoying Inchcape's indignation, Harriet said: "He said that he is the leader of the English colony."

"He did, did he? The old fool's in his second childhood. He spends his days in the bar at the Golf Club getting sustenance out of a bottle, like a baby. In his dotage; his anecdotage, I'd say. Ha!" Inchcape gave a laugh, cheered by his own wit, then he fell to brooding and, after a pause, said: "Leader of the English colony forsooth! I'll show him who's leader if he tries to order my men about."

Guy and Clarence exchanged smiles.

Harriet asked Inchcape: "If there were an invasion, if we had to leave here in a hurry, where would we go?"

Inchcape, still annoyed, answered shortly: "Turkey, I suppose."

"And from there?"

"Oh!" His tone became milder. "Make our way through Syria to the Middle East." He assumed his old joking manner. "Or we might try a little trek across Persia and Afghanistan to India." But he still spoke grudgingly. He interrupted himself to say: "But there'll be no invasion. The Germans have better things to do with their troops than spread them out over Eastern Europe. They'll need all they've got to hold the Western front."

Clarence stuck out his lower lip. He 'hmmd' a bit before remarking in a casual tone: "Nevertheless, the situation is serious. I bumped into Foxy Leverett today and he advised me to keep my bags packed."

"Then you'll keep them packed a long time." Inchcape now

shrugged the matter off. He might have been dealing with a junior-school fracas of which he had had enough.

The piccolo arrived, a scrap of a boy, laden with bottles, glasses and plates. Breathing loudly, he set the table.

Glancing up, Harriet found Clarence's gaze fixed on her. He looked away at once but he had caught her attention. She noted his long, lean face with its long nose, and felt it unsatisfactory. Unsatisfactory and unsatisfied. As she assessed him, his eyes came, rather furtively, back to her and now he found her gazing at him. He flushed slightly and jerked his face away again.

She smiled to herself.

Guy said: "I asked Sophie to join us here."

"Why, I wonder?" Inchcape murmured.

"She's very depressed about the war."

"Imagining, no doubt, that it was declared with the sole object of depressing her."

Suddenly all the perturbation of the garden was gathered into an eruption of applause. The name of the singer Florica was passed from table to table.

Florica, in her long black and white skirts, was posed like a bird, a magpie, in the orchestra cage. When the applause died out, she jerked forward in a bow, then, opening her mouth, gave a high, violent gypsy howl. The audience stirred. Harriet felt the sound pass like a shock down her spine.

The first howl was followed by a second, sustained at a pitch that must within a few years (so Inchcape later assured the table) destroy her vocal chords. People sitting near Ionescu glanced at him and at his women. Sprawled sideways in his seat, he stared at the singer and went on picking his teeth. The women remained impassive as the dead.

Florica, working herself into a fury in the cage, seemed to be made of copper wire. She had the usual gypsy thinness and was as dark as an Indian. When she threw back her head, the sinews moved in her throat: the muscles moved as her lean arms swept the air. The light flashed over her hair, that was strained back, glossy, from her round, glossy brow. Singing there among the plump women of the audience, she was like a starved wild kitten spitting at cream-fed cats. The music sank and her voice dropped to a snarl. It rose and, twisting her body as in rage, clenching her fists and striking back her skirts, she finished on an elemental screech that was sustained above the tremendous outburst of applause.

When it was over, people blinked as though they had survived a tornado. Only Ionescu and his women continued, to all appearance, unmoved.

Inchcape, not himself applauding, pointed in amusement at Guy, who, crying "Bravo, bravo!" was leaning forward to bang his hands together. "What energy," smiled Inchcape. "How wonderful to be young!" When there was silence again, he turned to Harriet and said: "She was a failure when she toured abroad, but here she's just what they like. She expresses all the exasperation that's eating these people up." As he turned in his seat, he suddenly saw Ionescu's party. "Oh ho!" he said, "Ionescu complete with harem. I wonder how his wife enjoyed the performance."

"You think," Harriet asked him, "she knows about Florica and her husband?"

"Dear me, yes. She probably has on record everything they have ever said or done during every moment they have spent together."

To encourage him, Harriet made a murmur of artless interest. Inchcape settled down to instruct her. He said: "Rumanian convention requires her apparent unawareness. Morality here is based not on not doing, but on recognising what is being done."

They had been served with a rich goose-liver paté, dark with truffles and dressed with clarified butter. Inchcape swallowed this down in chunks, talking through it as though it were a flavourless impediment to self-expression.

"Take, for instance, the behaviour of these women in company. If anyone makes an improper joke, they simply pretend not to understand. While the men roar with laughter, the women sit poker faced. It's ridiculous to watch. This behaviour, that fools no one, saves the men having to restrict their conversation when women are present."

"But the young women, the students, don't they rebel against this sort of hypocrisy?"

"Dear me, no. They are the most conventional *jeunes filles* in the world, and the most knowing. 'Sly', Miss Austen would have called them. If, during a reading in class, we come on some slight indecency, the men roar their enjoyment, the girls sit blank. If they were shocked, they would not look shocked: if they were innocent, they would look bewildered. As it is, their very blankness betrays their understanding." Inchcape gave a snort of disgust, not, apparently, at the convention but at the absurdity of the sex on which it was imposed.

"How do they become so knowledgeable so young?" asked Harriet, half listening to the talk between Clarence and Guy, in which she caught more than once the name of Sophie. Clarence, half in the party and half out of it, was taking a bite or two of paté.

"Oh," Inchcape answered Harriet, "these Rumanian homes are hot-beds of scandal and gossip. It's all very Oriental. The pretence of innocence is to keep their price up. They develop early and they're married off early, usually to some rich old lecher whose only interest is in the girl's virginity. When that's over and done with, they divorce. The girl sets up her own establishment, and having the status of divorcée, she is free to do what she chooses."

Harriet laughed. "How then is the race carried on?"

"There's a quota of normal marriages, of course. But surely you've heard the story of the Rumanian walking with his German friend down Calea Victoriei – the Rumanian naming the price of every woman they meet? 'Good heavens,' says the German, 'are there no honest women here?' 'Certainly,' replies the Rumanian, 'but – *very expensive!*' "

Harriet laughed, and Inchcape, with a satisfied smile, gazed over the restaurant and complained: "I've never before seen this place in such a hubbub."

"It's the war," said Clarence. "Eat, drink and be merry, for tomorrow we may be starving to death."

"Fiddlesticks!"

The second course arrived, a duck dressed with orange. As this was being carved, Inchcape said quietly to Harriet: "I see your friend Sophie Oresanu in the distance."

Not avoiding the underlying question, Harriet replied: "She is not my friend. I have never met her. What is she?"

"Rather an advanced young lady for these parts. Her circumstances are peculiar. Her parents divorced and Sophie lived with her mother. When the mother died, Sophie was left to live alone. That is unusual here. It gives her considerable freedom. She worked for a while on a student's magazine – one of those mildly anti-fascist, half-baked publications that appear from time to time. It lasted about six months. Now she thinks the Germans have marked her down. She's taking a law degree."

"Really!" Harriet was impressed by the law degree.

"It doesn't mean anything here," said Inchcape. "They all take law degrees. That qualifies them to become second assistant stamp-lickers in the civil service."

"Guy says the Rumanian girls are intelligent."

"They're quick. But all Rumanians are much of a muchness. They can absorb facts but can't do anything with them. A lot of stuffed geese, I call them. An uncreative people." While speaking, he kept his eye on a young woman who now mounted the platform and, stopping at the table and ignoring the others present, stared mournfully at Guy. He, talking, failed to notice her.

In a plaintive, little voice she said: " 'Allo!"

"Why, hello!" Guy leapt to his feet and kissed her on either cheek. Sophie suffered the embrace with a slight smile, taking in the company as she did so.

Guy turned cheerfully to Harriet: "Darling, you must meet Sophie. Sophie, my wife."

As Sophie looked at Harriet, her expression suggested she was at a loss to understand not only how he had acquired a wife, but how he had acquired such a wife. She eventually gave a nod and looked away. She was a pretty enough girl, dark like most Rumanians, too full in the cheeks. Her chief beauty was her figure. Looking at Sophie's well developed bosom, Harriet felt at a disadvantage. Perhaps Sophie's shape would not last, but it was enviable while it lasted.

Guy looked for another chair.

"Here," said Clarence, "take mine. I must go."

"No, no." Guy tried to hold him, but, after pausing uncertainly for a while, Clarence suddenly darted off.

"Now where's he gone?" Inchcape stared after Clarence, then gave Sophie a frown of annoyance, making it clear he thought her a poor exchange. Ignoring him, Sophie watched Guy reproachfully. It was some time before he noticed this, then he said:

"What's the matter?"

"Nothing," she said. "Nothing to be discussed in public." After a pause, she added: "Ah, this war! Such a terrible thing! It has made me so sad. When I go to bed at night, I am thinking of it: when I wake, I am thinking of it. Always I am thinking of it."

Inchcape filled a glass and put it in front of her. "Here," he said, "have a drink and cheer up." When Sophie ignored the wine, Inchcape turned his back on her and indicated the diners below.

"Down there," he said, "unless I'm much mistaken, there's a fellow who was at the Crillon when I stayed there some years ago. A Prince Yakimov. He used to be a very well known figure in Paris society."

While Inchcape spoke, Harriet heard Sophie's voice, uneven with tears: "How can he say to me 'Cheer up'? Is this a time to cheer up? It is very well, the 'stiff upper lip', if you are not sensitive. But me – I am very sensitive." Guy was trying to distract her with the menu. What would she eat? It was difficult to decide. She had just come from a party where she had eaten this and that; and was not hungry but perhaps she would have a little smoked salmon.

"Yakimov?" Harriet tried to sort that name out of her memory. "Which do you mean?"

"There, dining with Dobson. Haven't you met Dobson? Yakimov's the long, lean fellow, face like a camel. Not, I may say, that he's one for going long without a drink."

"I've seen him before. He came on our train."

This concentration of interest elsewhere was too much for Guy. Breaking through a new plaint from Sophie, he asked: "What are you talking about?"

"A man called Yakimov," said Inchcape. "Something of a *raconteur* and joker. There's a story about his painting the windows black."

Harriet asked: "Which windows? Why?"

"I've no idea. Being half Irish and half White Russian, he's said to have a peculiarly English sense of humour."

The three of them watched Yakimov, who, intent upon his food, was not recounting at that moment.

Petulantly Sophie broke in on them to ask: "What is a peculiarly English sense of humour?"

"A pleasant humour, I suppose," said Guy, "a good-humoured humour. Here a painful boot in the arse is called a Rumanian kick, and a dunt with the knee is called the English kick. That's the idea."

At the word 'arse' Sophie's face went blank, but only Harriet noticed it.

Guy said: "I'd like to meet Yakimov. Let's ask them over."

"Oh," Inchcape protested, "do we want Dobson here?"

Guy said: "I don't mind Dobson. He entered the diplomatic service so late in life, he is still reasonably human."

"An amateur diplomat, you might say. Drifted into the service after a rich and idle youth. I don't dislike him myself. If it costs him nothing, he'd as soon be pleasant as unpleasant."

Guy tore a sheet from a notebook and scribbled on it while Inchcape, having no part in the invitation, looked the other way. The note was taken by the waiter. Dobson wrote a line on it and sent it back.

"They're coming for coffee," said Guy.

"Ah!" Inchcape let his breath out and helped himself to wine.

Before retiring to bed that afternoon, Yakimov had sent to the station for his cases and handed most of his clothing over to the hotel valet.

Now, sauntering behind Dobson across the restaurant, his yellow waistcoat newly cleaned, the fine line of his check suit accentuated by skilful pressing, he had an air of elegance, even if rather eccentric elegance. When he reached the table to which he was being led, he smiled benignly upon it. After he had been introduced to the table, he picked up Harriet's hand, kissed it and said: "How delightful, when one has lived too long abroad, to meet an English beauty."

"I'm told you have a peculiarly English sense of humour," said Harriet.

"Dear me! Has poor Yaki's reputation preceded him?" Yakimov showed his gratification so simply, it dissipated Harriet's first suspicion of him – a suspicion based on nothing she could define. He repeated: "A peculiarly English sense of humour! I am flattered," and he looked to see if Dobson had overheard the tribute, but Dobson was talking to Guy. He said: "I was delighted to hear you chaps were back, but surprised they let you come." His nervous explosion of laughter softened his remark, but Inchcape's mouth turned down.

Dobson, who had walked trippingly, carrying himself so that his back line curved in at the waist and his front line curved out, was in young middle age, plump, dimpled, pink and white as a cupid. He was very bald but over his pate were pools of baby-soft fluff left by the receding hair.

Guy said: "I was ordered back here. The London office says we're in a reserved occupation."

"So you are," Dobson agreed, "but they don't think what a

worry it is for us chaps now having a lot of British nationals here without diplomatic protection." His laughter exploded again, joking and tolerant, but Inchcape was not amused.

He said: "I imagine that worry is part of your job."

Dobson jerked his head up, discomforted at being taken so seriously. He laughed again and Harriet understood why he seemed to Guy 'reasonably human'. This constant nervous laughter rippling over his occupational self-possession gave the impression he was more approachable than his kind. At the same time, she realised he was more than a little drunk. She decided he might be an easy acquaintance, but would not be easy to know.

Chairs were becoming scarce now. Guy had to tip the waiter before he would set out in search of more. When two arrived, Dobson lay on his as though about to slide off it, and stared at a slip of paper he held in his hand. It seemed so to bewilder him that Harriet looked over his shoulder. He was studying his dinner bill.

Yakimov placed his chair beside Harriet. To Sophie, on the other side of the table, the arrival of these newcomers was, apparently, an imposition scarcely to be borne.

Harriet said to Yakimov: "I saw you on the train at the frontier."

"Did you indeed!" Yakimov gave Harriet a wary look. "Not to tell a lie, dear girl, I was having a spot of bother. Over m'Hispano-Suiza. Papers not in order. Something to do with a permit. 'Fraid they impounded the poor old girl. Was just explaining to Dobbie here, that little frontier incident cleared me right out of the Ready."

"Where were you coming from?"

"Oh, here and there. Been touring around. Too far from base when trouble started, so came in to the nearest port. Times like these after all, a bloke can be useful anywhere. 'S'matter of fact, m'chance came this morning. Ra-ther an amusing story," he looked about him to gather in a larger audience and, seeing that Guy was ordering coffee for the party, he said: "How about a drop of brandy, dear boy?"

The waiter placed out some small brandy glasses. "Tell him to leave the bottle." Then, wriggling in his chair, trying to mould the seat more comfortably to his shape, he lifted his glass to Harriet, drained it and smacked his lips in an exaggerated play of appreciation. "Nourishment!" he said.

For a moment Harriet thought she saw in him an avidity, as though he would, if he could, absorb into his own person the substance of the earth; then he glanced at her. His eyes were guileless. Large, light green, drooping at the outer corners, they were flat-looking, seeming to have no more thickness than a lens and set, not in cavities, but on a flat area between brow and cheek.

He refilled his glass, obviously preparing to entertain the company. As Guy gazed expectantly at him, Sophie gazed at Guy. She plucked at his sleeve and whispered intimately: "There is so much I must tell you. I have many worries."

Guy, with a gesture, cut short these confidences, and Yakimov, unaware of the interruption, began: "This morning, coming down early, who should I see in the hall of the Athénée Palace but . . ."

Yakimov's normal voice was thin, sad and unvarying, the voice of a cultured Punchinello, but when he came to report McCann, it changed dramatically. As he reproduced McCann's gritty, demanding tones, he somehow imposed on his own delicate features the shield-shaped, monkey mug that must be McCann.

He told the whole story of his meeting with McCann, of the plight of the Poles outside the hotel, of the sleeping girl, the scarf that had been buried with the dead. Although he mentioned, apologetically, that he did not speak Polish, he produced the accent of the angry Pole.

Guy, in appreciation of this piece of theatre, murmured "Marvellous" and Yakimov gave him a pleased smile.

The others, though entertained, were disconcerted that such a story should be told like a funny anecdote, but when he opened his arms and said: "Think of it! Think of your poor old Yaki become an accredited war correspondent," his face expressed such comic humility at so unlikely a happening that they were suddenly won to him. Even Sophie's sullen mouth relaxed. He united them in the warmth of amusement and, at least for the time, they accepted him like a gift – their Yaki, their poor old Yaki. His height, his curious face, his thin body, his large, mild eyes, his voice and, above all, his humility – these were his components and they loved them.

Dobson had clearly heard the story before. Glancing up from the bill, he smiled at its effect. When the laughter had died down, Sophie, who had not laughed, took the floor with impressive seriousness: "It is not so difficult to be journalist, I think. I have been journalist. My paper was anti-fascist, so now things will be difficult for me. Perhaps the Nazis will come here. You understand?" As Yakimov blinked, appearing to understand nothing, she gave an aggravated little laugh: "You have heard of the Nazis, I suppose?"

"The Nasties, dear girl, that's what I call 'em," he giggled. "Don't know what went wrong with them. They seemed to start out all right, but they overdid it somehow. Nobody likes them now."

At this Inchcape gave a hoot of laughter. "The situation in a nut-shell," he said.

Sophie leant forward and gazed earnestly at Yakimov. "The Nazis are very bad men," she said. "Once I was in Berlin on holiday – you understand? – and a Nazi officer comes with big steps along the pavement. I think: 'I am a young lady, he will step aside for me', but no. Pouf! He brushes me as if I were not there and I am flung into the road with the traffic."

"Dear me!" said Yakimov.

As Sophie opened her mouth to talk on, Harriet broke in to ask Yakimov: "Are you the man who painted the windows black?"

"Why, yes, dear girl, that was poor Yaki."

"Won't you tell us the story?"

"Another time, perhaps. It's a trifle *outré* and happened long ago. Soon after m'schooldays, in fact."

Sophie, who had been watching Harriet sulkily, now smiled in triumph. Harriet realised, with surprise, that she saw this refusal as a point to her.

Harriet had failed to consider the possibility of a Sophie. Foolishly. There was always someone. There was also the fact that, whether Sophie had received encouragement or not, Guy's natural warmth towards everyone could easily be misinterpreted. She had herself taken it for granted that it was for her alone. (She had a sudden vivid memory of one of their early meetings when Guy had taken her claw of a hand and said: "You don't eat enough. You must come to Bucharest and let us feed you up.") They had slipped into marriage as though there could be no other possible resolution of such an encounter. Yet – supposing she had known him better? Supposing she had known him for a year and during that time observed him in all his other relationships? She would have hesitated, thinking the net of his affections too widely spread to hold the weighty accompaniment of marriage.

As it was, she had, in all innocence, been prepared to possess him and be possessed, to envelop and be enveloped, in a relationship that excluded the enemy world. She soon discovered that Guy was not playing his part. Through him, the world was not only admitted, it was welcomed; and, somehow, when he approached it, the enmity was no longer there.

"I imagine" – Inchcape was speaking to Yakimov, his ironical smile giving a grudging credit – "I imagine you were at Eton?"

"Alas, dear boy, no," said Yakimov. "M'poor old dad could not cough up. I went to one of those horrid schools where Marshall is beastly to Snelgrove, and Debenham *much* too fond of Freebody. But while we're on the subject, there's rather an amusing story about a croquet match played by the headmistress of a famous girls' school against the headmaster – an excessively corpulent man – of a very famous boys' school. Well . . ."

The story, vapid in itself, was made outrageously funny for his audience by the inflections of Yakimov's frail voice. Pausing on a word, speaking it slowly and with an accent of a slightly breathless disapproval, he started everyone, except Sophie, first into titters, then to a gradual crescendo of laughter. Sophie, her face glum, stared in turn at the reactions of the three male listeners – Guy saying "Oh dear!" and wiping his eyes, Inchcape with his head thrown back, and Dobson rocking in quiet enjoyment.

"But what sort of balls?" she asked when the story was over.

"Croquet balls," said Inchcape.

"Then I do not understand. Why is it funny?"

"Why," Inchcape blandly asked, "is anything funny?"

The answer did not satisfy Sophie. She said with some asperity: "That is an English joke, eh? Here in Rumania we have jokes, too. We ask 'What is the difference between a kitten and a bar of soap?' I think they are silly, such jokes."

"Well, what is the difference?" Guy asked.

Sophie gave him an irritated look and would not answer. He set about persuading her until at last she whispered in a petulant little voice: "If you put a kitten to the foot of a tree, it will climb up."

Her success surprised her. She looked around, suspicious at first, then, growing complacent, said: "I know many such jokes. We told them at school."

"Tell us some more," said Guy.

"Oh, they are so silly."

"No, they are very interesting." And after he had coaxed her to tell several more, all much alike, he began a dissertation on basic peasant humour, to which he related the riddles to be found in fairy-tales. He called on Yakimov to confirm his belief that Russian peasant tales were similar to all other peasant tales.

"I'm sure they are, dear boy," Yakimov murmured, his eyes vacant, his body inert, life extinct now, it seemed, except in the hand with which, every few minutes, he lifted the brandy bottle and topped up his glass.

Dobson, almost asleep, slid forward in his chair, then, half-waking, slid back again. Inchcape was listening to Guy, his smile fixed. It was late, but no one showed any inclination to move. The restaurant was still crowded, the orchestra played on, Florica was expected to sing again. Harriet, suddenly exhausted, wished she were in bed. Guy had told her that on hot summer nights the diners in these garden restaurants might linger on under the trees until dawn. This, however, was not a hot summer night. Gusts of autumnal chill came at intervals from outer darkness and hardened the summer air. Someone, earlier in the evening, had mentioned that the first snow had fallen on the peaks that rose north of the city. She hoped that discomfort, if nothing else, would soon set people moving.

She watched Yakimov drain the last of the bottle into the glass. He then began glancing about, his eyes regaining the luminous gleam of life. When a waiter approached, he made a minimal movement and closed his eyes at the bottle. It was whipped away and replaced at such speed, Harriet could only suppose Yakimov had over waiters the sort of magnetic power some people have over beast and birds. His glass newly filled, he sank back, prepared, Harriet feared, to stay here all night.

As for Guy, the evening's drinking had not touched on his energy. It had merely brought him to a garrulous euphoria in which discoveries were being made and flights taken into metaphysics and the moral sciences. Every few minutes, Sophie – happy and vivacious now – interrupted him possessively to explain what he was saying. Was it possible, Harriet wondered, that this talk was as fatuous as it seemed to her?

"One might say," Guy was saying, "that riddles are the most primitive form of humour: so primitive, they're scarcely humour at all, but a sort of magic."

Sophie burst in: "He means, like the sphinx and like the oracle. Oracles always spoke in riddles."

"Not the oracle at Delos," said Inchcape.

Sophie gave him a look of contempt. "The oracle was at Delphi," she said.

Inchcape shrugged and let it pass.

At midnight Florica came out to sing again. This time Guy was too absorbed in his own talk to notice her. Harriet looked towards Ionescu's table, but there was no one there. Florica, applauded with less vigour than before, departed and the orchestra strummed on.

Harriet yawned. Imagining she was accepting the situation indulgently, she watched Sophie and wondered: 'Is Guy really taken in by this feminine silliness? If I made all those grimaces and gestures as I talked, and interrupted and insisted on attention would he find it all attractive?' Almost in spite of herself, she said "I think we should go now."

Shocked by the suggestion, Guy said: "I'm sure no one wants to go yet."

"No, no," Sophie joined with him at once. "We do not go so soon."

Harriet said: "I'm tired."

"Tomorrow," said Sophie, "you have all day to sleep."

Inchcape stubbed his cigarette. "I would like an early night. I did not sleep much on the train."

"Well, let me finish this." Holding up his glass, which was full, Guy spoke in the tone of a child that begs to sit up ten minutes more.

Refilling his own glass, Yakimov said: "It's still very early, dear girl."

They sat another half-an-hour, Guy eking out his drink and trying to regain the rhythm of talk, but something was lost. An end-of-the-evening lameness was in the air. When, at last, they were agreed to go, there was still the business of finding the waiter.

Inchcape threw down a thousand-*lei* note and said: "That ought to cover me." Guy settled the rest.

They picked up a taxi in the Chaussée and started back. Sophie, whose flat was in the centre of the town, was dropped first. Guy descended with her and took her to her door where she talked at him urgently, holding to his arm. Leaving her, he called back to her: "We'll meet tomorrow."

Next Yakimov was taken to the Athénée Palace. Outside the hotel, he said: "Dear me, I'd almost forgotten. I'm bidden to a party in Princess Teodorescu's suite."

"Rather a late party," murmured Inchcape.

"An all-night party," Yakimov said.

Guy said: "When we find a flat, you must come to dinner with us."

"Delighted, dear boy," said Yakimov, who, as he struggled out of the taxi, was almost sitting on the step. Somehow he got down to the pavement and crossed it unsteadily. Pressing against the revolving doors, he waved back baby-fashion.

"I shall be interested," said Inchcape dryly, "to see what return you get for all this hospitality."

Reprovingly, Dobson spoke from his corner: "Yaki used to be famous for his parties."

"Oh, well," said Inchcape, "we'll see. Meanwhile, if you don't mind, I'd like to be dropped next."

The Pringles reached their room in silence, Harriet fearing complaint that she had broken up the party. A justified complaint. It was true she could sleep all day – and what did an hour or two matter in the face of eternity?

While she got into bed, Guy studied his face in the glass. He broke the silence to ask her: "Do you think I look like Oscar Wilde?"

"You do, a little."

He remained in front of the glass, distorting his face into the likeness of one famous film-star and another.

Harriet wondered if this was the moment to ask him about Sophie, and decided it was not. She said, instead:

"You're an incurable adolescent. Come to bed."

As he turned from the glass, he said with inebriated satisfaction: "Old Pringle's all right. Old Pringle's not a bad chap. Old Pringle's not a bad chap at all."

4

Yakimov found his dress clothes sponged, pressed and laid ready for him on his bed. When he changed, he put on one black shoe and one brown.

At the party someone would be sure to mention the fact that he was wearing odd shoes. He would then gaze down at his feet in surprise and say: "And do you know, dear boy, I have another pair at home exactly like these."

He believed this to be his most subtle party prank. He had not played it since dear old Dollie died, reserving it for those times when he was in the highest spirits. Now, so changed were his fortunes, he was ready for anything.

After he had dressed, he sat for a while re-reading a letter on which he was working. It was to his mother. In it he had already told her where he was to be found and had begged her to send his quarterly remittance as soon as possible. He was, he said, engaged on important voluntary war work, giving no details for fear she should be misled as to his need.

After a long reflective pause, he picked up his stub of pencil and added to please her: "Going tonight to Princess Teodorescu's bun-fight." Ordinarily the effort of one sentence would have brought him to a stop, but in his present mood his hand drove on. With some words written very large, some small, but all legible like the carefully written words of a child, he concluded: "All the best then, dear old girl, and keep your pecker up. Your Yaki is in the big times once again."

Filled with a sense of a task well done and pleasure ahead, he went down to meet Prince Hadjimoscos.

It had been for Yakimov a very satisfactory day. He was content, with a contentment he had ceased to experience since thrown penniless upon the world at Dollie's death. That afternoon, newly risen from his siesta, he had gone down to the hotel bar, the famous English Bar, where he had seen, as he hoped he might, someone he knew. This was an English journalist called Galpin.

Galpin, seeing Yakimov, had looked elsewhere. Unruffled, Yakimov had placed himself in view and said: "Why, hello, dear boy! We met last in Belgrade," then, before Galpin could reply, he added: "What are you drinking?" Whatever it was Galpin had been about to say, he now merely grunted and said: "Scotch."

Galpin was not alone. When Yakimov smiled around to ask what the others were drinking, they closed about him as an oyster closes about a pearl. He told the story of his encounter with Mc-Cann and received polite attention. "Think of it, dear boys," he said. "Your poor old Yaki become an accredited war correspondent!"

Galpin asked: "And did you get McCann's stuff out?"

"Naturally. Every word."

"Lucky for McCann," Galpin gazed glumly into his glass. It was empty.

Yakimov insisted on ordering a second round. The journalists accepted their drinks, then broke up to talk among themselves. They had been discussing the arrival in Bucharest of Mortimer Tufton, and now returned to the subject. Tufton, they said, had an instinct for coming events. When he arrived anywhere, the place became news. Yakimov was forgotten. He did not mind. He was happy that he could once again be a dispenser of hospitality. Having introduced himself as such, he might hope that in future no one would be actively rude to him.

Disgorged by the group, he came face to face with the local hangers-on of the bar that had been attracted over by the scent of Yakimov's largesse. They stared admiringly at him. He let them introduce themselves: Cici Palu, Count Ignotus Horvath and Prince Hadjimoscos. If there was in the smile with which he received them a trifle of condescension, it was very modest condescension. These, he knew, were his natural associates. He did not suppose they had any illusions about him, but it flattered him to be their patron. He ordered drinks for them. They all, as fashion required, took whisky, the most expensive drink in the bar. "After this," said Yakimov, "I must be on my way. I'm dining with my dear old friend Dobbie Dobson of the Legation."

At that the leader of the trio, Hadjimoscos, said: "I wonder, *mon cher Prince*, would you care to come to a little night party to be given by Princess Teodorescu in her hotel suite? There you will meet the true Rumanian aristocracy, as distinct from the politicians and parvenus that pretend to the *beau monde* these days. We are all so fond of the English."

"Dear boy," Yakimov beamed on him, "I would like nothing better."

The bar closed at midnight. Yakimov was to meet Hadjimoscos in the main room, where drinks were served while anyone remained to order them.

In the middle of the room, beneath the largest chandelier, were laid out on a table copies of every English newspaper of repute. Beside the table stood Hadjimoscos, drooping over a two-day-old copy of *The Times*. He was, Yakimov had discovered from Dobson, a last descendant of one of the Greek Phanariot families that had ruled and exploited Rumania under the Turks. He was small and slight; and had an appearance of limp softness as though his clothes contained not flesh and bone but cotton-wool. He wore very delicately made black kid slippers, on which he now slid soundlessly forward, putting out his small, white hands and placing one on each of Yakimov's hands. There they lay inert. In a small shallow voice he lisped: "How charming to see you again *cher Prince*." His face, though fretted over with fine lines like the face of an old woman, was still childish; his dark, small, mongoloid eyes were bloodshot; his skull showed waxen through the fine black strands of his hair.

The two men looked expectantly at one another, then Hadjimoscos turned his face aside, sighed and said: "I would so much like to offer you hospitality, but I find I have come without my wallet."

"Dear boy" – Yakimov suddenly remembered his position of power – "it is I who should offer it. What will you take?"

"Oh, whisky, of course. I never touch anything else."

They sat themselves on one of the tapestry sofas and Yakimov gave his order. Hadjimoscos, his head hanging as though he were confiding some disgraceful secret, said: "It is most awkward, my forgetting my money. The Princess is likely to start a table of *chemin* or some such play. I am devoted to play. Could you, *mon cher Prince*, lend me a few thousand?"

Yakimov fixed him with a concerned and regretful gaze:

"Would that I could, dear boy, but your poor old Yaki is living on tick at the moment. Currency regulations, y'know. Couldn't bring a *leu* with me. Waiting for m'remittance from m'poor old ma."

"Oh, la la!" Hadjimoscos shook his head and drained his glass. "In that case we may as well go up to the party."

The lift took them to the top floor of the hotel. A hotel servant stood on the landing to conduct the guests to Princess Teodorescu's drawing-room. On the way up, Hadjimoscos had remained silent: now, when Yakimov, bemused by the heat of the room and the reek of tuberoses, tried to take his arm, he eluded him. Yakimov came to a stop inside the doorway. The evening's drinking had blurred his vision. It seemed to him that the room, lit by black and gilded candles, stretched away in a funereal infinity. The floor looked a void, although it felt solid enough when tested with the foot. Realising that he trod a black carpet, that walls and ceilings were lost to view because painted black, he gained enough confidence to move forward. He saw Hadjimoscos in the centre of the room and, taking what looked like a short cut, he stumbled over a black velvet arm-chair. As he went down, several of the women guests drew attention to his fall by giving little artificial screams of alarm. He heard a voice cry ecstatically: "Hadji, *chéri*," and saw a head and neck floating in the air. The neck was strained forward, so that the sinews were visible. The face looked ravaged, not from age, but from a habit of unrelenting vivacity.

Hadjimoscos whispered savagely: "The Princess."

Yakimov picked himself up and was introduced.

"*Enchantée, enchantée*," cried the Princess. Something waved in front of Yakimov's face. Realising he was being offered a hand in a black velvet glove, he tried to seize and kiss it, but it was snatched away. Another guest had arrived.

Yakimov turned to speak, but Hadjimoscos was no longer there. Left un-anchored in the middle of the room, Yakimov peered about in search of a drink. As his eyes grew accustomed to the gloom he picked out small pieces of gilt furniture, but of the other guests he could see only faces and hands. He was reminded of Dollie's séances where ectoplasm had oozed out between the black curtains of the medium's cabinet.

He began to feel tired and befuddled. Cautiously he essayed out a little, feeling his way from one piece of furniture to another until he came upon a waiter carrying a tray. He sniffed at the glasses. He was about to take a whisky, when he was distracted by the larger glasses. "Ah, champers, dear boy," he said, "champers for me."

Smiling again, he moved cautiously about. Hadjimoscos was talking to two pretty girls. Approaching them, Yakimov heard Hadjimoscos say: "Think of it: one black shoe and one brown! I noticed them in the lift."

The younger girl gave a yelp. The other said: "*Les Anglais! Ils sont toujours sâouls.*"

Hadjimoscos's face, that had been agleam with mischief, straightened at the sight of Yakimov and assumed an enchanted smile. "Ah, there you are, *mon cher.*" He pressed Yakimov's arm. "Allow me to present you to my charming friends, Princess Mimi and Princess Lulie. Surnames do not matter."

Mimi, the younger girl, was very pretty in a babyish way. The other was sallow and drawn: her smile, that came reluctantly, was slight and did not linger long. They let him kiss their hands, then stood silent, examining him.

Hadjimoscos, still gripping Yakimov's arm, spoke effusively: "I was just saying, we must – a little later of course, when we are in the mood – play a delicious game called Snow White and the Seven Dwarfs. *Mon cher*, I *insist* that you be a dwarf."

"Not much good at games, dear boy."

"This is no ordinary game. We invented it ourselves. We choose an attractive girl – Mimi, say, or Lulie – and she is Snow White. Then we choose seven men to be the dwarfs. They leave the room and take off all their clothes. Inside the room, Snow White takes off hers. Then one at a time, the dwarfs enter and are confronted by Snow White. According to the reaction of each, so we name them – Happy, Sneezy, Grumpy and so on."

"And Dopey," Mimi cried, then clapped her hand over her mouth.

"Now promise me" – Hadjimoscos gave Yakimov's arm another squeeze – "*promise* me you will be a dwarf!"

Yakimov stepped back nervously. "Not me, dear boy. I'm no good at that sort of thing."

"How sad for you." Hadjimoscos spoke gravely, then, releasing Yakimov and excusing himself, he trotted off on his soft shoes to where Princess Teodorescu sat on a sofa embracing a young man with a large red moustache. Above the other noises of the room, Yakimov heard Hadjimoscos's whisper: "He said: 'I'm no good at that sort of thing'. " Yakimov was not disturbed. He was used to being quoted.

Suddenly Mimi, like a little clockwork doll that had been wound up, began chattering in French. Yakimov spoke French as well as he spoke English, but this Rumanian French confused him. He gathered she was speaking of a man who stood a few yards distant, a Baron Steinfeld, who was, it seemed, paying the rent of the apartment. Despite this, the Princess was devoting herself to a certain 'Foxy' Leverett, while the Baron was "*complètement* 'outsider'." As the girls bent together, Yakimov made off, thankful they were laughing at someone other than himself.

His move brought him to the Baron, who, showing all his large yellow teeth, greeted him courteously. Yakimov introduced himself.

"Ah, my dear Prince," said the Baron, "needless to say, I have heard of you. A great name. Was not your father equerry to the Czar?"

"Not to tell a lie, dear boy, *he was*." But even as Yakimov spoke he regretted what he said. The Baron had so eagerly awaited his reply, he feared it might be a trick question. He might be denounced to the party as an impostor. But the Baron, whose handsome high-coloured face was fixed in its eager smile, merely asked: "Are you an old friend of the Princess?"

"We met for the first time tonight. Hadjimoscos brought me."

"Ah!" Steinfeld nodded, then went on to speak, with relish and respect, of the Princess's ancient lineage: "She is descended from Dacian kings," he said. "She can trace a direct descent from Decebal, who defeated the Romans."

"Can she, indeed, dear boy?" Yakimov did his best to attend to Steinfeld while keeping his eye open for a waiter to refill his glass.

"The Teodorescu estates in Moldavia were once very fine, but now? Mortgaged and frittered away! Frittered away! These Princes, they think they can live in Paris or Rome and their lands will thrive without them. So feckless, yet so charming!" The Baron moved closer. "Now, my own little estate in Bessarabia is very well husbanded. We Germans, perhaps not so charming but, we understand to work. On my estate I make my own red wine, white wine, *tuică* and martini. The martini you can see in the shops. The King sells it in his own grocery store: Martini Steinfeld. It is excellent."

Yakimov, making an effort at approbation, said: "I suppose you make it from Italian recipes?"

"But naturally," said the Baron, "from raisins and recipes and herbs and all such things." As the Baron drew breath and started to talk again, Yakimov said: "Must get another, dear boy," and, ducking away, found himself in an ante-room where a buffet table stood laden with food.

The food was untouched, no invitation to eat having yet been given. Transfixed like one who has stumbled upon treasure, Yakimov murmured to himself: "*Dear boy!*" There was not even the presence of a waiter to curb his appetite.

He saw a row of roasted turkeys with breasts ready sliced, two gammons baked with brown sugar and pineapple, crayfish, salmon coated with mayonnaise, several sorts of paté, three sorts of caviare, many aspic dishes, candied fruits, elaborate puddings, bunches of hot-house grapes, pineapples and autumn raspberries, all set on silver plates and decorated with white catleyas.

Trembling like a man in dire hunger, Yakimov darted forward. He stuck a table-spoon into the fresh caviare, brought it out full and licked it clean. He decided he preferred the saltier variety to which he was used, and of this he took three spoonfuls. While he held some turkey slices in one hand, eating them like bread, he piled up a plate with salmon mayonnaise, quails in aspic, paté and creamed chicken, putting into his mouth as he went along oddments of anchovies, olives and sweets. When the plate would hold no more, he ate ravenously. About to set upon the puddings, he was interrupted by a step – a very light step. He stared guiltily, Hadjimoscos was at his elbow.

"Felt a trifle peckish," said Yakimov.

"Please!" Hadjimoscos smiled, making a gesture towards the food, but Yakimov felt it seemly to say:

"Thanks, dear boy, had about enough." Regretfully he put aside his plate.

"Then come back to the party. We are going to play baccarat. Everyone will be playing. There will be two tables, at least. *Do* come. We would not have you feel neglected."

At the word 'baccarat' there came down on Yakimov memory of the boredom he had suffered in the casinos to which Dollie used to drag him. He said: "Don't worry about me, dear boy. I'm quite happy here." He noticed some tiny pies standing on a hot-plate and, unable to control his longing, snatched one up and swallowed it. A scalding interior of mushrooms in cheese sauce poured into his throat. His eyes streamed.

Hadjimoscos's laugh was a hiss, his lips widened to disclose his white, small, unconvincing teeth. For a second he looked as vicious as a little puma, but he was all persuasion as he said: "The Princess is mad about play. She would never forgive me if I failed to include you."

"As I told you, dear boy, your old Yaki hasn't a *leu*. Cleaned out till m'remittance arrives."

"No one," said Hadjimoscos, "would refuse your IOU."

"Scarcely know how to play," said Yakimov.

"To learn is the matter of a moment."

Sighing, Yakimov gave a farewell glance at the buffet and, for the first time, noticed it was overhung by a portrait of an old boyar – no doubt some member of the great Teodorescu family. The boyar wore a fur turban of enormous size and a brocaded tunic beneath a mantle of fur. A pair of hands, white and delicate, rested on an embroidered cummerband, one thumb curled round the hilt of a heavily bejewelled dagger.

Yakimov was abashed, not by these accoutrements of wealth but by the face they surrounded – the long, corpse-pale nose and cheeks, the lips with their tattered fringe of beard, the heavy eye-lids beneath which a thread of iris peered malevolently.

He let himself be led away.

The lights had been switched on over two oval tables. A servant was shuffling the packs. A dozen or so people sat at one table and a few others stood about behind the chairs. Yakimov could see no rush to join in the play. The Princess and the red-haired 'Foxy' Leverett remained in an embrace on the sofa. Other couples were lying about in shadowed corners. The Baron, still grinning, stood at the table, but at such a distance that it was clear he did not intend to be drawn in.

Hadjimoscos, who had made another trip over to the Princess, returned with a bundle of notes. Their hostess, he announced, had a headache, so he would take the bank on her behalf. The bank was for 200,000 *lei*. He gave Yakimov a smile: "You see, *mon cher*, our game is modest. You cannot lose much. How many counters will you take?"

Yakimov, knowing the croupier received five per cent on the bank, made a wild bid to escape: "You'll need a croupier, dear boy. Why not let your poor old Yaki . . ."

"I am croupier," said Hadjimoscos. "It is the tradition here. Come now, how many chips?"

Resignedly Yakimov replied: "Give me a couple of thou."

Hadjimoscos laughed: "Each piece is for five thousand. We do not play for less."

Yakimov accepted five counters and handed over his receipt for twenty-five thousand *lei*. Hadjimoscos took his place before the shoe. As soon as he had drawn the cards, he became serious and businesslike. At first the game went much as Yakimov had expected, with the bank increasing steadily and an occasional win for the player on the right. Yakimov, on the left, frequently let his right to play pass on his neighbour. Despite this, he had lost twenty thousand *lei* in ten minutes. He was resigned to losing all his chips, but with his last five thousand he turned over a seven and a two. At the next *coup*, Hadjimoscos said: "I give." The player on the right held a king and a queen: Yakimov held a six and a two. When his next hand proved to be a nine and a ten, the punters began to bet on the left and Yakimov began to regain himself. He was even winning at baccarat: something he had never done before. He used his winnings to increase his bets.

As Yakimov's pile of chips grew, Hadjimoscos's manner became increasingly sharp and cold. He dealt with great speed and he brushed Yakimov's gains towards him in a disapproving way. Hadjimoscos's face, that ordinarily was as round as the face of a Japanese doll, lengthened and thinned until it might have been the face of the boyar portrayed above the supper buffet. Suddenly, he lifted the shoe and slapped it down again. With no trace of his usual lisp, he announced the bank was broken.

"I'll have to see the Princess," he said and hurried away. He returned to say the Princess had refused to replenish the bank. He went to the Baron's elbow and said: "*Mon cher Baron*, I appeal to you."

With an affable flash of teeth, the Baron replied: "Surely you know I never lend money." 'No wonder,' thought Yakimov, the Baron was "*complètement* 'outsider'."

Hadjimoscos began to appeal elsewhere, while Yakimov, his chips on the table, wished only that he could change them and go. Having little hope of this, he sat on. A withered little man, whose hands had trembled so, he could scarcely pick up his cards, now moved stealthily round the table and murmured to Yakimov: "*Cher Prince*, surely you remember me? I am Ignotus Horvath. We met in the English Bar. I wonder . . ." Horvath's hand, dark and dry as an old twig, hovered near Yakimov's chips. "A little loan. A mere ten thousand would do."

Yakimov passed them over, then heard a murmur at his other side. Turning warily, he met the black, astute gaze of a woman, lean with age, who leant towards him, attempting a charm that did not come easily to her. "I have had such misfortune . . ." she was beginning, when Hadjimoscos caught Yakimov's arm and gave him excuse to turn away.

Hadjimoscos said: "I deeply regret, *mon cher*. I must appeal to you."

Yakimov was prepared for this. "I am willing to take the bank," he said.

"Impossible," Hadjimoscos looked shocked. "The Princess is always the banker."

Realising he would be as likely to lose them by playing as by lending them, Yakimov handed over his winnings. He said: "Think I'll take a breather," and no one hindered him.

A waiter was carrying round glasses of wine. Yakimov asked for whisky but there was none. The drink was running out. This, he knew, was the time to go, but he was now so weary he could scarcely face the descent to his room. He decided to revive himself with one more drink. He took his glass to a sofa, settled down comfortably, and when the glass was empty, fell asleep.

Some time in the middle of the night he was violently wakened. Half a dozen people, Hadjimoscos among them, were pulling at him. When he was on his feet, they began to rip off his clothes. Bewildered, frightened and still half-asleep, he saw – scarcely believing he saw – that all the guests were naked and shunting each other in a circle round the room. Handled in a frenzied fashion, he looked about for aid. Perhaps 'Foxy' Leverett, a fellow Englishman, would rescue him – but Leverett was nowhere to be seen.

When they had exposed and laughed at his long, fragile body, his assailants rejoined the circle and pulled him into it. With the woman behind thumping his buttocks and the woman in front complaining of his lack of enterprise, he spent the rest of the night trudging dismally round, dressed in nothing but his socks and one black shoe and one brown.

5

IN FRONT OF THE UNIVERSITY STEPS, where Harriet waited at noon next day, the gypsies were conducting their flower-market. The baskets were packed as high as hay-cocks with the stiff, tall flowers of the season. Among all this splendour of canna lilies, gladioli, chrysanthemums, dahlias and tuberoses, the gypsies, perched like tropical birds, screeched at the passers-by *"Hey, hey, hey, domnule! Frumosă. Foarte frumosă.* Two hundred *lei* . . . for you, for you, only one fifty! For you, only one hundred. For you, only fifty . . ."* As the passers-by went on, unheeding, the cry followed, long-drawn, despairing as a train-whistle in the night: *"Domnule . . . domnule!"* to be plucked back with new vitality as a newcomer drew near. The bargaining, when it started, was shrill, fierce and dramatic. If a customer chose, as a last resort, to walk away, the gypsy would usually follow, looking, among the pigeon-shaped women on the pavement, long, lean and flashy, like a flamingo or a crane.

The gypsy women all trailed about in old evening dresses picked up from second-hand stalls down by the river. They loved flounced and floating chiffons. They loved colour. With their pinks and violets, purples and greens, their long, wild hair, and shameless laughter, they seemed to have formed themselves in defiant opposition to the ideals of the Rumanian middle class.

While watching the traffic of the gypsies, Harriet saw Sophie arrive among them and start bargaining sharply at one of the smaller baskets. When the deal was completed, she mounted the University steps, pinning one bunch of parma violets into the belt of her dress and another into her bosom. She started an animated waving, and Harriet, standing aside and unseen, looked and saw that Guy had appeared in the doorway. Sophie hurried to him, calling: "I say to myself I shall find you here, and I find you. Is it not like old times?" Her grievance, whatever it was, and the war – both were forgotten.

Guy, seeing Harriet, said: "Here's Harriet." It was a mere

statement of fact but Sophie chose to take it as a warning. She gasped, put a finger to her lip, looked for Harriet and, finding where she was, took on an air of elaborate unconcern. As Harriet joined them, Sophie gave Guy a consoling smile. He must not, said the smile, blame himself for the mishap of his wife's presence.

She said: "You go for luncheon, yes?"

"We were going to walk in the Cişmigiu," said Guy. "We might eat there."

"Oh, no," Sophie cried. "The Cişmigiu is not nice in this heat. And the café is too poor, too cheap."

Guy turned doubtfully to Harriet, looking to her to change their plans, but Harriet merely smiled. "I'm looking forward to seeing the park," she said.

"Won't you come with us?" Guy asked Sophie. When she complained that she could not, the sun was too much, she might get a headache, he took her hand consolingly and said: "Then let us meet for dinner tomorrow night. We'll go to Capşa's."

As they crossed the road to the park gates, Harriet said to Guy: "We cannot afford to go to expensive restaurants every night."

"We do so well on the black market," he said, "we can afford Capşa's once in a while."

Harriet wondered if he had any idea of what he could, or could not, afford on a salary of two hundred and fifty pounds a year.

A peasant had brought a handcart laden with melons into the town and tipped them out at the park gates. He lay among them, sleeping, his arms crossed over his eyes. The melons were of all sizes, the smallest no bigger than a tennis ball. Harriet said: "I've never seen so many before."

"That is Rumania," said Guy.

Repelled by their profusion, she had an odd fancy that, gathered there in a flashing mass of yellow and gold, the melons were not really inert, but hiding a pullulating craftiness that might, if unchecked, one day take over the world.

The peasant, hearing voices, roused himself and offered them the biggest melon for fifty *lei*. Guy was not willing to carry it about so they went on, passing out of the aura of melon scent into the earthy scent of the park. Guy led Harriet down a side-path that was overhung by a block of flats and pointing up to the first floor, that had a terrace before it, he said: "Inchcape lives there."

Enviously, Harriet saw on the terrace some wrought-iron chairs, a stone urn, a trail of pink ivy geranium, and asked: "Does he live alone?"

"Yes, except for his servant, Pauli."

"Will we be invited there?"

"Some time. He does not entertain much."

"He's an odd man," she said. "That edgy vanity! – what is behind it? What does he do with himself alone there? I feel there's something secret about him."

Guy said: "He leads his life, as we all do. What do you care what he does?"

"Naturally I'm interested."

"Why be interested in people's private lives? What they are pleased to let us know should be enough for us."

"Well, I just am. You're interested in ideas; I in people. If you were more interested in people, you might not like them so much."

Guy did not reply. Harriet supposed he was reflecting on the logic of her statement, but when he spoke she realised he had not given it a thought. He told her the Cişmigiu had once been the private garden of a Turkish water-inspector.

Brilliantly illuminated on spring and summer nights, it had a dramatic beauty. The peasants who came to town in search of justice or work saw the park as a refuge. They slept here through the siesta. They would stand about for hours gazing at the *tapis vert*, the fountain, the lake, the peacocks and the ancient trees. A rumour often went round that the King intended to take it all from them. It was discussed with bitterness.

"Will he take it?" Harriet asked.

"I don't think so. There's nothing in it for him. It is just that people have come to expect the worst from him."

In the last heat of the year, the greenery looked coarse and autumnal beneath a dust of light. The air was still. Noon weighed on everything. The great *tapis vert*, with its surround of leaf-hung poles and swags, its border of canna lilies and low bands of box, looked as unreal as some stage backdrop faded with age. A few groups of peasants stood about as Guy had described, but most of them had folded themselves into patches of shade and slept, faces hidden from the intolerable sun.

Everything seemed to give off heat. Harriet half expected the canna lilies, in great beds of sulphur, cadmium and red, to roar like a furnace. She stopped at the dahlias. Guy adjusted his glasses and examined the flowers, which were massive, spiked, furry, lion-faced, burgundy-coloured, purple and white, cinderous, heavy as velvet.

"Fine," he said at length.

She laughed at him and said: "They're like the invention of some ghastly interior decorator."

"Really!" Accepting the visible world because he so seldom looked at it, Guy was at first startled, then delighted, by this criticism of nature.

They followed a path that branched down to the lakeside. The water, glassy still, stretched out of sight beneath the heavy foliage of the lake-fed trees. The path ended beside a little thicket of chestnuts beneath which a small, derelict summer-house made a centre for commerce. Here the peasant who had any sort of stock-in-trade might begin a lifelong struggle up into the tradesman's class. One boy had covered a box with pink paper and laid out on it, like chessmen on a board, pieces of Turkish delight. There were not more than twenty pieces. If he sold them, he might be able to buy twenty-two. With each piece, the purchaser was given a glass of water.

"One eats," said Guy, "for the pleasure of drinking."

A man stood nearby with a weighing-machine. Another had a hooded camera where photographs could be obtained to stick on passports, or on the permits needed to work, to own a cart, to keep a stall, to sojourn in one town or journey to another.

At the appearance of the Pringles, some of the peasants lying on the ground picked themselves up and adjusted trays from which they sold sesame cakes, pretzels, matches and other oddments, and peanuts for the pigeons. Harriet bought some peanuts, and the pigeons, watching, came fluttering down from the trees to eat them. She was watched by some peasants standing near, whose eyes were shy and distrustful of the life about them. Newly arrived in the city, the men were still in tight frieze trousers, short jackets and pointed caps – a style of dress that dated back to Roman times. The women wore embroidered blouses and fan-pleated skirts of colours that were richer and more subtle than those worn by the gypsies. As soon as they could afford it, they would throw off these tokens of their simplicity and rig themselves out in city drab.

Three girls, resplendent in sugar-pinks, plum-reds and the green of old bottle glass, were posing for a photograph. They might have been dressed for a fair or a festival, but they drooped together as though sold into slavery. Seeing the Pringles watching them, the girls looked uneasily away.

As they passed among the peasants, Guy and Harriet smiled to reassure them, but their smiles grew strained as they breathed-in the peasant stench. Harriet thought: 'The trouble with prejudice is, there's usually a reason for it,' but she now knew better than to say this to Guy.

The path through the thicket led to the lake café, which was situated on a pier built out into the water. On this flimsy, shabby structure stood rough chairs and tables with paper tablecloths. The boards creaked and flexed when anyone walked across them. Just below, visible between the boards, was the dark and dirty lake water.

The Pringles, seated in the sun, breathed air that was warm and heavy with the smell of water-weed. The trees on the distant banks were faded into the heat blur. An occasional rowing-boat ruffled the lake surface and sent the water clopping against the café piers. A waiter came running, producing from an inner pocket a greasy, food-splashed card. The menu was short. Few people ate here. This was a place where the city workers came in the cool of evening to drink wine or ţuică. Guy ordered omelettes. When the waiter went to the hut that served as a kitchen, he switched on the wireless in honour of the foreigners. A loud-speaker over the door gave out waltz music.

The café was, as Sophie had said, poor enough, but it had its pretensions. A notice said that persons wearing peasant dress would not be served. The peasants outside, whether they could read or not, made no attempt to cross on to the pier. With the humility of dogs, they knew it was no place for them.

There were a few other customers, all men. Stout and hot-looking in their dark town suits, they sat near the kitchen where there was shade from the chestnut trees.

Guy, exposed out in the strong sunlight, took off his jacket, rolled up his shirt-sleeves and stretched his brown arms on the table so that they might get browner. He stretched his legs out lazily and gazed round him at the tranquil water, the tranquil sky, the non-belligerent world. For some time they sat silent listening to the music, the lap from the rowing-boats and the ping of chestnuts dropping on to the kitchen's iron roof.

"Where is the war now?" Harriet asked.

"As the crow flies, about three hundred miles away. When we go home at Christmas . . ."

"Do you really think we will?" She could not believe it, Christmas brought to her mind a scene, tiny and far away like a snowstorm in a globe. Somewhere within it was 'home' – anyway, England. Home for her was no more defined than that. The aunt who had brought her up was dead.

"If we could save enough, we could go by air."

She said: "We shall certainly have to save if we're ever to have a home of our own."

"I suppose so."

"And we can't save if we're going to eat all the time at expensive restaurants."

Guy looked away at this unwelcome conclusion and asked if she knew the name of the piece they were playing on the wireless.

"A waltz. Darling, we'll . . ."

He caught her hand and pinned it down. "No, listen," he insisted as though she were trying to deflect him from an enquiry of importance. "Where have I heard it before?"

"All over the place. I want to know about Sophie."

Guy said nothing, but looked resigned.

Harriet said: "Last night she said she was depressed because of the war. Was it only because of the war?"

"I suppose so."

"Nothing to do with your getting married?"

"Oh, no. *No*. She'd given up that idea ages ago."

"She once had that idea, then?"

"Well," Guy spoke in an off-hand way, perhaps to hide discomfort. "Her mother was Jewish, and she worked on this anti-fascist magazine . . ."

"You mean she wanted a British passport."

"It was understandable. I felt sorry for her. And, don't forget, I didn't know you then. Two or three of my friends married German anti-fascists to get them out of Germany and . . ."

"But they were homosexual. It was just an arrangement. The couples separated outside the registry office. You would have been landed with Sophie for life."

"She said we could get divorced straight away."

"And you believed her? You must be mad."

Guy gave a discomforted laugh: "As a matter of fact, I didn't really believe her."

"But you let her try and persuade you. You might have given in if you hadn't met me? Isn't that it?" She watched him as though he had changed before her eyes into a different person. "If anyone had asked me before I married, I would have said I was marrying the rock of ages. Now I realise you are capable of absolute lunacy."

"Oh, come, darling," Guy protested, "I didn't want to marry Sophie, but one has to be polite. What would you have done under the circumstances?"

"Said 'No' straight away. One doesn't complicate one's life unnecessarily. But she would never have tried it on with me. Knowing I was not susceptible, she disliked me on sight. With you, of course, she thinks she can get away with anything."

"Darling, don't be so harsh. She's an intelligent girl. She can speak half a dozen languages . . ."

"Did you lend her any money?"

"Well, yes. A few thousand."

"Did she pay it back?"

"Well – she didn't regard it as a loan."

Harriet enquired no further but said only: "I don't want to see her every night."

Guy stretched across the table and squeezed Harriet's arm. "Darling," he said, "she's sad and lonely. You can afford to be kind to her."

Half-heartedly, Harriet said: "I suppose I can," and let the matter drop.

They had eaten their omelettes and were waiting for coffee, when Harriet noticed two beggar children who had climbed up on the pier from the lake and were keeping out of the waiter's sight. The older child came crawling under the tables until it reached the Pringles, then it stood up, ragged, wet and dirty, thin as a gnat, and clutching the edge of the table with its bird-small hand, began the chant of "*Mi-e foame*".

Guy handed over his small coins. The child scuttled off and at once its place was taken by the younger child, who, hopping from one foot to the other, eyes on a level with the table-top, kept up, in a sing-song, what seemed to be a long, unintelligible story.

Having no more change, Guy waved it away. It flinched from his movement as from a blow, but, recovering at once, went on with its rigmarole. Harriet offered it a piece of bread, then an olive, then a piece of cheese. These offerings were ignored, but the whine went on.

After some minutes of this, Harriet, irritated, hunted through her bag and found an English sixpence. The child snatched it and ran. They had returned to the quiet that came of being surrounded not by land but water, when the music stopped abruptly. The silence was suddenly so dense that Harriet looked round, expecting something. At that moment a voice broke shrilly from the loud-speaker.

The men near the kitchen sat up. One jumped to his feet. A chair fell. The voice spoke again. The waiter came from the kitchen. Behind him, in singlet and trousers, very dirty, came the cook. The man who had jumped up started shouting. The waiter shouted back.

"Is it the invasion?" asked Harriet.

Guy shook his head. "It was something to do with Călinescu."

"Who is Călinescu?"

"The Prime Minister."

"Why is everyone so excited? What did the announcer say?"

"I don't know."

Taking advantage of the distraction, the elder beggar boy had come up under the very nose of the waiter and was now begging urgently, time being short. The waiter went to the rail and shouted down to a man who hired rowing-boats. The man shouted back.

"He says," said Guy, "that Călinescu has been shot. They announced that he is either dead or dying. We must go to the English Bar. That's where you get all the news."

They left the park by a side gate where a statue of a disgraced politician stood with its head hidden in a linen bag. Hurrying through the back streets, they came into the main square as the newsboys were calling a special edition of the papers. People were thrusting each other aside to seize them, and when they had read a line were throwing the papers away. The square was already littered with sheets that stirred slightly in the hot breeze.

Guy, pushing his paper under his arm, told Harriet: "He was assassinated in the Chicken Market."

As he spoke, a man standing nearby turned sharply and said in

English: "They say the Iron Guard is wiped out. Now such a thing happens! It can mean anything. You understand that? It can mean anything."

"What can it mean?" Harriet asked as Guy hurried her across the square.

"That the Germans are up to something, I suppose. We'll hear everything in the bar."

But the English Bar, with its dark panelling and palms in brass pots, was dismally empty. The hard shafts of sunlight falling in from high-set windows made the place look like cardboard. There must have been a crowd in recently because the air was heavy with cigarette smoke.

Guy spoke to the barman, Albu, a despondent, sober fellow regarded in Bucharest as a perfect imitation of an English barman. Where was everyone? Guy asked.

Albu said: "Gone to send news."

Guy, frowning with frustration, asked Harriet what she would drink. "We'll wait," he said. "They're sure to come back. This is the centre of information."

6

In an upper room of the hotel, Yakimov was roused to reluctant consciousness by the squawks of the newsboys in the square.

The day before, when he handed his British passport to the clerk, he had been asked if he wished to be awakened in the 'English manner' with a cup of tea. He had replied that he did not wish to be awakened at all but would like a half-bottle of Veuve Clicquot placed beside his bed each morning. Now, getting his eyes open, he saw the bucket and was thankful for it.

An hour or so later, having bathed, dressed and been served with a little cold chicken in his room, he made his way down to the bar. The bar was now crowded. Yakimov ordered a whisky, swallowed it and ordered another. When the drinks had steadied him a little, he turned slowly and looked at the group behind him.

The journalists were standing around Mortimer Tufton, who sat on the edge of a stool, his old, brown spotted hands clenched on the handle of his stick.

Galpin, noticing Yakimov, asked: "Any news?"

"Well, dear boy, it was quite a party."

"I'll say it was," said Galpin. "One hell of a party. And the old formula, of course: someone inside creates a disturbance and the bastards march in to keep order."

Yakimov stared at Galpin some moments before comment came to him, then he said: "Quite, dear boy, quite."

"I give them twenty-four hours." Galpin, sprawled with his back against the bar, was a string of a man in a suit that seemed too small for him. He had a peevish, nasal voice and, as he talked, he rubbed at his peevish yellow, whisky-drinker's face. Over his caved-in belly, his waistcoat was wrinkled, dirty and ash-spattered. There was a black edging of grease round his cuffs; his collar was corrugated round his neck. He sucked the wet stub of a cigarette. When he talked the stub stuck to his full, loose lower lip and quivered there. His eyes, that he now kept fixed on Yakimov, were chocolate-coloured, the whites as yellow as limes. He repeated: "Twenty-four hours. You wait and see," his tone aggressive.

Yakimov did not contradict him.

He was bewildered, not only by Galpin's remarks, but by the atmosphere in the bar. It was an atmosphere of acute discontent.

In a high, indignant voice, Galpin suddenly said to Yakimov: "You heard about Miller of the *Echo*, I suppose?"

Yakimov shook his head.

"As soon as it happened, he got into his car and drove straight to Giurgiu. He may have got across, and he may not, but he's not stuck here like a rat in a trap."

Galpin was clearly speaking not for Yakimov's enlightenment but from a heart full of bitterness. Letting his eyes stray about, Yakimov noticed the young couple called Pringle whom he had met the night before. There was something reassuring about Guy Pringle's size and the mildness of his bespectacled face. Yakimov edged nearer to him and heard him say: "I still don't see how the Germans will get here. The Russians have moved into Eastern Poland. They've reached the Hungarian frontier."

"My good chappie" – Galpin turned, expressing his bitterness in contempt – "the Nazis will go through the Russkies like a hot knife through butter."

Guy put an arm round his wife's shoulder and looked into her strained, peaky face. "Don't worry," he said to her, "I think we're safe."

A small man, grey-haired, grey-faced, grey-clad, more shadow than substance, entered the bar and, skirting apologetically round the journalists, handed Galpin a telegram and whispered to him. When the man had gone, Galpin said: "My stringman reports: German Embassy claims to have proof the murder was organised by the British Minister in order to undermine Rumania's neutrality. That gets a laugh." He opened and read the telegram and said: "So does this: '*Echo* reports assassination stop why unnews stop asleep query.' So Miller made it! Nice scoop for Miller! And a raspberry for the rest of us."

Tufton said: "There's safety in numbers. We couldn't all be flogging the dog."

Under cover of this talk, Yakimov whispered to Guy: "Dear boy, what *has* happened? Who's been assassinated?"

It so happened this whisper came out during a moment of silence and Galpin caught it. He turned to Yakimov, demanding in scandalised tones: "You mean to say, you didn't know what I was talking about?"

Yakimov shook his head.

"You hadn't heard of the assassination? You didn't know the frontier's closed, the international line is dead, they won't let us send cables, and no one's allowed to leave Bucharest? You don't know, my good chappie, that you're in mortal danger?"

"You don't say!" said Yakimov. Stealthily he glanced around for sympathy but was offered none. Trying to show interest, he asked: "Who assassinated who?"

The journalists made no attempt to reply. It was Guy who told him that the Prime Minister had been assassinated in the Chicken Market. "Some young men drove in front of his car, forcing him to stop. When he got out to see what was wrong, they shot him down. He was killed instantly. Then the assassins rushed to the broadcasting studios, held up the staff and announced he was dead, or dying. They didn't know which."

"Filled him full of lead," Galpin broke in. "He clung to the car door - little pink hands, striped trousers, little new patent-leather shoes. Then he slid down. Patches of dust on the side of his shoes . . ."

"You saw it?" Yakimov opened his eyes in admiration, but Galpin remained disapproving.

"It was seen," he added: "What the heck were you up to? Were you drunk?"

"Did have rather a heavy night," Yakimov admitted. "Your poor old Yaki's just levered head from pillow."

Tufton shifted impatiently on his stool. "Fortune favours fools," he said. "We were forced to tarry while he slumbered."

The hotel clerk entered the bar and announced that cables could now be sent from the Central Post Office. As the journalists jostled their way out, Yakimov imagined his ordeal was over. He was about to order himself another drink, when Galpin gripped his arm.

"I'll give you a lift," said Galpin.

"Oh, dear boy, I don't think I'd better go out today. Don't feel at all well."

"Are you doing McCann's job or aren't you? Come on."

Looking into Galpin's crabbed, uncharitable face, Yakimov dared not refuse to go.

At the post office he wrote on his form: "Very sorry to tell you the Prime Minister was . . ." then hesitated so long over the spelling of the word 'assassinated' that the office emptied and he was alone with Galpin. Galpin, his face solemn, said: "You've got the story, of course? Who's at the bottom of this? And so on?"

Yakimov shook his head: "Haven't a clue, dear boy."

Galpin tut-tutted at Yakimov's ignorance. "Come on," he said more kindly, "I'll give you a hand."

Taking out his fountain-pen, Galpin concocted a lengthy piece which he signed: 'McCann'.

"That'll cost you about three thousand," he said.

Yakimov gasped, dismayed. "But I haven't a *leu*," he said.

"Well, this once," said Galpin, "I'll lend you the cash, but you must have money for cables. The international line may be closed down for weeks. Trot along now and see McCann."

Next morning, as he went to the breakfast room, Yakimov saw Galpin and a Canadian called Screwby coming purposefully from the bar. Suspecting they were on the track of news, he tried to avoid them, but it was too late. Galpin had already seen him.

"There's a spectacle in the Chicken Market," said Galpin as though Yakimov would be delighted to hear it. "We'll take you in the old Ford."

Yakimov shied away: "Join you later, dear boy. Trifle peckish. Must get a spot of brekker."

"For Christ's sake, Yakimov," said Galpin unpleasantly, "I'm McCann's friend. I'll see him served right. You do your job." And, taking Yakimov's arm, he led him out to the car.

They drove through the Calea Victoriei towards the river Dâmbovita. Yakimov had been put into the uncomfortable back seat. Galpin, apparently satisfied by his submission, talked over his shoulder: "You've heard, of course, they got the chappies who did it?"

"Have they, dear boy?"

"Yah. Iron Guardists, just as I said. A German plot, all right: an excuse to march in and keep order, but they reckoned without the old Russkies. The old Russkies got in their way. The Germans couldn't march through them. But these Guardist chappies didn't realise. They thought, when the Germans got here, they'd be the heroes of the new order. No one'd dare touch them. They didn't even go into hiding. They were picked up before the victim was cold and executed during the night."

"But what about the King, dear boy?"

"What about him?"

"You said he said he'd get Călinescu."

"Oh, that! It's a complicated story. You know what these Balkan countries are like." Galpin broke off to nod out of the car window. "Tension's relaxed," he said.

Screwby gave the passers-by a knowing look and agreed that tension was relaxed.

"Not that most of them wouldn't rather have the Germans here than the Russians up on the frontier." Galpin nodded again. "Look at that fat bastard. Got pro-German written all over him."

Yakimov looked, half expecting to see a duplicate of Goëring, but he saw only the mid-morning Rumanian crowd out for its refection of chocolate and cream cakes. He sighed and murmured: "Don't feel so well. Hollow with hunger," but he was ignored.

They crossed the tram-lines and entered the road that sloped down to the river. Galpin parked the car on the quayside and Yakimov saw the enormous winding queue, compacted like gut, that filled the market area. It gave him hope. Even Galpin must think twice of joining it.

"Dear boy," he said, "we might wait all day."

Galpin sharply asked: "You've got your card, haven't you? Then follow me." He strode authoritatively into the multitude, holding up his card to proclaim his privileged position. No one questioned him. The peasants and workpeople gave way at the sight of him and Screwby and Yakimov followed in his wake.

A square had been cordoned off in the centre of the market place. It was guarded by a dozen or so police lolling about in their dirty sky-blue uniforms. They stood upright at the sight of Galpin. One of them examined his card, pretended to understand it, then began, importantly, to clear a viewpoint. The assassins were revealed.

Yakimov, who disliked not only violence but the effects of violence, hung back till ordered forward by Galpin. With distaste, fearing a loss of appetite, he looked at the bodies.

"Just been tumbled out of a lorry," said Screwby. "How many are there? I can see four ... five, six, I'd guess."

They looked like a heap of ragged clothes. The sightseers, kicking at them under the rail, had brought to view a head and a hand. On the head there was a bald spot, like a tonsure. One side of the face was pressed into the ground. The visible eye and nostril were clotted with blood; blood caked the lips together. The hand, growing dark and dry in the hot sun, was stretched out stiffly as though in search of aid. Blood, running down from beneath the sleeve, had stained the cobbles.

Galpin said: "That one wasn't dead when they pitched him out."

"How do you know, dear boy?" Yakimov asked, but received no reply.

Galpin put his foot under the rail and, stirring the heap about, uncovered another face. This one had a deep cut across the left cheek. The mouth was open, black with a vomit of blood.

Galpin and Screwby began scribbling in notebooks. Yakimov had no notebook, but it did not matter. His mind was blank.

Back in the car, he said to Galpin: "Dear boy, I'm faint. Wonder if you've a hip-flask on you?"

For answer Galpin started up the car and drove at speed to the Post Office. There they were given forms, but when Galpin presented his story he discovered that once again the stop was down. Nothing could be sent out. This was a relief for Yakimov, who had created five words ('They caught the assassins and . . .'). His eyes glazed with effort, he moaned: "Not used to this sort of thing. Simply must wet m'whistle."

"We're due at the press luncheon," said Galpin. "You'll get all you want there."

"But I'm not invited," said Yakimov, near tears.

"You've got your card, haven't you?" Galpin, his patience exhausted, said. "Then, for heaven's sake, come along."

With the quivering expectancy of an old horse headed for the stables, Yakimov followed the others into the desolate building which had been recently refurbished as a Ministry. They passed through a tunnelling of china-tiled passages to a room too high for its width, where, sure enough, food was lavishly displayed on a buffet table. The buffet was roped off. Before it stood several rows of hard chairs. It was to these the journalists were conducted.

Most of those present, being in Bucharest temporarily, to cover the assassination, had seated themselves unobtrusively at the back. Only Mortimer Tufton and Inchcape, now British Information officer, were in front. Tufton had placed his stick across the three chairs that separated them. He lifted it and motioned Galpin to sit beside him.

Inchcape sat askew, his legs crossed at the knee, an arm over his chairback and his cheek pressed back by his finger-tips. He looked sourly at Yakimov, who took the chair beside him, and said: "Something fishy about all this."

Yakimov, seeing nothing wrong but fearing to betray again his inexperience in the cunning world of journalism, murmured: "Quite, dear boy, quite!" His tone lacked conviction and caused Inchcape to wave an irritable hand at the buffet.

"Roped off!" he said. "Why? Never saw such a thing before at a public function. These people are nothing if not hospitable. And what are all these damned insolent flunkeys doing here? Are they on guard? Or what?" In an access of indignation, he jerked round his head and stared at the back rows.

There were, Yakimov now observed, a remarkable number of waiters; and these were smirking together as though involved in a hoax. Yet the food looked real enough. A side table was crowded with bottles of wines and spirits. Thinking he might get himself an apéritif, he motioned the nearest waiter and made a sign that seldom failed. It failed this time. The man, his lips twitching, lifted his face and appeared entranced by the fretted wooden ceiling.

Yakimov shuffled unhappily in his seat. Others shuffled and talked behind him. There were no new arrivals; time was passing; there was no sign of the Minister of Information. Inchcape's suspicion was extending itself through the room.

Suddenly Galpin said: "What's going on? Not a Boche or a Wop at the party. Nobody here but the friends of plucky little Rumania. And why are we being kept waiting like this?"

Tufton rapped with his stick on the floor. As the waiter looked up, he commanded: "Whisky."

One of the waiters, giving his fellows a sly, sidelong glance, replied in Rumanian.

"What the devil did he say?" asked Tufton.

Inchcape translated: "We must await the arrival of His Excellency Domnul Ionescu."

Tufton looked at his watch: "If His Excellency doesn't come within the next five minutes, I'm off."

The servants, expecting uproar, watched this exchange with interest and looked disappointed when nothing more resulted. The five minutes passed. Ionescu did not arrive, but Tufton remained in his seat. After a long pause, he said: "I suspect this is leading up to a reprimand."

"They'd never dare," said Galpin.

Yakimov's spine drooped. His hands hung, long, delicate and dejected, between his knees. He sighed repeatedly, like a dog kept too long on trust, and at one point told the world: "Haven't had a bite today." Placing his elbows on his knees, he buried his face in his hands and his thoughts wandered. There had been a time when he could dress up into an anecdote every incident of his life. Every situation became a comic situation. He had, he supposed, a gift for it. In those days he had entertained for the sake of entertaining. It delighted him to be the centre of attention. When times changed, he had entertained for any reward he could get. He told himself: 'Poor old Yaki has to sing for his supper.' Now he had lost interest in anecdotes. He felt no great inclination to entertain anyone. This working for food and drink was exhausting him. He only wanted sustenance and peace.

An electric bell rang in the room. The servants hurried to open the double doors. Yakimov roused himself hopefully. The journalists fell silent.

There was a further interval, then Ionescu entered, almost at a run. He stared, wide-eyed, at his guests and flapped his hands in humorous consternation that he should have kept them waiting so long. "*Comment faire mes excuses? D'être tellement en retard est inexcusable,*" he said, but he was grinning, and when he came to a stop in the middle of the room he appeared to be expecting applause. Being met with nothing but silence, he raised his brows; his eyes, black and small as currants, darted from face to face; his moustache twitched; he bit his lower lip as though he could scarcely keep from laughing outright.

He exuded a comic bewilderment that seemed to ask what could be the matter with them all. Hadn't he apologised? Suddenly sobering, he started to address the gathering in English:

"Gentlemen – and, ah yes, ladies! How charming!" He bowed at the two women present, one of whom was American, the other French. "Ladies and gentlemen, I should say, then, should I not?" He started to smile again, but, receiving no response, he shook his head to show bewilderment, and went on: "Yesterday afternoon, ladies and gentlemen, you were privileged to send your papers – cables. Was that not so?" He looked round in enquiry, moving his head with bird-like pertness. When no one replied, he answered himself: "Yes, it was so. And what cables! I may here and now tell you that in place of the fantasies handed in at the Central Post Office, the following announcement was sent to all papers . . ." He brought out a pair of heavily rimmed glasses and, placing them half-way down his nose, slowly searched his pockets. "Ah!" he said. He sobered again, produced a paper and, after gazing at it for some moments, read out unctuously: " 'Today Rumania with broken heart announces the tragic loss of her much loved son and Premier A. Călinescu, assassinated by six students who failed to pass their baccalaureate. While attempting to forgive this mad act of disappointed youth, the nation is prostrate with grief.' "

He stepped forward, bowed and handed the paper to Inchcape.

"I take it," said Galpin, "we'll get our money back?"

Ionescu gave his head a sharp shake: "No money back." He wagged a finger before his nose. "This is, as the English say, a little lesson. You have all been very naughty, you know." He moved back to the rope and, catching it with either hand, swung on it.

"Like a bloody parrot on a perch," whispered Galpin.

Ionescu's smile widened. "You must remember," he said, "you are guests of a neutral kingdom. Here we are peaceful. We wish no quarrel with our neighbours. While living here, you must behave like good children. Isn't it so?"

Turning in his chair, Tufton asked his neighbours: "How long's this nonsense going on?"

A voice from the back asked. "What fantasies? What's biting him?"

"Ah, dear friends," said Ionescu, "am I perhaps mistaken? Did no one here invent the story that the assassins were Guardists in German pay? That the Germans had planned an invasion? That a certain foreign diplomat was under house arrest, having been found in possession of a cheque with which to reward the assassins?"

"Is von Steibel under house arrest, or isn't he?" asked Tufton. Smiling, Ionescu said: "He is in bed with influenza."

"He's been ordered to leave the country, hasn't he?"

"Tomorrow he returns to Germany for a cure."

Questions now followed one another rapidly. In the confusion Ionescu straightened himself, raised his hands in alarm and waved for quiet: "A little moment, ladies and gentlemen. There is a more serious matter of which I am compelled to speak." His face grew grave and his voice became portentous. "This," he said, "is scarcely to be believed. Had I not seen with my own eyes the cable, I would have said such an invention was not possible."

Having made this statement, he paused so long that Galpin said: "All right. Let's have it."

Ionescu said: "A reputable journalist, representative of a famous paper, invented a story so scandalous I hesitate to speak of it. In short, he accused our great and glorious King, father of culture, father of his people, of being behind this fiendish murder. This journalist, we learn, is a sick man. He was wounded while driving out of Poland. He suffers, no doubt, a fever and we tell ourselves this story comes of delirium. No other explanation is possible. Nevertheless, as soon as he is capable, he will be ordered to leave."

Several present looked at Yakimov but Yakimov showed neither by expression or movement that he connected this reproof with anything he had permitted to be sent in McCann's name. Having administered this reproof, Ionescu relaxed and smiled again.

"Nearly three o'clock," said Tufton.

"One more little moment," said Ionescu. "We will now answer questions."

The American woman asked: "*M. le Ministre*, you have said the assassins were students. Isn't it possible they were Guardists, too?"

Ionescu smiled on her in pity: "*Chère madame*, was it not announced by His Glorious Majesty himself that not a single Guardist remains alive in this country?"

The French woman journalist now said: "It is widely rumoured that the assassins were in the pay of Germany."

Said Ionescu: "It is being widely rumoured that the assassins were in the pay of the Allied Powers. You must not believe café gossip, *madame.*"

"I never go to cafés," said the Frenchwoman.

Ionescu bowed to her: "Then you must permit me to take you to one."

Tufton broke in on this exchange to ask with ponderous slowness: "And may we enquire who executed the assassins – no doubt without trial?"

Ionescu grew grave again. He recited quickly: "The military, mad with grief and indignation at the murder of a beloved Prime Minister, seized the young men and, unknown to the civil authorities, shot them out of hand."

"Is that official?"

"Certainly."

Someone asked: "Are you aware the bodies are being displayed at this moment down in the market-place? Do you approve of that sort of thing?"

Ionescu shrugged: "The military here is powerful. We dare not interfere."

"I saw the bodies," said Galpin. "They looked to me pretty old for students."

"In this country we have students of all ages. Some remain at the university all their lives."

Galpin grunted and looked at Tufton. Tufton said: "We're wasting our time."

Galpin rose, and the rest, needing no further encouragement, began to leave their seats. Roused by the squeak of chairs, Yakimov started up in wild hope. He blundered forward into Ionescu.

"Permit me," said the Minister, unable to hold back the surge, and, unhooking the cord where it joined in the middle, he admitted his guests to the buffet.

With a restraint that was painful to him, Yakimov awaited his associates. Tufton was slow in getting to his feet. "A slap for Rumania's kind friends," he said to Galpin. "A playful slap, but a significant one. Something has reminded them that Hitler is uncomfortably close."

Galpin said: "Those bastards accepted our guarantee *after* the Germans occupied Slovakia."

Tufton was up now. As he began to limp towards the buffet, he said: "So did the Poles."

That evening the autumn set in. The Pringles, leaving their hotel restaurant, where the air was hot and heavy with smoke, came out into an unexpected freshness. Rain had fallen. In the distance, wetly agleam, were the cupolas of the Opera House, where the Prime Minister lay in state.

Guy was in an exuberant mood. He had been exuberant all evening. It was now accepted – in most cases unwillingly accepted – that only the Russian occupation of Eastern Poland had kept the Germans out of Rumania. It was also believed that the Russian move had been the result of foreknowledge of the German plot. All this seemed to Guy a triumph for his political ideals. He said to Harriet: "Even the Legation must realise now that the Russians know what they're doing." To hearten Harriet he drew in his notebook a map that proved that the Germans could reach Rumanian soil only by violating Hungarian neutrality.

"And they won't do that," he said. "Not yet awhile."

"Why not?"

"Because they've got enough on their plate already."

Harriet smiled, this new sense of security coming to her like a gift. As they reached the street, they took hands, electrified by the changed air, and ran towards the Opera House, from which light fell through open doors. A queue had been moving all day. Now there was no queue. They took the opportunity to enter.

Inside the vestibule, where grey stone figures flew and gestured, there was a smell of wet rubber from the soldiers' capes. The floor shone with footprints. Within the auditorium, that had been cleared of seats, the bier, lit by candles, hung with purple and silver, stood islanded in spacious gloom. At its head and foot stood priests, black-bearded, black-robed, veils falling from their high head-gear. They were muttering prayers.

When he came within sound of them, Guy whispered "Mumbo-jumbo", and would have turned on his heel had not Harriet held to his arm and led him to the coffin. There was nothing to be seen but the Premier's nose, grey-white, with a sheen like putty.

The Pringles paused for a moment, then went to look at the wreaths. These, of immense size, were propped in a wide circle round the bier. The two largest, gigantic, towering like idols in the gloom, stood side by side behind the coffin's head. They were shield-shaped, formed of red carnations, one swathed with red, white and blue ribbon; the other with black and red. The black and red ribbon carried a swastika.

Galpin was gazing at these rival expressions of grief, a grin on his face. At the sight of him, Guy hurried forward to ask: "What price the old Russkies now?"

Galpin's mouth bunched itself in self-congratulation. He stared up at the ceiling, that was as obscure as the roof of a cave, and said: "It all happened more or less as I said. Thanks to the Russkies, we're not in Gestapo hands at this moment."

"You think we're safe, then?" said Harriet.

"Safe?" Galpin's mouth collapsed again. He eyed Harriet in bleak ridicule. "Safe? – with the Russian army massing on the frontier? Believe me, they'll be here before the winter sets in."

Guy said: "We needn't worry. We're not at war with Russia."

"I hope they give you time to tell them that."

Out in the street again, Harriet attempted philosophy: "Wherever one is," she said, "the only thing certain is that nothing is certain."

Guy looked surprised. "There are several things of which I am completely certain," he said.

"What for instance?"

"Well." He considered the question a moment, then said: "Among other things: that freedom is the knowledge of necessity and there is no wealth but life. When you understand that, you understand everything."

"Even the universe? Even eternity?"

"They're unimportant."

"I think they're important." Rather resentfully, Harriet took her hand from his. "Imagine the possibilities of eternity. This life is limited, whatever you do with it. It can only end in death."

"All these religious concepts," said Guy, "are only a means of keeping the poor poor; and the rich rich. Pie in the sky. Accept the condition it has pleased God to put you in. I am not interested in eternity. Our responsibilities are here and now."

They walked a little apart, divided by the statements of their differences. Before them there shone on a street corner the glass prow of the café they had set out to visit. This was the Doi Trandafiri, said now to be the meeting place of those turned out of the demolished Napoleon. Guy imagined he would find there all sorts of old friends. Harriet feared that he would. Imagining him disappearing into their embrace, she felt eternity to be doubtful and the universe black in its inhuman chill. She slid her hand back into his.

She said: "We're together. We're alive – anyway, for the moment."

Squeezing her hand, he asked: "When shall we be more than that?"

He pushed through the doorway into brilliance and she left the question unanswered.

7

Inchcape had rented an empty shop, which he was fitting out as the British Information Bureau. The shop stood in the Calea Victoriei, immediately opposite the German Information Bureau. This, that he described as 'the rival establishment', displayed pictures of the Siegfried Line and troops on the march. Inchcape said that so far he had been sent only a bundle of posters proclaiming 'Britain Beautiful' and advising tourists to 'See Britain First'. He told the Pringles they might view Călinescu's funeral from one of the upper windows of this office, and invited them to come beforehand to his flat for a drink.

Inchcape, when the Pringles arrived, made a grimace of disappointment. He had hoped they could take their drinks out to the terrace. "But today," he said, "even the sky mourns."

He had switched on two yellow-shaded reading lamps in his sitting-room: now he went round switching on three more. While the Pringles watched him, he studied the effect of this imitation sunlight on the white walls, the delicate gold and white furniture, the white pianoforte, and the books on their white shelves, then he smiled to himself. He insisted, he said, that Harriet come out for just a moment and view the park. She went out with him to the terrace and from there he turned and smiled back at the radiant room.

In the wintry, out-of-doors light, the concrete face of the flats, designed to reflect the sun, looked blotched and gimcrack. The geraniums were shedding their flowers, but Harriet, feeling that admiration was important to her host, admired everything. He touched one of his collection of large-leafed, fleshy plants and said: "Soon they must all come indoors. And that, in a way, is a good thing." When she looked at him in enquiry, he explained: "The snow will come soon and here we shall be, tucked away safe and sound."

She still did not understand.

He gave an exasperated little laugh: "Surely, my dear child, you know that no one invades in the winter! The time to invade is the autumn – after the harvest and before the snow blocks the passes."

"Why not this autumn?"

"Invasions take time to prepare, and there are no preparations. The patrol 'planes report all quiet on all fronts."

"That is something to be thankful for."

Rather to her surprise, he touched her arm. "Didn't I tell you there was no cause for alarm? I do not for a moment believe that anyone wants to invade this country. If they do, it won't be for six or seven months. A lot can happen in that time."

He smiled, very amiably. He was, she felt, being more than necessarily pleasant to her, not because he liked women, but because he did not. She suspected, also, that he was relieved to find they could get on so well. She was relieved herself: but she imagined it would always be a relationship that called for careful handling.

While Inchcape leant over the rail and pointed down through the trees to his glimpse of the lake, Harriet heard someone talking quickly and excitedly in the room behind them.

"Who is with Guy?" Harriet asked.

"It's Pauli, my Hungarian. All the best servants here are Hungarian. The Saxons are also good, but dour. Mean people, the Saxons; not much liked; no fun."

Pauli came out to them, putting his hands over his face then dropping them to express his delight at the story he had to tell. He was young and very good-looking. He bowed to Harriet, then shot out a hand at her, almost touching her as he begged her to listen. Speaking rapidly in Rumanian, he told all over again the story he had been telling Guy.

Watching him, Inchcape's smile softened indulgently. When the story was finished, he gave Pauli's shoulder a small push, dismissive and affectionate. As he made off, Pauli turned several times to comment excitedly on his own story.

Pretending impatience, Inchcape called after him: "Where are the drinks?"

"Ah, ah, I go now and get," cried Pauli, shaking repentant hands in the air.

"That," said Inchcape, "is the latest story going round about the King. A drunk in a café was reviling the King – calling him lecher, swindler, tyrant; all the usual things – when a member of

the secret police, overhearing him, said: 'How dare you speak in
this manner of our great and glorious Majesty, your King and
mine?' 'But, but,' stammered the drunk, 'I was not speaking of
our King. Far from it. I was speaking of another King. In fact –
the King of Sweden.' 'Liar,' roared the policeman, 'everyone
knows the King of Sweden is a good man.' "

They returned to the room where Pauli was putting out bottles
and glasses. Realising his story was being retold, he stood grinning appreciatively until called away by a ring at the front door.

Clarence had arrived. He entered rather stiffly, greeting Guy
and Inchcape, but keeping his glance averted from Harriet.

"Ah," said Inchcape, now both his men were present, "I have
something to tell you: I shan't be able to view the funeral with
you." He rubbed his brow into his hand and laughed at the
absurdity of it all. "The fact is, your humble servant has been invited to attend the funeral. I shall be in one of the processional
cars."

Guy, too startled to restrain himself, said: "Good heavens,
why?"

"Why?" Inchcape was suddenly serious. "Because I am now in
an official position."

"So you are!" said Guy.

Clarence, staring down at the carpet, grunted once or twice.
This noise seemed to sting Inchcape, who said, off-handedly: "It's
a bore, but quite an honour for the organisation. The only other
members of the English colony invited are the Minister and
Woolley."

Clarence grunted again, then said with sudden force: "Talking
of honours, I hope you won't object to my accepting a little job
that's just been offered me by the Legation?"

"Oh! What would that be?"

"The administration of Polish Relief. A large sum has been
allocated by the Relief Committee at home and I've been recommended as a possible organiser. No salary. Just expenses and use
of car. What about it?"

"Why you?"

"I did relief work in Spain. I was with the Council in Warsaw.
I speak Polish."

"Humph!" Inchcape locked his fingers tightly together, examined them, then snapped them apart. "Let's have a drink," he said.

"So you don't object?" Clarence persisted.

"I *do* object." Inchcape swung round on him. "No one can do two jobs properly. You've been seconded by the British Council to our organisation. Now you're recommended for this work."

"It's war work. Someone must do it. I'll see the two jobs don't clash."

"They'd better not. Well, help yourselves. I must go." He went from the room, and a little later they heard him slam the front door as he left the flat.

At the sound, Clarence jerked his head up and accidentally caught Harriet's eye. He coloured slightly but seemed relieved that he had acknowledged her presence at last. His manner eased. As he poured out the drinks, he laughed and said: "When we were merely outcast purveyors of British culture, Inchcape outdid us all in contempt for officialdom. Now, what a change is here! The next thing, he'll be dining with Woolley."

Clarence was wearing a tie decorated with the small insignia of his college and a blazer with the badge of his old school. Before they left the flat, he wrapped himself up in a long scarf knitted in the colours of a famous rowing club.

Harriet could not refrain from laughing at him. "Are you afraid," she asked, "that people will think you do not belong anywhere?"

Clarence paused, challenged, then looked gratified as though it had occurred to him this might be not so much criticism as coquetry. Opening the front door, he said: "I have a weak chest. I have to take care of myself."

There was a gleam in his eye. Harriet was aware she had been, as she too often was, misunderstood.

The rain had started. To cross the road, they pushed their way through several rows of spectators waiting under umbrellas. The British Information Bureau, a small building, had its windows whitewashed. The painters were at work inside. Above, in Inchcape's office, the walls had been stripped and given a first coat of white distemper. In one corner there was a stack of new wood cut for shelves. Clarence took the Pringles into the small back room that had been allotted to him. Nothing had been done there. The walls were still covered with a dirty beige paper of cubist design. A table had been put in to serve as a desk. There was nothing on it but a blotting-pad and a photograph in a frame.

Guy picked up the photograph: "Is this your fiancée?"

"Yep. Brenda."

"A nice, good face."

"Um." Clarence seemed to imply he could offer no excuse for it.

They said no more about Brenda. Harriet went to the window and looked out at a large site being cleared in the parallel road, the new Boulevard Breteanu, that was being developed to draw the crowds off the Calea Victoriei. On either side of the site had been built wafer-thin blocks of flats, against which stood wooden lean-to sheds for the sale of vegetables and cigarettes. These had been put up by the peasants from the bug-ridden wood thrown out of the demolished houses. Other hovels stood about on the site, braced with flattened petrol cans, their vents protected with rags.

Clarence pointed out the skeleton of a new Ministry building that stood on the other side of the boulevard. Work on it had now come to a stop. The Minister had decamped to Switzerland with the Ministry funds. Meanwhile the workmen, left stranded, were camping in sheltered corners. Harriet could see them now, standing on the girders, gazing down into the street.

"Now it's growing cold," said Clarence, "they light bonfires and sit around them at night. Dear knows what they'll do when the winter comes."

Among the confusion below was a single rococo house, its stucco cracked and grey, its front door of engraved glass opening on to a pretty curve of broken steps, its garden a wasteland. Some-one was still living in it. At the windows hung thick lace curtains, as grimy as the stucco.

"Do you think we could find a house like that?" Harriet said.

As she spoke, some check in Clarence – a defensive prejudice against her, or perhaps mere shyness – broke suddenly, and he leant forward, smiling. "I'm fond of those old houses, too," he said, "but you can't live in them. They're alive with bugs. We're seeing the last of them, I'm afraid." He kept glancing sideways at her, awkwardly, half-smiling. "If Rumania had been as long under the Austrians as she was under the Turks, she might be civilised by now."

She noticed among his features, which before had had no special appeal to her, his sensitive and beautiful mouth. An occasional intentness in his glance made it clear to her that somehow there had been inaugurated an understanding, a basis for a relationship. It was an understanding in which she had no faith, a relationship she had no wish to pursue.

Their talk was interrupted by the distant thud-thud of a funeral march. The three hurried into the front room and, opening the windows leant out. The procession was appearing on the left and heading for the square. From there it would take a roundabout route to the station. Călinescu was to be buried on his own estate.

People were crowding out on to balconies, calling and waving to friends on other balconies. Despite the weather, there was an atmosphere of holiday. As the band drew near, the umbrellas, quilted below, moved towards the kerb: the police, wearing mourning bands on their arms, rushed wildly along in the gutter pushing them back again. A news-man on a lorry started turning his camera handle. The monstrous catafalque appeared, black and blackly ornamented with fringed draperies, ostrich feathers and angels holding black candles. It was drawn by eight black horses, weighted with trappings, the whites of their eyes flashing behind black masks. They slipped about on the wet road so that the whole vast structure seemed to topple.

The Prince walked behind it.

Ah! people shouted from balcony to balcony, this was just what they had expected. The King had been afraid to attend even in his bullet-proof car: yet there was the young Prince, walking alone and unprotected. It was felt that the crowd would give a cheer, were it an occasion for cheering.

Behind the Prince came the canopy of the Metropolitan. On either side the priests swept the watery streets with their skirts. The old Metropolitan with his great white beard, seeing the camera, plucked at his vestments, straightened his jewelled cross and lifted his face with mournful dignity.

The massed military bands, having changed from Chopin to Beethoven, went past uproariously. Then came the cars. Clarence and the Pringles looked out for Inchcape, but he could not be recognised among the anonymous, dark-clad figures within.

The tail of the procession crept past and hard upon it came the press of traffic released from the side streets. All in a moment, it seemed, even while the funeral was still thumping and wailing its way to the square, the Calea Victoriei was aswarm with cars hooting, dodging, cutting in upon each other, eager for life to return to normal.

The ranks of spectators broke up and people began crowding into bars and cafés. They swept past the neon-lit window of the German Information Bureau, which displayed a map of Poland partitioned between Germany and Russia. A swastika obliterated Warsaw. No one paused to give it a glance.

Confidence was growing again. The black market rate had dropped, so even Guy was inclined to agree they could not entertain Sophie every night. One Bucharest paper had expressed in a leader regret that Greater Rumania had not been given the chance to pit her strength against a mighty enemy. She would show the world how a war could be fought. Readers were reminded that in 1914 Rumania's gold had been sent for safety to Moscow. It had never come back again. Rumanian manhood was eager to redress this wrong – but would the opportunity ever come?

Clarence, drawing in his head and closing his window, said: "Now we've heard the last of Călinescu, let's go and get a meal."

But Călinescu was not to be so easily put out of mind. Three days of official mourning were proclaimed, during which the cinemas were to remain shut. When they opened, they showed a news-film of the funeral. For a week the giant coffin was carried by peasants through rain, to the family tomb, then, at last, the late Premier was replaced and forgotten. Forgotten also was the Iron Guard. Its members, declared Ionescu, had been wiped out to a man.

PART TWO

The Centre of Things

8

HARRIET PRINGLE, NO LONGER FEARING that she and her husband would have to flee at any moment, began to look for a flat, buy clothes and take an interest in the invitations that were arriving now that the university term had started. Among those invitations was one from Emanuel Drucker, the banker, whose son was Guy's pupil.

The rain came and went. At night the wind blew cold and the Chaussée restaurants moved their chairs and tables back to their winter premises. After a week of grey weather the sun shone again, but it was possible to sit out of doors only at mid-day.

To the north of the city, where before there had only been the sheen of sun and mist, mountains appeared, crevassed and veined with glaciers that looked like threads of cotton. One morning the highest peak was veiled with snow. Each day the snow grew a little whiter and spread further down the mountain-side. Although Guy laughed at Inchcape's theory of invasion, saying the Russians could come by the coastal plain any time they liked, Harriet was comforted by the thought of the high passes silting up with snow.

The day they were invited to luncheon with the Druckers was one of the last warm days of October. Harriet had arranged to meet Guy in the English Bar, but when she looked for him in the bar, he had not arrived. This did not surprise her, for she was beginning to realise that however late she might be for an appointment Guy could always be later.

The bar was not quite empty. Galpin sat at a table with a girl of dark domestic beauty, while Yakimov stood alone, disconsolately looking at them. Tufton and most of the visiting journalists had returned to their bases.

"Dear girl," Yakimov called when he noticed Harriet, "come and join poor Yaki in a whisky," his plaintive voice suggesting not the intimidating social background described by Inchcape, but a need for comfort.

She entered. The air was smoky and stifling, and she said: "Do you really like this bar? Hasn't the hotel a garden where we could sit?"

"A garden, dear girl?" He glanced around as though there might be a garden at his elbow. "I've seen one somewhere."

"Then let's look for it." Harriet left a message for Guy with Albu, and led Yakimov away.

The garden proved to be small, high-walled and accessible only through the French-windows of the breakfast room. Weather-worn tables and chairs stood under heavy trees. A few couples were sitting in secluded corners. The men glanced up at the newcomers in disconcerted surprise: the women, each of whom wore dark glasses, turned away. They all looked like people tracked down to a hide-out.

There were no flowers in the garden and no ornaments except, in the centre of the pebbled floor, a stone boy pouring an ewer of water into a stone basin. Sitting down beside the fountain, Harriet said: "This is better, isn't it?"

Yakimov murmured doubtful agreement and sat beside her.

There was a sense of pause in the air. The couples remained silent until Harriet and Yakimov began to speak. Harriet asked: "Who was that girl with Galpin?"

"Polish girl," said Yakimov, "Wanda Something. Came down here with McCann. Thought she was McCann's girl; now, apparently, she's Galpin's. I don't know!" Yakimov sighed. "Wanted to have a talk with Galpin about this mobilisation order. Y'know, I'm a journalist. Have to send stuff home. Important to discuss it, get it straight. Went up to them in the bar just now, said 'Have a drink', and got the nose bitten right off m'face."

He turned to stare at Harriet and she was surprised to see his eyes, set within the bewildered sadness of his face, become hard with grievance. He looked for the moment like an embittered child. Before she could speak, the waiter came to the table and she ordered lemonade. She said:

"Do you think it significant, the mobilisation order? Are they expecting trouble?"

"Oh no." Yakimov swept the thought aside with a movement of the hand. Galpin was forgotten now. Yakimov smiled with the delight of the entertainer. "You've heard about this frontier line the King plans to build round Rumania? Twice as strong as the Maginot and the Siegfried rolled into one? To cost a million million *lei*? The Imaginot Line, I call it, dear girl. *The Imaginot Line!*"

When Harriet laughed, he leant a little nearer to her and became gravely confiding. In the manner of an informed man, he said: "What I did think important was Hitler's peace plan. Said he had no more territorial ambitions. *Amazed* me when I heard they'd turned it down. Don't want to be critical, but I think Chamberlain slipped up there. No one wants this silly war, now *do* they?"

"But Hitler so often said he had no territorial ambitions. We couldn't possibly trust him."

"But we *must* trust him, dear girl." Yakimov's great eyes seemed to swim with trust. "In this life we have to trust people. It's the right thing to do."

Unable to think of a reply, Harriet drank her lemonade. Yakimov, his face relaxing after his effort at earnestness, said easily: "I wonder, dear girl, could you lend me a couple of thou?"

"What are 'thou'?"

"Why, mun, dear girl. Cash. Ready. Your poor old Yaki is broke until his remittance turns up."

She was so startled, her cheeks grew pale. She opened her bag and searching through it with flustered movements, found a thousand-*lei* note. "It is all I have," she said.

"Dear girl!" – he pocketed the note in an instant – "how can poor Yaki express his gratitude?" But Harriet did not wait to hear. As she rose and hurried from the garden, he called after her in hurt dismay: "*Dear girl!*"

She met Guy as he entered through the revolving door. He said: "What's the matter?"

She was too abashed to tell him, but after they had crossed the square, she had regained herself enough to laugh and say: "Prince Yakimov invited me to have a drink. I thought he was being kind, but all he wanted was to borrow some money."

Unperturbed, Guy asked: "Did you lend him any?"

"A thousand *lei*."

Now that Guy was treating the matter as unimportant, Harriet regretted her thousand *lei*. She said: "I hate lending money."

"Darling, don't worry about it. You take money too seriously."

She would have said that that was because she had never had any, but she remembered Guy had never had any, either. She said instead: "Yakimov is a fool. He was telling me we must trust Hitler."

Guy laughed. "He's a political innocent, but no fool."

They were approaching the back entrance to the park where the disgraced politician stood with his head in a bag. The Drucker family lived nearby in a large block of mansion flats owned by the Drucker bank.

Within the doorway of the block were two life-sized bronze figures holding up bunches of electric-light bulbs. There was an impressive stairway, heavily carpeted. The hall had an atmosphere of France, but smelt of Rumania. The porter, who, in hope of a tip, pushed his way into the lift with them, reeked powerfully of garlic, so that the air seemed filled with acetylene gas.

They were taken to the top floor. When the Pringles stood outside the great mahogany doors of the Druckers' flat, Harriet said: "I cannot believe that anything human exists behind these doors," but they opened even as Guy touched the bell and behind them stood Drucker and his sister and daughters. The actual opening of the door had been accomplished by a manservant, but Drucker's impulsive movement forward suggested that, had convention permitted a gentleman to open his own front door, he would have done it for Guy's sake.

At the sight of Drucker, Guy gave a cry of pleasure. Drucker shot out his arms and at once Guy threw wide his own arms. A tremendous babble of greetings, questions and laughter broke out while Guy, breathlessly trying to answer all that was asked of him, bent about him, kissing the women and girls.

Harriet stood back, watching, as she had watched the similar excitement in the *wagon-lit*.

It was Drucker himself – a tall, slow-moving man, stooping, heavy, elegant in silvery English tweeds – who came with outstretched hands to include her: "Ah, so charming a wife for Guy! *Si jolie et si petite!*" He gazed down on her with a long look of ardent admiration. He took her hands with confidence, a man who knew all about women. Added to the sensual awareness of his touch was a rarer quality of tenderness. It was impossible not to respond to him, and as Harriet smiled he nodded slightly in acknowledgement of response. He then called to his eldest sister, Doamna Hassolel.

Doamna Hassolel detached herself from Guy, giving a slight "Ah!" of regret. The animation of her face became restrained and critical as she was called to give attention to Harriet.

She was a small, stout, worn-faced woman with a decided manner. She took charge of the guests, apologising for the absence of the hostess, Drucker's wife, who was still at her toilette. Harriet was introduced to the younger sisters, Doamna Teitelbaum and Doamna Flöhr. The first had a worried thinness. Doamna Flöhr, the beauty of the family, was plump and would, in time, be as stout as the eldest sister. She examined Harriet with bright, empty eyes.

They moved into the living room. As soon as they had sat down, a servant wheeled in a trolley laden with hors-d'œuvres and the little grilled garlic sausages made only in Rumania. Harriet, having learnt by now that luncheon might be served any time between two o'clock and three, settled down to drink *ţuică* and eat what was offered her.

The room was very large. Despite its size, it appeared over-full of massive mahogany furniture and hemmed in by walls of so dark a red they were almost black. Hung on the walls, darker than the paper, were portraits heavily framed in gold. A vast red and blue Turkey carpet covered the floor. In the bow of the window, that overlooked the park, stood a grand pianoforte. Drucker's eldest daughter, a school-girl, sat on the stool, occasionally revolving on it and touching a note whenever she stopped before the keyboard. The younger girl, a child of nine, dressed in the uniform of the Prince's youth movement, stood very close to her father. When he had filled the glasses, he whispered to her. Shyly, she drew herself from his side to hand the glasses round.

The women talking in French and English, questioned Guy about his holiday in England – a journey that now seemed to Harriet to have happened long before – and all he and his wife had done since their arrival. Across the boisterous talk, Drucker smiled at Harriet but he was too far from her to draw her into the conversation. When she answered the questions that Guy referred to her, her voice sounded to her discouraging and remote. She had the sense of being isolated in this tumult of vivacious enquiry. Guy, flushed and excited, seemed as far from her as they were. The

first time he had visited here, he had been a stranger like herself
but he had been taken immediately into the family's heart. She,
she felt, was not what they expected; not what they felt she ought
to be. She would be a stranger here for ever.

They began to talk of the war. "Ah, the war!" The word flashed
from one to the other side of the little, quick-speaking women
with intonations of regret. Now they had touched upon this serious
subject, they turned to Drucker for comment.

He said: "Because of the war, we make much business: but still,
it is a bad thing."

Harriet glanced at Guy, wondering what he would think of this,
but whatever he thought, he was distracted from it by the entry of
Drucker's parents. They came in slowly, with an air of formal
purpose, the wife leaning on her husband's arm. Both were small
and very frail. Drucker hurried to them and led them carefully in
to greet Guy and meet Harriet. They had been born in the Ukraine
and spoke only Russian. The old man, slowly shaking Guy by the
hand, made a little speech in a voice so quiet it could scarcely be
heard.

Guy, delighted, brought out his four words of Russian – an
enquiry as to their health. This gave rise to wonder and congratulations, during which the old couple, smiling their ghostly smiles,
excused themselves and made their way out again.

Drucker said: "They tire very easily and prefer to eat in their
own drawing-room."

The flat, Harriet thought, must be very large. She later learnt
that the Drucker family occupied the whole of the block's top
floor.

Before the conversation could start again, Drucker's brothers-
in-law began to arrive from their offices. Hassolel, dry-faced and
subdued, dressed in silver-grey with white spats, arrived first but
had scarcely spoken before the two younger men came in together.
Teitelbaum wore several gem rings, a gold watch bracelet, diamond
cuff-links, a diamond tie-pin and a broad gold clip to hold down
his tie. His elderly, humourless manner made this jewellery seem
less an ornament than a weariness of the flesh. The two older men,
dispirited though they seemed, did their best to be affable, but
Flöhr made no effort at all. Though still in his thirties, he was bald.
His fringe of red hair and his striped chocolate-brown suit gave
him a flamboyance that did not seem to be part of his personality.

He took a seat outside the circle, apparently resenting the fact there were visitors in the room.

Guy had told Harriet that the brothers-in-law were all of different nationalities. Only Drucker held a Rumanian passport. It was evidence of Drucker's power in the country that the others – one German, one Austrian and one Polish – had been granted *permis-de-séjour*. They existed in his shadow.

The large skeleton clock over the fireplace struck two. Drucker's wife had not yet appeared. The door opened and the new arrival was the son Sasha, Guy's pupil. Doamna Hassolel explained that he was late because he had gone from the University to his saxophone lesson. When introduced to Harriet, he crossed the room to kiss her hand. He was a tall boy, as tall as his father, but thin and narrow-shouldered. As he bent over Harriet, the light slid across the black hair, which he wore brushed back from a low and narrow brow. Like his sisters, he resembled his father without being handsome. His eyes were too close together, his nose too big for his face, but because of his extraordinary gentleness of manner Harriet felt drawn to him. There was in him no hint of the family's energy and drive. He was like some nervous animal grown meek in captivity.

He left Harriet and went to shake hands with Guy, then he stood against the wall, his eyes half-shut.

Watching the boy, Harriet thought that were one to meet him in any capital in the world, one would think not 'Here is a foreigner' but 'Here is a Jew'. Though he would be recognisable anywhere, he would be at home nowhere except here, in the midst of his family. Despite the fact he did undoubtedly belong – as though to prove it his aunts had each as he passed given him a pat of welcome – there was about him something so vulnerable and unprotected that Harriet's sympathy went out to him.

After a while he whispered to Doamna Hassolel. She shook her head at him, then turned to the company: "He wants to play his gramophone but I say 'No, soon we must eat'." She reflected in her speech the family pride in the boy.

The rest of the family kept silent while Drucker and Guy discussed Sasha's progress at the University. He had been educated at an English public school and would be sent, when the war ended, to learn the family profession in the bank's New York branch.

The other men kept nodding approval of all Drucker said. There could be no doubt that it was he who gave them all status. Had a stranger asked: "Who is Hassolel? Who Teitelbaum? Who Flöhr?" there could be only one answer to each question: "He is the brother-in-law of Drucker, the banker."

When there was a pause, Teitelbaum said: "How fortunate a young man that can go to America. In this country, who can tell? Already there is general mobilisation and young men are taken from their studies."

"All the time now," said Doamna Hassolel, "we must pay, pay, pay that our Sasha may have exemption."

While the others spoke of Sasha, Drucker smiled at the little girl at his side so that she might know she was not forgotten. He gave her a squeeze, then said to Harriet: "This is my own little girl. She's so proud of her beautiful uniform." He fingered the silk badge on her pocket. "She is learning to march and shout 'Hurrah' in chorus for her handsome young Prince. Isn't she?" He gave her another squeeze and she blushed and pressed her face into his coat. As he smiled, there could be seen, behind the ravages of the years, the same sensitivity that on Sasha's face was unhidden and defenceless.

Feeling enough had been said about Sasha, Doamna Hassolel now questioned Guy about his friend David Boyd whom he had once brought to luncheon with them. Would David Boyd return to Rumania?

Guy said: "He planned to come back, but now I do not know. In war-time we have to do what we are told."

The sun, that had been for a while behind a cloud, burst through the window and lit the famous corn-coloured hair of Doamna Flöhr, who was said to have once been a mistress of the King. Peering short-sightedly at Guy, her head flashing unnatural fire, she cried: "Ah, that David Boyd! How he talked! He was a man who knew everything."

Guy agreed that his friend, an authority on the Balkans, was very knowledgeable.

"He was a man of the Left," said Teitelbaum. "What would he think, I wonder, of this German-Soviet Friendship Treaty?"

Everyone looked at Guy to see what he, another man of the Left, thought of it. He merely said: "I imagine Russia has a plan. She knows what she is doing."

Doamna Hassolel broke in quickly to say: "Never will I forget how David Boyd was talking of Vâlcov – how he rose at dawn and rowed out alone in the waterways and saw the thousands of birds, and how he saw a big bird called a Sea Eagle. It was so interesting. You would think he would be lonely and afraid in such places."

Guy said that David had travelled over all the Balkan countries and spoke the language of each.

"These Balkan countries are wild," said Doamna Hassolel. "They have dangerous wild beasts. I would not travel here. In Germany it was different. There Willi and I would take out walking sticks and . . ." She talked affectionately of life in Germany.

The clock had struck half past two before Doamna Drucker made her appearance. She had not met Guy before, having married Drucker only that summer, but she gave him her hand with barely a glance. She was a few years older than Sasha; not Jewish; a Rumanian beauty, moon-faced, black-haired, black-eyed, like other Rumanian beauties. She wore the fashionable dress of the moment, black, short, tight-fitting, with pearls, a large diamond brooch and several diamond rings. As she crossed to the chair, her body undulating with an Oriental languor, Drucker's gaze was fixed upon her. Settling like a feather settling, lolling there without giving a glance at the company, she expressed her boredom with the whole Drucker ménage. Her husband asked her if she would take *ţuică*. She replied: "*Oui, un petit peu.*"

When Drucker sat down again, the little girl patted his arm and whispered urgently to him, but now his attention was only for his wife. Unable to distract him, the child stood looking at her stepmother, her expression pained.

Luncheon was announced. Doamna Hassolel led the way to the dining-room. Drucker sat at one end of the table, but the other end was taken by Doamna Hassolel, who served from a great silver tureen a rich chicken soup made of sour cream. Doamna Drucker sat half-way down the table between Sasha and Flöhr.

Drucker, having Harriet at his hand, began to question her about her impression of Bucharest.

Looking admiringly at his wife, Guy said: "Apart from the Legation women, who have diplomatic immunity, Harriet is the only Englishwoman left here." Before he could say more, Doamna Hassolel interrupted rather sharply:

"Surely," she said, "Doamna Niculesco is here? She is an Englishwoman. You have met her?" She looked at Harriet, who said she had not. Harriet glanced at Guy, who dismissed Bella, saying: "Bella Niculesco is a tiresome woman. You would not have much in common."

At this Doamna Teitelbaum, whose cheeks hung like curtains on either side of the drooping arc of her mouth, said eagerly: "You do not like her? Me neither. Perhaps on you, too, she has tried the snub?"

The Drucker sisters, hoping for scandal, all turned to Guy, who innocently replied: "No, but I did upset her once – the only time I was taken to the Golf Club. Bella was supervising the hanging of a portrait of Chamberlain painted by some local artist. A ghastly thing. It was inscribed: 'To the Man who Gave us Peace in Our Time.' Chamberlain was holding the flower Safety and had the nettle Danger crushed beneath his foot. I said: 'What's that thing painted with? Treacle?' Bella Niculesco said: 'Mr. Pringle, you should have more respect for a great man.' "

This story did not meet with the acclaim it would have received in Guy's more immediate circle. Doamna Hassolel broke the silence by insisting that the Pringles must take more soup. Most of the members of the family had taken two or three plates. Doamna Flöhr had excused herself, saying she was slimming. Harriet tried to do the same.

"No, no," protested Doamna Hassolel, "it is not possible. If you grow more slim, you will disappear."

The soup was followed by sturgeon, then an entrée of braised steak with aubergine. The Pringles, supposing the entrée to be the main dish, took two helpings and were dashed by the sight of the enormous roast of beef that followed it.

"I went myself to Dragomir's," said Doamna Hassolel, "and ordered it to be cut 'sirloin' in the English fashion. We are told how you eat much roast beef. Now you must fill your plate, two, three times."

While the Pringles were silenced by food, the family grew relaxed and even more talkative. Doamna Flöhr said to Harriet: "You are looking for a flat?"

Harriet said she had started looking now it seemed they would stay.

"Ach," said Hassolel, "the Germans won't come here. The

Rumanians are clever in their way. Last war, they gained much territory. This time they will keep a foot in each camp and come out with even more."

Flöhr gave a snort of disgust. Speaking for the first time, he said: "Such a war! An unexploded squib of a war! What folly ever to start it. The great nations think only of power. They do not think of the ones who suffer for such a war."

In a conciliatory way, Guy said: "They say there will be financial collapse in Germany soon. That might shorten the war." He looked round for applause and met only shocked alarm.

Doamna Flöhr, moving anxiously in her seat, cried: "It would be terrible, such a collapse! It would ruin us."

Drucker, lifting his head tortoise-fashion out of his silence, said: "That is a rumour put around by the British. There will be no collapse." This firm assurance brought immediate calm. Harriet looked at Guy, but he, drowsy with food and wine, seemed unaware of the disturbance he had created. Or perhaps he preferred to seem unaware. It came into her mind that, where his friends were concerned, he was inclined to excuse anything.

Drucker, noticing her look, said quietly: "It is true our business is much dependent on German prosperity. But we made our connections long ago. We do not love the Germans any more than you, but we did not cause the war. We must live."

Doamna Hassolel broke in aggressively. "A banker," she said, "upholds the existing order. He is an important man. He has the country behind him."

"Supposing the order ceases to exist?" said Harriet. "Supposing the Nazis come here?"

"They would not interfere with us," Flöhr said with a swaggering air. "It would not be in their interests to do so. They do not want a financial débâcle. Already, if it were not for us, Rumania would be on her knees."

Teitelbaum added sombrely: "We could a dozen times buy and sell this country."

Drucker, the only member of the family who seemed aware that these remarks were not carrying Harriet where they felt she should go, lifted a hand to check them, but as he did so his youngest sister broke in excitedly to urge the pace:

"We work, we save," she said, "we bring here prosperity, and yet they persecute us." She leant across the table to fix Harriet with her reddish-brown eyes. "In Germany my husband was a clever lawyer. He had a big office. He comes here – and he is forbidden to practise. Why? Because he is a Jew. He must work for my brother. Why do they hate us? Even the *trăsură* driver when angry with his horse will shout: 'Go on, you Jew.' Why is it? Why is it so?"

The last query was followed by silence, intent and alert, as though, after some introductory circling over the area, one of the family had at last darted down upon the carcase of grievance that was the common meat of them all.

Drucker bent to his daughters and whispered something about "*grand-mère et grand-père*". They whispered back. He nodded. Each took an orange from the table, then, hand-in-hand, left the room.

The talk broke out again as the door closed after the children. Each member of the family gave some example of persecution. Drucker's long aquiline head drooped over his plate. He had heard it all before and knew it to be no more than truth. Guy, roused by the talk, listened to it with a crumpled look of distress. The only persons unaffected were Sasha and Doamna Drucker. Doamna Drucker looked profoundly bored. As for Sasha – the stories, it seemed, did not relate to him. His thoughts were elsewhere. He was the treasured fœtus in the womb that has no quarrel with the outside world.

"Yet you are not in danger here," said Harriet.

"It is not the danger," said Hassolel. "There is danger everywhere. It is the feeling, a very ancient feeling. In the Bukovina you will see the Jews wear fox-fur round their hats. So it was ordered hundreds of years ago to say they are as crafty like a fox. Today they laugh and wear it still. They are clever, it is true, but they live apart: they harm no one."

"Perhaps that is the trouble," said Harriet, "that they live apart. Your first loyalty is to your own race. And you all grow rich. The Rumanians may feel you take from the country and give nothing back."

Harriet had offered this merely as a basis for discussion and was startled by the tumult to which it gave rise. In the midst of it, Doamna Flöhr, near hysteria, shouted: "No, no, we are not to blame. It is the Rumanians. They shut their doors on us. They are selfish people. This country has everything but they do not want to share. They are greedy. They are lazy. They take everything."

Drucker, when he could be heard, said: "There is room for all here: there is food and work for all. The Rumanians are content to do nothing but eat, sleep and make love. Such is their nature. The Jews and the foreigners, they run the country. Those who do the work, make the money. Isn't it so? One might rather say of the Rumanians that they take and give nothing back."

This statement was greeted with nods and exclamations of agreement. Teitelbaum, his flat, depressed face looking newly awakened, said: "But we are generous, we Jews. We always give when we are asked. When the Iron Guard was powerful in 1937, the green-shirt boys came to the offices collecting for party funds. The Jewish firms gave twice, even three times, more than the Rumanians, and what was the gratitude? The Iron Guard made laws against us. Only last year there was a pogrom."

Hassolel was peeling an orange. Without looking up from this employment, he said heavily: "At the University our boy was thrown from a window. His spine was broken. Now he is in a sanatorium in Switzerland. Our daughter was medical student. In the laboratory the young men took off her clothing and beat her. She went to America. She is ashamed to come back. So, you see, we have lost both our children."

In the silence that followed, Hassolel went on peeling his orange. Harriet looked helplessly across at Guy, who had grown pale. He said suddenly: "When the Russians come here, there will be no more persecution. The Jews will be free to follow any profession they choose."

At these words, intended to comfort, the brothers-in-law turned on him faces so appalled that Harriet laughed in spite of herself. No one looked at her or spoke, then Doamna Hassolel began pressing people to take sweets and chocolates from the little trays round the table. Coffee was served. When he had drunk a cup, Teitelbaum declared slowly:

"The Communists are bad people. Russia has done great harm. Russia steals from Europe her trade."

At the appearance of this familiar argument, Guy recovered himself and laughed good-humouredly. "Nonsense," he said; "Europe suffers from an out-dated economy. Take this country where a million workers – that's one twentieth of the population – contribute half of the total yearly value of production. That means each worker carries on his back four adults – four male non-workers. And these workers are not only scandalously under-paid, they pay more than they should for everything they buy, except food. For food, of course, they pay too little."

"*Too little!*" The sisters were scandalised.

"Yes, too little. There is no country in the world where food is so cheap. At the same time, factory-made articles are priced out of all proportion to their value. So you get the wretched peasants labouring for a pittance and paying an absurd price for every article they buy."

"The peasants!" Doamna Drucker hissed in contempt and turned her head aside to suggest that when the conversation touched so low a level, it was time for her to depart.

"The peasants are primitive," said Guy, "and, under present conditions, they will remain primitive. For one thing, they receive almost no education: they cannot afford to buy agricultural machinery: they . . ."

Doamna Drucker, her face sullen with scorn, interrupted angrily: "They are beasts," she said. "What can one do for such creatures? They are hopeless."

"In one sense," Guy agreed, "they are hopeless. They have never been allowed to hope. Whatever has happened here, they have been the losers."

She rose from the table. "It is time for my siesta." She left the room.

There was an embarrassed pause, then Hassolel asked Guy if he had been that week to see Shirley Temple at the Cinema. Guy said he had not.

Hassolel sighed. "Such a sweet little girl! Always I go to see Shirley Temple."

"I also." Drucker nodded. "Always she reminds me of my own little Hannah."

When they returned to the sitting room, Sasha invited Guy to go with him into the small ante-room he used as a music-room. Drucker said to Harriet: "Excuse me a little moment," and went off, no doubt in search of his wife. Flöhr, muttering something about work, went too. From the music-room came the sound of a gramophone playing 'Basin Street Blues'.

Harriet, left alone with the Hassolels, the Teitelbaums and Doamna Flöhr, hoped the party would soon be over. But it was not over yet. A maid brought in some cut Bohemian glasses, red, blue, green, violet and yellow, and Doamna Hassolel began pouring liqueurs.

Doamna Teitelbaum, feeling perhaps that there had been too much of complaint at the meal, smiled on Harriet and said: "Still, you will enjoy life here. It is pleasant. It is cheap. There is much food. It is, you understand, *comfortable*."

Before she could say more the manservant entered to say Domnul Drucker's car was waiting for him. He was sent to find Drucker, who, when he entered, said he would drop Guy and Sasha back at the University. Harriet rose, ready to go with them, but the women clamoured:

"Not Doamna Pringle. Doamna Pringle must stay with us. She must stay for the 'five-o'-clock'."

"Of course she will stay," said Guy. Harriet gave him an anguished look but he did not see it. "She has nothing else to do. She would enjoy it."

Without more ado, he said his good-byes and was off with Drucker and Sasha, leaving her behind. There was a short pause, then Teitelbaum and Hassolel departed.

"You see," said Doamna Hassolel, "it is not yet half past four and they return to work. What Rumanian would work before five o'clock?"

The elder of the two Drucker girls came in to join her aunts. The women drew their chairs close together and sat with their plump, be-ringed hands smoothing their skirts over their plump, silk knees. Meanwhile they watched Harriet, somehow suggesting that even if she were formidable, she was outnumbered. They watched, she thought, with the purposeful caution of trappers.

The Drucker girl said: "She is pretty, is she not? Like a film star."

Now the men were all gone, Doamna Flöhr had taken a platinum lorgnette from her bag. She examined Harriet through it. "What age are you?" she asked.

"Thirty-five," said Harriet.

The women gasped. The girl tittered behind her hand. "We thought you were twenty," she said.

Harriet wondered when they had joined in coming to this conclusion. Doamna Flöhr looked puzzled and, pretending to fidget with the back of her dress, leant forward to take a closer look at Harriet.

Doamna Teitelbaum said in an extenuating tone: "Leah Blum, you remember, did not marry till she was thirty. Such happens, I am told, with Career Women."

The others laughed at the outlandishness of such women.

Doamna Hassolel said: "Here we say: at twenty, you marry yourself; at twenty-five, you must get the old woman to marry you; at thirty, the devil himself can't do it."

Harriet turned to Doamna Flöhr, because she was the youngest sister, and said: "What age are you?"

Doamna Flöhr started. "Here," she said, "women do not tell their ages."

"In England," said Harriet, "they are not asked to tell."

Doamna Hassolel now said: "How many children do you wish to have?"

"We shall probably wait until after the war."

"Then it will be too late."

"Surely not."

"But how many? Haven't you considered?"

"Oh, nine or ten."

"So many? Then you must start soon."

Harriet laughed and Doamna Teitelbaum, whose manner was more kindly than that of the others, said: "You are surely joking? You cannot be so old."

"I am twenty-two," said Harriet. "A year younger than Guy."

"Ah!" The others relaxed, disappointed.

Doamna Hassolel rang for the maid and gave an order. The maid brought in some jars of a sort of jam made of whole fruits.

Doamna Teitelbaum murmured her pleasure. "A little spoonful," she said, "I like so much gooseberry."

Harriet said: "I really must go." She started to rise, but the circle of women sat firm about her.

"No, no," said Doamna Hassolel, "you cannot go. Here already is the 'five-o'clock'."

A trolley was wheeled in laden with sandwiches, iced cakes, cream buns and several large flans made of sliced apples, pears and plums.

Harriet looked from the window. Rain was falling again. The wind was blowing it in sheets from the soaked trees. Doamna Hassolel watched her calmly as she returned to her chair.

9

WITH LATE NOVEMBER CAME THE *crivaţ*, a frost-hard wind that blew from Siberia straight into the open mouth of the Moldavian plain. Later it would bring the snow, but for the moment it was merely a threat and a discomfort that each day grew a little sharper.

Fewer people appeared in the streets. Already there were those who faced the outdoor air only for as long as it took them to hurry between home and car. In the evening, in the early dark, there were only the workers hurrying to escape the cold. Taxis were much in demand. Run cheaply on cheap fuel from the oil-fields that were only thirty miles distant, they charged little more than the buses of other capitals.

At the end of November there came, too, a renewal of fear as Russia invaded Finland. Although his friends were inclined to hold him responsible for the Soviet defection, Guy's faith did not waver. He and Harriet heard the news one night at the Athénée Palace, where Clarence had taken them to dine. They found as they left the dining-room that the main room had been prepared for a reception. The chandeliers were fully lit, the tables banked with flowers and a red carpet had been unrolled throughout the hall.

"Germans," said Guy when he saw the first of the guests. The Germans and the British in Bucharest knew each other very well by sight. This was Harriet's first real encounter with the enemy. Guy and Clarence pointed out to her several important members of the German Embassy, all in full evening dress, among them Gerda Hoffman, a stocky woman whose straw-coloured hair was bound like a scarf round her head. No one knew what her true function was, but a whispering campaign had given her the reputation of being the cleverest agent to come out of Germany.

A group of these Germans stood in the hall. Seeing the three young English people advance on them, they closed together on the red carpet so that the three had to divide and skirt them. As this happened, the Germans laughed exultantly among themselves. Harriet was surprised that people of importance should behave so crassly. Guy and Clarence were not surprised. This behaviour seemed to them typical of the sort of Germans sent out under the New Order.

"But they're certainly crowing over something," said Clarence. "I wonder what's happened. Let's ask in the bar."

In the bar they learnt of the invasion of Finland from Galpin, who said: "That's the beginning. The next thing, Russia'll declare war on us. Then the Huns and the Russkies will carve up Europe between them. What's to stop them?"

"A lot of things," said Guy, "I'm pretty sure the Russians won't commit themselves before they're ready."

Galpin looked him over with bleak amusement: "You think you know about Russia, the way the Pope knows about God. You wait and see. We'll have one or the other of the bastards here before you can say 'Eastern Poland'."

Guy laughed, but he laughed alone. The others were subdued by a sense of disaster.

The next morning, walking in the Cişmigiu, Harriet suffered again from uncertainty. She had made an appointment to see a flat, that mid-day. If they took it, they would be required to pay three months' rent in advance. She was unwilling to risk the money.

Guy said: "Don't worry. We'll be here at least a year."

They had the wintry park to themselves. When they reached the bridge, the wind came howling across the lake, carrying to them the icy spray from the fountain. They retreated and turned in among the flower-beds that displayed the last brown tattered silks of the chrysanthemums. A white peacock was trailing a few tail-feathers in the mud. Pigeon-down and some scraps of leaf spun along the path. The path curved and brought them to the chestnut thicket that led to the restaurant. Guy put his hand through Harriet's arm, but she was not responsive. He had promised to go with her and view the flat, but, having forgotten this promise, he had later arranged to give some special coaching to a student. The student's need seemed to him the greater.

"And I must see the landlord alone?" said Harriet.

"Oh no." Guy was delighted by his own resource. "I've rung up

Sophie and she has agreed to go with you." This he thought an altogether better arrangement, it being known that no English person could grapple unaided with the cunning of a Rumanian landlord.

It was an arrangement that did not please Harriet at all. Guy, as they walked, had been lecturing her on her unwisdom in not making better use of Sophie, who would, he knew, be only too delighted to help Harriet, if only Harriet would ask for help. Sophie had been very helpful to him when he was alone here. He was sure she was, fundamentally, a good-hearted girl. She had had a difficult life. All she needed was a little flattery, a little management....

Harriet, whom he seemed to imagine was absorbing this advice, said at the end of it no more than: "I'm *sick* of Sophie." After a pause, she added: "And we can't afford to go on feeding her."

Guy said: "Things will be easier when we have our own flat. Then we can entertain at home."

They had now strolled out of the trees and could see the café's wooden peninsula with the chairs and tables stacked up under tarpaulins. The kitchen was shuttered. A lock hung quivering in the wind. Guy asked Harriet if she remembered hearing here the announcement of Călinescu's assassination. Did she remember the heat, the quiet, the chestnuts falling on the tin roof? Rather sulkily, she replied that she did. Taking her hand, Guy said:

"I wish, darling, you liked Sophie better. She is lonely and needs a friend. You ought to get on well with her. She is an intelligent girl."

"She lets her intelligence trickle away in complaints, self-pity and self-indulgence."

"You are rather intolerant."

Before Harriet could reply to this, they heard a step behind them and glancing round saw a figure that was familiar but, so unlikely was the setting, unfamiliar.

"Good heavens," said Guy, glad of diversion. "It's Yakimov." Harriet said: "Don't let's talk to him."

"Oh, we must have a word." And Guy hurried out of reach of her restraint.

Yakimov, in his long full-skirted greatcoat, an astrakhan cap on top of his head, his reed of a body almost overblown by the wind, looked like a phantom from the First World War – a member of some seedy royal family put into military uniform for the purposes of a parade. As he tottered unhappily forward, his gaze on the ground, he did not see the Pringles. When stopped by Guy's exuberant "Hello, there!" his mouth fell open. He did his best to smile.

"Hello, dear boy!"

"I've never seen you in the park before."

"I've never been before."

"What a magnificent coat!"

"Yes, isn't it!" Yakimov's face brightened a little as he turned a corner of the coat to show the worn sable lining. "The Czar gave it to m'poor old dad. Fine coat. Never wears out."

"It's splendid." Guy stood back to admire the theatrical effect of the coat, his appreciation such that Yakimov's gaze went to Guy's coat in the hope of being able to return these compliments, but no return was possible.

Guy said: "It makes you look like a White Army officer. You should have a peaked cap. A sort of yachting cap."

"M'old dad had one; and a beard like Nicholas II." Yakimov sighed, but not, it seemed, over these glories of the past. His whole body drooped. Now he had come to a standstill, he seemed to lack energy to proceed.

Harriet, who had been watching him, felt forced to ask: "What is the matter?"

He looked up: "Not to tell a lie . . ." he paused, at a loss for a lie to tell. "*Not* to tell a lie, dear girl, I've been rather badly treated. Given the push. Literally." He laughed sadly.

"From the Athénée Palace?"

"No. At least, not yet. No, I . . . I . . ." he stared at the ground again, stammering as though his troubles were so compacted that they dammed the source of speech, then speech burst forth: "Given the push . . . flung out. Flung out of a taxi in a distant part of the town. Quite lost; not a *leu* on me: didn't know where to turn. Then someone directed me across this God-forsaken park."

"You mean, you couldn't pay the taxi?" Harriet asked.

"Wasn't my taxi, dear girl. McCann's taxi. McCann flung me out of it. After all I'd done for him." Yakimov's lips quivered.

Guy took his arm, and as they walked towards the main gate he persuaded Yakimov to describe exactly what had happened.

"McCann got me out of bed this morning at some unearthly

hour. Rang me up, and said he wanted to see me. Said he was in the hall, just leaving for Cairo. Well, dear boy, had to get m'clothes on. Couldn't go down in m'birthday suit, could I? Thought he was going to ask me to keep on the job. Didn't know whether to say 'yes' or 'no'. Hard work, being a war correspondent. Comes a bit rough on your poor old Yaki. Not used to it. Well, got myself titivated. 'Shall I accept the job, or shan't I?' kept asking m'self. Felt I ought to accept. War on, y'know. Man should do his bit. Thought I'd done a good job. If I couldn't get 'hot' news in the bar, always got a warmish version of it. Well, down I went – and there was McCann, fuming. But *fuming*! Said he'd be late for his 'plane. Bundled me into the taxi with him before I knew what was happening, and then started on me. And what do you think he said? He said: 'Might have known you hadn't a clue. All you could do was collect rumours and scandal'. "

"Really!" said Harriet with interest. "What scandal?"

"Search me, dear girl. I never was one for scandal. 'And you did yourself damned well,' he said. 'Two hundred thousand *lei* for a month's kip. What's my agency going to say when they have to pay that for the balderdash you've been sending home?' Then he stopped the cab, put his foot on m'backside and shoved me out." Yakimov gazed from one to the other of his companions, his green eyes astounded by reality. "And I've had to find m'way back here on m'poor old feet. Can you imagine it?"

"And he didn't pay you for the work you did?" Guy asked.

"Not a nicker."

"I suppose he paid the hotel bill?"

"Yes, but what has he said to the blokes there? That's what I'm asking m'self. Very worried, I am. Perhaps, when I get back, I'll find m'traps in the hall. It's happened before. I'd have to move to the Minerva."

"But that's a German hotel."

"Don't mind, dear boy. Poor Yaki's not particular."

They had reached the Calea Victoriei and there Yakimov looked vaguely about him. Recognising his whereabouts, he smiled with great sweetness and said: "Ah, well, we mustn't worry. We're in a nice little backwater here. We should get through the war here very comfortably." On this cheerful note, he set out to face the staff of the Athénée Palace.

Turning in the opposite direction, Harriet walked with Guy as far as the University gate. There he gave her two thousand-*lei* notes. "For lunch," he said. "Take Sophie. Go somewhere nice," and he went off with what seemed to her the speed of guilt.

Sophie opened the door in her dressing gown. Her face shone sallow for lack of make-up: her hair was pinched over with metal setting-grips.

In a high, vivacious voice she cried: "Come in. I have been washing my hair. Most times I go to the Athénée Palace salon, but sometimes – for an economy, you understand? – I do it myself. You have not been before in my *garçonnière*. It is not big, but it is convenient."

She talked them up the stairs. In the bed-sitting-room – an oblong modern room with an unmade bed and an overnight smell – she pushed some clothes off a chair and said: "Please to be seated. I am unpacking my laundry. See!" She lifted a bundle in tissue paper and gazed into it. "So nice! My pretty lingerie. I love all such nice things."

Looking round for a clock, Harriet noticed a photograph frame placed face downwards beside the bed. There was no clock, but Sophie wore a watch. Harriet asked the time. It was a quarter to twelve.

"The appointment with the landlord is at twelve o'clock," said Harriet.

"Ah!" Sophie, who was now unpacking her laundry, seemed not to hear. She lifted her underwear, piece by piece, with a sort of sensual appreciation. Smoothing down little bows, straightening borders of lace, she opened drawers and slowly put each piece away. When this task was completed, she threw herself on the bed. "Last night," she said, "I was out with friends, so this morning I am lazy."

"Do you think we could go soon?"

"Go? But where should we go?"

"Guy said you would come with me to see the landlord."

"But what landlord?"

Harriet explained her visit and Sophie, lying propped on one elbow, looked troubled: "He said you would call to see me. A friendly call, you understand, but he did not speak of a landlord." Sophie looked at her fingernails, then added as one who understood Guy better than Harriet did: "He arranges so many things, he forgets to explain, you know."

"Well, can you come?"

"But how can I? I must first have my bath. Then I must dress. It will take a long time because I meet a friend for lunch. And my fingernails. I must put on more varnish." Sophie spoke as though these activities might be a little selfish but were all the more endearing for that. She gave a laugh at Harriet's blank face and rallied her: "You can see the landlord by yourself. You are not afraid?"

"No." With a sense of giving Sophie a last chance, Harriet said: "The trouble is, I do not speak Rumanian."

"But the landlord will speak French. I am sure you speak very well French?"

"I hardly speak it at all."

"That is extraordinary, sure-ly?" Sophie's voice soared in amazement. "A girl of good family who cannot speak very well French!"

"Not in England." Harriet stood up.

Sophie encouraged her on the way out: "The landlord will not eat you. He will be nice to a young lady alone." She laughed, apparently delighted at the thought of it.

Harriet did not see Guy again until the evening. She told him she had come to an agreement with the landlord. She had taken the flat for six months.

"And what did Sophie think of it?"

"She did not see it."

"She dealt with the landlord, of course?"

"No, she could not come. She wasn't dressed when I called."

"But she promised to go with you."

"She said she hadn't understood."

Guy's expression left Harriet in no doubt but that Sophie had understood perfectly. He routed his dissatisfaction with a burst of admiration for Harriet: "So you did it all alone? Why you're wonderful, darling. And we have a flat! We must have a drink to celebrate." And Harriet hoped that for a few days, at least, she would hear no more of Sophie.

10

WHEN THEY MOVED INTO THE FLAT, the Pringles discovered that in negotiating with the landlord Harriet had not been as clever as they thought. Some of the furniture was missing. The bedside rug had been taken away. There were only two saucepans left in the kitchen. When telephoned, the landlord, with whom she had dealt in a mixture of English, French, Rumanian and German, told Guy he had explained to Doamna Pringle that these things would be removed from the flat.

They also discovered that if they wanted electricity, gas, water and telephone, they must settle the bills of the previous tenant, an English journalist who had disappeared without trace.

The flat was on the top floor of a block in the square. From the sitting-room, which was roughly coffin shaped, five doors opened. These led to the kitchen, the main bedroom, the balcony, the spare-room and the hall. The building was flimsy. What furniture remained was shabby, but the rent was reasonable.

When they took possession, on a day of exceptional cold, the hall-porter who brought up their luggage put a hand on the main radiator and grinned slyly. Noticing this, Harriet felt the radiator and found it barely warm. She told Guy to ask the man if it was always like this.

Yes, the flat was hard to let because it was cold. So the rent was low. The boiler, explained the porter, was not big enough to force the heat up to the top floor. Having made this revelation, he became nervous and insisted that the flats were of the highest class, each having attached to it not one servant's bedroom but two. He held up two fingers, pulling first one, then the other. *Two.* One was behind the kitchen, the other on the roof. Harriet said she had not noticed a bedroom behind the kitchen. The porter beckoned her to follow him and showed her a room some six feet long and three feet wide, which she had mistaken for a store cupboard. Guy surprised her by showing no surprise. He said most Rumanian servants slept on the kitchen floor.

When they had unpacked, they went out on to the balcony and surveyed the view that was their own. They faced the royal palace. Immediately below them, intact among the disorder left by the demolishers, was a church with gilded domes and crosses looped with beads. Apart from the Byzantine prettiness of this little church, and the palace façade, which had a certain grandeur, the buildings were a jumble of commonplaces, the skyline mediocre: and much was in ruins.

It was late afternoon. A little snow was falling from a sky watered over with the citrous gleams of sunset. Already, as the Pringles watched, the buildings were dissolving into dusk. The street-lamps came on one by one. At the entrance to the Calea Victoriei could be seen the first windows of the lighted shops.

A trumpet sounded from the palace yard. "Do you know what that says?" Guy asked. "It says: Come, water your horses, all you that are able. Come, water your horses and give them some corn. And he that won't do it, the sergeant shall know it: he will be whipped and put in a dark hole."

Harriet, who had not heard this jingle before, made him repeat it. As he did so, they heard a creak of wood below. The church door was opening and a light falling on to the snow-feathered cobbles. A closed *trăsură* drew up. Two women, like little sturdy bears in their fur coats and fur-trimmed snow-boots, descended. As they entered the church, they drew veils over their heads.

This incident, occurring there at their feet, beneath the balcony of their home, touched Harriet oddly. For the first time she felt her life becoming involved with the permanent life of the place. They might be here for six months. They might even be allowed a year of settled existence – perhaps longer. With so much time, one ceased to be a visitor. People took on the aspect of neighbours. There was a need to adjust oneself.

She said: "We could have done worse. Here we are at the centre of things," and she felt that, like herself, he was more impressed by that position than he cared to admit.

"We should buy things for the flat," she said. "Couldn't we go to the Dâmbovita?"

"Why not?" The term had ended. Guy was on holiday. With the high spirits of a move accomplished and refreshment due, he said: "First, though, we will go and have tea at Mavrodaphne's."

This was the newest, the most expensive, and so, for the

moment, the most fashionable of Bucharest cafés. The Pringles had visited it before, but this visit was a gesture of belonging. They were going where everyone went.

The café was situated in a turning off the Calea Victoriei. This was an old street that had been renovated with black glass, chromium and marble composites so that the buildings gleamed in the street lights. Within the brilliant windows were French gloves and trinkets, English cashmere garments and Italian leatherwork, tagged with exotic words like 'pulloverul', 'chic', 'golful' and 'five-o'clockul'. These shops stayed open until late at night.

The enormous windows of Mavrodaphne's were steamed over by inner heat and outer cold. A colony of beggars had already established rights in the shelter of the doorway. They lay heaped together, supping off the smell of hot chocolate that came up through the basement grating. They roused themselves in a hubbub when anyone passed inside. Within the door was a vestibule where a porter took the greatcoats of visitors and a piccolo, kneeling at their feet, removed their snowboots. This service was imposed. Customers were required to enter the better restaurants and cafés as they would enter a drawing room.

When the Pringles arrived, the whole vast area of the café, warm, scented, tricked out with black glass, chromium and red leather, was crowded for the 'five-o'clock', which for most people here meant coffee or chocolate, and cakes. Only a few had acquired the habit of drinking tea.

There seemed to be no vacant table. Wandering round in their search, Guy said: "We are sure to see someone we know," and almost at once they came upon Dobson, who invited them to join him. He had dashed out, he said, on some pretext, life in the Legation being now such that the girls had no time to make a decent cup of tea.

When the Pringles were seated, he asked: "You've heard about Drucker, of course?"

They, having spent their day packing and unpacking, had heard nothing. Dobson told them: "He has been arrested."

For some moments Guy looked blank with shock, then asked: "On what charge?"

"Buying money on the black market. Too silly. We all either buy or sell. They might have thought up a more substantial charge."

"What is the real reason for the arrest?"

"No one seems to know. I imagine it has something to do with his affiliations with Germany."

While they were talking, Guy was shifting to the edge of his seat, preparing, Harriet feared, to take some action. Not noticing this, Dobson chatted on, smiling as he did so: "I've heard for some time that Carol's been plotting to get his hands on the Drucker fortune. He can't do much because the bulk of it's in Switzerland. The Government could claim that the money had been deposited abroad contrary to Rumanian regulations, but that wouldn't cut much ice with the Swiss. No power on earth will get money out of a Swiss bank without the depositor's consent."

"So they may force Drucker to give his consent?" said Harriet.

"They may certainly try. Pressure *could* be brought to bear." Dobson gave a laugh at the thought. "Dear me, yes. We've felt for some time that Drucker was sailing too near the wind. His system of exchange was all in Germany's favour. The Minister of Finance told H.E. that the bank was ruining the country. Drucker claimed to be pro-British. You know what they said about him: that his heart was in England but his pocket was in Berlin . . ."

"The point was," Guy broke in, "he had a heart." Like Dobson, he spoke of Drucker in the past tense. He asked when the arrest had been made and was told "Early this morning."

"What about the other members of the family?"

Dobson had heard nothing about them.

As the waiter arrived to take their order, Guy rose. "I must go and see them," he said. "Sasha will be in a terrible state."

Harriet pleaded "Why not go after tea?", but Guy, looking like one on whom a heavy duty lay, shook his head and was gone. Harriet felt herself abandoned.

Dobson, startled by Guy's abrupt departure, turned and smiled on Harriet saying: "You will stay, won't you?" apparently so eager to retain her company that her composure was somewhat restored.

Feeling she might excuse Guy by echoing his concern for the Druckers, she said: "This is terrible news, isn't it?"

Dobson continued to smile: "Terrible for Drucker, of course, but you must remember his bank was serving the German cause."

Harriet said: "I suppose he'll soon buy his way out?"

"I don't know. This is a contingency against which he failed to provide. His wealth is outside the country. He could go to it, but it can't come to him."

The waiter brought tea and toast for Harriet, then, unasked, put on the table a plate of ball-shaped chocolate cakes pimpled over like naval mines. "Siegfrieds," he announced.

"Not our line," said Dobson, imperturbably, in English.

At once the waiter whipped away the plate, retreated a few steps, returned and put it down again. "Maginots," he said, and went off well satisfied by Dobson's amusement.

Beaming on Harriet, Dobson said: "I love these people. They have wit."

Harriet wondered if she would ever love them. She watched two girls, usually to be seen here, called, so Guy had said, Princess Mimi and Princess Lulie. They had just arrived and were making their way between the tables, faintly acknowledging their Rumanian friends. Keeping close together, their bodies seeming to melt and fuse, they had the air of lovers, too absorbed in each other to have other interests; but out of this confining intimacy, their glances strayed in search of someone to pay the bill. One of them saw Dobson. Somehow the fact of his presence was conveyed to the other. They moved towards him, all smiles now, then they noticed Harriet. The smiles vanished in an instant. They veered away.

Dobson glanced regretfully after them. "Charming girls!" he said.

"You prefer the Rumanians to other races?" Harriet asked.

"Oh no." Dobson talked quickly and willingly, used to doing his duty in important drawing-rooms. Harriet had heard people speak of his charm and she was grateful for it now she had been left on his hands, but she had noticed a curious thing about him. When he laughed – and he laughed very readily – his round, bright blue eyes remained as expressionless as the eyes of a bird. He was saying: "I love the French and the Austrians. And I simply *adore* the Italians. And," he added after a pause, "I've known some delightful Germans."

Harriet, feeling her conversation should be brighter, said: "Where do you think we met your friend Yakimov the other day?"

"Where? Do tell me?"

"Walking in the Cişmigiu."

"No, *never*! I can't believe it. Was he actually taking a walk?"

"Not voluntarily." She told the story of Yakimov's ejection from McCann's taxi and was gratified by Dobson's reception of it. His eyes grew damp and he shook all over his plump, soft body as he laughed to himself: "Ho-ho! Ho-ho-ho-ho-ho-*ho*!"

Her success was such, she felt she might safely question him about Yakimov, who had aroused her curiosity.

She asked: "Have you known Prince Yakimov long?"

"Oh *yes*. For years. He used to live in London, with Dollie Clay-Callard. They gave tremendous parties. Simply tremendous."

"I suppose you went to them?"

"Well, I went to one. It was fantastic. Out of doors in winter. The garden was floodlit and buried in artificial snow. We were told to wear furs, but, unfortunately, it was a muggy night and we were stifled. Yaki wore his sable-lined coat, I remember."

"The one the Czar gave his father?"

Dobson gave a burst of laughter: "The very one. And there was artificial ice. People skated and were pushed about in sleigh-chairs, carrying lanterns." He paused, reflected, and said: "Really, it was all rather charming. And there was a real Russian sleigh. At least Yaki said it was Russian. I wouldn't know. It was blue and gold and drawn by a pony with an artificial mane."

"Was everything artificial?"

"Everything that could be. The vodka was real enough. Dear me, I was younger then. I'd never seen anything quite like it. Soon afterwards Dollie and Yaki moved to Paris. Her money was running out. They couldn't live on that scale for ever."

"Where is Dollie now?"

"Dead, poor dear. She was much older than Yaki – twenty years or more. *And* looked it. But a wonderful old girl. We all loved her. We thought Yaki would inherit a fortune, but there wasn't a sou. Up to her eyes in debt. It must have been a shock to him."

"What did he do?"

"Travelled about. He never came back to England."

"So you never knew him really well?"

Dobson's eyes widened in surprise at this audacity, then he laughed again. "Oh, everybody knew Yaki." No one, it seemed, needed to know more than that.

She realised she was alarming him with this spate of questions, but there was one more she must ask: how did Yakimov live now? Perhaps suspecting what was coming, Dobson said quickly as she opened her mouth: "Here comes Bella Niculescu. *Such* a nice woman!"

Harriet let herself be distracted. She wanted to see Bella Niculescu.

Tall, broad-shouldered, her blonde hair knotted at the nape, Bella was a classical statue of a woman wearing a tailored suit. She was in the late twenties.

"She's very good-looking," said Harriet, thinking that Bella's over-stylish hat looked like a comic hat placed askew on the Venus de Milo. Behind her trotted a dark, moustached, little Rumanian Adonis. "Is that her husband?"

"Nikko? Yes. But surely you've met them?"

"No. She disapproves of Guy."

"Oh, nonsense," Dobson laughed, contradicting her with good-humoured confidence. "No one disapproves of Guy." He stood up to give his hand to Bella.

Bella's chief interest was in Harriet. When introduced, she said: "Someone told me that Guy had brought back a wife." Her tone and her use of Guy's Christian name seemed to Harriet an offer of friendship – one that Harriet felt inclined to accept.

Dobson, his admiring smiles now all for Bella, asked if the Niculescus would join him. But Bella refused. "We are meeting some Rumanian friends," she said, with a slight emphasis on the word Rumanian.

Dobson detained her with flattering interest: "Before you leave us, *do* tell us what lies behind Drucker's arrest. I'm *sure* you know."

"Well," – Bella straightened her shoulders, not displeased that the Legation came to her for information – "a certain lady – you can guess who! – discovered that Baron Steinfeld's holdings in Astro-Romano were in fact owned by Drucker. You know, of course, that all these rich Jews have foreign nominees so that they can avoid taxation. No need to tell you what those shares are worth at the moment! Well, the lady invited Drucker to supper and suggested he might care to make the holdings over to her as a Christmas present. He treated the suggestion as a joke. He had no holdings – in any case, Jews did not give each other Christmas presents, etcetera, etcetera. Then she tried other tactics. (I must say, I would have liked to have been a little mouse in the room, wouldn't you?) But Drucker, having a new young wife, was not susceptible. Then she became angry and said if he were not willing to hand over the shares, she would see they were confiscated. He thought, with his German connections, no one dared touch him – so he simply laughed at her. Twenty-four hours later he was arrested."

"I suppose," said Dobson, "the arrest could be something of an anti-German gesture."

"Oh, do you think so?" Bella's voice rose excitedly. "I must tell Nikko that. He'll be delighted. He's *so* pro-British." She waved to where Nikko had now joined his friends and said: "I must leave you. She gave her hand to Harriet. "I could never persuade Guy to come to my parties. Now you must bring him."

Harriet glanced after her as she went manoeuvring her broad and vigorous backside between the tables, and asked: "What does Nikko do?"

"Why nothing. He's married to Bella."

"You mean, she's rich?"

"Quite comfortably off."

Dobson had to return to the Legation. When he called the waiter, Harriet, knowing convention did not permit her to remain here alone, asked for her bill, which Dobson insisted on paying.

He had his car outside and offered her a lift, but she said she wanted to do some shopping.

As he was about to drive off, he said: "We don't get a moment to breathe these days, and now H.E. wants us to help with the decoding." He exploded with laughter at the thought of this humble employment.

Harriet remembered she had, when she first met him, decided he was difficult to know. She now thought she had been wrong. He was, she believed, as simply pleasant as he seemed.

She crossed over to a shop window in which she had seen an Italian tea-set of fine *sang-de-boeuf* china. She had suggested to Guy they might buy it with money given them as a wedding-present. Guy, who had no interest in possession, said: "Why waste money? When we leave here, we'll probably have to go empty handed." Now, in a mood to compensate herself, she looked defiantly at the tea-set, but, reflecting that she had been abandoned for the best possible motives by a husband made unreliable

only by his abysmal kindness, she went instead to the Calea
Victoriei and ordered an electric fire.

The wind had grown harder and there were occasional flurries
of snow. The sky, black and unrelenting as iron, hung like a
weight over the roof-tops. Not wishing to return to the empty
flat, she took a taxi down to the Dâmbovita. The market area
around the river had a flavour more of the East than of the West.
Guy had brought her here and shown her the houses, built in the
style of Louis XIII, once the mansions of Turkish and Phanariot
officials, now doss-houses where the poor slept twenty and thirty
to a room. The windows were still barred against thieves and
rebels. The Dâmbovita River, that ran between them, had no
beauty. Once navigable and the heart of the city, it was now
dwindling from some failure at source, leaving high banks of clay.
It was unused and in places covered to make a road.

When she left the taxi, she walked through the Calea Lipscani,
searching for a stall that sold decorated Hungarian plates. The
area was primitive, bug-ridden and brutal. Its streets, unlike the
fashionable streets, were as crowded in winter as in summer. The
gas-lit windows threw out a greenish glow. The stalls dripped with
gas flares. Harriet pushed her way between men and women who,
wrapped to the eyes in woollen scarves, were bulky with frieze,
sheep-skin and greasy astrakhan. The beggars, on home ground,
rummaging for food under the stalls, did not usually trouble to
beg here, but the sight of Harriet was too much for them.

When she stopped at a meat stall to buy veal, she became conscious of a sickening smell of decay beside her. Turning, she saw
an ancient female dwarf who was thrusting the stump of an arm
up to her face. She searched hurriedly for a coin and could find
nothing smaller than a hundred-*lei* note. She knew it was too much
but handed it over. It led, as she feared, to trouble. The woman
gave a shrill cry calling to her a troupe of children, who at once
set upon Harriet, waving their deformities and begging with
professional and remorseless piteousness.

She took the meat she had bought and tried to escape into the
crowd. The children clung like lice. They caught hold of her arms,
their faces screwed into the classical mask of misery while they
whined and whimpered in chorus.

Guy had told her she must try and get used to the beggars. They
could be discouraged by a show of amiable indifference. She had

not yet learned the trick and perhaps never would. Their persistence roused her to fury.

She reached the stall where the Hungarian plates were displayed and paused. At once the children surrounded her, their eyes gleaming at her annoyance, seeming to be dancing in triumph. She made off again, almost running, only wanting now to get away for them. At the end of the road she saw a *trǎsurǎ* and shouted to it. It stopped. She jumped on board and the children followed her. They clung to the steps, wailing at her, until the driver struck them off with his whip. As they dropped down, one by one, her anger subsided. She looked back at them and saw them still staring after the dispenser of hundred-*lei* notes – a collection of wretched, ragged waifs with limbs as thin as sticks.

Heavens above, how did one settle down to life in this society that Doamna Teitelbaum had recommended for its comfort? The day before, she had seen a peasant slashing his horse across the eyes for some slip of the foot. Though she was so shaken she could have murdered the man, she had to recognise what deprivation lay behind his behaviour.

Before she left England, she had read books written by travellers in Rumania who had given a picture of a rollicking, openhearted, happy, healthy peasantry, full of music and generous hospitality. They were, it was true, mad about music. Music was their only outlet. They made themselves drunk on it. As for the rest, she had seen nothing of it. The peasants in this city were starved, frightened figures, scrawny with pellagra, wandering about in a search for work or making a half-hearted attempt to beg.

The situation would have been simplified for her could she, like Guy, have seen the peasants not only as victims, but as blameless victims. The truth was, the more she learnt about them, the more she was inclined to share Doamna Drucker's loathing of them; but she would not call them beasts. They had not the beauty or dignity of beasts. They treated their animals and their women with the simple brutality of savages.

Driving now down the long, deserted Calea Victoriei, it seemed to her she could smell in the wind those not so distant regions of mountain and fir-forest where wolves and bears, driven by hunger, haunted the villages in the winter snow-light. And the wind was harsher than any wind she had ever known. She shivered, feeling isolated in a country that was to her not only foreign but alien.

A few yards past the University, she saw Guy walking, rather quickly, and stopped the *trăsură*. His face was creased and troubled. He said he was returning to Mavrodaphne's to look for her.

"Surely you didn't suppose I should still be there?"

"I didn't know." He obviously had not supposed anything at all. His mind had been elsewhere.

As he took the seat beside her, she said: "Did you see Sasha?"

He shook his head. He had gone to the flat but no one opened the door. He found the porter, who told him that the whole family had left that morning with a great deal of luggage. The servants had gone soon after. The flat was deserted. Asked about Sasha, the man could not remember having seen him with the others. Guy had then gone to the University, where there were, as usual, students sitting about in the common-room for want of anything better to do. There he learnt that the Drucker sisters, their parents, their husbands and the two girls had been seen at the airport boarding a plane for Rome, but Sasha and his step-mother had not been with them. There was a rumour that Doamna Drucker had gone to her father's estate in Moldavia.

Guy said: "Perhaps Sasha has gone with her."

Harriet said nothing but she thought it unlikely that Doamna Drucker would burden herself with Sasha.

"Wherever he is," said Guy, "I shall hear from him. He knows I will help him if I can."

Harriet was thinking of the panic that must have filled the household after Drucker's arrest, the hasty packing, the hasty departure.

"How did they get extra visas so quickly?" she asked.

"They must have been prepared. Drucker after all had been warned. If the arrest had not been made so quickly, he might have got away."

Thinking of the household with its solid furniture, the family portraits in their huge frames, a setting designed as a background for generations of Druckers, she knew she had been envious of its permanence.

'And yet,' she thought, 'that enclosed family was no more secure than we are.'

The *trăsură* was crossing the cobbles of the square. The driver turned to ask for direction.

Guy said to Harriet: "Where are we going to eat? Shall we go back to the hotel?"

She replied: "Tonight we are going to eat at home."

11

WHEN YAKIMOV RETURNED to the Athénée Palace after his conflict with McCann, he went to the English Bar and ordered himself a double whisky.

"Chalk it up, Albu, dear boy," he said.

When Albu 'chalked it up', he knew that his credit was still good. His anxiety vanished. A problem that need not be faced straight away was no problem to him.

At the end of the week he was presented with a bill. He looked at it in pained astonishment and required the manager to come to him. The manager explained that, as Yakimov was no longer backed by McCann's agency, he must settle a weekly account in the usual way.

"Dear boy," he said, "m'remittance should be here in a week or two. Difficult time. Posts uncertain. War on, y'know."

His quarterly remittance had, in fact, come and gone. Bored by the menu of the hotel, he had spent it on some excellent meals at Capşa's, Cina's and Le Jardin.

The manager agreed to let the account run on and it ran unquestioned until Christmas visitors began to fill the hotel. This time it was the manager who sent for Yakimov.

"Any day now, dear boy," Yakimov earnestly assured him. "Any day."

"Any day will not do, *mon Prince*," said the manager. "If you cannot pay, I must now present this matter to the British Legation."

Yakimov was alarmed. Galpin had told him: "These days you can be packed off under open arrest, third class and steerage, to Cairo, and there given the bum's rush into the ranks before you have time to say 'flat feet', 'conscientious objector' or 'incurable psychotic'."

Trembling slightly, Yakimov said to the manager: "Dear boy, no need to do that. I'll go there myself. M'dear old friend Dobbie

Dobson'll advance me the necessary. Just a question of asking. Didn't realise you were getting restless."

Yakimov was given another twenty-four hours. He did not go at once to Dobson, who was becoming less and less willing to lend him money, but first approached the hangers-on of the English Bar. Hadjimoscos, Horvath and Palu, as usual, together. He spoke first to Horvath:

"Dear boy, I have to settle a little bill. M'remittance is delayed. Never like to owe money. Wonder if you could manage to re-pay . . ."

Before he could finish, Horvath had spread hands so eloquently empty that Yakimov's words died in his throat. He turned to Hadjimoscos: "Do you think I could ask the Princess . . ."

Hadjimoscos laughed: "*Mon cher Prince*, rather ask the moon. You know the Princess. She is so irresponsible, one is made to smile. And it is the Rumanian habit never to repay a loan."

Yakimov moved his appealing eyes to Cici Palu, a handsome fellow who was said to do well out of women. Palu took a step back and glanced away with the air of one who sees and hears nothing that does not concern him. In desperation, Yakimov moaned: "Can no one lend me a *leu* or two ?" To encourage them, he tried to order a round. Albu shook his head. The others smiled, deprecating this familiar refusal, but their contempt was evident. Yakimov was now no more than one of them.

He was forced in the end to return to Dobson, who agreed to settle the bill on condition that he moved to a cheaper lodging.

"I was thinking of trying the Minerva, dear boy."

Dobson would not hear of the Minerva, or, indeed, of any other hotel. Yakimov must find himself a bed-sitting-room.

So, on the morning of the following Saturday, having been permitted a last breakfast in the dining-room, Yakimov departed the Athénée Palace. When he carried his own luggage through the hall, the porters looked the other way. Even had they been willing to attend him, attention would have been distracted from him by a new arrival who caused even Yakimov, burdened as he was, to pause and stare.

This was a white-haired, dark-skinned little crow of a man in a striped blue suit. He moved with a rattle of chains. One of his eyes was covered with a patch; the other swivelled about in keen and critical survey of all it saw. His left arm, with hand too small in its skin-tight glove, lay crooked across his breast. He wore a gold chain in a loop from button-hole to trouser pocket. Another heavier chain, attaching a walking-stick to his right wrist, struck repeatedly against the stick's silver mounting. Clearly unimpressed by the hall and its occupants, he strode to the reception desk and rapped out: "Any letters for Commander Sheppy?"

Galpin, on his way to the bar, gawped, and Yakimov said: "Striking figure, that! Who can he be?"

"Arrived last night," said Galpin. "Probably secret service. Nothing so conspicuous as your old-time member of the British Secret Service." Noticing Yakimov's luggage, he added: "Not leaving us?"

Yakimov nodded sadly. "Found a nice little place of m'own," he said and went out to his *trăsură*.

That morning the early snow hung like swansdown in the air. It was forming a gauze over the tarmac. The cold was intense.

The *trăsură* took Yakimov in the direction of the station. The coachman was a lean and fierce-looking fellow, no Skopitz. The horse was a skeleton roughly patched over with hide. As it was spurred by the whip, its bones, stretching and heaving, seemed about to fall apart. Blood trickled down its flanks from several open sores.

As he watched the skittish jig of its pelvis, a tear came into Yakimov's eyes, but he was not weeping for the horse. He was weeping for himself. He was retreating, most unwillingly, from the heart of Bucharest life to its seedy, unprofitable purlieus. He felt injured by circumstances. The world had turned against him since Dollie died. Now he had not even the last relic of their life together, his Hispano-Suiza. He found himself longing for it as for a mother.

The appearance of the station reminded him of the evening of his penniless arrival. How short his period of fortune had been! His tears fell.

Hearing a gulp and a sniff, the coachman turned and gave Yakimov a stare of crude curiosity. Yakimov brushed his sleeve across his eyes.

Beyond the station the roads were unmade. The horse stumbled in pot-holes, the carriage shook. Puddles, thinly sheeted over with ice, cracked beneath the wheels. Here the houses were mostly wooden shacks, but among them were blocks of flats, recently built but already turning into slums. The paint was scratched from the doors; washing hung on the balconies and women bawled down into the streets.

It was in one of these flats that Yakimov had found a room. The room had been advertised on a notice-board as '*lux nebun*' – insane luxury. Insane luxury at a low rent seemed just the answer to his problem.

He had come upon the block after searching the back streets for an hour or more. The servant, who opened the door an inch, gabbled something about 'siesta'. He pretended not to understand. The stone staircase, ventilated with open spaces, seemed colder than the street. He pushed open the door and edged his way into the oily heat of the flat's interior. He would not be moved out. Defeated, the servant tapped with extreme trepidation on a door, entered and was met with uproar. At last a man and a woman, both in dressing-gowns, peered out at Yakimov with angry hauteur. The man said: "What does this person here in our house?"

The woman replied: "Tell him at once to go."

It was some moments before Yakimov realised that, beneath the clotted disguise of accent, the two were speaking English to each other. He bowed and smiled: "You speak English? As an Englishman, I am flattered. I have called to see the room you advertised."

"An Englishman!" The wife stepped forward with an expression of such avidity that Yakimov quickly amended his status.

"Of White Russian origin," he said. "A refugee, I fear, from the war zone."

"A refugee!" She turned to her husband with an expression that said: 'That's just the sort of Englishman we *would* get.'

"The name is Yakimov. Prince Yakimov."

"Ah, a Prince!"

The room offered was small, cluttered up with Rumanian carved furniture and embroidered hangings, but warm and comfortable enough. He agreed to take it.

"The rent a month is four thousand *lei*," said the woman, whose name was Doamna Protopopescu. When Yakimov did not haggle, she added: "In advance."

"Tomorrow, dear girl." He touched her fat, grimy little hand with his lips. "Tomorrow a large remittance arrives for me at the British Legation."

Doamna Protopopescu looked at her husband, who said: "The

Prince is an English Prince," and so the matter was left for the moment.

Doamna Protopopescu had advised Yakimov the correct *trăsură* fare from the city's centre. Now, his bags safely on the pavement, he handed up the fare and a ten *lei* tip. The driver looked dumbfounded, then gave an anguished howl. He demanded more. Firmly Yakimov shook his head and started to gather up his bags. The driver flung the coins upon the pavement. Ignoring this gesture, Yakimov began to climb the stairs.

Swinging his whip above his head and haranguing the passers-by right and left, the driver leapt down and followed. Bounding and bawling, he caught up with his fare at the first landing.

Yakimov did not know what the man was saying, but he was shaken by the fury with which it was being said. He tried to run. He stumbled, dropped a case, then shrank in fear against the wall. The man did not attack him, but instead, as Yakimov crept on, kept beside him, banging his jackboots on the stairs, slashing his whip and causing so much noise that people came to their doors to see what was happening. Doamna Protopopescu and her servant peered over the third landing.

"How much did you give him?" she asked.

Yakimov told her.

"That was more than enough." At once her face became a mask of fury. She threw up her fists and, rushing at the driver, she screamed out a virulent stream of Rumanian. The man stopped in his tracks. She waved him away, very slowly, turning every few moments to fix Yakimov with a stare of sullen loathing. At this show of defiance, the servant ran after him, echoing her mistress's rage, while the mistress herself conducted Yakimov indoors.

"Dear girl, you were magnificent," said Yakimov as he sat panting on his bed.

"I said 'How dare you molest a nobleman' and he was afraid. So to deal with a filthy peasant." She flicked a hand, dismissing the matter, then said sharply: "And now, the money!"

"This evening," he promised her, "when the diplomatic post arrives, I'll stroll back to the Legation and pick up m'remittance."

Doamna Protopopescu's small black eyes bulged with suspicion. To greet her lodger, she had fitted herself into a short black dress that clung to the folds and wrinkles of her fat like a second skin. Her heavily whitened face sagged with annoyance like a flabby magnolia. She shouted through the door for her husband.

Protopopescu appeared, dressed in the uniform of an army officer of the lowest rank. He was a thin, drooping man with corseted waist, rouged cheeks and a moustache like that of a ringmaster, but he had nothing of his wife's fire. He said with a poor attempt at command: "Go this instant and get the money."

"Not now, dear boy." Yakimov settled down among the embroidered cushions. "Must have a bit of kip. Worn out with all this fuss." He closed his eyes.

"No, no!" cried Doamna Protopopescu and, pushing past her husband, she caught Yakimov by the arm and dragged him off the bed. "Go now. At once." She was extremely strong. She gave Yakimov a push that sent him headlong into the passage, then, closing the room door, she locked it and put the key in her handbag. "So! When you bring the money, I give the key."

Yakimov returned to the gnawing cold of the street. Where on earth could he find the money? He dared not approach Dobson who yesterday had lent him a last four thousand for the rent. Having no idea that Doamna Protopopescu could be so resolute, he had spent the money on a couple of excellent meals.

The pavements were freezing. He could feel the frost sticking to the broken soles of his shoes. He could not face the walk back to the main square and, realising he would have to learn to use public transport, he stood among the crowd waiting for a tramcar. When the tram came, there was an hysterical stampede in which Yakimov and an old woman were flung violently to the ground. The woman picked herself up and returned to the fray. Only Yakimov was left behind. When the next tram came along, he was prepared to fight. He was carried for a few *lei* to the city's centre. One could live here very cheaply, he realised, but who wanted to live cheaply? Not Yakimov.

He went straight to the English Bar and found it empty. Forced to search elsewhere, he crossed the square to Dragomir's food store, a refuge where a gentleman might sample cheese unchallenged and steal a biscuit or two.

The shop was decorated for Christmas. All about it peasants were selling fir trees from the Carpathians. Some trees were propped against the windows, some stood in barrels, some lay on the pavement among heaps of holly, bay and laurel. Great swags of snow-grizzled fir were tacked like mufflers about the shop front.

It was a large shop; one of the largest in Bucharest. Now it stood like a little castle embowered in Christmas greenery, its windows bright but burred with frost ferns.

A boar, on its feet, stood at the main entrance, its hide cured to a glossy blackness, its tusks yellow, snow feathers caught in its tough bristles. On either side of the door hung a deer, upside-down with antlers resting on the ground.

Yakimov sighed. These signs of festivity sent his thoughts back to Christmases at the Crillon, the Ritz, the Adlon and Geneva's Beau-Rivage. Where would he spend this Christmas? Not, alas, at the Athénée Palace.

As he entered the shop he found, crouched behind the boar, a heap of beggars, who set up a clamour at the sight of him that an assistant rushed out and kicked one, slapped another and attacked the rest with a wet towel. Yakimov slipped inside.

A little department at the door sold imports from England: Quaker Oats, tinned fruits, corned beef, Oxford marmalade – expensive luxuries eximious among luxury. These did not interest Yakimov, who made for the main hall, where turkeys, geese, ducks chickens, pheasant, partridge, grouse, snipe, pigeons, hares and rabbits were thrown unsorted together in a vast pyramid beneath a central light. He joined the fringe of male shoppers who went round with intent, serious faces examining these small corpses. This was not a shopping place for servants, nor even for wives. The men came here, as Yakimov did, to look at food, and to experience, as he might not, an ecstasy of anticipation.

He watched a stout man, galoshed, close-buttoned, Persian lamb on his collar, a cap in his hand, choose and order the preparation of a turkey still in its splendour of feathers. He swallowed hungrily as he watched.

This was not a good season for an onlooker. The counters that displayed shellfish, caviare and every sort of sausage were so hemmed in with customers he could see nothing of them. He wandered round with no more reward than the scent of honey-cured hams or the high citron fume of Greek oranges.

An assistant was sheering off the legs of live frogs, throwing the still palpitating trunks into a dustbin. Yakimov was upset by the sight, but forgot it at once as he peered into a basket of button mushrooms flown that morning from Paris. He put out a finger and brought it back tinged with the red dust of France.

In the cheese department, the sampling knife was in use. A little man in yellow peccary gloves, keeping an assistant at his heels, was darting about, nicking this cheese and that. As he waited, Yakimov eyed cheeses packed in pigs'-bladders, sheepskins, bark, plaited twigs, straw mats, grape pips, wooden bowls and barrels of brine. When he could bear it no longer, he broke off a piece of roquefort and would have put it into his mouth, but he realised he had been observed.

The observer was Guy Pringle.

"Hello, dear boy," said Yakimov, letting the cheese fall from his fingers into a bowl of soured cooking cream. "Difficult place to get served."

Guy, he saw, was not alone. Harriet Pringle had captured the assistant from the man in the peccary gloves. She seemed about to give an order, but at once the man, indignant at being deserted, began to demand attention. The assistant pushed past Harriet, almost bowling her over in his eagerness to assert his servility. "*Cochon*," said Harriet. The assistant looked back, pained.

Ever since the incident in the Athénée Palace garden, Yakimov had felt nervous of Harriet. Now, leaning towards Guy and whispering hurriedly, he said: "Your poor old Yaki's in a bit of a jam. If I can't lay m'hands on four thou, I'll have to spend the night on the streets."

Seeing Guy glance at Harriet, he added quickly: "Haven't forgotten. Owe the dear girl a thou. She'll get it soon's m'remittance turns up."

Guy took out the old note book in which he kept bank-notes and, leafing through it, found two thousand *lei*, which he handed to Yakimov. He said: "It's a pity you aren't a Polish refugee. I know the man who's administering relief."

"M'not exactly a Polish refugee, dear boy, but I'm a refugee from Poland. Got here through Yugoslavia, y'know."

Guy thought this fact might serve and gave him the address of the Polish Relief Centre, then mentioned that Yakimov had promised to visit them. Was he by any chance free on Christmas night?

"Curiously enough, I *am*, dear boy."

"Then come to dinner," Guy said.

Yakimov found the Relief Centre in a street of red, angular, half-built houses on which work had been abandoned for the winter. Builder's materials still lay about. Snow patched the yellow clay and the hillocks of sand and lime. Outside the one house that was nearly completed, a row of civilian Poles, in breeches and monkey-jackets, stood stamping their feet in the cold. Yakimov swept past them, wrapped in the Czar's greatcoat.

To the old peasant who opened the door, he said: "Prince Yakimov to see Mr. Lawson." He was shown straight into a room that smelt of damp plaster.

Clarence, seated behind a table, with an oil-stove at his feet and an army blanket round his shoulders, appeared to have a bad cold. When Yakimov introduced himself as a friend of Guy Pringle, Clarence looked shy, impressed apparently by the distinction of his visitor. Given confidence, Yakimov told how he had come down from Poland, where he had been staying on the estate of a relative. He had for a few weeks acted as McCann's deputy. When McCann left for Poland, Yakimov remained behind to collect a remittance which was being sent to him. The dislocations of war caused the delay of the remittance and so, he said: "Here I am on m'uppers, dear boy. Don't know where to look for a crust."

Strangely enough, Clarence did not respond as Yakimov had hoped to his story. He sat for some time looking at his fingernails, then said with sudden, startling firmness: "I cannot help you. You are not a Pole. You must apply to the British Legation."

Yakimov's face fell. "But, dear boy, I'm just as much in need as those blokes outside. Fact is, if I can't raise four thousand today, I'll have to sleep in the street."

Clarence said coldly: "The men outside are queuing for a living allowance of a hundred *lei* a day."

"You surely mean a thousand?"

"I mean a hundred."

Yakimov began to rise, then sank down again. "Never had to beg before," he said. "Good family. Not what I'm used to. Fact is, I'm desperate. The Legation won't help. They'll only send me to Cairo. 'S'no good to poor old Yaki. Delicate health. Been starving for days. Don't know where m'next meal's coming from." His voice broke, tears crowded into his eyes and Clarence, shaken by this emotion, put his hand into his pocket. He brought out a single note, but it was a note for ten thousand *lei*.

"Dear boy," said Yakimov, restored by the sight of it.

"Just a minute!" Clarence seemed rather agitated by what he

was doing. His cheeks reddened, he fumbled about looking for paper in a drawer. He took out a sheet and wrote an IOU. "I am lending you this," he said impressively, "because you are a friend of Guy Pringle. The money is from funds and must be paid back when your remittance arrives."

When the IOU was signed and the note had changed hands, Clarence, seemingly relieved by the generosity of his own action, smiled and said he was just going out to luncheon. Would Yakimov care to join him?

"Delighted, dear boy," said Yakimov. "*Delighted.*"

As they drove to Capşa's in the car which had been allotted to him, Clarence said: "I wonder if you know a Commander Sheppy? He's just invited me to a party. I don't know him from Adam."

"Oh yes, dear boy," said Yakimov. "Know him well. One eye, one arm – but keen as mustard."

"What is he doing here?"

"I'm told," Yakimov's voice dropped – "of course it's not the sort of thing one should pass round – but I'm *told*, he's an important member of the British Secret Service."

Clarence laughed his unbelief. "Who would tell you that?" he asked.

"Not in a position to say."

Capşa's was Yakimov's favourite among the Bucharest restaurants. As they passed from the knife-edge of the *crivat* into a lusciousness of rose-red carpeting, plush, crystal and gilt, he felt himself home again.

A table had been booked for Clarence beside the double windows that overlooked the snow-patched garden. To exclude any hint of draught, red silk cushions were placed between the two panes of glass. Clarence's guest, a thick-set man with an air of self-conscious pride, rose without smiling, and frowned when he saw Yakimov. Clarence introduced them: Count Steffaneski, Prince Yakimov.

"A Russian?" asked Steffaneski.

"White Russian, dear boy. British subject."

Steffaneski's grunt seemed to say 'A Russian is a Russian', and, sitting down heavily he stared at the table-cloth.

Defensively, Clarence said: "Prince Yakimov is a refugee from Poland."

"Indeed?" Steffaneski raised his head and fixed Yakimov distrustfully. "From where in Poland does he come?"

Yakimov, putting his face into the menu card, said: "I strongly recommend the crayfish cooked in paprika. And there is really a delicious pilaff of quails."

Steffaneski obstinately repeated his question. Clarence said: "Prince Yakimov tells me he stayed with relatives who have an estate there."

"Ah, I would be interested to learn their name. I am related to many landowners. Many others are my friends."

Seeing Steffaneski set in his deadly persistence, Yakimov attempted explanation: "Fact is, dear boy, there's been a bit of a misunderstanding. Left Poland before things started. Doing undercover work: saw trouble coming: was ordered to get away. White Russian, y'know. So, not to put too fine a point on it, your poor old Yaki had to take to his heels."

Watching him closely, Steffaneski was waiting for something to come of all this. When Yakimov paused, hoping he had given explanation enough, the Count said: "Yes?"

Yakimov said: "Got lost on the way down. Ended up in Hungary. Friend there, most generous fellow – Count Ignotus – invited me to stay on his estate. So, the fact was, the estate I spoke of was in Hungary."

"So you did not come down through Lvov and Jassy?" Steffaneski asked with apparent courtesy.

"No, just dropped straight down to Hungary."

"Through Czechoslovakia?"

"Naturally, dear boy."

"How then did you penetrate the German forces?"

"What German forces?"

"Can it be you did not encounter them?"

"Well." Yakimov looked appealingly at Clarence, who appeared embarrassed by these questions and answers. As Steffaneski began to harass Yakimov again, Clarence broke in to say: "He may have come through Ruthenia."

"Ruthenia?" Steffaneski jerked round to face Clarence. "Is Ruthenia not occupied, then?"

"I think not," said Clarence.

For some moments Clarence and the Count discussed, without reference to Yakimov, the possibility of his having passed unmolested through Ruthenia. Suddenly Steffaneski had another thought: "If he went through Ruthenia, he must have crossed the Carpathians." He returned to Yakimov. "You crossed the Carpathians ?" he asked.

"How do I know?" Yakimov wailed. "It was terrible. You can have no idea what it was like."

"I can have no idea? I drive with refugees from Warsaw to Bucharest! I am machine-gunned and I am bombed! I see my friends die: I help bury them! And you tell me I can have no idea!" With a gesture that implied life was real but Yakimov was not, he turned to Clarence and began to question him about Polish Relief.

Thankful to be left in peace, Yakimov gave his thoughts to the pilaff of quails which was being served.

Despite Yakimov's recommendation of the Moselle '34 and '37 Burgundy, Clarence had ordered a single bottle of Rumanian red wine. The waiter arrived with three bottles which he put down beside Yakimov, who gave him a look of complete understanding.

Steffaneski was describing a visit he had paid the day before to a Polish internment camp in the mountains. When he arrived at the barbed-wire enclosure he had seen the wooden huts of the camp half buried in snow. A Rumanian sentry at the gate had refused to admit him without sanction of the officer on duty. The officer could not be disturbed because it was 'the time of the siesta'. Steffaneski had demanded that the sentry ring the officer and the sentry had replied: "But that is impossible. The officer does not sleep alone."

"And so outside the camp I sit for two hours while the officer on duty sleeps, not alone. Ah, how I despise this country! One and all, the Poles despise this country. Sometimes I say to myself: 'Better had we stayed in Poland and all died together.' "

"I couldn't agree more, dear boy," said Yakimov, eating and drinking heartily.

Steffaneski gave him a look of disgust. "I was under the impression," he said to Clarence, "that our talk was to be private."

A second course of spit-roasted beef arrived and with it the second bottle of wine was emptied. Clarence spent some time explaining to Steffaneski how he was arranging with a junior Minister for the Poles to be shipped over the frontier into Yugoslavia, whence they could travel to join the Allied armies in France.

For permitting these escapes, the Rumanian authorities were demanding a fee of one thousand *lei* a head.

The beef was excellent. Yakimov ate with gusto and was examining the tray of French cheese, when Clarence noticed that the waiter was serving them wine from a new bottle.

"I ordered only one bottle," he said. "Why have you brought a second?"

"This, *domnule*," said the waiter, giving the bottle an insolent flourish, "is the third."

"The *third*!" Clarence looked bewildered. "I did not ask for three bottles."

"Then why did you drink them?" the waiter asked as he made off.

Consolingly, Yakimov said: "All these Rumanian waiters are the same. Can't trust them, dear boy . . ."

"But did we drink three bottles? Is it possible?"

"The empties are here, dear boy."

Clarence looked at the bottles beside Yakimov, then looked at Yakimov as though he alone were responsible for their emptiness.

When the coffee was brought, Yakimov murmured to the waiter: "Cognac." Immediately a bottle and glasses were put upon the table.

"What is this?" Clarence demanded.

"Seems to be brandy, dear boy," said Yakimov.

Clarence called the waiter back: "Take it away. Bring me my bill."

The cheese tray still stood beside the table. With furtive haste, Yakimov cut himself a long slice of brie and folded it into his mouth. Clarence and Steffaneski watching with astonished distaste, he said in apology: "Trifle peckish, dear boy."

Neither made any comment.

When the bill was paid, Clarence took out a notebook and noted down his expenses. Yakimov, whose sight was long, read as it was written:

Luncheon to Count S. and Prince Y.: *Lei* 5,500

Advance to Prince Y., British refugee from Poland: 10,000

For a moment Yakimov was discomforted at seeing his fantasy so badly recorded, then he forgot the matter. As they left the restaurant, his well-fed glow was like an extra wrap against the cold. He said to Clarence: "Delightful meal! Delightful company!"

He carried his smile over to Steffaneski, who was standing apart. Clarence barely responded.

Yakimov had expected the offer of a lift, but no offer was made. As Clarence and Steffaneski drove off without him, the glow began to seep from him. Then he remembered he had twelve thousand *lei*. He went into the *confiserie* attached to the restaurant and bought himself a little silver box full of raspberry pastilles. Holding this happily, he called a taxi and set out for his new lodgings, where he would sleep the afternoon away.

12

A FEW DAYS BEFORE CHRISTMAS, Bella Niculescu, meeting Harriet in the street, invited her to tea. Guy's only comment on this incipient friendship was: "She'll bore the arse off you."

Harriet said: "You scarcely know her."

"She's just a typical bourgeois reactionary."

"You mean, her prejudices are different from yours."

"You'll see for yourself," said Guy and, reminding her that they had been invited that evening to the Athénée Palace by a Commander Sheppy, he went to give a student private coaching. Harriet was left with doubts about her coming tea-party.

Bella's flat was in a new block on the Boulevard Brătianu. Walking there, Harriet felt the wind blow shrill across the desolate lots. Through the vents in the peasants' huts could be seen the flicker of lamps. The only crowds now were on the tramcars that clanked their way out of darkness into darkness. When she passed the vast black skeleton of the Ministry building, she saw a fire burning in a ground-floor corner. Beside it sat a huddle of workmen too old for the army and no use for anything else.

The blocks of flats rose out of the gloom like lighted towers. Their hallways, visible through glass doors, indicated the grandeur to which the designers of the boulevard had first aspired.

Harriet was shown into Bella's sitting-room. Low-ceilinged and very warm, it was carpeted in sky-blue and set about with walnut tables and blue upholstered arm-chairs. In the midst of this Bella, in a cashmere jersey and pearls, was seated before a silver tea-service.

Sinking into one of the chairs, Harriet said: "How comfortable!"

Bella replied: "It's cosy," as though Harriet had meant the reverse.

"This looks like English furniture."

"It *is* English furniture. Our wedding-present from daddy. He bought it for us from Maples. Everything came from Maples."

"And you brought it all this way? That must have been a business."

"It certainly was." Bella laughed, relaxing a little. "The amount it cost us in bribes, we might just as well have paid duty and have done with it."

While they were waiting for the tea to be brought in, Bella offered to show Harriet over the flat. They went first to Bella's bedroom, that contained a large double bed with highly polished walnut headboard and a pink counterpane braided, ruched, embroidered and embossed with satin tulips. Bella, touching out the collection of silver-backed brushes, silver-boxes and cut glass on her dressing table, said: "These peasant servants have no sense of anything."

She opened a door and disclosed a bathroom, as hot as a hothouse and closely packed with pink accoutrements.

"Delicious," said Harriet and Bella looked pleased.

"Now the dining-room!" she said and Harriet wished she had courage to tell her that she did not need to be impressed. She wanted to find herself in sympathy with Bella, who was, in a way, her own discovery – anyway, not a ready-made acquaintance imposed on her by Guy.

After luncheon with the Drucker family, she had said to Guy: "Your friends are disappointed in me. They expected you to marry someone exactly like yourself," but she had, she suspected, exceeded Bella's expectations.

In the dining-room, where Bella paused expectantly before a sideboard coruscant with silver and cut-glass, Harriet asked: "Do you use this stuff?"

"My dear, yes. Rumanians expect it. They look down on you if you can't make as big a show as they do." Bella smiled at the pretensions demanded of her, but her voice betrayed respect for them.

"The Pringle flat can provide nothing like this," said Harriet.

"Didn't you bring your wedding-presents?"

"We married in haste. We only got a cheque or two."

They had returned to the sitting-room, where tea awaited them. "Oh, I had a very big wedding," said Bella. "We came here with ten large packing-cases – *full*. Even the Rumanians were impressed. Still, you won't have to entertain them. The real Rumanians never mix with foreigners."

Harriet admitted they had been invited only to Jewish house-holds and Bella, gratified, was about to say more when she noticed something amiss among the silver on the tray before her. She stopped and her lips tightened. With a purposeful movement, she pressed a bell in the wall and waited. Her silence was intent. When the servant appeared, Bella spoke two words. The girl gasped and fled, to return with a tea-strainer.

"These servants!" Bella shook her head with disgust. Becoming suddenly animated, she talked at length about the sort of servants to be found in Rumania. She placed them in two categories: the honest imbeciles and the intelligent delinquents, the words 'honest' and 'intelligent' being, of course, merely relative.

"Which have you got?" Bella asked Harriet.

Inchcape's man, Pauli, had acquired for Harriet his cousin Despina. "She seems to me," said Harriet, "not only intelligent and honest, but very good-natured."

Bella grudgingly agreed that Hungarians were 'a cut above the others' but she had no doubt Despina 'made a bit' on everything she was sent out to buy. Harriet described how Despina, on being shown the cupboard that passed for a servant's bedroom in the Pringles' flat, had sunk to her knees and, kissing Harriet's hand, had said that at last she would be able to have her husband to live with her.

Bella saw nothing astonishing in this story. "She's very fortunate to have a room of any sort," she said, and almost at once returned to the subject of the real Rumanians whom Harriet was never likely to meet. "They're terribly snobby," she kept saying as she gave examples of their exclusiveness.

Harriet was reminded of Doamna Flöhr's claim that the exclu-siveness of the Jews was the exclusiveness of the excluded. What, she wanted to know, had the Rumanians to be so snobbish about? She said: "They must suffer from some profound sense of in-feriority."

Such an idea was new and strange to Bella. She looked bewil-dered as she asked: "But what are they inferior to?"

"Why, to us, of course; to the foreigners and the Jews who run the country for them because they are too lazy to run it for them-selves."

Bella, her mouth open, considered this point a moment, then she gave a gawp of laughter and said: "I don't know. Some of them still have a lot of money, but really, it's nothing compared with what people have in England and the States." A new vigour, roused by indignation, began to displace the careful refinement of her earlier speech: "And when you *do* get invited to their houses – the bother of it all! I can't tell you! Never a nice homey evening – always formality and everyone dressed up to the nines. All the time you have to think twice before you utter. And then this business of pretending you don't understand the men's jokes. Having to sit there like a dummy! My goodness, there's been times when I'd gladly go back to Roehampton. Anyone would think the women here were all bally virgins – and they're not, *believe me!*"

Exhilarated now by the daring of her own censure, Bella threw back her head, laughing and showing all her large, white, healthy teeth. Harriet laughed, too, feeling they had at last made contact.

"Here," said Bella, "have another cake. They're from Capşa's. I oughtn't to eat them; I'm putting on weight; but I do enjoy my food."

"Life here has its compensations," said Harriet.

"It certainly has. When I first arrived, the English wives were a bit snooty with me. They thought it a come-down to marry a Rumanian But my Nikko could show them a thing or two. He's shown me that Englishwomen know nothing at all."

Harriet laughed. "I expect they know something."

"Not much. Anyway, not the lot we had here. And now they're all coming back. Old Mother Woolley wrote to me, and what do you think she said? She said: 'My Joe's just like other men. With me away, his health suffers.' *I ask you!*" Bella threw back her head again and her bosom shook with laughter. "My Nikko says those old boys only started the scare to get rid of their wives." She wiped a tear from her eye. "Oh dear, it's a relief to talk to a woman of my own age – an Englishwoman, I mean – especially now Nikko's away."

"He's away?"

"Recalled to his regiment. His papers came yesterday and off he had to go. This morning I went round to see his senior officer. That man's a crook if ever there was one. It was only October last I arranged for Nikko to be released from service for six months, and here he is called up again. 'Ah, Doamna Niculescu,' said the officer 'I, too, have a senior officer.' 'And what does your senior

officer want?' I asked. 'Oh, the usual! One hundred thousand *lei*.'
I told him straight: 'If this war goes on for long, you'll bankrupt
me.' He just roared with laughter.''

"Your Rumanian must be very good?"

"I'm told it's perfect. I did languages, you know. I met Nikko
when I was at L.S.E. I speak French, German, Spanish and
Italian."

"So does Sophie Oresanu. I suppose you know her?"

Bella's face contracted significantly: "That little . . . um!"

"You really think she is . . . ?"

"I certainly do."

Harriet, confused by the liberal traditions of her generation,
had not been able to condemn Sophie so boldly, but now, hearing
Bella speak out without compromise – much, indeed, as Harriet's
aunt used to speak – Harriet was convinced by her certainty.

Bella said: "Nikko told me to say nothing, but really! The way
that girl runs after your husband! It's disgraceful. Quite frankly,
I don't think you should put up with it." She spoke rather breathlessly, in defiance of Nikko's ban. "It says a lot for Guy that there
hasn't been more gossip."

"Has there been gossip?"

"But of course there has. Can't you imagine it? In this place of
all places."

"I'm sure Guy doesn't realise . . ."

"I'm sure he doesn't. Still, he ought to have more sense. She's
the sort of girl who'd do anything for a British passport. If I were
you, I'd put a stop to it."

Harriet sat silent. Bella's statement that Guy should have 'more
sense' had struck her like a revealed truth.

When it was time for her to go, Bella came with her into the
hall, where the floor was tessellated in black and white. The white
walls were smooth as cream. Harriet said: "This is a very good
block. Ours is so flimsy, the wind seems to blow through
it."

Bella laughed. "You're in Blocşul Cazacul. That was built by
Horia Cazacu, whose motto is: *Santajul etajul*."

"What does that mean?"

"He's a financier but his income is chiefly from blackmail. It
more or less means 'Each blackmail builds a new floor'. Blocşul
Cazacul is bad even for Bucharest."

Feeling indebted to Bella for her friendly advances, Harriet asked her if she would be alone at Christmas.

"I'll be alone all right," said Bella. "Catch them asking me out without Nikko." The bitter amusement of Bella's tone disclosed her struggle to establish herself among the 'real' Rumanians.

Harriet squeezed her arm. "Then come and have supper with us," she said.

The public rooms of the Athénée Palace were crowded with visitors. On this, the first Christmas season of the war, war was forgotten. The threat of invasion had passed even from memory. Life here had always been uncertain and the people, like rabbits who have escaped the snare, recovered quickly. The Rumanian guests who sat drinking in the main room seemed to Harriet to exude confidence and self-sufficiency.

The new atmosphere had found expression in the Bucharest papers, which drew attention to the loss by Germany of the battle of the River Plate; and the fact that the Finns were making fools of the Russian invaders. Perhaps the threatening Powers were not, after all, so powerful! Perhaps the threat was all one great bluff! But, bluff or no bluff, Rumania had little to fear, being a richly provided country separated from the squabbles of others by a wall of snow-blocked mountains.

This attitude of self-congratulation did not persist into the breakfast room, where Dobson was introducing Commander Sheppy to those whom he had himself invited. There the air seemed edgy with uncertainties. Dobson, despite his charm, was a nervous host. When Harriet presented herself, he said: "You ought to meet Sheppy," but Sheppy was surrounded. "A little later, I think," said Dobson, dropping her and going to Woolley, who had entered behind her.

Guy, Inchcape and Clarence had not yet arrived. Among the other guests there was no one whom she knew well enough to approach. She took a drink and went to the French-window. Outside was the garden where she had sat in the sunlight with Yakimov only a short time before. Now the light from the room touched a bloom of snow on the north-east flanks of the trees. Somewhere outside in the darkness the boy was still emptying his urn. She thought she heard the tinkle of water, but could not be sure. Soon even moving water would be stilled to ice and the garden silent until spring.

A waiter, mistaking for a reprimand her interest in the world beyond the window, came fussily over and pulled the curtains. Then she had nothing to look at but the members of the business community gathered round the man who must be Commander Sheppy. She heard his voice come harsh and antagonising: "That, gentlemen, will be my problem." Then someone moved and she was able to see him.

Harriet noted the black eye-patch, the captive stick swinging and clattering beside him, the artificial hand held like an adornment, and smiled, thinking his manner that of someone who has taken a correspondence course in leadership. When she turned away she noticed Woolley at the bar and, crossing impulsively to him, said: " I hear your wife is returning. Now don't you think I was wise to remain in Bucharest?"

He stared at her, rebuking her with his long silence, then he said with decision: "No, I don't. If you want to know what I think of you staying here, after all it cost me to send my lady wife home – I think it wasn't playing the game." His brief nod underlined his opinion and he strode from her to join his associates round Sheppy.

At that moment Guy, Clarence and Inchcape arrived together. Guy and Clarence were at once seized upon by Dobson and taken to Sheppy. Inchcape was left, as Harriet had been, to find entertainment as best he might. He wandered over to Harriet, one eyebrow raised in a frown of bored enquiry.

"What've we been dragged here for?" he asked.

"No one seems to know."

"Which is Sheppy? I'm told he's an odd-looking cove."

Harriet pointed out Sheppy, who was now taking Guy, Clarence and some other young men to a corner of the room. When he had them to himself, he seemed to be lecturing them.

"What's he up to?" Inchcape stared over at the group. "And the chaps he has picked out – what have they in common?"

Harriet was about to say "Youth", but said instead: "They probably all speak Rumanian."

"So do I." Inchcape turned his back on Sheppy. "Well, I can't waste time here. I have people coming to dinner."

Sheppy did not keep the young men long. Clarence joined

Harriet and Inchcape, who at once asked him: "What's it all about?"

Clarence gave a provocative smile. "I'm not at liberty to say."

Inchcape put his glass to his lips and swallowed its contents. "I must be off," he said, and went with strides too long for his height.

Guy was still talking to the other young men. These were four junior engineers from the telephone company, an eccentric called Dubedat and an adolescent member of the English family Rettison that had lived in Bucharest for generations.

Harriet said: "Inchcape was wondering what you all had in common."

"The flower of the English colony," smirked Clarence.

"What *does* Sheppy want?" Harriet felt both pride and anxiety that Guy was among the chosen. "He really looks fantastic."

"Fact is, we don't know yet. He's calling us to a meeting after Christmas. I'd guess he's a 'cloak and dagger' boy – the lunatic fringe of security."

"What makes you think that?"

"He hinted he was here on a secret mission. But I shouldn't have told you that." Tilting back on his heels, displaying a diffident flirtatiousness, Clarence seemed to suggest she had wheedled a confidence out of him.

Harriet smiled it off but realised, whether she liked it or not, she had involved herself with Clarence. Nothing, she knew, would convince him she had not made a first move in his direction.

Impatiently she said: "What is Guy doing over there?" Guy was, in fact, talking enthusiastically to Dubedat.

Harriet had seen Dubedat about in the streets. He was a noticeable figure. He was said to have been an elementary-school teacher in England and had been 'thumbing' his way through Galicia when war broke out. He had walked over the frontier into Bessarabia. When the refugee cars came streaming down through Chernowitz, one of them gave him a lift. He called himself a 'simple lifer'. He had arrived in Bucharest in shorts and open-necked shirt, and for weeks wore nothing more. The *crivat* had eventually forced him into a sleeveless sheepskin jacket, but his legs and arms, remaining exposed, were whipped raw by the wind. When he walked in the street, his large, limp hands, mauve and swollen, swung about him like boxing-gloves on strings. Now, under Guy's regard, his face, hook-nosed, small-chinned, usually peevish, glowed with satisfaction.

Harriet asked Clarence: "Does Dubedat intend to stay in Bucharest ?"

"He doesn't want to go home. He's a conscientious objector. Guy is taking him on as an English teacher."

At this piece of news, Harriet moved to take a closer look at Dubedat, saying: "I'll go and see what they're talking about."

Guy was including in his audience the engineers, who stood together with the bashful air of obscure men unexpectedly given prominence. He was on a favourite subject – the peasants. Describing how they danced in a circle, their arms about each other's shoulders while they stared at their feet and stamped, he put out his own arms to the engineers. As they drew nearer, Dubedat's expression changed to one of hostility.

Guy said: "The peasants just go round and round, stamping in time to that hysterical music, until they're completely crazy with it. They begin to believe they're stamping on their enemies – the King, the landowner, the village priest, the Jew who keeps the village shop . . . And when they're exhausted, they go back to work. Nothing's changed, but they're not angry any more."

Harriet, having reached Dubedat's side, noticed the sour smell that came from him. He had been watching Guy's performance with his lips open so that she could see his yellow and decaying teeth. The creases of his nostrils were greasy and pitted with blackheads: there were crusts of scurf caught in the roots of his hair and grime beneath his fingernails. As he lit a new cigarette from the stub of an old one, she noticed the first and second fingers of his right hand yellowed by nicotine.

The engineers, having moved into the aura of Dubedat, began edging away again. Guy, however, was not worried. On the contrary he seemed like radium throwing off vitality to the outside world – not that he thought of it as the outside world. So spontaneous was his approach to it, he seemed unaware of any sort of frontier between himself and the rest of humanity.

Watching him, Harriet felt a wave of irritated love for him and heard this echoed by Clarence, who said behind her: "Let's get Guy away from here."

They had arranged to go that evening to see a French film at the main cinema and would have to leave soon. Harriet was about to speak to Guy, when young Rettison, on the fringe of the group, broke in in an accent that was peculiar to the Rettison family. He was a sleek, self-possessed and self-assertive young man who looked like a Rumanian. He said: "It has always been the same here. It was the same before the King became a dictator. It always will be the same. The English here criticise the King. They forget he is pro-British. We wouldn't have such a good time if he weren't here."

Guy said: "The King's pro-British because Britain is pro-King. That's the policy that's going to wreck us all."

The engineers glanced nervously towards Dobson, a representative of British policy, and Harriet said: "Darling, if you want to see the film, you must come now."

Guy wanted to see the film, but he also wanted to stay and talk. He looked like a baby offered too many toys.

"Come along," said Harriet and, to encourage him, she strolled on with Clarence out of the hotel. When Guy joined them he had brought Dubedat along too.

Clarence had his car with him. Harriet sat in the front seat beside him, while Guy sat with Dubedat in the back. As they drove across the square, Guy drew information from Dubedat. He asked him first where he came from.

Harsh and nasal, with a slight north country accent, Dubedat's voice came reluctantly from a corner. "I'm a scowse," he said. "From the dregs of the Liverpool soup."

He had won a scholarship to a grammar school, but at the school he had found not only the boys but the masters prejudiced against him. Everywhere he had gone, it seemed, he had met with prejudice.

"What sort of prejudice?"

"Social," said Dubedat.

"Ah!"

By the time they had reached the cinema, Guy was no longer interested in the film. "You go," he said to Harriet and Clarence. "I want to talk to Dubedat. We'll meet afterwards at the Doi Trandafiri."

Clarence protested, very annoyed, but Guy was too entranced to listen. Dubedat, looking smug, followed them across the road.

Clarence said: "It was Guy who wanted to see this film, not me."

"Would you rather go to the Doi Trandafiri?" Harriet asked.

"What! And listen to the confessions of Dubedat?"

The film was an involved and almost motionless domestic drama. Harriet's French was unequal to it and the Rumanian underlines did not help her much. It was preceded by a French news film that showed shots of the Maginot Line where trucks sped on rails through underground arsenals and barracks. There were vast stores of frozen meat and wine. A voice declared: "*Nous sommes imprenables.*"

"Let's hope so," said Clarence gloomily.

Behind the French lines soldiers filed through woods white with rime. They stood about, drinking from mugs and beating their arms for warmth while their breath clouded out on to the frozen air.

There was a little applause, but most of the time the audience shuffled and coughed, as bored by the war as were the idle men at arms.

Harriet and Clarence emerged, depressed, from the cinema. As they entered the Doi Trandafiri, an ancient beggar plucked at Clarence, repeating: "*Keine Mutter, kein Vater.*"

"*Ich auch nicht,*" replied Clarence and, cheered by his own wit, he turned smiling to Harriet: "I never give to beggars, on principle."

"On what principle?"

"They bring out the worst in me. They make me feel like a fascist."

Harriet laughed, but uneasily, recognising in Clarence something of herself. But because she loved Guy, she could feel safe. If she loved herself she would be lost indeed.

The interior of the Doi Trandafiri, with its yellow grained wood and horsehair sofas, the chess-sets and dominoes on the tables, the racks of newspapers mounted on batons, the faded photographs of writers, actors and painters, had a shabby, comfortable atmosphere of *Mitteleuropa.* It was a cheap café. In term-time it was crowded with students.

Guy and Dubedat were settled in the wide curve of the corner window. When the others sat down, Guy said delightfully: "Dubedat has been telling me he lives at the Dâmboviţa; actually in the Calea Plevna, with a family of poor Jews."

"The poorest of the poor," said Dubedat with glum satisfaction, "and the only decent folk in this dirty, depraved, God-forsaken capital." Fixing Clarence with a watery pink eye, he added, apparently in special reference to him: "A city of the plain."

"Oh, *really!*" Clarence, picking up a copy of the *Bukarester Tageblatt*, retired behind it in disgust.

Guy brushed aside the annoyance of the newcomers: "He doesn't mean any harm. You must hear about life at the Dâmboviţa." Guy swung round on Dubedat: "Tell them about the night the rats came in through the skylight."

Dubedat said nothing. Harriet was about to speak but Guy held up his hand. Gazing, aglow, at Dubedat, he coaxed: "Tell them about the mad beggar who drank silver polish."

Dubedat emptied his glass but remained silent. Clarence snorted behind his paper. When it became obvious that Dubedat was not to be persuaded, Guy, unaffected by rebuff, repeated his revelations for him while Dubedat, rather drunk, settled down into sleep.

They were as interesting as Guy promised, yet Harriet listened with impatience. At the same time she wondered whether she would have disliked Dubedat so much had his company not been forced upon her.

The difficulty of dealing with Guy, she thought, lay in the fact that he was so often right. She and Clarence could claim that their evening had been spoilt by the presence of Dubedat. She knew it had, in fact, been spoilt not by Guy's generosity but their own lack of it.

When it was time to go, Dubedat had to be roused and supported out to the car. They drove down through the Dâmboviţa area, which even at this hour was lively, with the brothels noisy and peasants and beggars wandering about in search of some night cover from the cold.

Wakened and questioned in the Calea Plevna, Dubedat managed to give his address. Guy said he would see Dubedat to his room on the top floor and wanted Clarence to come with him. Clarence insisted that they could not leave Harriet alone at such an hour, in this district.

When Guy and Dubedat had gone in, the other two sat for some time in silence. Suddenly, out of his thoughts, Clarence laughed and said in affectionate exasperation: "Guy is an extraordinary man with all this giving and expecting no return. Do you understand it?"

"It's partly pride," said Harriet, "and a habit of independence.

He wants to be the one to give because in the past he was always too poor to repay."

Upset by this rationalisation of Guy's virtue, Clarence sat up and said in reprimand: "He's a saint. In fact, a great saint. I often feel I'd like to give him something to show how much I admire him. But what can one give a saint?"

Considering this question in a practical way, Harriet said: "There are a great many things you could give him. Because he comes from a poor family, he has never had any of the presents that boys get as they're growing up. You could give him something useful – a set of hairbrushes or a fountain-pen or a shaving-brush . . ."

"Really!" Clarence interrupted with scorn. "Fancy giving Guy something like that! I thought of giving him a real present – two hundred pounds, say, so he would have something behind him if he needed it. But, of course, he wouldn't take it."

"I think he would. It would be wonderful."

"I couldn't offer it."

"Then why talk about it?"

Another long silence. Clarence sighed again. "I really want to do something for someone," he said, "but I let all my friends down in the end."

"Oh, well!" Realising that all this had merely been an exercise in self-mortification, Harriet left it at that.

When Guy returned to the car, he said: "We really must do something for Dubedat."

Harriet said: "What could we do? He's an exhibitionist. One should never separate an exhibitionist from his way of life."

"How else can he live?" Guy asked. "He has no money."

"Yet he smokes like a chimney."

"Oh, tobacco is necessary to him. From each according to his ability: to each according to his needs. We should offer him our spare room."

"I couldn't bear it," said Harriet, with such decision that Guy let the matter drop. She hoped she would hear no more of Dubedat, but next morning Guy mentioned him again: "We must ask him here on Christmas night."

"It's impossible, darling. The table only seats six. We've asked Inchcape and Clarence, and you asked Yakimov."

"That leaves room for one more."

"I've invited Bella."

"Bella Niculescu!"

"I suppose I can invite a friend?" said Harriet. "Nikko has been called to his regiment. Bella will be alone."

"All right." Guy could not fail to respond to Bella's situation, but he added: "What about Sophie?"

"Why should we ask Sophie?"

"She'll be alone, too."

"She's in her own country. She has friends. Bella's need is greater than Sophie's."

It was agreed at last that Sophie and Dubedat should be invited to come in after dinner. Both accepted when telephoned by Guy.

13

YAKIMOV WAS THE FIRST TO ARRIVE at the flat on Christmas night. He brought with him a thin, tall, narrow-shouldered, young man whom he introduced as Bernard Dugdale. Dugdale was a diplomat passing through Bucharest on his way to Ankara.

Barely touching Harriet's hand he sank into the only arm-chair and there he lay, seemingly lifeless except for his eyes, that roved around in critical appraisal of his surroundings.

Harriet hurried to Despina in the kitchen. When she explained there would be seven instead of six for dinner, Despina treated the emergency as a joke. She put a hand on Harriet's arm, squeezed it affectionately, then set off down the frosted fire-escape to borrow dishes from a neighbour's cook. When Harriet returned to the room, Inchcape and Clarence were entering from the hall. Yakimov, who had settled beside the electric fire with a glass of *tuică*, appeared abashed by the sight of Clarence.

Clarence said when introduced: "We have met before."

"So we have, dear boy. *So* we have!"

Inchcape, looking in amusement from one to the other, noticed Dugdale and suddenly stiffened. When he learnt that this stranger was a diplomat, he asked: "You came by train?" set on edge by the possibility that this young man might have been granted a priority flight over Europe.

Dugdale, weary but tolerant in his manner, admitted he had come by train: "A somewhat hazardous journey at the moment."

"In what way hazardous?" Harriet asked.

"Oh, one thing and another, you know." Dugdale implied that he had passed through perils the others could not even guess at.

When the introductions were completed, both Inchcape and Clarence seemed to withdraw from the party. It was some moments before Harriet realised they were annoyed at finding other guests present. The original plan had been for a 'family' party within the organisation and no one had told them of the change.

While standing, each stared down at the floor. When invited to sit down, Clarence took himself to the fringe of the group and remained silent, his head back against the wall. Inchcape, his legs crossed at the knee, turned up his elegant toe and stared at it, disguising his exasperation with an appearance of amusement.

Before anyone could speak again, Despina sped through the room, banging doors after her, to admit Bella. Bella entered with Nikko behind her.

Her Nikko, she explained, had been restored to her only half an hour before. As she apologised for bringing him unexpectedly, she beamed about in pride of him. Nikko was less composed than his wife. He was, no doubt on Bella's advice, dressed informally. He kept his head lowered while he glanced anxiously at the dress of the other men, then, reassured, he turned on Harriet, bowed and presented her with a bouquet of pink carnations.

When they were seated again, Inchcape, his lips depressed, looked under his brows at Clarence. Clarence, eyes wide, looked back. They were surprised at seeing, of all people, the Niculescus, and were, of course, displeased. Harriet was interested to note how similarly the two men reacted. Critical as each was of the other, there they both were withdrawn, suspicious and hard to mollify – not that she had time to mollify anyone at that moment.

Despina, enjoying her own resource, collected the smaller chairs from under the guests and took them to the table, then she sang out: "*Poftiţi la masă.*" On the table, among the Pringles' white china and napkins, were two yellow plates with pink napkins. Among the six chairs were the kitchen stool and the cork-topped linen box from the bathroom. This was the first dinner-party Harriet had ever given. She could have wept at its disruption.

When they were all seated, there was not much elbow room at the table. Nikko, pressed up against Yakimov, kept giving him oblique glances and at last blurted out: "I have heard of the famous English Prince who is so *spirituelle.*" Everyone looked at Yakimov, hoping for entertainment, but his eyes were fixed on Despina, who was carrying round the soup. When the bowl reached him, he filled his plate eagerly and emptied it before Guy had been served. He then watched for more.

Guy asked Nikko if there was any news of the Drucker family. Nikko, who had been for a short time an accountant in the Drucker bank, replied with satisfaction that there was none.

"And the boy?" Guy asked. "I have been hoping to hear from him."

"No one knows where he is," said Nikko. "He is not with Doamna Drucker, that is certain. He has disappeared. But of Emanuel Drucker I am told he is in a common cell with low criminals and perverts. Such must be very uncomfortable."

"Very indeed," murmured Inchcape with a sardonic smile.

"Who is this Drucker?" Dugdale asking, looking down with benign condescension upon Nikko.

Nikko swallowed and choked in his eagerness to reply: "This Drucker," he said, "is a big crook. A powerful lady – we do not name her – demanded of him certain holdings in Rumanian oil. He had been skinned before. Although he describes himself as pro-British, his business is with Germany – such a thing is not uncommon here – and he thinks Germany will protect him. So he refuses. He is arrested. He is jugged. Each minute a new charge is cooked for him – treason, forgery, plotting with Germany, plotting with Britain, black-market deals and so on. One would be enough. He is a Jew, so his possessions anyway are forfeit. His son has disappeared. His family has fled. His wife is demanding a divorce. The man himself? He will be in prison for life."

"Without trial?" Clarence asked, scandalised.

"Certainly not," said Nikko. "This is a democratic country. There will be a trial. A *great* trial. A trial that will squash him flat."

Dugdale gave a high neigh of a laugh. "Delicious!" he cried.

Clarence asked: "You are amused by a system of government that permits wrongful arrest, wrongful seizure of property and imprisonment for life on faked charges?"

Dugdale turned slowly to examine Clarence and smiled slightly at what he saw: "Aren't we in Ruritania?" he said. "What do you expect?"

Nikko, looking in consternation from Dugdale to Clarence, tried to reprove both at once: "This is not a bad country. Many people come here as guests. They make money, they live well, and still they criticise. One admires England. Another admires France. Another America. But who admires Rumania? No one. She is a cow to be milked."

The truth and vehemence of Nikko's statement brought the

table to a stop. After a silence, Harriet asked Dugdale if he thought he would enjoy Ankara.

"Things could be worse," he said. "My first appointment. I was offered Sofia – a deadly hole. However, I exerted a little pull and landed Ankara. It's an embassy. I'm not dissatisfied."

Yakimov, who had just filled his plate with turkey, taking most of the breast, said: "Let's face it, dear boy. An embassy is better than a legation." Having thus contributed to the conversation, he set about his food again.

Guy asked Dugdale what he imagined would be Germany's next move.

Dugdale answered in an authoritative tone: "In my opinion Germany has made her last move. Russia is the one we have to fear."

Yakimov, his mouth full, mumbled agreement.

"The next victim will be Sweden," said Dugdale, "then, of course, Norway and Denmark. After that the Balkans, the Mediterranean, North Africa – what's to stop them? The Allies and the Axis will watch helplessly, each unable to make a move for fear of bringing the other in on the side of Russia."

Guy began to say: "This is absurd. Russia has enough to do inside her own frontiers. What would she want . . ."

He was interrupted by Nikko, his brows raised in alarm. "But Rumania would fight," he said. "And the Turks, too. They would fight. At least I think so."

"The Turks!" Dugdale put a small potato into his mouth and swallowed it contemptuously. "We give them money to buy armaments, and what do they spend it on? *Education.*"

"Hopeless people!" Inchcape grinned at Clarence, who grinned back. Harriet was thankful they had, at last, decided to come down on the side of flippancy.

Despina had cut more turkey and was carrying the large serving dish round again. When she came to Yakimov, she held it so that the white meat was out of his reach.

"Just a *soupçon*, dear girl," he said with an air of wheedling intimacy and, stretching out his arms, he again took most of the breast. Only a few vegetables remained. He took them all. Despina, hissing through her teeth, attracted Harriet's attention and pointed to his plate. Harriet waved her on. Only Yakimov, intent on his food, remained unaware of Despina's indignation. He ate at speed, wiped his mouth with his napkin and looked around to see what was coming next.

Guy, having anticipated an evening of Yakimov's wit, now tried to encourage him to talk by telling stories himself. When his stories were exhausted, he started on limericks, occasionally pausing to ask Yakimov if he could not think of some himself. Yakimov shook his head. Despina having brought in a large mince pie, he could attend to nothing else.

Guy searched his mind for limericks and remembered one that he thought would seem particularly funny to the company. It concerned the morals of a British diplomat in the Balkans.

"That," said Dugdale coldly, "seems to me in rather bad taste."

"I couldn't agree more," said Yakimov heartily.

For some minutes there was no sound but that of Yakimov bolting down pie. He finished his helping before Despina had completed serving the others. "Hah!" he said with satisfaction and, unimpaired, looked to her for more.

As soon as was possible, Harriet motioned Bella to retire with her to the bedroom. There, not caring whether she was overheard or not, she raged: "How dare he snub Guy! The gross snob, wolfing down our food, and bringing that dyspeptic skeleton with him. When he gave his tremendous parties – if he ever gave them, which I doubt – he would not have dreamt of inviting us. Now he entertains his friends at our expense."

Bella was quick to echo this indignation: "If I were you, my dear, I wouldn't ask him here again."

"Certainly not," said Harriet, dramatic in anger; "this is the first and last time he sets foot in my house."

When the women returned to the room, the men were gathered round the electric fire. Guy was helping Yakimov to brandy. Dugdale, unperturbed, was sprawling in the arm-chair again. At the entry of the women, he lifted himself slightly and was about to drop back, when Harriet pushed the chair from him and offered it to Bella. He took himself to another chair with the expression of one overlooking a breach of good manners.

Inchcape smiled maliciously at Harriet, then turned to Yakimov and asked him: "Are you going on later to Princess Teodorescu's party?"

Yakimov lifted his nose from his glass. "I might," he said, "but those parties come a bit rough on your poor old Yaki."

To Harriet's annoyance, Guy was still trying to persuade Yakimov to talk. Yakimov seemed to be rousing himself, to be searching for jests through the fog of repletion, when there was a ring at the front door. Dubedat was admitted.

He made no concessions to the occasion. He had kept on his sheepskin jacket and to his personal smell was added the smell of badly cured skin. Looking, so Harriet thought, dirtier than ever, he surveyed the table grimly, aware the others had dined here and he had not.

At the sight of this new arrival, Dugdale rose and said he must go.

"Oh, no." Guy tried to detain him. "You have plenty of time to catch your train. You must have another brandy."

Guy began rapidly splashing brandy from glass to glass, but Dugdale stood firm. He had, he said, to collect his baggage from the cloak-room.

"Well, before you go," said Guy, "we must have 'Auld Lang Syne'."

Several people informed him that that was sung at New Year, but Guy said: "Never mind." His enthusiasm was such, the others rose and Dugdale let himself be drawn into the circle. When he had retrieved his hands, he said in a businesslike way: "Now, my overcoat."

While he was wrapping himself up, Yakimov sat down again and refilled his glass. Harriet, noticing this, said: "I imagine you will see your friend to the station."

"Oh, no, dear girl. Yaki isn't too well . . ."

"I think you should."

Even Yakimov recognised this as an invitation to go. Despondently, he gulped down the brandy and let himself be put into his coat.

When he and Dugdale had gone, Harriet and Bella freely expressed their indignation – an indignation that completely bewildered Guy.

"What are you two talking about?" he asked.

When they told him how he had been insulted, he burst out laughing. "I doubt whether Yaki even knew what he had said."

Harriet and Bella would have none of this, and Nikko backed them. While the other men sat complacently uninvolved in the situation, the two women insisted that he should never speak to Yakimov again.

Guy sat in silence, smiling slightly and letting the storm pass over his head. When at last it died down, Clarence said from the back of the room: "Yakimov came to the Relief Centre the other day presenting himself as a refugee from Poland. I lent him ten thousand."

"Oh," said Guy easily, "he'll pay it back."

Down in the street, Yakimov said: "Seems to me I was given the boot. Can't for the life of me think why."

Dugdale showed no interest. Calling a taxi, he said discouragingly: "I suppose you want to be dropped somewhere?"

"Athénée Palace, dear boy. Feel I ought to drop in on Princess T." As they drove across the square, he added: "I wonder, dear boy – end of the month and all that; bit short of the Ready – could you lend poor Yaki a *leu* or two?"

"No," said Dugdale, "my last five hundred went on tea."

"If you have any odd pennies or francs . . ."

Dugdale did not reply. When the taxi stopped, he opened the door and waited for Yakimov to descend.

Yakimov on the pavement said: "Delightful day. Thank you for everything. See you when you're back this way. Yaki's turn next."

Dugdale slammed the door on his speech and directed the taxi on. Yakimov pushed against the hotel door: the door revolved and he came out again. He stood for a moment looking after the taxi. Could he have brought himself to admit his address, he might have been driven all the way home.

He set out to walk. The Siberian wind, plunging and shrilling, stung his ears and tugged at the skirts of his coat. As he put up his collar and buried in it his long icicle of a nose, he murmured: "Poor Yaki's getting too old for his job."

Soon after the last of the Christmas guests had gone, the telephone rang in the Pringles' flat. Guy answered it. The caller was Sophie.

Sophie had not arrived, as expected, after dinner. Harriet went into the bedroom and left Guy to talk to her.

Sitting at her dressing-table, Harriet heard Guy's voice, concerned, solicitous, apparently pleading, and it renewed in her the anger Yakimov had aroused. Bella had said if she were Harriet, she would put a stop to that relationship. This, Harriet felt, was the moment to do it. She went into the sitting room and asked: "What is the matter?"

Guy was looking grave. He put his hand over the mouthpiece and said: "Sophie's in a state of depression. She wants me to go over and see her. Alone."

"At this time of night? Tell her it's out of the question."

"She's threatening to do something desperate."

"Such as?"

"Jump out of a window, or take an overdose of sleeping-tablets."

"Let me speak to her." Harriet took the receiver and said into it: "What is the matter, Sophie? You are being very silly. You know if you really intended to do anything like that, you would do it and not talk about it."

There was a long pause before Sophie's voice came, tearfully: "I will jump if Guy doesn't come. My mind is made up."

"Then go ahead and do it."

"Do what?"

"Why, jump, of course."

Sophie gulped with horror. She said: "I hate you. I hated you from the first. You are a cruel girl. A girl without heart." There came the thud of her receiver being thrown down.

"Now," said Guy severely, "I shall have to go. There's no knowing what she may do if I don't."

"If you go," said Harriet, "you won't find me here when you come back."

"You are being absurd," said Guy. "I expected more sense from you."

"Why?"

"Because I married you. You are part of myself. I expect from you what I expect from myself."

"You mean you are taking me for granted? Then you are a fool. I won't tolerate any more of this Sophie nonsense. If you go, I leave."

"Don't be a baby." He went into the hall and started to put on his coat, but his movements were uncertain. When he was ready, he stood irresolute, looking at her in worried enquiry. She felt a flicker of triumph that he realised he did not know her after all, then she choked in her throat. She turned away.

"Darling." He came back to the room and put his arms around her. "If it upsets you, of course I won't go."

At that, she said, "But you must go. I can't have you worrying about Sophie all night."

"Well!" He looked into the hall and then looked at Harriet. "I feel I ought to go."

"I know," she said, solving the problem as she had intended to solve it all along. "We'll go together."

The front door of Sophie's house was unlatched. The door into her flat was propped open with a book. When she heard Guy's step, she called in a sad little voice: "Come in, *chéri*." As he pushed wide the door, Harriet, behind him, could see Sophie sitting up in bed, a pink silk shawl round her shoulders. On the table beside her the picture that had been face downwards on Harriet's first visit now stood upright. It was a photograph of Guy.

Despite the smallness of her down-drooping smile, Sophie was much restored. She put her head on one side, sniffed and began to speak – then she noticed Harriet. Her expression changed. She turned on Guy.

"Your wife is a monster," she said.

Guy laughed at this statement, but it brought Harriet to a stop in the doorway. She said: "I'll wait for you downstairs."

She waited for about five minutes in the hallway of the house, then went out into the street. There she started to walk quickly, scarcely aware of the direction in which she went. For the first few hundred yards, feeling neither cold nor fear of the empty streets, she was carried on by a sense of injury that Guy should choose, after such a remark, to stay with Sophie: that he was, in fact, still with her.

Harriet was resolved not to go home. She found herself in the Calea Victoriei moving rapidly towards the Dâmboviţa, then she asked herself where she could go. In this country, where women went almost nowhere unescorted, her appearance, at this hour, luggageless, in an hotel would rouse the deepest suspicion. She might even be refused a room. She thought of the people she knew here – Bella, Inchcape, Clarence – and was disinclined to go to any of them with complaints about Guy. Inchcape might be sympathetic but would have no wish to be involved. Clarence would misunderstand the situation. Wherever she went, she would take with her an accusation of failure against Guy's way of life. She reflected that for her, and for Clarence, life was an involute process: they reserved themselves – and for what? With Guy it was a matter to be lived.

Contemplating in Clarence her own willingness to escape from living, she felt a revulsion from it. She had, she knew, done her worst with Sophie. She had made no attempt to flatter, she had not admitted herself to be vulnerable, she had not wanted Sophie's assistance. She had made none of those emotional appeals to which Sophie, once put into a position of power, might have responded with emotion.

Had she, she wondered, lacked charity? Had Sophie had some justification in seeing her as a monster?

She had withheld herself. Now she could not defend herself. She turned and walked slowly back to Sophie's house. She arrived at the doorstep as Guy came out. He took her hand and tucked it under his arm.

"That was nice of you," he said.

"What happened?"

"I told her not to be ridiculous. She really is as big an ass as Bella, and she's a great deal more of a nuisance."

PART THREE

The Snow

14

THE NEW YEAR BROUGHT THE HEAVY SNOW. Day after day it clotted the air, gentle, silent, persistent as time. Those who walked abroad – and these now were only servants and peasants – were enclosed in flakes. The traffic crept about, feeling its way as in a fog. When the fall thinned, the distances, visible once more, were the colour of a bruise.

Those who stayed indoors were disturbed by the outer quiet. It was as though the city had ceased to breathe. After a few days of this, Harriet, hemmed in by her surroundings, ventured down the street, but her claustrophobia persisted outside in the twilit blanket of snow, and she lost her way. She returned to the flat and telephoned Bella, who suggested they go together to Mavrodaphne's. Bella called for her in a taxi.

The two women had met several times since Christmas and a relationship that neither would have contemplated in England was beginning to establish itself. Harriet was becoming used to the limitations of Bella's conversation and did not give it much attention. Bella was easy, if unstimulating, company, and Harriet was glad, in the prevailing strangeness, of a companion from a familiar world.

In the café, while Bella described the latest misdoings of her servants, Harriet gazed at the café window, through which there was nothing to be seen but the mazing, down-soft drift of snow. Occasionally a shadow passed through it, scarcely distinguishable as a cab, or a closed *trăsură*, or a peasant with a sack over his head. More often than not the cabs stopped at Mavrodaphne's. The occupants, having sped the pavements, escaped the clamour of the beggars in the porch and entered the heady warmth with the modish air of hauteur. Turning their backs on the barbarities of their city, they saw themselves in Rome or Paris or, best of all, New York.

Bella raised her voice against Harriet's inattention. "*And*," she said, "I have to keep all the food locked up."

Recalled by Bella's aggravated tone, Harriet said: "Why bother? Food is so cheap here. It's less trouble to trust them." She regretted this remark as she made it. Tolerance, after all, should come of generosity, not expediency. Bella disapproved it for a different reason. She said:

"That attitude is unfair to other employers. Besides, one gets sick of their pilfering. If you'd had as much as I've had . . ."

When advising and informing the newcomer, Bella was as smug as an elder schoolgirl patronising a younger. Now she was in the presence of wealthy Rumanians, she reverted to refinement. Harriet could hear in her voice – especially in phrases like 'you daren't give them an inch', and 'the better you treat them the more they take advantage' – the exact inflections that had once made her aunt's dicta so irritating. For some moments it recalled an odd sense of helplessness, then she suddenly interrupted it.

"But what's the cause of all this?" she asked. "The poor aren't born dishonest any more than we are."

Bella looked startled. This was the first time Harriet had attempted to combat her. She tilted back her head and drew her fingers down her full, round throat. "I don't know." She spoke rather sulkily. "All I know is, that's what they're like." She bridled slightly and a flush spread down her neck.

In the uncomfortable pause that followed, Harriet saw Sophie enter. Hoping for diversion, she sat up, prepared to greet the girl, feeling she had come to terms with her; but when she raised a hand, she realised that only she had come to terms. Sophie had not. Sweeping past, with the sad averted smile of one who has been mortally wounded, Sophie joined some women friends on the other side of the room.

Rather out of countenance, Harriet turned back to Bella, who, given time to reflect, was saying defensively: "I know things aren't too good here. I noticed it myself when I first came, but you get used to it. You've got to, if you want to live here. You can't let things upset you all the time. There's nothing you can do about them. I mean, *is there*?"

Harriet shook her head. Bella was no reformer, but even if she had been prepared to beat out her brains against oppression, here she would not have changed anything. Having revealed her uncertainty in her situation, she looked rather shamefaced and for this reason Harriet warmed to her.

"No one can do much," said Harriet. "Nothing short of a revolution could force these people to change things. But why should you accept their absurd conventions? You are an Englishwoman. You can do what you like."

"You know," confided Bella, "when we talked that afternoon you came to tea, I remembered how free I was before I came here. And next day I wanted some things and I thought, 'Why shouldn't I go out and get them myself?' and I just took a shopping-basket from the kitchen and went out with it in my hand. I met Doamna Popp and *didn't she stare*!" Bella gave one of her vigorous laughs and Harriet liked her the more. Bella had felt satisfaction in instructing Harriet, and Harriet might find satisfaction in releasing Bella. To Harriet it seemed that to have found a sound basis for friendship with anyone as different from herself as Bella was a triumph over her own natural limitations.

When the snow stopped falling at last, the city was revealed white as a ghost city agleam beneath a pewter sky. The citizens crowded out again and the beggars emerged from their holes.

Beggars now were more plentiful than ever. Hundreds of destitute peasant families, their breadwinners conscripted, had been driven by winter into the capital, where, it was believed, a magical justice was dispensed. They would stand for hours in front of the palace, the law courts, the prefecture or any other large, likely-looking building. They dared not enter. When cold and hunger defeated them at last, they would wander off in groups to beg – women, children and ancient, creeping men. Lacking the persistence of professionals, they were easily discouraged. Many of them did no more than crouch crying in doorways. Some sought out the famous Cişmigiu, that stretched from its gates like a vast sheeted ballroom. Some slept there at night beneath the trees; others took themselves up to the Chaussée. Few of them survived long. Each morning a cart went round to collect the bodies dug from the snow. Many of these were found in bunches, frozen inseparable, so they were thrown as they were found, together, into the communal grave.

On the first morning that the air cleared, Guy and Clarence

were called by Sheppy to the Athénée Palace. At mid-day, when they were expected to leave the meeting, Harriet, anxious and curious, crossed the square to join them in the English Bar.

Wakening that morning she had seen the white light reflected on to the ceiling from the snowbound roofs. Emerging with a sense of adventure, she had been met by the *crivat*, blowing on a wire-fine note. In the centre of the square the snow was heaped like swansdown, its powdery surface lifting in the wind, but at the edge, where the traffic went, it was already as hard as cement. She walked round the statue of the old King, a giant snowman, shapeless and wild. The snow squeaked under her boots.

The cold hurt the flesh, yet even the most cosseted Rumanians had ventured out for the first sight of the city under snow. They trudged painfully, making for some café or restaurant, the men in fur-lined coats and galoshes, the women wrapped in Persian lamb, with fur snow-bonnets, gloves and muffs, and high-heeled snow boots of fur and rubber.

Outside the hotel the commissionaire stood, obese with wrappings, but the beggars were, as ever, half-naked, their bodies shaking fiercely in the bitter air.

As she passed the large window of the hair-dressing salon, Harriet saw inside, lolling on long chairs among the chromium and glass, Guy and Clarence having their hair cut. She went in to them and said: "Your meeting could not have lasted long."

"Not very long," Guy agreed.

"Well, what was it all about?"

He gave a warning glance towards the assistants and to deflect her interest said: "We are going to give you a treat."

"What sort of treat? When? Where?"

"Wait and see."

When they left the salon, Guy put on a grey knitted Balaclava helmet lent him, he said, by Clarence. It was part of an issue of Polish refugee clothing.

Clarence said: "Of course it must be returned."

"Really?" Harriet mocked him. "You imagine the Poles will miss it?"

"I am responsible for stores."

"It's a ridiculous garment," she said, dismissing it, and returned to the subject of Sheppy: "Who was he? What did he want? What was the meeting about?"

"We're not at liberty to say," said Guy.

Clarence said: "It's secret and confidential. I've refused to be in on it."

"But in on what?" Harriet persisted. She turned crossly on Guy. "What *did* Sheppy want with you?"

"It's just some mad scheme."

"Is it dangerous?" She looked at Clarence, who, self-consciously evasive, said: "No more than anything else these days. Nothing will come of it, anyway. I think the chap's crazy."

As they would tell her nothing, she decided she would somehow find out for herself. With this decision she changed the subject.

"Where are we going?"

"For a sleigh-ride," said Guy.

"No!" She was delighted. Forgetting Sheppy, she began hurrying the pace of the two men. They were approaching the Chaussée, that stretched broad and white into the remote distance. At the Chaussée kerb stood a row of the smartest *trăsurăs* in town. The owners had removed the wheels and fitted them with sleighs. The horses were hung with bells and tassels. Nets, decorated with pom-poms and bows, were stretched over the horses' hindquarters to protect the passengers from up-flung snow.

People were bargaining for sleigh-rides and about them were sightseers, and beggars battening on everyone.

"The important thing," said Harriet, "is to choose a well-kept horse." When they had found one rather less lean than the rest, she said: "Tell the driver we have chosen him because he is kind to his horse."

The driver replied that he was indeed a kind man and fed his horse nearly every day. Waving his rosetted whip in self-congratulation, he turned out of the uproar of the rank and sped away up the Chaussée to where the air was still and the wheels made no sound. In this crystalline world all was silent but the sleigh-bells.

On either side of the road the spangled skeletons of the trees flashed against a sky dark with unfallen snow. Across the snow-fields, that in summer were the *gradinas*, the wind leapt hard and bitter upon the sleigh. Its occupants shrank down among old blankets into a smell of straw and horse-dung, and peered out at the great plain of snow stretching to the lake and the Snagov woods.

They passed the Arc de Triomphe and came, at the furthest end of the Chaussée, upon an immense fountain that stood transfixed, like a glass chandelier, among mosaics of red, blue and gold.

As they reached the Golf Club, the driver shouted back at them.

"He says," said Clarence, "he'll drive us across the lake. I doubt whether it's safe."

Excitedly, Harriet said: "We must cross the lake."

They slid down the bank to the lake, that was a plate of ice sunk into the billowing fields, and the wind howled over their heads.

"Lovely, lovely," Harriet tried to shout, but she was scarcely able to breathe. Her ears sang, her eyes streamed, her hands and feet ached. Her cheeks were turned to ice.

The ice creaked beneath the sleigh and they were relieved to mount the farther bank and find themselves safely on solid ground. They had reached one of the peasant suburbs. The houses were one-roomed wooden shacks, painted with pitch, patched with flattened petrol cans, the doorways curtained with rags. Despite the antiseptic cold the air here was heavy with the stench of refuse. Women stood cooking in the open air. They waved to the sleigh, but the driver, unwilling that foreigners should observe this squalor, pointed his passengers to the cloudy whiteness of the woods and said: "Snagov. *Frumosa.*"

They came out to the highway at the royal railway station, which stood by the roadside, painted white and gold, like a booth at an exhibition. The road turned back to the town, so now the wind was behind the sleigh. The singing died in their ears. The horse was allowed to relax and they returned at a slow trot to their starting point.

When they reached the rank, Harriet noticed a young man, too large for a Rumanian, standing head and shoulders above the crowd and observing with an amused air the excitement about him.

Guy cried: "It's David!" and, jumping down from the sleigh, made for the young man with outstretched arms. The young man did not move, but his small mouth stretched slightly more to one side as he smiled and said: "Oh, hello."

"When did you arrive?" Guy called to him.

"Last night."

Harriet asked Clarence who this new arrival was.

"It's David Boyd," said Clarence, rather grudgingly.

"But you know him, don't you?"

"Well, yes. But I expect he has forgotten me."

Guy swung round and commanded Clarence forward: "Clarence. You remember David?"

Clarence admitted that he did.

"He's been sent out by the Foreign Office," said Guy, "the best thing they've ever done. At least there's someone to counteract the imbecilities of the Legation."

Harriet had heard that Guy and David Boyd looked remarkably alike, but their difference was apparent to her at once. They were large young men, identical in build, short-nosed, bespectacled and curly-haired – but David's mouth was smaller than Guy's, his chin larger. He wore a pointed sheepskin hat that had settled down on to the rim of his glasses so that the upper half of his face was snuffed out while the lower looked larger than it probably was.

"Were you thinking of taking a sleigh-ride?" Harriet asked him.

"No." Looking at her from under his eyelids, he explained that Albu, the barman, had heard Domnul Pringle and Domnul Lawson enquiring if the sleighs were out. Guy was delighted by this intimation that his friend had actually been searching for him. He said: "Let's all go and have lunch somewhere."

"I've arranged to meet a man . . ." began David.

Guy interrupted gleefully: "We'll all go and meet him."

David looked doubtful and Clarence, taking this fact to himself, said: "Don't worry about me. I'm going to a party being given by the Polish officers."

Guy swept on ahead with David while Harriet followed behind with Clarence. As they crossed the square, the two men in front, looking over-large in their winter wrappings, talked with an intimate animation. Guy was wanting to know what David had been sent out to do.

"Anything I can to help." Now that this first shyness had passed, David was voluble. His voice, rich, elderly and precise, the voice of a much earlier generation, came back to Harriet and Clarence in the rear: "I saw Foxy Leverett this morning – that fellow with the big red moustache. I said: 'When's this war going to begin?' And what do you think he said? 'Oh, things'll hot up soon. We'll give the Huns a biff. We'll give 'em a bloody nose.' "

Guy was stopped in his tracks by his own laughter. Harriet and Clarence, who had to step aside to skirt him, now walked ahead.

When they reached the Calea Victoriei, the talk of the other two was lost in the noise of the traffic.

David was meeting his friend in an old eating-house in a back street. When they reached the corner of this street, Clarence said: "I go straight on," and paused with Harriet, waiting for the others.

A barrel-organ stood at the street corner. A white-bearded peasant, bundled up in a sheepskin, was turning the handle, producing a Rumanian popular tune of the past, haunting and sad. Harriet had heard the same organ playing this tune several times before and no one had been able to tell her what it was called. Now, as they stood in a doorway sheltering from the cold she asked Clarence if he knew.

He shook his head. "I'm tone deaf," he said.

Harriet said: "That's the last barrel-organ in Bucharest. When the old man dies and there's no one to play it, that tune will be lost for ever."

Clarence stood silent, apparently reflecting, as Guy would never reflect, on the passing of things. "Yes," he said and as he smiled down on her his rare and beautiful smile, they touched, it seemed, a moment of complete understanding.

David and Guy came up, both talking together, exuding an air of engrossment in larger issues. David's voice rose above Guy's voice as he firmly said: "Although Rumania is a maize-eating country, it grows only half as much maize as Hungary. So we have here the usual vicious circle – the peasants are indolent because they're half-fed: they're half-fed because they're indolent. If the Germans *do* get here, believe me, they'll make these people work as they've never worked before."

"Clarence is going a different way," said Harriet when she got a chance.

"*No!*" Guy protested, not having grasped that Clarence was bidden elsewhere. He caught Clarence's arm, unwilling to let any-one pass from his sphere of influence. When Clarence explained where he was going, Guy demanded: "How long will your party go on for? Where will you be afterwards? We must meet again this evening."

Clarence, not yet recovered from the defensive disapproval with which he faced each new situation, murmured: "Well, it's a luncheon party. I don't know . . . I can't say," but before he left them he agreed to come to the Pringles' flat that evening.

Now Harriet had joined Guy and David, their conversation halted and started again on a more personal plane. David began asking about the people he had known when he was last in Bucharest. He spoke of each with an uncritical, indulgent humour, as though all human beings were for him more or less of a joke. Guy, not given to gossip, had not much to tell. Harriet was silent, as she tended to be with strangers.

"And how's our old friend Inchcape?" David asked.

Guy said: "He's fine."

"I hear he's risen in the world. Gets invited to Legation parties."

Guy laughed and said he believed that was true.

"When I was last in Cambridge," said David, "I met a friend of Inchcape – Professor Lord Pinkrose. They were up together. He was asking me about him. He said that Inch had been a remarkable scholar: one of those chaps who are capable of so much, they don't know what to do first. In the end they usually do nothing at all."

The restaurant was housed in an early nineteenth-century villa, with a front garden where bushes like giant heads set their chins upon the snowy lawn.

David, without a glance about him, talked his way up the front steps and entered as though he had never been away. They passed from the icy outer air into a hallway over-heated and scented by grilled meat. A stream of waiters were clattering and grumbling in and out of the four rooms. One of them tried to direct the three to a back room, but David, without bothering to argue, led the way to the main front room. The tables and chairs were rough. On the walls, papered in faded stripes, hung a few old Russian oleographs. From a dark ceiling hung a gilt chandelier laden with the grime of a decade. The place was noted for its excellent grilled veal.

When they were seated, David started at once to talk: "I saw Dobson, too, this morning – not a bad little chap. I always liked him, but the occupational disease is manifesting itself. I asked about the situation here. He said: 'Quite satisfactory. The Sovereign is with us.' I said: 'What if the people are not with the Sovereign!' 'Oh, I don't think we need worry about that,' said Dobson. When I asked him a few more questions, he h'md and hawed, then said, 'The situation's a bit complex for a newcomer!' "

"He probably doubted your ability to understand it," Guy said, rousing David to a paroxysm of snuffling laughter.

When there was a pause in the talk, Harriet asked him where he was staying and learnt with surprise that he was at the Minerva. "But that is the German hotel!"

David said: "I like to practise my German." Turning to Guy, he said: "And one picks up useful odds and ends of information. In the bar there, where the German journalists congregate, you get the same stringmen that take the news to the English Bar. One version goes to the Athénée Palace another to the Minerva. In that way our Rumanian allies keep in with both sides at once."

Guy, proud of his friend, now mentioned to Harriet that David spoke all the Slav languages.

David smiled down modestly. "My Slovene is a little rusty," he said, "but I can manage in the rest. I got through the first volume of *Anna Karenina* in the train. Now I find I haven't brought the second volume. I'll have to fly to Sofia to get it from the Russian bookshop. I'd like to know how it ends."

"Haven't you read it in English?" Harriet asked.

"I scarcely need to brush up my English."

If this were a joke, David gave no indication of the fact, but, sitting four-square on his chair, he stared down solemnly at the menu. His cap, when taken off, had left some snow in his curled black hair. As this melted and trickled down his cheeks, he thrust out his lower lip and caught the drops. His brow, visible now, was as massive as his chin.

Putting the menu down he said: "This policy of backing the established order, whether right or wrong, is not only going to lose us this country. When the big break-up starts, it will lose us concessions all over the world. In short, it'll be the end of us."

When on his own subject, David's manner lost its diffidence. He tended, Harriet thought, to address his listeners less like a conversationalist than a lecturer – and a lecturer wholly confident in the magnitude of his knowledge. His self-sufficiency was now evident. She remembered that his hobby was bird-watching. He was saying:

"Those F.O. dummies can't see further than the ends of their noses. For them the position inside the country is of no importance. The Sovereign right or wrong – that's all they know and all they need to know."

While David talked – and he talked at length – a waiter came and stood by the table. David was not to be interrupted, but when the man decided to move away, David seized and held him by the coat-tails while saying:

"I learnt on the train that German agents have settled in all over the country. They're working through the Iron Guard, buying grain, secretly, at double the usual rate. They said: 'See how generous we Germans are! With Germany as an ally, Rumania would be rich.' But could I persuade H.E. of this? Not for a moment. The Sovereign says the Iron Guard has ceased to exist and the Sovereign *must* be right."

The waiter, his patience exhausted, began to tug at his coat-tails. Turning irritably on him and shouting: "*Stai, domnule, stai*," David went on with his dissertation.

"Let us give our order," Harriet pleaded.

David jerked round on her and snapped: "Shut up."

"I won't shut up," she snapped back, and David, suddenly sniggering, looked down, all his diffidence returned. "We must order, of course," he said. "I suppose we'll have *Fleică de Braşov*." They gave their order and the waiter was released.

"Tell us what is going to happen here," said Guy.

"Several things could happen." David shifted his chair closer to the table. "There could be a peasant revolt against Germany, but we, of course, will see that does not happen. The Peasant Party is in opposition to the Sovereign, so it gets no support from us. I'm the only Englishman in this country who has met the peasant leaders . . ."

Guy interrupted: "I met them with you."

"Well, we're the only two Englishmen who have bothered to meet them: yet those men are our allies. They are our true allies. They would lead a rising on our behalf, but they are ignored and snubbed. We have declared ourselves for Carol and his confederates."

"Why are the peasants so despised?" Harriet asked.

"They suffer from hunger, pellagra and sixteen hundred years of oppression – all enervating diseases."

"Sixteen hundred years?"

"Rather longer." David now set out upon a history of Rumania's oppression, beginning with the withdrawal of the Roman legions in the third century after Christ and the appearance of the

Visigoths. He passed from the ravaging Huns to Gepides, Lango-
bards and Avars, to the Slavs and 'a race of Turkish nomads
called Bulgars'. "Then in the ninth century," he said, "the Mag-
yars swept over Eastern Europe."

"Isn't all this part of the migration of nations?" Harriet asked.

"Yes. Rumania is the part of Europe over which most of them
migrated. There were, of course, intervals – for instance, a brief
period of glory under Michael the Brave. That led to the most
wretched and tragic period of Rumanian history – the rule of the
Phanariots."

The waiter brought them soup. As David emptied his plate, he
followed the further misfortunes of the Rumanian people until the
peasant revolt of 1784. "Suppressed," he said, putting down his
spoon, "in a manner I would not care to describe during a meal."

Harriet was about to speak. David raised a hand to silence her.
"We come now," he said, "to the nineteenth century, when
Turkish power was waning and Rumania was being shared out
between Russia and Austria . . ."

They had ordered the veal grilled with herbs. It was brought to
the table on a board and there chopped into small pieces with two
choppers. Silenced by the noise, David frowned until it was over,
then started at once to talk again. He was interrupted by the arrival of a short, round-bodied, round-faced man who entered
quickly and came quickly to the table, smiling radiantly about him.

"Ah!" said David, rising, "here's Klein." Klein seized on both
his hands and, talking rapidly in German, displayed an ecstatic
pleasure in their reunion.

When introduced to the Pringles, Klein bowed from the waist,
saying: "How nice . . . how pleased to meet you!" but he looked
unsure of them until David said: "It's all right. They're friends."

The word 'friends' had, apparently, a special connotation. "Ah,
so!" said Klein, relaxing into the chair that Guy had brought to
the table for him. He had the fresh, snub, pink and white face of a
child. Had it not been for the fact he was bald and what hair he
had was grey, he might have passed for a very plump schoolboy –
but a super-subtle boy who, despite his smile of good humour, was
assessing everyone and everything about him. He accepted wine,
which he poured into a tumbler and mixed with mineral water, but
he would not eat. He had come, he said, from the first meeting of
a newly formed committee.

"An important committee, you understand. It exists to discuss the big demand Germany now makes on Rumania for food. And what did we do on the committee? We ate, drank and made funny remarks. There was such a buffet – from here to here," he indicated some twenty foot of the wall, "with roasts and turkeys, lobsters and caviare. *Such food!* I can tell you, in Germany today they have forgotten such food ever existed."

He laughed aloud while David, watching him, curled his lip in appreciation of this picture of the Rumanians in committee.

Klein gave Guy a smile, confiding and affectionate, and said: "I am, you understand, economic adviser to the Cabinet. I am called to this committee because each day Germany asks for more – more meat, more coffee, more maize, more cooking oil. Where can it all come from? And now she says: 'Plant soya beans.' 'What are soya beans?' we ask one another. We do not know, but Germany must have them. Every day come these requests – and each time they are more like demands. The Cabinet is nervous. They say: 'Send for Klein, Klein must advise us.' I am a Jew. I am without status. But I understand economics."

"Klein was one of the best economists in Germany," said David.

Klein smiled and twitched a shoulder, but did not repudiate this claim. "Here it is very funny," he said. "They call me in to advise. I say: 'Produce more: spend less.' What do they reply? They laugh at me. 'Ach, Klein,' they say, 'you are only a Jew. What can you know of the soul of our great country? God has given us everything. We are rich. Our land all the time produces for us. It cannot be exhausted. You are a silly little Jew.' "

As Klein laughed, his face flushed with mischievous glee, Guy laughed with him, delighted by this new acquaintance. And no one, Harriet was beginning to realise, enjoyed a new acquaintance more than Guy did. Aglow with interest in Klein, he neglected his food and, leaning forward, questioned him about his unofficial position in the Cabinet, then about his departure from Germany and arrival in Rumania two years before.

Klein's story was much like that of other refugee Jews in Bucharest except that his reputation as an economist had enabled him to stay in Germany longer than most. He had been warned in the end by a German friend that his arrest was imminent. He had walked empty-handed out of his Berlin flat, taken a train to the Rumanian frontier and, having had no time to buy the usual entrance permit, had crossed the frontier on foot after dark. He had been caught and spent six months in the notorious Bistriţa prison, where Drucker was now held. Friends had bought his release.

"But still," he said, "I have no permit to work. Still I am illegal. If I am not useful, then back I go to Bistriţa." He laughed happily at the prospect.

David, watching Guy's eager questioning of Klein, twisted his mouth with a quizzical amusement, pleased that he had brought them so successfully together. Harriet felt less pleased. She had heard a great deal about David Boyd, whom Guy regarded as an especial friend, one whose knowledge and conversation offered considerably more than the limited, personal concerns of Inchcape and Clarence. Now here was David, whose interests were, like his own, impersonal, social, economic and historical. She sighed at the thought of so much talk. It was not, she told herself, that she was unappreciative, but the impersonal quickly tired her. She felt a little out of it, a little jealous.

Perhaps sensing this, Klein turned smiling to her to include her. He said: "So here we all are Left-side men, eh? And Doamna Preen-gel? She, too, is Left-side?"

"No," said Harriet, "I am fighting the solitary battle of the reactionary."

Guy laughed to prevent Klein taking this seriously, and squeezed her hand.

Klein said: "You like Rumania, Doamna Preen-gel? It is interesting here, is it not?"

"Yes, but . . ."

"But it is interesting," Klein insisted. "And wait! It will become more interesting. Do you think the Allies can safeguard this country? I think not. It will be necessary to buy off the Germans with more and more food – with so much food, there will be a famine. If you stay, you will see the break-up of a country. You will see revolution, ruin, occupation by the enemy . . ."

"I don't want to stay so long."

"But you will see so much," Klein reasoned with her, "and all so interesting." He looked round the table as though offering them all a joyous future. "I say to this committee: 'Listen! In this country it is necessary that we have 200,000 wagon-loads of wheat in one year. This year, with the land workers mobilised, we shall have perhaps 20,000, perhaps less. It is necessary,' I say, 'that you demobilise those peasants and at once send them back to the land. If you do not, the people will starve.' And they laugh at me and say: 'We know you, Klein, you are of the Left. You do not look to the glory of Greater Rumania, you look to the welfare of the stupid, dirty peasants. Rumania is rich. Rumania cannot starve. Here, one day you throw seed on the ground, the next day it is bread. If we are short of wheat, merely it is necessary to stop exports.' 'If you do that,' I say, 'how will you make up the money?' 'All that is necessary,' they say, 'is a new tax.' I say: 'What can we tax? What is not already taxed?' And they laugh at me: 'Ha, Klein, it is for you to answer! You are economist.' "

Shaking with laughter at the thought of the trouble ahead, Klein put a hand to Harriet's shoulder. "Listen, Doamna Preen-gel: Rumania is like a foolish person who has inherited a great fortune. It is all dissipated in vulgar nonsense. You know the story the Rumanians tell about themselves: that God, when He had given gifts to the nations, found He had given to Rumania everything – forests, rivers, mountains, minerals, oil and a fertile soil that yielded many crops. 'Hah,' said God. 'This is too much,' and so, to strike a balance, he put here the worst people he could find. The Rumanians laugh at this. It is a true, sad joke!" said Klein, but he told it without any sign of sadness.

The meal was finished. Most of the other diners had left the restaurant; David, Guy and Klein however seemed prepared to stay all afternoon. After a while, Klein passed to stories of his life in prison. He gave the impression it had all been uproariously funny.

"And it was so interesting," he said, "so *interesting*! With such a lot of people crowded in a common cell, there was such a life, such stories, such feuds, such scandals. Always something happening. I remember one day the warders came in to beat a prisoner who was a little mad – in prison many get a little mad – and as they beat him, he screamed and screamed. This the warders did not like, so they put over his head a pillow of feathers. It stopped the screaming but when they took it off – what a surprise! The man was dead. Smothered! The warders stood like this . . ." Klein's mouth fell open and his eyes protruded, then he laughed: "And the prisoners – oh, they laughed so much!"

Klein went on to describe the cells slimed with damp, the floors deep in filth, the raped boys who, once corrupted, sold themselves for a few *lei*, and all the new crimes that came into existence in this community of men packed together with the hatreds, angers and lusts of propinquity.

"How terrible!" said Harriet.

Klein laughed: "But so interesting!" He explained that he had never been officially released but had made a condoned escape. "And when they told me I might escape, almost I did not wish to leave, it was so interesting. Almost I wished I might stay to hear the end of so many scandals and feuds, and plots and plans. It was like leaving a world."

At last the head waiter came himself and slapped their bill down in the middle of the table. When they had no choice but to go, Guy invited Klein and David to come back to the flat for tea, but they were going to the Minerva for a private talk. David agreed to call in later and Harriet, rather thankfully, took Guy home alone.

When they were indoors, he handed her a sealed envelope on which was written 'Top Secret' and said: "Sheppy gave these out. He says they're to be kept under lock and key. I'm afraid of losing mine. Put it away for me, somewhere safe."

Most of the drawers of the flat had locks but not one lock a key. Harriet put the envelope into a small drawer inside the writing-desk, saying: "It should be safe there. After all, we're the only people in the flat."

15

CLARENCE, RETURNING FROM HIS PARTY with the Polish officers, made his appearance after tea. He entered unsteadily, tried to cross the room and fell, instead, into a chair. Despina, who had admitted him, went out exploding with laughter.

"I want to get drunk," said Clarence.

Harriet said: "You are drunk."

He waved an arm laxly in the air. "Tell Despina to go out and bring back lots of beer."

"All right, where's the money?"

"Ha, you spoil everything," Clarence grumbled. He shut his eyes.

Despina now made an excuse to return and take another look at him. He shouted at her: "Hey, Despina, buy beer," and handed her a hundred *lei*.

"You won't get drunk on a hundred *lei*," said Harriet.

"I don't want to get drunk. I *am* drunk. I only want to stay drunk."

Guy, who had been reading, put down his book, saying: "Stop wrangling, you two," and produced a five-hundred-*lei* note. He sent Despina for the beer. While she was out, David arrived, his cap and shoulders white with snow. When he had taken off his outdoor clothes and settled by the fire, he noticed Clarence sprawling, eyes shut, sulky and uncomfortable, and asked with derision:

"What's the matter with Clarence?"

"He's drunk," said Harriet.

"Not exactly drunk," Clarence's beautiful and gentle voice came as though from a great distance, "but I hope to be."

Harriet said: "Do you want to get drunk, too, David?"

"I don't mind." David looked round for a drink.

"It's coming."

Despina came back with a boy carrying a crate of beer. Excited by the sight of it, Guy jumped up, saying: "Let's have a party. Let's invite everyone we can think of."

"Oh, no." Clarence roused himself. "There won't be enough," but Guy was already at the telephone ringing Inchcape. Inchcape said the snow was falling heavily; and he was in no mood to come out. Guy then tried to contact Dubedat, whom he thought might, for some reason, be at the Doi Trandafiri. While a piccolo was searching the café for Dubedat, Guy, with nothing to do but hold the receiver, reaffirmed his belief that Dubedat should be invited to move into the spare room.

"A man is made by his circumstances," said Guy. "If you want to change him, you must change his circumstances."

Harriet was aggrieved by Guy's persistence, yet felt an irritated respect for it. She replied sharply: "He can change his own circumstances. He's earning money now. You should not deprive him of initiative."

Her tone caused in the other two a slightly embarrassed stir, so that she felt annoyed both with herself and with Guy.

Learning that Dubedat was not to be found in the Doi Trandafiri, Guy rang the English Bar to see whom he could find there. David, impatient with the disconnected conversation that resulted, began to talk of a visit he planned to make to the peasant leader, Maniu, who had a house at Cluj. Clarence sighed ostentatiously and said: "Oh Lord!" When David gazed at him in surprised enquiry, he giggled and said: "Why don't you learn to talk to yourself David?"

David's left eyebrow rose, his small mouth turned to one side. Surveying Clarence's abandoned figure with amused contempt, he said: "Because, my dear Clarence, I don't want to talk to myself."

"Then you have more sympathy with others." After a moment Clarence, struck by his own wit, began to laugh helplessly.

David watched him with an expression that asked the world: 'Have you ever seen a more ludicrous sight?'

Suddenly aware of the irritated tedium in the room, Guy put down the receiver, jumped up and said: "More beer?" His return to the centre of things restored the atmosphere, and David, a full glass in his hand, asked: "Well, what's been happening here since war broke out?"

Guy said: "Apart from the assassination, nothing."

Clarence suddenly shouted: "Sheppy's Fighting Force."

There was a pause. David, his tone not much interested, his glance acute, asked: "What is Sheppy's Fighting Force?"

There was another pause, then Guy, torn between the need for discretion and the desire to entertain his friend, said: "We're supposed to keep quiet about it."

"David'll be dragged in," said Clarence. "Everybody'll be dragged in, except me. I opted out. I said to him," Clarence waved his glass about, "I said: 'I'm a pacifist. I'm not prepared to take life. I'd like to know exactly what you want us to do.' 'I'm not at liberty to tell you what you're expected to do,' said Sheppy. So I said: 'I think it would save time if I told you, here and now, I'm not at liberty to do it.' "

Laughing in spite of himself, Guy agreed: "He did say that."

Clarence, revivified by the beer and his own brilliance, burst in: "I said: 'I'm seconded from the British Council. The Council does not permit its members to take part in anything but cultural activities.' And Sheppy said" – here Clarence flung a finger into air and made a drunken effort to imitate Sheppy's peremptory tone – " 'You are called here as Englishmen – young, robust, patriotic Englishmen who ought to be on active service and for one reason or another are not. You are required to perform an important mission . . . ' 'I'm not robust,' I said, 'I have a weak chest.' " Here Clarence subsided again, giggling to himself.

Harriet, sitting forgotten outside the circle, saw David smile at Guy in innocent enquiry: "Who is this fellow Sheppy?"

"He's out here to organise a sort of private army."

"What does he expect to do?"

"It's all very hush-hush."

"Have you signed the Official Secrets Act?"

"Not yet."

"Then why worry? Anyway, he can't make you do anything."

"I know that. But he's right. We ought to be on active service and if we're not, we should do what we can."

"What is he like, Sheppy?"

So much had been revealed now, that Guy clearly felt there was little point in keeping back the rest. He did not interrupt as Clarence described Sheppy marching into the room where they were gathered at the Athénée Palace, hanging a map on the wall and demanding: "What have we here?" One of the telephone engineers, stepping forward and examining it, had said, as though making a revelation: "The Danube." "Right!" Sheppy had congratulated him. "Now," Sheppy went on, "I expect from you laddies implicit obedience. Two or three of my henchmen are being flown out and you must regard them as your superior officers. You'll be rank and file. Yours not to reason why, yours but to do and die. Right?" He had paused for agreement and been met with silence. He had gone on: "I'm not telling you much – security and all that – but I can tell you this. We're forming a Striking Force to strike the enemy where he'll feel it most. One place we'll strike him is the belly. Nearly four hundred thousand tons of wheat went from Rumania to Germany last year – and how did it get there? Along the Danube. Big plans are afoot. We'll be blowing things up. One of them's the Iron Gates. Remember, this isn't a lark: it's an adventure." He had brought his one hand down on the table and his one eye had jerked about from face to face. "There'll be lots of fun, and we're letting you in on it." Then he had drawn himself upright and assuming his machine-gun rattle, had shouted: "Be prepared. Await orders. Keep your traps shut. *Dis*-miss."

David waited until the end of Clarence's performance before saying: "The Iron Gates? What does he imagine they are? Real gates? Perhaps they hope to blow up the rapids and block the navigable passage close to the right bank. The Germans would soon clear that up." He gave a snuffling and derisory laugh. "This is 'cloak and dagger' stuff, of course. They take on these romantic old war-horses and say: 'If you succeed, you'll get no recognition. If you fail, you'll take the consequences.' That makes them grit their teeth. They love it."

At this, Harriet could keep quiet no longer. She said: "But Guy would be hopeless at this sort of thing. If he tried to blow up the Iron Gates, he'd be more likely to blow up himself. As for Clarence – trust him to get out of it."

Reminded of her presence and startled by her outburst, Guy said: "Darling, you must not repeat a word of this to anyone. Promise."

"Who would I repeat it to?"

Clarence said slowly: "Harriet is a bitch." After some moments, added reflectively: "I like bitches. You know where you are with them."

Harriet made no comment but she told herself she now knew what Clarence thought of her. The fantasy that had started on the day of Călinescu's funeral was running its course. The situation had its attraction. It was like being offered a second personality.

At the same time, seeing him as he lolled there, smugly smiling, she could have crossed the room and pushed him off the chair.

David, too, must have been feeling something of this, for he said: "Let's do something noteworthy."

He leant forward and smiled with reflective malice towards Clarence: "Let's de-bag him!" With a sudden, decided movement, he rose and began to advance on Clarence, stealthily, not wholly playfully. He gave a sideways glance at Harriet, knowing her an ally in this, and she jumped up at once, caught into the same impulse to ill-treat Clarence in some way.

"Come on," she said to Guy and he was drawn into the assault.

Clarence, his chair tilted back, sitting inert, with eyes closed, his head propped against the wall, seemed unaware that anything was happening until they were upon him, then, startled, he opened his eyes; his chair legs slipped and he went down, backwards, thumping his head against the floor. He gazed up at them, as though awakened from sleep, then, closing his eyes again, said dully: "What do I care?"

Although meeting with no resistance, David pinned his victim determinedly down like one dealing with a marauder. There was something vindictive in his movements. Clarence might have been an old enemy cornered at last. Harriet flung herself on him and held him down by his shoulders.

"Really!" Clarence gasped, making a feeble, almost idiotic, effort to escape. As he wrenched one hand free and tried to push Harriet away, she bit his fingers making him howl. Only Guy was treating the whole thing as a joke.

David began pulling off Clarence's trousers. Weighty and very strong, he worked with the concentrated gravity of an executioner. On his instructions, Guy pulled the trousers over Clarence's shoes. When they were off at last, David snatched at them and held them up in triumph. "What shall we do with them?"

"Put them on the balcony," said Harriet. "Make him go out and get them."

Clarence lay still, feigning unconsciousness.

As David went out on the balcony, the icy air came a moment into the room, then he returned and slammed-to the door. Sniggering, he said untruthfully: "I've thrown them into the street."

"What do I care?" Clarence mumbled again.

The force that had activated the others died as quickly as it had come. They sat around, watching Clarence as he lay in his underpants on the floor. When he did and said nothing, they started to talk among themselves and forgot about him.

After a while he began getting himself upright in stages. When in a sitting position, he shook his head and sighed, then rose slowly and went out on to the balcony. He remained out there in the snow, in the mid-winter cold, while he put on his trousers, then he returned to the room, closed the glass doors carefully, bolted them and, without a word went out to the hall. The others had stopped talking. They listened to Clarence's movements in the hall as he put on his coat. The front door shut quietly after him.

There was a silence, then Harriet said: "What is the matter with us? Why did we do that?"

"It was a joke," said Guy, though he did not sound sure of what he said.

"Really, we behaved like children," Harriet said and it occurred to her that they were not, in fact, grown-up enough for the life they were living. She asked: "What is wrong with Clarence? He told me once that he fails everyone."

With ponderous irony, David said: "Someone should dissect him and remake him nearer to the heart's desire."

Guy said: "I might be able to do it, if I had the time."

"Harriet could do it, I think." David smiled slyly at her.

Harriet grew pink, realising she had felt a pitying sympathy for Clarence as she had watched him picking himself up and taking himself so quietly, so unoffendingly, out of the flat. Both David and Guy were much younger than he and between them there was the understanding of an old friendship. Clarence could not have remained untouched by the fact the two had combined against him. She felt sorry for him, yet she disowned him, saying casually: "I don't want to remake him. Why should I?" and they went on to talk of other things.

16

THE NEXT MORNING, when alone in the flat, Harriet took out the envelope Guy had given her and opened it by rolling a pencil underneath the flap. Inside there was a print of a section through – what? An artesian well? Or, more likely, an oil well. Something else to be blown up. A blockage in the pipe was tagged with the one word: 'Detonator'. There was no written explanation of the diagram. She resealed the envelope and put it back into the drawer.

She heard no more about the Force until a few weeks later, when Guy telephoned from the University to say he would not be home for supper. He had been called to a meeting.

"Not one of Sheppy's meetings, I hope?" said Harriet.

Guy admitted it was, and added quickly that Clarence, who had refused to attend, had offered to take Harriet out to dinner. That, said Guy, would be nice for her. Clarence would take her to the new restaurant, Le Jardin, and Guy would meet them both later, in the English Bar.

Clarence called for Harriet while she was listening to the news. The Mannerheim Line had been breached but, except for the fighting on the Karelian peninsula, the war was at a standstill.

Clarence listened to such news as there was with a rather stern expression. He seemed to feel strain at being alone with Harriet, and Harriet, enjoying his embarrassment, talked vivaciously. She said that although there were people who still believed that 'something must happen soon', a good many now regarded the war as practically over. Anyway, no one gave it much thought these days. It had become like a background noise that could attract attention only by its cessation. The Jews were so confident, the black-market rate for sterling was lower than it had been before war started.

Clarence listened to all this with an occasional murmur, then picked up the book she had been reading. It was one of the D. H. Lawrence novels on which Guy was lecturing that term.

"*Kangaroo,*" he read out scornfully. "These modern novelists! Why is it that not one of them is really good enough? This stuff, for instance . . ."

"I wouldn't call Lawrence a modern novelist."

"You know what I mean." Clarence flipped impatiently through the pages. "All these dark gods, this phallic stuff, this – this fascism! I can't stand it." He threw down the book and stared accusingly at her.

She took the book up. "Supposing you skip the guff, as you call it! Supposing you read what is left, simply as writing." She read aloud one of the passages Guy had marked. It was the description of the sunset over Manly Beach: 'The long green rollers of the Pacific', 'the star-white foam', 'the dusk-green sea glimmered over with smoky rose'.

Clarence groaned through it, appalled at what was being imposed on him. "*I know!*" he said, in agony, when she stopped. "All that colour stuff – it's just so many words strung together. Anyone could do it."

Harriet re-read the passage through to herself. For some reason, it did not seem so vivid and exciting as it had done before Clarence condemned it. She was inclined to blame him for that. She turned on him: "Have you ever tried to write? Do you know how difficult it is?"

Well, yes. Clarence admitted he had once wanted to be a writer. He did know it was difficult. He had given up trying because, after all, what was the point in being a second-rate writer? If one could not be a great writer – a Tolstoy, a Flaubert, a Stendhal – what was the point in being a writer at all?

Disconcerted, Harriet said lamely: "If everyone felt like that, there wouldn't be much to read."

"What is there to read, anyway? Rubbish, most of it. Myself, I read nothing but detective novels."

"I suppose you do read Tolstoy and Flaubert?"

"I did once. Years ago."

"You could read them again."

Clarence gave another moan. "Why should one bother?"

"What about Virginia Woolf?"

"I think *Orlando* almost the worst book of the century."

"Really! And *To the Lighthouse*?"

Clarence wriggled in weary exasperation. "It's all *right* – but all her writing is so diffused, so feminine, so sticky. It has such an odd smell about it. It's just like menstruation."

Startled by the originality of Clarence's criticism, Harriet looked at him with more respect. "And Somerset Maugham?" she ventured.

"Goodness me, *Harry*! He's simply the higher journalism."

No one else had ever called Harriet 'Harry' and she did not like the abbreviation. She reacted sharply, saying: "Maybe Somerset Maugham isn't very good, but the others are. So much creative effort has gone into their work – and all you can say is 'Really!' and condemn them out of hand." She rose and put on her coat and fur cap. "I think we should go," she said.

Le Jardin, recently opened in a Biedermeier mansion, was the most fashionable of Bucharest restaurants and would remain so until the first gloss passed from its decorations. Situated in a little snow-packed square at the end of the Boulevard Brăteanu, its blue neon sign shone out cold upon the cold and glittering world. The sky was a delicate grey-blue, clear except for a few tufts of cirrus cloud. The moon was rising behind the restaurant roof, on which the snow, a foot thick, gleamed like powdered glass.

The interior of Le Jardin was the same silver-blue as the out-of-doors. The house had been gutted to make one vast room, and the proprietor, breaking away from the tradition of crimson and gilt, had trimmed it in silver with hangings of powder-blue. These cool colours, more fitted for summer than winter, were made appropriate by the sultry warmth of the room. The restaurant's *décor* had been described in the press as '*lux nebun*' – a challenge to the war world in which it had opened. But there, Harriet noted on arrival, was the usual Rumanian sight of a fat official, with his hat on, packing cream cakes into his mouth.

As Harriet passed between the tables with Clarence, there was a little murmur of comment: first, that she should make this public appearance with someone other than her husband, then the common complaint that English teachers – they were all regarded as 'teachers' – could afford to come to a restaurant of this class. In Rumania a teacher was one of the lowest-paid members of the lower-middle class, earning perhaps four thousand *lei* a month. Here was proof that the English teachers were not teachers at all but, as everyone suspected, spies.

When Harriet and Clarence were settled on one of the blue

velvet banquettes, Harriet returned to the subject of Clarence's writing. For how long had he tried to write? What had he achieved? To which publisher had he sent the results? Clarence squirmed under these questions, shrugged and was evasive, then admitted he had produced very little. He had planned a novel and written six pages of synopsis, very carefully worked out, but it had got no further than that. He could not visualise scenes. He did not know how to bring his characters to life.

"So you gave up? Then what did you do?" Harriet asked, for Clarence was nearly thirty and must have some sort of career behind him.

"I joined the British Council."

"You had a good degree?"

"Quite good."

He had been sent to Warsaw. Harriet questioned him about his two years there. Where Guy's memories would have been all of the conditions of the country and its people, Clarence's memories were personal, tender and sad. His face became wistful as he talked. Harriet, realising there was about him something poignant and unfulfilled, felt in sympathy with him.

In Poland he had fallen in love for the first time. He said: "It's extraordinary to look back on the things that used to be important to one. I can remember a night in Warsaw . . . I can remember standing under a street lamp and turning a girl's face to catch the light and shadow. As I did so, it all seemed significant. I don't know why. It would mean nothing now. And I remember walking with her to the Vistula and seeing the broken ice on the water. And we went through streets where they were building new houses, with everything half finished and the pavements muddy, with planks across them. But she wouldn't have me. She turned up at the office one day and said she was engaged to someone else. I believe she'd had this other man all along. I'll never forget it."

"I'm sorry," said Harriet.

"Why be sorry? At least I was alive then. I could feel." He reflected on this, then said: "I've never had the woman I wanted. I always seem to want bitches and they always ill-treat me."

"What about your fiancée?"

He shrugged. "She's a good girl, but, really, she stirs nothing in me. With her, there's nothing to fight against. She's just a punching bag. So am I, for that matter. Anyway, who knows what will happen? The last time I wrote to her, I said: 'It may be ten years before I get home again.' "

"You think that? And Brenda is willing to wait?"

"I suppose so." Clarence sighed deeply. "But I did advise her to marry someone else."

"After Poland, where did you go?"

"Madrid. I was there when the civil war broke out. The British were being evacuated and I jumped a lorry going to Barcelona. I offered myself to the International Brigade, but I was pretty sick. I'd caught a chill on the way. I've always had this trouble with my chest. When I got better, I was put in charge of a refugee camp, where I was more use than I would have been in the lines. But I wanted to fight. Not fighting was a sort of sacrifice."

"Anyway, it let you preserve your integrity intact."

Clarence kept his head hanging for some moments, then, hurt, he said quietly: "I might have expected you to say something like that." He suddenly gave a half-laugh of satisfaction that she had fulfilled his worst expectations, then he said: "Someone had to look after the camp."

"A woman could have done the job."

He raised his brows, considered this, then drawled: "No, not really," but he did not enlarge on his denial.

"So there were no bitches there!"

"Oh yes, there was one – a magnificent bitch. An English girl looking after a crowd of evacuee children. She did exactly what she liked. She slept with anyone she wanted. Even with me. Yes, one night she pointed at me and said: 'I'll have you,' and I followed her out." Clarence sat for a while silent, smiling at the memory of it.

"Nothing came of that, I suppose?"

"What could come of it? She had a Spaniard she was mad about. One of the English fellows went on leave to Paris and she ordered him to bring her back an evening dress. When he brought the dress, he gave a party, thinking she would dance with him: but she just ignored him and danced all night with the Spaniard. I like tough women. Women of character."

"You like being pushed around."

"Not necessarily." He sat withdrawn for a while, before he said: "In Spain there was colour and heat and danger. Things were significant there. Life should be like that."

"There is danger here."

"Oh!" He shrugged his contempt of the present.

Throughout the meal Clarence pursued his memories, that were all much alike. Contemplating those worlds of delight from which he felt himself excluded, he said several times: "Life should be like that." When he had talked himself out and was waiting for the bill, Harriet asked him: "You like feeling dissatisfied with yourself. Why is that?"

Clarence stuck out his lower lip but did not reply.

"For you do like it," she insisted. "You enjoy revealing your worst aspects."

He said: "We all get corrupted. Even Guy."

"In what way is Guy corrupted?"

"Before he married he owned hardly anything. He had no room of his own, not even a cupboard. People used to put him up: they loved having him. He didn't mind where he slept. He'd sleep on the floor. Now you're surrounding him with bourgeois comforts. You're corrupting him."

"I thought he used to share a flat with you."

"Well, he did last spring, but when he first came here he had literally nothing. I've never seen a man with so few possessions."

"Now you're blaming him for having a home like everyone else."

The waiter arrived. Clarence, as he started to settle the bill, repeated obstinately: "You're corrupting him."

Harriet said: "He must have wanted to be corrupted or he would never have got himself married. A single man can go round sleeping on floors. A married couple are less welcome."

Clarence did not reply. When they left the restaurant, Harriet realised he was rather drunk. She suggested they leave the car and walk to the hotel. He replied brusquely: "I drive best like this," and shot them with a series of violent movements round the corner and across the square. They jerked to a standstill outside the Athénée Palace.

They were late, but Guy was not in the bar and Albu had seen nothing of him. Harriet and Clarence decided to wait for him. The journalists – only a handful of whom were still in Bucharest – were in the telephone boxes in the hall. Harriet, alert now for the excitement of alarm, said: "I believe something has happened."

"What could happen?" Clarence was gloomily ordering brandy.

Yakimov stood alone at the bar, holding an empty glass. Harriet was careful not to meet his gaze, but she had noticed a change in him. He was a down-at-heel, uncared-for figure very different from that she had met first in the garden restaurant. Then he had been allowed to dominate the scene, now it did not seem possible he could dominate anything. He was sallow, rheumy, crumbled – a man in defeat. When he sidled up to Harriet saying: "Dear girl, how nice to see a human face," he looked so abject that she had not the heart to turn her back on him.

Drooping against the bar, holding the empty glass out at an angle that prevented its being overlooked, he sighed and said: "Haven't been feeling too good. Bitter weather. Tells on your poor old Yaki."

Harriet asked coldly if he had seen Guy. He shook his head.

"Has anything happened?"

"Not that I know of, dear girl." He glanced over his shoulder, then, stepping nearer, confided despondently: "Just had m'head bitten off by m'old friend, Prince Hadjimoscos. He was off to some party or other. I said: 'Take me along, dear boy,' and what d'you think he said? 'You're not invited.' Not invited! I ask you! In a town like this. But I don't let it worry me. It's just anti-British feeling. It's growing, dear girl. I can feel it. Haven't been a war correspondent for nothing. They're beginning to think the Allies are too far away."

"I'm surprised they didn't think it long ago."

Albu had put two glasses of brandy on the counter. Yakimov eyed them, and Clarence, with resigned annoyance, asked him if he would take a drink.

"Wouldn't say 'No', dear boy. Whisky for me."

Having accepted his drink, he began to talk. Veering between complaint and a tolerant acceptance of suffering, he described how his friends Hadjimoscos, Horvath and Palu had all been horrid to him. There was only one explanation of it – anti-British feeling. After a while, realising that this despondent talk was not holding his audience, he made a visible attempt to pull himself together and give some entertainment in return for his drink.

"Went to see Dobson this morning," he said. "Heard most amusing story. Foxy Leverett came out of Capşa's last night, saw the German Minister's Mercedes parked by the kerb, got into his Dion-Bouton, backed down the road, then raced forward and crashed the Mercedes. Devil of a crash, I'm told. When the police came up, Foxy said: 'You can call it provoked aggression.' "

As he finished this story, the journalists began to return. Looking at the Polish girl who had entered with Galpin, he said, half to himself: "There's that dear girl!" His large eyes fixed on Wanda, he bent towards Harriet and said: "You've heard that Galpin's got her attached to some English paper?" Yakimov's tone subtly expressed derogation of the sort of paper that would employ Wanda. "Charming girl, but so irresponsible. Sends home all sorts of rumours and gossip, doesn't care where she picks up the stuff . . ." His voice faded as the two approached.

Harriet, glad to drop Yakimov, asked Galpin if there were any news.

"Uh-huh." Galpin nodded his head, his expression glum. Among the journalists now ordering at the bar, there was the excitement of a situation come to life.

"What is it?"

"Just heard Hungary's mobilising. German troops flooding in. We've been trying to get Budapest all evening but the lines are dead. It's my belief that this time we're for it."

Harriet felt the pang of fear. Now, after six months in Rumania, she reacted more sharply to news of this sort than she would have done when she first arrived. In a small voice, she said: "But aren't the passes blocked with snow?"

"Oh, that old theory! Do you think snow could keep out mechanised forces?"

"The Rumanians said they would fight."

"Don't make me laugh. Have you ever seen the Rumanian army? A bunch of half-starved peasants."

Without waiting for the order, Albu had handed Galpin a double whisky. Now, taking a gulp at it, Galpin grew flushed and stared at Harriet as though angry with her: "What do you think will happen here? Fifth column risings. This place is stiff with fifth columnists – not only those German bastards, but thousands of pro-Germans and chaps in German pay. And there's all those hangers-on of the German Legation. They're not here for their health. There're two big German establishments here – and a regular arsenal in each of them. We're all marked down. Yours truly with the rest. Make no mistake about it. We're just sitting on a time-bomb."

Harriet had grown pale. As she put her hand to the bar counter, Clarence drawled with exaggerated calm: "What are you trying to do, Galpin? Scare the wits out of her?"

Galpin now swung his angry stare on to Clarence, but he was slightly disconcerted by this reproof. He drank to give himself time, then he said: "We've got to face facts. The women oughtn't to stick around if they can't face facts. And you chaps'll have to face them, too. Everyone thinks you're agents. Don't quote me, but the chances are you'll wake up one night with a gun in your belly."

"I'll worry about that when it happens," said Clarence.

Yakimov's eyes had grown round. "Is this really true about Hungary?" he asked in shocked surprise.

"True enough for my paper."

"Meaning," said Clarence, "you and the others have just cooked it up?"

"Meaning nothing of the sort. Ask Screwby here. Hey, Screws!"

Screwby loped slowly over from the other side of the room, his smile wide and simple. Appealed to, he scratched one cheek of his large, soft, heavy face and said: "Yah, there's something to it all right. Budapest's closed down. Can't get a squeak from them. That means a 'stop' and a 'stop' can mean anything. Something'll happen tonight, and that's for sure."

Harriet said anxiously: "We must try and find Guy."

"First," said Clarence, "have another drink."

"After all," Yakimov tried to soothe her, "we can't do anything. Might as well have a couple while we're able. Doubt if we'll get much in dear old Dachau." He giggled and looked at Clarence. Clarence ordered another round. When it was drunk, Harriet would stay no longer.

As they crossed the hall, the hotel door started to revolve. Harriet watched it hopefully but it was only Gerda Hoffman, 'trying to look', Harriet thought, 'as fatal and clever as she's reputed to be'. The train of Germans that followed her appeared to be in the highest spirits; congratulating themselves, it seemed to Harriet, on the elements of victory.

"I wish we were safely out of this country," she said.

"You'll get leave in the summer," said Clarence. "Only five more months."

They drove to the Doi Trandafiri. Guy was not there. They did a round of several other bars, but could see nothing of him. Harriet was mystified by his disappearance. In the end she said she would go home. When Clarence left her at the door of Blocşul Cazacul, he said: "I expect he's up there waiting for you." This now seemed so probable that Harriet was the more disturbed to find the flat dark and silent and the bedroom empty.

She was suddenly convinced that Guy's disappearance had something to do with the scare about Hungary. Perhaps Sheppy had already taken him off on some sabotaging expedition. Perhaps he had already injured himself – or been arrested – or seized by the fifth columnists. Perhaps she would never see him again. She blamed herself that she had not gone immediately to Inchcape and asked him to interfere: now she went to the telephone and dialled his number. When he answered, she asked if Guy were with him. He had seen or heard nothing of Guy that evening.

She said: "There's a rumour that Germany has invaded Hungary. Do you think it's true?"

"It could be." Inchcape took the news lightly. "It doesn't mean they'll come here. Hungary is, strategically speaking, more important to Germany than Rumania is. It simply means the Germans are straightening out their Eastern front."

Harriet, in no mood to listen to Inchcape's theories, broke in rather wildly: "Everyone thinks they'll come here. All the journalists think so. And Guy has disappeared. I'm afraid he's gone to Ploeşti with Sheppy on one of these insane sabotage plans."

"What insane sabotage plans?" Inchcape spoke with the mild patience of one out to discover something, but Harriet did not need to be manoeuvred. She was keeping nothing to herself. All she wanted now was to seize Guy back from disaster.

She answered: "Putting detonators down the oil wells. Blowing up the Iron Gates . . ."

"*I see*! That's what he's up to, is he? Indeed! Well, don't worry, my dear child. Leave this to me, will you?"

"But where is Guy? Where is *Guy*?"

"Oh, he'll turn up." Inchcape spoke impatiently, the question of Guy's whereabouts being, in importance, a long way behind the threat to his dignity contained in Sheppy's use of his men.

As Harriet put down the receiver, she heard Guy's key in the lock. He entered singing, his face agleam with the cold. "Why, hello!" he said, surprised at seeing her standing unoccupied beside the telephone.

"Where on earth have you been?" she asked. "We were meeting you in the English Bar." She was guilty and cross with relief.

"I glanced in and there was no one there, so I walked down to the Dâmboviţa with Dubedat."

"Couldn't you have waited? Can't you wait for me even for ten minutes? Do you know that German troops are pouring into Hungary? They may invade Rumania tonight."

"I don't believe it. I bet you got this from Galpin."

"I did, but that doesn't mean it isn't true."

"These rumours are never true."

"One day one will be true. This sort of phoney war can't go on for ever. Someone's got to move some time and we'll be trapped. Galpin says the place is full of fifth columnists. He says you'll wake up one night with a gun in your belly. We'll be sent to Dachau. We'll never be free . . . we'll never go home again . . ." As he reached her, she collapsed against him crying helplessly.

"My poor darling." He put his arms round her, astonished. "I didn't realise you were getting nervous." He put her into the armchair and telephoned the Legation, where Foxy Leverett was on duty. He learnt that the rumours had derived from nothing more than a breakdown on the line to Budapest. This had now been righted. Foxy had just rung Budapest and found all quiet there.

While undressing, Guy grumbled about Galpin, Screwby "and the rest of the riff-raff we've got here calling themselves journalists. They're utterly irresponsible. A story at any price. What does it matter so long as they can startle people into buying the paper?"

Harriet, sitting up in bed, red-eyed, limp and relieved, said: "You shouldn't have gone off with Dubedat without leaving a message. You should have known I'd be worried."

"Surely you weren't worrying about me, darling? You know I'm always right."

She said: "If the fifth columnists came for you, I'd murder them, *I'd murder them.*"

"I believe you would, too," he said indulgently as he pulled his shirt over his head.

17

IT WAS A WINTER OF UNUSUAL COLD in Western Europe. The cinema newsreels showed children snowballing beneath Hadrian's Arch. Rivers were transfixed between their banks. A girl pirouetted on the Seine, her skirt circling out from her waist. The Paris roofs spilled snow in puffs, like smoke. The Parisians carried gasmasks in tin cylinders. An air-raid warning sounded and they filed down into the Métro. The streets were empty. A taxi-cab stood abandoned. Then everyone came up again, smiling as though it were all a joke. ('And perhaps it is a joke,' Yakimov thought, 'perhaps this will go down in history as the joke war.') St. Paul's appeared briefly with a feather-boa of snow. A glimpse of Chamberlain and his umbrella gave rise to a flutter of applause. At once the film was interrupted and a notice appeared on the screen to say public demonstrations of any kind were forbidden. The audience watched the rest of the film in silence.

Yakimov, in the cheapest seats, was reminded by these pictures of the fact that he would sooner or later have to return to the streets of Bucharest, where the hard ridges of frozen snow bit through his shoes and the wind slapped his face like a sheet of emery paper.

He had taken to the cinema when finally prevented from bedding down at the Athénée Palace. He had managed at first to maintain not only some sort of social life there, but a semblance of residence. Unwilling to take the long journey each afternoon back to his lodgings, he would slip upstairs when the bar closed and settle himself in any bedroom he found with a key left in the lock. If there was a bathroom attached, he would take a bath, then sleep the afternoon away. When caught, as he often was, by the room's rightful owner, he apologised for having mistaken the number. "All these rooms look alike," he would explain. "Your poor old Yaki belongs on the floor below."

But suspicions were roused; complaints were made. He was caught, and recognised, by one of the porters who knew he had no bedroom on the floor below. The manager warned him that, caught again, he would be forbidden entry to any part of the hotel. After that, he was found stretched out on one of the main room sofas. He was warned again. He then tried sleeping upright in an arm-chair, but the guests objected to his snoring and the waiters roughly awakened him.

Hounded, as he put it, from pillar to post, he went, when he could afford it, to the cinema. When he could not afford it, he walked to keep himself awake.

Morning and evening, he joined the mendicant company of Hadjimoscos, Horvath and Cici Palu, and stood with them on the edge of one or the other of the groups at the English Bar. Sometimes, ignoring insults, stares of disgust, excluding backs and shoulders, they had to stand about an hour or more before someone, out of embarrassment or pity, invited them in on a round. They expected nothing from *habitués* like Galpin and Screwby, and got nothing. They had most to hope for from the casual drinker, an English engineer from Ploeşti or a temporary American visitor elated by the black-market rate in dollars. When Galpin, seeing the three at his elbow, said "Scram", an American newspaperman said: "Oh, I guess we owe the local colour a drink."

Sometimes, to encourage patronage, one of the group would offer to buy a round, then, the order given, would discover he had come out without any money. It was surprising how often some bystander would lend, or pay, out of shame for the tactics of the group. Albu refused to pour these drinks until the money was produced, but what he thought of it all, no one knew. While the pantomime of pocket-patting and consternation was going on, he would stand motionless, his gaze on a horizon not of this world.

Something in Albu's attitude disturbed Yakimov. Not the bravest of men, he was often painfully upset by the audacity of the others, and yet he clung to them. It was not that they welcomed him – it was simply that he was not welcomed by anyone else. He, who had once been the centre of Dollie's set, was now without a friend.

He could not understand why Hadjimoscos, Horvath and Palu were 'horrid' to him; why there was always a hint of derision, even of malice, in their attitude towards him. Perhaps the fact that he had once been in the position of patron had marked him down for all time. They had once deferred to him, now they need defer no longer. And there had been the incident of Hadjimoscos's teeth. Returning drunk from a party, Hadjimoscos, sick in a privy, had spewed out his false teeth. Yakimov, in attendance, had flushed them away before he realised what had happened. At least, that had been Yakimov's story – and he had told it widely, and unwisely, round the bar. Hadjimoscos could not contradict it because the teeth were missing, and remained missing until a new set could be made. He had no memory of what had become of them. Too late, Yakimov became aware of the displeasure in Hadjimoscos's mongoloid eyes – a displeasure that gave them a truly frightening glint. He murmured: "Only a little joke, dear boy," but it was after that that Hadjimoscos refused to take him to parties, always giving the excuse that he had not been invited.

The trio also, it seemed, resented Yakimov's attempts to repay drinks with amusing talk. In front of him, Hadjimoscos said with disgust to the others: "He *will* tell his dilapidated stories! He *will* insist that he is not what he seems!"

The second accusation referred to the fact that, when asked what he was doing in Bucharest, Yakimov would reply: "I'm afraid, dear boy, I'm not at liberty to say." In reply to someone who said: "I suppose it's your own government you're working for," he mumbled in humorous indignation: "Are you trying to insult poor Yaki?"

A rumour had reached the Legation that Yakimov was working for the Germans, and Dobson, taking the matter up, had traced it back to Hadjimoscos. Dropping into the English Bar and inviting Hadjimoscos to a drink, he had remonstrated pleasantly: "This is a very dangerous story to put around."

Hadjimoscos, nervous of the power of the British Legation, protested: "But, *mon ami*, the Prince is a member of some secret service – he himself makes it evident. I could not imagine he worked for the British. They surely would not employ such an *imbécile!*"

"Why do you say he 'makes it evident'?" Dobson asked.

"Because he will take out a paper – so! – and put to it a match with fingers shaking – so! – then he will sigh and mop his brow and say: 'Thank God I have got rid of that'."

Yakimov was ordered to the Legation. When Dobson repeated his conversation with Hadjimoscos, Yakimov was tremulous with fear. He wailed pathetically: "All in fun, dear boy, all in innocent fun!"

Dobson was unusually stern with him. "People," he said, "have been thrown into prison here for less than this. The story has reached Woolley. He and the other British businessmen want you sent under open arrest to the Middle East. There you'd go straight into the ranks."

"*Dear boy!* You'd never do that to an old friend. Poor Yaki meant no harm. That old fool Woolley has no sense of humour. Yaki often plays these little japes. Once in Budapest, when flush, I got a cage of pigeons and went down a side street like this . . ." As he lifted a wire tray from Dobson's desk and moved with exaggerated stealth round the room, the sole flapped on his left shoe. "Then I put down the cage, looked around me, and let the pigeons fly away."

Dobson lent him a thousand *lei* and promised to talk Woolley round.

Had Yakimov been content to eat modestly, he could have existed from one remittance to the next, but he was not content. When his allowance arrived, he ate himself into a stupor, then, penniless again, returned, a beggar, to the English Bar. It was not that he despised simple food. He despised no food of any kind. When he could afford nothing more, he would go to the Dâmbovița and eat the peasant's staple food, a mess of maize. But food, rich food, was an obsessive longing. He needed it as other men need drink, tobacco or drugs.

Often he was so reduced he had not even the bus fare to and from his lodging. Walking back at night through streets deserted except for beggars and peasants who slept, and died of cold in their sleep, in doorways or beneath the hawkers' stalls, he often thought of his car, his Hispano-Suiza, and plotted to retrieve it. All he needed was a Yugoslav transit visa and thirty-five thousand *lei*. Surely he could find someone to lend him that! And he felt, once the car was his again, his whole status would change. It was heavy on petrol and oil, of course, but they were cheap here. He would manage. And with this dream he would trudge through the black, wolf-biting night until he found refuge in the syrupy heat of the Protopopescus' flat.

There he was comfortable enough, though things had not gone so well at first. For several nights after he settled in, he had been bitten by bugs. Awakened by the burning and stinging itch they produced, he had put on the light and seen the bugs sliding out of sight among the creases of the sheets. His tender flesh had risen in white lumps. Next morning the lumps had disappeared. When he spoke to Doamna Protopopescu, she took the matter badly.

"Here buks, you say?" she demanded. "Such is not possible. We are nice peoples. These buks have come with you."

Yakimov told her he had come straight from the Athénée Palace. Not even pretending to believe him, she shrugged and said: "If so, then you have imaginations."

Having paid his rent in advance and being without money to pay elsewhere, he had no choice but to suffer. He produced one or two dead bugs, the sight of which merely increased Doamna Protopopescu's scorn. "Where did you find such?" she demanded. "In bus or taxi or café? In all places there are buks."

Aggrieved beyond measure, he set his mind to work and, the next night, threw back the covers and gathering the bugs up rapidly, dropped them one by one into a glass of water. Next morning, smiling and pretending to click his heels, he presented the glass to his landlady. She examined it, mystified: "What have you?"

"Bugs, dear girl."

"Buks!" She peered into the glass, her face sagging further in its bewildered exasperation, then, suddenly, she was enlightened. She flew into a rage that was not, thank God, directed at him. "These," she cried, "are Hungarian buks. Ah, filthy peoples! Ah, the dirty mans!" It transpired that, in order to accommodate a lodger, the Protopopescus had bought a bed in the seedy market near the station. The salesman, an Hungarian, had sworn it was a clean bed, as good as new, and now what had been discovered! "Buks!"

Doamna Protopopescu's usual movements were indolent. Her body was soft with inertia and over-eating, but now, in her rage, she displayed the animal vigour of her peasant forebears. She turned the bed on its side and glared into the wire meshes beneath it. Yakimov, looking with her, could see no sign of bugs.

"Ha!" she menaced them, "they hide. But from me they cannot hide."

She bound rags to a poker, dipped it in paraffin and set it alight. As she swept the flames over the springs and frame of the bed, she hissed: "Now, I think no more buks. Die then, you filthy Hungarian buks. Ha, buks, this is for you, buks!"

Yakimov watched her, impressed. That night he slept in peace. The incident drew them together. It broke down the barrier of strangeness between them – a process maintained by the fact that Yakimov had to pass through the Protopopescus' bedroom to reach the bathroom.

The Protopopescus had probably imagined that, at the most, a lodger would require a bath once or twice a week. They had not allowed for his other bodily needs. When, directed by the maid, Yakimov first found his way through the bedroom, the Protopopescus were still in bed. Doamna Protopopescu lifted a bleared face from the pillow and regarded him in astonished silence. No comment was made on his intrusion then, nor at any other time. If they were in the bedroom when he passed through, the Protopopescus always behaved in the same way. On the outward journey they ignored him. As he returned, they would suddenly show awareness of him and greet him.

Often Doamna Protopopescu was alone in the room. She spent much of her day lying on her bed dressed in her kimono. Yakimov was delighted to observe that she did everything a woman of Oriental character was reputed to do. She ate Turkish delight; she drank Turkish coffee; she smoked Turkish cigarettes; and she was for ever laying out a pack of frowsy, odd-faced cards, by which she predicted events from hour to hour. He sometimes stopped to watch her, amused to note that when the cards foretold something displeasing, she would snatch them all up impatiently and, in search of a more acceptable future, set them out again.

She entered his repertoire of characters, and at the bar he told how coming out of the bathroom and anticipating recognition, he had said: "*Bonjour*, doamna and domnul lieutenant Protopopescu," only to realise too late that, although on the chair lay the familiar padded uniform and the grimy male corsets, and on the floor were an officer's spurred riding boots, the figure beside Doamna Protopopescu was that of a man much younger than her husband.

"So now," he concluded, "I merely say '*Bonjour*, doamna and domnul lieutenant', and leave it at that."

The flat, its windows sealed for the winter, smelt strongly of sweat and cooking. The smell in the Protopopescus' bedroom was overpowering, yet Yakimov came to tolerate it, indeed to associate it with the comforts of home.

One morning, when he paused to watch his landlady laying out her curious cards, he essayed a little joke. He handed her a *leu*, turned to the side imprinted with a corn cob and said: "A portrait of our great and glorious Majesty, King Carol II. You, dear girl, may not recognise the likeness, but there are many dear girls who would."

Doamna Protopopescu's immediate reaction was to display the blankness with which Rumanian middle-class women out-faced impropriety, then her peasant blood got the better of her. She spluttered, and as she handed back the coin she made an 'away with you' gesture that encouraged him to relax at the hips until he was sitting, or nearly sitting, on the bed-edge. When he did reach the point of sitting down, she gave him a swift, calculating glance and said: "Tell me now some sinks about Inklant. Do I say it right: Inklant?"

A sort of friendship grew up despite the fact Yakimov was very nervous of his landlady. A few days after his arrival in the flat, he had been awakened by an uproar outside his door. Protopopescu's batman, sent to the house to do some chores, had been caught stealing a cigarette. Doamna Protopopescu was beating him with her fists while he, doubled up and shielding his head with his arms, howled like a maniac: "Don't beat me, *coănită*, don't beat me." Ergie the maid, standing by, caught Yakimov's startled eye and laughed. The scene was a common-place to her.

Though, after that, he often heard the howls of the batman or Ergie or Ergie's consumptive daughter, who slept in the kitchen with her, Yakimov could not get used to these rows. While closeted with Doamna Protopopescu, Yakimov would often look at her little beringed paw and reflect upon its strength.

At first, he saw the bedroom as something of a refuge from the English Bar, where he spent so many hours standing about, hungry, thirsty and often tired. In Doamna Protopopescu's room he could sit down; and, by sitting long enough, by gazing with the concentration of a hungry dog at everything that went into her mouth, Yakimov could obtain from her a piece of Turkish delight, a cup of coffee, a glass of *ţuică*, or even, but rarely, a meal. Doamna Protopopescu was not generous. Whatever Yakimov received, he had to earn by an hour or more of what she called 'English conversation'.

He did not object to chatting to her. What he found intolerably tedious was the fact that he was expected to pick up her errors of grammar and pronunciation, and wrestle for their correction. If these corrections were not frequent, she became suspicious. She would let him talk on indefinitely without reward.

Her pronunciation he found beyond mending. She had no ear. When she repeated a word after him, he would hear for an instant an echo of his own cultivated drawl, then, at once, she would relapse. Like many members of the Rumanian middle classes, her second language was German. Yakimov complained in the bar: "Bloke I know says English is a low German dialect. Since I've met Doamna P. I've come to believe it."

The ruthlessness with which she kept him to his task soon deprived the occasions of charm. Yakimov was driven to reflect how cruelly he was required to labour for the sustenance that was, surely, a human right.

Fortunately no more than tuition was required of him.

Doamna Protopopescu's kimono was of black artificial silk printed over with flame-coloured chrysanthemums. It was a decayed and greasy-looking garment, smelling of the body beneath. Sometimes one of her big breasts would fall out and she would bundle it back with the indifference of habit. Clearly – thank God! – she did not see Yakimov as a man at all. His comment at the bar was: "That dear girl exists only for the relaxation of the warrior."

When she talked, it was usually about herself or her husband, who was, she said, impotent. "But here," she explained, "all men are impotent at thirty. In youth, they know no restraint." She never spoke more openly of the fact that she had acquired a second bed-fellow, but frequently said: "Here it is not nice to have more than one lover at a time."

Occasionally she complained, in the usual Rumanian fashion, of the country's two despised components – the peasants and the Jews.

"Ah, these peasants!" she said one day, after a particularly furious fracas with the batman, "they are but beasts."

"So little is done for them," said Yakimov in the approved English style.

"True." Doamna Protopopescu sighed at the magnanimity of her agreement. "The priest, who should do all – he does nothing. He is the village bull. The women dare not refuse him. But were he other, would they learn? I doubt. It is the nature everywhere of the workers that they are the dregs, the sediments."

"Oh, I don't know," said Yakimov. "Some of them are rather sweet."

"*Sweet!*" Aghast at the word, she looked at him so that he feared she was about to strike him.

As for the Jews, they were, according to Doamna Protopopescu, to blame for all the ills of the world. They were particularly to blame for the war, that was causing the rise in prices, the shortage of artisans and the stagnation in French fashions.

Attempting to lighten the tone of the talk, Yakimov said: "Ah, dear girl, you should have met my dear old friend, Count Horvath. He had the finest Jew-shoot in Hungary."

She nodded. "So, in Hungary they shoot Jews! They have wisdom. Here they do not shoot them. In Rumania it is always so – the nature is too soft." As she spoke her whole face drooped with greed, inertia and discontent.

Yakimov, disconcerted, said: "They do not really shoot Jews. It was only a joke."

"A joke, heh?" In her disgust, she thrust into her mouth a piece of Turkish delight so large it left round her mouth a fur of sugar.

He had been in the house some weeks before he dared venture into the kitchen. Then, returning supperless one night to a silent flat, he opened the door and switched on the light. All about him the walls heaved as cockroaches, blackbeetles and other indigenous insects sped out of sight. He was tip-toeing towards a cupboard, when a movement startled him. He saw that Ergie and her daughter were lying on a pallet wedged between gas-stove and sink. Ergie had raised her head.

"A glass of water, dear girl," he whispered and, drawing a glass, was forced to drink the wretched stuff before going hungry to bed.

18

A FEW DAYS AFTER HARRIET HAD TOLD INCHCAPE of Sheppy's sabotage plans, the Pringles quarrelled for the first time. Guy's safe return had put all thought of Sheppy from her head. She was as surprised as Guy when one morning Inchcape entered their flat with a swagger and, stripping off his gloves and smacking them across his palm, laughed at Guy in triumph.

"Well, I've just left your friend: the mysterious Commander Sheppy." Inchcape rapped the words out in Sheppy's own style: "I think I've put him straight on a few points. I've informed him that, whosoever he may be, he has no jurisdiction over my men."

Guy said nothing, but looked at Harriet. Harriet looked out of the window.

Inchcape, enjoying himself, swung half a circle on his heel and stretched his lips in an angry smile. "Our permits to live and work here," he said, "are issued on the undertaking we do not get mixed up in any funny business. I can well understand your wanting to do something more dramatic than lecturing, but the situation does not permit. It *simply* does not permit. Whether you like it or not, you're in a reserved occupation. You're here to obey orders. *My* orders."

Guy still said nothing, but took down the *ţuică* bottle and started to look for glasses. Inchcape held up his hand: "Not for me." Guy put the bottle back.

Inchcape began fitting his gloves on again: "If you want to help out at the Legation with a bit of decoding or clerical work, no one will object. Clarence has his Poles. No objection. No objection whatsoever." His gloves on, he stood for some moments gazing in at the pleated white silk lining of his bowler hat, then added: "H.M. Government decided that our job is here. It's our duty to do it, and to stay here, doing it, as long as humanly possible. I'm willing to bet that Sheppy's outfit will be kicked out of Rumania before it's had time to turn round. Well!" He jerked his head up and his smile relaxed. "No need for you to see Sheppy again. I've dealt with him. You'll get no more notices of his meetings. And I can tell you one thing – you're well out of it.'' He put on his hat, tapped it, and, swinging round with grace, took himself off.

Guy gave Harriet another look. "Yes," she agreed, "I did tell him. It was that night you were out with Dubedat. I thought Sheppy had got hold of you. I was frightened."

Guy, without speaking, went to the hallway for his coat. As she began to move towards him, he opened the door. "I must hurry," he said.

Harriet was hurt by his coldness: "But aren't we going to walk in the park?"

"I won't have time. I have a students' meeting. David will be in the Doi Trandafiri at one. You can come there if you like."

When he had gone, Harriet, more desolate than at any time before her marriage, picked up a red kitten that was now her companion in the flat, and held it for comfort to her throat.

The kitten had been a stray, found wandering one night in the snow. Guy thought it might be one of the wild cats that lived in the half demolished buildings in the square, but it had been a long way from the buildings. The Pringles took it home. It became at once Harriet's cat, her baby, her totem, her *alter ego*. When anyone else picked it up, it turned into a mad little bundle of pins. Guy was frightened of it, and the kitten, sensing that it had the upper hand with him, would bite him savagely. When he was seated, forgetful of it, it would fly up the back of his chair and land, all teeth and claws, in the thickness of his hair. He would cry for Harriet to remove it.

Guy applauded Harriet, who, picking up the kitten with all the confidence in the world, was never bitten or scratched. "The thing," she said, "is not to be nervous." To the kitten she said: "You may bite other people, but I'm different. You don't bite me," and the kitten, fixing her with its curious stare, seemed to realise they met on equal terms.

Guy, though he remained nervous of it, was proud of the little creature that changed into a fury in his hands. He admired its red-gold colour and the way it would hurtle like a flying cat from one end of the flat to the other. Despina, always eager to echo admiration, said it was a most exceptional cat in every way. If the Pringles had to leave Rumania, she would take it and care for it herself.

Harriet, standing now gazing through the French-windows at

the snow-crowned palace, imagining herself abandoned by Guy, felt for the kitten a passion of tenderness as though it were the only love left to her. She said to it: "I love you. I love you with all my heart." The kitten seemed to take on a look of serious enquiry. "Because you are wild," she added, "because you are warm; because you are living." And, of course, because Guy had turned against her.

She reflected that he had asked Klein to try and discover what had happened to Sasha Drucker and because of this was meeting him with David at the Doi Trandafiri. He had never, as she felt inclined to do, let the matter drop. He was faithful to his friends, but (she told herself) indifferent to her. All these people – David, Klein, the Druckers, Dubedat and a host of others – were his faction: he bound them to himself. She had no one but her little red cat.

Almost at once, she revolted against the situation. Putting the cat down, she dialled Clarence's number at the Propaganda Bureau and said to him: "Guy was taking me for a walk in the park, but he has had to go to a meeting. Won't you take me?"

"Why, yes of course I will." Clarence sounded only too glad of an excuse to leave his office. He came round at once for her and drove her to the park.

It was the beginning of March. The wind was relaxing a little. More and more people were walking abroad, and once again nurses were bringing children to play in the open air. No new snow had fallen for two weeks, but the old snow, blackened and glacial, lingered on. It was lingering too long. People were tired of it.

As Harriet walked with Clarence along the path that lay under Inchcape's balcony, they looked up and saw the summer chairs and flower-baskets heaped with snow. Icicles hung firm as a fringe of swords from every edge. Yet there was a smell in the air of coming spring. Any day now rain would fall instead of snow, and the thaw would begin.

When they reached the dove-cotes, they stopped to watch the apricot-coloured doves that were already perking up their be-draggled tail-feathers, dipping their heads and languishing their soft, gold-glinting necks from side to side. The air was full of their cooing. Behind them the snow was sliding from the branches of a weeping willow. A false acacia, buried all winter, was appearing again, hung over with pods that looked like old banana skins.

Under the chestnut trees by the lake some children were feeding the pigeons. A solitary salesman, with nuts and sesame cakes, stood with his hands under the arms of his short frieze jacket, and slowly raised one knee at a time in a standstill march, his feet so bound with rags he seemed to have gout in both of them. The children were bundles of fur. The little girls wore ear-rings; they had necklaces and brooches over the white fur of their coats and bracelets over the cuffs of their fleecy gloves. A little boy with a gold-topped cane struck the ground authoritatively, agitating the pigeons that fluttered up and, after flying a half-circle of protest, settled down quickly before the food could disappear. Between bites, they moaned and did a little love-making.

Suddenly excited by the coming spring, Harriet felt her quarrel with Guy was of no importance at all. As they crossed the bridge, from which they could see the dusty ice of the waterfall, she paused and leant on the rail and said: "Everything is wonderful. I want . . . I want to be . . ."

Clarence concluded smugly: "What you are not?"

"No. What I am. The 'I' that is obscured by my own feminine silliness. In some ways, I suppose I am just as absurd as Sophie or Bella."

Clarence laughed. "I suppose you are. Women are like that, and one likes them like that."

"No doubt you do. But I don't imagine I exist to enhance your sense of superiority. I exist to satisfy my own demands on myself, and they are higher than yours are likely to be. If you don't like me as I am, I don't care."

Clarence was unruffled. "You mean, you do care," he said, "that's the trouble. Women want to be liked. They can never be themselves."

"And you, my poor Clarence, can never be anything but yourself." She moved to the other side and looked to the widening lake, from which the snow had been swept. The restaurant was now no more than a cape of snow, but someone had crossed it – the footsteps were cleanly cut – and brought out the wireless set. It was playing across the ice. The music was a Russian waltz and there were half a dozen skaters pressing forward against the wind, turning and lifting feet to the waltz rhythm. This end of the lake was so overhung with trees that it seemed enclosed, like a room.

The branches, lacy with frost, glimmered an unearthly silver-white against the pewter colours of ice and sky.

Clarence crossed over to her. Staring down at the scored and riven surface of the lake, he said soberly: "There are things one can never leave behind."

"Such as?"

"One's childhood. One can never recover from that."

As they turned back on their tracks, she knew he wanted her to question him, and asked, not very willingly: "What sort of childhood had you?"

"Oh, a perfectly ordinary one – at least, it would have seemed ordinary to anyone outside it. My father was a clergyman." After a pause, he added: "And a sadist."

"You really mean that? A sadist?"

"Yes."

The wind was behind them now. Released from its stinging onslaught, they walked slowly, feeling almost warm. Harriet did not know what to say to Clarence, who looked sombre and in-drawn, possessed, it seemed, by the memory of childhood as by the memory of an old injustice. She would have chosen to say: "Don't think about it: don't talk about it," but, of course, the thing he needed was to talk. She had a pained sense that something was about to be inflicted on her.

"But worse than that – worse than my father, I mean – was life at school. My father sent me there because the headmaster was a believer in corporal punishment. He believed in it, too."

At the age of seven, Clarence had been beaten for running away from the school. Afterwards, when he lay in bed 'blubbing', he did not know what it was he had done wrong. All he had known was that he wanted to return to his mother. Harriet thought of a child of seven – a child the same age, she imagined, as the boy who had frightened the pigeons with his gold-topped stick. It was scarcely possible to imagine anyone even slapping so young a child, yet Clarence insisted he had been savagely beaten, beaten with all the fury and vigour of revenge.

After a while, he said, he had learnt to 'put up a show'. He had hidden his fears and uncertainties beneath the front he had retained until now, but the truth was that, over the years, his nerve had been broken. His home had offered him no escape from misery. His mother, a gentle creature who feared his father more than Clarence did, had been merely an object of pity, a weight on his emotions – yet, he said, she had been someone to whom he could talk. She had died when he was ten and he felt she had made her escape. She had abandoned him. His happiest times had been those Sundays when he had been permitted to cycle out on the moors with a friend.

"You got on well with the other boys?" Harriet asked.

Clarence looked sullen a moment, withdrawn from this question, then he answered it obliquely: "It's always that sort of school where boys are bullied. It had a tradition of brutality. It was transmitted by the masters."

"But you weren't actually ill-treated by the other boys?"

For reply, he shrugged his shoulders. They were walking down the main path beside the *tapis vert*. In this wind-swept area, which they had to themselves, the snow had drifted so thickly it was impossible to tell where the flower-beds ended and the paths began. Clarence kept tripping on small hedges, keeping no watch where he went, as he described those evenings when, cycling back from the moors, he had grown sick at the sight of the school gates and the sunset reddening the bricks of the school buildings. In time he had acquired a desolate resignation to his position – the inescapable position of victim. Even now, he said, even here in Bucharest, the summer Sunday light, the closed shops, the sound of the bell of the English Church, could bring back that sick hopelessness. It filled him with a sense of failure, and that sense would haunt him all his life.

They were nearing the Calea Victoriei. Harriet could hear the squeak of motor-horns, yet, as they walked isolated on the path, she had the sense of being in a limbo with Clarence. When she thought back on the scene, it seemed to her the snow had been reddened by the desolation of those sabbath sunsets. Though his story of childhood did not relate in any way to hers, its misery seemed altogether too familiar. As she grew depressed, he began to emerge from memory and to smile. She felt that by his confidences he had been making a claim on her. Involuntarily, she took a step away – not only from Clarence but from the unhappy past that overhung him. He had, she felt, been marked down by fear.

He did not notice her movement. Still confiding he said: "I need a strong woman, someone who can be ruthlessly herself."

So Clarence believed her to be that sort of woman! She did not repudiate his belief but knew she was nothing like it. She was not strong, and she certainly felt no impulse to nurse a broken man. She would rather be nursed herself. At the gate, she said she was meeting Guy at the Doi Trandafiri.

Clarence frowned down at his feet and complained: "Why *does* Guy go to that place?"

"He likes people. He likes being pestered by his students."

"Incredible!" drawled Clarence, but, as Harriet went on, he kept beside her.

The café was as crowded as ever. Guy was nowhere to be seen. Harriet said: "He's always late," and Clarence grunted agreement. They had to stand for some minutes before a table was vacated.

Almost as soon as they had sat down, David and Klein entered. Guy came hurrying in behind them. Because of the estrangement, she saw him newly again: a comfortable-looking man of an un-harming largeness of body and mind. His size gave her an illusion of security – for it was, she was coming to believe, no more than an illusion. He was one of those harbours that prove to be too shallow: there was no getting into it. For him, personal relationships were incidental. His fulfilment came from the outside world.

Clarence, meanwhile, had been talking to her, continuing his story as though there had been no interval between the park and the café. As he stared at her, resentful of her inattention, she knew he was one who, given a chance, would shut her off into a private world. What was it they both wanted? Exclusive attention, no doubt: the attention each had missed in childhood. Perversely, she did not want it now it was offered. She was drawn to Guy's gregarious good humour and the open world about him.

She watched him as he came up behind David and Klein and, stepping between them, put his arms about their shoulders. Klein glanced back smiling, at once accepting this as a normal greeting, but David, though he was Guy's intimate, looked confused and, flushing slightly, began to talk away his own confusion. In a moment, Guy saw her and, leaving the others, came hurrying towards her between the crowded noisy tables through the hot and smoky air. He put out his left hand, smiled and squeezed her hand. The estrangement was forgotten.

"Who is this Klein?" Clarence asked, as though the approaching stranger brought intolerable tedium.

"A source of information," said Guy. "One of David's contacts."

When they were all seated, Clarence, doubtful and suspicious, made his usual defensive retreat into silence, but only Harriet noticed. Guy was eager to hear what Klein had discovered about the Druckers.

He had not discovered much. He said: "It seems that Sasha was taken with his father."

"You mean he was arrested?"

"One cannot say that." Klein's face creased with amusement. "This, you must remember, is a civilised country. There was no charge against the boy."

"Then what do you think has happened to him?"

"Who can say! He is not in prison. If he were, I think I would discover it. A prisoner cannot be totally hidden."

"Perhaps he is dead," said Harriet.

"A body must be disposed of. Here secrecy is not so easy. The people are given to talk. Besides, why should they kill the boy? They are not such bad people. They would not kill without reason. All I can say is, no one has seen him since his father's arrest. He has disappeared. But something I have discovered that is very interesting. Very interesting indeed!" He leant forward, grinning. "I have discovered that the Drucker money in Switzerland – a great sum – is banked in the name of Sasha Drucker. Is that not interesting? So, I think he is alive. In Switzerland the banks hold very tightly to money. Even the King could not demand it. It can be withdrawn only by the authority of this young Drucker or his legal heirs. He is an important boy."

"He is indeed!" David agreed. "Perhaps he is being held somewhere until he gives his authority."

Klein shot out his hands in delighted enquiry: "If so, where? Here we have not the Middle Ages. For our Cabinet the situation must be very difficult. Here is an innocent young man – a man so simple, young and innocent that no capital charge could be trumped against him. To hold him without a charge! That would not be civilised, not Occidental! Yet – a young man of such importance! How could they afford to let him leave the country?" Klein sat shaking with laughter at authority's predicament.

Guy frowned to himself, perplexed and concerned. "But what have they *done* with him?" he asked the table.

"Why?" Klein opened his pale eyes. "What do they matter to you, these Druckers? They have made much money – illegal money. They have lived well. Now they are not so well. Need you weep?"

"Sasha was a pupil of mine. The Druckers treated me kindly. They were my friends."

Klein smiled mockingly into Guy's face. "Tell me," he said, "how do you reconcile such friendship with your ideas on international finance?"

David snuffled and sniggered at this question, his mouth curling up under his nostrils. With his head down, he looked up in ironical enquiry at Guy, but before Guy had found a reply, Klein, relenting, said: "All things, all people – all are so interesting."

Clarence leant towards Harriet, speaking to her as though she were alone: "I must say, I think Guy squanders himself on a lot of people who aren't worth it."

"Well, you don't do that," said Harriet with some derision.

"Neither do you."

Harriet put up her hand, warding off this private controversy, so that she could listen to Klein, who had now left the Druckers and was talking of the country's internal situation.

"The King," he announced, "is granting an amnesty to the Iron Guardists."

David and Guy were astounded by this news. There had been no indication in the press, not even a rumour, that this would be possible.

"The amnesty is already signed," said Klein, speaking quietly, "but not yet announced. Wait. Tomorrow or the next day you will hear of it."

"But why should he grant an amnesty?" David asked.

"Ah, it is interesting. The war is ending in Finland. Any day now the Russians will be free to advance themselves elsewhere. And where will they advance? Here the Cabinet is very nervous. To whom can they look for help? Would the Allies defend Rumania against Russia? If so, how would it be possible? But Germany! Germany could do it, and *would* do it, at a price. Already the question has been asked: What price? What does Germany demand? And she has answered: First, grant an amnesty to the Iron Guard."

Clarence drawled crossly: "But I thought there was no Iron Guard left."

"You believed that? My friend, there are many Guardists, but they are hidden. And in Germany, too, there are many. They fled there in 1938 after Codreanu and his legionaries were shot. In Germany they were made welcome. They have been drilled. They have been trained in the concentration camps. They have become more Nazi than the Nazis. The Germans wish them to return here, for here they will be useful."

"But surely," Clarence protested, "no one wants fascism here. Rumania is still pro-British. There'd be an uproar. There might even be risings."

"Britain is loved," said Klein. "The majority would choose a liberal Government if they had nothing to lose by it. But Russia is feared too much. Great fear can cast love out. Stay here and you will see it happen."

David said: "I told the Legation a year ago that we'd lose this country if we didn't change our policy."

Clarence asked, sulkily: "What change of policy could make any difference now?"

"Now, very little. We've left it too late." David's agreement was heated. "But we need not play Germany's game for her." Taking possession of the talk, David spoke with force and feeling: "We support a hated dictatorship. We snub the peasant leaders. We condone the suppression of the extreme Left and the imprisonment of its leaders. We support some of the most ruthless exploitation of human beings to be found in Europe. We support the suppression of minorities – a suppression that must, inevitably, lead to a break-up of Greater Rumania as soon as opportunity arises."

"Perhaps the opportunity won't arise."

"Perhaps it won't. It depends on the conduct of the war. The war will have to move sometime. The deadlock can't continue and I don't believe there is a chance of a truce. If the Allies could break through the Siegfried Line and advance into Germany, then they might, without particular injury to British interests, continue their policy here indefinitely. As it is we're doing the fascists' job for them. At the first indication of a possible German victory, the whole vast anti-Communist movement here would rise against us."

"Do you expect us to support the Communists?" Clarence asked.

"Certainly not. My complaint is that, when we could, we did nothing to establish a liberal policy that could save the country from either extremity – Left or Right."

"I think you take too black a view of things," mumbled Clarence.

"You, I can see," said David, "would agree with H.E. The old duffer describes my reports as 'alarmist' and files them away and forgets about them."

"Hum!" said Clarence, hiding his annoyance under an expression of superior doubt, then he jumped up, claimed he had a luncheon appointment, and went without saying his good-byes.

David looked after him, smiling in amused pity. "Poor old Clarence," he said. "He's a bit of a half-baked intellectual, but a good fellow, really. Yes, quite a good fellow!" and he returned to his condemnation of British policy in Rumania.

PART FOUR

The Fall of Troy

19

THE IRON GUARD AMNESTY WAS ANNOUNCED as the thaw set in. The thaw, arriving late, bringing with it deluge and floods, was the more discussed. The announcement of the amnesty led, not to uproar and revolt as Clarence had predicted, but to a change in the Cabinet and the appointment among the new Ministers of the Guardist leader Horia Sima. The King assured the Allies they need have no fears. The amnesty meant nothing. A few new jokes went the rounds of the cafés. The Rumanians, it seemed, were prepared for anything now.

But the thaw was another matter. As the snow melted and ran from eaves and balconies, the whole city dripped beneath a leaden sky. Most people went about under umbrellas. When the iced surfaces on roads and pavements began to crack, people sank, without warning, deep into slush. Soon the roads were nothing but slush, ice-cold and filthy, that was sprayed by the speeding traffic on to the passers-by.

The sky grew darker and sank lower until it split beneath its own weight and the rain fell in torrents. Rivers overflowed their banks. Whole villages were drowned in a night. Conscripted peasants, having begged leave to help their families, wandered about in search of their homes, finding nothing but a waste of waters. The destitute survivors crowded into the city to replace the beggars that winter had killed.

The Finnish peace treaty was signed. Russia was free for another adventure. The citizens of Bucharest, cooped up in cafés, watching the downpour, passed round rumours of invasion. A reconnaissance 'plane was said to have sighted troops crossing the Dniester. Refugees were streaming towards the Pruth. Detailed descriptions were given of atrocities committed by Russian troops on Rumanian and German minorities. People went fearful to bed and rose to find everything much as they had left it. The rumours of yesterday were denied, but repeated the day after.

During this time there appeared in Bucharest an English teacher called Toby Lush who declared that all Bessarabia was in a ferment, the Russians being expected that very night.

It was thought at first that Lush came from the University of Jassy. Clarence and the Pringles felt much sympathy for any Englishman in a frontier town since hearing that the British Council lecturer at Ljubljana had been seized in the street one night by a German patrol car, taken over the frontier into Austria and never heard of again. However, when they started to talk to Lush, they discovered he came not from Jassy but from Cluj. He had thought that, things being as they were, he would be safer in the capital. After a fortnight, during which all the frontiers remained unviolated, he rather sheepishly said farewell to his new acquaintances, got into his car and returned to his pupils in Cluj.

One morning before Easter, when a gleam was lightening the puddles and the chestnut buds were breaking, Yakimov stood in the Calea Victoriei and stared into the window of a small restaurant. He was indifferent to the indications of spring. He was indifferent, too, to the gypsies, crowding back to their old pitch with baskets full of snow-drops, hyacinths, daffodils and mimosa, who were calling out excitedly to passers-by as though to old friends. One of them slapped Yakimov's arm, spinning him round and greeting him with fervour: "*Bună dimineață, domnule,*" and he smiled, murmuring vaguely: "Dear girl," before he returned to his contemplation of the raw steaks and pork chops behind the glass.

He was without a hat, and his hair, fine, fair and in need of a cut, stirred in the cold March wind. Though the pavement snow was reduced now to a thin layer of something like wet and dirty sugar, his shoes were soaked. The hem of his coat, becoming unstitched, dipped down to his heels. He had a cold in his head; but none of this meant much compared with the fact he was tormented by a longing for food.

Guy, going home for luncheon, saw him and stopped and spoke. He drew his gaze slowly from the chops and tried to look blank. "How nice to see you, dear boy," he said. His voice was hoarse.

"Aren't you well?" Guy asked.

"Touch of *la grippe*." He tried to blow his nose without taking off a glove and the hard, wet, broken leather, prodding his inflamed nostrils, brought a tear to his eye.

Guy said: "Are you eating anywhere in particular?"

"Why, no, dear boy." At the prospect of food, Yakimov began to shake slightly and a second tear followed the first. He sniffed and said: "Not to tell a lie, I've been rather let down. Was luncheoning with my old friend Hadjimoscos, but apparently he's been called to his estate."

"Good heavens, has he an estate?"

"Heavily mortgaged, of course." Yakimov shifted hastily from the estate back to the subject of food. "Bit short of the Ready, dear boy. M'remittance held up again. Was just wondering what I'd do for a bite."

"Why not come back and eat with us?"

"Delighted." All pretences fallen in the emotion of the moment, he tripped as he turned and had to catch Guy's arm for support. Walking towards the square, Yakimov's sufferings poured from him.

"Difficult times," he said. "Your poor old Yaki's homeless. Been turned out. Thrown out, in fact. Literally thrown out by m'landlady. A terrible woman. Terrible. And she's kept all m'belongings."

"She can't do that." Guy was indignant, but on reflection added: "Unless, of course, you owe her some rent."

"Only a few *lei*. But that wasn't the main trouble, dear boy. It was a ham-bone I found lying about. Feeling a bit peckish, I picked it up – and she caught me with the bone in m'hand. You know what's on a ham-bone, dear boy! Scarcely a mouthful, but she went mad. *Mad.* She hit me, kicked me, beat me over the head, screamed like a maniac: then she opened the front door and shoved me out." He shuddered from cold or fear and glanced about as though in danger of renewed attack. "Never knew anything like it, dear boy."

"But you got your coat."

"Happened to be wearing it. It happened last night. I'd just come in." He touched the coat with love. "Did I tell you the Czar gave this coat to m'poor old dad?"

"Yes. Where are you staying now?"

"Nowhere. I just spent the night tramping the streets, dear boy. Just tramping the streets."

When Guy brought Yakimov into the flat, Harriet, who had been sitting by the electric fire, rose without a word, went into her bedroom and slammed the door. She remained so long that Guy went after her. She turned on him angrily, saying: "I've told you I will not have that man in the flat."

Guy reasoned with her: "Darling, he's ill; he's hungry; he's been turned out of his lodgings."

"I don't care. He insulted you. I won't have him here."

"When did he insult me?"

"On Christmas night. He said your limerick was in bad taste."

"Really, darling!" Guy laughed at her absurdity. "Listen! He's not well. I've never before seen him looking so thin and ill."

"I don't care. He's a scrounger and a glutton."

"Yes, you do care." Guy, holding her by the shoulders, shook her affectionately. "We must help him, not because he's a good person but because he needs help. You understand that." She let her head fall forward against his chest and, pleased by her capitulation, he gave her a final squeeze and said: "Come into the room. Be nice to him."

When Harriet entered the sitting-room, Yakimov looked apprehensively at her. He put her hand to his lips and said: "How kind of Beauty to feed her poor old Yaki."

Harriet, sufficiently recovered to be polite, was touched, in spite of herself, by Yakimov's appearance. He looked ill, aged and underfed.

He ate fiercely, saying nothing throughout the meal. When replete and revived, he looked up brightly. "Dear boy," he said to Guy, "I could put you on to a good thing. Had hoped to do the like for m'old friend Dobson, but he's been out of sight these last weeks. Keep dropping in on him but his secretary says he's busy, for some reason. Want him to get me a Yugoslav transit visa, then all I need's m'train-fare, a few thou and a C.D. number-plate. Once there I'd redeem m'poor old Hispano-Suiza and drive her back. Anyone who financed the trip would be quids in. With a C.D. number-plate, there's a packet to be made running stuff over frontiers. Take currency, for instance . . ."

"I'm sure Dobson couldn't get you a C.D. number-plate," said Harriet.

'M'sure he could, dear girl. Dobson's an old friend, deeply indebted to poor Yaki. And he'd get his whack. Now you, dear boy, if you could let Yaki have a few *lei* – thirty-five thousand, to be exact – I'd see you didn't lose by it."

Guy laughed, not taking the scheme seriously, and said he and Harriet were going to the mountains for Easter. They would need all the money they could spare for the holiday.

Yakimov sighed and swallowed down his coffee.

Guy turned to Harriet. "The flat will be empty while we're away," he said. "Couldn't we let Yaki stay here?"

She gave him a look and said coldly: "Why ask me?"

"He could look after the kitten."

"Despina will look after the kitten."

"Well, it's always a good thing to keep a place lived in."

"We're not leaving until tomorrow."

"There's the spare room."

"With no bed in it."

Yakimov broke in eagerly: "Anything will do for me, dear girl. The arm-chair, the floor, the odd mattress. Your poor old Yaki'll be thankful to have a roof over his head."

Guy looked steadily at Harriet, trying to melt her with consciousness of Yakimov's plight. She got to her feet impatiently: "Very well, but he must find somewhere to go before we get back."

She returned to the bedroom, from where she heard Guy lending Yakimov the money to pay off Doamna Protopopescu and regain his possessions.

"I suppose you wouldn't come and face her with me?" Yakimov asked.

No. Guy would do many things, but he would not do that.

After the two men had left the flat, Harriet wandered about, feeling fooled. She had refused to take in Dubedat, so this time Guy, grown cunning, had not given her the chance to refuse. He had circumvented her with her own compassion. Yakimov had been dishonestly imposed on her. She felt furious.

She went to the arm-chair where the red kitten lay sleeping, and, as though to assert the true seat of her compassion, she held it to her face, saying: "I love you." She kissed it wildly. "And I don't love anyone else," she said.

20

THE THAW HAD REACHED the mountain village of Predeal just before the Pringles. The snow was wet and sliding wetly down from the rock faces above the houses. The hotels were emptying as the skiers went to the higher alps. On Easter Saturday the rain began.

Guy cared for none of this. He intended, he said, to produce a play and the choice was among *Macbeth*, *Othello* and *Troilus and Cressida*, copies of which he had brought with him. He had spoken of this intention during the winter, but Harriet had hoped nothing would come of it. Now, she realised, it had attained reality for him.

"I shall put it on at the National Theatre," he said.

She looked at *Troilus and Cressida* and saw it contained twenty-eight speaking parts. Dismayed, caught into the difficulties of such a production as into the toils of a prophetic dream, she tried to reason with him, but he simply laughed, seeing no difficulties at all.

She said: "Very few of the students are good enough to play Shakespeare."

"Oh, they'll only take minor parts. There are other people – friends, the chaps at the Legation . . ."

"Do you really think the Legation men will have time for amateur theatricals?"

Guy merely replied: "There'll be nothing amateur about my production."

"And the costumes! The expense, the work – and then, perhaps, no one will come." She spoke with an anguish which made him laugh at her.

"It will be tremendous fun," he said. "Everyone will come to it. You wait and see. It will be a great success."

His confidence reassured her, but at the same time she suffered the possibility of failure. She tried to persuade him to moderation: "Why not just do a reading in the lecture hall?"

"Oh no. We must do the thing in style. Rumanians only respond to snob appeal."

"And when are you thinking of starting it?"

"As soon as we get back."

It was late afternoon when the Pringles returned to their Bucharest flat. Two days before they had sent Yakimov a warning telegram. When they entered the sitting-room, there was no sign of him.

"There you are!" Guy congratulated himself. "He's gone. I knew we'd have no trouble with him."

Harriet, not so sure, went into the bedroom. She was stopped as she entered by its heavy, unfamiliar smell. The curtains were pulled close. She threw them open. The windows were shut. She opened them, then, looking round at the disordered room, saw on the bed, cocooned in blankets, huddled knees to chin, head buried, Yakimov, in the depths of sleep. She went and shook him angrily.

"Wake up."

He came to consciousness slowly. She pulled the covers from his face and one eye looked at her with an injured expression.

"Didn't you get our telegram?" she asked.

He dragged himself up, trying to smile. "Dear girl, how delightful to see you back! Did you enjoy your trip? Tell Yaki all about it."

"We expected you would be gone before we returned."

"Yaki is going: going this very day, dear girl." His face, swollen and damp from sleep, the skin pink like scar tissue, turned resentfully to the open window. "Dreadfully chilly," he said.

"Then get up and dress. The bed linen will have to be changed."

Wincing at the cold, Yakimov came from under the covers, revealing pyjamas, torn and very dirty, made of flame-coloured *crêpe de Chine*. "Sick man," he murmured as he found, and tremulously covered himself with, a tarnished dressing-gown of gold brocade. "Better take a bath." He hurried off and shut himself in the bathroom.

Despina had appeared by now, expressing delight at the Pringles' return, but holding up her hands to warn her mistress that there had been catastrophe in her absence. The red kitten was dead.

"No!" Harriet cried, Yakimov and every other annoyance forgotten in the face of this news.

Despina, nodding in sombre sympathy, related how the kitten had died. One morning, when she was cleaning the room, it had gone on to the balcony and run along the balustrade to the balcony of the next-door flat. There the servant ("a Rumanian, of course," said Despina meaningfully) had hissed at it and flicked it back with a duster. Startled, it had lost its footing and fallen nine floors to the cobbles below. Despina went down and found it dead. It had, she was sure, died instantly.

Harriet wept. The loss seemed to her unendurable. She stood crouched together, weeping with intent bitterness, in agony, as though the foundations of her life had been taken from her. Guy watched her helplessly, amazed at so much grief.

"And the servant did it!" she burst out at last. "The beastly peasant."

Guy remonstrated: "Darling, really! The girl didn't realise what she was doing."

"That's the trouble. They have the equipment of humans and the understanding of beasts. That is what one hates." She wept again. "My kitten, my poor kitten!" After a while, she blew her nose and asked: "And where was Yakimov when it happened?"

"Ah, that one!" Despina spoke scornfully. "He was asleep."

"He would be asleep." Harriet's anger with the peasant servant was now carried over to Yakimov and Despina tried to divert her by encouraging it.

"What has he done," she asked, "but eat, eat, eat and, sleep, sleep, sleep!" She had, she said, spent all the housekeeping money the Pringles had left with her. She had managed to obtain credit at a shop where she was known to have English employers, but the credit was limited. On Easter Sunday Yakimov had invited in guests – another Prince and a Count – and had demanded a fine meal. Despina, afraid for the honour of the Pringles, was at her wits end. She had gone to Domnul Professor Inchcape and borrowed two thousand *lei*.

"Did you tell him why you needed the money?" Harriet asked. Despina nodded.

"And what did he say?"

"He laughed."

"I bet he did."

Despina broke in with another grievance, speaking so rapidly that Harriet could not follow her. Guy translated in a deprecating tone: "He wanted her to wash some clothes. She refused."

"Good for her."

"A mountain of clothes," cried Despina.

"He's leaving today," Harriet promised her and sent her to make tea.

When the tea was brought in, Yakimov appeared, dressed. His demeanour was so nervous that Harriet could say nothing. Despina had bought some iced cakes for the homecoming and he ate his way through them with absentminded sadness. After tea he sat on, huddled over the fire. Harriet, longing to see the back of him, asked where he had found a room.

"Haven't found one yet, dear girl."

"You've left it very late."

"Not been fit to trudge around."

"Aren't you going now?"

He answered brokenly: "Where is poor Yaki to go?"

Despina was working in the bedroom. Harriet, half imagining Yakimov might take himself off in her absence, went to speak to her. A few minutes later Guy came in and spoke to her, quietly and urgently: "Darling, be charitable."

At the word, something turned over inside Harriet in self-accusation, yet she said: "This is my home. I can't share it with someone I despise."

"He has no money. No one will take him in unless he pays in advance. Let him stay. It doesn't cost us anything to let him sleep in the chair."

"It does. It costs me more than you could ever guess. Go and get rid of him."

"Darling, I can't. The fact is, I've already told him he can stay."

She turned her back on him and went over to the dressing-table, reflecting, in a sort of dazed wonder, on how it was that Guy, seemingly reasonable and the most gentle of men, always got his own way.

Guy, accepting her silence as agreement, said with confiding cheerfulness: "You know, darling, it would really pay us to keep Yaki here, where we have a hold on him."

"You mean you may get back some of the money he owes you?"

"No, the money's not important. It's the play. He's ideal for Pandarus. His voice is the very voice of Pandarus. He could make my production."

"Oh, that damned production!"

"If we turn him out," Guy went on happily, "he'll be found wandering and ordered out of the country. If we keep him, he'll have to behave. And I'll make him work. You wait and see."

She replied with decision: "I don't want him here," and, sweeping past Guy, she returned to the sitting-room, where she found Yakimov settled into the arm-chair with the *ţuică* bottle.

21

A FEW DAYS LATER, Guy invited his friends in to a first reading of *Troilus and Cressida*. Before they arrived, Harriet opened the French-windows on to the balcony, Outside, an azure light glinted over the cobbles and silvered the roofs. The days were growing long and warm, and the evening crowds were coming out again. The murmur of the traffic, muted for months by snow, came distinct and new through the open windows. For the first time that year, she left the doors open.

Guy was cutting an old Penguin edition of the play. It was evident, from the businesslike manner in which he answered her, that he was excited.

Harriet had been told she could read Cressida. Yakimov, for whom a camp-bed had been bought and placed in the spare room, was beginning to realise that Guy seriously intended him to take the part of Pandarus. He was expected to learn it by heart When the order had first been given him, he had dismissed it with a smile: "Can't possibly, dear boy. Always was a poor scholar. Never could remember anything."

"I'll see you learn it," Guy replied, and when Yakimov put the matter from his mind, Guy, suddenly and with an astonishing firmness, made it clear that if Yakimov wished to remain in the flat he must play Pandarus. This persuaded him to read the part. Before the night of the first rehearsal, Guy took him through it half-a-dozen times.

Guy, he realised, had complete faith in his ability as a producer. He seemed to have an equal faith in Yakimov. Yakimov himself, with no faith at all, could have wept to find Guy, usually so easygoing, turned to task-master – and no lenient task-master, either. By the evening of the reading he was beginning to remember the lines in spite of himself. He did not know whether to be relieved or sorry. Rising a little out of a nadir of depression, he did his best to greet the visitors. Finding himself treated as one who had an important part in the proceedings, his spirits rose and he began to feel rather pleased with himself.

Inchcape, when he entered, pressed a hand down on Yakimov's shoulder and said: "Good Pandarus – how now, Pandarus?"

"I have had my labour for my travail," Yakimov automatically replied, and at Inchcape's crow of amusement his old easy smile returned.

Guy had had the play typed and duplicated and was now handing out copies to each person who arrived. Soon all the men were present. Bella had been invited and was coming in after a cocktail party. The room became noisy with talk. One of the men was telling a funny story about Hitler's conduct of the war, when Guy called everyone to attention. His manner suggested that the war might be a joke, but this production was not. Rather to Harriet's surprise, the talk stopped at once. The company seated itself and looked to Guy for instructions. He said: "Cressida will read her first dialogue with Pandarus."

Calmly, Harriet moved out on to the floor, mentioning that, unlike most of the girls she had known at school, she had never been ambitious to go on the stage.

Guy frowned at the levity of this approach. Aloof and patient, he said: "Will you please begin."

Yakimov read: "Do you know a man if you see him?" to which Harriet replied with the gaiety of repartee: "Ay, if I ever saw him before, and knew him."

Harriet thought she did rather well. They both did well. Yakimov, who scarcely needed to be anything other than himself, spoke in his delicate, insinuating voice, only accentuating a little, now and then, its natural melancholy or note of comic complaint.

At the end Guy said no more than "All right," then, pointing to Dubedat, said: "Thersites."

As Dubedat ambled out, the bugle sounded from the palace yard, and Harriet began the old chant of "Come, water your horses . . ."

"Please!" Guy commanded her and, silenced, she raised an eyebrow at David, who started to snuffle. Ignoring this, Guy repeated: "Thersites," and Dubedat, his legs still scaled from the ravages of winter, came on to the floor in his new spring outfit of T-shirt and running shorts.

"Begin reading Act Two, Scene One. I'll do Ajax for the moment."

Dubedat read Thersites with a Cockney snivel that was only a slight exaggeration of his normal speech. At the end of the scene, he was applauded, but Guy, not so easily satisfied, said: "The voice will do. But the part calls for venom, not complaint."

Swallowing convulsively, Dubedat set out again, reading at a great rate, but Guy stopped him: "Enough for now. I'd like to hear Ulysses."

Inchcape, whom Harriet was certain would refuse to take a part, now got to his feet with a look of deep satisfaction. Hemming and huffing in his throat, he took a step or two into the middle of the room, and, with feet elegantly planted, shoulders back, looking even now more audience than actor, he said with a smile: "I'm an old hand with theatricals. I always produced the school play. Of course we never attempted anything as frisky as this "

"Act One, Scene Three," said Guy. "The long speech: 'What glory' etcetera."

Still smiling, matching his tone to his smile, Inchcape read with a dry and even humour that Guy accepted, anyway for the moment. "All right," he nodded and Inchcape, taking a step back, twitched up his trousers at the knees and lowered himself carefully back into his seat.

Clarence and David were not yet cast. Guy now suggested that David might attempt Agamemnon.

David's lips parted in alarm. As he came out slowly into the middle of the room, snuffling down at his feet, Harriet saw he was not only amused at the position in which he found himself: he was pleased. After some hesitation, he began to read, pitching his elderly don's voice on too high a note so that he sounded querulous.

Guy broke in on him: "Give it more voice, David. Don't forget you're the General of the Grecian forces."

"Oh, am I? So I am!" Moving his feet nervously, he pushed his glasses up his nose and started again on a deeper note.

Harriet and Yakimov, their star positions fixed in a firmament otherwise chaotic, sat together on the arm-chair, Harriet on the seat, Yakimov on the arm. They had nothing to say to each other, but she felt him relaxed as the impossible had become for him possible, and even, maybe, enjoyable.

Harriet had been feeling a painful anxiety on Guy's behalf. She would have been glad for the production to collapse first rather than last, so sure was she it must collapse sometime.

Now she was beginning to realise she might be wrong. Contrary to her belief, people were not only willing to join in, they were grateful at being included. Each seemed simply to have been awaiting the opportunity to make a stage appearance. She wondered why. Perhaps they thought themselves under-employed here, in a foreign capital, in time of war. Perhaps Guy offered them distraction, a semblance of creative effort, an object to be achieved.

Guy's attitude impressed her, though she had no intention of showing it. He had the advantage of an almost supernatural confidence in dealing with people. It seemed never to occur to him they might not do what he wanted. He had, she noted with surprise, authority.

In the past she had been irritated by the amount of mental and physical vitality he expended on others. As he flung out his charm, like radium dissipating its own brilliance, it had seemed to her indiscriminate giving for giving's sake. Now she saw his vitality functioning to some purpose. Only someone capable of giving much could demand and receive so much. She felt proud of him.

David, coming to the end of a long speech, looked uncertainly at Guy.

"Go on," said Guy. "You're doing splendidly," and David, shouldering importance like a cloak, went ahead with renewed enjoyment.

Bella, arriving in a suit of black corded silk, hung with silver foxes, was asked if she would play Helen.

"Is it a long part?" she asked.

"No."

"Thank goodness for that!" she exclaimed over-fervently.

Inchcape, bending towards her, said: "You are Helen of Troy. We ask only that you should be beautiful. Yours is the face that launched a thousand ships."

"Dear me!" said Bella. She threw off her furs and her cheeks grew pink.

She took the floor, read her exchange with Pandarus and came, flushed and serious, to sit near Harriet. She was, Harriet was beginning to realise, a woman of considerable competence. She knew nothing of acting; she never had been on a stage; her movements were stiff, yet she had done well.

"What about Troilus?" Inchcape asked. "Who can we get for him?"

Guy replied that he was hoping to cast one of the Legation staff for the part. He was waiting for the Minister's approval.

"And Achilles?" asked Inchcape. "Rather a tricky part!"

"I've one of the new students in mind, young Dimancescu, a good-looking boy and a junior fencing champion. He went to an English public-school before the war."

"Indeed! Which?"

"Marlborough."

"Excellent!" said Inchcape. "Excellent!"

Harriet burst out laughing. She said: "Most of your actors have only to play themselves."

Guy turned on her frowning. "Just try and keep quiet," he said.

His annoyance startled her into silence. Guy called the men to read in a group, himself taking the parts still uncast, and avoiding those scenes in which Cressida appeared.

Next day in the students' common-room, Guy held a meeting of those students he proposed using in his production. While he was out, Dobson telephoned to say the Minister would permit any of his staff who wished to take part in the play.

"He approves, then?" Harriet said, surprised.

"He thinks it a splendid idea," said Dobson. "Showing the flag and all that. Cocking a snook at the Boche."

So Harriet had been wrong again. She said to Guy when he returned: "This is wonderful, darling," but he was not responsive. He was, she supposed, absorbed in his production, and the fact made her feel misgiving like a child whose mother is too occupied with the outside world. Still, she was caught in a sort of wonder at the growing reality of the play.

"You are rather remarkable," she admitted. "You make it all seem so easy. You just ignore difficulties that would have brought me completely to a stop."

His only reply was: "I'll take Yaki with me tomorrow. We'll have to start rehearsing seriously."

"And me?"

"No." He was sitting on the edge of the bed tugging at his shoes, trying to get them off without undoing the laces. As he did so, he gazed out of the window with a frown of decision: "I think you'd be more useful doing the costumes."

"Do you mean instead of playing Cressida?"

"Yes."

She was, at first, merely bewildered: "But there isn't anyone else to play Cressida."

"I've already got someone."

"Who?"

"Sophie."

"You invited Sophie to play my part before you'd even told me?" She was dumbfounded. This treatment seemed to her monstrous, but she told herself she was not hurt. She did not care whether she was in the production or not. After a pause she asked: "Did you tell Sophie that I was to have played the part?"

"No, of course not."

"But someone else might have told her."

"They might, of course. What does it matter?"

"You don't think it matters if Sophie learns she has pushed me out of the play?"

"She hasn't pushed you out of the play. It had nothing to do with her. It was simply obvious to me that we couldn't work together. You would never take the production seriously." He started looking about for his slippers. "Anyway, no producer can do a proper job with his wife around."

After she had absorbed the situation she tried to explain it away. Guy, she supposed, found her presence frustrating. She had not actually ridiculed his position – but he feared she might. She made him apprehensive. Her presence spoilt the illusion of power.

After a long interval, she said: "I suppose I deserve it."

"Deserve it? What do you mean?"

"I made no attempt to understand Sophie, or to behave, so I brought out the best in her. I suppose I could have played up to her; shown sympathy or something. I didn't. I was to blame. Now you are giving her an opportunity to get her own back."

"Darling, you are absurd!" Though he laughed at her ideas, he was clearly disconcerted by them. "You can't possibly believe that!" He frowned down at her, his frown affectionate yet perplexed. He put a hand on her shoulder and gave her a slight shake as though seeking to shake her into a semblance of something more comprehensible. He said: "It was only that I had to have someone else. Sophie is suitable. You must agree. You would have done quite well, but I knew I couldn't produce you. The relationship would have got in the way."

She let the matter drop. It was only later when everyone she knew was in it that she began to feel hurt at being out of the production. More than that, she was jealous that Guy should be producing Sophie in one of the chief parts of the play. Unreasonably, she told herself. She could no longer doubt that Guy had been perfectly honest about his relationship with Sophie. Innocent and foolish as he was, the idea of marriage to Sophie had. been, nevertheless, attractive as an idea rather than a reality. He was not, in fact, one to make a marriage of self-sacrifice. He was a great deal more self-protected – perhaps from necessity – than most people realised. Realising it herself, she could only wonder at the complexity of the apparently simple creature she had married.

22

THE SPRING SHOWERS WASHED AWAY the last vestiges of the snow. With each reappearance the sun grew warmer. More and more people came out at evening to stroll in the streets. Up the Chaussée, where the chestnut branches were breaking with green, the chatter of the crowd could be heard above the traffic. Despite the delights of the season, it was a disgruntled chatter.

The Cabinet had inaugurated internal retrenchment in order that exports to Germany might be increased. To save petrol, taxis were forbidden to cruise in search of fares: they could be picked up only at given points – an unheard-of inconvenience. Food prices were rising. The new French silks were appearing in the shops at an absurd price. Imported goods were growing scarce and would, it was rumoured, soon disappear altogether. In panic, people were buying many things they did not want.

Guy was not much interested when Harriet described the sense of grievance in the city. His worries were elsewhere. There was, she thought, a sumptuous aloofness about his manner these days. His preoccupation was the deeply contented preoccupation of the creator: he was not to be shaken by trivialities. Even Inchcape, coming in one breakfast time – his usual time for unexpected visits – could rouse little curiosity in Guy, although he made it evident that his news was likely to please Guy less than it pleased him.

He would not sit down, but strolled about the room laughing in high delight at what he had to tell. "Well, well," he said. "Well, *well*!"

The Pringles, knowing that, given encouragement, he would only procrastinate further, waited in silence to hear it.

At last he relented. "You've heard what's happened to your friend Sheppy?" he asked.

They shook their heads.

"Ha!" squawked Inchcape; then, coming to it at last: "He's been arrested."

"No!" said Harriet.

"*Yes*. Down by the Danube. The ass was caught with the gelignite on him."

"Trying to blow up the Iron Gates?"

"Something like that. They were caught in a river-side bar, shouting drunk, talking quite openly about bringing Danube shipping to a standstill. They imagined, because Rumania is supposed to be a British ally, the Danube bargemen would be happy to help sabotage their own livelihood. What a pack of fools! Anyway, they're all under lock and key now. 'A fair cop,' I believe the expression is."

"Who got caught with him? Anyone we know?"

"No, none of the local conscripts were there; only the top brass. This was Sheppy's first expedition – and his last." Inchcape slapped his thigh, crowing at the thought of it. "The first and last sally of Sheppy's Fighting Force."

Harriet smiled at Guy, but Guy might have been a thousand miles removed from the whole matter. She asked Inchcape: "What will become of them?"

"Oh!" Inchcape twisted his mouth down in his ironical smile. "No doubt the F.O. will get them out. They're *much* too valuable to lose."

Rumania did not want a diplomatic incident just then. Sheppy and his 'henchmen' were flown back to England. After that came official denial that he had ever existed. No saboteur, it was stated, could slip past the net spread wide by Rumania's magnificent body of security police. But the story had got around and it added to the general sense of insecurity and victimisation. The press began to write openly of the injustices being suffered by a peaceful nation in someone else's war.

Harriet could now read enough in the Rumanian papers to realise how rapidly Rumania's too distant allies were passing out of favour. No one had been reassured by Chamberlain's declaration that "Hitler has missed the bus". If it were true that England was now an impregnable fortress, then "*tant pis pour les autres*" said *L'Indépendence Romaine*. The fact that Germany, without making any move, was now receiving seventy per cent of all Rumanian exports was not, said *Timpul*, any cause for self-congratulation. Germany's demands would increase with her needs.

What she was not given she would come and take. *Universul* wrote slightingly of those who used Rumania in time of peace but in war-time not only abandoned her defenceless, but sought to sabotage her resources. When, oh when, they all wanted to know, could the great, generous-hearted Rumanian people, now left to buy off the enemy as best they might, again look forward to those summers of joyous frivolity they had known before this senseless war began?

Harriet, a member of an unfavoured nation, felt shut out from Guy's world to face the painful situation alone. With little else to do, she often dropped in at the Athénée Palace to look at the English papers. They were exceptionally dull, concerned usually with some argument about mine-laying in Norwegian waters.

The hotel was as dull as the papers. It was an inert period between seasons: a time of no news when the journalists were elsewhere. Nothing was happening in Bucharest. Nothing, it seemed, was happening anywhere in the world. And, despite all the apprehension, it was likely enough nothing would happen.

But in Bucharest, anyway, apprehension was not groundless. The political atmosphere was changing. A notice appeared under the glass of the café tables to say it was forbidden under threat of arrest to discuss politics And arrest, it was said, might lead one to the new concentration camp being organised on the German model by Guardists trained in Dachau and Buchenwald. People said the camp was hidden somewhere in the remote Carpathians. No one could say exactly where.

One showery morning, as she came from the hotel, Harriet was struck by the appearance of a young man sheltering beneath the lime trees that over-reached the garden wall.

The rain had stopped. The young leaves flashed their green against a sky of indigo cloud. The cloud was breaking. A gleam touched the wet tarmac. The young man, although neither beggar nor peasant, remained by the wall with nothing to do apparently but stand there. He was dressed in the city grey much worn by the middle classes, but he was unlike any middle-class Rumanian Harriet had ever seen. He was hard and thin. His was a new sort of face in this town. Looking at his hollowed cheeks, meeting his unfriendly gaze, she told herself he must be one of the Guardist youths newly returned from Germany. He looked at the moment not so much dangerous as ill-at-ease. Here he was, returned to a city grown unfamiliar to him, a destroyer, perhaps, but for the moment powerless.

After she had seen this one, she began to see others like him. They stood about the streets, their pallid, bony faces sometimes scarred like the faces of German duellists. They watched the pampered crowds with the contempt, and uncertainty, of the deprived. They were waiting as though they knew their day would come.

To Guy, Harriet said sombrely: "They're a portent. The fascist infiltration."

"They're probably not even Guardists," Guy said.

"Then what are they?"

"I wouldn't know."

He was cutting down Ulysses's speeches in his copy of *Troilus and Cressida*, giving all his mind to the job, determined not to let outside things distract him.

Harriet had been comforted a little by Clarence's indignation when he found she was no longer in the cast. He left a rehearsal to telephone her, vehemently demanding: "*Harry*, what is this little bitch doing in your part? Have you walked out of the show?"

"No, I was put out."

"Why?"

"Guy said he couldn't work with me. He said I didn't take him seriously."

"Why should you? It's only a footling end-of-term show, anyway. If you're not in it, I don't want to be in it."

Harriet reacted sharply to this. It was important to her that Guy's project should succeed. "You must stay in," she insisted. "He will need everyone he can get. And it will probably be quite good."

Clarence, who had been given the sizeable part of Ajax, did not argue about this, but grumbled: "It's awful having Sophie around. She's beginning to queen it insufferably." He said he had no intention of attending all the rehearsals. Between his work for Inchcape and his work with the Poles, he was much too busy.

The truth was, as Harriet knew, he did almost nothing at the Propaganda Bureau and very few Poles remained. The camps were almost empty. Of the officers who had entertained him on several wild occasions, scarcely one remained. They had all been smuggled over the frontier to join the fighting forces in France. Clarence, who had organised these escapes, had worked himself out of work. He needed distraction. He invited Harriet to have dinner with him next evening. There was in his giving and her acceptance of this invitation a certain revolt against Guy and the importance he gave to his production.

Next morning at breakfast, when Guy announced another day of rehearsals, Harriet asked: "Must you keep at it like a maniac?"

"It's the only way to get it done."

His method revealed to her what she least expected to find in him – a neurotic intensity.

She said: "I'm going out to dinner with Clarence tonight."

"Oh, good! And now I must get Yaki up."

"When can we hope to get rid of that incubus?" Harriet crossly asked.

"I expect he'll find a room when his remittance comes. Meanwhile, he must be fed and housed and accepted, like a child."

"A pretty cunning child."

"He's harmless, anyway. If the world was composed of Yakimovs, there'd be no wars."

"There'd be no anything."

It was the morning of the 9th of April. Guy and Yakimov had just left when the telephone rang. Lifting the receiver, Harriet heard Bella crying to her: "Have you heard the news?"

"No."

"Germany has invaded Norway, Sweden and Denmark. I've just heard it on the wireless." Bella spoke excitedly, expecting excited response. When Harriet did not give it, she said: "Can't you *see*! It means they aren't coming here."

"It doesn't mean they won't come."

Harriet, though disturbed, imagining any move to be a danger signal, understood Bella's relief. The blow had fallen elsewhere. For Rumania there was, if not a reprieve, a stay of execution. Standing by the balcony door, Harriet could see the square and roofs pearl-white beneath the vast white misted sky. From different points miniature dark figures were converging on the newsboys like ants on specks of food. She could hear the mouse-squeaks of the boys calling a special edition. Wanting to share the situation with someone, she said to Bella: "Let's meet at Mavrodaphne's."

"Oh, I can't," said Bella. "Guy has called a rehearsal. I must go. Rehearsals are such fun."

Harriet went out and bought a paper. The invasion was announced in the stop press with a statement made by the Minister of Information to the effect that the news need rouse no apprehension in Rumanian hearts. Carol, the Great and Good, Father of Culture, Father of his People, had nearly completed the mighty Carol Line and soon Rumania would be surrounded by a wall of fire that would repel any invader.

People stood in groups about the paper-sellers talking loudly. Harriet could hear the agitated staccato of their voices as they called to one another: "*Alors, ça a enfin commencé, la guerre?*" "*Oui, ça commence.*" Her own fears renewed, she crossed the square and started to walk up the Chaussée. As she went, the sun that had been inching its way through the mist, broke out, suddenly resplendent, unrolling light like golden silk at her feet. All in a moment, the sky became cloudless and blue with the blue of summer. Piccolos were running out with poles to pull the blinds down over Dragomir's windows. All over the façades of buildings striped awnings were being lowered – red and yellow, blue and white, fringed, tasselled and corded – while windows and doors were opening and people were coming out on to balconies. The balcony plants could be seen now to be swelling and spreading and growing green. Already there were little bowers of tender shoots that would, by late summer, become bedraggled tangles of coarse creepers. The cement walls, blotched and grey when the sky was grey, now gleamed like marble.

Up the Chaussée, where the women, unprepared for this sudden brilliance, were holding up handbags to shield their eyes, people were distracted from the war news. The cafés were putting chairs out in gardens and on pavements. Even as the chairs were placed in position customers were sitting down on them, beginning, without delay and with a new gaiety, the outdoor life of summer.

When Harriet reached the building that was supposed to be a museum of folk art, she saw some paintings were on show. She went inside. Rumanians did not express themselves well in paint. Indeed, there were no pictures in Bucharest worth looking at except the King's El Grecos, nine in number, bought for a song before El Greco returned to fashion, and these were not on show to the public. The exhibitors at the salon were mediocre, imitating every genre of modern painting, but they were numerous. She was able to spend a long time looking at them. When she came out, she walked back across the square into the Calea Victoriei and, passing through the parrot-land of the gypsy flower-sellers, reached the British Propaganda Bureau. No one was looking at the pictures of British cruisers that curled and yellowed in the sun, but there was a crowd round the German Bureau opposite. Curiosity propelled her across the road.

The window was filled with a map of Scandinavia. Arrows, three inches wide, cut from red cardboard, pointed the direction of the German attack. In the crowd no one spoke. People stood awed by the arrogant swagger of the display. Harriet, trying to look indifferent to it, made for the University building. It was now nearly luncheon time, so she might, with reason, call for Guy.

The main door of the University building lay open but there was no porter inside. Term did not begin until the end of April. The vaulted, empty passages looked bleak and smelt of beeswax and linoleum. Harriet was guided by the distant sound of Guy's voice saying:

" 'Indeed, a tapster's arithmetic may soon bring his particulars therein to a total.' " Cressida, he went on to explain, was making fun of Troilus. A tapster's arithmetic being notoriously limited, the particulars could not be very great. "Now again," he said, beginning the speech in a bantering manner.

The words were taken up and repeated in the same manner – this time by a female voice. Sophie's voice. Harriet heard it with a pang of jealousy so acute she stopped in her tracks. She was about to retreat – but what point in retreating? Sooner or later, she had to face Sophie in this part.

She went on slowly. The door stood open at the end of the corridor. She came to it silently, expecting a crowd of players among whom she could enter unnoticed, but only Sophie, Yakimov and Guy remained.

The common-room, dark-panelled and without windows, was large and gloomy. It was lit by a central dome. The three stood under the dome. Guy had one foot on a chair and his script on his knee, the other two were performing before him. No one noticed Harriet as she took a seat by the wall.

As Sophie and Yakimov went through speech after speech, with Guy interrupting and enforcing constant repetitions, she began to realise she could not have tolerated for long the tedium of rehearsals. She might not have required to be interrupted so often or to receive so many explanations of the words she spoke – but these interruptions and explanations were no hardship to Guy. He delighted in them. In fact he probably preferred a Cressida who would be entirely of his own making.

As for the other two . . . Yakimov and Sophie? She realised that what would be tedium to her was to them self-aggrandisement.

Sophie, of course, had never lacked vanity. She had the usual Rumanian face, dark-eyed, pasty and too full in the cheeks, but her manner of seating and holding herself demanded for her the deference due to a beauty. Now that her self-importance seemed justified, there was a flaunting of this demand. All the attention must be for her. When Guy gave it to Yakimov, she wanted it back again, interrupting the rehearsal every few minutes to ask: "*Chéri*, don't you think here I might do this?" or "Here, while he is saying this, I make like so? You agree? You agree?" posturing her little backside, imbuing all her moves and *moues* with a quality of sensuous and lingering caress. She seemed to be in a state of inspired, almost ecstatic, excitement about it all. She wriggled with sex.

Although she could not refrain from flirting even with Yakimov, for Guy she kept a special look, inciting and conspiratorial, which did not, Harriet noted, appear to disconcert him. He accorded Sophie now exactly the same kindly but unemotional sympathy he had accorded her when she imagined herself neglected, injured and suicidal.

While Sophie attacked direction, Yakimov responded to it. Though he appeared to have taken on size and substance, he did exactly what Guy required him to do. Harriet could imagine Guy's satisfaction in producing from Yakimov the version of the performance he would have chosen to give himself. She could feel between the two men a warmth of mutual approval. Yakimov received the acclaim which Sophie sought, with the result that there was in her demanding interruptions a querulousness that roused Harriet's sympathy. She, too, was beginning to feel excluded.

Suddenly Guy picked up his script and said: "We'll stop now."

When they became aware of her, Harriet said: "You've heard they've invaded Norway and Denmark?"

Oh yes, everyone had heard that by now. Guy had already discounted the news. "It was to be expected," he said. "Once we started mining Norwegian waters, Germany had no choice but to invade."

"Perhaps we mined them because Germany was planning to invade."

"Perhaps!" Guy did not want to discuss the subject further.

Harriet marvelled at his ability to turn his back on the news. For herself, she always faced anxieties, believing that, unfaced, they would leap upon her and devour her. Perhaps Guy would not face what he was not in a position actively to combat. She should be glad, she supposed, that he had this production as a bolt-hole.

What annoyed her was that Yakimov and Sophie, to play up to him, were echoing his unconcern. They were set apart from the implications of the invasion: they were people with more important matters in mind. Harriet felt particularly irritated with Sophie, who was, she knew, as liable to panic as any other Rumanian.

Guy said: "We'll go and have a drink." As they left the dark University hall and came out to the dazzle of day, he exclaimed: "Isn't it wonderful!"

Sophie laughed shortly: "How ridiculous the English are about the sun! In England they hold up their faces, so . . ." she goggled absurdly up at the sky, "and say..." she cooed absurdly: " 'Oh, the sun, the sun!' Here, I can tell you, we get sick of the sight of it."

Harriet asked her how she was enjoying her part in the play. Her only answer was a shrug and a sulky down-droop of her full lips. Was it possible that, despite her advantage. she resented Harriet's appearance on the scene? Had she imagined that, having displaced Harriet in the part, she might displace her altogether? "Really!" thought Harriet, "the girl is ridiculous!"

As Guy made to cross the road, Sophie paused and asked where they were going. He answered: "To the Doi Trandafiri." Fretfully, she said: "I don't want to go there. It's always so crowded."

"Oh well," said Guy. "We'll see you later."

As Sophie went off, looking angry, Harriet said: "If you don't make a fuss of your poor leading lady, you'll be losing her."

"I don't think so." Guy spoke easily. "She's enjoying herself too much."

In the café, he said: "I want to hear Yakimov in a few scenes."
They read three scenes and between each Guy bought Yakimov a
ţuică.

At the end, Yakimov asked: "How was I?" and there was in
the question a tremulous anxiety.

"Splendid," said Guy, his approval so whole-hearted that Yakimov's cheeks grew pink.

Gratified, Yakimov breathed: "Dear boy!" and was for a
moment bemused like a child becoming aware of its own qualities.

Harriet noticed a change in him, not great, but radical. Guy
had roused in him a will to excel.

"You know," said Guy, "you have the makings of a great
actor."

"Have I?" Yakimov's question was modest, but not disclaiming. He fixed on Guy eyes glowing with admiring gratitude.

"But you must learn your lines."

"Oh, I will, dear boy. Don't fear, *I will.*"

As Harriet watched, it seemed to her this nebula of a man, so
long inert, was starting slowly to evolve.

23

A WEEK AFTER THE GERMAN INVASION of Denmark and Norway, Inchcape displayed in the British Propaganda Bureau window a map of the Scandinavian countries with the loss of the German destroyers at Narvik restrainedly marked in blue. In time came the landings of British troops at Namsos and Andalsnes.

In the window opposite, the red arrows of Germany thrust the Norwegians back and back. One day the Allies announced an advance, another the Germans announced an Allied retreat. Merely a strategic retreat, said the British News Service. The Germans, advancing up the Gudbranstal, claimed they had joined up with their Trondheim forces. The British admitted a short withdrawal.

Every morning the passers-by, lured by these first remote moves in the war, crossed the road to compare window with window; but it was the blatant menace of the giant red arrows that held the crowd. The pro-British faction of the press predicted a British counter-attack that would finish the Germans once and for all. But even while this prediction was being made, the Germans reached Andalsnes. Four thousand Norwegians had surrendered; the politicians fled; the Allies took to the sea. It was suddenly a German victory.

The map with the red arrows disappeared. The window remained empty. No one was much impressed. The move had not, after all, been the beginning of events. It seemed a step into a cul-de-sac. The audience waited for more spectacular entertainment.

At the beginning of May, Harriet had to face her task of dressing the players. Inchcape had written to the London office and obtained a small grant towards the production. Most of this money was required for the hire of the theatre and theatre staff. What remained could be expended on the costumes. Harriet had been envisaging some such gorgeous display as she had seen in London productions of Shakespeare. The money she had in hand would barely cover the cast in sack-cloth.

She found that costumes could be hired from the theatre and went with Bella to see those made for a production of *Antony and Cleopatra* some ten years before. They had been used on every possible occasion since and were threadbare and elaborately ugly.

"Filthy, too," said Bella, who had been examining them keenly. She twitched her fingers in distaste. "Can you see Helen in that pea-green plush?"

Feeling discouraged, like a child set a task beyond its years, Harriet, who had not wanted the task in the first place, tried to hand it back to Guy. Guy, adept at delegating work, simply laughed at her. "Don't make difficulties, darling. It's all quite simple. Don't have armour – actors hate it, anyway. Just suggest it. Hire a few helmets, swords and so on from the theatre. Hire the cloaks, too. Put the Greeks into skirts and corselets – quite easy to make with canvas. The Trojans, being Asiatics, could wear tights – they're the cheapest things possible."

"But the Rumanians would be bewildered."

"They'd love it. A new idea – that's all they want."

Having, with a few words, reduced the task to an absurdity, Guy swept off, leaving her with the sense that she had made a great deal of fuss about nothing.

Clarence offered to drive her wherever she wanted to go. One evening in early May they drove to a suburb where there was a factory that made theatrical tights. Harriet, when called for, found Clarence's associate Steffaneski in the car. Clarence was combining the trip to the factory with some Polish business. The two passengers greeted one another rather blankly. Neither found the other easy company and each had regarded this occasion as his own. Clarence, who had nothing to say, seemed equally displeased with both of them. It was as though the presence of each had caused a rift between himself and the other. It occurred to Harriet that Clarence was the friend of the solitary personality, and he wanted to be the only friend. He was the friend of Harriet and the friend of Steffaneski – but not of both together. Siding, as he did, with the misfits, he was troubled now by not knowing with which to side. His face was glum.

As they drove out through the long grey low-built streets that stretched towards the country, Harriet, who thought the Count the least occupied of men, broke the silence by suggesting he might take part in the play.

He turned from her in morose scorn. "I have not," he said, "time for such things. I do not make play while the war is fought."

"But you can't fight here."

Steffaneski, suspecting he was being teased, gave an exasperated twitch of the lips.

In this area of Bucharest the buildings were of all wood. These were not the shacks of the very poor, but roomy, well-built shops and houses like those in a Middle West shanty town. The wide, unmade road, under water in spring, was still a quagmire, with stretches of standing water reddened by the evening sun.

The car rocked and squelched, then came to a standstill. Clarence pressed the accelerator. The wheels turned in the mud but did not move forward.

"We're here for the night," said Clarence.

"Perhaps Count Steffaneski would get out and push," said Harriet.

The Count stared, unhearing, from the window. Clarence, un-amused by Harriet's humour, was becoming acutely irritable, when, unexpectedly, the wheels caught and the car lunged forward.

They found the address Harriet had been given. She had hoped for a theatrical workroom, a sort of studio perhaps, with some-thing of the self-contained creative life she most missed in Bucha-rest. What she found was a large wooden hut like a garage. Inside there was a single room where a dozen peasants, some still at the level of peasant dress, were working on knitting machines. There was not even a chair to offer the customer. The light was failing. Some oil-lamps hung from the rafters and the air was heavy from a smoking wick.

A gaunt little man, wearing peasant trousers but a jacket that was part of an old morning suit, came forward, unsmiling, and raised his brows. As he stood beside Harriet, silent and expres-sionless, she could not tell whether or not she were conveying her needs to him. She had written down the sets of measurements in metres and, beside each, the colour required. When she finished speaking, he nodded. She could not believe he had grasped it all so quickly. When she tried to explain further, he bent, touched his ankle and drew his hand up to his waist.

"*Da, da, precis,*" she agreed.

He nodded again and waited for her to go.

She went, doubtfully.

"All right?" Clarence asked as he started the car again.

"I don't know." She could not believe that the man had grasped so rapidly what had been conveyed in very poor Rumanian.

On the way back, Clarence turned into an alleyway, a deep rift of mud, and stopped at a warehouse, another wooden hut, its doors held with a padlock. It housed the goods sent out from England for the relief of the Poles. Harriet, when she followed the men in, gazed about in wonder at the bales of linen, the sheets, blankets and pillows, the shirts and underwear, the crates of knitted garments.

"What are you going to do with it all?" she asked.

Clarence said: "That is what we have come here to decide."

Harriet, wandering round and examining things, waited for a discussion to take place, but neither of the men said anything.

Harriet fingered a pile of shirts and suggested they could let Guy have some of them. "He only owns three," she said.

Clarence thrust out his lower lip, looking wary and important. After some reflection, he said: "I might *lend* him a few."

"Yes, do." Harriet began picking out the largest shirts.

"Just a minute." Clarence strode over to her with an air of nervous decision, obviously afraid she would get the better of him, and said: "I will lend him two."

She gave a laugh of derisive annoyance. "Really, Clarence, are you sure you can spare them?" Clarence looked the more obstinate.

Steffaneski, consciously aloof from their quarrel, said: "Is it not to be decided what we do with this stuff?"

"It might be sold to the Rumanian army," said Clarence.

The suggestion, tentative as it was, was accepted without hesitation: "Agreed. Now I wait in the car." Steffaneski strode out, leaving Harriet and Clarence to face one another, each in a state of sparking annoyance.

"What about underwear?" Harriet began turning over a pile of vests.

Clarence pushed her away: "I have to account for these things."

"Guy has almost no underwear."

The more Harriet persisted, the more obstinate Clarence became; the more she felt his obstinacy, the more she persisted. At last, Clarence said: "I'll lend him two vests and two pairs of pants."

She accepted this offer defiantly, knowing he expected her to refuse.

When they left the warehouse, Clarence locked the doors ostentatiously. Harriet, smiling with anger, carried her prizes to the car, where Steffaneski, one shoulder hunched against a window, sat biting the side of his left thumb. He stared into the distance.

Returning to the city's centre, no one had anything to say. When they reached the cross-roads and the statue of the boyar Cantacuzino, it was late twilight. The office workers were fighting their way on to the trams. In the Calea Victoriei the car was held up by the crowd round the window of the German Propaganda Bureau.

Harriet said: "There's a new map in the window." Without speaking, Clarence stopped the car and got out. Rising tall and lean above the heads of the Rumanians, he stood for some moments and gazed into the window, then turned in a business-like way and opened the car door. "Well, it's begun," he said.

"What do you mean?" Harriet asked.

"Germany has invaded the Lowlands. They've overrun Luxembourg. They're already inside Holland and Belgium. They claim they're advancing rapidly."

As he got into the car, neither Harriet nor Steffaneski spoke. Chilled with nervous excitement, she reflected that while they had been wrangling about shirts and underwear this news had been waiting like a tiger to pounce on them.

"This comes of the folly of Belgium," said Steffaneski. "They would not permit a Maginot Line to the sea. Now" – he struck his finger across his throat – "Belgium is *kaput*." He sounded more angry than anything else.

"Not yet," said Harriet.

"Wait. You know nothing. But I – I have seen the Germans advance."

"Yes, but not against British troops."

"Wait," said Steffaneski again, his face impassively grim.

Clarence hooted his way round the crowd. The windows of Inchcape's office were dark. Clarence smiled at Harriet, reconciled to her in the exhilaration that comes when outside events take over one's life. She smiled back.

"This time," he said, "it'll be a fight to a finish. Let's go and have a drink."

24

FOR YAKIMOV THESE WERE BLISSFUL DAYS. Each morning his breakfast was brought into his room. He had persuaded Guy that he could 'study' best in bed and Guy had persuaded Harriet to let him be served there. He was awakened too early, of course. The tray was slapped down angrily by Despina, who then threw up his blind, startling him out of sleep, and slammed his door as she departed. Her attitude was a pity. He could have put her to good use, cleaning and pressing his clothes: but she was not to be won. Faithfully she reflected Harriet's disapproval of him.

Harriet herself behaved as though unaware of his presence in the flat. He had always been nervous of her, but now, knowing that while Guy needed him, Guy would protect him, he no longer attempted to placate her. He merely avoided her.

Those mornings when Guy did not force him up for an early rehearsal, he would lie on after breakfast, dozing, a copy of *Troilus and Cressida* open on the counterpane. His room had two doors, one opening on to the hall, one on to the living-room. Through the delicious apathy of half-sleep, he could hear Despina complete her work in the room, and hear the front door close as Harriet left the flat. When both were out of the way, he would rouse himself and bath and dress in comfortable solitude.

Yakimov did not care to appear alone for meals in the flat. Understanding this, Guy, if too occupied with a rehearsal to break it, would send him out for sandwiches. When they returned for meals together, Yakimov would sit at the table silent in Guy's shadow. The plainness of the Pringle food was regrettable. He saw things in the shops for which he longed – a very thick, green variety of asparagus, for instance, about which he attempted a hint one day: "Am told it's excellent, dear girl; and cheap at the moment. This is the season for it," but it did not appear. As a result of this limited diet, he was constantly hungry, not for food, but for rich food. Whenever he could borrow the money he went to a restaurant to eat alone. Dobson had refused to lend him any more, but he was able to persuade an occasional 'thou' out of Fitzsimon, the good-looking third secretary who was to play Troilus, and Foxy Leverett, who was cast as Hector.

Guy had forbidden Yakimov to borrow from students, but when pestered by one of them to explain his brilliance as an actor he would take the chance to whisper rapidly: "Wonder, dear boy, could you spare a *leu* or two?" and seize what was offered and make off with the celerity that Bacon preferred to secrecy.

He could also make a little pocket-money when he dined out with the Pringles. Guy, who over-tipped in a manner Yakimov thought rather ill-bred, always left a heap of small coins on the table for the piccolo. Yakimov, insisting that Guy precede him from the table, would pocket all he could gather up as he passed.

Guy was absurdly careless with money. One noonday, when they were rehearsing alone, Yakimov saw him pull out with his handkerchief two thousand-*lei* notes. Retrieving, and borrowing, these unseen, Yakimov excused himself and went to Çina's, where he sat on the terrace eating the asparagus of which he had been deprived and heard the orchestra play in the elegant *chinois* stand over which the Canary creeper was breaking into flower.

What he experienced in these days was what he had experienced with Dollie, the consolations of security. When he did not know where his next meal was coming from, he was usually too driven by hunger to feel pity for himself. Now, as he lay in bed, contemplating his profound need for care and protection, a tear would often trickle down his cheek; a luxurious, an enjoyable tear. He had found again in Guy the figure of the provider. More than that, Guy gave him, as Dollie had failed to give, the comfortable sense that he was earning his keep. And he was not only secure in the flat, he was secure in the country. The Legation was on his side. He was doing a job for British prestige. Should his *permis de séjour* be cancelled, Foxy or Fitzsimon would see that it was renewed. Above all, he had become again what he had been in the old days – a personality.

He was modest in acceptance of praise. When Foxy Leverett said: "You're magnificent, dear fellow. How do you do it?", when the large-bosomed girl students crowded round him squealing: "You are *so* good, Prince Yakimov; tell us how you are so good," he shook his head, smiling, and said: "I really do not know," that being no less than the truth.

Since the term began, the junior students had been left to Guy's staff of English teachers; the seniors had been absorbed into the play. Only a few had speaking parts; the others, cast as soldiers and attendants, were called to all rehearsals so that they might improve their diction and their knowledge of the play. Guy frequently lectured them, elucidating its obscure passages. They formed an ever-present background to the production – and Yakimov was their hero.

His success as Pandarus surprised him less than it surprised anyone else. He had always nursed the belief that if he ever tried to exert himself the result would be remarkable. At school, where he had been the droll of the class, one of the masters had said: "Yakimov is such a fool, he must be a genius." And Dollie had often said: "There's more to Yaki than you think."

He had always supposed that success called for effort, and effort was something he particularly disliked. It was the ease of his triumph that surprised him. Guy had given him no more than a push and he had stumbled forward into achievement. He was charmed by his success, and assured. He began to believe not only in the present, but the future. Something, he was sure, would come of his performance as Pandarus. He would live off it for the rest of his life.

Had he been pressed to define what might come of it, he would have looked back no further than to the days when he had been a war correspondent. He had a hankering after the privileges and prominence of that position, and, more than anything, for an expense account that would permit him once more to revel in unlimited food and drink. Perhaps someone would invite him to become a war correspondent again!

Meanwhile, he stood unobtrusively at Guy's elbow, accepting drinks from his admirers with murmurs of gratitude. Guy was the centre of the group. Guy did the talking. Yakimov told himself: 'The dear boy likes the limelight' – this observation being no more critical than that which he had once made about Dollie: 'The dear girl likes her own way.' He did no more than speak a warning to himself: he wanted to keep his place. For this reason, quite seriously and admiringly he spoke of Guy these days as 'the impresario', flattering him with the exotic importance of the appellation.

The group usually drank in the Doi Trandafiri. For some

reason, Guy was not willing to go to the English Bar, which Yakimov much preferred. The only advantage he could see in the Doi
Trandafiri was that the drinks were cheaper – and that was no
advantage when one was not paying for them.

One day before the German 'take-over', having acquired a little
money, he could not resist dropping into the English Bar to show
himself hastily, a man much in demand elsewhere, to Hadjimoscos, Horvath and Cici Palu. The three noted his appearance with
cold and narrow nods. He had just enough to buy a round of
ţuică, thus coaxing out of them a meagre show of affability.
Hadjimoscos asked: "And where, dear Prince, have you been,
away from us all this time?"

"I'm taking part in a play," he replied with satisfaction.

"*A play!*" Hadjimoscos's smile grew wide with malice. "Have
you then found employment in the theatre?"

"Certainly not," said Yakimov, shocked. "It is an amateur
show. Several important members of the British Legation are
taking part."

The others looked at one another. They pretended to hide their
scorn under an air of bafflement. How very bizarre the English
were! As a result, Yakimov felt it necessary to imply that the play
was a cover for something more important – something to do
with the secret service. Hadjimoscos raised his eyebrows. Horvath and Palu looked blank. Yakimov opened his mouth, but was
saved from further folly by the entrance of Galpin, taut and
jumpy with news. There was a general movement of enquiry. All
present, except Yakimov, became alert with expectancy. Yakimov
was bewildered to see Hadjimoscos, Horvath and Palu united
with the rest.

"They're across the Meuse," Galpin announced. "The Dutch
Army has just capitulated."

Yakimov did not know who was across the Meuse, but having
heard rumours of their rapid advance through Holland, he supposed 'they' must be the Germans. He said: "Why so alarmed,
dear boy? They're not coming our way."

No one took any notice of this remark. Yakimov felt completely
outside the society of the bar, that, occupied with the movements
of a far-off army, had no interest in Yakimov or his performance
in a play. Discomforted, he left, with no desire to return, under-

standing now why Guy preferred to make his own world at the Doi Trandafiri and attend only to his production.

Rehearsals were becoming intensive. Guy had announced that the theatre was booked for the night of June 14th. That gave the players a month in which to perfect themselves. They had no time to brood on present anxieties. They lived now to pursue a war of the past. The common-room at rehearsal time was always crowded with students. Some came who had no part in the play; others were not even in the English faculty. The production had become a craze among them. Yakimov was talked about throughout the University. His arrival in the common-room would give rise to a fury of whispering. Some of the students would call out as at the entry of a hero. He would smile around, radiating good-will over his admirers, seeing no one very clearly.

The only others accorded anything like this reception by the students were Guy, Sophie and Fitzsimon. Guy was not only producer but a popular figure in his own right. Sophie was one of them. Fitzsimon was acclaimed for his extraordinary good looks and his easy, casual manner admired by the girls, whom he ogled with exaggerated eye movements whenever Sophie let his attention wander. When he announced that 'on the night' he intended to gild his hair, the girls gave little screams of shocked excitement. He took his part more seriously than anyone had hoped.

Most members of this enclosed fellowship had forgotten the war altogether, but even here reality sometimes intruded. One or other of the Legation members would throw in the bad news – there was no good news these days – with the humour of one whose duty it is to keep calm: "Just heard the bastards have taken Boulogne" or "Those blighters have got Calais now."

"*Calais!*"

Even to Yakimov this was the fall of a neighbour. Yet what could be done about it? Nothing. It was a relief for them all to turn their attention to the fall of Troy.

Before the end of May, Yakimov had memorised all his lines. Guy let him make his speeches without interruption. After the first complete run-through, Guy looked round at the thirty-seven men and women of the cast, and as they looked anxiously back at him, said: "It's shaping. Cressida is good. Helen, Agamemnon, Troilus, Ulysses, Thersites – good. Pandarus – very good. The rest of you will have to work."

One day Harriet broke in on them with the smell of outdoor anxiety still about her, startling them back to the present.

Guy, running his fingers through his hair, had been lecturing his audience on the character of Achilles, who, offered the alternative of a long life spent in peaceful obscurity and a short life of glory, chose the latter. In Homer, Guy was saying, Achilles was the ideal of the military hero: but Shakespeare, whose sympathies had been with the Trojans, had depicted him as a fascist whose feats were performed by fascist thugs. Young Dimancescu, standing hand on hip, idly playing with a foil, was smiling a wan, warped smile, satisfied by this interpretation of his part. He turned this smile, lifting his brows a little in surprise, as Harriet walked in to the middle of the room, Clarence behind her.

Guy paused, brought to a stop by something in her manner. He asked: "What is the matter?"

She said: "The British troops have left Europe. They've got away."

What she had brought was news of the Dunkirk evacuation.

"They say it was wonderful," she said. "Wonderful." Her voice broke.

Yakimov looked in a puzzled way at Guy. "What is it, dear boy?" he asked. "A victory?"

"A sort of victory," said Clarence. "We've saved our army."

But the students, crowding up against Harriet and the circle round her, glanced at one another and started to whisper among themselves. Evidently to them it was no sort of victory. The Allied armies, that existed, among other things, for the protection of Rumania, had disintegrated. The French were being routed; the English had fled to their own island: the rest had capitulated. Who was to protect Rumania now?

Harriet, in the centre of the floor, did not move until Guy put his hand to her elbow and gave her a slight push, gently impatient. "We must get on," he said.

She stood for a moment, frowning at him, seeming unable to keep him in focus, then she said: "I suppose you'll come home some time."

As she went, Clarence started to follow her, but Guy called to him: "Clarence, I want you." Clarence paused, about to excuse himself, then was caught under Guy's influence. He said: "Very well," and Harriet returned alone to the uneasy streets.

25

INCHCAPE'S SERVANT, Pauli, made a model in a sand-box of the British Expeditionary Force queueing for embarkation on the Dunkirk beaches. The little ships stood in a sea of blue wax. Inchcape put it in the window of the Propaganda Bureau. Though it was skilfully made, it was a sad-looking model. The few who bothered to give it a glance must have thought the British now had nothing to offer but a desperate courage.

In Bucharest the most startling effect of events was the change in the news films. French films ceased to arrive. Perhaps there was no one left with the heart to make them. English-speaking films were blocked by the chaos of Europe. What did come, with triumphant regularity, were the U.P.A. news films.

People sat up at them, aghast, overwhelmed by the fervour of the young men on the screen. There was nothing here of the flat realism of the English news, nothing of the bored inactivity which people had come to expect. Every camera trick was used to enhance the drama of the German machines reaping the cities as they passed. Their destructive lust was like a glimpse of the dark ages. The fires of Rotterdam shot up livid against the midnight sky. They roared from the screen. The camera backed, barely evading a shower of masonry as tall façades, every window aflame, crashed towards the audience. Bricks showered through the air. Cathedral spires, towers that had withstood a dozen other wars, great buildings that had been a wonder for centuries, all toppled into dust.

Clarence, sitting beside Harriet, said in his slow, rich voice: "I bet these films are faked."

People shifted nervously in their seats. Those nearest glanced askance at him, fearful of his temerity.

The cameras moved between the poplars of a Flemish road. On either side stood lorries, disabled or abandoned, their doors ripped open and their contents – bread, wine, clothing, medical supplies, munitions – pulled out and left contemptuously in disarray. In the main streets of towns from which the inhabitants had fled, the invaders sprawled asleep in the sunshine. These were the golden days, the spring of the year. Outside one town, among the young corn, tanks lay about, disabled. Each had its name chalked upon it: *Mimi, Fanchette, Zephyr.* One that stood lop-sided, its guns rakishly tilted, was called *Inexorable.*

On the day that news came of the bombing of Paris, a last French film reached Bucharest, like a last cry out of France. It showed refugees trudging a long, straight road; feet, the wheels of perambulators, faces furtively glancing back; children by the road-side drinking in turn from a mug; the wing of a swooping plane, a spatter of bullets, a child spread-eagled on the road. The French film cried: "Pity us"; the German film that followed derided pity.

Out of the smoke of some lost city appeared the German tanks. They followed each other in an endless stream into the sunlight, driving down from Ypres and Ostend. A signboard said: *Lille –* 5 *kilomètres.* There seemed to be no resistance. The Maginot Line was being skirted. The break-through had been so simple, it was like a joke.

And the fair-haired young men standing up in their tanks came unscathed and laughing from the ruins. They held their faces up to the sun. They sang: "What does it matter if we destroy the world? When it is ours, we'll build it up again."

The tanks, made monstrous by the camera's tilt, passed in thousands – or, so it seemed. The audience – an audience that still thought in terms of cavalry – sat watching, motionless, in silence. This might of armour was a new thing; a fearful and merciless thing. The golden boys changed their song. Now, as the vast procession passed, they sang:

> "*Wir wollen keine Christen sein,*
> *Weil Christus war ein Judenschwein.*
> *Und seine Mutter, welch ein Hohn,*
> *Die heisst Marie, gebor'ne Kohn.*"

Someone gasped. There was no other noise.

Harriet, alone this time, at a matinée, surrounded by women, felt they were stunned. Yet, as she left in the crowd, she heard in its appalled whispering a twitter of excitement. One woman said: "Such beautiful young men!" and another replied: "They were like the gods of war!"

It was strange to emerge into the streets and see the buildings standing firm. Harriet now had somewhere to go. She went straight to the Athénée Palace garden, that had become a meeting-place for the English since they were dispossessed of the English Bar.

The bar itself had been occupied by the Germans one morning at the end of May. The move was obviously deliberate. It was a gesture, jubilantly planned and carried out by a crowd of journalists, businessmen and members of the huge Embassy retinue. The English – only three were present at the time – let themselves be elbowed out without a struggle. The Germans had the advantage of their aggressive bad manners, the English the disadvantage of their dislike of scenes.

Galpin was the first of the three to pick up his glass and go. Before he went, he spoke his mind. "Just at the moment," he said, "I can't stomach sight, sound or stench of a Nazi." He walked out and his compatriots followed him.

There were more Germans in the vestibule. Germans were crowding through the public rooms into the dining-room. Some sort of celebratory luncheon was about to take place. Galpin, trying to escape them, marched on, drink in hand, until he found the garden – a refuge for the routed.

The next day the Germans were back again in the bar. Apparently they had come to stay. Galpin returned to the garden: anyone who wanted him was told they could find him there. Most of the people who came in search of news had not known before that the hotel garden existed.

Galpin now spent most of his day there. It was there that his agents brought him news of Allied defeats and an occasional item of Rumanian news, such as the enforced resignation of Gafencu, the pro-British Foreign Minister, whose mother had been an Englishwoman. Other people came and went. As the situation, growing worse, became their chief preoccupation, they began to sit down and wait for news; each day they stayed longer and longer. They were drawn together by the one thing they held in common – their nationality. Because of it, they shared suspense. The waiter, understanding their situation, did not trouble them much.

Clarence, Inchcape, Dubedat and David looked in between work and rehearsals, but not, of course, Guy and Yakimov. It was thought to be a sign of those strange times that the English, the admired and privileged, the dominating influence in a cosmopolitan community, should be meeting in so unlikely a place.

The summer was established now. The city had come out of doors anticipating three months or more of unbroken fine weather. The heat would eventually force it in again, but for the moment the open air cafés were crowded all day.

Galpin had taken over as his own a large, rough, white-painted table that stood by the fountain in the centre of the garden. When Harriet arrived from her cinema matinée, she found installed there with Galpin and Screwby the three old ladies who always formed the afternoon nucleus of the group. These were retired governesses who lived by giving English lessons. They took classes for Guy in the morning and for the rest of the day had nothing to do but face disaster. They chose to face it in company. They greeted Harriet like an old friend.

As she sat down, she asked, as everyone always asked on arrival: "Any news?"

Galpin said: "There's a rumour that Churchill has made a statement. It may be relayed later."

The three old ladies had ordered tea. Harriet took some with them. She was sitting, as she usually sat, nearest to the stone boy who poured his ewer of water into a stone basin. At first she had been irritated by this monotonous tinkle, then, recognising in it a symbol of their own anxiety, she adopted it into her own mind – a vehicle of release. It had become a part of these hot, lime-scented improbable summer days in which they learnt of one defeat after another. She knew she would never forget it.

"Very nice tea," said Miss Turner, the eldest lady, who usually spoke only to mention the household of a wealthy Rumanian whose children she had educated. She mentioned it now: "We used to have tea like this in the old days. The Prince was most generous in every way. He never stinted the nursery – and that's rare, I can tell you. When I retired he gave me a pension – not a very big pension, it's true; I could not expect it. But adequate. He was a most thoughtful, perceptive man for a Rumanian. He used to say to me: 'Miss Turner, I can see that you were born a lady.' "
She turned her pale, insignificant, little face towards her neighbour Miss Truslove, and nodded in satisfaction at the Prince's perception. She then gave a pitying glance at the third woman, to whom she always referred, behind her back, as 'poor Mrs. Ramsden',

for she had long made it clear to everyone that the fact she had been 'born a lady' placed her in a category of human being higher than that occupied by Mrs. Ramsden, who so obviously had not.

Mrs. Ramsden whispered to Harriet: "The pension's only good here, of course. She won't have a penny if we have to skedaddle."

Having listened for a week to the conversation of these women, Harriet knew that what they dreaded most was the disintegration of their adopted world. Everything they had was here. Such relatives as remained to them in England had forgotten them. If they were driven out of Rumania, they would find themselves without friends, homes, status or money.

"I haven't got a pension," said Mrs. Ramsden, "but I've got me savings. All invested here. I'll stay here. Whatever happens, I'll take me chance." A stout woman, noted for her enormous feathered hats, she was the most lively of the three. She had come to Bucharest when widowed, after the First World War. She had never gone home again. She frequently told the table: "I'm sixty-nine. You'd never believe it, but I am."

Now she said: "When Woolley packed us all off last September, I was that home-sick, I cried my eyes out every night. Istanbul is a dirty hole. I'd never trust meself there again. Might end up in one of them hair-eems." She brought her hand down heavily on the knee of Miss Truslove and suddenly shouted: "Whoops!"

Miss Truslove was looking disturbed. In her mournful little voice, she said: "I wouldn't care to stay on here, not with a lot of Germans about."

"Oh," said Mrs. Ramsden, "you never know your luck."

Galpin had at first seemed resentful of Mrs. Ramsden and her vitality. When she first settled herself at the table, her hat shifting and shaking as though barely anchored on her head, her blouse of shot-silk creaking as though about to split, he asked discouragingly: "No private pupils this afternoon, Mrs. Ramsden?" She answered briskly: "Not one. English is out these days. Everyone's learning German."

Now he turned on her with scorn: "You don't imagine you can stay here under a German occupation, do you? Any English national fool enough to try it would find himself in Belsen double quick."

At this Miss Truslove started sniffing, but as she searched for her handkerchief, she was distracted, as was Galpin, by the appearance of the Polish girl, Wanda.

Wanda had broken with Galpin. She had lately been seen driving with Foxy Leverett in his de Dion Bouton. People, surprised at this sight, sought to explain it away. Foxy, still a frequent companion of Princess Teodorescu, had, they said, been ordered to associate with Wanda and try to persuade her to moderate the irresponsible nonsense she was sending to her paper as news. Whatever their relationship, she had been much alone since Foxy had had to give his time to the play. Now here she was, turning up in the garden, like the rest of them.

"I'll be damned!" said Galpin, his eyes staring out at Wanda so that the whole of the chocolate-brown pupil could be seen, merging at top and bottom into the bloodshot yellow of the sclerotic.

She had made something of an entry in a tight black dress and shoes with very high heels. Her bare back and arms were already burnt brown. Ignoring Galpin, she greeted Screwby. "Any news?" she asked. There was none.

The women, recognising in her the same tense consciousness of peril that united them all, moved round to make room for her. She sat, leaning forward over the table, her brow in her hand, her lank hair falling about her, and stared at Screwby. She was a silent girl, whose habit it was to fix in this way any man who interested her. She asked: "What is going to happen? What are we going to do?" as though Screwby had but to open his lips and their dilemma would be solved.

Screwby made no attempt to play the rôle allotted him. He grinned his ignorance. Galpin began to talk rather excitedly, trying to give the impression that Wanda's entry had interrupted one of his stories. He started half-way through a story Harriet had heard from him several times – how, when a newspaper-man in Albania, he had attempted to break into the summer palace and interview the Queen, who had been newly delivered of a child.

"I wasn't going to be kept out by that ridiculous little toy army round the gates," he said.

"And did you see her?" Mrs. Ramsden played up to him.

"No. They threw me out three times. Me – who'd gone round Sussex collecting two pints of mother's milk a day for the Ickleford quads."

Wanda's silent presence made Galpin's talk more aggressive

and grotesque. As he talked, he watched her, his eyes standing from his head like aniseed balls. She ignored him for an hour, then rose and went. He stared after her glumly. "Poor thing," he said. "I feel sorry for her. Really I do! She hasn't a friend in the place."

They stayed on in the garden until the evening, when the scent of lime was strongest. Galpin had his portable wireless-set and repeatedly tried to get the promised report of Churchill's speech. The bats were darting about overhead. Mrs. Ramsden bent down, frightened for her hat.

"They have to be cut out if they get in," she said, adding: "But it's not just *them*: it's what they leave behind."

The trees grew dark beneath a sky sheened like a silver plate. Unlike most other café gardens, the hotel garden was not illuminated. The only light came from the hotel windows. The possibilities of the garden had never been exploited. Grass grew in tufts from the pebbled floor. No one bothered to brush from the tables the withering lime-flowers. Except for a few clandestine Rumanian couples who sat where they would be least observed, the English usually had the place to themselves.

At last the speech began. The Rumanian couples rose out of the shadows and moved silently forward to hear Churchill promise that England would never surrender. "We shall fight on the beaches," he said. "We shall fight in the fields."

Mrs. Ramsden bowed her face down into her hands. Her hat fell off and rolled unnoticed under the table.

Each day the crowd round the German Bureau window saw the broad arrows of the German advance stretch farther into France. One crossed the Somme and veered south towards Paris. The spectators said that surely, some time soon, there must be a stop. No one could contemplate the loss of Paris.

Harriet passed the window on her way to Bella's flat. She need not have gone up the Calea Victoriei or, going that way, she could have kept to the other pavement. Instead she brushed through the crowd, giving the arrows a glance which was meant to be indifferent, and went on with her head in the air.

Bella, as Harriet entered her drawing-room, cried: "What do you think?" giving Harriet, for a second, a pang of hope, but Bella's excitement was merely a state of mind produced by her success as Helen. All she had to say was: "They've still got that portrait of Chamberlain hanging up at the club. Him and his flower Safety. I called in the servants and ordered them to take it down at once. I made them put it face to the wall in the toilet."

The dressmaker was delivering the woman's costumes, and Bella had insisted that Harriet come to see the final fitting.

The dress, made from cheap white voile from which peasant women made their blouses, was of classical simplicity. Bella had been displeased to find all the female characters were to dress alike. She wanted to have her own costume made, contemplating something rather fine in slipper satin. Now, having to put on the voile dress, she thrust out her lower lip and walked to and fro before the glass of her gigantic wardrobe, giving petulant little tugs at the bodice and skirt.

The dressmaker, on her knees, sat back on her heels and watched. She had been the cheapest Harriet could find – a tiny creature, very thin, smelling of mouldy bread. Her face, which had one cheek full and one caught-in like a deformed apple, was dark yellow and heavily moustached. She twitched nervously when Bella paused near her and, raising her hands appealingly, began to talk. Ignoring her, Bella said: "Well, all I can say is, we're going to look like a lot of vestal virgins. Of course, I've got plenty of jewellery – but the others! I don't know, I'm sure."

"Must you wear jewellery?"

"My dear, I am Helen of Troy. I am a queen." She turned sideways, drew back her head and, with a stately and reflective air, observed the line of her fine bosom and her bare, round, white arm. The dress had an elegance and perfection scarcely to be found among the best English work: "I think we need a little colour – a square of chiffon. A big hankie, perhaps. A nice blue for me, or perhaps a gold. Other colours for the other girls."

Bella's face had softened, but Harriet felt depressed. She saw her designs now as stark and insipid. She felt she had spoilt the play. The dressmaker tried to speak again. Harriet asked:

"What does she want?"

"She wants to be paid."

Harriet began getting out the money. Bella said: "She's asking a thousand *lei*. Give her eight hundred."

"But a thousand is nothing. It's barely ten shillings."

"She doesn't know that. She'll take eight hundred. A Rumanian would give her half that."

Harriet had nothing smaller than a thousand-*lei* note. The woman accepted it with a show of bashful reluctance, but as soon as it was in her hand she bolted to the door. Bella, near the door, shut it before she could reach it, then sternly demanded the two hundred *lei* change. The woman, her face drawn, whined like a professional beggar, then began to weep. Bella held out her hand, unrelenting.

Harriet said: "*Bella!* She's earned her money. We don't want a row over a couple of bob. Let her go."

Bella, startled by this appeal, moved from the door and the woman fled. They could hear her scrabbling with a lock, then, as she went, leaving the front door open, the click of her heels as she sped down the marble staircase.

"Really!" Bella grumbled in self-excuse. "You can't trust them an inch. They always take advantage of foreigners. If you'd had as much to do with them as I have, you'd be just as sick of them."

Before Harriet went, they found the dressmaker had abandoned the parcel of costumes which she was supposed to deliver to the other female players.

"There, look at that!" said Bella. "We'll have to get a man to take it to the University."

"I'll take it," said Harriet.

"No, no." Bella held it firmly. "I'll take it," she said, "I'm not ashamed to be seen carrying a parcel."

When Clarence drove her back to the knitting factory, Harriet found the tights completed and exactly as she had ordered. On the way back he called again at the Polish store and came out with an armful of shirts and underwear. He put these on her lap. "For Guy," he said.

"Why wouldn't you give me these before?"

"Because you were being so bloody-minded. Don't you realise – if you treated me properly, you could get anything in the world you wanted from me?"

That afternoon, when Harriet sat with the others in the Athénée Palace garden, the news of the Italian declaration of war on the Allies was brought out by an Italian waiter who sometimes served them. He beamed over the English faction at the table, saying several times: "You are surprise, eh? You are surprise?"

Galpin replied: "We are not surprised. We're only surprised

there aren't more of you hungry hyenas trying to get in on some-one else's kill."

The waiter did not understand or, if he did, he was unaffected. He merely said: "Now it is we, the Italians, who will go abroad to look at picture galleries." He gave a flick of his cloth at the lime-flowers on the table and went off singing a snatch, laughing on a high note of triumph.

26

THE DRESS REHEARSAL of *Troilus and Cressida* was to take place after the theatre closed on the night of Thursday, the 13th of June. From then until midnight on Friday the theatre and its staff were hired by the English players. Harriet was invited to this final rehearsal, which was called for eleven p.m.

Clarence, who was taking her out to supper, called for her in the early evening. He said: "There's some sort of scare on. The police are stopping people and examining their papers."

"What are they looking for?"

"Spies, I suppose."

The crowds were out walking as usual in the streets. Police were moving among them in sky-blue knots of three or four. Police vans stood at the kerbs. No one seemed much alarmed. The situation was too desolating to cause excitement.

For Bucharest, the fall of France was the fall of civilisation. France was an ideal for all of those who struggled against their peasant origin. All culture, art and fashion, liberal opinion and concepts of freedom were believed to come from France. With France lost, there would be no stay or force against savagery. Except for a handful of natural fascists, no one really believed in the New Order. The truth was evident even to those who had invested in Germany: the victory of Nazi Germany would be the victory of darkness. Cut off from Western Europe, Rumania would be open to persecution, bigotry, cruelty, superstition and tyranny. There was no one to save her now.

An atmosphere of acute sadness overhung the city, something near despair. Indeed, it was despair. Harriet and Clarence drove up to the Chaussée in what seemed the last sunset of the world.

The *grădinăs*, that all winter had been a waste of snow, were alive now with lights and music. Here there was an attempt to believe that life was going on as usual. People were strolling beneath the chestnuts and limes that, in full leaf, were still unblemished by the summer heat. Harriet and Clarence left the car and joined the crowd, walking as far as the Arc de Triomphe. Around them they could hear, in several languages, expression of the bewilderment they felt themselves. People were asking one another what had happened inside France. What confusion among the French forces, what failure of spirit, had enabled an enemy to make this rapid advance? "It is the new Germany," said a woman. "No one can withstand it."

Clarence laughed shortly and said: "Steffaneski's gloating a bit. He said he had to hear enough about the three weeks' war in Poland. Now we can reflect on the fact that Holland and Belgium have capitulated and the English been forced out of Europe all within eighteen days. He doesn't give France another week."

"What do you think?" Harriet asked.

"I don't know." Clarence spoke slowly, putting up a show of reflective calm. "The Germans reached the Marne in the last war. The French fought like madmen to save Paris. They went to the front in taxis; every man in Paris turned out; and the line held. It could happen again."

As they approached the Arc de Triomphe, the crowds thinned. Three little peasant girls, not yet in their teens, wearing embroidered dresses and flowers in their hair, suddenly appeared in front of them, and, dancing backwards, began chanting something at Clarence. Harriet thought they were begging, but they were not using the beggar's whine, and they occasionally gave Harriet mischievous side-glances of great liveliness.

"What do they want?" she asked.

"Why," said Clarence, "they're offering themselves, of course. They're whores."

"They can't be. They're children."

Clarence shrugged. With his chin down, his lower lip thrust out, he looked from under his brows at the girls who were dancing before him, sometimes scattering apart and sometimes bunching together and giggling at whatever they were suggesting.

"They're a lot more cheerful than most peasants," Harriet said, laughing.

Clarence grunted. "They haven't yet learnt what life is like."

"It's odd they should approach you when I'm here."

"They're inexperienced. They know no better."

Aware they were being discussed, the girls shrieked with laughter, but they had begun to look about them for more promising material. Seeing a group of men together in the distance, they suddenly ran off, squeaking among themselves like a flock of starlings.

Harriet, her mind elsewhere, said: "That was rather amusing."

"You think so!" Clarence sombrely asked.

They went to one of the smaller garden restaurants, where the dusk was clotting in the trees. It was the time of the year when the evenings were most delightful – as warm as summer but still scented and moist with vegetation. Out here, beyond the houses, the whole sweep of the sky was visible from the iris-blue of the horizon up to the zenith, that was the rich, bloomed purple of a grape. There were a few stars of great size and brilliance.

A small orchestra was playing in the garden. When it came to a stop, neighbouring orchestras could be heard wailing and sobbing in response like birds. Somewhere in the distance Florica rose to her top note. But the music soothed no one. The diners glanced from table to table, aware of themselves and those about them, all gathered helplessly here in a time of disaster. Only the lovers at secluded tables remained untouched in their private worlds outside the flow of time.

Clarence sighed and said: "I wonder what will become of us. We may never get home again. I imagine your parents are pretty worried."

"I haven't any parents," said Harriet. "At least, none to speak of. They divorced when I was very small. They both remarried and neither found it convenient to have me. My Aunt Penny brought me up. I was a nuisance to her, too, and when I was naughty she used to say: 'No wonder your mummy and daddy don't love you.' In fact, all I have is here."

She wondered what it was she had. Looking up through the leaves at the rich and lustrous sky, she felt resentment of Guy because he was not here. She told herself he was a man who could never be present when needed. This was a time they should be together. Looking at the budding canna lilies and breathing in the scent of the box, she thought she should be sharing with Guy these enchantments that gave so keen an edge to suspense.

They had ordered their food. When the wine waiter came, Clarence said: "Well, if we die tomorrow, we can at least drink well." He chose an expensive Tokay.

Harriet thought that, after all, she was not alone. She had someone. It was a pity she could feel no more for Clarence than that. It was, she thought, a charade of a relationship, given an added dimension by the uncertainty in which they existed. It had to serve for what she missed with Guy. And did Guy realise she missed anything at all?

She wondered if he had any true awareness of the realities of life. That morning Dobson had rung the flat to say that British subjects must get transit visas for all neighbouring countries against a possible sudden evacuation. Guy said: "You'll have to get them. I'm much too busy with the play." She felt his escape from reality the less excusable because it was he who, in their few pre-war days together, had been the advocate of an anti-fascist war, a war that would, he knew, come down like a knife between him and his friends in England. He had often quoted: "So I drink your health before the gun-butt raps upon the door." Well, here was the gun-butt – and where was Guy? He would be dragged off to Belsen protesting that he could not go because he was too busy.

Clarence, watching her, asked her what she was smiling at. She said: "I was thinking of Guy." After a pause, she asked him: "Did you know that Guy once thought of marrying Sophie to give her a British passport?"

"Surely not?"

"He *thought* of it. But I doubt if he would ever have done it. He might be a natural teacher but he's not taking on, on a permanent basis, the teacher-pupil relationship. No, when it came to marriage, he chose someone he thought would not make too many demands. Perhaps the trouble is, I make too few."

Clarence looked at her keenly but his only comment was to say in a tone of high complaint: "Guy picks up with the most extraordinary people. Take Yakimov, for instance. Now, there's a mollusc on the hull of life, a no-man's-land of the soul. I doubt if Guy will ever shake him off. You've got him for life now."

Harriet, refusing to be upset, said: "I think Guy saw him as a subject for improvement. He could turn him into something, even if it were only an actor. You know what Guy is like. I've heard you say he is a saint."

"He may be a sort of saint but he's also a sort of fool. You don't believe me? You'll find I'm right. He can't see through people as you can. Don't be misled by him."

Harriet said: "He's not a fool, but it's true, he can suffer fools.

That's his strength. Because of that, he'll never have a shortage of friends."

"There's a streak of the exhibitionist in Guy," said Clarence. "He likes to feel himself at the centre. He likes to have a following."

"Well, he certainly has got a following."

"A following of fools."

"That's the only sort anyone can hope to have. The discriminating are lonely. Look at me. When Guy is occupied, I have no one but you."

Clarence smiled, taking this as a compliment.

The fiddler from the orchestra was wandering round playing at each table in turn. When he reached Clarence and Harriet, he bowed with significant smiles, certain they were lovers. He struck his bow across the strings and, working himself into an immediate frenzy, produced poignant howls from his instrument. It was all over in a moment, a rapid orgasm, then he bowed again, and Clarence gave him a glass of wine. He held up the glass first to Clarence, then to Harriet, congratulating them – on what? Probably on their non-existent passion.

Clarence's beautiful, gentle mouth sank sadly as he gazed into his glass. When he had drunk enough, Harriet noted, forbearance took the place of self-criticism. He now felt love and pity for his own sufferings.

She said: "You should get married."

"One can't just marry for marrying's sake."

"There's always Brenda."

"Brenda is twelve hundred miles away," he said. "I don't know when I'll see her again, and I don't know that I want to. She isn't what I need."

Harriet did not ask him what he needed, but he was now drunk enough to tell her: "I need someone strong, fierce, intolerant and noble." He added: "Someone like you."

She laughed, rather uneasy at so direct an approach. "I don't recognise myself. I'm not strong. I suppose I'm intolerant – a bad fault. I have no patience with people. Sophie told Guy he had married a monster."

"Oh, Sophie!" Clarence spoke the name with contempt.

Harriet said: "I sometimes think I shall end up a lonely, ragged, mad old woman trailing along the gutter."

"Why should you?" Clarence tartly asked. "You've got Guy. I suppose you'll always have Guy."

"And he'll always have the rest of the world."

When they drove up the Calea Victoriei, they saw that the illuminations had been switched off in the Cişmigiu. The park, where people walked in summer until all hours, was now silent and deserted, a map of darkness in the heart of the subdued city.

Clarence said: " 'The Paris of the East' mourning her opposite number."

In contrast, the German Bureau window was brilliant with white neon, and still drew its audience. They saw, as they passed, the red arrows, open-jawed like pincers, almost encircling the site of Paris.

When they entered the theatre, they entered an atmosphere so removed from the outside tension that it might have been that of another planet. Every light was lit in the foyer. People were hurrying about, all, it seemed, so hypnotised by Guy and his production that reality had lost substance for them. They were possessed by a creative excitement, anticipating fulfilment, not defeat.

Even Clarence was caught, as he entered, into this atmosphere. He said: "I must leave you. Guy wants us dressed and ready by eleven o'clock," and he hurried off into a maze of passages to find the dressing room assigned to him.

Harriet, after standing uncertainly awhile, went in search of a familiar face, but the people she met brushed past her, too wrapped up in their players' world to recognise her. Only Yakimov, on his way to the stage in pink tights and a cloak of rose coloured velvet, stopped and said: "What's the matter, dear girl? You look worried."

"Everyone's worried," she said. "The Germans have almost reached Paris."

"Really!" He looked concerned a moment, then someone called him, his face cleared, and he left her for more important matters.

She hoped she might be needed to advise on the wearing of the costumes, but she was only the designer. The wardrobe mistress, a student, pins in her mouth, needle and cotton in hand, was surrounded by enquiries and complaints. Harriet stood beside her a while, hoping to be consulted, but the girl, with a brief shy smile, indicated that she could cope very well on her own.

Harriet had never encouraged the students. She had, indeed,

resented their possessiveness and their demands on Guy's time, so now she knew she had only herself to blame if they received her with respect rather than cordiality.

She came at length on Bella, who was sharing a dressing-room with Andromache and Cassandra. The girls were dressing unobtrusively in the background while Bella, already dressed, sat before the glass, critically yet complacently examining her face, that was richly coloured in creams, buffs, pinks and browns. Her hair, that had grown more golden since Harriet last saw it, was caught into a golden tube and hung in a tail down her back.

Harriet said: "I've brought the chiffons."

"Oh, darling!" Without taking her eyes from the glass, Bella stretched a hand in Harriet's direction and wriggled her fingers. "How sweet of you!" She threw her voice back to the girls: "*Atenţiune!* Doamna Pringle has brought us some gorgeous chiffons." Bella, it seemed, had taken on with her status of actress the elevated camaraderie of the green-room.

When Harriet had distributed the chiffons, she made her way back to the immense auditorium, with its gilt and claret-coloured plush, that was lit only by the light from the stage. She took a seat in the row behind Fitzsimon, Dobson and Foxy Leverett, who were dressed ready for the rehearsal. Dobson and Foxy were advising Fitzsimon that he must ensure his success in the leading rôle by padding out the front of his tights.

"– certainly stuffing in some cotton-wool," said Foxy, gleeful at the thought. "The girls here like to see a teapot."

On the stage Guy, dressed as Nestor, but not made up, was haranguing a line of peasants who blinked bashfully into the glare from the footlights.

Harriet whispered to Dobson: "What is going on?"

"They're the stage-hands," said Dobson. "Guy spent the afternoon explaining what was required of them and putting them through it, but just now, when he started the rehearsal, they were hopeless. They're just indifferent, of course. They think anything will do for a pack of foreigners."

Driven into one of his rare fits of anger, Guy had lined the men up before him. Some were in dark, shabby suits like indigent clerks, others in a mixture of city and peasant dress; one man, so thin that he had an appearance of fantastic height, wore on the point of his head a conical peasant cap. Some stood grinning in a sort of foggy wonder at being addressed, and forcibly addressed, by a foreigner in their own language. One or two looked dignified and pained: the rest stood in a stupor, any language, even their own, being barely comprehensible to them.

From what she could catch of his words, Harriet gathered that Guy was impressing on the men that tomorrow evening a great company of Rumanian Princes, aristocrats and statesmen, foreign diplomats and distinguished personages of every nationality and kind, was to be present. This was to be a tremendous occasion when every man must do not only his best, but more than his best. He must achieve a triumph that would stun the world with admiration. The honour of this great national theatre was at stake; the honour of Bucharest was at stake – nay, the honour of the whole of Rumania was in their hands.

As Guy's voice rose, the three Legation men stopped talking among themselves and listened.

The stage-hands shuffled and coughed a bit as the force of their responsibility was revealed to them. One, a short, stout, ragged peasant with a look of congenital idiocy, grinned, unable to take Guy seriously. Guy pointed at him. "You!" he cried. "What do you do?"

The man was a scene-shifter.

A job of supreme importance, said Guy. A job on which depended the success or failure of the whole production. Guy looked to him for his full support. The peasant grinned from side to side, but, meeting no response from his fellows, his grin faded.

"And now," said Guy, stern but satisfied that by the force of his personality he had made them attend to him: "Now . . ." and towering with his height and bulk over even the tallest of them, he began to go again through the drill of scene and lighting changes which he had worked out.

Harriet stared up at Guy, her heart melting painfully in her breast, and asked herself what it was for – this expense of energy and creative spirit. To produce an amateur play that would fill the theatre for one afternoon and one evening and be forgotten in a week. She knew she could never give herself to such an ephemeral thing. If she had her way, she would seize on Guy and canalise his zeal to make a mark on eternity. But he was a man born to expend himself like a whirlwind – and, indeed, what could one do but love him?

At midnight, while the stage-hands were still being put through their duties, Harriet went home to bed. She heard Guy and Yakimov return some time in the middle of the night. They were gone again before breakfast. That morning there was to be a final rehearsal in the theatre.

When she left the house, people seemed to be in a state of subdued confusion. They were wandering about asking each other what was happening. The red arrows had come to a stop in the window of the German Bureau. Were the German forces at a standstill? Some thought there was a lull for strategic reasons. Others said the French had pulled themselves together and were holding the line round Paris. Whatever the news might be, the Rumanian authorities, 'to avert panic', were withholding information and had cut the international lines.

Harriet went to the Athénée Palace garden. No one there had much to say. Even Galpin was silenced by the sense that they were approaching an end.

"What's going to happen to us all?" Miss Truslove asked out of the great nothingness of their thoughts.

"That," said Galpin, "is anybody's guess."

After an interval, during which the fountain's trickle was as monotonous as silence, Mrs. Ramsden said: "Well, there's the play tonight. That's something to look forward to."

"Do you think anyone will come?" asked Harriet, fearful now that there would be no audience at all.

"Of course they will," said Mrs. Ramsden. "Sir Montagu will be there. The Woolleys are going. Oh, everyone's turning up. It's *the thing*, I can tell you."

Miss Truslove said: "It's nice to have something to distract us."

The others nodded agreement. Even Galpin and Screwby had booked seats.

"Haven't been inside a theatre for months," said Galpin.

Screwby said: 'Haven't been in one for years."

"An English play," said Mrs. Ramsden. "For us here, that's quite an intellectual treat." She sighed and said: "I do like an evening at the theatre."

The morning was hot and growing hotter. The sun rose until it was poised directly over the lime trees. The English group at the table, meshed in a shifting, glimmering pattern of light and shade, was bemused with heat and half-sleep.

Harriet, lolling in her chair beside the fountain, lost sense of the garden altogether and seemed to pass into an English landscape of fields, some fallow, some furrowed, all colourless through mist. A few elms rose out of the hedges into a milky sky. The scene was so vivid, she shivered slightly in the English air, then a lime-flower dropped on to the table before her and she was returned, startled, to the sunlight. She picked up the flower and stared at it to cover the pricking in her eyes.

She remembered her arrival in Rumania, and her first long days of sunlight. That had been a difficult time, yet she thought of it nostalgically because the war had barely begun. She saw herself as she had been, nervous, suspicious and isolated among strangers; jealous of Guy's friends and of his belief that he owed his chief allegiance to the outside world. Unmarried, she had been a personality in her own right. Married, she saw herself coming in, if at all, somewhere in Guy's wake.

It occurred to her that it was only during these last weeks she had become reconciled to the place. She had faced uncertainty without Guy. Those who faced it with her had become, through the exalted concord of their common fears, old friends.

She stayed with them until early evening, then went back to her flat to dress for the evening performance.

27

ONLY STUDENTS had been admitted to the matinée performance of *Troilus and Cressida*: the seats were cheap. For the evening performance the price of seats was such that wonder had been aroused, bringing in a great many rich Rumanians and Jews who could not afford not to be seen in the audience. The profits were to be contributed towards a scheme devised by Guy and Dubedat for the housing of poor students. The fact roused more wonder than the price of the seats, for few Rumanians could believe that a group of people, even English people, would work so hard and so long at no profit to themselves.

Nikko, having formally asked Guy's permission to escort Harriet to the play, called for her at half-past seven. In his waisted dinner-jacket, with his beautifully tied bow, he looked like a dark, angry little male cat. He seemed ready to hiss. Instead he smiled brilliantly and kissed her hand.

"Harry-ott, a token of esteem!" He presented her with a rose from the King's flower-shop. "I do not often go there. I would not myself encourage a King who is not only a gangster but a common shopkeeper, but tonight, when I passed the window, I saw the rose and thought of Harry-ott."

He went on smiling, but he was on edge and, as Harriet poured him a drink, he burst out: "I am not one to speak of money. Like the English, I think it not *chic* to speak of money, but . . ." he drew up his shoulders and spread his hands like fins. "For weeks I am grass widow. I have no wife – and now what do they say? 'Domnul Niculescu, please pay five thousand *lei* to see Doamna Niculescu walk upon a stage.'" He gave a gulp of disgusted laughter and tried to look amused. "It is funny, is it not?"

Harriet said: "There were no free seats. The proceeds are for charity."

"The poor students, you mean? Ah, Harry-ott, cast half an eye around. There are too many poor students. Every son of a peasant-born priest or schoolmaster must go to the University. All seek to be lawyers. Believe me, there are already too many lawyers. There is not the work for them. What we need are artisans." Here he interrupted himself: "But this is no time for solemn talk. I take a beautiful lady to a great occasion. It is rather a time for levity. Come, the taxi awaits."

In the taxi, he asked: "You have heard the news?"

"No. Is there news?"

"Madame has demanded a speed-up of the Drucker trial. She is afraid the German influence may squash it. A trial could be embarrassing to Germany."

"So the German influence may save Drucker?"

"Indeed not. Nothing can save Drucker. For him, if it is not Bistriţa, then it will be Dachau. He is no use now to Germany or anyone else."

"Then I do not understand – what is Madame afraid of?"

"Without a trial, his oil holdings cannot be seized by the State. They would remain the property of Doamna Drucker."

Harriet was thankful to see the theatre foyer full. "A brilliant audience," said Nikko as they took their seats. He rose frequently to bow from the waist in this direction and that, his bared teeth white beneath the black bar of his moustache. Between bows, he indicated to Harriet the titles about them. Among these were a great many princes and princesses. "Of great family," whispered Nikko, "but almost all on their uppers. I wonder who paid for their seats!" Among them was Princess Teodorescu with her Baron.

"Ah, Harry-ott," said Nikko, "you can be proud. And reflect also, Harry-ott, we are even now the ally of England. We come to show sympathy."

Every seat was taken before the curtain rose. Harriet smiled about her in relief at the sight. She even smiled at Woolley, who, sitting with his arms folded high on his chest, turned his chin on to his shoulder and accorded her a brief nod.

Sir Montagu and his party appeared in the royal box. The audience rose while 'God Save the King' was played as a dirge. This was followed by the Rumanian national anthem, after which the orchestra slid into a waltz that faded with the fading of the lights. The crimson curtains glowed. Between them appeared a student, wrapped to the chin in a black cloak, who spoke the Prologue. He had been well rehearsed. As he backed out of sight, members of the audience whispered congratulations to the parents. The father half-rose to bow his acknowledgments. Harriet watched this interruption anxiously. Fortunately the rise of the curtain brought it to a stop – and there, standing languidly, hand on hip, was Fitzsimon in white and gold, padded out as Foxy Leverett had advised, his looks enhanced with a golden wig.

The audience gasped. Heads went together. A twitter of excitement passed like a breeze over the stalls. The impression was such that some of the women began to applaud before they realised what they were applauding. Fitzsimon stood with a fine air of disconsolate virility, waiting for silence. His eyes moved slowly over the women in the front rows. When satisfied by the expectant hush, he fixed his gaze on Princess Teodorescu, sighed and said:

> "Call here my varlet; I'll unarm again;
> Why should I war without the walls of Troy,
> That find such cruel battle here within?"

No one noticed Yakimov until he asked: "Will this gear ne'er be mended?" conveying in his light, epicene voice a world of bawdy insinuation while moving towards the footlights with a gentle confidingness that was bewilderingly innocent.

The audience stirred, not knowing how to take it until Sir Montagu gave a guff of appreciation and the Rumanians relaxed. Once reassured, they took wholeheartedly to Yakimov. He, for his part, had given himself at once, never for a moment doubting their response. In little more than a moment, they loved him. After his first speeches, they were scarcely breathing for fear of missing a nuance of impropriety. The women enjoyed themselves under cover of darkness while the male laughter burst out repeatedly without restraint.

Harriet watched him intently, drawn in in spite of herself. This was 'your poor old Yaki' – the same that had entranced the dinner-table that first night in Bucharest. 'Your poor old Yaki,' she thought. 'My poor old Yaki. Anyone's poor old Yaki, providing they're doing the paying,' yet that was not wholly just, for now it was Yakimov who was making repayment. Guy had befriended him and Guy was being rewarded. Yakimov had learnt his part; he was giving himself without stint. He was helping to make Guy's production, and Harriet was thankful to him.

His exit led to a tumult of applause and comment that held up the action for several moments. Harriet remained tense, watching Fitzsimon, who accepted the delay good-humouredly. When at last he held up a hand and, smiling, said: "Peace, you ungracious clamours! peace, rude sounds!" the laugh accorded him left no doubt but that the audience was on the side of the players. Harriet felt about her the willingness to be pleased. Unless something went badly wrong there was nothing to fear.

She relaxed gradually as the scenes passed, not only without mishap, but with gathering pace. The show was succeeding with its own success and she was warmed to all those who were doing so well: Dubedat, Inchcape, David – and the men from the Legation whom she had supposed would treat the whole thing as a joke.

As for Sophie! Sophie's performance was beyond expectations. As she sauntered and swayed with little meaningful looks and gestures, letting her pink chiffon drift, like a symbol of her own sexual fragrance, about Troilus or her manservant or, indeed, any male who happened to be near, Harriet realised the girl was a born Cressida, a 'daughter of the game'. Even in her scenes with Pandarus she was not overshadowed. The two enhanced and complemented each other, a scheming partnership of niece and uncle set to devour the guileless and romantic Troilus.

Nikko turned excitedly in his seat, trying to read her name on the programme. "Who is she?" he asked. "Is it Sophie Oresanu?"

"Yes."

"But she is *charming*!"

The interval came after Pandarus had conducted the lovers to 'a chamber with a bed'.

In the bar, where Nikko had to struggle for drinks, Harriet, wedged into the crowd, listened to the comment about her. She heard mention of Clarence ("You would not think, to see him in the street, that Mr. Lawson could be so comic") and Dubedat, who, with his snivel schooled to virulence, was declared to be "*très fort*".

"And that young Dimancescu!" exclaimed a woman. "Such a beautiful English! And in manner the English aristocrat, no?" recalling Dimancescu's throw-away indifference and the wearily drooping eyelids that had been lifted once, in rapid rage, when Patroclus had missed his cue.

"And Menelaus!"

"Ah ha, Menelaus!" A titter passed among the men, for Dobson, unable in his Greek dress of skirted corselet to emulate the effect created by Foxy Leverett and Fitzsimon, had managed to suggest that, even had his dress permitted, his part called for no such display. He conveyed, with rueful and apologetic smiles that appealed to the Rumanian sense of humour, his unenviable position.

When Nikko returned to Harriet with two glasses of whisky, he was congratulated on Bella's performance. Her appearance had caused no small sensation.

One of the men said: "She looked like Venus herself." She had indeed, Harriet thought, looked like a Venus of a debased period; a great showy flower without scent.

The student who had played Paris, not very well, had been completely dwarfed by his impressive paramour as she swept to the centre of the stage, keeping her profile well in view. Yakimov, who had excelled in this scene, had carried the weight of Bella's playfulness, glossing the exchange with the ebullience of wit.

Someone in the audience, having consulted his programme, had whispered in amazement: "Is it possible this lady is a Rumanian?"

"Yes, yes," another whisper answered him and Nikko had been scarcely able to contain his pride.

Now, as he received congratulations, his face was so contracted with bliss that he seemed about to weep.

The congratulations were carried over to Harriet as those in their circle reflected on Guy's playing of the not very rewarding part of Nestor. Someone praised him with the words: "You would have thought him truly ancient," while Nikko said in wonder: "But, Harry-ott, your husband knows how to act!"

Pressed for expert opinions on this performance and that, Harriet found she could not sort out her impressions. She had been too fearful of failure and now, grateful for success, she said only: "They were all good."

There was general agreement.

"A production of genius," Nikko concluded. "We are having, I may say, our money's worth."

In the second half, as Inchcape gave himself with the full force of his histrionic irony to his exchange with Achilles, the vice-consul sniggered in the row behind Harriet and said: "By Jove, Ulysses is just old Inchcape to the life."

And there, Harriet thought, lay the strength of the production. Except for Yakimov and Guy, no one was called upon to act very much. Each player was playing himself. She had, she remembered, criticised this method of casting, yet, with the material in hand, what else would have been possible? And the audience accepted it: indeed seemed to find this heightened behaviour more impressive than acting. When the final curtain fell, the actors who received most applause were those who had been most themselves. For Yakimov there was an almost hysterical acclaim. The curtain rose and fell a dozen times, and there could be no end until Guy came forward and thanked everyone – the audience, the actors and, above all, the theatre staff, that had 'co-operated so magnificently'. When he retired, the audience began to file out.

"By Jove," said the vice-consul again, "never knew Shakespeare wrote such jolly stuff. That play had quite a story to it."

On the wave of great good humour, laughing, calling to one another, the members of the audience made their way to the street. They must have looked to the passers-by like maniacs.

Abject faces stared into the lighted foyer. Someone spoke into the happy crowd that was emerging: "Paris has fallen."

Those in front fell silent. As the news was passed back, the silence followed it. Before most people had reached the pavement, despondency had hold of them.

The vice-consul was now ahead of Harriet. His companion, a Jewess, turned to him and, making boxing movements with her little fist, she sadly asked: "Why is it you Allies cannot fight more good?"

Harriet said: "I'd forgotten Paris."

"I, too," said Nikko.

They had all forgotten Paris. Chastened, they emerged into the summer night and met reality, avoiding each others' eyes, guilty because they had escaped the last calamitous hours.

28

INCHCAPE WAS GIVING a party in his flat for the English players and those of the students who had speaking parts. Harriet and Nikko, the first to arrive at his flat, were welcomed by Pauli, who, if he had heard the news, appeared unaffected by it.

The room, with its many gold-shaded lamps and displays of tuberoses, was hot and pungent. There was nothing to drink but *ţuică* and Rumanian vermouth. The food comprised some triangles of toast spread with caviare. Harriet asked Pauli to make her an Amalfi. As he was shaking up the mixture, he told the visitors that Domnul Professor Inchcape had given him a ticket for the matinée. Although he had not understood much of the play, he had thought it all wonderful, wonderful, wonderful. He began strutting around, taking off one actor after another – the professor, and Domnul Boyd, and Domnul Pringle. He gave the impression of being a big man like Guy or David, a general in a general's cloak. He went on for a long time, entertaining Inchcape's guests in Inchcape's absence.

Harriet laughed and applauded, but her mind was on the fall of Paris. She had a sense of remoteness from the members of the cast when they arrived in jubilant mood, still caught up in the excitement that had carried them through the evening.

Nikko ran at once to his wife and caught both her hands. "*Dragă*," he cried, "but you were magnificent. Everyone was saying to me: 'How beautiful, your Bella! How rightly named!' "

There was something febrile about the laughter with which Bella accepted this praise. She turned to Harriet, ready to accept more, and Harriet said: "You have heard the news?"

"Oh, my dear, yes. Isn't it terrible!" She spoke on a high note and swept away, leaving Harriet with the certainty she had said the wrong thing.

Guy, in the midst of his company, had the vague benevolence that came of contentment and physical exhaustion. When Harriet went to him, she slid her arms round him and squeezed his waist in love and thankfulness that the play was over and his companion-ship would be restored to her.

She said: "The show was a tremendous success. The audience forgot all about France."

"It wasn't too bad," he agreed, his modesty that of a man well satisfied with his achievement. He went on to criticise the pro-duction. It had, he thought, been full of minor faults, but one must learn from experience. "When I do another . . ." he began.

"Oh, surely not another?"

Bewildered by her demur, he said: "But I thought you enjoyed it," and turned aside in search of more encouraging praise. He found it at once. It was being given on all sides. Harriet did her best to join in, but she was outside their union that resulted from weeks of contiguity – besides, she was in the real world, they were not. She could not emulate their high spirits.

She looked around for Nikko, but he was in attendance on his wife, growing drunk on the overflow of congratulations. She retreated to the terrace doorway and stood there, half in the room, half out, watching the clamour within.

Yakimov was wandering round, his face vacant and happy, holding out his glass to be refilled, receiving congratulations with "Dear girl, how kind," "Dear boy, what nice things you say!" but not bestowing them. He looked a little anaesthetised by his suc-cess; and so, for that matter, did the others. They were like travel-lers unwillingly returned from brilliant realms, not yet adjusted to their return.

The room was dividing into two groups, one centred upon Sophie, the other upon Bella. Bella had seated herself on an arm-chair, with Nikko on one of the arms. She plucked at Yakimov and he let himself be pulled down to her other side. Having organised the students into a semi-circle at her feet, she appeared to be holding court again, but it was really Yakimov who was the heart and centre of attention. The students gazed at him, waiting for him to speak, and when Dubedat, chewing glumly at the caviare, asked disgustedly: "What's this stuff?" and Yakimov replied: "Fish jam, dear boy," they rolled about in their delight. Encouraged, he began to rouse himself and talk. Harriet could not hear what he was saying, but she saw Bella break in on the acclaim by slapping him and saying with mock severity: "Behave yourself."

Sophie, who had changed into a black velvet evening dress but was still wearing stage make-up, was attended by all the men from the Legation and, Harriet noted rather jealously, Clarence.

Guy, David and Inchcape stood together between these groups. When Inchcape noticed Harriet alone, he crossed to her and said: "Let us go out to the terrace."

Outside, a breeze came cool and moist from the trees, and there was a scent of geraniums. The park was still in mourning, a cloudy darkness starred at the heart with the lights of the lake restaurant.

When they reached the rail and looked over it, Harriet realised that the path below was a-rustle with people walking in silence in the darkness. She began to speak of them, but Inchcape showed no inclination to listen.

"The situation's serious, of course," he said, "but we haven't much to worry about. The Germans are too busy to bother us. I think we're lucky to be here," and before Harriet could contest this optimism, he went on to ask her opinion of each performance in the play.

When Yakimov, Sophie, Guy, David, Dimancescu had been given their due, Inchcape remained expectant.

"And Dubedat was good," said Harriet.

"Remarkable!" Inchcape agreed. "He certainly knows how to exploit his natural unpleasantness."

Inchcape still waited, and Harriet, suddenly realising what was amiss, said: "And your Ulysses, of course, was tremendous – that slightly sour manner edged with wit: the tolerance of experience. People were very impressed."

"Were they, now!" Inchcape smiled down at his small, neat feet. "Of course, I hadn't much time for rehearsals."

Pauli came out on the terrace, eagerly summoning his master. Sir Montagu had arrived. Inchcape snorted and gave Harriet a wry smile that could not hide his satisfaction: "So the old charmer's turned up after all!"

He hurried inside and Harriet followed him. Sir Montagu was standing in the middle of the room, leaning on his stick. His face, dark, handsome and witty, with thick folds of skin on either side of a heavy mouth, was like the face of some distinguished old actor. He was smiling round at the girls.

Fitzsimon, on the sofa, holding Sophie in a casual clinch that she tried to make look like an embrace, suddenly saw his chief and sprang to his feet. Sophie slid to the ground. She looked furious until she saw who was the cause of her fall, then she began to rub her buttocks with rueful humour.

" 'Evening, sir," said Fitzsimon. "Good of you to patronise the show, sir."

"I must say, I enjoyed myself." Sir Montagu looked at Sophie then smiled at Fitzsimon. "Very nice," he said. "Nice, plump little partridges. Very fond of 'em m'self. Sorry to be late. I had to offer our condolences to the French."

"And how were the French, sir?" Dobson asked.

"Apologetic. The Rumanians have sent us their condolences. They think the war's over. I told them it's only just begun. No more demmed allies round our necks. Now the real fighting can begin."

During the laughter and applause that followed, Inchcape approached the Minister, who held out his hand. "Congratulations, Inchcape. Fine show. Clever fellows you've got on your staff; very clever fellows! And I must say" – he gave a long look first at Fitzsimon, then at Foxy Leverett – "I admired the mixed grill put up by the Legation."

"All my own, sir," said Fitzsimon with a smirk.

"Indeed!" Sir Montagu smiled in bland disbelief. "Very enviable, if I may say so."

Inchcape had gone to a corner cupboard. After some clinking of hidden bottles, he came back with half a tumblerful of whisky, which Sir Montagu, watched respectfully by the whole room, drained in two gulps. After that he excused himself, nodded his good-nights and limped out.

"See you to your car, sir." Dobson followed at his heels.

"Oh," screamed Sophie while the Minister was still within earshot, "*what* a sweetie-pie!"

Now, with his chief safely come and gone, Fitzsimon became animated. He went to the pianoforte and started to thump out the tune of the 'Lambeth Walk'.

Guy and David were standing playing chess on the piano-top with some valuable ivory chess-men while Inchcape hovered about them, apparently afraid something might get broken.

Clarence, his expression gentle and bemused, saw Harriet and came over to her. He was, she realised, rather drunk. He put a

hand to her waist and led her out to the terrace away from the
growing uproar of the room.

The students were on their feet now and dancing while Dubedat,
loudly and tunelessly, bawled a Münich version of the 'Lambeth
Walk'.

> "Adolf we say, that's easy.
> Do as you darn well please-ee.
> Why don't you make your way there,
> Go there, stay there?
>
> When the bombs begin to fall,
> Behind our blast-proof, gas-proof wall,
> You'll find us all,
> Having a peace-time talk.
>
> If you walk down Downing Street,
> Where the Big Four always meet,
> You'll find us all,
> Having a peace-time talk."

Peering down over the rail at the end of the terrace, Harriet
said: "Do you realise there are people still walking in the park?
They don't know what's going to happen now. They're afraid to
go home."

Clarence looked down on the moving darkness and said: "This
is a bad time to be alone," adding, after a pause: "I need someone.
I need you. You could save me."

She did not feel like discussing Clarence's personal problems
just then. She said: "What do you think will happen to us? I wish
we had diplomatic protection like the Legation people."

Clarence said: "According to my contract, the Council's bound
to get me back to England somehow or other."

"You're fortunate," she said.

"You could come with me."

The din from the room was growing. The ferment of the party,
that had been precariously balanced, tilting for moments over the
verge of depression, had now righted itself. A new abandon had
set in. Some of the students were stamping out a *horă* while others
were clapping in time and shouting to encourage them. Fitzsimon
was still at the pianoforte attempting to produce *horă* music while
Sophie, beside him, sang shrill and sharp in imitation of Florica.

Harriet said: "Let's go and watch." She tried to move, but Clarence caught her elbow, determined to retain her attention. He kept repeating: "You could save me."

She laughed impatiently: "Save yourself, Clarence. You said that Guy is a fool. There may be ways in which that sort of fool is superior to you. You show your wisdom by believing in nothing. The truth is, you have nothing to offer but a wilderness."

Clarence stared at her with sombre satisfaction. "You may be right. I've said that Guy was a sort of saint. The world has not been able to tempt him. He may be something – but I'll never be able to change now."

"You're like Yakimov," said Harriet. "You belong to the past."

He shrugged. "What does it matter? We're all down the drain, anyway. Where are we going if we lose England?"

"Home. And we won't lose England."

"We won't get home. Here we are, stuck on the wrong side of Europe. Pretty soon the cash'll run out. We'll be paupers. No one will start a relief fund for us. We'll . . ."

As Clarence's voice dropped with despondency, the noise from the room was such that Harriet could scarcely hear what he was saying. Suddenly both Clarence and the music were interrupted by a Rumanian voice that screamed above everything else with a rage that was near hysteria: "*Linişte! Linişte!*"

Startled, Clarence released Harriet. As she escaped, she heard him complaining behind her: "I think you've treated me pretty badly."

When she reached the room, she saw a little ball of a woman, wearing a dressing-gown, her hair in curlers, who had entered and was storming at Inchcape's astonished guests:

"What is it you make here, you English? You have lost the war, you have lost your Empire, you have lost all – yet, like a first-class Power, you keep the house awake!"

For a moment the English were stunned by this attack, then they surged forward calling out: "We've lost nothing yet." "And we're not going to lose." "We shall win the war, you wait and see."

Bella's voice, indignant but still lady-like, rose from the back of the room. "The English have never lost a battle," she cried.

David amended this with an amused reasonableness: "That's not quite true. We lose battles, but we do not lose wars."

This authoritative statement was taken up by the others. "We never lose wars," they shouted, "we never lose wars."

The woman, unnerved, took a step backwards, then retreated rapidly, as Rumanians tended to retreat before assault. When she reached the hall door, she bolted through it and Pauli, laughing, slammed it after her.

"Rule Britannia," commanded Fitzsimon as he re-seated himself at the pianoforte.

There were no more interruptions. The party went on until daybreak. By that time the park was deserted and silence had come down over Inchcape's room. A number of guests had left. The rest, encouraged by Inchcape, prepared to follow them. Yakimov had slipped off his arm-chair and was lying unconscious on the floor. Inchcape agreed to let him stay there until he waked, so the Pringles left with David.

As they reached the street, the dawn was whitening the roofs. Wide-eyed and wakeful from lack of sleep, Harriet suggested they stroll up to the German Bureau and see what had been done to the map of France. When they reached the window, they saw the dot of Paris hidden by a swastika that squatted like a spider, black on the heart of the country.

They stood staring at it a while. Soberly, Guy asked: "What do you think will happen here? What are our chances?"

David pursed his mouth, preparing to talk, then he gave his snuffling laugh. "As Klein says, it will be very interesting! The Rumanians had hoped to do what they did last time – keep a foot in both camps. But the Germans have put the lid on that. What they're organising here is one gigantic fifth column. The King hoped to rally popular support for the defence of the country, but too late. He's lost the trust of everyone. The régime cannot last."

"You think there'll be a revolution?"

"Something of the sort. But, worse than that, the country itself will fall apart. Rumania cannot preserve her great fortune. She has been too foolish and too weak. As for our chances . . ." He laughed again. "They depend on knowing when to get away."

Guy took Harriet's arm. "We'll get away all right."

She said: "We'll get away because we must. The great fortune is life. We must preserve it."

They turned from the map of France with the swastika at its centre and walked home through the empty streets.

The Spoilt City

To Ivy Compton-Burnett

PART ONE

The Earthquake

1

THE MAP OF FRANCE had gone from the window of the German Propaganda Bureau and a map of the British Isles had taken its place. People relaxed. There was regret that the next victim was to be their old ally, but it might, after all, have been Rumania herself.

The end of June brought a dry and dusty heat to Bucharest. The grass withered in the public parks. Up the Chaussée, the lime and chestnut leaves, fanned by a breeze like a furnace breath, curled, brown and papery, and started falling as though autumn had come. Each day began with a fierce, white light splintering in between blinds and shutters. When people ate breakfast on the balconies, there was a smell of heat in the air. By noonday, the ingot of the sun dissolved in the sky as in a vat of molten silver. The roads, oozing tarmac, shimmered with mirages. The dazzle hurt the eyes.

During the afternoon, the hot air concentrated between the cliff-faces of buildings, seemed visible and tangible in the ochre dust-fog. Deadened by it, people slept. When the offices closed for the midday meal, the tramway cars were hung with clerks fighting their way home to darkened bedrooms. At five, when the atmosphere was like felt, the offices reopened, but the rich and the workless remained inactive until evening.

It was evening when rumours of the ultimatum spread. The streets were full of people strolling in the light of early sunset.

Passers-by, keeping an eye on the map in the German Propaganda Bureau window, were speculating on how long the British could hold out, when they learnt of the Russian demand and Britain was forgotten.

The demand had not, of course, been officially announced. The evening papers did not mention it. As usual with any cause for alarm, the authorities were trying to keep it secret, but in Bucharest nothing could be kept secret for long. The Soviet Minister had scarcely delivered the ultimatum when details of it were brought to the foreign journalists in the Athénée Palace Hotel. Russia required the return of Bessarabia and, with it, a segment of the Bukovina on which she had no real claim. The ultimatum was due to expire at midnight on the following day.

Within minutes of its reception in the hotel, the news reached the crowded streets and passed to restaurants and cafés. Apprehensions quickened at once into ferment, for panic was an incipient condition in the capital. People became possessed by an hysteria of alarm.

That evening Guy Pringle, a lecturer in English at the University, was sitting in Mavrodaphne's with his wife, Harriet. Someone, entering at one end of the large, brilliant café, shouted across the room and at once disorder spread through it like a tidal wave. People leapt to their feet and, shrill with grievance, bawled right and left, stranger protesting to stranger. The Pringles could hear them blaming the Jews, the Communists, the defeated allies, Madame Lupescu, the King and the King's hated chamberlain, Urdureanu – but blaming them for what?

Harriet, a dark, thin girl who had grown thinner during their months in this disintegrating society, was set on edge now by any unnatural stir. She said: "It must be the Germans. We shall be trapped," for there were always rumours of a German invasion.

Guy attempted to make an inquiry at a neighbouring table. At once, the man to whom he spoke, recognising an Englishman, accused him in English: "It is Sir Stafford Cripps who has done this thing."

"What thing?"

The man said: "He has made the Russians take our Bessarabia."

"And," added his female companion, "steal our Bukovina with its beautiful beech forests."

Guy, a large young man whose mild and guileless air was enhanced by spectacles, answered with his usual good humour, pointing out that Cripps, having arrived in Moscow only that morning, had scarcely had time to make anyone do anything; but the other turned impatiently from him.

Harriet said: "You might suppose that no one had ever thought the Russians a danger before," whereas, in fact, the Communists with their ungodly Marxist creed, were more dreaded here than the Nazis.

Hearing English spoken, an elderly man leapt up from a nearby table and reminded everyone that Britain had guaranteed Rumania. Now that Rumania was menaced, what were the British going to do? "Nothing, nothing," he screamed in rage. "They are finished," and he made a lunge towards the Pringles with his tussore parasol.

Harriet looked uneasily about her. When, ten months before, she had first arrived in Bucharest, the British here had been respected: now, on the losing side, they were respected no longer. She half feared actual attack – but no attack came. A certain sentiment, even affection, persisted for the once great, protecting power which was believed to be doomed.

Unwilling to show fear by taking themselves off, the Pringles sat still amid a hubbub which suddenly changed its tenor. A man had risen and, attracting attention by the reasonable quiet of his speech, asked if their fears might not be premature. It was true that the British could do nothing for Rumania, but what of Hitler? Hadn't the King recently changed his allegiance? He could now call on German aid. When the Führer heard of this ultimatum, he would force Stalin to withdraw it.

Ah! The shouting died down. People, taking up this reassurance, nodded to one another. Those who had been most fearful, became in a moment cheerful and hopeful. Those who had complained loudest were now loud with confidence. Nothing was lost yet. Hitler would protect them. For once the King was in favour. His cunning, from which the country had so long suffered, was now applauded. He had declared for the Axis at just the right moment. There was no doubt about it, he was going to prove himself the saviour of his country.

This sudden euphoria spread as rapidly as the earlier panic. The Pringles walked home through streets in which people were congratulating each other as though upon a victory. But next morning the refugee cars began to arrive from the north. Grey with dust and strapped over with baggage, they looked much as the Polish cars had looked when they drove into Bucharest ten months before.

They brought the German land-owners of Bessarabia who, warned by the German Legation, had fled, not in fear of the Russians but of the peasants who hated them. Their appearance brought a new wave of anxiety, for if anyone had been told of Hitler's intentions, they must have been told.

The Pringles' flat overlooked the main square. During the

morning, people began to fill the square, standing silently and gazing towards the palace.

Prince Yakimov, an Englishman of Russian origin, whom Harriet unwillingly tolerated as a guest in the flat, came back from his haunt, the English Bar, and said: "Everyone's very optimistic, dear girl. I'm sure a solution will be found," and when he had eaten he retired to untroubled sleep.

Guy was supervising end-of-term examinations and did not come home to luncheon. During the afternoon, Harriet went out to the balcony and saw the crowds still standing beneath the torrid sun. The siesta was the traditional time for making love, but no one had heart now for sleep or love. There was still no official confirmation of the ultimatum, but it was known that the King had summoned the Crown Council. The ministers were unmistakable in their white uniforms. Everyone saw them arrive.

Immediately below Harriet's balcony was a small Byzantine church with golden domes and crosses looped with beads. Its door creaked continually as people entered to pray for help in this time of crisis.

The church was surrounded by buildings left partly demolished when the war brought the King's "improvements" to an end. Beyond these ruins was the sun-scorched square with the waiting crowds and the palace where state officials came and went. Cars were crowded within the palace railings. New arrivals had to park outside.

Harriet could smell her hair toasted by the sun. The heat was a burden on her head. Yet she stood for a while watching a peasant crossing the cobbles below her. He was a vendor of chickens. A cage of live birds hung on either side of him from a yoke across his shoulders. Every few minutes he lifted his head and squawked like a fowl. A servant shouted to him from one of the lower balconies, then appeared down in the street. Together vendor and buyer examined the chickens, stretching out their wings and poking at their breasts. In the end, one chosen, the peasant, amid a cackling and flurry of feathers, wrung its neck.

Harriet went back to the room. When she came out again, the peasant was sitting on the church step, the chicken plucked, the feathers about his feet. Before he went on his way again he pulled a piece of sacking over each cage to protect his birds from the sun.

At five o'clock there was a movement among the crowd as office workers started back to offices. A little later, when the newsboys began crying a special edition, the whole square came to life. Harriet hurried down to discover the news. People were pressing against the boys, snatching the papers and leafing frantically through them. One man, coming to the last page, shook his paper in the air, then throwing it to the ground, stamped wildly upon it.

Harriet feared this meant that Bessarabia was lost, but when she bought a paper, the headlines stated that the Prince had passed his baccalaureate with 98.9 marks out of a possible hundred. The King, though pale and apparently anxious, had left the Council Chamber to congratulate his son. Everywhere about her she could hear the words "*bacalaureat*", "*printul*", "*regeul*" being spoken with derisive anger, but there was no news of Bessarabia.

As the sunset threw its reds and purples across the sky, the waiting crowds grew restless. Time was passing. Those in the square had been mostly men of the working classes. With evening, women appeared, their light clothes glimmering in the twilight. The first breath of cool air brought the prosperous Rumanians out for the promenade. Though they walked from habit into the Calea Victoriei and the Boulevard Carol, they were drawn back again and again to the square, the centre of tension.

When Guy returned from the University, Harriet said they must eat quickly, then go out and discover what was happening.

In the street, meeting people they knew, they learnt that the King had appealed to Hitler, who had promised to send a personal message before the ultimatum should expire. Everyone was suddenly hopeful again. Inside the palace, the King and his ministers were awaiting the message. The King was reported to have said: "We must look to the Führer. He will not fail us in our hour of need."

Darkness was falling. A bugle sounded in the palace yard. As though it were a call to arms, a man in the square started to sing the national anthem. Others took it up, but the voices were sparse, choked by uncertainty, and soon died away. Inside the palace the chandeliers sprang alight. Someone shouted for the King. The cry was taken up, but the King did not appear.

The moon rose, bland and big, and floated above the city. All the time there was a slamming of car doors as people came and went at the palace. One of the arrivals was a woman. Immediately the story went round that an attempt had been made on the life of Madame Lupescu, who had fled from her villa in Alea Vulpache and had come to the King for protection.

There was a new stir at the arrival of Antonescu, a proud man, out of favour since he had supported the Iron Guard leader. It was said that, recognising the situation as desperate, the General had begged an audience with the King. The press in the square grew. Something would happen now. But nothing happened and soon the General drove away again.

The next time they approached the Athénée Palace Guy said: "Let's go in and have a drink." If there were any real news it would immediately be brought there.

The area outside the hotel was packed with the Bessarabian cars, many of them still loaded with trunks and suitcases, rolled carpets and small, valuable pieces of furniture. Within the hall, beneath the brilliant lights, were heaped more trunks, cases, carpets and rich possessions. As the Pringles picked their way through them, they came face to face with Baron Steinfeld, one of the Bessarabians, more often in Bucharest than on his estate. The Pringles, who had met him only once, were surprised when he accosted them. They had thought him a charming man, but he was charming no longer. His square, russet-red face was distorted, his large teeth bared; he spoke with such anguished rage, his words seemed to be shaken from him: "I have lost everything. But everything! My estate, my house, my apple orchard, my silver, my Meissen ornaments, my Aubusson rugs. You cannot imagine, so much have I lost. You see here these things – they were all brought by the lucky ones. But I – I was in Bucharest, so I lose all. You English, what are you doing that you fight against the Germans? It is the Bolsheviks you must fight. You must join with the Germans, who are good men, and together you must fight these Russian swine who steal my everythings."

Shocked by the change that had come over the baron, Guy did not know what to say. Harriet began: "Bessarabia isn't lost yet . . ." but paused, confused, as the baron broke down, saying through tears: "I have even lost my little dog."

"I am sorry," said Harriet, but the baron raised a hand, rejecting pity. What he wanted was action: "It is necessary to fight. Together we must destroy the Russians. Do not be fools. Join with us before it is too late." On this dramatic note, he pushed out through the swing door and left the Pringles alone.

Hall and vestibule were deserted. Even the booking-clerk had gone out to watch events in the square, but a sound of English voices came from the next room.

Guy said: "The journalists are back in the bar."

The bar – the famous English Bar—had been, until a month before, the preserve of the British and their associates. The enemy had been kept out. Then, on the day Calais fell, a vast crowd of German businessmen, journalists and legation officials had entered in a body and taken possession. The only Englishmen present – Galpin, and his friend Screwby – had retreated before this triumphant, buffeting mob and taken themselves to the hotel garden. Now they were back again.

Galpin was one of the few journalists permanently resident in Bucharest. An agency man, living at the Athénée Palace and seldom leaving it, he employed a Rumanian to scout for news, which was brought to him at the hotel. The other journalists in the bar had flown in from neighbouring capitals to cover the Bessarabian crisis.

As the Pringles entered, Galpin seized on them and began at once to describe how he had marched into the bar at the head of the new arrivals and called to the barman: "Vodka, *tovarish*."

Whether this was true or not, he was now drinking whisky. He let Guy refill his glass, then, glancing towards the dispirited Germans who had been pushed into a corner, he toasted the ultimatum: "A slap in the eye for the bloody Boche," apparently seeing the Russian move as a British triumph.

Surely, Harriet thought, it was rather the Allies who were being flouted. They had condoned the Rumanian seizure of the Russian province in 1918 and now in 1940 it was their weakness that prompted the Russians to demand it back again.

When she started to say this, old Mortimer Tufton, staring aloofly over her head, cut her short with: "The Paris Peace Conference never recognised the annexation of Bessarabia."

Tufton, after whom a street in Zagreb had been named, was a noted figure in the Balkans. He was said to be able to scent the coming of events and was always on the spot before they occurred. Informed, dry, consciously intimidating, he had the manner of a man accustomed to receiving deference, but Harriet would not let herself be put down. "You mean that Bessarabia was never really part of Greater Rumania?"

She gave a false impression of confidence and Tufton, snubbing her for her sex and impudence, answered casually: "One could say that," and turned away from her.

Disbelieving, but lacking knowledge with which to contend against him, she looked for support to Guy who said: "The

Soviets never recognised Bessarabia as Rumanian. They're perfectly justified in taking it," and, elated by the sudden, unusual popularity of the country which interpreted his faith, he added: "You wait and see. Russia will win this war for us yet."

Tufton gave a laugh. "She may win the war," he said, "but not for us."

This was too much for the journalists, who ridiculed the idea of Russia winning any war, let alone this one. A man who had been in Helsinki spoke at length of "the Finnish fiasco". Galpin then said the reputed power of Soviet armour was one huge bluff and described how during the war in Spain a friend of his had run into a Soviet tank which had buckled up like cardboard.

Guy said: "That's nonsense, an old story. Every hack journalist with nothing better to write up was putting it around." Now that his ideals were attacked, he was on the defensive, no longer mild but ready to argue with anyone. Harriet, though the ideals were too political and disinterested to appeal to her, was prepared to take his side; but Galpin shrugged, giving the impression he thought the whole thing unimportant.

Before Guy could speak again, Mortimer Tufton, who had no patience with the conjectures of inexperienced youth, broke in with a history of Russian-Rumanian relations, proving that only Allied influences had prevented Russia from devouring the Balkans long ago. Rumania, he said, had been invaded by Russia on eight separate occasions and had suffered a number of "friendly occupations", none of which had ever been forgotten or forgiven. "The fact is," he concluded, "the friendship of Russia has been more disastrous to Rumania than the enmity of the rest of the world."

"That was Czarist Russia," said Guy. 'The Soviets are a different proposition."

"But not a different race – witness this latest piece of opportunism."

Catching his small, vain, self-regarding eye fixed severely upon her, Harriet, deciding to win him, smiled and asked: "To whom would *you* award Bessarabia?"

"Hmmm!" said Tufton. He looked away, appearing to swallow something astringent in his throat, but, mollified by her appeal, he gave the question thought. "Russia, Turkey and Rumania have been squabbling over that particular province for five hundred years," he said. "The Russians finally got it in 1812 and held on to it until 1918. I imagine they kept it rather longer than anyone else managed to do, so, on reflection . . ." he paused, hemmed again, then impressively announced: "I'd be inclined to let them have it."

Harriet smiled at Guy, passing the award on to him, and Galpin nodded, confirming it.

Galpin's dark, narrow face hung in folds above his rag of a collar. Elbow on bar, sourly elated by his return to his old position, he kept staring about him for an audience, his moving eyeballs as yellow as the whisky in his hand. As he drank, his yellow wrist, the wrist-bone like half an egg, stuck out rawly from his wrinkled, shrunken, ash-dusty dark suit. A wet cigarette stub clung, forgotten, to the bulging, purple softness of his lower lip and trembled when he spoke.

"The Russkies are sticking their necks out demanding this territory just when Carol's declared for the Axis."

Guy said: "I imagine the declaration prompted them to do it. They're staking their claim before the Germans get too strong here."

"Could be." Galpin looked vague. He preferred to be the one to theorise, "Still, they're sticking their necks out." He looked for Tufton's agreement and when he got it grunted, agreeing with himself, then added: "If the Germans ever attacked them, I wouldn't give the Russkies ten days."

As they were discussing the Russian war potential, in which Guy alone had faith, a small man in dilapidated grey cotton, an old trilby pressed against his chest, sidled in and nudged Galpin. This was Galpin's scout, a shadow who lived by nosing out news, takin one version of it to the German journalists at the Minerva, and another to the English in the Athénée Palace.

When Galpin bent down, the scout whispered in his ear. Galpin listened with intent interest. Everyone waited to hear what had been said, but he was in no hurry to tell them. With a sardonic, bemused expression, he took out a bundle of dirty paper money and handed over the equivalent of sixpence, which reward was received with reverent gratitude. Then he paused, smiling around the company.

"The eagerly awaited message has arrived," he said at last.

"Well, what is it?" Tufton impatiently asked.

"The Führer has asked Carol to cede Bessarabia without conflict."

"Hah!" Tufton gave a laugh which said he had expected as much.

Galpin's close companion, Screwby, asked: "This is a directive?"

"Directive, nothing," said Galpin. "It's a command."

"So it's settled," said Screwby bleakly. "No chance of a scrap?"

Tufton scoffed at him: "Rumania take on Russia single-handed? Not a chance. Their one hope was Axis backing if they stood firm. But Hitler doesn't intend going to war with Russia – anyway, not over Bessarabia."

The journalists finished their drinks before making for the telephones in the hall. No one showed any inclination to hurry. The news was negative. Rumania would submit without a fight.

When they left the hotel, the Pringles were surprised at the quiet outside. The Führer's command must be known to everyone now, but there was no hint of revolt. If there had been a show of anger, it was over now. The atmosphere was subdued. A few people stood outside the palace as though there might still be hope, but the majority were dispersing in silence, having recognised that there was nothing more to be done.

After the tense hours of uncertainty, acceptance of the ultimatum had probably brought as much relief as disappointment. Whatever else it might mean, it meant that life in Bucharest would go on much as before. No one would be called upon to die in a desperate cause.

Next day the papers were making the best of things. Rumania, they said, had agreed to cede Bessarabia and the northern Bukovina, but Germany had promised that after the war these provinces would be returned to her. Meanwhile, in obeying the Führer's will, she was sacrificing herself to preserve the peace of Eastern Europe. It was a moral victory and the officers withdrawing their men from the ceded territory might do so with breasts expanded and heads held high.

Flags were at half-mast. The cinemas were ordered to shut for three days of public mourning. And the rumour went round that the Rumanian officers, now pelting down south, had abandoned their units, their military equipment and even their own families, in panic flight before the advancing Russians. By the end of June, Bessarabia and the northern Bukovina had become part of the Soviet Union.

When the Pringles next visited the English Bar, Galpin said: "Do you realise the Russian frontier is less than a hundred and twenty miles from here? The bastards could be on top of us before we'd even known they'd started."

2

HARRIET HAD IMAGINED that when the term ended they would be free to go where they pleased. She longed to escape, if only for a few weeks, not only from the disquiet of the capital, but from their uncertain situation. She thought they might leave Rumania altogether. A boat went from Constanza to Istanbul, and thence to Greece. Excited by the prospect of such a journey, she appealed to Guy, who said: "I'm afraid I can't go just now. Inchcape's asked me to organise a summer school. In any case, he feels none of us should leave the country at the moment. It would create a bad impression."

"But no one spends the summer in Bucharest."

"They will this year. People are afraid to leave in case something happens and they can't get back. As a matter of fact, I've already enrolled two hundred students."

"Rumanians?"

"A few. The Jews are crowding in. They're very loyal."

"I should say it's not just loyalty. They want to get away to English-speaking countries."

"You can't blame them for that."

"I don't blame them," said Harriet but, disappointed, she was inclined to blame someone. Probably Guy himself.

Now she was coming to know Guy, she was beginning to judge him. When they had married ten months before, she had accepted him, uncritically, as a composite of virtues. She did not demur when Clarence described him as "a saint". She still might not demur, but she knew now that one aspect of his saintliness was composed of human weaknesses.

She said: "I don't believe Inchcape thought of this school. He's lost interest in the English Department. I believe it's all your idea."

"I discussed it with Inchcape. He agreed that one can't spend the summer lazing around while other men are fighting a war."

"And what is Inchcape going to do? I mean, apart from sitting in the Bureau reading Henry James."

"He's an old man," said Guy, deflecting criticism as much from himself as from his superior. Since Inchcape, who was the professor, had become Director of Propaganda, Guy had run the English Department with the help only of three elderly ex-governesses and Dubedat, an elementary school-teacher, marooned in the Balkans by war. With uncomplaining enthusiasm, Guy did much more than was expected of him; but he was not imposed upon. He did what he wanted to do and did it, Harriet believed, to keep reality at bay.

During the days of the fall of France, he had thrown himself into a production of *Troilus and Cressida*. Now, when their Rumanian friends were beginning to avoid them, he was giving himself up to this summer school. He would not only be too busy to notice their isolation, but too busy to care about it. She wanted to accuse him of running away – but how accuse someone who was, to all appearances, steadfast on the site of danger, a candidate for martyrdom? It was she, it seemed, who wanted to run away.

She asked: "When does the school start?"

"Next week." He laughed at her tone of resignation, and, putting an arm round her, said: "Don't look so glum. We'll get away before the summer ends. We'll go to Predeal."

She smiled and said: "All right," but as soon as she was alone she went to the telephone, looking for comfort, and rang up the only Englishwoman she knew here who was of her generation. This was Bella Niculescu, who had very little to do and was usually only too ready to talk. That morning, however, she cut Harriet off abruptly, saying she was dressing to go out to luncheon. She suggested that Harriet come to tea that afternoon.

Harriet waited until nearly five o'clock before venturing into the outdoor heat. At that time a little shade was stretching from the buildings, but in the Boulevard Breteanu, where Bella lived, the buildings had been demolished to make way for blocks of flats, only two or three of which had been built when war brought work to a stop. The pavements were shadeless between the white baked earth of vacant lots.

In summer this area was a dormitory for beggars and unemployed peasants, and the dust-filled air carried a curious odour, sweetish, unclean yet volatile, distilled by the sun from earth saturated with urine and ordure.

Bella's block rose sheer from the ground like a prow from water. Against its side-wall a peasant had pitched a hut for the sale of vegetables and cigarettes. Several beggars sleeping in the shade of the hut made an attempt to rouse themselves at Harriet's step and whined in a half-hearted way. One of them was well known to her. She had seen him first on her first day in Bucharest: a demanding, bad-tempered fellow who, recognising a foreigner, had thrust his ulcerated leg at her like a threat and refused to be satisfied with what she gave him. At that time she had been horrified by the beggars, especially this beggar. Having just journeyed three days to the eastern edge of Europe, she had seen him as a portent of life in the strange, half-Oriental capital to which marriage had brought her.

Guy had said she must become used to the beggars; and, in a way, she had done so. She had even become reconciled to this man, and he to her. Now she handed him the same small coins a Rumanian would have given and he accepted them, sullenly, but without protest.

The smells of the boulevard did not enter the block of flats, which was air-conditioned. In its temperate, scentless atmosphere, Harriet's head cleared, and, stimulated and cheerful, she thought of Bella to whom she could look for companionship during the empty summer ahead. She contemplated their meeting with pleasure, but as she entered the drawing-room she realised something was wrong. She felt so little welcome that she came to a stop inside the door.

"Well, take a pew," Bella said crossly, as though Harriet were at fault in awaiting the invitation.

Sitting on the edge of the large blue sofa, Harriet said: "It's beautifully cool in here. It seems hotter than ever outside."

"What do you expect? It's July." Bella pulled a bell-cord, then stared impatiently at the door as though she, who chattered so easily, were now at a loss how to entertain her guest.

Two servants entered, one with the tea, the other with cakes. Bella watched, frowning in a displeased fashion, as the trays were put down. Harriet, discomfited, also found herself at a loss for conversation and looked at an early edition of the evening paper which lay beside her on the sofa. When the girls went, she made a comment on the headline: "I see Drucker is to be tried at last."

Bella inclined her head, saying: "Personally, I'd let him rot. He made out he was pro-British, but his rate of exchange was all in favour of Germany. Lots of people say his bank was ruining the country." She spoke tartly, but in a refined tone reminding Harriet of their first tea-party when Bella, fearing that her guest might

have pretensions to family or wealth, had overwhelmed her with
gentility. Eventually set at ease, Bella had revealed a hearty appetite for gossip and a ribaldry which Harriet, in need of a friend,
had come to enjoy. Now here was Bella, a great classical statue of
a woman in an unnatural pose, again barricaded behind her best
electro-plated tea-service. For some reason they were back where
they had started from.

Harriet said: "I met Drucker once. His son was one of Guy's
students. He was a warm-hearted man; very good-looking."

"Humph!" said Bella. "Seven months in prison won't have improved his looks." Unable to repress superior knowledge, she took
a more comfortable pose and nodded knowingly. "He was a
womaniser, like most good-looking men. And, in a way, that's
what did for him. If Madame hadn't thought he was fair game,
she'd never have tried to get him to part with his oil holdings.
When he refused her, she took it as a personal affront. She was
furious. Any woman would be. So she went to Carol, who saw a
chance to get his hands on some cash and trumped up this charge
of dealing in foreign currency. Drucker was arrested and his
family skedaddled."

Pleased by her own summary of the circumstances leading to
Drucker's fall, Bella could not help smiling. Harriet, feeling the
atmosphere between them relaxing, asked: "What do you think
they will do to him?"

"Oh, he'll be found guilty – that goes without saying. He'll have
to forfeit his oil holdings, of course; but there's this fortune he's
got salted away in Switzerland. Carol can't take that, so if
Drucker makes it over he might get off lightly. Rumanians are
quite humane, you know."

Harriet said: "But Drucker can't make it over. The money's in
his son's name."

"Who told you that?" Bella spoke sharply and Harriet, unable
to disclose the source of it, wished she had kept her knowledge to
herself.

"I heard it some time ago. Guy was fond of Sasha. He's been
trying to find out what became of him."

"Surely the boy bolted with the rest of the family?"

"No. He was taken away when they arrested his father, but
apparently he's not in prison. No one knows where he is. He's
just disappeared."

"Indeed!" Used to being the authority on things Rumanian,

Bella was looking bored by Harriet's talk of the Druckers, so Harriet changed to a subject which was always of interest. "How is Nikko?" she asked.

Conscripted like the majority of Rumanian males, Bella's husband was usually on leave. It was Bella's money that bought his freedom.

"He's been recalled," she said bleakly. "They're all in a funk, of course, over Bessarabia."

In the past Harriet would have heard this news on arrival and it would have kept Bella in complaints for an hour or more.

"Where is his regiment at the moment?" Harriet encouraged her.

"The Hungarian front. That damned Carol Line, not that there's anything anyone could call a line. A fat lot of good it would be if the Huns did march in."

"I expect you'll be able to get him back?"

"Oh, yes. I'll have to cough up again."

Bella had nothing more to say and Harriet, attempting to keep some sort of conversation going, spoke of the changing attitude of the Rumanians towards the English, saying: "They treat us like an enemy – a defeated enemy: guilty but pitiable."

"I can't say I've noticed it," said Bella, her tone aloof: "But, of course, it's different for me."

There was a long silence. Harriet, exhausted by her attempts to break down Bella's restraint, put down her teacup, saying she had shopping to do. She imagined Bella would be relieved by her departure, but, instead, Bella gave her a troubled look as though there was still something to be resolved between them.

They went together into the hall where Harriet, making a last approach, suggested they might, as they often did, meet for coffee at Mavrodaphne's. "What about tomorrow morning?" she said.

Bella put her large, white hands to her pearls and stared down at the chequered marble floor. "I don't know," she said vaguely as she placed her white shoe exactly in the centre of a black square. "It's difficult."

Knowing that Bella had almost nothing to do, Harriet asked impatiently: "How, difficult? Whatever is the matter, Bella?"

"Well . . ." Bella paused, watching the toe of her shoe, which she turned from side to side. "Me being an Englishwoman married to a Rumanian, I have to go carefully. I mean, I have to think of Nikko."

"But, of course."

"Well, I think we'd better not be seen together at Mavrodaphne's. And about ringing each other up: I think we should stop while things are as they are. My phone's probably tapped."

"Surely not. The telephone company is British."

"But it employs Rumanians. You don't know this country like I do. Any excuse and they'd arrest Nikko just to get a bribe to release him. It's always being done."

"I don't honestly see . . ." Harriet began, then paused as Bella gave her a miserable glance. She said: "But you'll come and see me sometimes?"

"Yes, I will." Bella nodded. "I promise. But I'll have to be careful. I must say, I wish I'd never appeared in *Troilus*. It was a sort of declaration."

"Of what? The fact you are English? Everyone knows that."

"I'm not so sure." Bella drew back her foot. "My Rumanian's practically perfect. Everyone says so." She jerked her face up, pink with the effort of saying what she had said, and her look was defiant.

Six, even three, months ago, Harriet would have despised Bella's fears; now she felt compassion for them. The time might soon come when the English would have to go and Bella would be left here without a compatriot. She had to protect herself against that time. Harriet touched her arm: "I understand how you feel. Don't worry. You can trust me."

Bella's face softened. With a nervous titter, she took a hand from her pearls and put it over Harriet's hand. "But I *will* drop in," she said; "I don't expect anyone will notice me. And, after all, they can't deprive me of my friends."

3

THAT EVENING, on their way to the Cişmigiu Park, the Pringles met Clarence Lawson.

Clarence was not one of the organisation men. He had been seconded to the English Department by the British Council and at the outbreak of war had gone with Inchcape into the Propaganda Bureau. Bored by the work, or lack of work, there, he had taken on the administration of Polish relief and organised the escape of interned Polish soldiers.

Guy said to him: "We're going to have a drink in the park. Why not come with us?"

Clarence, as tall as Guy but much leaner, drooped sadly as he considered this proposal and, rubbing a doubtful hand over his lean face, said: "I don't know that I can."

As he edged away a little, apparently feeling the pull of urgent business elsewhere, Harriet said: "Come on, Clarence. A walk will do you good."

Clarence gave her an oblique, suspicious glance and mumbled something about work. Harriet laughed. Aware of his eagerness to be with her, she took his arm and led him up the Calea Victoriei. As he went, he grumbled: "Oh, all right, but I can't stay long."

They walked through crowds that, having accepted the loss of Bessarabia, were as lively as they had ever been. Harriet was used to the rapid recovery of these people who had outworn more than a dozen conquerors and survived eight hundred years of oppression, but now she thought they looked almost complacent. She said: "They seem to be congratulating themselves on something."

"They probably are," said Clarence. "The new Cabinet has repudiated the Anglo-French guarantee. The new Foreign Minister was a leader in the Iron Guard. So now they know exactly where they are. They're really committed to Hitler and he must protect them. They think the worst is over, and – " he pointed to the placard of the *Bukarester Tageblatt* which read: FRIEDEN IM HERBST – "they think the war is over, too."

At the park gate, he paused, murmuring: "Well, now, I really think I . . ." but as the Pringles went on, ignoring his vagaries, he followed them.

Passing from the fashionable street into the unfashionable park, they moved from hubbub into tranquillity. Here, as the noise of the street faded, there was nothing to be heard but the hiss of sprinklers. The air was sweet with the scent of wet earth. Only a few peasants stood about, admiring the spectacle of the *tapis vert*. The only flowers that thrived in the heat were the canna lilies, now reflecting in their reds and yellows and flame colours the flamboyance of the sunset sky.

Down by the lakeside, the vendors of sesame cake and Turkish delight stood, as they had stood all day, silent and humble beneath the chestnut trees. Beyond the trees, a little gangway led to a café which was chiefly used by shop assistants and minor clerks. It was here that Guy had arranged to meet his friend David Boyd.

As they crossed the flexing boards of the artificial island, Harriet could see David sitting by the café rail in the company of a Jewish economist called Klein.

Guy and David had met first in 1938 when they were both new-comers to Bucharest. David, a student of Balkan history and languages, had been visiting Rumania. He reappeared the following winter, having been appointed to the British Legation as an authority on Rumanian affairs. The two men, of an age and physically similar, resembled each other in outlook, both believing that a Marxist economy was the only remedy for the feudal mismanagement of Eastern Europe.

At the sight of the new arrivals Klein leapt to his feet and advanced on them with arms wide in welcome. The Pringles had met him only twice before, but at once Guy, like a fervent bear, caught hold of the stout, little, pink-cheeked man, and the two patted each other lovingly on the back. David snuffled his amusement as he watched this embrace.

When released, Klein swung round excitedly to greet Harriet, the flush rising from his cheeks to his bald head. "*And* Doamna Preen-gal!" he cried. "But this is nice!" He wanted to include Clarence in his rapture, but Clarence hung back with an uneasy grin.

"So nice, but so *nice!*" Klein repeated as he offered Harriet his seat by the rail.

The evening was very warm. Guy had been walking with his

cotton jacket over his arm and his shirt-sleeves rolled up, a state of undress which the Rumanians regarded as indecent. The café patrons, though shabby, sweaty, and only a generation or two away from the peasantry, were all tightly buttoned up in the dark suits that indicated their respectability. They looked askance at Guy, but Klein took off his jacket, revealing braces and the steel bracelets that held up the sleeves of his striped shirt. He also removed his tie from under his hard collar, laughing at himself as he said: "In this country they do not dress for taking off the coat, but here, I ask you, what does it matter?"

Meanwhile David, who had raised himself slightly in greeting, now slumped back into his chair to indicate it was time for these pleasantries to cease and serious talk to begin again. Chairs were found. Everybody was seated at last.

David, his bulk enhanced by a linen suit that had shrunk in the wash, his large square dark face glistening with sweat, pushed his glasses up his moist nose and said to Klein: "You were saying . . . ?"

Called to order, Klein surveyed the company and said: "First you must know, Antonescu has been flung into jail."

"For speaking the truth again?" David asked.

Klein grinned and nodded.

Harriet did not know what David's occupation was at the Legation, and if Guy knew he kept his knowledge to himself. David was often away from Bucharest. He said that he went to watch the bird life of the Danube delta.

Inchcape claimed that once, in Brașov, he had recognised David under the disguise of a Greek Orthodox priest. He had said: "Hello, what the devil are you up to?" and as the other swept by had received the reply: "*Procul, o procul este, profani.*" Whether this story, and all it implied, was true or not, David, whose subject was Balkan history, was noted for his inside knowledge of Rumanian affairs, some of which was obtained from associates like Klein.

"It is such a story!" Klein said, and ordered another bottle of wine. While the glasses were filled, he paused, but kept his brilliant glance moving from one to the other of his companions. When the waiter was gone, he asked: "What am I? An illegal immigrant, let out of prison to advise the Cabinet. What do I know? Why should they heed me? 'Klein,' they say, 'you are a silly Jew.' "

Rather impatiently, David interrupted to ask: 'But what was the cause of Antonescu's arrest?"

"Ah, the arrest! Well – you know he went to the palace on the night of the ultimatum. He asked to see the King and was prevented. Urdureanu prevented him. The two men came to blows. You heard that, of course? Yes, to blows, inside the palace. A great scandal."

"Was he arrested for that?"

"Not for that, no. Yesterday he received a summons from the King himself. Being fearful that from emotion he could not speak, he wrote a letter. He wrote: 'Majesty, our country crumbles about us.' Now, did I not say that the country would crumble? You remember, I described Rumania as a person who has inherited a great fortune. From folly, he loses it all."

"What else did Antonescu say?' Clarence asked, his slow, deep voice causing Klein to glance round in surprise.

Delighted at hearing Clarence speak, Klein went on: "Antonescu said: 'Majesty, I cry to you to save our nation,' and begged the King to rid himself of the false friends about his throne. When he read the letter, the King instantly ordered his arrest. It is for Urdureanu a great victory.'

Klein sounded regretful and Guy asked: "Does it matter? Urdureanu is a crook, but Antonescu is a fascist.'

Klein stuck out his lower lip and rocked his head from side to side. "It is true," he said. "Antonescu supported the Iron Guard, but, in his way, he is a patriot. He wishes to end corruption. How he would act in power one cannot tell."

"He would just be another dictator," Guy said.

The talk turned to criticism of the King's dictatorship, out of which Clarence suddenly said: "The King has his faults, but he's not insensitive. When he knew Bessarabia was lost, he burst into tears."

"Crying over the oysters he's eaten – or, rather, got to cough up," David said, sniffling and snuffling with amusement at his own wit.

"Anyone can cry," said Harriet. "In this country it doesn't mean much."

Clarence gave her a pained look and, tilting his chair back from this unsympathetic company, drawled: "I'm not so sure of that." After a pause in which no one spoke, he added: "He's our only friend. When he goes, we'll go – if we're lucky enough to get away."

"That's true," David agreed; "and we can thank ourselves for it. If we'd protected the country against the King instead of the King against the country, the situation here would have been very different."

Klein stretched out his short, plump, shirt-sleeved arms and beamed about him. "Did I not tell you if you stayed it would be interesting? You have not seen a half. Already this new Cabinet arranged to ration meat and petrol." As the others looked at him in astonishment, he threw back his head and laughed. "This new Cabinet! Never have I laughed so much. First they repudiate the Anglo-French guarantee. That is easy, everyone feels big work is done – but then, what to do? One has an idea. 'Let us,' he says, 'order for each of us a big desk, a swivel chair, a fine carpet!' 'Good, good!' they all agree. Then rises the new Foreign Minister. Once he was a nobody, now he is the great man. He calls to me to approach. He says, 'Klein, give me a list of our poets.' I bow. 'You will have them in what order?' I ask. 'Sometimes such a list is put in order of literary merit. How naïve! How arbitrary! Why not in order of height, of weight, of income, or the year they did their military service?' 'So,' says the Foreign Minister, 'so we will have it: the year they did their military service. I propose now that these poets write poems to the great Iron Guard leader Codreanu, who is dead but in spirit still lives among us. Domnul Prime Minister, what opinion have you of this proposition?' 'Hm, hm,' mumbles the Prime Minister. What can he say? Was not Codreanu the enemy of the King? 'The opinion I have . . . the opinion I have . . . oh!' He sees me and looks very stern. 'Klein,' he says, 'what opinion have I of the proposition!' 'You think it is good, Domnul Prime Minister,' I tell him."

Klein's stories went on. The others were content to let him talk.

The sunset was fading. Electric light bulbs of different colours sprang up along the café rail. A last tea-rose flush coloured the western sky, giving a glint to the olive darkness of the water. Harriet watched the trees on the other side of the lake as they drew together in the twilight, sombre and weighty as the trees in an old tapestry.

"The other day," said Klein, "in marched His Majesty. 'I have decided,' he said, 'to sell to my country my summer palace in the Dobrudja. It will be like a gift to the nation, for I am asking only a million million *lei*.' 'But,' cried the Prime Minister, 'when Bulgaria takes the Dobrudja, they will take the palace as well.' 'What!' cried the King. 'Are you a traitor? Never will Bulgaria take our Dobrudja. First will we fight till every Rumanian is dead. I will lead them myself on my white horse.' And everyone leaps up and cheers, and they sing the national anthem; but when it is all over, they find they must buy the palace for a million million.'"

Harriet, laughing with the rest, kept her face turned towards the lake from which came a creak of oars and the lap of passing boats. She looked down on a creamy scum of water on which there floated sprays of elder flower, flat-faced and lacy, plucked by the boatmen and thrown away. A scent of stocks came from somewhere, materialising out of nothing, then passing and not returning. The wireless was playing "The Swan of Tuonela", bringing to her mind some green northern country with lakes reflecting a silver sky. About them, she thought, were the constituents of peace and yet, sitting here talking and laughing, they were, all of them, on edge with the nervous city's tension.

She began to think of England and their last sight of the looped white cliffs, the washed white and blue of the sky, the sea glittering and chopped by the wind. They should have been stirred by the sight, full of regrets, but they had turned their backs on it, excited by change and their coming life together. Guy had said they would return home for Christmas. Asked how they took life, they would have said: "Any way it comes." Chance and uncertainty were part of it. The last thing she would have wanted for them was a settled life lived peaceably in one town. Now her attitude had changed. She had begun to long for safety.

". . . and then the new Prime Minister makes a great speech." Klein raised his hand and gazed solemnly about him. "He says: 'Now is the time for broad issues. We do not worry about trifles . . .' then, suddenly, he stops. He points to the things on his table. His eyes flash fire. 'Cigarettes,' he cries, 'pastilles, mineral water, indigestion tablets, aspirin. Auguste,' he calls, 'come here at once. How many times I say to you what must be on my table? Tell me, Auguste, where is the aspirin? Ah, so! Now I speak again. This, I say, is the time for broad issues . . .'"

A gipsy flower-seller, trailing around her an old evening dress of reseda chiffon, came to the table and placed some tight little bunches of cornflowers at David's elbow. She said nothing, but held out her hand. He pushed them aside and told her to go away.

She remained where she was, silent like a tired horse glad to stand rather than move, and kept her hand out. If they ignored her, she might stand there all night. "Oh, for God's sake," said David in sudden, acute irritation, and he gave her a few *lei*. Shyly, with an ironical grin, he slid the flowers over to Harriet.

The park was now in darkness. During the early summer it had been illuminated, but the lights had been switched off when Paris fell and never switched on again. The café floating, an island of brilliance on the water, drew the boats towards it. Though poor, it had its pretensions. It did not admit peasants in peasant dress, but these were allowed to hire the cheap and shabby boats. Now, stopping just beyond the water's luminous verge, the boatmen gazed with envious respect at the patrons in their city suits.

Klein was saying: ". . . then the Prime Minister says: 'Here is the report. Domnul Secretary, never must this report be shown to Herr Dorf. You understand?' The secretary writes across the report: 'Never to be shown to Herr Dorf.' One minute later the door opens and in comes Herr Dorf. The secretary holds the report to his chest. Never will he show it; first will he die. But what does the Prime Minister say? 'No,' he says, 'Herr Dorf shall see the report. Always I play with my cards on the table.' "

At Guy's shout of laughter, the nearest boatload realised that here were foreigners. The opportunity was too good to miss. Their oars touched the water: they drifted into the light. The man in the middle seat began to do some simple acrobatics, then managed, clumsily, to stand on his hands. While this was going on, his companions stared expectantly towards the English. The acrobatics over, they began singing together a sad little song, after which they made diffident attempts to beg. Harriet, the only one who had been aware of the performance, threw some coins. They lingered awhile, hoping for more but lacking the courage to ask, then at last took themselves off.

The talk had now moved to the Drucker trial. It was Klein who had obtained for Guy the little information he had about Sasha Drucker's disappearance. He grimaced now as the others questioned him about the trial, saying he was not much interested in this Drucker "who had lived well and now was not so well".

"Will the Germans protect him?" Guy asked.

Klein shook his head.

"As his business was with Germany," said Clarence, "the trial could be interpreted as an anti-German gesture?"

Klein laughed. "A gesture perhaps, but not anti-German. They try to show him Rumania is still a free country. She is not afraid before the world to bring this rich banker to justice. And the trial diverts people. It keeps their minds off Bessarabia. But the Germans, what do they care? Drucker is no use now. Ah, Doamna Preen-gal" – as Klein leant towards Harriet a pink light coloured his cheek – "was I not right? I said if you stayed here it would be interesting. More and more is it necessary to buy off the Germans with food. Believe me, the day will come when this" – he touched the saucers of sheep-cheese and olives that came with the wine – "this will be a feast. You are watching a history, Doamna Preen-gal. Stay, and you will see a country die."

"Will you stay, too?" she asked him.

He laughed again – perhaps because laughter was the only answer to life as he saw it: but it occurred to her, for the first time, that his was the laughter of a man not completely sane.

Speaking seriously, David asked him: "Can you stay? Are you safe here?"

Klein shrugged. "I doubt. The old ministers would say to me: 'Klein, you are a Jew and a rogue. Make the budget balance,' and they would joke with me. But the new men do not joke. When I am no longer of use, what will they do to me?"

"Are you ever afraid?" Harriet asked.

"But I am always afraid," Klein laughed, and taking Harriet's hand, stared at her. "Perhaps," he said, "Doamna Preen-gal should not stay too long."

An hour or so later, Clarence was still with them, though he had had nothing to say since his remark about the Drucker trial. When they left, he let Guy go ahead with David and Klein, and loitered behind, hoping Harriet would join him. She had seen very little of him, since at the party given for Guy's production of *Troilus and Cressida* she had been unable to take seriously the suggestion she should return to England with him. Now their friendship was, as she supposed, at an end, she found herself regretting it. Usually silent under the pressure of competitive talk, she did not enjoy the audience Guy liked to have around him. With a single companion, however, she talked readily enough and, herself the child of divorced parents, neither of whom had found it convenient to give her a home, she had felt a rather unwilling sympathy for Clarence, whose childhood had been wretched. She did not want to share his distrust of the world. She had rallied him, scoffed at him, but the sympathy had been there nevertheless. Now, as she walked with him, she felt his distrust turned against her. He had accused her of encouraging him and rejecting him – and perhaps she had. They passed in silence under the chestnut trees, avoiding the peasants who had settled down to spend the night there, and turned into a side lane, overhung by aromatic trees, where the air, damp and cool, was occasionally scented by unseen flowers.

To start him talking she asked if he were busy, though she knew he was not. He answered, rather sullenly: "No," and added after a long pause: "I don't know what I'm doing here at all.

"Since Dunkirk the Bureau's been at a standstill. That doesn't worry Inchcape, of course. He never did do much. What have we ever had to propaganda, apart from the evacuation of the Channel Islands and the loss of Europe?" He laughed bitterly.

"What about the Poles?"

"They're practically all gone. I've worked myself out of work."

"Why not come back to the English Department? Guy needs help."

"Oh!" Clarence sighed. She could visualise his face drawn down with guilty dejection as he said: "I loathe teaching. And the students bore me to tears."

"Then what are you going to do?"

"I don't know. I might get some decoding at the Legation."

"I thought you despised the Legation and everyone in it."

"One has to do something."

Clarence, keeping his distance as they walked on the narrow path, was putting up a show of detachment from her; an unconvincing show. From sheer need for distraction she was tempted to make a gesture to regain him, but she did nothing. A romantic, he was never likely to be content with the prosaic companionship which was all she had to offer.

They were approaching the park gate and could hear the traffic of the main road. Clarence slowed his pace, unwilling, now that he had started talking, to leave the park's encouraging cover for the interruptions and buffetings of the street.

Sighing again and saying reflectively: "I don't know!" he let his thoughts wander into the metaphysical byways that skirted his self-pity and self-contempt. "How much easier life must be when one has that little bit of extra something that tips one to the manic rather than the depressive side."

"You think it's just a matter of chemistry?"

"Well, isn't it? What are we but a component of chemicals?"

"Surely something more."

Not wanting to leave the particular for the general, he said: "The truth is, I've been frustrated all my life. I'll die of it. But I'm dying already. The beginning of death is ceasing to desire to live."

"Oh, we're all dying," Harriet answered him impatiently.

"Some of us are alive – anyway, for the moment. Look at Guy!"

They both looked ahead at Guy whose white shirt could be seen glimmering through the darkness. His voice came to them. He was on to his favourite subject – the sufferings of the peasants, the sufferings of the world. Sufferings, Harriet thought, that would remain long after Guy had talked himself into his grave. Catching the word "Russia," she smiled.

Clarence had caught it, too. On a high, complaining note of inquiry, as though the question had never occurred to him before, he asked: "What *is* the basis of his love affair with Russia?"

She said: "I think it's the need to put his faith into something. His father was an old-fashioned radical. Guy was brought up as a free thinker, but he has a religious temperament. So he believes in Russia. That's another home for little children above the bright blue sky."

"In fact," said Clarence, "he's simply what the psychologists call 'a rebel son of a rebel father'."

This idea was new to Harriet. She might consider it later but was not prepared to let Clarence dismiss Guy so easily. She said: "There's more to it than that," and there probably was more to it. When Guy was growing up the mills and mines were idle. The majority of the men he knew, his own father among them, had been on the dole. He had watched his father, a skilled man, highly intelligent, decline and become, through despair and the illness brought by despair, unemployable. He had resented this waste of human energy and became absorbed in the politics of the wasteland and the welfare of the wasted.

Mildly scornful, Clarence went on: "And David's another one. They both imagine that life can be perfected by dialectical materialism."

She said: "David is more realistic, and probably more rigid."

"And Guy?"

"I don't know." It was true, she did not know. She had discovered, but still could not elucidate, the resolute impracticability of Guy's way of life. She said: "I told him once that when I married him, I thought I was marrying the rock of ages. I pretty soon found he was capable of absolute lunacy. For instance, he once thought of marrying Sophie just to give her a British passport."

Harriet's tone of criticism at once caused Clarence to change his attitude. He said reprovingly: "Still Guy is not like most of these left-wing idealists. He doesn't just talk, he does things. For instance, he visited the political prisoners in the Vacaresti jail. Quite a risky business in a country like this."

"When did he do that?" Harriet asked, alarmed.

"Before the war. He took them books and food."

"I hope he doesn't do it now?"

"I don't know. He doesn't tell me."

He did not tell Harriet either. She realised he resented her intervention in his activities and could be secretive. She felt resentful, too, thinking that when he was out of the flat – which he often was – he might be up to anything.

"He's an idealist, of course," Clarence said.

"I'm afraid he is."

"You're becoming critical of him."

"It's not that I'm no longer grateful for his virtues, but they extend too far beyond me. He's too generous, too forbearing, too easily called upon. People feel they can call on him for anything, but he's always somewhere else when I need him."

"Yet what better could you find?"

She did not attempt to answer this question. Her feeling was that she had been taken in, and too easily: perhaps because he was so unlike herself. In early adolescence she had been skinny and charmless. Feeling unwanted, she had been both aggressive and withdrawn, so her aunt had nagged at her: "Why can't you make yourself pleasant to people? Don't you want them to like you?" Whether she wanted it or not, she soon learnt not to expect it. When she did make an effort to please, it seemed to her she aroused not liking but suspicion. Being unsuccessful in the world herself, she had to find someone who would be successful for her. And who better than Guy Pringle, that large, comfortable, generous, embraceable figure? But she should have recognised warning signs. There was, for instance, the fact that he had so few possessions. She had put this down to poverty, but quickly discovered that when he was given anything he promptly lost it. She began to suspect that he saw possessions as a tie. They revealed too much. They defined their owner and so limited him. Guy was not to be defined or limited or held in fee.

There was, she admitted, an emotional shyness about him, but his elusiveness came from a deeper cause than that. And yet, as Clarence had asked, what better could she find? She envisaged a creature similar, but dependent; someone she could compass; her own possession; a child, she supposed. That might be permitted one day, but Guy insisted that at the moment their circumstances were too insecure for children. Was that a reason or an excuse? After all, children were possessions. They, too, defined and limited their possessors.

Meanwhile, Clarence was saying: "I believe in Guy. I think you're lucky to have found him. He has integrity, but I suppose that's the trouble. You're trying to destroy it."

"What do you mean?"

"You're filling him with middle-class ideas. You make him bath every day and get his hair cut."

"He has to grow up," Harriet said. "If he hadn't married me, he'd probably have wasted his life as a sort of eternal student, living out of a rucksack. I think he was probably thankful for an excuse to compromise."

"That's just the point. One is corrupted by compromise. And respectability is compromise. Look at me. I went to an expensive school where I was flogged like a beast. I wanted to revolt and I dared not. I wanted to fight in Spain and I dared not. I could have entered any profession I chose: I chose nothing. That was my revolt against my own respectability – and it led to nothing. I compromised with respectability and was corrupted."

"I expect it would have been the same whatever happened. You offer yourself to be corrupted."

He considered this in silence for some moments, then concluded: "Anyway, I'm lost. I let everyone down. I'd even let Guy down."

"I doubt it."

"Why are you so sure?"

"You don't mean enough to him."

"Hah!" said Clarence in sombre satisfaction that she should diminish him in this way.

The others had come to a stop at the gate. Seeing Harriet and Clarence appear, they were about to pass through when someone darted out of the shadows and accosted them. David and Klein went on, but Guy remained talking to the newcomer.

Clarence distastefully asked: "What lame duck has Guy picked up now? Is it a beggar?"

"It doesn't look like a beggar," Harriet said. Despite their dissension, she and Clarence were at once united in disapproval of Guy's readiness to encourage everyone and anyone.

As soon as they were within earshot, Guy called excitedly to Harriet: "Who do you think this is?"

Harriet did not know and she could see no reason for excitement. The man, about whom nothing was familiar, wore the decayed and dirty uniform of a conscript. When she had seen him moving in the distance, she had thought he was young. Now, in the uncertain light from the main road, he had an appearance of decrepitude found in poverty-stricken old age.

He was tall, skeletal, narrow-shouldered and stooped like a consumptive. His head, that had been shaved, was beginning to show a greyish stubble. The face, grey-white, with cheeks clapped in on either side of a prominent nose, would have seemed the face of a corpse had not the close-set, dark eyes been fixed on her, alive in their apprehensive anguish of need.

She was repelled by such misery. She wanted to go out of sight of it. She shook her head.

"But, darling, it's Sasha Drucker."

She did not know what to say. Sasha, when she saw him nine months before, had been the well fed, well dressed son of a wealthy man. Now he smelt of the grave.

"What has happened to him? Where has he been?"

"In Bessarabia. When his father was arrested, he was taken to do his military service. He was sent to the frontier. When the Russians marched in, the Rumanian officers just took to their heels. There was disorder and Sasha got away. He's been on the run ever since. He's starving. Darling, he must come back with us."

"Yes, of course."

Too shocked to say anything else, she moved out of the aura of Sasha's desperation and walked ahead with Clarence, wondering. When Sasha was fed, where was he going?

As they crossed the square towards the Pringles' block, Harriet, feeling the need of some other presence to share the burden of Sasha's condition, asked Clarence to come in.

"No fear," he said, rejecting responsibility.

"What on earth are we going to do with this boy?" she asked on a note of appeal, but she could expect neither help nor sympathy from Clarence that evening. He laughed. "Put him in with Yakimov," he said as he made off.

There was nothing to eat in the kitchen except bread and eggs. In this heat, in a country where refrigerators were almost unknown, fresh food had to be bought each day. While she made an omelette, Harriet could hear from the cupboard-sized room next door the snores of Despina, the maid, and Despina's husband.

As Sasha ate the omelette with apologetic eagerness, a little colour came into his face. He looked, Harriet thought, like a sapling devastated by storm. She had remembered Sasha Drucker as a dark, gentle, protected youth, the darling of a large family, who had the gentle and unsuspecting air of a domestic animal. Now when he glanced at her, he did so with the wary look of the hunted.

Opposite him, watching him, Guy's face was constricted with concern for the boy. He was deeply hurt by Sasha's condition. He turned to Harriet and said in the persuasive tone she had come to suspect: "We can put him up somewhere, can't we? He can stay?"

She said: "I don't know," exasperated that Guy spoke openly in this way. She felt the realities of the situation should be privately discussed before any decision could be taken. Where, for instance, was Sasha to be put?

Sasha himself sat silent. Ordinarily, he would surely have shown some reluctance to be forced on her hospitality like this, but now she was his only hope. When he had eaten, he looked at her and smiled with an agonised emptiness.

Guy offered him the arm-chair. "Make yourself comfortable."

Sasha shifted diffidently, not rising. "I would prefer this wooden chair. You see . . . I have lice."

"Would you like a bath?" said Harriet.

"Yes, please."

When she had given him towels and shown him the bathroom, she returned to the room free to confront Guy. "We can't possibly have him here," she said. "Our position is insecure enough. What would happen if we were caught harbouring a deserter – especially Drucker's son?"

Guy stared at her and asked with a suffering expression: "How can we refuse? He has nowhere else to go."

"Has he no other friends?"

"No one who would dare take him in. He's at the end of his tether. We can't put him out on the street. We must let him sleep here, anyway for tonight."

"Well, where?"

"On the sofa."

"What about Yakimov?"

Guy looked disconcerted. Blustering a little, he said: "Oh, Yaki's all right," but he knew Yakimov was not all right. They dare not trust him.

Seeing the consternation on Guy's face, Harriet pitied him, but the impasse was of his own making. He had persuaded her to take in Yakimov much against her will; and she could not help feeling some satisfaction as she waited for him to offer a solution. He had none to offer.

He asked unhappily: "Can you think of anyone who would give him a bed?"

"Can you?" There was a long pause while Guy's face grew more troubled, then she said: "You could tell Yakimov to go."

"Where could he go? He hasn't a penny."

During the silence that followed, Harriet reflected on their diversity. Guy, typically, wanted Sasha in the flat without giving any thought to the problem of having him there. She, perhaps, was over-conscious of difficulty. If it rested with Guy alone, there might be no difficulties. He would have trusted Yakimov and Yakimov might have proved trustworthy. She was annoyed at the same time, seeing his willingness to have Sasha here as a symptom of spiritual flight – the flight from the undramatic responsibility to one person which marriage was.

Guy gave her a pleading look as though she could, if she would, reveal a solution. And there was a solution. Pitying him at last, she said: "There's a room of some sort on the roof: a second servant's bedroom."

"That belongs to us?"

"It belongs to the flat. We couldn't use it without telling Despina. She keeps some of her things there."

"Darling!" In his relief, his face glowed with delight in her. He sprang up and threw his arms round her shoulders. "What a wife! You're wonderful!"

Which, she told herself, was all very well: "He can only stay one night. You must find somewhere else for him. I'm not sure we can trust Despina."

"Of course we can trust Despina."

"What makes you think so?"

"She's a decent soul."

"Well, if you think it's all right, you must go and wake her up. She knows where this room is. I don't."

Guy, about to go happily off to tell Sasha that all was well, paused, blankly surprised at being given the onerous task of waking Despina.

"You wake her," he cajoled her, but she shook her head.

"No, you must wake her."

As he moved reluctantly towards the kitchen, she almost said: "All right, I'll do it," but checked herself and for the first time in their married life stood firm.

4

YAKIMOV HAD PLAYED PANDARUS in Guy's production of
Troilus and Cressida. The play over, his triumph forgotten, he was
suffering from a sense of anti-climax and of grievance. Guy, who
had cosseted him through it all, had now abandoned him. And
what, he asked himself, had come of the hours spent at rehearsals?
Nothing, nothing at all.

Walking in the Calea Victoriei, in the increasing heat of midday,
his sad camel face a-run with sweat, he wore a panama hat, a suit
of corded silk, a pink silk shirt and a tie that was once the colour
of Parma violets. His clothes were very dirty. The hat was brim-
broken and yellow with age. His jacket was tattered, brown beneath the armpits, and so shrunken that it held him as in a brace.

During the winter he had felt the ridges of frozen snow through
the holes in his shoes: now he felt, just as painfully, the flagstones'
white candescence. Steadily edged out to the kerb by the vigour of
those about him, he caught the hot draught of cars passing at his
elbow. He was agitated by the clangour of trams, by the flash of
windscreens, blaring of horns and shrieking of brakes – all at a
time when he would ordinarily have been safe in the refuge of
sleep.

He had been wakened that morning by the relentless ringing of
the telephone. Though from the lie of the light he could guess it
was no more than ten o'clock, apparently even Harriet was out.
Damp and inert beneath a single sheet, he lay without energy to
stir and waited for the ringing to stop. It did not stop. At last,
tortured to full consciousness, he dragged himself up and found
the call was for him. The caller was his old friend Dobbie Dobson
of the Legation.

"Lovely to hear your voice," Yakimov said. He settled down in
anticipation of a pleasurable talk about their days together in
Troilus, but Dobson, like everyone else, had put the play behind
him.

"Look here, Yaki," he said, "about those transit visas . . ."

"What transit visas, dear boy?"

"You know what I'm talking about." Dobson spoke with the edge of a good-natured man harassed beyond endurance. "Every British subject was ordered to keep in his passport valid transit visas against the possibility of sudden evacuation. The consul's been checking up and he finds you haven't obtained any."

"Surely, dear boy, that wasn't a serious order? There's no cause for alarm."

"An order is an order," said Dobson, "I've made excuses for you, but the fact is if you don't get those visas today you'll be sent to Egypt under open arrest."

"*Dear boy!* But I haven't a bean."

"Charge them to me. I'll deduct the cost when your next remittance arrives."

Before he left the flat that morning, it had occurred to Yakimov to see if he could find anything useful in it. Guy was careless with money. Yakimov had more than once picked up and kept notes which his host had pulled out with his handkerchief. He had never before actually searched for money, but now, in his condition of grievance, he felt that Guy owed him anything he could find. In the Pringles' bedroom he went through spare trousers and handbags, but came upon nothing. In the sitting-room he pulled out the drawers of sideboard and writing-desk and spent some time looking through the stubs of Guy's old cheque-books which recorded payments made into London banks on behalf of local Jews. In view of the fact Drucker was awaiting trial on a technical charge of black-market dealing, he considered the possibility of blackmail. But the possibility was not great. Use of the black market was so general that, even now, the Jews would laugh at him.

In the small central drawer of the writing-desk he came on a sealed envelope marked "Top Secret." This immediately excited him. He was not the only one inclined to suspect that Guy's occupation in Bucharest was not as innocent as it seemed. Affable, sympathetic, easy to know, Guy would, in Yakimov's opinion, make an ideal agent.

The flap of the envelope, imperfectly sealed, opened as he touched it. Inside was a diagram of a section through – what? A pipe or a well. Having heard so much talk of sabotage in the English Bar, he guessed that it was an oil well. A blockage in the pipe was marked "detonator". Here was a simple exposition of how and where the amateur saboteur should place his gelignite. This was a find! He resealed and replaced the empty envelope, but the plan he put into his pocket. He did not know what eventual use he might make of it, but he would have some fun showing it around the English Bar as proof of the dangerous duties being exacted from him by King and country. He felt a few moments of exhilaration. Then as he trudged off to visit the consulates the plan was forgotten, the exhilaration was no more.

The consulates, taking advantage of the times, were charging high prices. Yakimov, disgusted by the thought of money wasted on such things, obtained visas for Hungary, Bulgaria and Turkey. That left only Yugoslavia, the country that nine months before had thrown him out and impounded his car for debt. He entered the consulate with aversion, handed over his passport and was – he'd expected nothing better – kept waiting half an hour.

When the clerk returned the passport, he made a movement as though drawing a shutter between them. "*Zabranjeno*," he said.

Yakimov had been refused a visa.

It had always been at the back of his mind that when he could borrow enough to remit the debt, he would reclaim his Hispano-Suiza. Now, he saw, they would prevent him doing so.

As he wandered down the Calea Victoriei, indignation grew in him like a nervous disturbance of the stomach. He began to brood on his car – the last gift of his dear old friend Dollie; the last souvenir – apart from his disintegrating wardrobe – of their wonderful life together. Suddenly, its loss became grief. He decided to see Dobson. But first he must console himself with a drink.

During rehearsals, to keep a hold on him, Guy had bought Yakimov drinks at the Doi Trandifiri, but Guy was a simple soul. He drank beer and *ţuică* and saw no reason why Yakimov should not do the same. Yakimov had longed for the more dashing company of the English Bar. As soon as the play was over, he returned to the bar in expectation of honour and applause. What he found there bewildered him. It was not only that his entry was ignored, but it was ignored by strangers. The place was more crowded than he had ever known it. Even the air had changed, smelling not of cigarettes, but cigars.

As he pushed his way in, he had heard German spoken on all sides. Bless my soul, German in the English Bar! He stretched his neck, trying to see Galpin or Screwby, and it came to him that he was the only Englishman in the room.

Attempting to reach the counter, he found himself elbowed back with deliberate hostility. As he breathed at a large man

"Steady, dear boy!" the other, all chest and shoulders, threw him angrily aside with "*Verfluchter Lümmel!*"

Yakimov was unnerved. He lifted a hand, trying to attract the attention of Albu, who, because of his uncompromising remoteness of manner, was reputed to be the model of an English barman. Albu had no eyes for him.

Realising he was alone in enemy-occupied territory, Yakimov was about to take himself off when he noticed Prince Hadjimoscos at the farther end of the bar.

The Rumanian, who looked with his waxen face, his thin, fine black hair and black eyes, like a little mongoloid doll, was standing tiptoe in his soft kid shoes and lisping in German to a companion. Relieved and delighted to see a familiar face, Yakimov ran forward and seized him by the arm. "Dear boy," he called out, "who *are* all these people?"

Hadjimoscos slowly turned his head, looking surprised at Yakimov's intrusion. He coldly asked: "Is it not evident to you, *mon prince*, that I am occupied?" He turned away, only to find his German companion had taken the opportunity to desert him. He gave Yakimov an angry glance.

To placate him, Yakimov attempted humour, saying with a nervous giggle: "So many Germans in the bar! They'll soon be demanding a plebiscite."

"They have as much right here as you. More, in fact, for they have not betrayed us. Personally, I find them charming."

"Oh, so do I, dear boy," Yakimov assured him. "Had a lot of friends in Berlin in '32," then changing to a more interesting topic: "Did you happen to see the play?"

"The play? You mean that charity production at the National Theatre? I'm told you looked quite ludicrous."

"Forced into it, dear boy," Yakimov apologised, knowing himself despised for infringing the prescripts of the idle. "War on, you know. Had to do m'bit."

Hadjimoscos turned down his lips. Without further comment, he moved away to find more profitable companionship. He attached himself to a German group and was invited to take a drink. Watching enviously, Yakimov wondered if, son of a Russian father and an Irish mother, he could hint that his sympathies were with the Reich. He put the thought from his mind. The British Legation had lost its power here, but not, alas, over him.

The English Bar was itself again. The English journalists had re-established themselves and the Germans, bored with the skirmish, were drifting back to the Minerva. The few that remained were losing their audacity.

Hadjimoscos was again willing to accept Yakimov's company, but cautiously. He would not join him in an English group – that would have been too defined an attachment in a changing world – but if Yakimov had money he would stand with him in a no-man's land and help him to spend it.

Yakimov, though not resentful by nature, did occasionally feel a little sore at this behaviour. Practised scrounger though he was, he was not as practised as Hadjimoscos. When he had money, he spent it. Hadjimoscos, whether he had it or not, never spent it. With his softly insidious and clinging manner, his presence affected men like the presence of a woman. They expected nothing from him. By standing long enough, first on one foot then on the other, he remained so patiently, so insistently *there*, that those to whom he attached himself bought him drinks in order to be free to ignore him.

Yakimov, entering the bar that morning, saw Hadjimoscos with his friend Horvatz and Cici Palu, all holding empty glasses and watching out for someone to refill them.

He bought his own drink before approaching them. Seeing them eye the whisky in his hand, he began, in self-defence, to compl in of the high cost of the visas he had been forced to buy. Hadjimoscos, smiling maliciously, slid forward a step and put a hand on Yakimov's arm. "*Cher prince*," he said, "what does it matter what you spend your money on, so long as you spend it on yourself!"

Palu gave a snigger. Horvatz remained blank. Yakimov knew, had always known, they did not want his company. They did not even want each other. They stood in a group, bored by their own aimlessness, because no one else wanted them. To Yakimov there came the thought that he was one of them – he who had once been the centre of entertainment in a vivacious set. He attempted to be entertaining now: "Did you hear? When the French minister, poor old boy, was recalled to Vichy France, Princess Teodorescu said to him: '*Dire adieu, c'est mourir un peu.*' "

"Is it likely that the Princess of all people would be so lacking in tact?" Hadjimoscos turned his back, attempting to exclude Yakimov from the conversation as he said: "Things are coming

to a pretty pass! What do I learn at the *cordonnier* this morning?
Three weeks to wait and five thousand to pay for a pair of hand-
made shoes!"

"At the *tailleur*," said Palu, "it is the same. The price of English
stuff is a scandal. And now they declare meatless days. What, I
ask, is a fellow to eat?" He looked at Yakimov, for all the world
as though it were the British and not the Germans who were
plundering the country.

Yakimov attempted to join in. "A little fish," he meekly suggested, "a little game, in season. Myself, I never say no to a slice
of turkey."

Hadjimoscos cut him short with contempt: "Those are *entrées*
only. How, without meat, can a man retain his virility?"

Discomfited, casting about in his mind for some way of gaining
the attention he loved, Yakimov remembered the plan he had
found that morning. He took it out. Sighing, he studied it. The
conversation faltered. Aware of their interest, he lowered the
paper so it was visible to all. "What will they want me to do
next!" he asked the world.

Hadjimoscos averted his glance. "I advise you, *mon prince*," he
said, "if you have anything to hide, now is the time to hide it."

Knowing he could do nothing to please that morning, Yakimov
put the plan away and let his attention wander. He became aware
that a nearby stranger had been attempting to intercept it. The
stranger smiled. His shabby, tousled appearance did not give
much cause for hope, but Yakimov, always amiable, went forward and held out his hand. "Dear boy," he said, "where have we
met before?"

The young man took his pipe out from under his big, fluffy
moustache and spluttering like a syphon in which the soda level
was too low, he managed to say at last: "The name's Lush. Toby
Lush. I met you once with Guy Pringle."

"So you did," agreed Yakimov, who had no memory of it.

"Let me get you a drink. What is it?"

"Why, whisky, dear boy. Can't stomach the native rot-gut."

Neighing wildly at Yakimov's humour, Lush went to the bar.
Yakimov, having decided his new acquaintance was "a bit of an
ass," was surprised when he was led purposefully over to one of
the tables by the wall. He did not receive his glass until he had sat
down and he realised something would be demanded in return
for it.

After a few moments of nervous pipe-sucking, Lush said: "I'm here for keeps this time."

"Are you indeed? That's splendid news."

With his elbows close to his side, his knees clenched, Lush sat as though compressed inside his baggy sports-jacket and flannels. He sucked and gasped, gasped and spluttered, then said: "When the Russkies took over Bessarabia, I told myself: 'Toby, old soul, now's the time to shift your bones.' There's always the danger of staying too long in a place."

"Where do you come from?"

"Cluj. Transylvania. I never felt safe there. I'm not sure I'm safe here."

It occurred to Yakimov that he had heard the name Toby Lush before. Didn't the fellow turn up for a few days in the spring, bolted from Cluj because of some rumour of a Russian advance? Yakimov, always sympathetic towards fear, said reassuringly:

"Oh, you're all right here. Nice little backwater. The Germans are getting all they want. They won't bother us."

"I hope you're right." Lush's pale, bulging eyes surveyed the bar. "Quite a few of them about though. I don't feel they like us being here."

"It's the old story," said Yakimov: "infiltrate, then complain about the natives. Still, it was worse last week. I said to Albu: 'Dry Martini' and he gave me three martinis."

Squeezing his knees together, Lush swayed about, gulping with laughter. "You're a joker," he said. "Have another?"

When he returned with the second whisky, Lush had sobered up, intending to speak what was on his mind: "You're a friend of Guy Pringle, aren't you?"

Yakimov agreed. "Very old and dear friend. You know I played Pandarus in his show?"

"Your fame reached Cluj. And you lodge with the Pringles?"

"We share a flat. Nice little place. You must come and have a meal with us."

Lush nodded, but he wanted more than that. "I'm looking for a job," he said. "Pringle runs the English Department, doesn't he? I'm going to see him, of course, but I thought perhaps you'd put in a word for me. Just say: 'I met Toby Lush today. Nice bloke,' something like that." Toby gazed earnestly at Yakimov, who assured him at once: "If I say the word, you'll get the job tomorrow."

"If there's a job to be got."

"These things can always be arranged." Yakimov emptied his glass and put it down. Lush rose, but said with unexpected firmness: "One more, then I have to drive round to the Legation. Must make my number."

"You have a car? Wonder if you'd give me a lift?"

"With pleasure."

Lush's car was an old mud-coloured Humber, high-standing and hooded like a palanquin.

"Nice little bus," said Yakimov. Placing himself in an upright seat from which the wadding protruded, he thought of the beauties of his own Hispano-Suiza.

The Legation, a brick-built villa in a side street, was hedged around with cars. On the dry and patchy front lawn a crowd of men – large, practical-looking men in suits of khaki drill – were standing about, each with an identical air of despondent waiting. They watched the arrival of the Humber as though it might bring them something. As he passed among them, Yakimov noted with surprise that they were speaking English. He could identify none of them.

Lush was admitted to the chancellery. Yakimov, as had happened before, was intercepted by a secretary.

"Oh, Prince Yakimov, can I help you?" she said, extruding an elderly charm, "Mr. Dobson is so busy. All the young gentlemen are busy these days, poor young things. At their age life in the service should be all parties and balls, but with this horrid war on they have to work like everyone else. I suppose it's to do with your *permis de séjour*?"

"It's a personal matter. *Ra*-ther important. I'm afraid I must see Mr. Dobson."

She clicked her tongue, but he was admitted to Dobson's presence.

Dobson, whom he had not seen since the night of the play, raised his head from his work in weary inquiry: "Hello, how are you?"

"Rather the worse for war," said Yakimov. Dobson gave a token smile, but his plump face, usually bland, was jaded, his eyes rimmed with pink; his whole attitude discouraging. "We've had an exhausting week with the crisis. And now, on top of everything, the engineers have been dismissed from the oil-fields."

"Those fellows outside?"

"Yes. They've been given eight hours to get out of the country.

A special train is to take them to Constanza. Poor devils, they're hanging around in hope we can do something!"

"So sorry, dear boy."

At the genuine sympathy in Yakimov's tone, Dobson let his pen drop and rubbed his hands over his head. "H.E.'s been ringing around for the last two hours, but it's no good. The Rumanians are doing this to please the Germans. Some of these engineers have been here twenty years. They've all got homes, cars, dogs, cats, horses . . . I don't know what. It'll make a lot of extra work for us."

"Dear me, yes." Yakimov slid down to a chair and waited until he could introduce his own troubles. When Dobson paused, he ventured: "Don't like to worry you at a time like this, but . . ."

"Money, I suppose?"

'Not altogether. You remember m'Hispano-Suiza. The Jugs are trying to prig it." He told his story. "Dear boy," he pleaded, "you can't let them do it. The Hispano's worth a packet. Why, the chassis alone cost two thousand five hundred quid. Body by Fernandez – heaven knows what Dollie paid for it. Magnificent piece of work. All I've got in the world. Get me a visa, dear boy. Lend me a few thou. I'll get the car and flog it. We'll have a bean-feast, a royal night at Cina's – champers and the lot. What d'you say?"

Dobson, listening with sombre patience, said: "I suppose you know the Rumanians are requisitioning cars."

"Surely not British cars?"

"No." Dobson had to admit that the tradition of British privilege prevailed in spite of all. "Mostly Jewish cars. The Jews are always unfortunate, but they *do* own the biggest cars. What I mean is, this isn't a good time to sell. People are unwilling to buy an expensive car that might be requisitioned."

"But I don't really want to sell, dear boy. I love the old bus. . . . She'd be useful if there were an evacuation."

Dobson drew down his cheek and plucked at his round pink mouth. "I'll tell you what! One of us is going to Belgrade in a week or so – probably Foxy Leverett. You've got the receipt and car key and so on? Then I'll get him to collect it and drive it back. I suppose it's in order?"

"She was in first-class order when I left her."

"Well, we'll see what we can do," Dobson rose, dismissing him.

Outside the Legation, the oil-men were still standing about, but the Humber had gone. As Yakimov set out to walk back through the sultry noonday, he told himself: "No more tramping on m'poor old feet. And," he added on reflection, "she's worth money. I'd make a packet if I sold her."

5

A WEEK AFTER THE VISIT to the park café, Harriet, drawn out to the balcony by a sound of rough singing, saw a double row of marching men rounding the church immediately below her. They crossed the main square.

Processions were not uncommon in Bucharest. They were organised for all sorts of public occasions, descending in scale from grand affairs in which even the cabinet ministers were obliged to take part, to straggles of school-children in the uniform of the Prince's youth movement.

The procession she saw now was different from any of the others. There was no grandeur about it, but there was a harsh air of purpose. Its leaders wore green shirts. The song was unknown to her, but she caught one word of it which was repeated again and again on a rising note:

"*Capitanul, Capitanul. . . .*"

The Captain. Who the captain was she did not know.

She watched the column take a sharp turn into the Calea Victoriei, then, two by two, the marchers disappeared from sight. When they were all gone, she remained on the balcony with a sense of nothing to do but stand there.

The flat behind her was silent. Despina had gone to market. Yakimov was in bed. (She sometimes wished she could seal herself off, as he did, in sleep.) Sasha – for he was still with them despite her decree of "one night only" – was somewhere up on the roof. (Like Yakimov, he had nowhere else to go.) Guy, of course, was busy at the University.

The "of course" expressed a growing resignation. She had looked forward to the end of the play and the end of the term, imagining she would have his companionship and support against their growing insecurity. Instead, she saw no more of him than before. The summer school, planned as a part-time occupation, had attracted so many Jews awaiting visas to the States, he had had to organise extra classes. Now he taught and lectured even during the siesta time.

On the day the oil engineers were expelled from Ploesti, the Pringles, like other British subjects, received their first notice to quit the country. Guy was just leaving the flat when a buff slip was handed him by a *prefectura* messenger. He passed it over to Harriet. "Take it to Dobson," he said. "He'll deal with it."

He spoke casually, but Harriet was disturbed by this order to pack and go. She said: "But supposing we have to leave in eight hours?"

"We won't have to."

His unconcern had made the matter seem worse to her, yet he had been proved right. Dobson had had their order rescinded, and that of the other British subjects in Bucharest, but the oil engineers had had to go.

At different times during the day, Harriet had seen their wives and children sitting about in cafés and restaurants. The children, becoming peevish and troublesome, had been frowned on by the Rumanians, who did not take children to cafés. The women, uprooted, looked stunned yet trustful, imagining perhaps that, in the end, it would all prove a mistake and they would return to their homes. Instead, they had had to take the train to Constanza and the boat to Istanbul.

Despite the Rumanian excuse that the expulsion had been carried out on German orders, the German Minister was reported to have said: "Now we know how Carol would treat us if we were the losers."

Well, the engineers, however unwillingly they may have gone, had gone to safety. Harriet could almost wish Guy and she had been forced to go with them.

While she stood on the balcony with these reflections in mind, the city shook. For an instant, it seemed to her that the balcony shelved down. She saw, or thought she saw, the cobbles before the church. In terror she put out her hand to hold to something, but it was as though the world had become detached in space. Everything moved with her and there was nothing on which to hold. An instant – then the tremor passed.

She hurried into the room and took up her bag and gloves. She could not bear to be up here on the ninth floor. She had to feel the earth beneath her feet. When she reached the pavement, that burnt like the Sahara sand, her impulse was to touch it.

Gradually, as she crossed the square and saw the buildings intact and motionless, the familiar crowds showing no unusual alarm, she lost her sense of the tremor's supernatural strangeness. Perhaps here, in this inland town with its empty sky ablaze and the sense of the land-mass of Europe lying to the west, earthquakes were common enough. But when, in the Calea Victoriei, she came on Bella Niculescu, she cried out, forgetting the check on their relationship: "Bella, did you feel the earthquake?"

"Didn't I just?" Bella responded as she used to respond: "It scared me stiff. Everyone's talking about it. Someone's just said it wasn't an earthquake at all, but an explosion at Ploesti. It's started a rumour that British agents are blowing up the oil-wells. Let's hope not. Things are tricky enough for us without that."

The first excitement of their meeting over, Bella looked disconcerted and glanced about her to see who might have witnessed it. Harriet felt she had done wrong in accosting her friend. Neither knowing what to say, they were about to make excuses and separate when they were distracted by a lusty sound of singing from the distance. Harriet recognised the refrain of *"Capitanul."* The men in green shirts were returning.

"Who are they?" Harriet asked.

"The Iron Guard, of course. Our local fascists."

"But I thought they'd been wiped out."

"That's" what we were told."

As the leaders advanced, lifting their boots and swinging their arms, Harriet saw they were the same young men she had observed in the spring, exiles returned from training in the German concentration camps. Then, shabby and ostracised, they had hung unoccupied about the street corners. Now they were marching on the crown of the road, forcing the traffic into the kerb, filling the air with their anthem, giving an impression of aggressive confidence.

Like everyone else, the two women silenced by the uproar of *"Capitanul,"* stood and watched the column pass. It was longer than it had been that morning. The leaders, well dressed and drilled, gained an awed attention, but this did not last. The middle ranks, without uniforms, were finding it difficult to keep in step, while the rear was brought up by a collection of out-of-works, no doubt converted to Guardism that very morning. Some were in rags. Shuffling, stumbling, they gave nervous side-glances and grins at the bystanders and their only contribution to the song was an occasional shout of *"Capitanul."* This was too much for the Rumanian sense of humour. People began to comment and snigger, then to laugh outright.

"Did you ever see the like!" said Bella.

Harriet asked: "Who is this '*capitanul*'?"

"Why, the Guardist leader – Codreanu: the one who was 'shot trying to escape', on Carol's orders, needless to say. A lot of his chums were shot with him. Some got away to Germany, but the whole movement was broken up. Who would have thought they'd have the nerve to reappear like this? Carol must be losing his grip."

From the remarks about them, it was clear that other onlookers were thinking the same. The procession passed, the traffic crawled after, and people went on their way. From the distance the refrain of "*Capitanul*" came in spasms, then died out.

Bella was saying: "They tried to make a hero of that Codreanu. It would take some doing. I saw him once. He looked disgusting with his dirty, greasy hair hanging round his ears. *And* he needed a shave. Oh, by the way,' she suddenly added, "you were talking about that Drucker boy. Funny you should mention him. A day or two after, I got a letter from Nikko and he'd been hearing about him too. Apparently they only took him off to do his military service. (I bet old Drucker had been buying his exemption. Trust *them*!) Anyway, the boy's deserted and the military are on the look-out. They've had orders to find him at all costs. I suppose it's this business of the fortune being in his name. They'll make him sign the money over."

"Supposing he refuses?"

"He wouldn't dare. Nikko says he could be shot as a deserter."

"Rumania's not at war."

"No, but it's a time of national emergency. The country's conscripted. Anyway, they're determined to get him. And I bet, when they do, he'll disappear for good. Oh, well!" Bella dismissed Sasha with a gesture. "I'm thinking of going to Sinai. I'm sick of stewing in this heat waiting for something to happen. My opinion is, nothing will happen. You should get Guy to take you to the mountains."

"We can't get away. He's started a summer school."

"Will he get any students at this time of the year?"

"He has quite a number."

"Jews, I bet?"

"Yes, they are mostly Jews."

Bella pulled down her mouth and raised her brows. "I wouldn't encourage that, my dear. If we're going to have the Iron Guard on the rampage again, there's no knowing what will happen. They beat up the Jewish students last time. But they're not only anti-Semitic, they're anti-British." She gave a grim, significant nod then, when she was satisfied that she had made an impression, her face cleared. "Must be off," she cheerfully said. "I've an appointment with the hairdresser." She lifted a hand, working her fingers in farewell, and disappeared in the direction of the square.

Harriet could not move. With the crowd pushing about her, she stood chilled and confused by perils. There was the peril of Sasha under the same roof as Yakimov, a potential informer – she did not know what the punishment might be for harbouring a deserter, but she pictured Guy in one of the notorious prisons Klein had described; and there was the more immediate threat from the marching Guardists.

Her instinct was to hurry at once to Guy and urge him to close down the summer school, but she knew she must not do that. Guy would not welcome her interference. He had put her out of his production on the grounds that no man could "do a proper job with his wife around". She wandered on as a preliminary to action, not knowing what action to take.

When she reached the British Propaganda Bureau, she came to a stop, thinking of Inchcape, who could, if he wished, put an end to the summer school. Why should she not appeal to him?

She stood for some minutes looking at the photographs of battleships and a model of the Dunkirk beaches, all of which had been in the window a month and were likely to remain, there being nothing with which to replace them.

She paused, not from fear of Inchcape but of Guy. Once before by speaking to Inchcape she had put a stop to one of Guy's activities and by doing so had brought about their first disagreement. Was she willing to bring about another?

Surely, she told herself, the important point was that her interference in the past had extricated Guy from a dangerous situation. It might do so again.

She entered the Bureau. Inchcape's secretary, knitting behind her typewriter, put up a show of uncertainty. Domnul Director might be too busy to see anyone.

"I won't keep him a moment," Harriet said, running upstairs before the woman could ring through. She found Inchcape stretched on a sofa with the volumes of *A la Recherche du Temps Perdu* open around him. He was wearing a shirt and trousers. Seeing her, he roused himself reluctantly and put on the jacket that hung on the back of the chair.

"Hello, Mrs. P.," he said with a smile that did not hide his irritation at being disturbed.

Harriet had not been in the office since the day they had come here to view Calinescu's funeral. Then the rooms had been dilapidated and the workmen had been fitting shelves. Now everything was painted white, the shelves were filled with books and the floor close-carpeted in a delicate shade of grey blue. On the Biedermeier desk, among other open books, lay some Reuter's sheets.

"What brings you here?" Inchcape asked.

"The Iron Guard."

He eyed her with his irritated humour: "You mean that collection of neurotics and nonentities who trailed past the window just now? Don't tell me they frightened you?"

Harriet said: "The Nazis began as a collection of neurotics and nonentities."

"So they did!" said Inchcape, smiling as though she must be joking. "But in Rumania fascism is just a sort of game."

"It wasn't a game in 1937 when Jewish students were thrown out of the University windows. I'm worried about Guy. He's alone there except for the three old ladies who assist him."

"There's Dubedat."

"What good would Dubedat be if the Guardists broke in?"

"Except when Clarence puts in an appearance, which isn't often, I'm alone here. I don't let it worry me."

She was about to say: "No one notices the Propaganda Bureau," but stopped in time and said: "The summer school is a provocation. All the students are Jews."

Although Inchcape retained his appearance of urbane unconcern, the lines round his mouth had tightened. He shot out his cuffs and studied his garnet cuff-links. "I imagine Guy can look after himself," he said.

His neat, Napoleonic face had taken on a remote expression intended to conceal annoyance. Harriet was silenced. She had come here convinced that the idea of the summer school had originated with Guy – now she saw her mistake. Inchcape was a powerful member of the organisation in which Guy hoped to make a career. Though she did not dislike him – they had come to terms early on – she still felt him an unknown quantity. Now she had challenged his vanity. There was no knowing what he might not say about Guy in the reports which he sent home.

When in the past she had been critical of Inchcape, saying: "He's so oddly mean: he economises on food and drink, yet spends a fortune on china or furniture in order to impress his guests," Guy had explained that Inchcape's possessions were a shield that hid the emotional emptiness of his life. Whatever they were, they were a form of self-aggrandisement. She realised the summer school was, too.

Knowing he could not be persuaded to close it, she decided to placate him. "I suppose it *is* important," she said.

He glanced up, pleased, and at once his tone changed: "It certainly is. It's a sign that we're not defeated here. Our morale is high. And we'll do better yet. I have great plans for the future . . ."

"You think we have a future?"

"Of course we. have a future. No one's going to interfere with us. Rumanian policy has always been to keep a foot in both camps. As for the Germans, what do they care so long as they're getting what they want? I'm confident that we'll keep going here. Indeed, I'm so confident that I'm arranging for an old friend, Professor Lord Pinkrose, to be flown out. He's agreed to give the Cantecuzene Lecture."

Meeting Harriet's astonished gaze, Inchcape gave a grin of satisfaction. "This is a time to show the flag," he said. "The lecture usually deals with some aspect of English literature. It will remind the Rumanians that we have one of the finest literatures in the world. And it is a great social occasion. The last time, we had eight princesses in the front row." He started to lead her towards the door. "Of course, it calls for a lot of organisation. I've got to find a hall and I'll have to book Pinkrose into an hotel. I'm not sure yet whether he'll come alone."

"He may bring his wife?"

"Good heavens, he has no wife." Inchcape spoke as though marriage were some ridiculous custom of primitive tribes. "But he's not so young as he was. He may want to bring a companion."

Inchcape opened the door and said in parting: "My dear child, we must maintain our equilibrium. Not so easy, I know, in this weather, when one's body seems to be melting inside one's clothes. Well, goodbye."

He shut the door on her, and she descended to the street with a sense of nothing achieved.

Shortly before the Guardists passed the University, Sophie Oresanu had come to see Guy in his office. The office had once been Inchcape's study, and the desk at which Guy sat still held Inchcape's papers. The shelves around were full of his books.

Sophie Oresanu, perched opposite Guy on the arm of a leather chair, had joined the summer school with enthusiasm. She now said: "I cannot work in such heat," leaning back with an insouciance that displayed her chief beauty, her figure. She pouted her heavily darkened mouth, then sighed and pushed a forefinger into one of her full, pasty cheeks. "At this time the city is terrible," she said.

Guy, viewing Sophie's languishings with indifference, remembered a conversation he had overheard between two male students:

"*La* Oresanu is not nice, she is *le* 'cock-tease'."

"*Ah, j'adore le* 'cock-tease'."

He smiled as she wriggled about on the chair-arm, flirting her rump at him. Poor girl! An orphan without a dowry, possessed of a freedom that devalued her in Rumanian eyes, she had to get herself a husband somehow. Remembering her grief when he had returned to Bucharest with a wife, he said the more indulgently: "The other students seem to be bearing up."

She shrugged off the other students. "My skin is delicate. I cannot tolerate much sun."

"Still, you're safer in the city this summer."

"No. They say the Russians are satisfied there will be no more troubles. Besides" – she made a disconsolate little gesture – "I am not happy at the summer school. All the students are Jews. They are not nice to me."

"Oh, come!" Guy laughed at her. "You used to complain that because you are half-Jewish, it was the Rumanians who were 'not nice' to you."

"It is true," she agreed: "No one is nice to me. I don't belong anywhere. I don't like Rumanian men. They live off women and despise them. They are so conceited. And the women here are such fools! They want to be despised. If the young man gives them *un coup de pied*, they do like this." She wriggled and threw up her eyes in a parody of sensual ecstasy. "Me, I wish to be respected. I am advanced, so I prefer Englishmen."

Guy nodded, sympathising with this preference. He had avoided marrying her himself, but he would have been delighted could he have married her off to a friend with a British passport. He had attempted to interest Clarence in her unfortunate situation, but Clarence had dismissed her, saying: "She's an affected bore," while of Clarence she said: "How terrible to be a man so unattractive to women!"

"Besides," she went on, "it is expensive, Bucharest. Every quarter my allowance goes, pouf! Other summers, for an economy, I let my flat and go to a little mountain hotel. Already I would have taken myself there, but my allowance is spent."

She paused, looking at him with a pathetic tilt of the head, expecting his usual query: "How much do you need?"

Instead, he said: "You'll get your allowance next month. Wait until then."

"My doctor says my health will suffer. Would you have me die?"

He smiled his embarrassment. Harriet had forced him to recognise Sophie's wiles and now he wondered how he had ever been taken in by them. Before his marriage, he had lent Sophie what he could not afford, seeing these loans, which were never repaid, as the price of friendship. With a wife as well as parents dependent on him, he had been forced to refuse her. His refusal had kept her at bay for the last few months and he was acutely discomforted at the prospect of having to refuse her again.

Leaning forward with one of the persuasive gestures she had effectively used in *Troilus*, she said: "I worked hard for the play. It was nice to have such a success, but I am not strong. It exhausted me. I have lost a kilo from my weight. Perhaps you like girls that are thin, but here they say it is not pretty."

So that was it! She wanted a return for services rendered. He looked down at his desk, having no idea, in the face of this, how to reject her claim. He could only think of Harriet, not certain whether the thought came as a protection or a threat. Anyway, he could use her as an excuse. Sophie knew she could get nothing out of Harriet.

He was beginning to recognise that Harriet was, in some ways, stronger than himself. And yet perhaps not stronger. He had a complete faith in his own morality and he would not let her override it. But she could be obdurate where he could not, and though he stood up to her, knowing if he did not he would be lost, he was influenced by her clarity of vision; unwillingly. It was probably significant that he was physically short-sighted. He could not recognise people until almost upon them. Their faces were like so many buns. Good-natured buns, he would have said, but Harriet did not agree. She saw them in detail and did not like them any the better for it.

He was troubled by her criticism of their acquaintances. He preferred to like people, knowing this fact was the basis of his influence over them. The sense of his will to like them gave them confidence: so they liked in return. He could see that Harriet's influence, given sway, could undermine his own successful formula for living and he felt bound to resist it. Yet there were occasions when he let her be obdurate for him.

While these thoughts were in his mind Sophie's chatter had come to a stop. Looking up, he found her watching him, puzzled and hurt that he let her talk on without the expected interruption.

As she concluded in a small, dispirited voice: "And I need only perhaps fifty thousand, not any more," she dropped all her little artifices and he saw the naïveté behind the whole performance. He had often, in the past, thought Sophie unfairly treated by circumstances. She had been forced, much too young, to face life alone with nothing but the weapons her sex provided. He thought: "The truth is, she's not much more than a scared kid," thankful nevertheless that he did not have fifty thousand to lend her.

He said as lightly as he could: "Harriet looks after the family finances now. She's better at it than I am. If anyone asks me for a loan, I have to refer them to her."

Sophie's expression changed abruptly. She sat upright, affronted that he should bring Harriet in between them. She rose, about to take herself off in indignation when a sound of marching and singing distracted her. They heard the repeated refrain "*Capitanul*".

"But that is a forbidden song," she said.

They reached the open window in time to see the leading green shirts pass the University. Sophie caught her breath. Guy, having talked with David's informants, was less surprised than she by this resurgence of the Iron Guards. He expected an appalled outcry from her, but she said nothing until the last stragglers had passed, then merely: "So! We shall have troubles again!"

He said: "You must have been at the University during the pogroms of 1938?"

She nodded. "It was terrible, of course, but I was all right. I have a good Rumanian name."

Remembering her annoyance with him, she turned suddenly and went without another word. She apparently had not been much disturbed by the spectacle of the marching Guardists, but Guy, when he returned to his desk, sat there for some time abstracted. He had seen a threat made manifest and knew exactly what he faced.

When they had discussed the organisation of the summer school, Guy had said to Inchcape: "There's only one thing against it. It will give rise to a concentration of Jewish students. With the new anti-Semitic policy, they might be in a dangerous position."

Inchcape had scoffed at this. "Rumanian policy has always been anti-Semitic and all that happens is the Jews get richer and richer."

Guy felt he could not argue further without an appearance of personal fear. Inchcape, who had retained control of the English Department, wanted a summer school. His organisation must do something to justify its presence here. More than that, there was his need to rival the Legation. Speaking of the British Minister, he would say: "The old charmer's not afraid to stay, so why should I be?" If anyone pointed out that the Minister, unlike Inchcape and his men, had diplomatic protection, Inchcape would say: "While the Legation's here, we'll be protected too."

Guy knew that Inchcape liked him and, because of that, he liked Inchcape. He also admired him. With no great belief in his own courage, he esteemed audacious people like Inchcape and Harriet. Yet he tended to pity them. Inchcape he saw as a lonely bachelor who had nothing in life but the authority which his position gave. If a summer school made Inchcape happy, then Guy would back it to the end.

Harriet, he felt, must be protected from the distrust that had grown out of an unloved childhood. He would say to himself: "O, stand between her and her fighting soul," touched by the small, thin body that contained her spirit. And he saw her unfortunate because life, which he took easily, was to her so unnecessarily difficult.

He picked up a photograph which was propped against the ink-stand on his desk. It had been taken in the Calea Victoriei: one of those small prints that had to be provided when one applied for a *permis de séjour*. In it Harriet's face – remarkable chiefly for its oval shape and the width of her eyes – was fixed in an expression of contemplative sadness. She looked ten years older than her age. Here was something so different from her usual vivacity that he said when he first saw it: "Are you really so unhappy?" She had denied being unhappy at all.

Yet, he thought, the photograph betrayed some inner discontent of the confused and the undedicated. He replaced the photograph with a sense of regret. He could help her if she would let him; but would she let him?

He remembered that when he had set about her political education, she had rebuffed him with: "I cannot endure organised thought," and, having taken up that position, refused to be moved from it.

Before she married, she had worked in an art gallery and been the friend of artists, mostly poor and unrecognised. He had pointed out to her that were they working in the Soviet Union they would be honoured and rewarded. She said: "Only if they conformed." He had argued that in every country everyone had to conform in some way or other. She said: "But artists must remain a privileged community if they're to produce anything important. They can't just echo what they're told. They have to think for themselves. That's why totalitarian countries can't afford them."

He had to admit that she, too, thought for herself. She would not be influenced. Feminine and intolerant though she might be in particular, she could take a wide general view of things. Coming from the narrowest, most prejudiced class, she had nevertheless declassed herself. The more the pity, then, that she had rejected the faith which gave his own life purpose. He saw her muddled and lost in anarchy and a childish mysticism.

What did she want? The question was for him the more difficult because he was content. He wanted nothing for himself. Possessions he found an embarrassment, a disloyalty to his family that had to survive on so little. While he was taking his degree, he had worked as a part-time teacher. His mother had also worked. Between them they had paid the rent and kept the family together.

He had envied no one except the men without responsibilities who had been free to go and fight in Spain. These men of the

International Brigade had been his heroes. He would still recite their poetry to himself, with emotion:

> "From small beginnings mighty ends:
> From calling rebel generals friends,
> From being taught at public schools
> To think the common people fools,
> Spain bleeds, and Britain wildly gambles
> To bribe the butcher in the shambles."*

The marching Guardists that morning had brought to his mind the Blackshirts and their "Monster Rally" in his home town. That was when his friend Simon had been beaten up and he had recognised the fact that one day he, too, would have to pay for his political faith.

Simon had arrived late and sat by himself. When the rest of them, sitting in a body, attempted to break up the meeting they were frogmarched into the street. Simon, left alone, had with a fanatical, almost hysterical courage, carried on the interruptions unsupported. The thugs had had him to themselves. They had dragged him out through a back door to a garage behind the hall. There he was eventually found unconscious.

At that time the stories of fascist savagery were only half believed. It was a new thing in the civilised world. The sight of Simon's injured and blackened face had appalled Guy. He told himself he knew now what lay ahead – and from that time had never doubted that his turn would come.

While he sat now at his desk, confronting his own physical fear, his door opened. It opened with ominous slowness. He stared at it. A tousled head appeared.

With playful solemnity, Toby Lush said: "Hello, old soul! I'm back again, you see!"

Harriet, walking home with all her fears intact, allayed them with the determination to act somehow. If she could not surmount one danger, she must tackle another. There was the situation at home – at least she need not tolerate that.

She must make it clear to Guy that they could not keep both Yakimov and Sasha. He had brought them into the flat. Now it

* Acknowledgements are due to Mr. Edgell Rickworth for kind permission to print his lines.

was for him to decide which of the two should remain, and to dismiss the other.

When, however, she entered the sitting-room and found Yakimov there, awaiting his luncheon, she decided for herself. Sasha was the one who needed their help and protection. As for Yakimov, only sheer indolence kept him from fending for himself. And she was sick of the sight of him. Her mind was made up. He must go. She would tell him so straightaway.

Yakimov, sprawled in the arm-chair, was drinking from a bottle of *ţuică* which Despina had brought in that morning. He moved uneasily at the sight of her and, putting a hand to the bottle, excused himself: "Took the liberty of opening it, dear girl. Came in dropping on m'poor old feet. The heat's killing me. Why not have a snifter yourself?"

She refused, but sat down near him. Used to being ignored by her, he became flustered and his hand was unsteady as he refilled his glass.

Her idea had been to order him, there and then, to pack and go, but she did not know how to begin.

His legs were crossed and one of his narrow shoes dangled towards her. His foot shook. Through a gap between sole and upper, she could see the tips of his toes and the rags of his violet silk socks. His dilapidation reproached her. He lay back, pretending nonchalance, but his large, flat-looking, green eyes flickered apprehensively, looking at her and away from her, so she could not speak.

He tried to make conversation, asking: "What's on the menu today?"

She said: "It is a meatless day. Despina bought some sort of river fish."

He sighed. "This morning," he said, "I was thinking about *blinis*. We used to get them at Korniloff's. They'd give you a heap of pancakes. You'd spread the bottom one with caviare, the next with sour cream, the next with caviare, and so on. Then you'd cut right through the lot. Ouch!" He made a noise in his throat as at a memory so delicious it was scarcely to be endured. "I don't know why we don't get them here. Plenty of caviare. The fresh grey sort's the best, of course." He gave her an expectant look. When she made no offer to prepare the dish, he glanced away as though excusing her inhospitality with: "I admit there's nothing to compare with the Russian Beluga. Or Osetrova, for that matter."

He sighed again and on a note of yearning, asked: "Do you remember ortolans? Delicious, weren't they?"

"I don't know. Anyway, I don't believe in killing small birds."

He looked puzzled. "But you eat chickens! All birds are birds. What does the size matter? Surely the important thing is the taste?"

Finding this reasoning unanswerable, she glanced at the clock, causing him to say: "The dear boy's late. Where *does* he get to these days?" His tone told Harriet that, having been dropped from Guy's scheme of things, he was feeling neglected.

She said: "He's started a summer school at the University. I expect you miss the fun of rehearsals?"

"They were fun, of course, but the dear boy did keep us at it. And, in the end, what came of it all?"

"What could come of it? I mean, so far from home and with a war on, you could not hope to make a career of acting?"

"A career! Never thought of such a thing."

His surprise was such, she realised he had probably looked for no greater reward than a lifetime of free food and drink. The fact was, he had never grown up. She had thought once that Yakimov was a nebula which, under Guy's influence, had started to evolve. But Guy, having set him in motion, had abandoned him to nothingness, and now, like a child displaced by a newcomer, he scarcely knew what had happened to him.

He said: "Was happy to help the dear boy."

"You'd never acted before, had you?"

"Never, dear girl, never."

"What did you do before the war? Had you a job of any sort?"

He looked slightly affronted by the question and protested: "I had m'remittance, you know."

She supposed he lived off a show of wealth: which was as good a confidence trick as any.

Conscious of her disapproval, he tried to improve things: "I did do a little work now and then. I mean, when I was a bit short of the ready."

"What sort of work?"

He shifted about under this enquiry. His foot began to shake again. "Sold cars for a bit," he said. "Only the best cars, of course: Rolls-Royces, Bentleys . . . M'own old girl's an Hispano-Suiza. Finest cars in the world. Must get her back. Give you a run in her."

"What else did you do?"

"Sold pictures, bric-à-brac . . ."

"Really?" Harriet was interested. "Do you know about pictures?"

"Can't say I do, dear girl. Don't claim to be a professional. Helped a chap out now and then. Had a little flat in Clarges Street. Would hang up a picture, put out a bit of bric-à-brac, pick up some well-heeled gudgeon, indicate willingness to sell. 'Your poor old Yaki's got to part with family treasure.' You know the sort of thing. Not work, really. Just a little side-line." He spoke as though describing a respected way of life, then, as his shifting eye caught hers, his whole manner suddenly disintegrated. He struggled upright in his seat and, with head hanging, gazing down into his empty glass he mumbled: "Expecting m'remittance any day now. Don't worry. Going to pay back every penny I owe . . ."

They were both relieved to hear Guy letting himself into the flat. He entered the room, smiling broadly as though he were bringing Harriet some delightful surprise. "You remember Toby Lush?" he said.

"It's wonderful to see you again! Wonderful!" Toby said, gazing at Harriet, his eyes bulging with excited admiration, giving the impression that theirs was some eagerly awaited reunion.

She had met him once before and barely remembered him. She did her best to respond but had never been much impressed by him. He was in the middle twenties, heavy-boned and clumsy in movement. His features were pronounced, his skin coarse, yet his face seemed to be made of something too soft and pliable for its purpose.

Sucking at his pipe, he turned to Guy and jerked out convulsively: "You know what she always makes me think of? Those lines of Tennyson: 'She walks in beauty like the night of starless climes and something skies.' "

"Byron," said Guy.

"Oh, crumbs!" Toby clapped a hand over his eyes in exaggerated shame. "I'm always doing it. It's not that I don't know: I don't remember." He suddenly noticed Yakimov and crying: "Hello, hello, hello," he rushed forward with outstretched hand.

Harriet went into the kitchen to tell Despina there would be a guest for luncheon. When she returned, Toby, with many irrelevant guffaws, was describing the situation in the Transylvanian capital from which he had evacuated himself.

Although Cluj had been under Rumanian rule for twenty years, it was still a Hungarian city. The citizens only waited for the despised regime to end.

"It's not that they're pro-German," he said, "they just want the Hunks back. They shut their eyes to the fact that when the Hunks come the Huns'll follow. If you point it out, they make excuses. A woman I know, a Jewess, said: 'We don't want it for ourselves, we want it for our children.' They think it'll happen any day now."

Toby was standing by the open French window, the dazzle of out-of-doors limning his ragged outline. "I can tell you," he said, "the only Englishman among that lot, I had to keep my wits about me. And what do you think happened before I left? The Germans installed a Gauleiter – a Count Frederich von Flügel. 'Get out while the going's good,' I told myself."

"Freddi von Flügel!" Yakimov broke in in delighted surprise. "Why, he's an old friend of mine. A dear old friend." He looked happily about him. "When I get the Hispano, we might all drive to Cluj and see Freddi. I'm sure he'd do us proud."

Toby gazed open-mouthed at Yakimov, then his shoulders shook as though giving some farcical imitation of laughter. "You're a joker," he said and Yakimov, though surprised, seemed gratified to be thought one.

While they were eating, Harriet asked Toby: "Will you remain in Bucharest?"

"If I can get some teaching," he said. "I'm a free-lancer, no organisation behind me. Came out on my own, drove the old bus all the way. Bit of an adventure. The fact is, if I don't work, I don't eat. Simple as that." He gazed at Guy, supplicant and inquiring. "Hearing you were short-staffed, I turned up on the doorstep."

The question of his employment had obviously been raised already, for Guy merely nodded and said: "I must see what Inchcape says before taking anyone on."

Harriet looked again at Toby, considering him not so much as a teacher as a possible help in time of trouble. She had noticed his heavy brogues. He was wearing grey flannel trousers bagged at the knees and a sagging tweed jacket, much patched with leather. It was the uniform of most young English civilians and yet on him it looked like a disguise. 'The man's man!' The last time he had arrived in Bucharest, during one of the usual invasion scares, he had fled from Cluj in a panic: but she was less inclined to condemn panic since she had experienced it herself. How would he react to a sudden Guardist attack? All this pipe-sucking masculinity, this casual costume, would surely require him, when the time came, to prove himself "a good man in a tight corner". She looked at Guy, who was saying: "If Inchcape agrees, I might be able to give you twenty hours a week. That should keep you going."

Toby ducked his head gratefully, then asked: "What about lectures?"

"I would only need you to teach."

"I used to lecture at Cluj – Mod. Eng. Lit. I must say, I enjoy giving the odd lecture." Toby, from behind his hair and moustache, gazed at Guy like an old sheepdog confident he would be put to use. Harriet felt sorry for him. He probably imagined, as others had done before him, that Guy was easily persuadable. The truth was, that in authority Guy could be inflexible. Even if he needed a lecturer, he would not choose one who mistook Byron for Tennyson.

"The other day," Yakimov suddenly spoke, slowly and sadly, out of his absorption in his food, "I was thinking, strange as it must seem, I haven't seen a banana for about a year." He sighed at the thought.

The Pringles had grown too used to him to react to his chance observations, but Toby rocked about, laughing as though Yakimov's speech had been one of hilarious impropriety.

Yakimov modestly explained: "Used to be very fond of bananas."

When luncheon was over and Yakimov had retired to his room Harriet looked for Toby's departure, but when he eventually made a move Guy detained him saying: "Stay to tea. On my way back to the University, I'll take you to the Bureau to meet Inchcape."

Harriet went into the bedroom. Determined to incite him to act while the power to incite was in her, she called Guy in, shut the door of the sitting-room and said: "You must speak to Yakimov. You must tell him to go."

Mystified by the urgency of her manner and unwilling to obey, he said: "All right, but not now."

"Yes, *now*." She stood between him and the door. "Go in and see him. It's too risky having him here with Sasha around. He must go."

"Well, if you say so." Guy's agreement was tentative, a playing for time. He paused, then said: "It would be better if you spoke to him."

"You brought him here, you must get rid of him."

"It's a difficult situation. I was glad to have him here while he was rehearsing. He worked hard and helped to make the show a success. In a way, I owe him something. I can't just tell him to go now the show's over, but it's different for you. You can be firm with him."

"What you mean is, if there's anything unpleasant to be done, you prefer that I should do it?"

Cornered, he reacted with rare exasperation: "Look here, darling, I have other things to worry about. Sasha is up on the roof. Yakimov's not likely to see him and probably wouldn't be interested if he did see him. So why worry? Now I must go back and talk to Toby."

She let him go, knowing nothing more would be gained by talk. And she realised it would always be the same. If action had to be taken, she would have to be the one to take it. That was the price to be paid for a relationship that gave her more freedom than she had bargained for. Freedom, after all, was not a basic concept of marriage. As for Guy, he did not want a private life: he chose to live publicly. She said to herself: "He's crassly selfish" – an accusation that would have astounded his admirers.

She went over to the window and leant out. Looking down the drop of nine floors to the cobbles below, she thought of the kitten that had fallen from the balcony five months before. The scene dissolved into a marbling of blue and gold as her eyes filled with tears, and she suffered again the outrageous grief with which she had learnt of the kitten's death. It had been her kitten. It had acknowledged her. It did not bite her. She was the only one who had no fear of it. Possessed by memory of the little red-golden flame of a cat that for a few weeks had hurtled itself, a ball of fur and claws, about the flat, she wept: "My kitten. My poor kitten," feeling she had loved it as she could never love anything or anybody. Guy, after all, did not permit himself to be loved in this way.

She did not return to the room until she heard Despina taking in the tea things. Toby was saying: "But someone's certain to march in here sooner or later. I suppose the Legation'll give us proper warning?"

Guy did not know and did not seem much to care. He said:

"The important thing is not to panic. We must keep the school going."

Toby ducked his head in vehement agreement. "Still," he said, "one must keep the old weather eye open."

Yakimov had appeared for tea in his tattered brocade dressing-gown and when Guy and Toby went off to see Inchcape there he still was, his apprehensions forgotten, comfortably eating his way through the cakes and sandwiches that were left. Well, here was her opportunity to say: "You have been living on top of us since Easter. I've had enough of you. Please pack your bags and go." At which Yakimov, with his most pitiful expression, would ask: "But where can poor Yaki go?" There had been no answer to that question four months before, and there was no answer now. He had exhausted his credit in Bucharest. No one would take him in. If she wanted to get rid of him, she would have to pack his bags herself and lock him out. And if she did that, he would probably sit on the doorstep until Guy brought him back in again.

When he had emptied the plates he stretched and sighed: "Think I'll take a bath." He went, and she had still said nothing. Knowing herself no more capable than Guy of throwing Yakimov out, she had thought of a different move. She would go and see Sasha. The boy probably imagined that they, like the diplomats, were outside Rumanian law. She could explain to him that by shelter-ing him Guy ran the same risk as anyone else. Then what would Sasha do?

The problem of their responsibility lay between desperation and desperation. The only loophole was the possibility that Sasha could think of a friend who might shelter him, perhaps a Jewish school-friend. Or there was his stepmother, who was claiming maintenance from the Drucker fortune. Somebody surely would take him in.

She went out to the kitchen. Despina was on the fire-escape, bawling down to other servants who had a free hour or so before it was time to prepare dinner. Feeling anomalous in these regions, Harriet slipped past her and started to ascend the iron ladder, but Despina missed nothing. "That's right," she called out. "Visit the poor boy. He's lonely up there."

Despina had adopted Sasha. Although Despina had been told that he must not come into the flat, Harriet had several times heard them laughing together in the kitchen. Despina scoffed at her fears, saying she could pass the boy off to anyone as her relative. Sasha was settling into a routine of life here and would soon, if undisturbed, become, like Yakimov, an unmovable part of the household.

The roof, high above its neighbours, was in the full light of the lowering sun. The sun was still very warm. Heat not only poured down on to the concrete but rose from it.

A row of wooden huts, like bathing-boxes, stood against the northern parapet, numbered one for each flat. Harriet, as she reached the roof-level, could see Sasha sitting outside his hut, holding a piece of stick which he had been throwing for a dog. The dog, a rough, white mongrel, apparently lived up here.

As soon as he saw her, Sasha got to his feet while the dog remained expectant, swaying a tail like a dirty feather.

She explained her visit by saying: "How are you managing up here? Is Despina looking after you?"

"Oh, yes." He was eagerly reassuring, adding thanks for all that was done for him. The fact of his presence being a danger to them seemed not to have occurred to him.

While he talked she looked beyond him through the open door of the hut where he was living. The hut had no window and was ventilated by a hole in the door. On the floor was a straw pallet that Despina must have borrowed for him, a blanket, some books Guy had brought up and a stub of candle.

Before she left England she would have believed it impossible for a human being to survive through the freezing winter, the torrid summer, in a cell like this. She had discovered in Rumania that there were millions to whom such shelter would be luxury. She took a step towards it but, repelled by the interior smell and heat, came to a stop saying: "It's very small."

Sasha smiled as though it were his place to apologise. He had been here only a few days but he was already putting on weight. When she had seen him on the night of his reappearance, she had been repelled by his abject squalor. Now, clean, wearing a shirt and trousers Guy had given him, the edge of fear gone from his face, his hair beginning to show like a shadow over his head, he was already the boy she had first met in the Drucker flat.

He was rather an ugly boy with his long nose, close-set eyes and long drooping body, but there was an appeal about his extreme gentleness of manner, which on their first meeting had made her think of some nervous animal grown meek in captivity. Because of this, he seemed completely familiar to her.

Feeling no restraint with him, she put out her hand and said: "Let us sit on the wall," and jumping up, she settled herself on the low parapet that surrounded the roof. From here she could see almost the whole extent of the city, the roofs gleaming through a heat-mist that was beginning to grow dense and golden with evening. Sasha came and leant against the wall beside her. She asked him what he passed for among the servants who slept in the other huts.

He said: "Despina says I come from her village."

He looked nothing like a peasant, but he might be the son of some Jewish tallyman. Anyway, no one, it seemed, took much notice of him. Despina said the kitchen quarters of Bucharest harboured thousands of deserters.

"How long had you been in Bucharest when we met you?" she asked.

"Two nights." He told her that he had separated from his company in Czernowitz and stowed away in a freight train that brought him to the capital. On the night of his arrival, he had slept under a market stall near the station, but had been turned out soon after midnight by some beggars whose usual sleeping place it was. The next night he had tried to sleep in the park, but there had been one of the usual spy scares on. The police, in their zeal, had tramped about all night, forcing him repeatedly to move his position.

He had not known what had happened to his family. When in Bessarabia, he had written to his aunts but received no reply. When he reached Bucharest, he had looked up at the windows of the family flat and seeing the curtains changed, realised the Druckers were not there. In the streets he had caught sight of people he knew, but in his fear of re-arrest dared approach no one until he saw Guy.

While he talked, he glanced shyly aside at her, smiling, all the misery gone from his gaze.

She said: "You know that your family have left Rumania?"

"Guy told me." If he knew they had taken flight immediately, without a backward glance for him or his father, he did not seem much concerned.

She decided the time had come to mention the possibility of his finding another shelter. She said: "Your stepmother is still here, of course. Don't you think she could help you? She might be willing to let you live with her."

He whispered: "Oh, no," startled and horrified by the suggestion.

"She wouldn't hurt you, would she? She wouldn't give you away?"

"Please don't tell her anything about me."

His tone was a complete rejection of his stepmother. So much for her. Then what about the possible friends? She said: "You must have known a lot of people in Bucharest. Isn't there anyone who would give you a better hiding-place than this?"

He explained that, having been at an English public school, he had no friends of long standing here. She asked, what about his University acquaintances? He simply shook his head. He had known people, but not well. There seemed to be no one on whom he could impose himself now. Jews did not make friends easily. They were suspicious and cautious in this anti-Semitic society, and Sasha had been enclosed by a large family. The Druckers formed their own community, one which depended on Drucker's power for its safety. His arrest had been the signal for flight. If they had hesitated, they might all have suffered.

Watching him, wondering what they were to do with him, Harriet caught Sasha's glance and saw her questions had disturbed him. He had again the fearful, wary look of the hunted, and she knew she was no better than Guy at displacing the homeless. Indeed, she was worse for, unlike Guy, she had been resolved and had failed. When it came to a battle of human needs, her resolution did not count for much.

Glancing away from her, Sasha saw the dog, stick in mouth, patiently awaiting his attention. He put out his hand to it.

The extreme gentleness of his gesture moved her. She suddenly felt his claim on her and knew it was the claim of her lost red kitten, and of all the animals to whom she had given her love in childhood because there had been no one else who wanted it. She wondered why Yakimov had not moved her in this way. Was it because he lacked the quality of innocence?

She said to Sasha: "There's someone living with us in the flat, a Prince Yakimov. We have to keep him for the moment, he has nowhere else to go, but I don't trust him. You must be careful. Don't let him see you." She slid down from the wall, saying as she left him: "This is a wretched hut. It's the best we can do for the moment. If Yakimov leaves – and I hope he will – you can have his room."

Sasha smiled after her, his fears forgotten, content like a stray animal that, having found a resting-place, has no complaint to make.

Next morning only *Timpul* mentioned the "trickle of riffraff in green shirts that provoked laughter in the Calea Victoriei". By evening this attitude had changed. Every paper reported the march with shocked disapproval, for the King had announced that were it repeated the military would be called out to fire on the marchers.

The Guardists went under cover again, but this, people said, was the result not of the king's threat but an address made to the Guardists by their chief, Horia Sima, who was newly returned from exile in Germany. He advised them to leave off their green shirts and sing "*Capitanul*" only in their hearts. The time for action was not yet come.

Their leading spirits again hung unoccupied about the streets, sombre, shabby, malevolent, awaiting the call. These men, whom it seemed only Harriet had noticed in the spring, suddenly became visible and significant to everyone, giving rise to fresh excitements and apprehensions, and renewed terror among the Jews.

PART TWO

The Captain

6

THE NEXT TIME HARRIET WENT UP to see Sasha she took with her a bowl of apricots and a copy of *L'Indépendence Romaine*. The paper contained the date on which Drucker's trial would begin, an announcement overshadowed by the news that the Hungarian premier and his foreign minister had been granted an audience with the Führer. What were the Hungarians after?

Harriet, eating her supper alone, made her way through the leading article on Transylvania: "*le berceau de la Nation, le coeur de la Patrie*". No mention was made of Hungary's old claim to this territory, but at the end the article asked: Had the Rumanian people not suffered enough in their efforts to preserve Balkan peace? Was yet another sacrifice to be demanded of them? And answered: No, yet again no. If rumours of such a sacrifice were circulating they must be instantly suppressed.

The Pringles had been invited to dine that evening with a Jewish couple who, granted a visa to the United States, wanted to know how to conduct themselves in the English-speaking world. Invitations of this sort were frequent. Though Guy knew no more about the States than he had learnt from American films, he was always happy to give advice, but Harriet was becoming bored with listening to it. She said: "You go. They don't really want me," for at the back of her mind was the intention to see Sasha again.

As she climbed up the iron ladder to roof-level, she was startled by the grandeur of the sky from which plumes of puce and crimson had been pulled downwards by the setting sun. The concrete glowed like marble, but for all the richness of the light the air was heavy, almost thunderous, though thunder was rare here.

Sasha was sitting on the parapet, an intent and solitary figure, scribbling on something. As she stepped up on to the roof, she saw him lift his head and stare towards the cathedral which, built on high ground, overlooked the city. Its golden domes were afire now and the whole building stood like an embossed enamel against the luminous darkness of the lower sky.

At the sound of her step, he jerked his head round and his face brightened at the sight of company, so she ceased to feel any need to account for her visit.

She asked where the dog was.

He said: "It didn't live here. Despina was keeping it for someone. Now it has gone home."

"Do any of the servants sleep on the roof?"

"No, there's no one but me."

As she had thought, these advertised 'second servant rooms' were merely an attempt to smarten the jerry-built, ill-planned block. No one needed or could afford the extra staff.

She felt sorry for the boy alone up here. She put the apricots on the parapet and said: "Those are for you," then she looked at his sketch of the cathedral done on the concrete with a lump of rough charcoal Despina had found for him somewhere. She said: "It's quite good."

"Is it?" he asked eagerly. "You really like it?" so surprised and trusting of her judgement that she felt ashamed of her unthinking praise, and looked at it again. It was boldly done, the rough surface of the parapet giving the lines a comic distortion.

"Yes, it is good," she confirmed her own judgement and he smiled in naïve pleasure.

"If you like this," he said, "you'd like some things I saw in Bessarabia. They were super."

As she hoisted herself on to the wall, she asked: "Where were you in Bessarabia?"

He had been on the frontier, in a fortress that was as bare, cold and ill-lit as it would have been in the Middle Ages. There was nothing at all in the district but a village that comprised two rows of desolate huts with a pitted mud track running between. The whole area had been raided so often, it was like the environs of a volcano: only the most desperate would make a home there. In winter it had been swept by gales and blizzards and in spring, when the snow melted, it became a quagmire.

"The village was jolly queer," he said. "All the people living there were Jews."

"Why did they live there, of all places?"

"I don't know. Perhaps they'd been driven out of everywhere else."

She had imagined she would have difficulty in persuading him to talk about his experiences, but it seemed he had already put them at a distance. He had adopted Guy and Harriet in place of his family so, feeling protected again, he could chat away as though nothing had ever happened in his life to check his confidence. While he talked, she wondered at the simplicity of a nature able so rapidly to regain itself.

"And what about these things you saw? Were they drawings?"

"No. Paintings. They were shop-signs."

He described the Jews of the villages – the men gaunt wraiths in their tattered caftans, the women wearing black woollen wigs over heads shaven because they suffered from some skin disease which had died out elsewhere. They were sly and obsequious, and Sasha, who had always known Jews who were the richest members of the community, had been amazed to find any as debased as these.

"They couldn't even read," he said. "They were terribly poor – but they could do these paintings."

"What were they like?"

"Oh – sort of fantastic. People, animals and things, in the most super colours. I'd always go and look at them when I could."

He spoke as though the shop signs had been his only entertainment and she asked: "Did you have any friends in the army?"

"I knew a boy in the village. His father kept the place where the soldiers went to drink *ţuică*. It was just a room, very dirty, but all the soldiers said the man was an awful crook and making lots of money."

Sasha described the boy, thin, white-faced, in a black skull-cap, knickerbockers that fastened below the knee and black stockings and boots. Tufts of red down were appearing on his glazed white cheeks, and red ritual curls hung before his ears. "You never saw anyone look so funny," Sasha said.

"But all the Orthodox Jews look like that," Harriet said. "Surely you've seen them down the Dâmboviţa?"

Sasha shook his head. He had never been near the ghetto area. His aunts would not allow him to go there.

"Did you speak to the boy?" Harriet asked.

"I tried, but it wasn't much good. He only spoke Yiddish and Ukrainian, and he was very shy. Sometimes he'd run away when he saw me in the street."

"But hadn't you friends among the soldiers?"

"Well . . ." Sasha sat silent for some moments, staring down and rubbing the palm of his hand on the rough edge of the wall. "Yes, I did have a friend." He spoke as though making an admission painful to him. "He was a Jew, too. He was called Marcovitch."

"Did he run away with you?"

Sasha shook his head, then after a moment said: "He died."

"How did he die?"

Sasha said nothing for some minutes, and she saw there was an area of experience, unnaturally imposed upon his natural innocence, to which he would not willingly revert. She said persuasively: "Tell me what happened."

"Well . . ." He spoke casually, like one old in knowledge. "You know what it is like here. If anything happens, they say: 'It's the Jews.' In the army it was the same. They blamed the Jews for Bessarabia. They said we called in the Russians because of the new laws against us. As though we could!" He looked at her and laughed. "Just silly, of course." His self-conscious attempt at sophistication made her realise how young he was.

"Did they ill-treat you?" she asked.

"Not very much. Some of them were quite decent, really. It was beastly for everyone, being conscripted. The barracks were full of bugs. When I first went there I was bitten so much, I looked as though I had measles. And every day maize or beans, but not much. There was money for food, but the officers kept it."

"Is that why you ran away?"

"No." He picked up his charcoal and began darkening the lines of his drawing that had started to disappear with the light. "It was because of Marcovitch."

"Who died? When did he die?"

"After we were ordered out of Bessarabia. We were on the train and he went down the corridor and he didn't come back. I asked everyone, but they said they hadn't seen him. While we were waiting at Czernowitz – we stayed on the platform three days because there were no trains – they were saying a body had been found on the railway-line half-eaten by wolves. Then one of the men said to me: 'You heard what happened to your friend, Marcovitch? That was his body. You be careful, you're a Jew, too.' And I knew they'd thrown him out of the train. I was afraid. It could happen to me. So in the night, when they were all asleep, I ran down the line and hid in a goods train. It took me to Bucharest."

While they were talking, the sound of the last post came thin and clear from the palace yard. The sunset clouds had stretched and narrowed and faded in the sky, leaving a zenith of clear turquoise in which a few stars were appearing. The square below was lit not only by its lamps but by a reflection from the sky that was like a sheen on water.

She thought she had made Sasha talk enough and Guy might soon be back. She slid down from the wall and said: "I must go, but I'll come again." Before she left, she handed Sasha the paper. "It says your father's trial starts on August 14th. The sooner it is over, the better. After all, he may be acquitted."

Sasha took the paper, which could not be read in this light, and said: "Yes," but his agreement was simply politeness. He knew as well as she did that the law required Drucker's conviction before his oil holdings could be forfeit to the Crown. What hope then of an acquittal?

As she set out across the roof area, Sasha went to his hut. When she turned to descend, she could see he had already lit his candle and, kneeling, was bent over the paper that was spread on the ground before him.

7

YAKIMOV SAW THE GREAT YELLOW CAR outside the Legation as soon as he turned into the road. The hood was down, hidden beneath a panel, so there was nothing to break the long, fine line from nose to tail. His eyes filled with tears. "The old girl herself," he said. As he added: "I love her," he scarcely knew whether he referred to the Hispano-Suiza or to Dollie, who had given it to him.

The car was now seven years old, but he had taken care of it as he had never taken care of himself. He opened the bonnet and examined the engine. When he closed it, he patted the stork that flew down-drooping wings from the radiator cap. He walked round the car, noting that the body was dusty but no worse, and the pigskin leather of the seats was in "good shape". "Bless the old Jugs," he thought. "They haven't treated her so badly."

He spent so long rejoicing over the car that Foxy Leverett noticed him from a window and came out to give him the keys.

"She's a beaut," said Foxy.

Even during the days of triumph in *Troilus*, Yakimov had not received much attention from Foxy, who accorded the same off-hand goodwill to everyone. Now, acknowledging a compeer in the owner of a Hispano-Suiza, he became voluble: "Went like a bird. The worst road in Europe, but she did a steady sixty. If I hadn't got the Dion-Bouton, I'd make you an offer."

"Wouldn't sell her for a king's ransom, dear boy," Yakimov said, adding with a hint of hauteur: "In this part of the world I'd never get what she's worth. The chassis alone cost two and a half thou, sterling. Body by Fernandez. Wonderful work. Had one before this. Lovely job. Body built all of tulip wood. You should have seen it. Had m'man then, of course. He kept it like a piece of Chippendale."

Yakimov talked for some time, too elated to feel the sweltering sunlight. Foxy, his hair and moustache the colour of marigolds, his eyes as blue as the eyes of a china doll, turned peony-pink under the heat. When Yakimov paused he cut short his reminiscences by saying: "I put two hundred litres in the tank at Predeal. There's plenty left."

"I'm in your debt, dear boy." Yakimov became more subdued. "Don't know what I owe, but it'll all be settled when m'remittance shows up."

"That's all right," said Foxy.

His nonchalance prompted Yakimov to try his luck: "Like to get her cleaned, dear boy. Wonder if you could spare a thou?"

Foxy's moustache twitched, but, trapped and making the best of it, he pulled out some notes and handed one over.

"*Dear boy!*" Yakimov took it gratefully. "Y'know," he said, "if you'd get me a C.D. plate, there's no end to the stuff we could run in and out. And not only currency, mind you. There's a demand here for rhino horn – aphrodisiac, y'know. You can get it in Turkey. And hashish . . ."

With a guffaw of derisive laughter, Foxy turned on his heel and shot back into the chancellery.

Yakimov climbed into the car and started it up – the Hispano was an extravagance: despite its size and power it was designed to seat only two persons – and as he gazed along the six-foot bonnet, he saw his status restored and his old glory returned to him. He had not driven for eleven months. He took himself to the Chaussée for a trial run. Discomposed at first by the delirium howl of passing cars, he steadily regained his old confidence and felt the impulse to outstrip them. He rounded the fountain at the extreme end of the Chaussée, then, returning, pressed down on the accelerator and saw with satisfaction that he was touching ninety. Unperturbed by the klaxons that bayed about him like a hungry pack, he swung into the square, circled round it and stopped outside the Pringles' block. Having had no tea, he was, he realised, a trifle peckish.

After tea he dressed in such items of decent clothing as remained to him. In the Athénée Palace that morning, he had noticed the main rooms were being decorated for a reception.

The Rumanians these days were in a buoyant mood, for the Hungarian ministers had left Munich apparently having achieved nothing. When this was reported, Hadjimoscos soberly told his circle: "The Führer said to them: 'Do not forget, I am Rumania's father, too.' Such a sentiment is very gratifying, don't you think? Baron Steinfeld tells me it is thanks to the fine fellows in the Iron Guard that we stand so high in German favour."

To Yakimov the Guardists were merely the murderers of Calinescu. He had been amused by the fact they claimed still to be led by a young man two years in his grave. He seized upon this mention of them to make a joke: "I take it, dear boy, you refer to the non-existent members of the totally extinguished party which is led by a ghost?"

Hadjimoscos stared coldly at Yakimov a moment before he said: "Such quips are not *de rigueur* in these times," and paused impressively before adding: "They are not even safe."

Yakimov was used to Hadjimoscos' changes of mood and had to accept them. That morning he had listened in silence while the reception was discussed with a respect he found bewildering in view of the fact no one present had been invited. It was to be an Iron Guard reception, held in defiance of the King, to promulgate the growing power of the party.

"Under the circumstances," Hadjimoscos said, with knowing complacency, "it is not surprising that people like us, members of the old aristocracy, have received no *official* invitation, but I am confident it will be indicated to us that our presence is desired."

Yakimov was surprised that any sort of gathering could be given in defiance of the King, but told himself: "Hadji is pretty cute. Hadji knows which way the wind blows," and that evening, although he had not been invited, he prepared to attend the reception himself.

The hotel was only a hundred yards away, but when he set out he took the Hispano as an earnest of past opulence, a visa to better times. As he drew up outside the hotel, Baron Steinfeld was arriving with Princess Teodorescu, both in full evening dress, and he was a trifle disconcerted, not having realised the occasion merited such a rig, but was gratified to see the Baron eyeing the Hispano with interest.

The Princess had not recognised Yakimov since last September, when Hadjimoscos had brought him to her party; but now she lifted the tail of one of her silver-fox furs and waggled it playfully as she called to him: "Ah, *cher prince*, you have been a long time out of sight." Yakimov sped towards her and kissed her hand in its rose-coloured glove. The Princess was noted for the directness of her approach and now, without preamble, she said: "*Cher prince*, I want so much tickets for the Drucker trial."

In the failing light, the runnels of her handsome, haggard face seemed filled with ink. Her eyes, within their heavily darkened lids, were fixed avidly on Yakimov as she explained: "I received, of course, my two-three tickets, but always my friends are asking me: 'Please get for me a ticket.' What can I do? Now you, *mon prince*, are *journalist*. You have many tickets, isn't that so? Do for me a little favour. Give me two-three tickets!"

The tickets for the trial had been allotted to persons of importance, who now were selling them for enormous sums to persons of less importance. Yakimov, needless to say, had none, but he smiled happily. "Dear girl, of course, I'll do what I can. 'Fraid I've given mine away, but I'll get more. There are ways and means. Leave it to your Yaki."

"But how kind!" said the Princess and as a mark of favour she off-loaded her foxes into Yakimov's arms. Delighted by this hot and heavy burden, he said: "We must get a lead for these, dear girl," and the Princess smiled.

As they strolled to the hotel, the Baron said: "It is remarkable, don't you think, that the Germans have not yet made their invasion of the British Isles?" His tone suggested that it was not only remarkable but unfortunate. When Yakimov said nothing, the Baron went on: "Still, there are grave newses from England. They say that racing under Jockey Club rules has been given up. Clearly all is not well there." He turned appealingly to Yakimov. "Surely it is time to end this foolish disagreement between our great countries. You are a prince of old Russia: cannot you induce your English friends to turn their armours against the Soviets?"

Yakimov looked as though he could, but did not feel he should. "Don't want to start any more trouble, do we?" he said. They had reached the red carpet and then he was able to change the subject. "Bit of a do on, I see."

"A reception given by the Iron Guard leaders," said Steinfeld. "An important occasion. Horia Sima is to be present."

The vestibule was banked with carnations, tuberoses and ferns. A notice informed the public that only ticket holders would be admitted to the main salon, which could be seen through the glass doors already very crowded. Hoping to identify himself with the occasion, Yakimov said: "I hear that my dear old friend Freddie von Flügel has been appointed Gauleiter in Cluj. He has asked me up to stay with him."

"Gauleiter? Indeed! A position of power," said Steinfeld, but the Princess was less impressed: "Surely," she said, "you are an Englishman? Is it correct, in time of war, to visit the enemy?"

The Baron brushed this query aside: "People in our position can dispense with such *convenances*," he said, and Yakimov agreed with enthusiasm.

They were approaching the salon entrance where some young men stood on guard. Yakimov, keeping close to his companions, still had hope of entering under their auspices, but the Princess was having none of that. He had been rewarded enough. She stopped, took her furs out of his arms, and said: "Well, toot-el-ee-ooh, as you English say. Do not forget my two-three tickets," and she handed the furs to Steinfeld. Yakimov knew himself dismissed.

He watched as the couple reached the salon entrance. There they were stopped and made to produce their invitations. There was no sign of a buffet inside and the guests were drinking wine. Deciding the "do" looked a pretty poor one, Yakimov went into the English Bar.

At this moment the Pringles, crossing the square, heard behind them the furious and persistent hooting of an old-fashioned motor-horn. They moved to the pavement. The hooting persisted. Supposing it was some sort of anti-British demonstration, they did not look round. Britain was rumoured to be trying to sell her oil shares to Russia and the Rumanian Cabinet had declared it would take steps to prevent any such perfidy. Anti-British feeling was growing stronger.

The hooting, drawing nearer, demanded attention, and the Pringles turned to see an old, mud-coloured car being driven at them by Toby Lush. Toby grinned. Inchcape had approved his appointment and he had started work at the University. He stopped the car. Confident of welcome, he thrust out his disordered, straw-coloured head and shouted "Hello, there!"

"Why, hello," said Guy.

Beside Toby sat Dubedat. Between the two assistant teachers there had sprung up one of those close, immediate friendships that puzzle everyone but the pair concerned. Harriet had not only been puzzled by it, but rather annoyed. Seeing Toby as a comrade in danger, she had been prepared to accept him into her circle, but she was not prepared to accept Dubedat.

Sitting now in the sunken car seat, Dubedat did not greet the Pringles but stared straight ahead, his profile, with its thin hooked nose and receding chin, taut and disapproving as ever.

They had stopped in the centre of the square, beside the statue of the old king who rode a horse too big for him. Cars were parked round the pediment. Toby said: "I'll leave the jalopy here and stretch my legs."

The Pringles had been invited by David to the English Bar and it was evident the two assistant teachers were coming with them. Harriet looked at Guy and as he avoided her eye she knew he had invited Toby to join them. If she had asked him 'Why?' he would probably have replied "Why not?" Surely anyone would agree that it was better to drink with several people than with just one or two?

Guy, delighted to have more company, walked ahead with Toby while she, left to follow with Dubedat, found herself wondering, not for the first time, whether life with Guy was not more often an irritant than a pleasure.

She glanced at Dubedat, noticing a smile lingering round his lips – "like the grime left by bath-water," she told herself – and felt sure he was aware of her irritation. That irritated her more. He had nothing to say. She did not attempt to break the silence.

Dubedat, an elementary school-teacher from Liverpool, had been "thumbing" his way through Galicia when war broke out and been given a lift in one of the refugee cars that streamed down to Bucharest when Poland collapsed. Describing himself as a "simple-lifer", he had gone about Bucharest in shorts and open-neck shirt until the winter wind forced him into a sheepskin jacket.

His appearance had improved since those early days. He had been teaching at the University for nearly a year now and as a result of prosperity had given up the "simple-life" outfit, and was wearing a suit of khaki twill. It looked very grimy. He no longer lived in the Dâmbovita area, but had rented a modern flat in the centre of the city. Toby had moved in with him. Guy used to excuse Dubedat, saying that his old lodging did not give him opportunity to wash, but it seemed to Harriet that his personal aroma was much as it used to be. Or was it merely an emanation of her own dislike of him?

Ahead, Toby, moving with exaggerated strides, was giving crows of nervous laughter. Despite the heat, he still wore his tweed jacket with its patches of leather. As he walked, he scuffed his brogues in the dust, one shoulder drawn up, his fists bagging out his pockets. She heard him say: "Don't want to be a bottle-washer all my life."

"Even in these times," Guy replied, "we must expect a lecturer to have a degree."

Dubedat, beside Harriet, snorted his private disgust at this statement.

They had reached the hotel, where the striped awning was out, the carpet down and a gigantic Rumanian flag hung the length of the façade. People had gathered round to watch events. A lorry arrived and from it jumped a dozen young men in dark suits, who at once began pushing back the docile onlookers and forming a cordon of six on either side of the pavement. Before anyone could inquire into this behaviour, a Mercedes drew up and a man alighted – a small, lean man of unusual appearance. The cordon at once flung up arms in a fascist salute, sharp, businesslike and un-Rumanian, and the new arrival responded, holding the salute dramatically for some moments, his head thrown back so all might see his hollow, bone-pale face and lank, black hair.

Guy whispered: "I believe that's Horia Sima."

Whoever he was, he was clearly an intellectual and a fanatic, someone totally different from the lenient, self-indulgent Rumanian males now strolling in the Calea Victoriei. He dropped his arm, then strode to the swing door. He gave it a push, treating it as an unimportant impediment, but the door was not to be coerced. It creaked round slowly and he was forced, in spite of himself, to shuffle in at its pace. The young men, following after, did no better.

Harriet, as she watched, could hear Toby gasping nervously at his pipe. "Never seen the like," he said, The English party, much sobered, entered the hotel hall as the Guardists went striding into the main salon.

David was in the hall. Guy asked him: "Was that Horia Sima?"

David nodded. "He's joining the Cabinet. That's the excuse for the reception, of course, but it's really a gesture of defiance. I wonder how His Majesty's going to take it." David gave Dubedat an unenthusiastic "Hello," then looked blankly at Toby whom he had never seen before.

Guy introduced them, saying: "Toby comes from Cluj. I thought you might be interested to hear what's going on there."

"Oh!" said David, and he said nothing more.

They went into the bar, where Guy bought a round of drinks.

Toby had evidently heard of David, for he kept close to him, and with eyes bulging excitedly asked: "Is it true they're starting concentration camps in the Carpathians?"

"I've never seen them myself," David said, keeping his gaze on his glass.

Toby continued to ask questions about the country's situation and its dangers, receiving answers that were brief and discouraging, while Dubedat stood on one side, obviously annoyed by Toby's eagerness and David's lack of it.

As soon as Guy entered the conversation, Dubedat took the opportunity to pluck at his friend's arm, at which Toby turned with a jerk and, seeing Dubedat's frown, asked in a fluster: "What is it, old soul? What's the matter?" Hissing through his teeth so he looked like an angry rat, Dubedat made a movement of the head that directed Toby to step aside with him. Puffing and spluttering in apprehension, Toby let himself be led off.

"Where did you pick up that impossible ass?" David asked Guy.

Guy looked surprised. "He's working for me. He's not a bad chap."

David lowered his voice. "I've something to tell you. Klein has gone."

"He's left the country?"

"No one knows. He might have been arrested, but I don't think so. I think he's crossed the frontier into Bessarabia. There's a secret route over the Pruth: thousands are going, I'm told. Anyway, I doubt whether we'll ever see him again."

Guy nodded in a sad approval of this escape and Harriet thought of how Klein had several times advised her to wait and see the break-up of a country – "revolution, ruin, occupation by the enemy – all so interesting"; but he had not waited himself. She felt disconsolate at this flight, as though an ally had abandoned them.

While the others talked, she glanced around the bar, seeing, but avoiding seeing, Yakimov, who was with his Rumanian friends. Clarence was sitting alone at one of the tables. She had heard nothing from him since their evening in the park and now when she looked at him he avoided meeting her eye.

Something in the odd turn of his head made her think of those boys described by Klein who, violently raped during their first days in prison, had acquired a taste for the indignity and afterwards offered themselves to all comers. Clarence, too, had been raped. His spirit had been broken by physical violence. As Harriet made a move towards him his eyes slid sideways, his expression became furtively defensive as though at a threat of chastisement both feared and desired.

Galpin entered briskly, his girl-friend Wanda at his heels. He wore an air of waggish self-congratulation that meant news. Harriet returned to hear what he had to say.

The heat of the day hung clotted in the bar. Although Rumanian convention did not permit men to appear in any sort of undress, they might, in mid-summer, wear their jackets cape-fashion. In Hadjimoscos' group, only Yakimov was lax enough to do this. His tussore coat, hanging limp and frayed from his shoulder-bones, permitted his neighbours to note that the silk of his shirt had rotted away under the armpits. The shirt was a deep Indian yellow, and he wore with it not a tie but a neckcloth of maroon velvet. The neckcloth seemed to Hadjimoscos excessively daring and he had been brought to tolerate it only by the assurance that it came from the most expensive outfitters in Monte Carlo.

Hadjimoscos merely changed for the summer from a suit of dark wool to one of dark alpaca. He said he had never before spent a summer in Bucharest and he frequently described the heat as *incroyable*. That evening he was in low spirits, as were Palu and Horvatz. No one had indicated to them that their presence was desired at the reception. Yakimov had spent most of his thousand *lei* on drinks for his companions, but their gloom persisted. "It looked a pretty dull party to me," he said.

Ignoring Yakimov, Hadjimoscos moaned to Palu and Horvatz: "We may take it that we members of the old aristocracy are not in favour."

"Oh, I wouldn't say that," said Yakimov, "The Princess was invited."

For some reason this remark, intended to console, merely angered Hadjimoscos who turned on Yakimov, saying: "The Princess, I can assure you, was invited merely as the companion of Baron Steinfeld. Since his losses in Bessarabia the Baron has thrown himself heart and soul into the Nazi cause, with the result that, unlike us members of the old aristocracy, he is *très bien vu* with the Guard."

"Really, dear boy," Yakimov protested out of his bewilderment: "I don't know what you're all so worried about. Apparently these Guardists were put down by the King – a lot of them were shot or something. How could they suddenly become so impor-

tant? What do you care whether they invite you to their junket-
ings or not?"

"Believe me," Hadjimoscos said, "the day is fast coming when
those they do not recognise may as well be dead."

Impressed by the solemnity of Hadjimoscos' statement, Yakimov began for the first time to think seriously about the Iron
Guard. He remembered how, during his brief period as a journalist, he had, on Galpin's advice, written dispatches condemning in
violent language the murderers of Calinescu. The chief villain had
been someone called Horia Sima. The dispatches had not been
allowed to leave the country. What had become of them? A chill
pang struck the pit of his stomach, and as he stood like the others
with an empty glass in his hand he began to feel as gloomy as they
did.

"Well, well," Galpin said throwing his thumb back over his
shoulder, "if that lot knew what I know, there'd be no reception
tonight."

Everyone looked expectantly at him.

David asked, smiling: "What's happened now?"

"The Rumanian ministers have been summoned to Salzburg –
the Hunks and Bulgars, too. Herr Hitler is ordering them to settle
their frontier problems."

"Is that all?" said Harriet.

"It's enough," said Galpin sharply: "What are Rumania's
frontier problems? Simply other people's demands. All she wants
is to hang on to what she's got. Now, you wait and see! There's
going to be trouble here."

David's smile had changed to a look of startled interest. "When
did you hear this?" he asked.

"A moment ago. The Cabinet's been summoned. I met my
scout in the square. He's got a contact in the palace. It's hot news,
but I needn't try to send it. The authorities are trying to keep it
secret. Look at them," he said, and they all looked through the
open door of the bar at the guests passing on their way to the
main salon. "The poor bastards! They think they've got on to the
band-wagon. They're calling it the New Dawn. And here's their
Führer once again demanding a sacrifice in the interests of Balkan
peace."

David sniggered into his glass. "Perhaps the Führer is not
finding world dictatorship so easy after all. I imagine, if he could

he'd shelve all these problems until the war was over, then settle them his own way. But Hungary and Bulgaria are not having that. They are demanding immediate payment for their support."

"What about Rumania?" Harriet asked.

"She's not in a position to demand anything."

Clarence had joined them to ask what the excitement was all about. When she told him that the Rumanians had been summoned to a conference at Salzburg, he shrugged slightly, having expected worse. She, too, felt that in a world so full of dangers those that did not immediately affect them could be put on one side.

He remained on the fringe of the group and Harriet, realising he was more dispirited than usual, said: "What's the matter?"

He looked up, responding at once to her sympathy: "Steffaneski left this morning. He's going to try to join Weygand. That's the last of my Poles."

"We'll all have to go sooner or later."

"He was my friend." Clarence hung his head, repudiating consolation.

Harriet said: "You have other friends." He did not reply but after a moment, nodding at Guy and David, he said: "They'll go on talking all night. Why don't you come and have supper with me?"

She recognised this as a peace offering and refused it regretfully: "David has invited us out, so I'm afraid . . ."

"Oh, don't apologise." Clarence turned his face away. "If you don't want to come, someone else will."

Harriet laughed. "Who for instance?" she asked.

Clarence sniffed and smirked, so she realised, not without a touch of pique, that he really had some substitute up his sleeve. She could see he was waiting for her to ask who it was. Instead she moved away from him, giving her attention elsewhere, and found herself listening to Dubedat, who had by now had several drinks handed to him.

Taciturn when sober, garrulous when drunk, he was keeping Toby away from the others with a stream of talk. His subject at the moment was poverty, his own poverty, a condition which he had once flaunted as a virtue.

Before the war he had climbed arduously into a scholarship worth £150 a year. He had become an elementary school-teacher. Remembering his description of the Dâmbovita Jews as "the poorest of the poor and the only decent folk in this dirty, depraved, God-forsaken capital", Harriet realised that his attitude, like his dress, was changing. Now he was saying: "God, how I hate poverty. It's not only an evil, it's a disease and if you don't get rid of it, it becomes an incurable disease. It rots your guts. You become gutless. You crawl. You don't give a damn for yourself. Any way of escaping it is excusable. When you're poor you can only afford to mix with people as poor as yourself. If they're stupid, they bore you. If they're intelligent, they're discontented and depress you. So you never escape. Your nose is kept firmly down in the dirty water of reality. It's the greatest destructive force in the world, poverty. Half the world's intellect has been blunted or destroyed by it. None of us escape from it whole. Even the elephant hides are marked by it."

All this was spoken rapidly, in a hectoring tone that Harriet recognised as the tone in which he had played Thersites in Guy's production of *Troilus*. He had excelled in the part, and something of it seemed to have entered into him. Here, she thought, was a transformed Dubedat, a Dubedat who had found eloquence.

The main salon must have overflowed, for the guests could now be seen standing about in the hall. Soon the hall was also crowded. Suddenly the occupants of the bar were startled to hear a chorus of singing from both salon and hall. Community singing at an Athénée Palace reception!

People looked at one another as they recognised the song which the members of the Iron Guard had been advised to sing "only in their hearts".

"*Capitan-ul, Capitan-ul,*" came from the resplendent guests outside.

Before any of the English could say anything the man whom Galpin called his scout appeared struggling in through the press at the bar door. Once through, he paused to straighten out his wrinkled cotton jacket, then sidled over to Galpin. Galpin bent down to receive the news, his eyes roving about with intent attentiveness.

"Well," he said when all had been told, "this is really something! Didn't I tell you there'd be trouble? A voice has been raised, a solitary but significant voice – and it has called on the King to abdicate."

His listeners gazed at him, too startled to comment. He went on to explain that, seeing the Cabinet ministers arriving, people had collected outside the palace. "Then the news began leaking out. People realised the next question was going to be Transylvania – and suddenly someone bawled out '*Abdicati*'."

David said: "Good God!"

"What happened then?" Guy asked.

"Nothing – that's the extraordinary thing. Everyone bolted, of course. They probably expected the guards to shoot, but they did nothing. There wasn't a murmur from the palace . . ."

Wanda broke in anxiously: "But the King would not abdicate? No?" She spoke so seldom that everyone stared at her and she turned her eyes from one to the other with an expression of dramatic agony.

Accredited to an English Sunday paper that did not inquire too closely into the truth of what it printed, she had recently lost her job because the news she was sending bore no relation of any kind to the news being sent by other journalists. The result was that she had turned to Galpin for help and their relationship, once broken, had been renewed.

She was wearing a black Schiaparelli suit like a man's dinner suit, lightened by a tie of very bright pink. The heels of her shoes were also pink, and so overrun that her feet slipped sideways. She had tilted a miniature top-hat over one eye and from under it her hair streamed to her waist like pitch. She was as grimy as ever and dramatically beautiful, and as she looked at Clarence he looked back with bleak and lustful gloom murmuring: "I don't know," which meant, Harriet knew: "How is it other men can get women and I can't?"

When she looked at David, he sniggered and answered her: "Who knows? I hear he keeps a plane ready in the back-yard just in case. You can't really blame these Balkan kings if they're a bit light-fingered. They never know from one day to the next what's going to happen."

Wanda gave a gasp of disgust at David's levity and turned her tragic, inquiring gaze on Galpin, who said: "No need to worry about Carol. He and his girl-friend have got vast sums salted away abroad. Anyway the Germans will keep him here. It takes a crook to hold this country together."

David's mouth dipped in contempt of Galpin's predictions and he contradicted them authoritatively: "The Germans will not keep him here. They're not taken in by his conversion to totalitarianism. They know it's mere expediency. The new men in

Germany are, in their way, idealists. They're not like the old-fashioned diplomats who don't care how dishonest a man is so long as he's playing their game. They're dedicated men who'd hand Carol over to the firing-squad without a blink."

"But this is terrible," Wanda moaned: "He is such a splendid king with his helmet and his white cloak and his beautiful white horse."

"It may be terrible," David indulgently agreed, "but he's brought it on himself. He tried to play off the powers one against the other – and he didn't succeed. As for us, we haven't done much better. We could have bought up the Iron Guard any time we liked. Had we given a hint of recognition to the Peasant Party, they would have been with us. It's not too late. Maniu could still start a pro-British rising in Transylvania. But, even now, all the Legation is worrying about is how to keep in with the bloody sovereign."

Wanda sparked with exalted indignation. "You are an Englishman," she accused him. "You have a great empire and a fine king, and yet you want your Legation here to rouse a rabble of peasants! Is it possible?" Excited into unusual volubility, she gazed again from one to the other of the circle, and cried: "The last words I write to my paper were: 'At the word of command, every man in Rumania will rise to defend the throne.' "

Snuffling happily to himself, David murmured to Guy: "Just what you'd expect from the Poles. They still sing 'Poland has not perished yet'!"

Whether or not the news of the Salzburg conference had reached the reception, the singing went on. Harriet saw the view from the bar door was blocked by the backs of men standing in a row, shoulder to shoulder, across the doorway.

There was a pause outside, then the voices of the Guardists rose in the *Horst Wessel*. Someone gave a command, and gradually this song was also taken up by the guests.

From the other side of the bar Hadjimoscos' voice rose in admiring awe: "Such a demonstration of loyalty I have never before heard."

"I think we ought to go," said Harriet.

David agreed: "It is a bit sinister."

They took their leave of Galpin and moved towards the door. Guy, glancing round to include all his faction, noticed that Clarence was lingering uncertainly behind. "Coming with us?" he asked.

"I don't know. I . . ." Clarence looked at Harriet, but when she did not wait to listen, he followed after her.

They reached the row of bodies wedged across the door. Beyond could be glimpsed the glitter of the women guests, the white shirt-fronts of the men. Here was Bucharest's wealthiest and most frivolous society standing, grave-faced, almost at attention, singing the Nazi anthem.

David bent to the ear of the central figure blocking the doorway and said: "*Scuză, domnuli.*" The figure remained rigid. David repeated his request and, when it was ignored, put his hand on the man's shoulder and shook it.

Angrily the man half turned his face to say: "*Hier ist nur eine private Gesellschaft. Der Eintritt ist nicht gestattet.*"

Amused and reasonable, David replied: "*Wir wollen einfach heraus.*"

The man jerked his face away with the word "*Verboten*".

David looked round. "We are – how many?" Noting Clarence, Dubedat and Toby in the rear, he made a grimace of humorous resignation and said: "The more the merrier, I suppose. Well, come along. Put your shoulders against these fellows and when I say 'Shove', let's all shove."

"Wait," said Harriet, "I know a better way." She unclasped a large brooch of Indian silver and held the pin at the ready. Before anyone could intervene – Clarence breathed "*Harry!*" in horror – she thrust the pin into the central backside. Its owner skipped forward with a yelp, leaving a space through which she led her party.

As the Rumanians observed this incident the *Horst Wessel* faltered, but nobody smiled.

Having reached the vestibule, the men wanted to get away quickly, but Harriet felt a desire to linger on the scene of triumph. The occasion, she felt, called for some sort of demonstration. She moved towards the table where the newspapers lay.

Guy said warningly: "Harriet!" but she went on.

At one time the table had displayed copies of every English journal published; now among the German and Rumanian newspapers there still remained the last copy of *The Times* to reach Bucharest. It bore the date June 12th 1940. Harriet picked it up and began to read a report of the French retreat across the Marne, but the paper was too limp and ragged to remain upright. As its pages sagged, she saw she was being watched by a woman whose face was familiar to her.

Guy caught her elbow. "Come along," he said, "you're being silly."

The woman, plainly dressed in black, was holding a glass as though unaware she held it. Her flat, faded, colourless face seemed to have on it the imprint of a heel. About her was an atmosphere of such unhappiness, it affected the air like a miasma.

Harriet said: "Yes, I am being silly . . ." As she let Guy lead her away, she remembered who the woman was: Doamna Ionescu, the wife of the ex-Minister of Information who had been pro-British but was pro-British no longer.

The singing had gathered strength again, but everyone watched the English party as it went.

"Well," said Clarence out in the square, "this may be Ruritania, but it's no longer a joke."

Guy looked about for Dubedat and Toby. The pair had not waited to support Harriet; they had fled. Half-way across the square Dubedat could be seen strutting at an indecorous speed while Toby, shoulders up, head down, hands in pockets, pinching himself with his own elbows, was scurrying like a man under fire.

8

Occasionally when Yakimov overslept in the afternoon, he would awake to find the Pringles had gone out and Despina – to spite him – had cleared away the tea things. When this happened on one of the molten days of late July, he suddenly felt to the full the deterioration of his life and could have wept for it. There had been a time when the world had given him everything: comfort, food, entertainment, love. He had been a noted wit, the centre of attention. Now he did not even get his tea.

He threw himself into the arm-chair in a state of revolt. No one had loved him since Dollie died. Perhaps no one would ever love him again – but why should he have to suffer as he did suffer in this wretched flat, in this exhausting heat? He wanted to get away.

A bugle call, coming from the palace yard, said: "Officers' wives have puddings and pies, soldiers' wives have skilly," and he thought: "Precious few puddings and pies we get these days." He did not entirely blame Harriet for that. Food was abominable everywhere in Bucharest these days.

Pushing his chair back as the lengthening fingers of sunlight burnt his shins, he asked himself: why did he live – why did anyone live – here, on this exposed plain, where one was fried in summer and frozen in winter? And now starved! Nothing to eat but fruit.

Apricots! He was sick of the sight of apricots.

That morning he had seen a barrow laden with raspberries – a great mountainous mush of raspberries – the peasant asleep beneath it. The man had probably walked all night to bring his produce to town, but the market was glutted. The raspberries were rotting in the heat and the man's shirt was crimson with the dripping juice.

In his youth, in a reasonable country, Yakimov had said he could live on raspberries. Now he dreamt of meat. If one got any here, it was the flesh of an old ewe or of a calf so young it was nothing but gristle. What he wanted was steak or roast beef or pork! – and he thought he knew where he could get it.

When he told the Baron that Freddi von Flügel had invited him to stay, it had been just "a little joke". He had heard nothing from Freddi, but that was no reason why Yakimov should not visit him. Freddi had received a great deal of Dollie's hospitality. Why should he not return it now that he was in "a position of power" and poor old Yaki was on his uppers?

Yakimov had practically made up his mind to set out – the only thing that detained him was the need for money. He had studied maps of Transylvania and realised the journey from Bucharest to Cluj was a long one. He would have to spend the night on the road. He would have to eat. In short, he would have to wait until his remittance turned up.

When he had mentioned to Hadjimoscos that he planned to drive to Cluj, Hadjimoscos had been discouraging. Apparently, as a result of some wretched conference being held in Salzburg, Cluj was now in disputed territory and liable to change hands any day. After hearing that, Yakimov had begun to inquire of Galpin and Screwby about the progress of the conference, and soon came to the conclusion that nothing was happening at all. And he had been right. Even Hadjimoscos now agreed with him that the Conference would probably drag on until the war put a stop to the whole business.

Meanwhile, he had to remain here in a comfortless flat where he was not wanted by the hostess, and the host, having made use of him, had scarcely time to throw him a word. His acute sense of hardship was suddenly aggravated by a sound of laughter coming from the kitchen: and his curiosity was aroused.

The laughter had not been the usual sniggering of servants. He had heard Despina laugh, he had heard her husband. This was unfamiliar laughter. Who had she got in there? It occurred to him to put his head into the kitchen and make some jocular reference to tea.

The kitchen door had a glass panel. He approached quietly and looked in. Himself hidden by the lace curtain, he could see Despina and a young man sitting at the table preparing vegetables for the evening meal. A young man, eh! Despina was married to a taxi-driver who was more often out than in. Well, well! The two at the table were chattering in Rumanian. The fellow started laughing again.

Yakimov opened the door. At the sight of him, the young man's laughter stopped abruptly. Yakimov had the odd sensation that the youth knew who he was and was afraid of him. Surprised at this, he essayed in English – his Rumanian was poor – a leading inquiry: "Believe we've met before, dear boy?"

The young man stammered out: "I don't think so." Looking ghastly, he managed to get to his feet and stood there trembling as though stupefied by fear. He was as long and lean as Yakimov himself, and unmistakably Jewish.

"Are you staying with the Pringles?" Yakimov asked.

"No," the young man said, then added: "I mean, yes." After a moment, encouraged by Yakimov's courtesy of manner, he added more easily: "I'm on a visit."

Yakimov was puzzled, not because the boy spoke English – English was widely spoken among Bucharest Jews – but because he spoke it with the accent of an English public school. Where had he come from? What was he doing here? But before Yakimov could make further inquiries, Despina broke in in the high, abusive tone she always adopted with Yakimov. He gathered she was claiming the young man as her nephew.

An educated Jew Despina's nephew! A likely story. It roused Yakimov's suspicions. He looked at the boy, who nodded, his colour returning, as though relieved at hearing this explanation of his presence.

Yakimov said: "You speak English extremely well."

"I learnt at school."

"Indeed!" With no excuse for lingering longer, Yakimov made his request for tea and retreated. Despina shouted after him: "*Prea târziu pentru ceai*," and before he reached the sitting room door he heard her hooting with laughter. She thought she had fooled him. His suspicion deepened.

He went into the bathroom and filled the bath. Lying in the water, he reflected on the presence of the young man in the kitchen. He could only suppose the fellow was some fugitive of the troubled times whom Guy was keeping under cover. He felt a vague jealousy, then, remembering the plan of the oil-well he had found in Guy's desk, it came to him that the young man in the kitchen might be a British spy. His jealousy changed to disapproval and concern.

He often himself hinted that he was engaged in espionage, but everyone knew that was just a little joke. This was a serious matter. He thought: "If Guy gets caught, it'll be a bad look-out for him," then he realised, with indignant alarm, that it would be a bad look-out for all of them. He, poor old Yaki, innocently involved in this fishy business, would have to suffer with the rest.

Spies were shot. Even if he were not actually shot, he would be ordered out of the country. And where could he go? Bad as things were here, Bucharest was the last outpost of European cooking.

Levantine dishes upset his stomach. He could not bear the luke-warm food of Greece.

Worse than that, he would never reach Cluj and dear old Freddi. He would not even have the harbour of this flat but, ageing and penniless, would have to face the unfriendly world again.

He sat up, all pleasure gone from the bath, and considered the possibility of safeguarding himself by acting as informer. That would never do, of course. "Lucky for the dear boy," he told himself, "that Yaki's not one to give the game away."

The Salzburg Conference did not outlast the war, but petered out in failure by all parties to agree. Yakimov, like almost everyone else in Bucharest, decided that that was the end of the matter.

"What did I tell you, dear boy?" he said to the few persons willing to listen. "I've been a journalist, y'know. I've a nose for how these things will shape," and he was happy that nothing stood between him and his visit to Freddi but the need for a little cash.

The Transylvanian question forgotten, interest in the Drucker trial returned. *L'Indépendence Romaine* predicted that the trial would be "*l'évenement social le plus important de l'été*".

In every café and restaurant that Harriet visited, she heard talk of Drucker. People discussed his origins and the origins of his fortune and his love of women. She heard women envying his young second wife who, having reverted to her maiden name and started an affair with the German military attaché, was claiming, and would probably receive, fifty per cent of her husband's estate.

Galpin had a story of how Drucker, when first placed in the common prison cell, had been held down and raped by old lags. There were a great many similar stories. Harriet realised that among all this talk Drucker's own identity was lost. No one doubted the innocence of this friendless man, but that factor did not bear discussion. No one could help him. He was a victim of the times.

As for the war, it was at a standstill. Events, it seemed, were becalmed in the oppressive, dusty, windless heat of midsummer.

People believed the worst was over. A euphoria, one of the periodic intermissions in its chronic disease of dread, possessed the city. Gaiety returned.

Then, in a moment, the mood changed. The Pringles, out walking after supper, heard among the crowds the shrill ejaculations of panic. The newsboys came shrieking through the streets with a special edition. Those who did not already know learnt that the Führer had called another conference. The Hungarian and Rumanian ministers, ordered to Rome, were required to reach speedy agreement.

The sense of outrage was the more violent because only that morning the new Foreign Minister had broadcast a speech of the highest optimism. He had pointed out that in 1918 the Germans had been as weak as the Rumanians, and today, by their energy and determination, they ruled the world. The implication had been that Rumanians might do likewise – yet here they were ordered to reach agreement with an enemy whose sole intention was to eat them up.

Gabbling in their rage, people shouted to one another that they had been betrayed. Rumania was to be divided among Russia, Hungary and Bulgaria. The whole of Moldavia would be handed to the Soviets as the price of Russia's neutrality. The Dobrudja, of course, would go to Bulgaria. Even now the Hungarians were marching into Transylvania.

Word went round that the Cabinet was sitting, then that the King had summoned his generals. Suddenly people were convinced that Rumania would fight for her territory and they began shouting for war. As they swarmed towards the square to demonstrate the defiance of the moment, Guy and Harriet made their way to the English Bar, where Galpin was in a state of excitement. His scout had brought the news that Maniu, the leader of the Transylvanian peasants, was making a speech calling on the King to defy Hitler and defend what was left of Greater Rumania. "This means war," said Galpin, "this means war."

On the way home, Harriet said: "Do you think they will fight?"

"I doubt it," said Guy, but the violence of feeling about them seemed to be such that they went to bed in a half-expectation that they would awake to find the country in arms.

Next morning all was quiet and when Guy telephoned David he learnt that Maniu had indeed made an impassioned speech demanding that they hold Transylvania by force, but he had been ridiculed. The new Guardist ministers had pointed out that while the Rumanian army was defending the western front Russia would march down from the north. It was their belief that only by implicit obedience to Hitler could they hope for protection from the arch-enemy, Russia. At this an old statesman had burst into tears and scandalised everyone by crying out: "Better to be united under the Soviets than dismembered by the Axis."

But the Rumanians, harried themselves, decided to harry someone. Next morning, as Guy was leaving for the University, a messenger handed him a second order to quit the country within eight hours.

He gave it to Harriet, saying: "I haven't time to deal with this. Go and see Dobson."

"But supposing we have to go?" she protested.

He said, as he had said last time: "We won't have to go," but Harriet did not find Dobson so reassuring.

When she entered his office with the paper, he sighed and said: "We're getting a lot of this bumf at the moment." He rubbed a hand over his baby-soft tufts of hair and gave a laugh that deprecated his own weariness. "I wonder," he said, as though the matter were not of much importance one way or the other, "do you really *want* to stay? The situation is tricky, you know. There's a pretty steady German infiltration here. Whether you realise it or not, they're taking this country over. I very much doubt whether the English Department will be permitted to reopen when the autumn term begins."

Harriet said: "We're not supposed to leave without orders from London."

"That's theoretical, of course. But if Guy's work here is finished . . ."

"He doesn't see it as finished. At the moment he's running the summer school and he's extremely busy."

"Oh, well!" Dobson gave his head a final rub and said: "I'll see what I can do. But don't be too hopeful."

She returned to the flat to await a call from him, not hopeful, indeed prepared for the possibility that they would be given no choice but to go. Whether she liked it or not, their going would cut through a tangle of anxieties.

Wandering round the room, examining their possessions, wondering what to take and what to leave, she looked into the writing-desk drawers and came upon the envelope marked "Top

Secret". As she took it up, the flap fell open and she saw there was nothing inside. Some moments passed before she could remember what it had contained.

The previous winter a certain Commander Sheppy – described by David as "a cloak and dagger man" – had come to Bucharest to organise the young men of the British colony into a sabotage group. His intention had ended abruptly with his arrest and deportation. All that had remained of "Sheppy's Striking Force" was a plan, handed out to the men, a copy of which had been inside this envelope; a section through an oil well, intended to show the inexperienced saboteur where to place a detonator. Both Guy and Harriet had forgotten its existence. Now, here was the envelope unsealed and empty. The plan had disappeared.

This fact bewildered her, then it began to work on her imagination and she was chilled.

As soon as Guy came in to luncheon, she said: "Someone has stolen the oil-well plan Sheppy gave you."

She remembered as she spoke that she was supposed not to know what had been inside the envelope, but Guy had forgotten that. He said merely: "But who would take it?"

"Perhaps Yakimov."

"That's unlikely."

"Who then? Surely not Despina or Sasha. It means someone has been in while we were out. The landlord perhaps. Despina says he's a member of the Iron Guard. And probably has a key." The realisation brought down on her a painful sense of doom and Guy, seeing her distraught, changed his attitude and said: "It *could* have been Yakimov . . ."

"Then you had better speak to him."

"Oh, no, that would give the whole thing false importance. Better say nothing, but you could try and be nicer to him. Let him see we trust him."

She said, exasperated in anxiety: "You think that will make a difference? If Yakimov isn't grateful now, he never will be. In fact, he's resentful because you take no notice of him. Why didn't you leave him to fend for himself? You interfere in people's lives. You give them a false idea of themselves, an illusion of achievement. If you make someone drunk, he's likely to blame you when he wakes up with a hangover. Why do you do it?"

Buffeted by this attack, he remonstrated: "For goodness' sake! The plan might have been taken months ago. We can't tell who took it – but whoever it was, if he'd wanted to make trouble we'd have heard by now."

She thought this equivocal comfort.

After Guy had gone to the University, she threw herself on to the bed, oppressed by the sense of events becoming too much for her. A few days earlier Despina, treating the matter as a joke, had described Yakimov's discovery of Sasha in the kitchen. "But I was ready for him," she said. She had told him the boy was her nephew and he had believed it. "The imbecile!" she cried, tears of laughter in her eyes, but Harriet could not believe that Yakimov had been so easily deceived. She had hoped he would mention the incident himself, so she could tell him that Sasha was one of Guy's students; but he did not mention it, and his silence disturbed her more than any questioning could have done.

Suddenly, with the thought of Sasha in her mind, she sat upright, shocked by the realisation that when they went they would have to leave him behind. What would become of him? Where could he go?

Thinking of Sasha's trust in them, his dependent innocence and need, she was stricken by her own affection for the boy. She could no more abandon him than she could abandon a child or a kitten. But he was not a child or a kitten to be carried to safety: he was a grown man who could not leave the country without a passport, exit visa and transit visas, and he was a man for whom every frontier official would be on the watch.

It had been in her mind that their going, if they had to go, would cut through a tangle of anxieties. Now all these anxieties were forgotten in her concern for Sasha.

She put her feet to the ground in an impulse to rush up to him, to insist that he think of someone, anyone, whom they could approach on his behalf, but stopped herself. They had had this out. There was no one, so what point in alarming the poor boy?

She was still sitting on the bed edge, brooding on this problem, when the telephone rang. Dobson said: "It's all right. I've been through to the *prefectura* and told them H.E. requires Guy's presence here. The order's rescinded."

"Thank goodness for that," she said with a fervour that must have surprised him.

"By the way," he said before he rang off, "you're wanted at the Consulate. Just a formality. No particular hurry. Drop in when you get a chance."

The next afternoon, Guy having no classes, they went to the Consulate.

The Vice-consul, Tavares, shouted: "Come in, come in, come in." Elaborately casual and cheerful, he said: "It's like this . . ." He opened a drawer and pulled out some roneoed sheets, which he threw down in front of Guy and Harriet. "Every British subject required to fill one in. Never know these days, do you? So, just for the records, we want a few details: religion, next-of-kin, whom to notify in the event of death (as it were!), where to send kit, etcetera, etcetera. *You* understand!"

"Yes," said Harriet.

When the forms were filled, Tavares noticed that Guy had failed to disclose his religion. Guy said he had no religion. Tavares laughed off this revelation: "What were you baptised?" he asked.

"I wasn't baptised."

Tavares flicked a finger to show that nothing could surprise him. "Must put something," he said. "Y'wouldn't want to be planted without ceremony. Why not put 'Baptist'? Baptists don't get baptised."

In the end, Guy put in "Congregational", having been told that old soldiers who claimed this denomination were able to avoid church parades.

Walking home, Harriet said: "Why didn't you tell me you'd never been baptised?"

"I didn't think of it. But you knew I was a rationalist."

"But no one's *born* a rationalist."

"In a way, I was. My father would not let me be baptised."

"This means when we die we'll be in different places. You'll be in limbo."

Laughing, Guy said: "I don't think so. We'll be in the same place, don't worry. A hundred years from now we shall be exactly where we were a hundred years ago – which is nowhere at all."

But Harriet was not satisfied. She brooded over their post-obitum separation all during tea, then suddenly, when Yakimov had gone off to have a bath, she lifted the teapot and poured cold tea over Guy's head. While he sat stolidly acceptant of her follies, she said: "I baptise thee, Guy, in the name of the Father and of the Son and of the Holy Ghost," which was all she knew of the baptismal service.

9

HARRIET HAD NEVER HEARD the word "*abdică*" before the night of the Guardist reception, now she heard it everywhere. The King had been deposed for his misdeeds once before. The concept of deposition was not new, yet people seized upon it as though it were a prodigious solution of their problems. During the apprehensive days of the Rome Conference they talked of nothing else.

The King had always had his enemies – if he ever emerged from the palace, it was in a bullet-proof car – but to most people he was only one knave of many, and a shrewd, diverting knave, the hero of half the jokes that went around. This attitude changed overnight. Suddenly, he diverted no one. He was the bane of the country. True he had been clever: he had declared for the Axis – but too late. *Too late.* He had been too clever. He had played a double game and lost. Anyway, Hitler loathed and distrusted him. The country was paying for his sins. He must be abjured, for with such a man on the throne there could be nothing ahead but disaster.

These opinions were so widespread that they penetrated even to the King's apartments.

He was induced to broadcast, a thing he did seldom and never very well. The radio vans were already outside the palace when the Pringles were having breakfast. Another van, with a loud-speaker on its roof, stood beside the statue of Carol the First. It had been announced that the King would speak at ten o'clock; he came to the microphone shortly before noon.

During the morning a few dozen idlers hung round the loud-speaker van, and when the speech began it gathered in a few more. The listeners showed no enthusiasm, appearing to have nothing to do but listen, and Harriet, watching them from the balcony, switched on her radio set for the same reason. She had heard a broadcast by the King a year before (when he had promised that Rumania would never suffer defeat) and had little hope of under-standing his halting Rumanian, but when he started to speak she realised he had been very thoroughly coached for this occasion.

He pronounced each word with an earnest deliberation, in a charged voice, so she imagined him shocked into a painful sobriety.

While he was talking, she watched a file of young men who came out of the Calea Victoriei and crossed the square, carrying banners and distributing leaflets. Whatever their message was, it aroused more interest than the King, who was, she gathered, promising his people that whatever sacrifices they might be called upon to make, he would be beside them, whatever their sufferings, he would be there to suffer with them. Dramatically, his voice breaking with emotion (much as he had made the promise that Rumania would never suffer defeat), he promised that he would never abdicate.

As he spoke the words "*Nu voi abdică niciodată*", the young men reached the palace railing, where they came to a stop and stood with banners held in view of the palace windows.

Harriet had no doubt who these young men were. They were members of the Iron Guard. The Guardists did not wear uniform or march in formation or sing "*Capitanul*", but they had started to possess the streets, Having noted the first insecure few who had come from Germany after the spring amnesty, she marvelled at the numbers who were crowding back with all the confidence in the world and gathering adherents – the indigent and the afflicted. Once lost in the back streets, these men now swaggered through the Calea Victoriei while timorous passers-by stood aside to let them pass.

The speech over, Harriet decided to take a closer look at the Guardist banners. The sun stood overhead. The square was clearing under the onslaught of midday heat, but the young men remained steadfast. Harriet, long-sighted, stopped near the statue and saw that one banner called on the King to abdicate. Another demanded the arrest of Lupescu, Urdureanu, the Chief of Police, and other despoilers of the country. The third promised that once the King and his followers were cast out, the Axis would return Bessarabia to the Rumanian people.

Harriet was not the only one who chose to read these demands from a safe distance. People about her were murmuring in amazement and trepidation. And she, too, was amazed that this demonstration could proceed in full view of the palace without a movement from the guards.

Inside the palace someone was pulling down the cream-coloured blinds, masking the windows one after another – perhaps against the sun, perhaps against the sight below. Nothing else happened.

Before returning, Harriet walked past the young men to receive a pamphlet – a manifesto headed "*Corneliu Zelea Codreanu*" – which she hurried home to read while awaiting Guy's return. She settled down to it with a dictionary.

The truth (said the manifesto) could now be told. Codreanu had not been shot while trying to escape. He had been assassinated by order of the King. His death had come about in this way.

The Iron Guard, also called the Legion of the Archangel Michael, had gained sixty-six seats at the election of 1937. The King, insanely jealous of Codreanu's power, had at once dissolved all parties and declared himself dictator. At this, Hitler had said: "For me there exists only one dictator of Rumania and this is Codreanu." Codreanu had won the love and confidence which the King, corrupt instigator of a corrupt regime, had lost. Young, noble, saintly, tall, of divine beauty, Codreanu had been directly inspired by the archangel Michael to redeem his country by forming the Iron Guard. He possessed a mysterious power which was felt by all who approached him. When he appeared, dressed in white, on his white horse, the peasants at once recognised him as the archangel's envoy on earth. His purpose was to unite all Rumanians in brotherhood, not only the living but the souls of the unborn and the dead . . .

Harriet hastened on to the tragic end. Skipping the suppression of the Iron Guard, the evidence of the forged letter and the farcical trial in which Codreanu was found guilty of high treason, for which he was imprisoned, she reached the cold November night on which Codreanu and his thirteen comrades were taken in trucks, bound and gagged, to the forest of Ploesti, where each in turn was strangled with a leather strap. At Port Jilava, acid was poured over the bodies; they were burnt, and what remained was buried in a grave which was sealed with a massive slab of concrete.

Yet all these precautions had been in vain. Codreanu was an immortal. Even now his spirit was moving through the land, regathering forces . . . inspiring . . . exhorting . . . leading . . . and so on.

Harriet had read enough. Her imagination excited by this romance of a young leader murdered by a jealous King, she thought of the men who had handed it to her in the square. Bare-headed and dark-skinned, wearing singlets or cheap shirts without collars, they may have been artisans. They were scarcely more than peasants. Guy, seeing the Guardist groups pushing through the streets, had said: "How rapidly they are gathering in their kind: the hopeless, the inadequate, the brute." And yet, she thought, they were the only people in this spoilt city whose ideals rose above money, food and sex. Why should the brute not be infused with ideals, the hopeless given hope, the inadequate strength?

She was stimulated, too, by the revelation of a mystical strain in this pleasure-loving people. It was easy to see how a visionary like Codreanu could excite half-starved and superstitious peasants, but one supposed that the townspeople would find the King, with his mistresses, his chicanery and his love of money, a more likely projection of themselves. Or were all people at variance with themselves? Anyway, it had been here in Bucharest, during the funeral of Guardists killed in Spain, that people had given Codreanu so frenzied a welcome that the King determined to kill his rival and stamp out the whole Guardist movement.

When Guy came in, Harriet was impatient to talk about Codreanu, but he showed no interest. He had heard all the stories before.

"You must admit," she said, "that the Iron Guard concepts are not so very different from your own."

Guy glanced up sharply and, with a gesture, indicated that here and now, in the absurdity of this statement, he could pin down the root trouble of the world. "Codreanu," he said, "was a murderer, a Jew-baiter and a thug. He had a following of nonentities who wanted only one thing – power at any price."

"But if, having power, they could remake the country . . ."

"Do you imagine they could? The incompetence of Carol's set would be as nothing compared with the incompetence of Codreanu's bunch of thugs."

"Well, one could give them a chance."

"Before the war there were quite a lot of sentimentalists like you. They did not realise that while they were being mesmerised and misled by the romantic aspects of fascism, they were being made to sell their souls . . ."

Having used this phrase inadvertently, he paused, and Harriet, feeling ignorant and something of a fool, leapt in with: "If the fascists make you sell your soul, the communists make you deny it."

Guy grunted and picked up a newspaper. She knew he had no use for religion, seeing it as part of the conspiracy to keep the rich powerful and the poor docile. He was prepared to discuss very little that did not contribute towards a practical improvement in mankind's condition. Harriet's own theories, of course, were too simple-minded to matter.

At the moment he held up the paper to screen him from any more of her nonsense. She said to provoke him: "Clarence says you're merely the rebel son of a rebel father."

"Clarence is an ass," Guy said, but he put the paper down. "In fact I could say I reacted against my father. The poor old chap was a bit of a romantic. He imagined the moneyed classes were the repository of culture. He used to say: 'That's their function, isn't it? If they don't safeguard the arts, what the hell do they do?' When I began to meet rich people I was shocked by their ignorance and vulgarity."

"Where did you meet these rich people?"

"At the University – the sons of local manufacturers. They weren't aristocrats, it's true, but they were rich. And not first-generation rich, either. They were the country-house-owning class of the Midlands. They were always talking about 'parvenus', but even the most intelligent of them preferred the fashionable to the good."

She laughed. "They're much like everyone else. How many people do love the highest when they see it? They just about tolerate it if they're told often enough that it's the right thing."

He agreed and was about to go back to his paper when she said: "But did you know these people well? Did you go to their houses?"

"Yes. I suppose I was taken up by them – in a way. At first they wouldn't believe I was a genuine member of the proletariat. I was too big and untidy. According to them I should have been a bony little man in a dark suit, permanently soul-sick. When they found I was quite genuine, they adopted me as their favourite member of the working class."

"And you didn't mind? You liked them? You liked the Druckers?"

He had to admit it was true. He could not help liking people who liked him. They became, and remained, his friends.

"But," he said, "I know that humanity's superiority depends on a few persons of intellectual and moral structure: people like my father, for instance, who almost never have money or power, and have no sense at all of their own importance."

With that, Guy went back to his students; and Harriet, as soon as the heat began to relax, took herself up to the roof to talk to Sasha.

Guy had said once that, although she was nearly twenty-three, she still had the mentality of an adolescent. Perhaps her relationship with Sasha was a relationship of adolescents.

Guy's all-knowingness, his lack of time for any sort of fantasy, was frustrating her. She felt gagged. Sasha, on the other hand, had unlimited time. He did not say much himself, but he listened to her with the intent interest of someone new in the world. He was delighted to be entertained, watching her with warm, attentive eyes that made her feel whatever she said was pertinent and exciting. He believed – or rather, his silent extrusion of sympathy led her to believe he believed – that he, as she did, related life to eternity rather than to time.

Now when Guy was out she had somewhere to go. During the day, she had occupation enough. It was in the evening, the time of relaxation, when the changing light, giving a new spaciousness to the city, induced a sense of solitude, that she thought of Sasha who was lonely, too.

That evening, when she went to see him after tea, she spoke of Codreanu, saying: "He loved the peasants. He gave them this idea of a nation united in brotherhood. Surely the important thing was that people believed in him?"

Sasha listened uneasily. "But he did terrible things," he said. "He started the pogroms. My cousin at the University was thrown out of a window. His spine was broken."

That was the reality, of course. "But why did the reality have to be that?" she said. The ideals had been fine enough. They had been formulated to combat a corrupt régime in which the idle, self-seeking and dishonest thrived. Why then, she wanted to know, must they degenerate into a reality of blackmail, persecution and murder? Were human beings so fallible and self-seeking that degeneration was inevitable?

Guy, who had dismissed pretty sharply any suggestion of a flirtation with the Legion of the Archangel Michael, knew the answer to human fallibility: it was a world united under left-wing socialism. Sasha did not know the answer.

To please her, he was trying to consider the problem with

detachment, but as he looked at her his soft, vulnerable, loving gaze was troubled.

She remembered the moment at the Drucker table when one of his aunts had asked: "Why do they hate us?" Drucker had sent the little girls out of the room, but he did not send Sasha. Sasha had to be prepared for reality. However much his wealth might protect him, he could not be protected from prejudice. But, of course, he had not been prepared. Enclosed and loved as he had been, he could not relate their stories of persecution to himself.

He said: "The peasants are very simple people. It wouldn't be difficult to make them believe in Codreanu. They'd believe in anything," and he gazed appealingly at her as though to say: "Let that explain away the mysterious influence of Guardism and all that came of it." In short: "Let us talk of something else." He probably wanted to talk about the peasants who had shown him, at times, a rough kindness. They had respected him because he spoke English, though they could scarcely believe he had actually been to England. England they held to be a sort of paradise, the abode of titans.

He described how they stood, as patient as their own beasts, all day on guard in the midsummer heat, clad in winter clothing. Money was allotted for the purchase of cotton uniforms but it was misspent somewhere. Who were they to complain?

"What did they guard?" Harriet asked.

"Oh, a bridge or a railway-station or a viaduct. It was silly. When the Russians came, the officers just piled into cars and drove away. We didn't know what to do . . ."

She saw his face change as this mention of the army's flight recalled Marcovitch. By now she had heard other stories – of the Orthodox Jew whose skull had been kicked in "like a broken crock"; and the distinguished folklorist who, having been beaten by his sergeant, had appeared next day wearing a medal. "So you have decorated yourself!" said the sergeant. "No," replied the scholar, "the King decorated me," for which piece of impertinence he had been struck violently across the face.

Nothing very terrible had happened to Sasha himself, but, unprepared as he was, he had been appalled at this treatment of his scapegoat race. He had run away.

He said: "I can remember some of the songs the peasants sang. The folklorist used to collect them."

As he talked, she looked over the parapet and saw Guy crossing the square on his way home. In the early days of their marriage, she would have sped down the stairs; now she leant still and watched him, thinking of Sasha's theory that Guardism had grown not from the power of its founder but the credulity of his followers. She felt that the argument had, as arguments often did, come full circle. Wonders were born of ignorance and superstition. Do away with ignorance and superstition and there would be no more wonders, only a universe of unresponsive matter in which Guy was at home, though she was not. Even if she could not accept this diminution of her horizon, she had to feel a bleak appreciation of Guy, who was often proved right.

She broke in on Sasha to say: "I'm afraid I must go now."

He smiled, as uncomplaining and unquestioning as the peasants, but as she went he said forlornly: "I wish I had my gramophone here."

"You should be studying," she said, for at her suggestion Guy had set him some tasks: an essay to write, books to read. The books lay scattered over the ground. He had opened them, but she doubted whether he had done much more. "Why not do some work?"

"All right," he said, but as she turned to descend the ladder she saw he had picked up his charcoal and was scribbling idly on the wall.

10

One morning, while the city quivered like a mirage in the August heat, Harriet came face to face with Bella in the Calea Victoriei. Bella gave a smile and hurried into a shop. So she had not gone to Sinai after all, but had remained here, like everyone else, the prisoner of uncertainty and fear.

The Rome Conference had broken down. This time no one imagined that that was the end of the matter. There would be another conference. When it was announced, there was no stir and no more talk of defiance. The new Cabinet had announced complete fealty to the Führer and the Führer required a peaceful settlement. A settlement of any kind could only mean Rumania's loss. Around the cafés and bars this fact was beginning to be accepted with a half-humorous resignation. What else was there to do? Yakimov, inspired by the tenor of conversation about him, had thought up a little joke. "*Quel débâcle!*" he said whenever opportunity arose: "As you walk cracks appear on the pavement," and even Hadjimoscos had not the heart to snub him.

The young men still stood with their banners on the palace pavement, supported now by an admiring crowd. As for the King, having made his speech, his declaration of constancy, he had retired into silence, and a song was being sung which David did his best to put into English verse:

> "They can have Bessarabia. We don't like corn.
> The best wheaten bread's the stuff in our New Dawn.
>
> Let them have the Dobrudja. Ma's palace, anyway,
> Has been sold to the nation for a million million *lei*.
>
> Who wants Transylvania? Give it 'em on a plate.
> Let them take what they damn well like. I'll not abdicate."

The last phrase "*Eu nu abdic*" was the slogan of the moment. Jokes were told and the point was "*Eu nu abdic*". Riddles were asked and the answer was always "*Eu nu abdic*". However recondite, it was the smartest retort to any request or inquiry. It always raised a laugh.

In the face of the threat to Transylvania, no one gave much thought to the southern Dobrudja, but the story went round that the old minister who had wept over Bessarabia, had wept – probably from habit – when the Bulgarian demand was received. He reminded the Cabinet that Queen Marie's heart was buried in the palace at Balcic and the queen had believed her subjects would safeguard it with their lives. He stood up crying: "To arms, to arms," but no one, not even the old man himself, could take this call seriously. The queen, though barely two years dead, symbolised an age of chivalry as outmoded as honour, as obsolete as truth.

The transfer of the southern Dobrudja was announced for September 7th.

That, Harriet thought, was one frontier problem peaceably settled, but when she made some comment of this sort to Galpin, he eyed her with the icy irony of one who has good cause to know better.

They had met on the pavement outside the Athénée Palace and Galpin was carrying a suitcase. "For my part," he said, "I'm keeping a bag ready packed and my petrol-tank full."

"Oh?"

He crossed to his car and put the case into the boot, then remarked in a milder tone: "I thought it darn odd they were willing to settle for that mouldy bit in the south when they could grab the whole coast."

"Do you mean they *are* grabbing the whole coast?"

"They and one other. I expect it was arranged months ago. When the Bulgars take the south, the old Russkies will occupy the north. *Between* them they'll hold the whole coastal plain. It's a Slav plot."

When Harriet did not look as alarmed as he felt she should be, he said on a peevish note: "Don't you see what it means? Rumania will be cut off from the sea. The Legation plan is to evacuate British subjects from Constanza. You'll be one of the ones to suffer. There'll be no escape route."

"We can go to Belgrade."

"My dear child, when the Germans march this way, they'll take Yugoslavia *en route*."

"Well, we can go by air."

"What, the whole blessed British colony? I'd like to see it. And anyway, when there's trouble the air service is the first thing to pack up. I've seen it time and again. Well, I'm taking no risk. When I get wind of the invasion, I'm into the flivver and off."

"Ah, well,' said Harriet, attempting to lighten the situation, "perhaps you'll take us with you?"

Galpin's eyes bulged. "I don't know about that. I've got baggage. I've got Wanda. The Austin's old. The road over the Balkans is bad. If we broke a spring, we'd be done for." Looking as though she had attempted to take an unfair advantage, he got into the car, slammed the door and drove away.

When she reached the flat, the telephone was ringing. Inchcape was looking for Guy. "Tell him I'll be in after luncheon," he shouted and she felt the jolt of his receiver violently replaced.

He arrived while the Pringles and Yakimov were still at table. Guy had scoffed at Galpin's story of a Slav plot, saying the Russians would not seize territory on which they had no claim. Even if they did occupy the northern Dobrudja, that would not prevent British subjects leaving from Constanza.

Yakimov brought out his "*Quel débâcle!*" joke and showed an inclination to sit and talk, but Inchcape walked about the room with such a show of impatience that it eventually came to Yakimov that he was not wanted. When he went, Inchcape swung a chair round, sat astride it and said: "They're trying to get us out. They want us to go."

"Who wants us to go?" Guy asked. "The *prefectura* or the Legation?"

"The Legation. They're trying to thin out the British colony. They want to get rid of what they call the 'culture boys'."

"Because of this Dobrudja business?" Harriet asked.

"That among other things. Dobson had the cheek to suggest we've outlived our usefulness here. He said: 'You must realise that having you around means extra work for us.' That's all they're worrying about."

"Do you mean it's a definite order?"

"An attempt at one." Inchcape lit a cigarette and stamped angrily on the match. "But they can't expel us without good reason. Their first move is to get us to close down the English Department. Once they do that, they can say: 'What is the point of your being here?' I'm determined to stay open."

Guy nodded his support and Harriet wondered if any mention

had been made of the Propaganda Bureau, which, inactive in its heyday, was now moribund. Before she could ask, Inchcape stubbed out his cigarette, two-thirds unsmoked, into a saucer, and said: "When I was summoned to the Legation this morning, I insisted on seeing Sir Montagu."

"What happened then?" Guy asked.

Inchcape, his hand shaking, lit another cigarette. The war between nations was forgotten. He was waging his old war against the Legation. "I was called in, ostensibly about these notices to quit which we keep getting. Dobson said: 'We think it would be better if the summer school closed down.' I refused to discuss it with him. I demanded to see one of the top brass. They tried to fob me off with Wheeler. In the end, believe it or not, I got in to the old charmer himself. And what do you think he said? 'Summer school?' he said. 'What summer school?' I told him that before we could stop work we'd have to get a direct order from our London office. That's not likely to come in a hurry. No one at home has any real idea of what's going on here."

"And – ?"

"The old boy blustered a bit. I stood firm. So he said: 'If you stay, you do so at your own risk. I don't guarantee to get one of your fellows out of here alive.' "

"What about Woolley and the other businessmen?"

"He said they could look after themselves. They've got cars. When the time comes, they can drive into Bulgaria. He said: 'You chaps without cars won't find it so easy. The trains will be taking troops to the frontier. The civilian aircraft will be commandeered by the army. There won't even be a boat if Constanza's in Russian hands.' I said it was a risk we were prepared to take." Inchcape looked for confirmation to Guy.

Guy said: "Of course."

"Why?" asked Harriet.

"Because we have a job to do," Guy said: "While we're of any use here, we must stay."

"Exactly," said Inchcape. He sat down again, calmed by Guy's support. "Besides," he said, "there's the Cantecuzeno Lecture in the offing. Pinkrose is being flown out. He's getting a priority flight to Cairo. That's not granted to everyone. I shall certainly be here to welcome him."

"What else did Sir Montagu say?"

"He tried persuasion. 'You can only speak for yourself,' he

said. 'The other men should be consulted.' I said: 'I know my men.
I can speak for them.' 'Nevertheless,' he said, 'they should get
together and discuss the situation. Let Dobson have a word with
them!' I could see the wily old bastard thought I'd keep you in the
dark, so I said: 'Very well. I'll call a meeting this very evening.
Anyone can attend. I know my men, I know what they'll say.' "
Inchcape gazed intently at Guy, who again nodded his support.
Inchcape stood up, satisfied: "The staff-room at six, then."

"Can I come?" Harriet asked.

Inchcape looked round, surprised that she should feel concerned in this. "If you like," he said, then he turned to Guy again.
"Alert the others. Dubedat, Lush and the old ladies. I think you'll
find they're all behind us. No one wants to lose his job."

By six o'clock the haze was lifeless and yellowish, like a thin
smoke over the inert streets. The heat was stale and without fervour. The shops, though open, seemed asleep.

In the Calea Victoriei one pavement baked in the honey-yellow
sun, the other was Prussian blue. Harriet walked in the shade
until she reached the German Propaganda Bureau and there,
before crossing the road, she paused. The map of France had
appeared and disappeared in less than a month, but the map of
the British Isles had remained so long, people were losing interest
in it. Harriet was the only one looking in the window. She said to
herself: "They'll never get there," and saw that among the towns
ringed with flames was the one where she had been born – a town
she hated. Her eyes filled with tears.

On the other side of the road the gipsies, rousing themselves
from behind their great baskets, were squirting their flowers with
water from old enema bulbs. The sweet and heavy scent of tuberoses hung about the University steps. "Doamna, doamna,"
screeched the gipsies as Harriet made her way up.

When she passed into the building's gothic gloom, she could
hear Guy's voice. He was still in the lecture-room. She went back
to sit on the balustrade and watch the street waking up. When the
students came out she was surprised that they dispersed so quickly.
She waited, expecting more to come, but instead Guy came out
to look for her.

She said: "Why are there so few students?"

"Numbers have dropped off," he admitted. "It's quite usual.
Some of them get bored. Come along. The meeting has begun."

He hurried ahead of her down the long main passage that was too narrow for its height, and opened the common-room door. Inchcape was saying: ". . . a ridiculous state of affairs. The fact is, the Legation's trying to close down the summer school. I've called you all here to discuss it. After all, it's your bread and butter."

Elegant in a grey silk suit, he was sitting on the common-room table with one foot latched into a chair-rung. He smiled as he mentioned the malapert Legation. Apparently his rancour had gone, but his hands were gripping the back of the chair and he watched intently as the Pringles took their seats.

Clarence, stretched in the arm-chair from Guy's office, slid an oblique glance at Harriet as she sat down beside him. Frowning, he slid lower in the chair and began biting the side of his right forefinger. Toby caught her eye and grinned as though a particular understanding existed between them. The three women teachers watched Guy warmly. Dubedat kept his gaze fixed on Inchcape who, as soon as the room was settled again, said: "I happen to have good news up my sleeve. It came in just before I left the Bureau." As everyone fixed him expectantly, he smiled, holding the situation a moment before he said: "When our friend Dobson arrives, we may find the Legation has changed its tone."

Harriet wondered, was it possible that the war had ended? Miraculously and yet, of course, unsatisfactorily. No, the war couldn't end with the enemy unbeaten.

"I've just heard," Inchcape went on, "that last night the R.A.F. bombed Berlin."

"Why, that's splendid!" Guy said. Everyone murmured agreement, but they had clearly expected more.

"It *is* splendid. It means we're hitting back," said Inchcape. "This is the first time the German civilian has tasted this war. It is only a question of time before we're keeping them busy in the west, an eastern front will be out of the question."

Mrs. Ramsden gave an "ah!" of appreciation.

"A lot of things can happen before that day comes," Dubedat sombrely said.

"I'm not so sure," Inchcape pushed the chair from him and folded his arms. His smile suggested that he could, if he wished, justify his confidence. The others waited, but he said no more.

Feeling the silence begin to drag, Guy stood up. The women teachers turned to him as though he were about to solve something. He said: "The important thing is for us to stay. I mean, we should not run away. There are too many people here who need our support."

"I agree," Clarence's voice came rich, resonant and magnanimous from the depths of his chair.

The door fell open. "I do apologise," Dobson said as he hurried through it, his linen suit rumpled, a large patch of damp between his shoulder-blades. "They keep us at it day and night." He did not look at anyone but opened his eyes in amusement at things as they were and searched for a handkerchief. His face and head were pink. Beads of moisture stood among the downy hairs that patched his skull.

Inchcape stretched out his legs and jerked himself upright. "The floor is yours," he said.

Finding his handkerchief, Dobson patted all over his head. "Well now!" He smiled round with an appearance of easy faith in the good sense of those about him. "There isn't much to be said. I'm speaking for H.E., needless to say." At this, he stopped smiling and became serious. "Things are becoming unstuck here. You can see it for yourselves. Even His Majesty isn't feeling too secure on his throne. No one can be certain what will happen next. Our guess is that the Germans are planning to overrun the place. There's a pretty consistent pattern of events these days. A fifth column – in this case it would be the Iron Guard – creates trouble, giving Axis troops an excuse to march in and keep order. If this happens here, you may be given a chance to get out; then again, you may not. If you did get a warning, you might still fail to get transport. In any case, you'd probably have to abandon all your stuff. It could happen any time – next week, tomorrow, even tonight . . ." He looked round gravely and, meeting despondent eyes, smiled in spite of himself. "I don't want to scare you" – he swallowed his smile – "but there's not much point in waiting till it's too late. The English Department has done its bit. *Troilus and Cressida* was a simply splendid effort. The production boosted morale just when a boost was needed. I might say" – he gave a giggle – "you stuck to your posts like Trojans. Still" – he straightened his face again – "your work here is over. You must see that. H.E. thinks the department should close down and the staff pack up and get away in good order."

Having spoken, he glanced at Inchcape, restoring him to the centre of the attention. Inchcape did not move. Staring down at his white buckskin shoes, his hands clasped before him, he conveyed a modest intent to influence no one. After a long pause, he glanced up and from side to side, inviting independent opinion. Mrs. Ramsden's vast hat, trimmed with pheasant feathers, swung about as she looked for the next speaker, and her taffeta creaked. When no one else spoke, Miss Turner, the eldest of the three, said in her plaintive little voice: "We do know that things are bad here, but surely now that our aeroplanes have raided Berlin . . . I mean, surely that makes a difference?"

Dobson, leaning courteously towards her, explained as to a child: "We are all delighted about the raid. It's enormously good for our prestige, of course, but the situation here has deteriorated much too far to be affected by it. The truth is – we have to face it! – Rumania is, to all intents and purposes, in enemy hands."

Miss Turner looked sorrowfully at Inchcape, hoping for more favourable comment, but Inchcape had nothing to say. Guy again rose to his feet: "We've all known for some time that our situation here is precarious. In spite of that, we've chosen to stay. Probably we are a trouble to the Legation, but the point is . . ."

"My dear fellow," Dobson expostulated, "we're concerned for your safety."

"I am just twenty-four," Guy said. "Clarence, Dubedat and Lush are all of military age. Our contemporaries are in uniform. I do not think we're in any more danger here than we would be in the Western Desert."

Having decided what he would say, Guy said it with firm directness, but Harriet, watching him, realised he was under strain. He pressed the lower edge of his right palm against his brow and held it there as though for support. Coming from a provincial University and a background of poverty, he did not find it easy to withstand the majesty of the British Minister and his Legation.

He paused, then said quickly, almost aggressively: "I think we should remain in Bucharest while there is a job to be done."

"Here, here!" said Mrs. Ramsden.

"But *is* there a job to be done?" Clarence's tone had changed now to languid indecision. "What can we do – or the Legation, either, for that matter – remnants of a discredited force in what is virtually an enemy-occupied country?"

Guy said: "It's true, the British have failed here; but if we can stay to the end, we may give someone something to believe in during the time ahead. There are many people here in much greater danger than we are. For them we represent all that is left of Western culture and democratic ideals. We cannot desert them."

"Be reasonable, Pringle!" Dobson spoke amiably enough: "What have you got here now? A handful of Jewish students."

Guy answered: "While the Jewish students are loyal to us, we must remain loyal to them."

Dubedat, his face expressionless, was picking at an eye-tooth with one of his long dirty fingernails. Toby, pipe-sucking just behind him, leant forward and whispered something. Dubedat frowned him into silence.

Inchcape, bland now and smiling, sauntered forward, saying: "We must also remember the Cantecuzeno Lecture. Professor Lord Pinkrose is being flown out."

"Who the hell is Professor Lord Pinkrose?" Clarence asked. Lying there, supine, vacillating between truculence and sentiment, he was, Harriet realised, more drunk than sober.

Still smiling, Inchcape looked about him. "Does anyone need me to answer that?" he asked.

"The students are the first consideration," said Guy, dogged now in combating Legation indifference to his cause.

Harriet felt a stab of pride in him, yet felt, at the same time, some resentment that his first consideration was not their own safety. She knew, were it not for Sasha she would be concerned for nothing but getting Guy away before it was too late. Trapped here by her sense of responsibility for him, she was near to resenting Sasha too. And, she thought, it was Guy's easy, almost feckless willingness to adopt the world that had brought the boy into their home.

She did not really imagine that the Legation could persuade them to go 'in good order'. She had faith in Inchcape's determination to remain while there was any excuse for remaining, but she saw now that the problem of Sasha must be settled somehow. They must, when the time came, be free to go without a qualm.

Inchcape had taken the centre of the room again and was saying: "Pinkrose is out of the top drawer. That sort of thing goes down well with the Rumanians."

Apparently it also went down well with Dobson. He was already retreating. He had not been impressed by Guy's appeal for loyalty to the students, but here he was nodding in reverent approval as Inchcape enlarged on the social importance of the lecture and the lecturer. She was surprised that Dobson did not comment on the fact that the London office knew no better than to fly out this professor. Inchcape, of course, had kept them in ignorance of the true situation here – not wantonly, but from sheer unwillingness to face it. She smiled a little bleakly as it occurred to her that, thanks to Inchcape's vanity, Lord Pinkrose might end like the rest of them, in a German concentration camp.

"The lecture's a consideration, I agree," Dobson said, "though I'm sure H.E. would advise you to warn Lord Pinkrose what to expect here. If he knew the risks, he might think twice about coming . . ."

"I doubt that, I doubt that," Inchcape broke in affably.

"Well," Dobson concluded, "I suppose if your men are set on staying we'll have to let them stay, anyway for a while. But" – he turned to Mrs. Ramsden, Miss Turner and Miss Truslove – "the ladies are another matter. H.E. says he cannot accept liability for unmarried English ladies. That is, ladies without menfolk to look after them."

A moan passed among the three women. The feathers on Mrs. Ramsden's hat quivered as though set on wires. They looked at Dobson, who was beaming so pleasantly upon them, then turned to Inchcape for succour, but Inchcape, in high spirits at his victory, was willing to concede the women teachers. "On this point," he said, "I agree with His Excellency. I am sure you ladies would not wish to feel you were in the way here. Apart from that, your work is coming to an end. How many students enrolled for the summer school? Some two hundred. Now we've got – how many?" He cocked an inquiring eye at Guy, who answered reluctantly:

"About sixty. But the school is in five grades."

"It can be reorganised. The fact is," Inchcape looked at the women teachers, "your jobs will soon be folding up. You'd be better off elsewhere."

"We don't want to go," said Mrs. Ramsden.

"It's up to you, of course," Dobson said agreeably, "but when you next receive an order to quit I shall not be able to claim that your presence here is essential. It would be better for you to go in your own good time."

"But look here!" Mrs. Ramsden spoke with vigour, "We had all this when the war began. Mr. Woolley gave his general order for the ladies to leave Rumania. He sent his wife home. Dozens of others went at the same time and most of them never came back. We three went to Istanbul. We had to stay in a *pension* – a hole of a place, filthy dirty *and* expensive. We were miserable. We just sat about with nowhere to go and nothing to do. We spent all our savings – and for nothing, as it turned out. In the end we came back again. This is where we belong. Our homes are here. We're only old girls. The Germans wouldn't touch us."

"And I have my little income here," said Miss Turner, whose complexion had the bluish pallor of skimmed milk. "The Prince lets me have it, you know. I looked after his children for twenty years. I can't take this money out of the country. They won't let me. If I leave here, I'll be penniless."

"We'd rather stay and risk it," said Mrs. Ramsden.

"Dear lady," Dobson patiently explained, "if the Germans come in, they won't let you stay in your homes. You'll be sent to prison camps, somewhere like Dachau, a terrible place. You might be there for years. You'd never survive it."

Miss Truslove was dabbing at her eyes with a cotton glove. She spoke with an effort: "If I have to go away again, it'll kill me . . . kill me." Her speech ebbed and became a sob.

Inchcape patted her shoulder, but he was not to be moved. "In war-time," he said cheerfully, "we must all do things we don't like."

Miss Turner plucked at his sleeve: "But surely you said . . . this raid on Berlin . . ."

"Alas, that doesn't mean the end of the war," and he made a little gesture dismissing the whole subject.

Miss Truslove, near weeping, began struggling with her gloves. She moaned: "I can't get them on. I can't get them on."

Watching the old ladies, seeing them pitiable, Harriet knew nevertheless that Dobson was right. Mrs. Ramsden might eke out a few years in a prison camp, but Miss Turner and Miss Truslove, frail and nervous creatures, would be doomed. They were not looking so far ahead. Catching her eye, Mrs. Ramsden said: "I'm sure Mr. Pringle doesn't want us to go. I'd like to speak to him but" – she looked wistfully at Guy, who was talking to Dobson – "I suppose I shouldn't worry him now."

Harriet said: "Professor Inchcape is still in charge of the department. I'm afraid he has the last word."

As they moved off, they glanced back at Guy, hoping he would see them and somehow save them. But what could he do? He kept his back to them, probably in painful consciousness of their plight, and, with no excuse for lingering, they went.

Behind Harriet, Toby was talking about Cluj – the dangers he had foreseen there and his own wisdom in getting away before the present crisis developed. He claimed that the professor had attempted to "bully-rag" him with all sorts of threats into keeping his contract, but Toby knew that as a foreigner he could plead *force majeure*. It was typical of Toby's stories. He led one to believe he had always been involved in such a morass of University politics, only a very wily fellow could have survived. It occurred to her, as she glanced round at his soft, fleshy face, his soft chin slipping back from under his moustache, hearing him say in self-congratulation: "A chap's got to survive," that he might well survive where the rest of them would not.

Suddenly Dubedat stepped briskly over to Dobson and broke into his talk with Guy. "About this Slav plot," he said as though he had no time to waste: "is there any basis for believing we'll be cut off from Constanza?"

Dobson, abashed for only a moment, answered lightly: "So far as we know, none at all," then turning from this intrusion, continued his conversation with Guy: "Hitler cares nothing for Balkan politics. He is interested only in Balkan economics. He has ordered the Rumanians to settle these frontier problems simply to keep them busy until his troops are free to march in. That could be any day now."

Dubedat glanced at Toby and made a movement with his head. He left the room. Toby followed him without a word.

The porter came to ask if he could lock up. Inchcape led Dobson, Clarence and the Pringles from the building. On the terrace, they paused in the greenish glow of evening. As the swaddling bands of heat loosened and the air moved and cooled, people were crowding out of doors. This was the pleasantest hour of daylight. Dobson offered a lift to whomsoever should want it, but the others preferred to walk. "I must be off then," he said, and with his front line curving out before him he ran trippingly down the steps.

Waiting till he was out of earshot, Inchcape laughed. "The day is ours," he said.

Guy was not responsive. His face was creased with concern for the victims of their victory. He said: "Perhaps we could give Mrs. Ramsden and the others introductions to our representative in Ankara? They're good teachers. He could use them."

"Why not? Why not?" said Inchcape, adding at once: "Now

how are we to entertain Pinkrose? I'm afraid he's a bit of a stick."

Harriet leant on the balustrade, gazing down into the flower-baskets. As she had expected, Clarence made his way over to her, though slowly and, she felt, unwillingly. When he reached her, she said: "Will we ever get away?"

Clarence was not in a sympathetic mood. "You're free to go any time," he said. "You haven't even a job to keep you here."

"I have a husband. Even if I were willing to go without him, he couldn't afford to keep two homes going."

"You could get work of some sort."

"That's not so easy in a foreign country. Anyway, I'm staying while Guy stays."

The gipsies, excited by the growing crowds, were darting about in their chiffon flounces, accosting people with shrieks of "Dom-nuli . . . domnuli . . . domnuli."

Harriet noticed Sophie standing among the flowers in a yellow dress cut to enhance her large bosom and small waist. Whom was she waiting for? She looked up and, noting Clarence above her, began moving from basket to basket with the peculiar precision of someone conscious of the limelight. She smiled admiration all about her, then paused at a basket packed with rosebuds. She picked one out, sniffed at it ecstatically, then held it at arm's length. Harriet half-expected her to stand on the point of one foot and pirouette. Instead, she approached the vendor.

The summer before, Harriet had watched Sophie bargaining for violets. Then she had bargained sharply; now she was all art-less sweetness. When the gipsy named a price, she made a little movement of hurt protest but, helpless in a world where even beauty had a price, she paid without argument.

Harriet looked at Clarence. Clarence was watching Sophie with a peculiar smile. "Is she waiting for you?" Harriet asked.

"I suppose so." Clarence smirked, knowing he had surprised her: "Sophie seems to have become attached to me for some reason. She said the other day that when I'm drunk I have a dangerous look."

"Oh, really!" Harriet laughed with more irritation than amuse-ment: "I've seen you drunk often enough, but I've never seen you dangerous."

Clarence grunted, saying after a pause: "Sophie says you have no heart. I'm sure she isn't right."

"Do you want a woman with a heart?"

"No. I want someone as tough as old boots. In fact I want you. I knew you were my sort of woman the first time I set eyes on you. You could save me."

"You'd do better with Sophie."

Guy called to Harriet and he and Inchcape descended the steps. She followed with Clarence. Sophie, down on the pavement, showed surprise at seeing Clarence, but it was all spoilt by Clarence's reluctance to see her. She had to catch his arm. "I have had," she said, "a little chat with Mr. Dubedat and Mr. Lush. Ah, how nice is Mr. Lush! So straightforward, so honest, so simple and so kind of heart. A true representative of England, I would say." Her glance at Guy and Inchcape suggested they might well take a lesson from Mr. Lush, then she smiled at Clarence. Mumbling, shamefaced, he asked where they were going.

"I like so much Capşa's," said Sophie. "The garden there is so nice."

Clarence looked at Inchcape and the Pringles, but there was no escape. As they went in one direction, he was led off in the other.

11

DRUCKER'S TRIAL HAD BEEN TWICE POSTPONED, then suddenly, at the end of August, it was announced for the following day.

There was consternation among ticket-holders given less than twenty-four hours in which to arrange the luncheon and cocktail parties attendant upon such an occasion. Princess Teodorescu, with so many friends to be transported to the court-house, was forced to appear herself in the Athénée Palace foyer and commandeer every car-owner with whom she could claim acquaintance. Among them was Yakimov. Delighted to be drawn into the fun, if only in the capacity of chauffeur, he spent his last hundred *lei* getting the Hispano cleaned.

These were the dog days of summer when, at noon, the sky was like an open furnace, but Yakimov was not much discomposed by the heat. He walked nowhere. He would drive the distance between the Pringles' flat and the hotel, even though the Hispano accelerated so rapidly, he was scarcely started before he must stop again. He enjoyed what he called "the cut and thrust" of Bucharest traffic. He had regained all his old skill as a driver. Foxy Leverett, seeing him pull up outside the Athénée Palace, said: "You ride that car, old boy, as though you're part of it." Although he had to admit that drink and misfortune had bedevilled his nerves, he could, when he chose, keep 'the old girl' going at a steady hundred.

On the first morning of the trial he rose early and, bathed and dressed in his best, reported at the hotel lobby.

Galpin was there, watching preparations. "Going to the trial?" he asked.

"Why, yes, dear boy," smiled Yakimov.

The English journalists were the only ones not invited and Galpin said glumly: "A waste of time, the whole slapstick. His Majesty won't get a penny out of it."

"You mean he can't confiscate the oil holdings?"

"I mean he'll be out on his ear."

Before Yakimov had time to be perturbed by this prediction, he was seized on by Baron Steinfeld, who ordered him to escort Princess Mimi and Princess Lulie. The two girls were clearly displeased at being relegated to Yakimov, who could only hope that the sight of the Hispano, newly polished, its chrome asparkle, would console them. Mimi, indeed, gave him a cold smile, but Lulie kept her narrow, sallow face averted and her eyes fixed on the distance. Even when crushed with him in the seat, the girls maintained an aloof silence. He pressed the starter. The engine whirred and died. He pressed it again. Again the engine whirred and died, whirred and died.

The girls gazed blankly through the windscreen.

The indicator marked "*Essence*", broken some years before, stood permanently at "*demi*", but the tank was empty. He had been driving on Foxy's two hundred litres and had completely forgotten the need to replenish them.

Lulie, dropping her eyelids, murmured: "*Quel ennui!*"

"We'll have to take a taxi," Mimi said and looked at Yakimov, but Yakimov had no money for a taxi. He jumped from the car, promising to be back "in a brace of shakes", and hurried to the bar, where he set about trying to borrow money. Galpin did not lend money. No one else had any money to lend. By this time the lobby had cleared. The other cars had started off. When Yakimov emerged again, still penniless, the princesses had disappeared.

He stood for a long time beside the car, mourning over it and begging help of everyone known to him who entered or left the hotel – but there was no one in Bucharest these days who was willing to lend him anything.

In the end he had to leave the car where it stood, immediately outside the hotel entrance, and after two days the manager ordered him to move it.

He had begged Dobson to make him an advance on his remittance and had been reminded that the whole sum had gone on his visas and the cost of retrieving the Hispano from the Yugoslavs. Yakimov's heart sank. However would he get to Freddi?

"Couldn't you lend your Yaki a thou or two?"

"No," said Dobson. Guy also said: "No." This was the end. The days of his refulgence were over for ever. He was not only penniless, he was nearly in rags. He had only two things left in the world – his car and the sable-lined greatcoat which the Czar had given his father.

He would have to sell the car. Having made that decision, he was suddenly gleeful. He would be in the money again. He would "make a packet". With this thought in mind, he set out to visit car salesrooms, which confirmed what Dobson had said. Only a few persons could afford to run a car like the Hispano, and those few were all Jews. As Jewish cars were being requisitioned by the army, it was unlikely anyone would buy it at all.

At last a salesman, whose window was at the junction of the Calea Victoriei and the Boulevard Breteanu, lent Yakimov a can of petrol with which to bring the car to the shop. "*C'est beau,*" he admitted when he saw it, but he would not buy. He agreed to display the car and would try to sell it for Yakimov. So it was driven into the large triangular window and left there.

Yakimov received no sympathy in the bar for the loss of the Hispano. When it had first appeared in Bucharest, Hadjimoscos had refused to go out and look at it, implying with a gesture that his life had been littered with such cars. Now he said: "Even were there no requisitions, only a fool would buy an Hispano. It eats up the *essence* and is without accommodation. No doubt, too, there will be many such cars for sale. The English, having failed to protect us, now run away to protect themselves."

Yakimov, quite bewildered, said: "It's true, dear boy, that a few old ladies have gone – Mrs. Ramsden and that lot – but . . ."

"I do not refer to old ladies," Hadjimoscos, agleam with malice, spoke very distinctly. "I refer to Mr. Dubedat and Mr. Lush."

"Lush and Dubedat? I'm sure you're mistaken, dear boy."

"I think not. They were seen leaving the town with very much luggage. People say they are no longer at the University."

Knowing nothing of this, Yakimov could only shake his head. When he returned to luncheon, he said to Guy: "There's a *canard* going round that Lush and Dubedat have packed their traps and hopped it. Not true, I'm sure."

Guy said nothing.

"They're still here, aren't they?" Harriet asked.

Guy shook his head. "I'm afraid they *have* gone."

"You said nothing about it. When did they go?"

"I've been expecting them to turn up. They told me they were going away for the week-end. I took their classes on Monday, then, when they weren't back on Wednesday, I sent a porter round to their flat. There was no one there, but the hall-porter there told him they'd paid off their servant and taken all their stuff away.

This morning they heard at the Consulate that Toby's old car has been found abandoned on the quayside at Constanza."

"They've bolted! They've gone to Istanbul."

After a pause, Guy said: "I suppose one can't blame them."

"Why can't one blame them?"

"They don't belong to the organisation. It's chance employment for them. Why should we expect them to take such a risk?"

"And now you have no help at all? You're alone at the University!"

"I'll manage somehow," said Guy.

That was all that was said in front of Yakimov. When he had retired, Harriet said: "With all these things happening, I have a feeling we won't be here much longer."

"Oh, I don't know. Things could settle down."

"I'm getting worried about Sasha."

Guy, preoccupied, said: "He's all right up there, isn't he?"

"Yes, he's all right. But what is going to happen to him if we go."

"We'll have to think about that. Would Bella take him in?"

"Bella? You're crazy."

"You said she was a decent sort."

She laughed at the fact Guy had simply taken her word for it, and said: "So she is, in a way, but one couldn't expect her to take in a Jewish deserter whom she has never met. Anyway, left alone here, she'll have her own problems. What about your students? Isn't there one who would hide him?"

"Several would, I'm sure," he said, then on reflection, he added: "But would it be fair to ask them? Besides, they're all hoping to get away. He would merely exchange one temporary refuge for another."

"Then what do you suggest?"

"Nothing at the moment." Mildly exasperated by her persistence, he added: "Now that Lush and Dubedat have gone, I have to rearrange all the classes. We can discuss this problem of Sasha when we have more time."

"All right," she said, wondering as she did so whether he had ever given any thought to it. How much feeling had he for Sasha? He had been fond of the boy when they were master and pupil. He had been grateful to the Druckers for extending their friendship to him while he was alone here. But how involved was he now? She felt the trouble was that Guy was fond of too many people.

Allegiance was a narrow business. She had almost ceased to expect it from him. It would be as difficult, she thought, to tie him down on Sasha's behalf as on her own.

Her long silence caused him to say: "Don't worry. We're not leaving tomorrow. We'll think of something." When she still did not speak, he went round the table, took her hands and pulled her up. "You don't trust me enough," he said.

She slid her arms round his waist and felt reassured by the nearness of his warm, muscular body. "Of course I trust you," she said and, their dissensions forgotten, they went into their room. But Guy could not forget the time for long. With all the work of the summer school on his hands, he would not even wait for tea.

As he was dressing, she said: "Couldn't I take some of the classes for you?"

He shook his head doubtfully: "You've no experience of teaching, you're quite unqualified and it's more difficult than you think."

12

When Guy left, Harriet, fretted by the peculiar insipidity of life at that hour, went out to the balcony and looked over the empty square. The air was furred with heat. On the pavement the Guardist youths with their banners and pamphlets, were still trying to rouse revolt. Although a sense of revolt agitated the nerves like an electric storm that would not break, the city was lethargic, the palace dormant, its white blinds drawn down against the tedium of the afternoon.

A third conference had broken down and now the Transylvanian question was being discussed in Vienna. People had begun again to believe it would be solved by proving insoluble. Yakimov, repeating the opinion of the bar, had said: "Dear girl, it'll all trickle out in talk, talk, talk."

It was barely five o'clock, but already the light had an autumnal richness. The height of summer was past. The dahlias were ablaze in the Cismigiu. Up the Chaussée, the trees were parched, their few leaves dangling like burnt paper, as they had been the first time she saw them. The brilliant months had gone down in fear and expectation of departure.

She had been married a year. It was, as Guy liked to point out, a pre-war marriage. With a sadness that seemed an emanation of the deepening, dusty colour of the air, she thought perhaps it might not, after all, prove to be what it had seemed at first, an eternal marriage. She could imagine the loosening of the bond. Guy had said to her: "You can't trust me enough," yet he had not had cause to say that when, after three week's acquaintance, she had crossed Europe with him. If she did not trust him now, if, left on her own, she sought companionship elsewhere, he had himself to blame.

At that moment, she remembered that Sasha had asked her to do something for him. He had asked her to try and see his father.

Drucker was, for the moment, the most talked-of man in Bucharest; the *u* sound of his name seemed constantly in the air. Despina's husband had brought in the information that at different times of the day the accused man could be seen entering and leaving the back entrance of the court-house. Despina, always eager to impart news, had run at once to tell Sasha. The next time Harriet had gone up on the roof, she had found him awaiting her in great excitement. He began eagerly to beg to be allowed to go, that very evening, to see his father leave the court, and perhaps even accost him.

Harriet had been appalled at the suggestion. "It's out of the question," she said. "The military police are looking for you. They might be waiting there for you, and there's the danger someone might recognise you, especially if you spoke to him . . ."

He had interrupted eagerly: "I could stand where no one would see me. I could just look at him."

"Wherever you stood, someone might see you. The risk is too great."

Used to his gentle compliance, she was surprised when he persisted, his face becoming vivid with his eagerness to go. She reasoned with him as with a child that must be protected against its own rashness.

After a few minutes, his fervour suddenly collapsed. He looked so desolate that she felt guilty and wondered how much of her own opposition came of a will to control him. In a way Guy had eluded her, but Sasha was not only her pet and dependent, he was her prisoner. Nevertheless, she could not permit him to walk into a trap.

Watching her, he said: "If you won't let me go, will you go yourself? If you saw him, you might be able to speak to him."

Startled by this suggestion, Harriet said: "If I went, what could I say."

"Tell him I'm with you. Say: 'Don't worry about Sasha. We are looking after him.' "

That had been yesterday morning. Although she had not agreed to go, she had not actually refused. She discovered that Drucker left the court-house at midday, returned at three o'clock and left again at six o'clock, but she made no attempt to see him at any of those times. If she did go, she knew she would not speak to him. For one thing, his warders would probably not permit such a thing. For another, the English were conspicuous here. She must not give the outside world cause to connect her with the Druckers. Apart from all that, she had no wish to seem to gape at a man who had suffered the rigours of nine months in a Rumanian prison.

She decided she could not go. Yesterday evening, when Sasha was expecting her to bring him news of his father, she had failed to visit him. As she wondered how she could excuse her dereliction, she suddenly felt that he had not asked so much of her. Turning to her image of Guy, she protested: "If you give your devotion to others, why shouldn't I?"

She started out immediately after tea. As she crossed the square she noticed the blinds were being raised in the palace and cars were entering through the palace gates. She could see from their white uniforms that the new arrivals were Crown councillors. The square, too, was coming to life. People were strolling in from the side-streets and gathering on the pavement outside the palace rail. Their pace suggested not so much an event as hope of one.

By the time she had reached the main road, the newsboys were out. She bought *L'Indépendence Romaine* and read two lines in the stop press. Agreement had been reached in Vienna. Terms would be announced.

No time was given for the announcement, but people were coming out into the streets, all, for some reason, lively, as though expectant of good news.

The trial was again of secondary importance. On previous days, crowds of spectators had gathered to view the ticket-holders and the famous forty-nine witnesses called against the accused. This evening there were scarcely a dozen round the front entrance. At the back, in an area of small warehouses and workrooms still at work, there were some six or eight. They were discussing the news of the Transylvanian settlement and took no notice of Harriet.

A smell of salt fish hung in the air and the narrow, cobbled pavements were gritty with sand. A windowless van was at the kerb, its doors open to receive Drucker, who was due to appear at any minute. Harriet stood behind a group of clerks and gathered from their conversation that the prevailing optimism was based on the fact that Rumania had been acknowledged as a partner of the Axis. The Führer would see that she received fair treatment. One clerk said they might have to cede a province or two, but no more. In his opinion the German minorities in Transylvania favoured the Rumanian cause because the Rumanians, as a people, were more amenable than the arrogant, independent Hungarians.

The court door was thrown open and two warders emerged. Harriet, who had seen Drucker only once, ten months before, remembered him as a man in fresh middle age, tall, weighty, elegant, handsome, who had welcomed her with a warm gaze of admiration.

What appeared was an elderly stooping skeleton, a cripple who descended the steps by dropping the same foot each time and dragging the other after. The murmurs of "Drucker" told her that, whether she could believe it or not, this was he. Then she recognised the suit of English tweed he had been wearing when he had entertained the Pringles to luncheon. The suit was scarcely a suit at all now. As he approached, she noticed his trousers were so worn at the knees that she could see, as it bent against the cloth, the white bone of his knee-cap, but the broad herringbone pattern showed through the grime.

From the bottom step he half-smiled, as though in apology, at his audience, then, seeing Harriet, the only woman present, he looked puzzled. He paused and one of the warders gave him a kick that sent him sprawling over the narrow pavement. As he picked himself up, there came from him a stench like the stench of a carrion bird. The warder kicked at him again and he fell forward, clutching at the van steps and murmuring "*Da, da*," in zealous obedience.

As soon as the van doors closed on him, Harriet, unconscious now of the ferment of the pavements, hurried back to the Calea Victoriei. By the time she reached the end of it, she had decided she could safely deceive Sasha. He was never likely to see his father again.

There was now a considerable crowd in the square. Approaching her block of flats, she glanced up at the roof and saw Sasha on the parapet, staring down towards her. When she reached him, she was able to say convincingly: "Your father looked very well."

"You really saw him?" He had jumped down at the sight of her and brushed his cheeks with the back of his hand, but she could see he had been crying. He asked eagerly: "And were you able to speak to him? Did you tell him I was living here."

"Yes of course."

"I am sure he was pleased."

"Very pleased. I can't stay, I'm afraid. Guy is bringing a friend in to supper," and she went to avoid answering further questions.

The friend was David Boyd whom Harriet had not seen since their last meeting in the English Bar. He had then gone for a "bird-watching week-end", which had become so protracted that Guy had at last telephoned the Legation to ask for news of him. Foxy Leverett's secretary would say nothing but "The Legation is not alarmed by Mr Boyd's absence."

When David telephoned that morning Harriet had felt relief at his safe return, realising he had become important to her as one of their small and dwindling community. His sound nerves were comforting. And he was Guy's friend. Whoever might desert them, David, she was sure, would stay to the end.

While awaiting the men, she heard a sound of agitation in the square and was about to send Despina to discover the cause of it, when Guy and David came in through the front door. David was talking loudly: "It's exactly what Klein predicted. You remember his image of the great fortune? Well, this is the last of it down the drain. The country is falling to pieces."

As they entered the room the two men, both large, their dissimilarities masked by sunburn, looked remarkably alike. They differed only in the colour of their hair. Guy had become bleached by the sun, David had remained very dark. His black curls glistened with moisture, and moisture lay along the ridge of his large dark chin. Both were carrying their jackets caught under their elbows. They had been walking and their shirts were soaking. A smell of sweat entered with them.

Guy said: "The terms of the settlement are out. Rumania has to cede the whole of Northern Transylvania: the richest part of it."

"Quite a nice bit of territory," David said, snuffling in delight: "Area about seventeen thousand square miles, population two and a half millions. But it means more than that. The Rumanians are emotional about Transylvania, 'the cradle of the race'. This means trouble – as I imagine His Majesty will soon discover."

Harriet asked: "What's happening outside now?"

"People are weeping in the streets."

Harriet, shocked, felt like weeping herself. If asked, she would have said she expected nothing different and yet she had, she realised, ingested the baseless, febrile hopes that had lately possessed the Rumanians.

While they ate supper the sun slipped down behind the sunset clouds, heaped, livid, in the west, their gloom hung over the square. The crowds seemed muted now as by catastrophe. Even the traffic had stopped. Harriet, with little appetite for food, felt, as she had felt after the earthquake, a desire to be in the open and touch the ground.

She said: "But are the Rumanians bound to accept this?"

"What else can they do?" David asked. "The terms were dictated by Ribbentrop and Ciano. The Rumanian ministers were told that if they did not accept, their country would immediately be occupied by German, Hungarian and Russian troops."

"The Rumanians might fight," said Harriet.

Eating heartily, exhilarated by events, David said in tolerant amusement at her folly: "A war between Rumania and Germany would be like the life of primitive man: nasty, brutish and short."

"Why are the Rumanians being treated in this way?"

"They must be asking that themselves. I suppose they're being made to pay for their old friendship with Britain. There's also a story going round that Carol, while pretending to play ball with Hitler, was in fact trying to form a military alliance with Stalin."

"Do you think that's true?" Guy asked.

"Whether true or not, it will be believed. Carol is a clever man whose behaviour from beginning to end has been that of a fool. The worst thing is that this division is not going to solve any of the Transylvanian problems. Hitler is simply cutting the baby in half. But what does he care? He's keeping the Hunks quiet; and if he ever wants their help, he'll probably get it."

They took their coffee out on to the balcony where the twilight had almost turned to dark. The chandeliers were alight inside the main rooms of the palace. A great crowd filled the square. The stunned silence was breaking now and a sense of perturbation came up upon the air. The shadows below were moving; someone was addressing them, then a single tenor voice was lifted in the national anthem that began "*Treasca Regili*" – Hail the King!

The first words were scarcely out when the singing was lost in a hubbub of angry shouting. The word "*abdică*" rose above the uproar and was taken up and repeated in different parts of the square, gathering volume until it seemed all the country's protest was resolved into the single demand that the King be king no longer.

13

THE WEEK THAT FOLLOWED was a trying one for Yakimov. Whenever, on his way to and from the bar, he tried to cross the square, he was harangued and buffeted by people demonstrating for or against the King – usually against. Leaflets were pushed into his hand in which Carol was condemned as a traitor. The Guardists declared they had proof of his attempt to form an alliance with Russia. This shocking act of treachery, they said, had alienated their German friends. In view of this the Axis decision on Transylvania had been a just one. The country had paid for the sins of its ruler.

The Guardists, however, were the only ones who had a good word for the Axis these days. So this, people said, was how the Führer treated his children! This was their reward for sending their beasts, crops and oil to Germany! The truth was, Hitler had failed in his attempts to invade Britain, and had turned, in spite, against Rumania! Yakimov had actually seen a swastika torn from a car and trodden underfoot, but the sight had merely increased his trepidation at these disturbances. "*Quel débâcle!*" he said, "*quel débâcle!*" and it was no longer a little joke.

Hadjimoscos especially upset him by describing the frightful consequences should the King be dethroned. Ignored by the Guardists and having nothing to hope for from them, Hadjimoscos had become a fervent royalist. The departure of the King, he declared, would bring "absolute anarchy". "We of the old aristocracy," he said to Yakimov, "would be the first to suffer. You, as a member of the English ruling class, would face immediate arrest. The Guardists are frantically anti-British. I would not put it past those fellows to erect the guillotine. It will be *la Terreur* all over again, I assure you. We are in this together, *mon prince*," and he gave Yakimov's arm a squeeze, for the Rumanians, in their bitterness against Germany, were remembering their attachment to their old ally.

Britain had declared against the division of Transylvania and suddenly everyone was saying that, in spite of everything,

Britain would win the war and restore all Rumania's possessions. And perhaps she would! But not in time to save poor Yaki.

Sunday afternoon being a time when everyone was free, the commotion in the square was much greater than usual. Someone, bawling in the midst of the crowd, was rousing so much anger that Yakimov was prompted to make a detour, but he felt too tired. Bemused from his siesta and the dense heat, he slipped into the crowd and moved vaguely towards the hotel. The going was easy for a dozen yards, then he began to strike impassable knots of people. He changed direction again and again, each time finding the press growing thicker about him. When he glimpsed the speaker – a young man flinging himself wildly about on a platform – he realised he was going in the wrong direction. He attempted retreat, but the ranks had closed in behind him. Here people were not only compacted but, in full hearing of the frenzied oratory, were in a state of furious excitement. Tense, inflamed, straining and shouting, they had no awareness of Yakimov, who, murmuring apologies, began trying to edge out through any crack he could find.

Suddenly, it seemed to him, his neighbours went mad. They not only shouted, they threw up their arms, shook fists, stamped feet, and he, inadvertently struck and jolted, could only cower and plead: "Steady, dear boy, steady!" As the turbulence grew about him, there was a violent surge forward and Yakimov was carried with it, so tightly held that he could not raise his arms. He felt stifled, not only by the pressure on his frail chest and belly, but by the heat of the crowd and its reek of sweat and garlic. Feeling that his lungs had collapsed, so he could not even call for help. In terror, knowing that if he lost consciousness he would be dragged down and trampled underfoot, he reached out and clung to the man in front of him. This was a large black-bearded priest whose veiled headgear had been dodging about before Yakimov's eyes like a ship's funnel in a gale. The priest was howling with the rest of them – something to do with Transylvania, of course – while Yakimov, certain the killing was about to begin, hung round his shoulders, pleading in a whisper: "For God's sake, save me, Let me out."

He was thinking: "This is the end for Yaki," when he felt a slackening of the frenzy about him. Warning shouts were coming from the edge of the crowd. In a moment, the speaker had dropped from his platform and disappeared into anonymity. People began straining round, and as calls of "*Politeul*" passed among them the struggle turned outwards. Caught in this new movement, Yakimov, almost dead of compression and fear, held like a drowning man to the priest, who stood still, anchored by sheer weight in the current.

Through the thinning crowd Yakimov could see the reason for the dispersal. The police were preparing to turn hoses on the demonstrators. As the jets of water were raised, he tried to run with the rest, but now the priest to whom he had clung, clung to him, seizing and gripping his hand to hold him upright as men pelted past them, bouncing against them like boulders in an avalanche. Yakimov, thrown in every direction by these blows, felt as though his arm was being wrenched from its socket. He cried to be released, but the priest held to him, all the while grinning reassuringly at him with gigantic, grey-brown teeth.

The square cleared. No one remained by Yakimov and the protector from whom he was still struggling to escape. Both of them were soaked. At last the priest thought it safe to let go his hold. Smiling the smile of a benefactor, he brushed Yakimov down, patted him on the back and sent him on his way.

Yakimov made straight for cover. Stumbling, trembling, dripping with water, he fell into the English Bar, which at that time of day was packed with journalists. Galpin and Screwby were there together with old Mortimer Tufton and the visitors from neighbouring capitals who always turned up when trouble was in the air.

Yakimov did not wait to see if anyone would offer him a drink. He went to the bar and bought one for himself. He longed to talk of his experience, but those around were too busy discussing what had occurred to notice someone who had been in the midst of it. He swallowed his *țuică*, then, trembling and sweating and seeking comfort, he stood as near as he dared to Galpin.

When Galpin bought a round of drinks, a glass came accidentally to Yakimov, who gulped it down before anyone could take it from him. Short of a drink, Galpin looked round to account for it and, noticing Yakimov, shot out an arm and seized him. "I've been looking for you," he said.

Terror following on terror, Yakimov cried: "I didn't mean to. I thought it was meant for me."

"Pipe down. I'm not going to eat you." Still holding to him,

Galpin led him out of the bar into the lobby. "I want you to do a little job for me."

"A *job*, dear boy?"

"You did a job for McCann once, remember? Well, I want you to give me a hand. I suppose you've heard that the Hungarians march into Transylvania on the fifth. I ought to get to Cluj to see the take-over, but I've got to stay here in case the balloon goes up. So I want you to go to Cluj for me."

Yakimov's immediate thought was of Freddi, but all the spirit had been shaken out of him. "I don't know, dear boy," he said, hesitant. "It's a long journey, and with the country in revolt . . ."

"You'd be a lot safer there than here," Galpin assured him. "*This* is where the trouble will be. It's all centred round the palace. Cluj is unaffected. Good food, charming place, nice people. Restful journey. All expenses paid. Could you ask for more?"

"What would I have to do?"

"Oh, just keep your eyes and ears open. Get the atmosphere of the place. Look around, tell me what's going on." When Yakimov still showed no enthusiasm, Galpin added: "I helped you when you needed help. You want to help me, don't you?"

"Naturally, dear boy."

"Well, then . . . You'd only be away a couple of nights. I must have the news hot."

Yakimov, recovering as the attraction of the trip took hold of him, said: "Delighted to go, of course. Delighted to help. And, I may say, you've come to the right man. I've a friend there in a very important post. Count Freddi von Flügel."

"Good God! The bloody Gauleiter?" Galpin's yellow eyeballs started out at Yakimov. "You can't go and see *him*." Then as Yakimov's face fell, he added quickly: "It's up to you, of course. After all, he's a friend of yours. That makes a difference. Go and see him if you want to, but leave me out of it." Galpin drew out a note-case. "I'll advance you five thousand for expenses. If that doesn't cover things, we'll settle up when you get back."

Yakimov held out a hand, but Galpin, on reflection, put the case back again. "I'll give it to you when you leave. That'll be Wednesday. Give them time to get steamed up. You'd better take the midday train. I'll call for you eleven-thirty, take you to the station myself. Come along." He gripped Yakimov as though intending to keep him in custody until he went: "I'll buy you another drink."

14

AWAKENED BY EXCITEMENT on Wednesday morning, Yakimov was up and dressed before ten o'clock. The idea of Cluj now possessed him. His one thought was to get to safety, Freddi and good food; his one fear that transport might stop before he could set out.

The disturbances during the last days had been an agony to him. There had been constant uproar in the square. Shots had been fired at the palace. Rumours of every sort had gone round. Antonescu had been summoned to the palace and ordered to form a government. He had said he would not serve under a non-constitutional monarchy. At this, he had been sent back to prison again.

Yakimov had scarcely hoped to reach Wednesday alive. And now at last it was Wednesday. The square was quiet. The King was still in his palace and so far as Yakimov was concerned, all was right with the world.

Harriet was still at the breakfast table when he made his early appearance. She had just heard on the radio that the Drucker trial had ended late the previous evening. Drucker had been found guilty and sentenced to three terms of imprisonment for different currency offences: seven years, fifteen years and twenty-five years to run consecutively. She added these up on the margin of a newspaper and discovered that the banker was to be imprisoned for forty-seven years. And nobody cared, nobody was interested. The court had been almost empty when sentence was pronounced. The trial which was to be "the major social occasion of the summer", had become a hurried, paltry affair, precipitated by crisis and fear of invasion.

Harriet was astonished when Yakimov told her he was leaving for Cluj. It had never entered her head that he might take himself off, even for a couple of nights.

She said: "Do you think it's a good idea leaving Bucharest at a time like this?"

"Yaki will be all right. Going on important business, as a matter of fact. Could call it a mission."

"What sort of mission?"

" 'Fraid I can't divulge, dear girl. Hush-hush, you understand? But between you and me and the gate-post, I've been told to keep m'eyes and ears open."

"Well, I hope you don't end up in Bistrita."

He gave a nervous laugh. "Don't frighten your poor old Yaki."

When he had finished breakfast – one of those wretched skin-flint meals that made him impatient for Freddi's hospitality – he went back to his room to pack. Most of his clothing was now beyond repair. He picked out the best of it and filled his crocodile case. When he took his passport from a drawer, he found, folded inside it, the plan of the oil-well which he had taken from Guy's desk. Not knowing what else to do with it, he put it into his pocket. He was forced, for fear of rousing Galpin's suspicions, to leave behind his sable-lined greatcoat; but, if need be, his old friend Dobbie could send it on to him through the diplomatic bag.

Yakimov travelled in the dining-car. Even had he wished to sit anywhere else, there would have been no room for him. He had arrived to find every carriage of the midday train crowded and the corridors made impassable by peasants packed together, their feet entangled in their gear. The dining-car was locked. At either entrance affluent-looking men, carrying brief-cases, stood awaiting admission. A few minutes before twelve the doors were unlocked. The men elbowed one another in and Yakimov went in with them. "There you are," said Galpin, "You'll do the trip in style." Yakimov found a seat and was well satisfied.

Luncheon was served at once; a wretched luncheon. A Hungarian complained and the head waiter shouted at him: "You'll get nothing at all when your German friends follow you into Transylvania."

Some deplorable coffee followed: there was no sugar. Now that beet was being exported to Germany, sugar was becoming scarce in Rumania. When the meal ended, the stifling heat of the car became weighted by cigarette smoke. It was past three o'clock. The train still stood in Bucharest station. There was no explanation of the delay and no one seemed perturbed by it. It was enough for the passengers that they were on a train that must move some time, while outside there were vast and agitated numbers of those who were not on any train at all.

The meal was paid for, the tables cleared. Conversation failed in the oppressive heat and one by one the men – Yakimov among them – folded their arms on the wine-stained, rumpled cloths, dropped down their heads and slept among the crumbs. Most of them did not know when the train started.

Somehow or other it crawled up into the mountain. Yakimov was awakened when the waiters brought round coffee and cakes. Anyone refusing these refreshments was told he must give up his seat.

Munching the dry, soya-flour cakes and sipping the grey coffee, Yakimov gazed out at the crags and pines of the Transylvanian Alps. The train stopped at every small station. People on the platform were wearing heavy clothing, but the air, unchanged inside the carriage, remained warm, flat and clouded like stale beer. Depressed by the magnificence of the scenery, Yakimov hid his face in the dusty rep window curtain and went to sleep again.

The afternoon faded slowly into evening. Every half an hour or so, coffee was served, each cup weaker than the last. Yakimov began to worry as his money dwindled. He knew he should leave the car but, seeing at either end of the carriage the doorways packed with men only too ready to displace him, he stayed where he was.

At Braşov a seat became vacant and the first of those waiting hurried into it. He slapped down a brief-case and a large weighty bag, took off his silver-coloured Homburg and sat down, an important-looking Jew. Despite his importance, he could not refrain from nervously opening and shutting the brief-case, taking out papers, glancing at them, putting them back and so bringing Yakimov to full wakefulness. Yakimov sat up, yawning and blinking, and the Jew, looking critically at him, said: "*Sie fahren die ganze Strecke, ja?*"

When he discovered that Yakimov was English, his manner changed, becoming confiding though overweening. He took out a Rumanian passport and waved it at Yakimov. "You see that?" he said. "It is mine since two years. For it I pay a million *lei*. Now" – he struck it contemptuously with the back of his fingers – "what is it now? A ticket to a concentration camp."

"Surely not as bad as that?" Yakimov said.

The Jew sniffed his contempt. "You English are so simple. You cannot believe the things that happen to others. Have you not seen those madmen of the Iron Guard? In 1937 what did they do? They took the Jews to the slaughter-house and hung them on meat-hooks."

"But you're going to Cluj," said Yakimov. "When the Hungarians come in, you can get a Hungarian passport."

"What!" The Jew now looked at him with anger as well as contempt. "You think I go there to live? Certainly not. I go to close my branch office, then I come away double-quick. The Hungarians are terrible people – they are ravening beasts. Now it is very dangerous in Cluj."

"Dangerous?" Yakimov was startled.

"What do you think?" the Jew scoffed at him: "You think the Rumanians hand over like gentlemen. Naturally, it is dangerous. There are shootings in the streets. The shops are boarded up. No one has food . . ."

"Do you mean the restaurants are closed?"

The Jew laughed. He slapped his bag and said: "Here I bring my meat and bread."

Noting Yakimov's glum expression, he spoke with relish of raping, pillage, slaughter and starvation. The Rumanians had introduced land reform. Under the Hungarians the peasants would have to give up their small plots.

"So," said the Jew, "they are running wild in the streets. Already people have been killed and the doctors are packing their hospitals and leaving. They will attend no one. It is a terrible time. Did you not ask why the train came so late from Bucharest? It was because there was so much rioting. They feared the train would be wrecked."

"Dear me!" said Yakimov to whom it was now clear that Galpin had chosen the safer part.

"You go perhaps on business?"

"No, I am a journalist."

"And you do not know how are things in Cluj?" The Jew laughed and looked pityingly at Yakimov, while outside a gloomy twilight fell on a landscape in which there was no sign of life. Dinner was served, the worst Yakimov had ever eaten. He grudged the cost of it, especially as he was left with barely enough to pay for a night's lodging.

In the grimy ceiling of the car a few weak bulbs appeared. The landscape faded away, and now there was nothing to look at but the weary faces of other passengers.

About midnight they began rousing themselves, hoping for the journey's end. No coffee had been served since dinner. The kitchen had closed down, yet the train dragged on for another two hours.

When they reached Cluj, Yakimov rose to bid his companion goodbye, but the Jew, having collected his possessions some time before, was already up and fighting his way off the train. Most of the other dining-car passengers were doing the same thing, so that in a few minutes Yakimov found himself alone. The platform, when he reached it, was dark and empty of officials or porters. The offices were shut and padlocked. A soldier with a rifle at the station entrance re-roused Yakimov's apprehensions.

Outside the station he saw the reason why the others had left in such a hurry. There were no taxis, but there had been half a dozen ancient *trăsurăs* which had been commandeered and were moving off. Those who had failed to snatch one had to walk. It was surprising how few people there were. The train must have emptied at stations along the line and Yakimov set out with only a handful of other persons towards the town. These dispersed in different directions, so that soon he knew from the silence that he was alone.

He had expected mobs and riots, but now he feared the road's emptiness. It was a long road hung down the centre with white globes of light that were reflected in the glossy tarmac. The pavements were dark. Anything might lurk in the hedges. He was relieved when he reached the first houses. Almost at once he found himself in the cathedral square which, Galpin had told him, was the centre of the town. The main hotel was here. Galpin had promised to telephone and book him a room. Seeing its vestibule lighted, he told himself thankfully that they had waited up for him.

When he entered and gave his name the young German clerk made a gesture of hopelessness. No one could have telephoned because the telephone equipment was being dismantled; not that a call would have made any difference. The hotel had been full for days. Every hotel in Cluj was full. Rumanians were coming here to settle up their Transylvanian affairs. Hungarians were crowding in to seize the business being relinquished by others. "Such is the take-over," said the young man. "There is not a bed to be found in the whole town." Looking sorry for Yakimov, who looked sorry for himself, he added: "At the station you could sleep on a bench."

Yakimov had another idea. He asked the way to the house of Count Freddi von Flügel. Seeming pleased that Yakimov had this refuge, the young German came to the hotel entrance with him and showed him a white eighteenth-century Hungarian house that stood four-square not a hundred yards away.

Despite the heat of the night, all the shutters of the house were closed. Its massive iron-studded door made it look like a fortress. Yakimov hammered on this door for five minutes or more before a grille opened and the porter inside, speaking German, ordered him to be off and return, if he must return, in the morning. Yakimov, putting his hand in the grille to prevent its being closed on him, said: "*Ich bin ein Freund des Gauleiters, ein sehr geschätzter Freund. Er wird entzückt sein, mich zu begrüssen.*" He repeated these statements several times, becoming tearful as he did so, and they slowly took effect. The door was opened.

The porter motioned him to sit on a stone seat in a stone hall that was as cold as a cellar. He sat there for twenty minutes. Having come from the summer night, wearing his silk suit, he began to shiver and sneeze. There was nothing to distract him but some giant photographs of Hitler, Goring, Göebbels and Himmler, which he contemplated with indifference. To him they were nothing but the stock-in-trade of someone else's way of life. If Freddi were "in with that lot", then all the better for both of them.

At last, at last, a figure appeared at the top of the stone staircase. Yakimov jumped up crying: "Freddi."

The Count, doubtful, frowning, descended slowly, then, recognising Yakimov, he threw open his arms and sailed down with rapid steps, his yellow brocade dressing-gown floating out about him. "It is possible?" he asked. "Yaki, *mein Lieber!*"

Tears of relief filled Yakimov's eyes. He tottered forward and fell into Freddi's arms. "Dear boy" – he spoke on a sob – "so many bridges gone under the water since we last met!" He held to his old friend fervently, breathing in the strong smell of gardenia that came from his person. "Fredi," he murmured, "Fredi!"

The emotional moment of reunion past, von Flügel stepped back and contemplated Yakimov with misgiving. "But is this wise, *mein Lieber*? We are now, you know, in opposite camps."

Yakimov, with a gesture, swept such considerations aside.

"Desperate situation, dear boy. Just arrived from Bucharest to find the hotels full. Not a bed to be got in Cluj. Couldn't sleep in the street, y'know."

"Certainly not," von Flügel agreed: "I am only hoping for your sake you were not followed here. Have you eaten?"

"Not a bite, dear boy. Not a morsel all day. Poor old Yaki's famished and dropping on his poor old feet."

The Count led the way upstairs and, opening a door, snapped on switch after switch. Chandeliers of venetian glass sprang into light throughout an immense room.

"What do you think of my lounge?" He spoke the word as though it had an exotic chic. Yakimov, not much interested in such things, looked round at the purple and yellow room with its vast gilded chimney-piece flanked by life-size plaster negroes naked except for the chiffon loin-cloths playfully placed about their immense pudenda.

"Delightful!" Yakimov limped to a sofa and sank down among the cushions. "Crippled," he said: "Crippled with fatigue."

"I designed it all myself."

"And hungry as a hunter," Yakimov reminded him.

As his host moved about, admiring and touching his own possessions, Yakimov, impatient for a drink, looked at Freddi more critically. How changed he was! His hair, that had once fallen like silk into his eyes, was now cut *en brosse*. His features, never distinctive, were lost in wastes of mauve-pink flesh – and he had grown a shocking little moustache that stood out like a yellow scab on his upper lip. His famous blue eyes were no longer blue: they were pink. Yet Freddi had been recognisable at once from his movements, that were, as they always had been, curiously fluid.

Meeting Yakimov's eye, von Flügel giggled. Yakimov recognised the giggle, too. That and the features were all that remained of the golden boy of 1931.

"How well you are looking!" said Yakimov.

"You, too, *mein Lieber*. Not a day older."

Well satisfied, Yakimov unlaced his shoes saying: "They're killing me." He shook them off, then, looking down at his feet, saw his socks were tattered and dark with sweat, and shuffled his shoes on again. "Trifle peckish," he said when Freddi had made no move.

Freddi tugged an embroidered bell-pull. While they waited,

Yakimov's roving eye noted a tray of bottles. "How about a little drinkie?" he said.

"So remiss of me!" Von Flügel poured out a large brandy. Yakimov took it as his due. Freddi had done very well out of old Dollie when her fortunes were high and his were low.

"And what brings you to Cluj?" von Flügel asked.

"Ah!" said Yakimov, his attention on his glass.

"I suppose I should not ask?"

Yakimov's smile confirmed this supposition.

There was a sharp rap on the door. Von Flügel sat up and straightened his shoulders before commanding: "*Herein.*"

A young man marched in, uniformed, muscular, conveying, without any hint of expression, a virulent annoyance. Yakimov did not like his face, but von Flügel leapt up, fluid and giggling once more, and saying: "Axel, *mein Schatz!*" went close to the young man and talked at him in a persuasive whisper until something was agreed. When Axel slammed his way out, von Flügel explained: "The poor boy's a little put out. We brought him from his bed. The cook is a local man. He goes home after dinner and I am then dependent on the boys."

When Axel returned, he brought a plate of sandwiches, which he put down with the abruptness of the unwilling and went off slamming the door again.

Yakimov, deliciously infused with brandy, settled down to the sandwiches, which were rough but contained some sizeable chunks of turkey. He silenced Freddi's apologies, saying: "Poor Yaki's used to living rough."

When he had eaten, the Count, who had been watching him with a waggish expression, went over to a corner that was cut off by a Recamier couch. "I have some amusing curiosities I really must show you," he said.

Yakimov lifted himself wearily out of the cushions. Von Flügel, having drawn aside the couch, beckoned his friend into the corner and handed him a magnifying glass. On either wall hung a Persian miniature. Yakimov examined them, tittering and saying: "Dear boy! Dear boy!" but he had no interest in that sort of thing and hoped he was not in for a night of it.

"Over here, over here," said von Flügel, leading him across the room to a tall cabinet set with shallow drawers. "You must see my Japanese prints."

"Oh, dear!" said Yakimov, taking the prints handed to him: "One must sit down to enjoy such things."

He tried to return to the sofa, but von Flügel held to him, pulling him here and there between the purple and yellow armchairs, and opening Chinese lacquer cabinets to display his collection of what he called "delectable *objets*".

As the effect of the brandy wore off, Yakimov became not only bored but cross. He had forgotten that Freddi was such a silly.

"Being in an official position," said von Flügel, "discretion is forced upon me, but one day I hope to have all my things out and displayed about the lounge."

"Lounge!" Yakimov said: "Where did you pick up that awful house agent's jargon?"

"Am I being vulgar?" asked von Flügel, too excited to care. "I *must* show you my Mexican pottery."

When Yakimov had been shown everything, von Flügel seemed to imagine he was the one who had earned a reward. He said in a tone of humorous complaint: "You still haven't told me what you are doing in Cluj."

Yakimov, sinking into his seat, said: "First I must have a drink, dear boy." His glass full, he sipped at it in better humour. "If I told you I was a war correspondent," he said, "you wouldn't believe me."

Freddi looked surprised. "A war correspondent! In which zone?"

"Why, in Bucharest, dear boy."

"But Rumania is not at war."

Yakimov thought this a quibble. "Anyway," he said, "I was a newspaper man."

"Indeed!" Von Flügel smiled encouragement.

Sitting with hands folded in his lap, he looked, thought Yakimov, like a benign old auntie, and his heart warmed to his friend. He giggled: "You and Dollie used to think that Yaki wasn't too bright. Well, I reported that Calinescu business for an important paper."

Von Flügel lifted a hand in astonished admiration. "And you come here to report the return of the Hungarians to their territory?"

Yakimov smiled. Delighted by the impression he was making, he felt a need to improve on it. He said: "I might as well tell you, this assignment is just a cover. My real reason for being here is . . . Well, it's pretty hush-hush."

Von Flügel watched him intently and, when he did not add to this revelation, said: "You are evidently a person of consequence these days. But tell me, *mein Lieber*, what exactly do you *do*?"

Not knowing the answer to this question, Yakimov backed down an old retreat route: "Not at liberty to say, dear boy."

"May I hazard a guess?" von Flügel archly inquired. "Then I would say you are attached to the British Legation."

Yakimov raised his eyes in astonishment at the accuracy of von Flügel's guess. "Between ourselves," he said, "speaking as one old friend to another, I'm on the *inside*. I know a thing or two. As a matter of fact, there's very little I don't know."

Von Flügel nodded slowly. "You work, no doubt, with this Mr. Leverett?"

"Old Foxy!" Yakimov immediately regretted his exclamation, which was, he realised, a betrayal of his ignorance. Von Flügel smiled and said nothing. Yakimov, discomforted by a sense of lost advantage, stared into his empty glass for some moments before it occurred to him that he had in his possession the means of re-establishing interest in himself. He drew from his hip pocket the plan he had found in Guy's desk. "Got something here," he said. "Give you an idea . . . not supposed to flash it about, but between old friends . . ."

He handed the paper to Freddi, who took it smiling, looked at it and ceased to smile. He stared at it on both sides, then held it up to the light. "Where did you get this?" he asked.

Disturbed by the change in Freddi's tone, Yakimov put out his hand for the paper. "Not at liberty to say."

"I'd like to keep this."

"Can't let you do that, dear boy. Not mine really. Have to give it back . . .'

"To whom?"

This question was put abruptly, in a hectoring tone that pained and bewildered Yakimov. If he had forgotten Freddi could be a silly, he had never known that Freddi could be a beast. He said with hurt dignity: "This is all very hush-hush, dear boy. 'Fraid I can't tell you anything more. Really must have the paper back."

Von Flügel rose. Without answering Yakimov, he crossed over to one of his cabinets, put the plan into it and locked the door.

Uncertain whether or not this was a joke, Yakimov protested: "But you can't, dear boy. I must have it back."

"You may get it before you leave." Von Flügel put the key into his pocket. "Meanwhile, we shall find out if it is genuine."

"Of course it's genuine."

"We shall see."

During this exchange von Flügel's manner had been stern and unamused, now it changed again. Advancing on Yakimov, he clasped his hands under his chin and his gait became a caricature of himself. Yakimov, watching him, was embarrassed by behaviour that he could only describe as odd. His embarrassment changed to fear when von Flügel, reaching him, stood over him with the malign stare of an old crocodile.

"Whatever is the matter, dear boy?" Yakimov tremulously asked.

"What is this game? You take me for a simpleton, perhaps?"

"However could you think that?"

"Does one enter a lion's den and say: 'Eat me. I am a juicy steak'?"

Von Flügel's whole attitude expressed menace, but to Yakimov it seemed such a deplorable performance that he imagined at any moment the whole thing would collapse into laughter. Instead von Flügel went on with increasing grimness: "Does one come to a Nazi official and say: 'I am an enemy agent. Here is my sabotage plan. Hand me, please, to the Gestapo.' "

"Really, dear boy, the *Gestapo!*"

"Yes, the *Gestapo!*" Von Flügel savagely imitated Yakimov's outraged tone. "What else do I do with a British spy."

Yakimov, for the first time, felt genuine alarm. There seemed to be nothing left of his old friend Freddi. What he saw beside him was indeed a Nazi official who might hand him over to the Gestapo. At the thought he almost collapsed with fear. "Dear boy!" he pleaded on a sob.

Freddi, a stranger and a dangerous stranger, had become the interrogator. "What little trick do you come here to play? What do you call it? The double bluff? We can soon discover. I have in this house a number of strong young men with fists."

"Oh, Freddi," Yakimov whimpered, "don't be unkind. It was only a joke between friends."

"That plan wasn't a joke."

"I told you it didn't belong to me. I pinched it. Just to amuse you, dear boy."

"You said you belonged to British Intelligence."

"No, dear boy, not in so many words. Can you see poor Yaki as a secret agent? *I ask you!*" Crouching in the sofa corner, watching with the perception of terror, Yakimov saw uncertainty on von Flügel's face, but not conviction. If he, von Flügel, could change into a Nazi official, then what might Yakimov not become in these strange times? Gradually von Flügel's face softened with contempt. He sat down. Speaking in the tone of one who will brook no further nonsense, he asked: "Where did you get that plan?"

Yakimov in his relief was not only willing to answer, but to answer more than he was asked. He was, he explained, a lodger in the flat of Guy Pringle, an Englishman who lectured at the University. He had found the plan in the flat and had borrowed it, just for fun. "Meant no harm," he said: "Didn't really know what it was, but I had m'suspicions. Queer comings and goings in that flat, I must say . . ." As he went on for some time about his suspicions and the "queer types" whom the Pringles entertained, he reminded himself of how he had worked to make Guy's production, but when it was over Guy had abandoned him. He said: "If you ask me, Pringle's a Bolshie."

Von Flügel nodded calmly and asked: "What sort of 'queer types'?"

"There's that fellow David Boyd. Now *he* works with Leverett and no one knows what he does. And there's a very strange chap hangs around the kitchen. He pretends he's related to the servant but he speaks English like a gent. The Pringles have kept him under cover. He was in a blue funk when I walked in on him."

Von Flügel set his teeth on his lower lip and appeared to reflect on this. He asked at last: "What are you doing in the apartment of such people?"

"Went there in all innocence, dear boy. Thought them very nice at first."

Von Flügel nodded and spoke portentously: "Charm is the stock-in-trade of such persons. It is intended to put you off your guard."

Yakimov nodded. He had, indeed, been put off his guard – and who better able to do that than Guy Pringle? He began to feel justified in giving the game away to Freddi. Freddi was a friend, a dear old friend, and Yaki had done no more than warn him. "When I saw that plan, I felt I ought to show it to you," and Yakimov ran happily on about the suspicious character of everyone he had seen there, the suspicious nature of everything that had ever occurred.

Von Flügel, still distant and severe, listened without much comment, but at the end he said: "One thing I would say to you: remove yourself from that flat at the earliest date. More, I would say remove yourself from Bucharest. I say it for your own good."

Yakimov nodded meekly. He had no wish to do anything else. He felt, now that he had re-established himself in Freddi's favour he might settle in here very comfortably. He lay back and closed his eyes. Exhausted, physically and emotionally, he felt himself sifting like a feather down through the softness of the earth. He heard von Flügel say: "Come. I will show you to your room," but had no time to reply before he was lost in sleep

The next morning confirmed his belief that life with Freddi would comply with his needs. After he had taken his bath, he and Freddi, in dressing-gowns, lay in long chairs to take breakfast on the balcony. The coffee was pre-war coffee, the food was excellent. Freddi was his old charming self. There were, unfortunately, a number of those horrid young men about, but Axel was the only one whom Freddi treated indulgently. With the others he was the stern commandant of *das Braune Haus*.

His memory of the previous night left him with an uneasy sense that he had been a trifle unfair to poor old Guy, but lying in his valetudinarian languor he could not worry unduly. After all, Guy *had* been unfair to him.

Breakfast over, the two men remained in the early sunlight, looking down at an ancient Citroën piled with furniture and bedding, that was being dragged to the station by a mule. All the petrol, Freddi explained, had been plundered by the outgoing Rumanians, who now refused to send in fresh supplies. "A hopeless people!" said Freddi. In a side-street a queue of people could be seen outside a shuttered bakery. From somewhere in the distance came a sound of shooting. Yakimov made movements as though he were thinking of getting up. "I should dress," he said. "I'm supposed to be getting the tempo of the town."

"So you really are a journalist?" said Freddi.

"In a manner of speaking. Not an aristocrat's occupation, I'm afraid."

"This is not an aristocrat's war."

Yakimov struggled to a sitting position.

"Is this activity really necessary?" Freddi asked. "The streets are unsafe. I would not recommend that you wander about. Such news as there is we can get from the boys." He rang a bell and a young man entered at once. "Ah, here is Filip. Filip, what is the news?"

Filip recited the latest incidents. A man resembling the Hungarian Consul had been set upon by Rumanian peasants and been left unconscious with an eye kicked out. Some people who had queued all day before a grocery store, finding the shop empty and the grocer gone to Braşov, had set fire to the shop, and the family living above had been burnt to death. There had been trouble at the hospital where Hungarian doctors had accused Rumanian doctors of removing equipment which had originally been Hungarian. One doctor, pushed over a balcony, had broken his neck.

As this recital of disorders went on, Yakimov nervously twitched his toes and murmured: "Dear me!"

"Don't be alarmed," said von Flügel: "These are the little inconveniences of change. No food, no petrol, no telephone, no public transport. The cafés are closed. Soon the lights will go out, the water will be cut off, the gas will cease to come through the pipes – but here all is well. We are well stocked with food and drink. There is a great range in the kitchen that burns wood. There is a well in the courtyard. We could withstand a seige." He glanced at Yakimov. "Perhaps you would care to make some notes."

"I forgot m'little notebook."

Von Flügel ordered Filip to bring pen and paper. When these were in Yakimov's hands, von Flügel explained how necessary it was to take Transylvania out of the control of the feckless, incompetent Rumanians and hand it over to the shrewd, hardworking Hungarians. At the end of an hour Yakimov had written, in his uneven hand, at the top of the sheet of paper: "The Takeover – A Good Thing."

This done, von Flügel said: "Surely it is not too early for an aperitif?"

Yakimov fervently agreed it was not.

His future still unsettled, he now mentioned the tiresome fact that he was supposed to be returning to Bucharest on the Orient Express that very night. "Not to tell a lie, dear boy," he added confidingly, "I don't really want to go back there. The food is atrocious and there's always some sort of rumpus going on. You advised me to leave Rumania, so I've decided I'd like to stay here."

"Here? In Cluj?" Von Flügel stared at him. "It's out of the question. When the Rumanians withdraw, this will be virtually Axis territory."

Yakimov smiled persuasively. "You could take care of old Yaki."

For a moment von Flügel looked aghast at this suggestion, then he said in a decided tone: "I could do nothing of the sort. As a member of the old régime I have to go very carefully myself. I could not possibly protect an enemy alien." He turned with a stern expression but, seeing Yakimov's gloomy face, relaxed. "No, no, *mein Lieber*," he said more kindly, "you cannot stay here. Return as you have arranged to Bucharest tonight. I will send Axel to obtain for you a *wagon-lit*. As soon as you arrive, put your affairs in order and take yourself to safety without delay."

"But where can I go?" Yakimov asked, near tears.

"That, I fear, you must decide for yourself. Europe is finished for you, of course. North Africa will go next. Perhaps to India. It will be some time before we get there."

For the rest of the day, Yakimov ate and drank with a mourning sense of farewell to the might-have-been. Towards evening, von Flügel, indicating that his friend must prepare for departure, said that Axel would give him sandwiches for the journey. Von Flügel himself had been invited that evening to a dinner given in his honour by the Hungarian community, so could not see Yakimov to the station.

"One thing, *mein Lieber*," he said as Yakimov got sadly to his feet: "you know the carpet-shop opposite Mavrodaphne's? When I was last in Bucharest, I saw there a very fine Oltenian rug. Thinking it a little expensive, I unwisely delayed its purchase, now I wish I had taken it. I wonder, would you buy it for me and have it delivered to the German Embassy?"

"Why, certainly, dear boy."

"You cannot mistake it: a black rug with a pattern of cherries and roses. Mention my name and they will produce it. It was about twenty-five thousand. Should I give you the money now?"

"It would be as well, dear boy."

Von Flügel opened a drawer that was filled with decks of new five-thousand-*lei* notes. He carefully peeled off five of these and held them just out of Yakimov's reach. He said: "I had better take your address in Bucharest, just in case . . ."

Yakimov gave it readily and the notes were handed over. "By the way," he said, "you still have that plan I showed you last night."

"I'll post it to you tomorrow. Now don't forget the rug. A *black* rug with cherries and roses, a delightful piece. And don't linger in Bucharest. I can tell you, in strictest confidence, Rumania's next on the list."

The friends parted amicably, Yakimov with regrets, von Flügel with a slightly off-hand urbanity. In a hurry to dress, he told the chauffeur to drive Yakimov to the station and return without delay.

As the car crossed the square in the evening light, the black wing of a plane, bearing the words '*România Mare*' dipped over the cathedral spire. Crowds of peasants were gathering at the street corners, running in groups this way and that, ready to make a stand but lacking leadership. They shouted at the sight of von Flügel's Mercedes and shook their fists.

The chauffeur, a Saxon, laughed at these gestures. He told Yakimov that the peasants had believed that Maniu was arriving to incite a revolt against the Vienna award. A deputation had waited all day at the station, then learnt that Maniu was at his house outside Cluj, having come by road. They rushed to see him and found him packing up his belongings. Saying he could do nothing, he advised them to return peacefully to their houses and accept the situation.

"So they are disappointed," said the chauffeur complacently, "And Domnul Maniu no doubt is sad."

"No doubt he is," said Yakimov, who was sad himself.

The long road to the station was crowded with townspeople and peasants making their way to the trains. They swarmed in front of the car with their belongings on carts and barrows, ignoring the hooting of the Mercedes that had slowed to a crawl.

"Hah, these Rumanians!" said the chauffeur with contempt. "In 1918 they drove out the Hungarians with much brutality, now they fear revenge."

The Orient Express, on which Yakimov had his sleeper, was due in soon after eight o'clock. The chauffeur congratulated Yakimov on being in good time, handed him his bag and left him to push his way in through the crowd that heaved and struggled about the station entrance.

When he at last reached the platform, he could scarcely get on to it. It was piled with furniture, among which the peasants were making themselves at home. Several had set up spirit-stoves on tables and commodes, and were cooking maize or beans. Others had gone to sleep among rolls of carpet. Most of them looked as though they had been there for hours. There was a constant traffic over gilt chairs and sofas, the valued possessions of displaced officials. Now that the train was due, dramatic scenes were taking place. Hungarian girls had married Rumanians and, as the couples waited to depart, parents were lamenting as though at a death. Yakimov stepped over two women who, howling into each other's faces, were lying in an embrace at the very edge of the line. He made his way through the *melée* until it began to thin at the platform's end, and there he waited.

Time passed. The express did not come. After an hour or more, he tried to inquire when it was expected, but whichever language he spoke seemed to be the wrong one. His Rumanian was answered with "*Beszélj magyarul,*" and his Hungarian with "*Vorbeşte româneşte,*" and his German with silence. Wandering about, he came on the Jew whose acquaintance he had made in the dining car, and learnt that the train was signalled two hours late. It might arrive about ten o'clock. At this Yakimov took himself back to the end of the platform where he found a vacant armchair, an imitation Louis XIV piece, not comfortable but better than nothing, and ate his sandwiches.

Darkness fell. Two or three lights came on, leaving shadowy areas lit only by the blue flames of the spirit stoves. Suddenly, amazingly, a train came in – a local train of the poorest class. A fierce energy at once swept through the peasants. Gathering up their possessions, they flung themselves at the doors only to find they were locked. Without pause they set to smashing the windows. Once inside, the men hauled up their women, children and baggage with roars that threatened death to any official who should restrain them. The air was filled with screams of anger and fear and the cracking of flimsy woodwork.

Yakimov watched in dismay. He knew this could not be the express but he suffered acute trepidation, realising what would happen when the express did come in.

The local train filled up in a minute, then the peasants began clambering to the carriage roofs, pulling their families after them. The uproar drowned the warning whistle. The train moved off with women and children hanging by arms and legs, unable to make the muscular effort to mount farther. Their shrieks rose even above the clamour of those left behind, who ran down the line, howling despair and threats until brought to a stop by rifle-fire from a bridge. When the train had gone, there were plaints and groans, but no one, it seemed, was seriously hurt, and everyone climbed back to the platform and settled down to wait again.

A clock struck in the distance. It was eleven. Yakimov stood up, certain the express would be coming at any moment, but half an hour later he sat down again, growing more apprehensive with the passing of time. A second local train came in and was charged like the last one. While it stood at the platform, another train arrived and stopped out of sight on the next line. People began shouting to one another that this was the express.

Yakimov, trembling in painful anxiety, waited for the local train to draw out, but it did not draw out, then came a cry that the express was leaving. People ran in either direction alongside the train that blocked the way and Yakimov ran with the rest. Stumbling over slag-heaps and rails, he rounded the hot, fire-breathing engine of the local train and reached the express. Its engine had been shunted off: the carriages remained. He found the *wagon-lit* and climbed up, but the door was locked. He thumped on the glass, shouting "*Lassen Sie mich herein*" to people standing in the corridor. They watched him, but no one moved. Suddenly the *wagon-lit* began to move. Clinging to the door-handle, his suit-case between his legs, Yakimov was swept into darkness. Then the *wagon-lit* stopped with a jerk that almost threw him off the steps. They were out in the bare and windy countryside. Knowing if he climbed down he would be lost, he hung sobbing with fear on the step while the carriage started back, as though galvanised by an electric shock. He was thankful to see the station again. The *wagon-lit* stopped: he climbed down between the two trains. At once the local train drew out. The foot-plate grazed him; the engine, at the back, passed him in a shower of sparks, and he screamed in panic. The express had reassembled itself. He ran to the rear where he could see the light of an open door. He reached it, threw his bag in and climbed after it. He was in terror lest someone should prevent him from entering, but there was no one to prevent him. This was the back way into the dining-car. He looked into the kitchen. The cook, a little gollywog of a man, was cutting up meat. Stunned and humbled, like one who has come into peace out of a raging storm, Yakimov stood and smiled on him. The meat looked dark, stringy and tough, but the cook was working at it with the absorption of an artist. Gently, affectionately, Yakimov asked if he might pass through. The man waved him on without a glance.

The blinds were pulled down inside the car. There were a number of vacant seats. The diners, again all men, sat talking, indifferent to the shrieks outside. When he was safely seated, Yakimov pulled aside his blind and glanced out at the crowds running helplessly up and down the line. Someone spoke to a waiter, who explained that the train was locked, inviolate, because the morning express had been besieged by peasants who had not had the money to pay the fare. They had refused to get off and had to be carried to Brasov. That must not happen again.

Someone on the line, seeing Yakimov looking out, thumped the window and cried piteously to be allowed in. He felt now as disassociated as the other diners. Anyway what could *he* do?

There were more shots and cries and a heavy pelting of feet. Faces seemed to press against the glass and stay there a moment, like wet leaves, before disappearing. Then the train began to move. People ran beside it, gesticulating, their mouths opening and shutting, but there was no hope for them. Something – a stone, probably – struck the window beside Yakimov. He let the blind drop and gave his order to the waiter. When he had eaten, he rose to find his berth and found that the door into the rest of the train was locked. He appealed to the waiter, but no one was empowered to open it. At last, weary of argument, he returned to his seat, put his head down on the table and slept.

The return journey took even longer than the outgoing one. The express had been due into Bucharest next morning. It actually reached the capital as darkness fell. Yakimov had had to spend the whole time in the dining-car, again taking meal after meal, paid for with Freddi's money.

At Bucharest station, there were no porters. No one collected tickets. The place was deserted except for the newly arrived passengers who remained at the entrance, whispering together, reluctant to emerge. Yakimov looked out. The street, usually swarming at this hour and adazzle with flares, was deserted, but he could see nothing to fear. The worst of it was there were no taxis or *trăsurăs*. Another long walk! He hung around awhile, hoping someone would explain their apprehensions, but no one

spoke to him and nothing happened. He decided to set out. H
went alone.

The stalls of the Calea Grivitei were shut and abandoned. The
pavements were empty. Occasionally he saw figures in doorways,
but they slid back out of sight before he reached them. The town
was unnaturally silent. He had never before seen the streets so
empty.

At last, at the junction of the Calea Victoriei, he came on a
group of military police with revolvers at the ready. One of them
ordered Yakimov to stop. He dropped his bag in alarm and put
up his hands. An officer came forward and sternly asked what he
was doing out of doors. The question frightened him; he realised
that his fellow-passengers had known something he had not
known. He started to explain in German – the safest language
these days – how he had arrived on the Orient Express and was
walking home. What was wrong? What had happened? He received no reply to his questions but was ordered to produce his
permis de séjour. He handed it over with his passport. Both were
taken under a lamp-post and examined and discussed, while a
soldier kept him covered. The discussion went on for a long time.
At intervals one or other of the men turned to stare at him, so he
feared he would be arrested or shot out of hand. In the end his
papers were restored to him. The officer saluted. Yakimov might
proceed, but must make a detour to avoid crossing the main
square.

Obediently he went down a side-street into the Boulevard
Breteanu and, adding about half a mile to his walk, reached the
Pringles' block, still very agitated. The hall was in darkness. The
porter had been conscripted some time before and not replaced.
As Yakimov made his way up in the lift, he was suddenly convinced that the invasion had begun. The city not only seemed
empty, it was empty. People had fled. He would find the Pringles
had gone with the rest.

At the thought he might find himself deserted in a German-
occupied country, he almost collapsed. To think he could have
stayed on the express and been carried right away to safety! His
self-pity was acute.

He was shaking so he could scarcely get his key into the lock.
The flat, when he entered it, was in darkness, but there were
voices inside. Reassured at once, he switched on the sitting-room
light.

"Put that light off, you damned fool," someone whispered from the balcony.

He switched the light off, but the moment's illumination had shown him Harriet standing against the jamb of the balcony door and Guy and David Boyd lying on the balcony floor, peering out through the stonework of the balustrade. It was David who had spoken.

Yakimov tiptoed in. "Whatever is going on, dear boy?" he asked.

In reply, David said: "Shut up. Do you want them to take a pot at us?"

Yakimov crouched against the doorway opposite Harriet, and looked out into the square. At first he could see nothing. The square, like the streets, was deserted, the lights shining on cobbles and stretches of tarmac bare of everything but the marks of tyres. The palace was in darkness.

After a long interval of silence, Yakimov whispered to Harriet: "Dear girl, do tell Yaki what is happening!"

She said: "The army has been called out. They're expecting an attack on the palace. If you look over there" – she pointed to the entrance to the Calea Victoriei – "you can see the tip of a machine-gun. There are soldiers all over the place."

Peering out, he began to see a movement of shadows among shadow. The first shop in the Calea Victoriei was visible and from its doorway heads were stretched. There were other movements among the scaffolding and half-demolished buildings in the square. These movements were all made cautiously, in silence. He heard a distant sound of singing.

"Who is going to attack the palace?"

Yakimov spoke piteously, feeling that no one wanted to tell him anything.

"We don't know," Harriet answered. "We think it must be the Iron Guard, but there've only been the usual rumours and confusion."

"It couldn't be the revolution, could it?"

"It could be anything. There was a lot of shouting for the King to abdicate, then the police went round clearing the streets and the military came out. David came in and said there was this rumour of an attack on the palace. That's all we know."

"The King won't abdicate, will he?"

Overhearing this question, David snuffled gleefully. "You wait and see," he said.

Yakimov picked up his bag and went into his bedroom. He sank down on to his bed, weary yet unable to contemplate rest. His consternation came not only from Hadjimoscos' predictions of anarchy and the guillotine, but from the fact that the word "revolution" had always fluttered him. Revolution had destroyed his family fortunes and sent his poor old dad into exile. He had grown up with his father's stories of the downfall of the Russian monarchy and the appalling end of the Russian royal family. Yakimov imagined that in a short time now, perhaps in an hour or two, the workers would abandon trains, planes and ships. The military would requisition petrol. They would all be stuck.

Freddi had warned him not to linger in Bucharest and Freddi had said that Rumania was next on the list.

Everyone had always said that the Germans could not afford trouble here. A rising would be the signal for an immediate German occupation. It occurred to Yakimov that in casting suspicion on Guy – rather meanly, he realised, but he had no time for compunction now – he could have brought trouble on himself, for here he was, one of a discredited household, and he might not get time to prove he had not been implicated.

His thoughts went to the Orient Express which he had just left, and which always stood at least an hour in the Bucharest station. Why not hurry back to it? He had walked safely here, and could as safely return. And, for once, with Freddi's money on him, he was "well heeled".

Saying: "Now or never, dear boy," he jumped up and began pulling out the oddments of clothing that were left in the drawers. He stuffed his bag full.

He did everything quietly. He felt a need to keep his departure secret, not from any fear of being detained, but from a nervous sense of shame that, having given old Guy away, he was now himself doing a bolt. Were he to try and explain his going, he might somehow betray his betrayal.

His window opened on to the balcony. As he crept about, he could hear David Boyd whisper: "Here they come. Now we'll see something." There was a noise outside. He moved across to the window and looked into the square. A line of soldiers stood blocking each end of the road which ran from it. Their rifles were poised to fire.

The noise was growing. Evidently a mob of some sort was making for the palace. Yakimov could only hope that the fracas here would draw attention from the side-streets by which he would reach the station.

Before he left he took down his sable-lined greatcoat which hung behind his door. With coat, suitcase and what was left of Freddi's twenty-five "thou", he tiptoed from the flat. Down in the street he heard the rifles fire, and he ran towards the Boulevard Breteanu.

He reached the station unaccosted and unharmed. The Orient Express, ignorant of the events that Yakimov had left behind, was still awaiting the passengers that, strangely, did not arrive. Having acquired Yakimov, it seemed content, and almost immediately set out for Bulgaria. At the frontier there was a slight altercation because he had no Rumanian exit visas, but a thousand *lei* put that right.

He obtained a berth in the almost empty sleeping-car and next morning awoke to the safety of Istanbul.

PART THREE

The Revolution

15

DURING THE FIRST DAYS OF SEPTEMBER the murmur of the crowded square had become for Harriet as familiar as the murmur of traffic. Shortly after Yakimov had set out for Cluj, it suddenly became a hubbub, there were new shouts of "*Abdica*" and a sound of breaking glass. Here, she thought, was uprising at last. When she went out to look, the crowd was in a ferment and the police were getting their hoses ready for action. The threat was enough. The uproar died down, but people did not disperse. This time they were not to be moved. If they might not speak, they could remain, a reproach to the despoilers within the palace.

Harriet remembered, when they took the flat, she had said to Guy: "We are at the centre of things." Now it seemed they were at the centre of trouble.

A little later, when the office workers had been added to the mob, there was a sudden burst of cheering. Guy had just come in and he joined Harriet on the balcony. With her long sight she could see a man in army uniform standing, hand raised, on the palace steps. Guy could see nothing of this but heard the crowd yelling in a frenzy of jubilation.

"Can it be the King?" said Harriet. "Has he done something to please them at last?"

Guy thought it unlikely. Despina came running into the room, waving her arms and shouting that something wonderful had happened. Antonescu had been brought a third time from prison and a third time offered the premiership – on his own terms. He had accepted, and at once demanded the resignation of Urdureanu.

Now, cried Despina, striking her fist into her palm, the country would be set right.

That, apparently, was everyone's opinion. Antonescu was being treated as a hero. His car could scarcely get out of the palace gate for the press of admirers. When it disappeared into the Boulevard Elisabeta, everyone began to move off as though there were nothing left to wait for.

By early evening, the resignation of Urdureanu was announced. Guy and Harriet, going out to meet David, felt a change in the air. The sense of mutinous anger had gone and near-elation had taken its place. And this, they felt, was merely a beginning. As Despina had said, the country would now be set right. One man, parting from a friend shouted: "*En nu abdic,*" raising laughter among all who heard him. The friend answered that Antonescu would make him change his mind.

David had invited the Pringles to eat with him and was waiting for them in the English Bar. He suggested they go to Cina's on the square. They could seldom afford this restaurant, but the evening was a special one.

"Anything may happen," he said, "And if it does, we shall have a ring-side seat."

The day had been very hot and the evening was as warm as mid-summer. The garden tables were all taken by people who seemed to be awaiting an event.

"Would it be the abdication?" Guy asked.

David sniggered and said: "It seems to be expected."

They were given a table by the hedge. Sitting in wicker chairs beneath the ancient lime trees, they watched the passers-by strolling in an amiable way about the square. Two or three dozen people, the remnants of the morning crowd, stood round the statue of Carol I. Suddenly everyone was on the alert. People began running towards the palace. The diners in the garden became excited and began shifting about in their seats and demanding information from the waiters. When the waiters could tell them nothing, they complained as though the news were being unjustly withheld from them. Several people called for the head waiter, an old man who knew everyone. Entering the garden he held up a hand and said in gentle, smiling reproof: "A decree, merely a decree," then quietly gave details to the waiters who went round from table to table repeating them.

The decree had cancelled the royal dictatorship, leaving the King with nothing but the right to wear decorations and present them to others. When required to sign it, he had raged like a madman and accused Antonescu of high treason, but he had been forced to sign in the end.

"Alas, the poor old Great and Good!" said David. "He's become a mere figurehead. And now what will the General do? He can't rule alone. He'll have to call on the Iron Guard or the army, and I imagine he knows the army too well to trust it."

Guy said: "You think we're in for an Iron Guard dictatorship?"

David shrugged: "I can't see any alternative."

So their position, Harriet thought, was more precarious than ever.

As the foliage clotted above their heads, strings of coloured lamps were lit among the branches. Within the palace, where the King had been stripped of everything but his decorations, appeared the galaxies of the chandeliers. Above the palace, a single star, embedded in the cerulean satin on the sky, shone with great brilliance. The roofs were lustrous with the last radiance from the west.

Suddenly, in the middle of the garden, the orchestra stand sprang alight and the musicians, in white blouses and velvet knee breeches, filed between the tables, bowing to right and left. They climbed into the stand: there was a howl from the violin, a pause and then a frenzy of music was released upon the diners.

Harriet thought of the last time they had eaten here. It had been mid-winter and, sitting beside the double window, their table had been lit by the sheen from the garden which, fleeced with snow, had looked small and intimate. Two broken-down cane chairs were outside on the terrace, their seats cushioned with snow. Snow picked out the delicate traceries of the chair backs and limned every curve and indentation of the roofing of trees. Beneath the trees, caged in the complex of branches, was the snow-capped orchestra-stand, a piece of chinoiserie, lacquered in gold and yellow. Who, seeing it now, hung with lights and leaves and flowers, could think that in a little while it would be left forlorn.

Last autumn Inchcape had told Harriet that an enemy never invaded in the winter. He had said: "The snow will come soon and here we shall be, tucked away safe and sound."

She felt a nostalgia for the snow which recalled for her some enchantment of childhood, a security she had known before her childhood changed. But the times had changed. Last autumn the Germans had been two frontiers away. This autumn, when the snow blocked the passes, it would enclose a host of Germans and the whole of the Iron Guard.

The Pringles awoke next morning to quiet. The Guardists had already taken up their position by the palace-rail but they stood there alone. The other inhabitants of the city were content to leave matters to Antonescu.

Despina, coming in with the breakfast things, talked excitedly about this champion who had risen to right everyone's wrongs. He had been the only one who dared oppose the King and he had suffered for his opposition. Now he had triumphed. He was the ruler. As for the King – she made a gesture as though she would jerk her hand off her wrist. The King was "nobody".

Whether the King was nobody or not, Harriet thought, he had been the ally and protector of the English community. She was not sorry that he was still on the throne.

Neither was Guy. If he felt no enthusiasm for the King, he felt less for Antonescu who had, from necessity, been set up as a symbol of honest strength in the midst of perfidy and confusion. People saw him as a solution simply because there was no solution. They might have cause to regret their illusion.

The day passed without incident. To most people it seemed the situation had been resolved so they were astonished when the police appeared in force that evening and ordered everyone off the streets.

The Pringles, on their way to the English Bar, found themselves encompassed in the square. They hurried to reach the hotel before they could be turned back, but the revolving door was locked. No one could leave or enter. They ran to the glass door of the hairdressing shop: that, too, was bolted. The windows began to fill with the faces of guests inside. Harriet saw Clarence looking out at them and waved to him. Could he not obtain their admission? He shook his head in bewildered helplessness.

Galpin, Screwby and other journalists were peering out of a side window. A porter thrust his way in front of them and pulled down a blind.

The emptied square looked vast, the cobbles reflecting the rosy gleams of the sunset. In the hotel, the palace, Cina's and the other buildings, all blinds had been pulled down, their pallid surfaces imposing a sabbatical void upon the evening.

A police officer, seeing the Pringles, the only civilians now at large, told them to go home. Guy asked the reason for this police action and was told that martial law had been declared.

"Why?" Guy asked. "What is happening?"

The officer shrugged and looked blank, then unable to keep his knowledge to himself, he said an attack was about to be made on the palace.

"By whom?"

The officer did not know.

As the Pringles passed out through the cordon, troops were arriving in lorries. A tank, painted sky-blue, had stationed itself outside the hotel. Machine-guns were being set up wherever there was cover. In the street outside the entrance to the Pringles' block a military van with a loudspeaker was demanding not only that everyone stay indoors, but that the blinds be drawn and balconies vacated. Anyone found in the street after half-past six would be in danger of arrest.

Entering the flat some fifteen minutes after leaving it, the Pringles were delighted to find that David had arrived during their absence and was peering out through the balcony door.

"What is happening?" Harriet asked.

"A *coup*, I imagine," said David. "Organised by the general. He's divested the King but Lupescu and Urdureanu are still in the palace biding their time. In fact, people who know are laughing at the decree. The King will simply wait until he can seize power again. So we have this attack on the palace. A put-up job, but it may work."

"It's a revolution?"

"A sort of revolution. If we get down out of sight we'll be able to see everything."

There was no sound from the square. Traffic had stopped. Darkness fell and still nothing happened. The two men lay peering through the stone tracery while Harriet pressed against the door-jamb. There was no sign of life below. Everyone, police as well as military, was concealed in shadow. The horseman on his giant horse sat in solitude. About him the lights were reflected on a world of polished ebony.

The silence of the waiting town had no undertones. It was as complete as the silence of the country.

At last Harriet, cramped and bored, went out to the kitchen. The servants were all on the roof awaiting events. Harriet made sandwiches and took them into the room. The three sat cross-legged to picnic on the balcony floor. When Harriet returned to her position by the door-jamb, she said: "I can hear singing." The song was no more than a pulse in the air. As they listened,

Yakimov arrived. The singing grew louder. With it came the sound of marching. The marchers were coming from the centre of the town. The singing stopped, cut short by an order, and there was a sound of shouting instead. The shouts grew nearer. An order was given in the square. The shadows came suddenly to life.

"Now," said David, "we should see something."

Soldiers with rifles at the ready were running out of the darkness to range themselves across the junctions of the Calea Victoriei and the Boulevard Elisabeta.

The noise of approaching feet and voices came like a rush of water, and soon it was possible to pick out individual threats to the King, Lupescu and Urdureanu. There was a repeated call of death to the King.

The marchers were now very near. Another order was given in the square. The soldiers ranged across the Boulevard Elisabeta raised their rifles. The marchers came on. An officer bawled again. The soldiers fired into the air. The report brought the uproar to an immediate stop. There was a moment of silence, then the scuffle of retreat – but, retreating, the marchers raised their voices in a song of defiance. It was "*Capitanul*".

The soldiers remained in position, but there were no more orders. "*Capitanul*" became again a pulse on the air, then faded out of hearing.

Guy and David rose to their feet. Guy said: "Let's have a drink."

Harriet asked: "That was a poor sort of revolution?"

"It was enough," said David. "Antonescu can now say: 'You're in mortal danger. I cannot protect you. You must go.' " Guy poured out the *ţuică* and David held up his glass: "Farewell to the King. He'll be gone before morning."

Later the story went round that that night Carol wrote on his dinner menu: "*Auf Wiedersehen*", resigned to going but certain his country must in the end recall so sharp-witted a King.

16

THE FOLLOWING MORNING Harriet could hear the babble in the square before she was out of bed. The city was celebrating.

During breakfast, Despina darted in and out of the room with stories shouted up to her by the other servants. The King, she said, had refused to sign the abdication order until 4 a.m., and then only after a squabble about the pension he would receive. He had been driven at once to Constanza in a German diplomatic car and put on board his yacht. Lupescu and Urdureanu had gone with him, but the palace was not empty. There was a new King, Michael; young, handsome and good, he would rule benignly, like an English king.

Meanwhile, people were pouring into the square from every side street, many of them peasants who had come from the country, the men in white frieze, the women brilliant as oriental birds in the dresses they wore only on feast days and holidays. It was clear that no one would work today. Harriet said to Guy: "Surely you need not go to the University?" but he thought he ought to put in an appearance, and took himself off as usual.

Harriet was still at the table when she heard "*Capitanul*" being sung beneath the balcony. She ran out, her coffee-cup in her hand, and gazed down on the ranks of green-clad men who were marching round the church below her. They cut through their audience, straight across the square to the palace, where the guards, who the night before had fired over their heads, now raised arms in the fascist salute.

As they lined up in their hundreds before the palace, the crowd surged about them, kissing their hands and slapping their backs.

The jubilation so stimulated the air that she felt jubilant herself. Yet what was there to rejoice about? The new régime might mean a fresh start, but the lost provinces were still lost. The country must still obey the demands of its voracious ally.

Harriet was recalled by shouts of "*Cornita*". Despina had been out and now, aglow with all the sensations, congratulations and fantasies of the market-place, stood in the room with one hand behind her back. As Harriet entered, she whipped out her hand with a flourish and presented a roast of meat.

It was Friday, a meatless day. "Special for the abdication," she said: "and it is not veal, it is beef." They had not eaten beef since early spring. "Now the King is gone," she cried, "there will be no more meatless days. We shall eat roast beef for every meal," and she said that when a peasant, recognising her as Hungarian, had refused to serve her, she had shouted: "*Sitie kiansinlai blogi*," and overthrown his basket of tomatoes. The bystanders were in such a state of revelry that they treated the incident as a joke.

"Is no one sorry the King has gone?" Harriet asked.

Despina shrieked with laughter at the idea. "No one, no one. A robber, a cheat, a lecher – such was the King! Away with him!" She made a rude gesture of dismissal and described how Carol and Lupescu, about to leave the palace with boxes of jewels and bags of gold, had been seized by Horia Sima and flown to Berlin where the Führer waited to repay old scores. "*O să-le taie gâtul*," she said, sweeping a finger across her own throat.

"Is this true?" Harriet unbelievingly asked.

True? Of course it was true. Everyone was talking about it.

An uproar from the square sent Harriet hurrying out with Despina at her heels. The young King was standing on the main balcony of the palace – a tall young man in army uniform, his ministers behind him. As he lifted a hand in greeting, the crowd howled its enthusiasm. For the first time, Harriet saw men and small boys clambering over the statue of Carol the Great. Soldiers, making way for the cars that were trying to reach the palace, shook hands on all sides with excited members of the crowd.

When the new King retired, those near the palace railing, made bold by the good-fellowship of the times, ventured inside. Soon, people were strolling in and out of the gates and round the small ornamental lawns as freely as in a public park.

Despina gasped in astonishment. Never, never, she said, had such a thing been done before.

Harriet felt she must go out and see these wonders at closer range, but as she was about to leave the flat, there was a ring at the door. Bella had called.

Harriet had heard nothing from her since their chance meeting in the Calea Victoriei. Now, her arms full of flowers, she threw herself on Harriet with more animation than she had ever shown before. Handing her a bunch of roses as though the occasion were one of rejoicing for them both, she said: "Oh, the excitement. It's wonderful. Wonderful," then seeing that Harriet was holding bag and gloves, she shouted: "But you can't go out. You might be attacked. Carol was pro-British, so the English are terribly unpopular. It'll pass of, of course – but, just at the moment, you're safer indoors."

"You weren't attacked."

"Oh, I'm different. I have Rumanian papers and I speak German. My German is so good the shopkeepers fall over themselves to serve me."

Harriet took her out to the balcony where she settled into a deck-chair, saying: "Why go out when you've got a front row seat?"

Her skin apricot, her hair bleached by the sun, Bella was looking extremely handsome and seemed almost intoxicated by the night's happenings. "How wonderful to have a strong man in power!" she said. "Everyone is saying that Rumania will regain all her territory."

"What makes them think that?"

"Because Antonescu is a real dictator. He knows how to deal with Hitler and Musso. He's one of them. I don't mind betting, within three months, this country will be on its feet again."

"What about the Iron Guard? They could cause a lot of trouble."

"Not them." Bella hooted at the thought of them. "The general will stand no nonsense from that rabble. Their leaders are all dead. People are saying they're like potatoes: the best of them are underground."

Bella's confidence was such she almost conveyed to Harriet her belief that there was nothing to fear: their world would settle down again. She felt cheered by Bella's visit that brought back to her the pleasures of their companionship. In this city a woman could go nowhere alone but two women, chaperoning each other, were free to do what they liked. She said:

"When this is all over, let us start going again to Mavrodaphne's."

"Yes, let's," Bella heartily agreed. She looked up eagerly as Despina, who had run out to a cake-shop, set down a tray of coffee and cream cakes. "How much do you pay that girl?" she asked when Despina had gone.

"A thousand a week."

"Merciful heavens! That's as much as a schoolmaster gets. You spoil them. I've told you before. It makes things difficult for the rest of us."

A fresh burst of cheering greeted Michael's reappearance on the balcony.

"He's a nice boy," said Bella, "but not as colourful as his father. It's a pity about Carol, really. They say that when Antonescu shouted at him: 'You must abdicate,' he burst into tears and said: 'But I haven't done so badly.' It made me feel quite sorry for him."

"He had a gift for bursting into tears at the right moment," Harriet said.

Bella seemed to resent this. She said: "He was very virile."

"David Boyd says all these stories about his virility were put out by the palace."

"David Boyd!" said Bella with contempt. "A lot he knows about it." To restore Bella's good humour Harriet appealed to her for information: "What do you think has happened to Carol?"

"Nobody knows for sure," Bella nodded towards the palace. "He may still be over there," she said.

The Guardists, in full throat, appeared out of the Calea Victoriei.

"There's that bloody song again," said Bella. "But, you wait and see! The general will make mincemeat of that lot once he's established."

The Guardists, a small contingent, were leading a long procession of priests and nuns. Bella explained that it was St. Michael's Day – not only the name-day of the new king but the day of Michael Codreanu, the Iron Guard saint. This coincidence must have impressed the crowds, for they watched in a respectful silence until suddenly there was renewed uproar. A man was leaving the palace on foot. Bella started up.

"Good heavens," she said, "that's Antonescu himself. People are going mad. I must go down and see the fun."

As Harriet made to rise, Bella put a hand on her shoulder. "No, you stay here," she commanded. "I'll keep in touch. I'll ring up every day and give you the news."

As soon as she saw the lift descend with Bella in it, Harriet ran down by the stairs. Because of Bella's fears for her Harriet avoided the square, taking the first turning into the Boulevard Elisabeta. She had imagined the shops would be shut, but except for the sense of heightened activity life went on as usual. The peasants had brought in their produce on barrows. The restaurants were open. In the café gardens people sat beneath striped umbrellas drinking morning coffee.

In the Calea Victoriei, however, the new force was manifesting itself. Young men and women, pushing their way boisterously through the crowds, were handing out Guardist leaflets. A group of girls, flushed, rather wild in their appearance, and still rather bashful of their own importance, were going from shop to shop distributing posters. As fast as they were delivered, the posters appeared in the windows, portraying a romantically handsome young man, long-haired, large-eyed, dark as a gipsy, beneath which were the words: CORNELIU ZELEA CODREANU – PREZENT. This was an idealised image of the captain who was ever present among his followers.

Soon the face of Carol's enemy, who had been, until a few weeks before, a despised traitor, was exhibited everywhere as national hero, martyr and saint.

When Harriet entered the University, she knew at once that the building was empty, or almost empty. The porter had probably taken the day off. She went down the corridor. The lecture-room door stood open. No one had pulled down the blinds. Midday poured hot and heavy on to the vacant seats.

She found Guy in his office. He was sitting over some exercise-books, apparently intent, but jerked his head round when she entered. Hoping for a student, he looked surprised to see her. He said: "They've all taken a holiday."

"Why didn't you come home?"

"There were three classes this morning. Someone might have turned up for one of them."

"The Iron Guard is out in force today."

"I heard them. You weren't anxious about me, were you?" He took her hand affectionately. "No need to worry. The Guardists won't cause trouble at the moment. They don't want to spoil their chance of coming to power."

"Well, you needn't stay here any longer. Let's walk across the park."

He stood up, then thought to look at his watch. "The last hour has only just begun," he said. "I must allow a bit more time. Someone might turn up."

"They won't. They dare not risk it."

But Guy would not give up hope. He strolled round the room,

humming to himself, and Harriet, suffering for him, said: "I'll go out and wait on the terrace."

He remained inside some ten minutes longer. When he appeared he said in a jaunty way: "Come along, then. Let's go to the park."

The heat swelling in the air, pressed like an eiderdown on the senses, but there was no lull in the excitement. The gipsies were cock-a-hoop among their flower baskets, shrieking about them as though the day were a triumph for their race.

The park was full of peasants. As usual most of them were grouped in wonder, gaping at the *tapis vert*. Its grass was still trimmed and watered, but the swagged surround was losing its shape. The general neglect was evident. The hedges were unclipped, weeds and grass grew in the beds. The cana lilies and gladioli fell unstaked across the paths. The dahlias, that last year had been a firework display, were lost in a jungle of dead flowers and foliage.

The Pringles took the path that dropped down to the lake café. Peasants were sitting in the shade of the chestnuts, but stiffly, arms round knees, self-conscious here in the city, exuding, for all the festivity of their dress, a mute sense of endurance. In the past there had always been half a dozen men here selling sesame cakes and Turkish delight, but sweetmeats were rare and expensive now, and only one man remained. He held a tray of peanuts.

Guy and Harriet crossed the bridge to the café and sat where they usually sat, by the rail. Guy had brought a batch of exercise-books with him and while they waited for the wine he had ordered, he brought out his fountain-pen and set to work on them. Harriet had been given a copy of the Guardist news-sheet *Capitanul*. She now made her way through the leading article which was a laudation of General Antonescu. The general, called as a witness at the trial of Codreanu, had been asked if he considered Codreanu to be a traitor. He had crossed the court-room, seized hold of Codreanu's hand and said: "Would General Antonescu give his hand to a traitor?" As a result of this act, the Guardists claimed him for their own.

She put the pamphlet aside and watched Guy at work. She felt no inclination now to protest or interrupt. She was beginning to suspect that while Inchcape ignored truth, Guy merely pretended to ignore it. Perhaps it was for her sake he would not admit the hopelessness of their situation here. Anyway, she realised that while they remained he must make a show of having a job to do. He must believe that he was needed.

She looked away across the hazy, dirty water. Sitting here, a year before, they had thought of the war as a compact area of conflict about three hundred miles distant.

Rumania then had been sleek and prosperous, a land of plenty. Even this café, one of the cheapest, had given plates of olives, cheese and gherkins when one bought a glass of wine. Now those things were scarce. She seemed to remember the water, beneath its haze of heat, as translucent as crystal. Now it smelt of weed. The crusted surf round the café held captive floating bottles, orange-peel, match boxes and paper bags. As for the café itself, it reflected in its greyish weathered timbers, its crippled chairs, its dirty table papers, the decay of the whole country.

She sighed, feeling in the gummy September heat all the tedium of the year repeating itself. Guy, thinking she was bored, said: "Nearly finished," but she was not bored. Becoming conditioned to Guy's preoccupation, she was learning the resort of her own reflections. With him, in any case, talk was too general for intimacy. He despised the metaphysical and the personal. He did not gossip. She was beginning to believe that what he had lacked was a fundamental interest in the individual – a belief that would astonish him were she to accuse him. But she did not accuse him. Once she had believed that finding him, she had found everything: now she was not so sure. But here they were, wrecked together on the edge of Europe as on an island and she was learning to keep her thoughts to herself.

When he put down his pen, Guy picked up the news-sheet and pointed out the name of the editor. It was Corneliu Zelea Codreanu. Then followed the names of the editorial board.

"All dead," said Guy. "At every meeting these names are called out first and someone answers '*Present*'. No wonder the Iron Guard is called 'the legion of ghosts'."

"Still," said Harriet, "they have a sort of idealism . . ."

"Yes, indeed," Guy laughed, rising to his feet. "If they come to power, the same crimes will be committed, but only for the best possible reasons."

They crossed the bridge over the lake and walked through open parkland to the rear gate where stood the statue of a disgraced politician. Ever since Harriet had been in Bucharest, the head of the politician had been hidden in a linen bag. Today the bag had been removed. The politician – a short, stout man with head thrown back, one foot advanced, one hand extended in a Dantonesque gesture, was revealed as snub-nosed, his features clustered together like a bunch of radishes. No name was engraved upon the pediment.

Just outside the gate stood the mansion block where the Druckers had lived. The family had occupied the whole of the top floor. In those days the curtains in the great out-curving corner window had been of plum-coloured velvet, now they were of pink brocade. All the Drucker possessions, including, no doubt, the plum-coloured curtains, had been forfeit to the crown.

Carol had got the trial over in good time and sold the Drucker oil holdings to Germany. Nobody cared. The whole affair had passed into oblivion.

Seeing her glance up at the top floor flat, Guy said: "I have been thinking about Sasha. And I've talked over the problem with David. The only answer, it seems to me, is: when we go, we must take him with us."

"How can we do that? They would never let him out of the country."

"Of course he would have to have a passport in another name, but these things can be arranged. Clarence had a whole department at work forging papers for the Poles. He must know someone who would help."

"Darling, you're wonderful!" she said, delighted by this suggestion, "I didn't believe you would give the matter a thought." She caught his arm, filled with all her old admiration for him and said: "Will you speak to Clarence?"

"Better if you speak to him. He'll do anything for you."

She was not sure of that. She felt some misgivings, but the very simplicity of the solution seemed to have extinguished the problem. It was as though a lock that would not open had fallen off in her hand.

Outside, the rejoicings, in which they had no part, were still going on. Listening to them, she felt that here she and Guy had no part in life. They existed off dangers peculiar to their small community. Even the problem of Sasha – which had been, like the secret cache of an alcoholic, something to which to resort in desperate times – was gone. What purpose was left to them? She felt a longing for England where the danger might be greater, but was shared by all.

David called in and the three sat on the balcony. There was a great deal of calling for the King. Plaudits greeted every arrival at the palace. Someone in the crowd was letting off fireworks. Guardist vans were relaying a radio speech in which Horia Sima described the *coup d'état* as yet another New Dawn.

"Dear me!" said David. "We seem to be getting a new dawn every day. But that," he snuffled, "is, after all, in the nature of things."

A rocket went up: a very small one that petered out on a level with the balcony. David snuffled again. "Do you realise," he said, "that in less than two months, Rumania has lost forty thousand square miles of territory? And with it, six million of her population? The drop in national income will be in the region of five hundred million sterling. Not a self-evident cause for rejoicing, would you say?"

Behind the palace the sky was aflame. Soon drifts of cloud, fine as smoke, dampened the autumnal fire and lights came on in the royal apartments. The sunset grew bleary. The bugle sounded from the palace yard. Harriet felt comforted by its familiarity. Kings came and went, and the nations fell, but men and horses must have rest.

17

NEXT MORNING THE GAIETY was gone and only a few peasants wandered about the square.

Bella, as she had promised, rang Harriet and described how the previous night the Guardists, grown drunk on the day's adulation, had marched through the ghetto area shouting threats to the Jews.

"We don't want all that again," she said.

This surprised Harriet who had never discovered in Bella much concern for the Jews. Bella explained that she was worried on her own behalf. In this country of dark-haired Latins, the Jews, contrary as ever, were notably blond or red-haired. As a result, Bella had always been suspect. So apparently, was Guy, the more so as he was reputed to favour his Jewish students.

Bella said: "It's no good telling people that in England it's the other way round. They don't want to believe you. They hate the thought of Jews having dark hair. It's different, of course, with educated Rumanians: the sort we mix with. They've travelled and seen for themselves. But these Guardists are riff-raff. They know nothing. They're ignorant as dirt."

"What about Antonescu? Isn't he red-haired?"

"Yes, he's got Tartar blood, but they all know who he is. No one's likely to make a mistake about him. It's different for me. Last time they caused trouble, I never went out alone. You'd better be careful."

"But I am dark," said Harriet.

"Well, you'd better keep Guy indoors."

Before Bella rang off, Harriet suggested they might meet for coffee somewhere. Bella said: "Not today. Not just yet. Better let things settle a bit." She was willing to visit Harriet, but it was another thing to be seen in her company.

Harriet, when she went out shopping, sensed misgiving in the streets. The meat shops were empty. All the stocks for the coming week had been sold to mark yesterday's rejoicings – and now the rejoicings were over. When would there be more meat? Who could tell? What were people to eat this week-end? No one knew. People were asking what had, in fact, happened? They had exchanged one dictator for another: the known for an unknown who might bring the Iron Guard in his wake.

As though to enhance the anti-climax, Sunday was declared a Day of Atonement. Bucharest must atone for its slaughter of Codreanu and his comrades; for its pro-British past; and its frivolity. The church bells tolled from dawn till late at night. Cinemas, cafés, restaurants, even the English Bar, were closed. Every Rumanian, wherever he might be, was required to kneel down at eleven in the morning and pray to the Guardist martyrs for forgiveness. Processions of black-clad priests, heads bowed, trailed around all day in the glutinous heat.

The gloom was enlivened for the Pringles by a telephone call from Galpin. He wanted Yakimov. Yakimov was not in his room.

"Where's he got to?" Galpin angrily demanded.

Harriet did not know. For the first time, it occurred to her that she had seen nothing of him since Thursday evening. "Wasn't he in the bar yesterday?" she asked.

"No. Look here!" Galpin's tone was severely accusing. "He's got five thousand of mine. *And* I paid his fare to Cluj."

"He won't get far on five thousand."

"He'd better not try," Galpin said and his receiver was violently replaced.

Harriet went to ask Despina when she had last seen Yakimov. Despina, having been on the roof when he returned from Cluj, had seen nothing of him since the morning of his departure. She said his bed had not been slept in.

Harriet, puzzled, began to wonder whether indeed Yakimov had returned; or whether his brief appearance in the shadowy room had been but a conjuration of the evening's drama.

When she spoke to Guy he said confidently: "Yaki wouldn't go without telling us."

"Then where is he?"

Before Guy had found an answer to this question, Galpin came thumping on the door of the flat. He pushed his way in, apparently imagining the Pringles were hiding Yakimov. "He's had my money," shouted Galpin, "and I want my news."

In Yakimov's room, Galpin threw open the cupboards and pulled open the drawers so Harriet saw that, apart from some scraps of cast-off clothing, all Yakimov's possessions had gone.

Even his sable-lined greatcoat was missing from its hook. "He wouldn't take that if he were coming back," she said.

"The bastard!" Galpin shouted. "He's vamoosed. If I ever see him again, I'll scrag him."

When Galpin had gone, Guy said consolingly: "He'll be back."

"Well, he won't be back here," said Harriet with decision. "I want this room for Sasha."

Guy, torn between the claims of his two protégés, looked disconcerted.

Harriet said: "It is much safer for all of us to have Sasha inside the flat."

Guy agreed. Suddenly enthusiastic, throwing all doubts aside, he said: "But of course the boy must have the room. He can't spend the winter on the roof. What does he do all day? I haven't had time to see him lately. Is he still studying?"

"He reads and draws, but he's lazy. Down here you can keep an eye on him and he can have the wireless. He's fond of music."

Guy nodded. "He used to play the saxophone. We must do something for him. I wish we could borrow a gramophone." Suddenly beset by the urgency of Sasha's case, he said: "Let's bring him down straightaway," and sped off as he spoke. When he came back with Sasha, he was more elated by the move than the boy himself.

Despina had tidied the room. "It's super," Sasha said, then added as he sat down on the edge of the bed: "Jolly nice to have a real bed," but Harriet felt he scarcely cared where he was as long as someone stood between him and the discomforting world outside.

As he was arranging papers and pencils on the bedside table, she noticed he had brought down among his other things, his military uniform.

She said: "Did you have any sort of papers? I mean, a passport or *permis de séjour*?"

"I have this." He searched the uniform jacket and produced the *carte d'identité* issued to conscripts.

She saw it contained what she wanted, Sasha's photograph and said: "This is evidence against you. I had better destroy it." She took it to the kitchen where she unpeeled the photograph and put it into her handbag. The card she tore into fragments and burnt in an ash-tray.

That evening Sasha sat down to supper with them. While they ate, they listened to the news, or what served for news these days. It consisted, on this occasion, of an indictment of Carol, who was described as the Pandora's Box from which all Rumania's evils had sprung. But, listeners were reminded, Hope had been imprisoned at the bottom of the box, and Hope, in the shape of General Antonescu, was in the studio. He would address the country.

Antonescu came at once to the microphone. Speaking in simple biblical language, he promised that once the country had expiated its sins, it would be restored to greatness. No one need fear. The new régime would bring neither bloodshed nor recriminations. For every useful member of Society, regardless of race or creed, there would be an ordered and protected life.

"Do you think we can count on that?" Harriet asked.

"Why not?" said Guy. "We haven't lost the war yet; and we may not lose it. The British are known to have great powers of survival. Antonescu doesn't want to antagonise us, and while our Legation is here, we're a recognised community."

Harriet asked Sasha what his family had thought of Antonescu. Sasha shook his head vaguely, apparently never having heard of him. "Despina says he's quite decent," he said.

Sasha had watched the revolution from the roof. What had he made of it all? He certainly had not been disturbed. It probably never entered his head that events could jeopardise his protected position. As for the fate of Rumania, why should that mean anything to him? Although he had been born here, he was no more emotionally involved with the place than were the Pringles themselves. Reflecting on his English schoolboy slang that at once placed and displaced him, she thought wherever he was, he would belong nowhere.

Guy's students, reassured by the general's speech, turned up in force at the University on Monday morning, but Sunday's gloom still hung in the air. Cinemas and theatres were to remain shut for the rest of the week. Although they had been ordered to return to work, thousands of people still kept half-hearted holiday, wandering the streets as though waiting for a sign that their disorganised world would become normal once again.

Bella had telephoned Harriet that morning, excited because she had been right in suspecting that Carol had not left immediately after his abdication. He had, in fact, remained in the palace another twenty-four hours, then gone by rail, taking a train-load of valuables.

"And all the El Grecos," Bella said, scandalised.

"But weren't they bought by his father?"

"Yes, with public money. Of course, Lupescu and Urdureanu went with him. One of the waiters on the train is putting it round that the three of them squabbled all the way, blaming each other for what had happened. At the frontier, the Iron Guard machine-gunned them and they had to lie on the floor. Just think of it!" said Bella, giggling as she thought of it herself.

Harriet expressed some concern that the ex-King and his followers should have been all day in the palace listening to the rejoicings over their downfall.

"Oh," said Bella, "don't you fret your fat over that lot. They'll live in luxury with the cash they've salted away. Nikko says it was a mistake, letting them go. They should have been arrested and tried and forced to disgorge. The Iron Guard needs some diversion. There's no knowing what they'll get up to now."

Bella seemed less confident that the Iron Guard could be kept from power. "After all," she said, "who else is there? Maniu's pro-British and Bratianu's anti-German. I can't see Hitler standing for either of them. And," she glumly added, "we've got these wretched refugees pouring into the town, filling up the hotels and cafés, and putting up prices again."

"What will happen to them?"

"God knows," said Bella.

The trains had stopped for two days when the news of the revolution reached Transylvania and most of the refugees were only now reaching the city. Those that filled the hotels and cafés were the fortunate few. The majority, the dispossessed peasants, had had to shelter beneath the trees of the park and up the Chaussée. Arriving during an interregnum, they received less consideration than the Poles had done. No one was empowered to deal with them. They spent their days standing dumbly before any large building where power might reside. Imagining that justice must eventually be brought out to them, they were prepared to wait days and weeks: and they probably would have to wait, for the Cabinet had not yet been appointed. The *prefectura* and ministries were empty of important people. The senior civil servants were spending their days with the processions of penitents that followed the priests and nuns about the streets.

Harriet, when she went out, took a *traşura* up the Chaussée as far as the fountain that marked the edge of the town. She was on her way to visit Clarence who lived in a new block on an unfinished boulevard. Never having been there before, she had difficulty in finding it. She might have telephoned him and arranged to meet him in the English Bar, but felt an unexpected call would be more likely to impress him with the urgency of her request.

When Harriet asked for Domnul Lawson his cook, a grimy woman with a sly manner, pointed, grinning, at the balcony as though to say: "He's there, where he always is." Harriet found him lying on a long chair, a copy of the *Bukarester Tageblatt* on the floor beside him. He wore a heavy white sweater across the chest of which was embroidered the word "Leander". His eyes were shut. He did not open them until she said: "Hello, Clarence," then he started up, confused by the sight of her, and was immediately on the defensive. In a complaining tone, he explained: "I'm supposed to rest. The mornings are getting chilly. With my weak chest, I have to be careful."

The balcony was in the shade, overlooking open fields from which came a hint of breeze. Swallowing back a derisive comment, Harriet mildly said: "I'm sorry if I disturbed you."

He gave her a suspicious glance. Seeing she was serious, he said: "I suppose you've heard? The blitz on London has begun."

She had not heard the news that morning. Looking down at the German paper, she asked: "What does it say?"

"According to this rag the whole city's aflame. They say the fire service could not cope. They claim tremendous damage done, thousands of casualties and so on. Probably a lot of lies – but who knows?"

"If we get back, there may be nothing to get back to."

He shrugged and dragged himself out of his chair. "How about a drink?"

While he went into the room and called to the servant for glasses, Harriet remained on the balcony, shocked by what she had heard. On the other side of the road there was a cornfield. The corn, a second or third crop, not more than a foot high, was still grey-green. Its freckling of poppies gave the vista a look of spring, but the mountains were visible in the distance – a sign that the summer haze was lifting and autumn had begun. There was even a glint of snow on the highest peak.

Clarence called her. She went into the room and looked about at the dark, carved furniture, the painted plates and the cloths and cushions embroidered in blue and red cross-stitch.

"Peasant stuff," said Clarence: "I bought it from the previous owner for a few thousand. I got the cook as well. She sleeps with her husband and three children in the kitchen. Not an ideal arrangement but if I'd got rid of them, they'd have nowhere to sleep at all."

"Do peasants have furniture as good as this?"

"Some do, but even the most prosperous have a miserable diet."

He handed her a glass of ţuică. She looked about her thinking that in this small room, which was exposed and overlighted like a birdcage on a wall, she would suffer from both claustrophobia and agoraphobia. Clarence, however, seemed content.

He said: "The flat suits me. I live, eat and sleep in one room, but I don't mind. I like to have all my needs within reach. But I'm getting rid of it. I haven't told anyone yet: I'm leaving."

"Leaving Rumania?"

"Yep."

"Oh!" Harriet, who on the long drive up the Chaussée had thought of Clarence gratefully as one who stood with them in peril, now felt a drop in spirits. She said: "You think it's time to go? That something is going to happen here?"

"I'm not worrying about that. It's simply that I've nothing to do here."

"What about your job at the Propaganda Bureau?"

"You know as well as I do, the Bureau is a farce."

"When will you go?"

"Oh, no hurry."

That was a relief, anyway. She asked: "And where will you go?"

"Egypt, perhaps. Brenda cabled me last week."

Brenda, Clarence's fiancée, was in England. When Harriet first saw her photograph, she had said: "A nice, good face," but Clarence showed no enthusiasm. He said now: "She's joined some sort of women's naval service and is going to Alexandria. She wants me to meet her there and get married."

"Why not?"

"Why not, indeed?"

"You now have Sophie to think about, of course."

"To hell with Sophie. Would you condemn me to that? Brenda at least would respect me."

Harriet smiled. "For what?"

Satisfied that he had provoked her raillery, he lay back in his chair and sombrely echoed her: "For what?" He thrust out his lower lip then, after some moments, said: "The gall of frustration has poured for years into my system. I'll die of it in the end." He gave her a long, brooding look, intended to be darkly significant, so she had difficulty in not laughing outright.

She decided to ask his help before things deteriorated further. Changing her tone, appealing to his generosity, she said: "I've come to ask your help. Before you go, there's something you must do for us."

"Ah!" Clarence looked down into his glass. He did not move but his attitude had become wary. After a long pause, he asked: "What?"

"We have to try and get someone out of the country."

"Not Yakimov?"

"Yakimov's gone."

"Indeed? He never paid back that ten thousand he got from the Polish fund."

"He never paid back anything. We're worried about Sasha Drucker. If we have to go, what will happen to him?"

"You were a couple of fools to keep him in the first place."

"Well, we did keep him and now we have to look after him."

"Why? He's not a child. Surely he can look after himself? He belongs here: he must have friends . . ."

"He hasn't. Anyway, his friends would be Jews. They couldn't help him."

Her urgent advocacy made Clarence sit up, sobered and vexed. He said sharply: "I can imagine Guy busy-bodying himself about this fellow. But why are you involved?"

Harriet reflected on the complex of instincts that caused her to protect such dependent innocents as Sasha and the red kitten but did not suppose Clarence would be satisfied by any attempt to explain them. After some moments, she said: "We can't just abandon him here. You must see that. We thought, if we could get him a passport of some sort, he could come with us."

Clarence stared blankly at her.

"Guy says you had someone who forged passports for the Poles."

Seeing where this was leading, Clarence smiled to himself. "They were made by Poles for Poles." He shifted in his chair, throwing one leg over the arm, and explained with superior patience: "The whole set-up was organised inside the Polish army: the Rumanian government connived at it. In those days, Rumania was our ally and the Poles were escaping to join the allied forces in France. The Rumanians did quite well out of it. They were paid so much per escape. It ran into thousands. This fellow of yours is a different matter. He's a deserter from the army and all the frontier officials would be on the look-out for him."

"Is there anyone left of the people you had working for the Poles?"

Clarence made a movement suggesting that even if there were, he personally was taking no risks.

"You *might* help, Clarence. *Please.* If you could get him a pass-port and drive him over the frontier into Bulgaria . . ."

Clarence interrupted her with an angry laugh. "My dear child, do you realise what you're asking? If I were caught with this fellow in my car, I'd stand a fair chance of ending my days in a Rumanian prison."

She said with persuasive sweetness: "At least, get me the pass-port."

Clarence stared from the window, his expression sullen, his glass forgotten in his hand. He had once said to her: "If you treated me properly, you could get anything you wanted from me," but she had, of course, to reckon with Clarence's ideas of proper treatment. They changed with his moods. He now said coldly:

"You can be very charming when you want something."

"Well, I don't want something for myself. I want to help this poor boy."

"Why? What do you care about Sasha Drucker?" He turned on her a stare of black resentment that made clear to her the fact that he might do something for her but would do nothing for Sasha. He would do even less when it was she who pleaded for him. It would have been better had Guy made the appeal.

She stood up. "We've taken him in," she said. "We feel for him as for a child who has a right to the elements of a reasonable life. That's all."

Clarence got slowly to his feet. She waited, but he remained silent, embarrassed, but sustained by his obstinate jealousy.

She took out Sasha's photograph and put it on the table, making a last plea: "Will you think about it?"

In acute exasperation, he burst out: "Think about *what*? You're asking the impossible. I can do nothing."

She left the photograph, feeling it might speak for itself, and went, saying nothing more.

She walked the two miles back to the centre of the town. For most of the way she felt empty with disappointment, then her old anxiety began seeping back again. What had seemed so simple a solution of the problem had proved no solution at all. When, after luncheon, she had Guy to herself, she told him of Clarence's refusal to obtain the passport. Giving an explanation not too painful to her own vanity, she said: "You might suppose he was jealous of the boy."

Guy laughed. "He probably is. He has always been very devoted to me, investing me with the qualities he lacks himself."

"You mean, he's probably jealous of your befriending Sasha?"

"What else?"

Leaving it at that, Harriet said: "Perhaps you're right. But what are we to do now?"

"We're not dependent on Clarence. God help us if we were. We'll try someone else."

"Who?"

"I don't know. I'll speak to David. Leave it to me and don't worry."

Towards the end of the week, the Pringles, about to enter the Athénée Palace, met Princess Teodorescu and Baron Steinfeld emerging. The baron was ordering a string of hotel servants who were carrying luggage out to his Mercedes. The princess stared furiously at the Pringles, making them feel that their appearance at that moment was the final outrage of an outrageous day. The baron, however, greeted them as though feeling some need to explain his departure. "We go to the mountains," he said. "We go late, we go in fear, but we escape the heat. If we stay, we melt away."

"*Hör doch auf*," said the princess, pushing him towards the car.

The Pringles, surprised not so much by this belated departure as the fluster attending it, mentioned it to Galpin when they went into the bar.

"They're escaping the heat, are they?" Galpin twisted his lips down in an ironical smile. "I bet they're not the only ones," and he went on to explain that the Guardists, having broken into

Lupescu's house, had that morning found a box of letters which incriminated some of the most famous names in the country.

"They've been pretending, the whole lot of them, that they've been Guardist all along. They now refer to Lupescu as 'the dirty Jewess', but she's got the laugh on them, all right. She left this box of letters, open, bang in the middle of her bedroom floor. They're from people like Teodorescu all addressing her as '*ma souveraine*' and 'your majesty' and saying they couldn't wait for the day when she would be crowned queen. It's damned funny, but the Iron Guard isn't amused. Humour isn't in fashion these days. I bet there'll be quite a few of the upper crust moving out of Bucharest to escape the heat."

The papers announced that the city's atonement would end on Sunday, the day Queen Helen, the Queen Mother, was returning from exile to reside with her son in Bucharest.

Sunday's pageantry began with the clatter of horses. The Queen's own regiment, out of favour since her departure, was galloping across the square in frogged uniforms and busbies, pennants flying, to meet her at the station. The whole city was in the streets to cheer them. Antonescu had promised new order, new hope, renewed greatness, and all, it was believed, would return with the wronged Queen who was the very symbol of the country's exiled morality. Here was the resolution for which everyone was waiting.

The noise brought Despina from the kitchen. She ran through the room to join Guy, Harriet and Sasha on the balcony, shrieking with delight at the hussars and the flags and the ferment of the square. Here was a new beginning indeed! But even while the dust of the horsemen still hung in the air, the sound of "*Capitanul*" could be heard swelling from the Calea Victoriei.

The Iron Guard had been silent during the week of atonement. There was a general belief that they were being discouraged while Antonescu was seeking some other agent to police his régime. Whether this was true or not, here they were and something in their bearing had changed. There had always been a touch of defiance about all their marching and singing in the past, but now it was exultant. When they finished "*Capitanul*", they started on the National Anthem, linking the tunes as though they had a peculiar warranty for both.

Harriet said: "I've never heard them sing that before."

The leading Guardists were cheered, automatically, accepted as part of the day's entertainment, but as the ranks passed stern-faced and contemptuous of the audience, the applause dwindled. People were uncertain what response was required of them, and gradually silence came down.

Guy said: "I don't like the look of this," and after a moment, he turned and went into the room.

The Guardists were still passing when a new interest revivified the crowds. The old Metropolitan, bejewelled like an Indian prince, had appeared walking beneath a golden canopy. His followers, who had spent the week trailing round the streets as penitents, in black, were now exultant in cloth of gold. As this dazzling procession appeared in the square, the crowd surged towards it, leaving the Guardists to jackboot their way unheeded.

Sasha, excited by everything he saw, leaned out over the ledge while Despina clapped her hands, jumping up and down and crying: "*Frumosa, frumosa, frumosa.*"

Long after they had circled the square, the priests could be seen, agleam in the sunlight, climbing the rising road to the cathedral. A sound of gunfire announced the Queen's arrival. At once all the bells of the city rang out and cheers, relayed from the station, were redoubled by cheers from the crowd below. The clangour and chorus of bells cheering drowned the Guardists who lifted their heads, bawling in an effort to be heard.

Harriet looked into the room to say: "The Queen is coming," and Guy, who had been talking on the telephone, put down the receiver. "I've just rung the Legation," he said. "The Iron Guard is in power."

"You mean the whole of the Cabinet is now Guardist?"

"Yes, except for one or two military men and experts. Guardists have been appointed to all the important ministries."

"What will happen now?"

"Chaos, I imagine."

She took advantage of his disturbed expression to say: "You must close the summer school."

He was about to speak when the cheers started up in the square again and they returned to the balcony to see the hussars escorting the Queen and her son, who were in a gilded coach covered with roses. The coach passed through the square, then went on its way to the cathedral. There was sudden silence, then came the sibilant murmur of the mass relayed through the loudspeakers and as though a wind had passed over it, the crowd sank to its knees. Harriet could see the women pulling out handkerchiefs and weeping in an excess of emotion.

From somewhere in the remote distance there still came on the air the monotonous throb of "*Capitanul*".

18

Hotel Splendide Suleiman Bay,
Istanbul.

Dear Boy [wrote Yakimov]:

Is the old girl sold? If so, get Dobbie to remit cash through bag. Your Yaki is in low water. Food here poorish. Kebabs and so on. The English Colony a funny lot. When I tell them I'm a refugee from the oil fields, no one seems to believe me.

Don't delay
With the lei,

Your poor old needy Yaki.

Crossing to the corner of the Boulevard Brateanu, Harriet saw the Hispano still in the window, looking immovable, like a museum exhibit. She went in to inquire whether anyone was showing interest in the car. The salesman glumly shook his head.

Each of the showroom windows displayed a portrait of Codreanu. The same portrait stared out from the windows opposite, the empty windows of Dragomir's, the largest grocery shop in Europe. Queues waited for such food as there was.

The windows rattled as across the square, at sixty miles an hour, a fleet of Iron Guard motor-cyclists sped on their way to the Boulevard Carol where the richest men in Rumania lay under house arrest, awaiting the results of Horia Sima's enquiry into the origins of all private fortunes. Nothing might be moved from their houses. An armed guard stood at every gate.

Suicides were occurring daily. One of the first was of the Youth Movement leader, decorated last June by Hitler. Unable to account for a missing twelve million *lei*, he had shot himself. The police had gone on strike. Their work, they said, was too dangerous. Those who were in power one day, were in prison the next; those who had been in prison, were now in power. The Guardists had taken over and patrolled the streets with revolvers in their holsters.

As the motor-cyclists roared past, the salesman raised one eyebrow and one shoulder. Who these days would buy such a symbol of private wealth as this Hispano?

Bella, when she telephoned that morning, had said: "These Guardist police are worse than no police at all. All they do is go round the offices collecting for party funds. And not only the Jewish offices, either. They don't care whose money they take. They call it cleaning up public life, but even if you find a burglar in your house, you can't get a Guardist to come and arrest him. I hope you're staying indoors. Things'll settle down, of course, but, if I were you, I wouldn't go out yet awhile."

Had Harriet taken Bella's advice she would, like Carol's financiers and Chief of Police and Chief of Secret Police, have been a prisoner in her own home. As it was, made restless by insecurity, she wandered about the streets and went each day to meet Guy as he left his classes. She imagined he would be less liable to attack if he were with a woman.

Stories were going round that thousands of people had been arrested and thousands executed.

People caught leaving the country were sometimes arrested, sometimes merely stripped of their valuable possessions and allowed to proceed.

"That Ionescu's gone," said Bella. "Him that used to be Minister of Information. He overbalanced trying to face all ways at once. He became a Guardist but he knew he was for it. His children were carrying little fur muffs. Muffs! – at this time of the year, I ask you! Naturally they roused suspicion. The customs men tore them to pieces and found them stuffed with jewellery and gold. I always thought him to clever by half."

Another who went was Ionescu's mistress, the singer Florica. She reached Trieste and then turned round and came back again. She was reported as having said: "I thought of my country and knew that at such a time I could not leave it."

But, as Bella pointed out, she was a gipsy and no true Rumanian, so her behaviour was, as one might expect, peculiar.

Harriet, as she walked about in the sticky autumnal heat, saw no open signs of persecution, not even of the Dambôviţa Jews. What she did see, daily, were processions of Cabinet ministers, civil servants, officers of the armed services, priests, nuns and schoolchildren following the most impressive funerals. For the Guardist leaders were busy disinterring their Martyrs. Raised in batches to which were given heroic names like the Decemvirii and the Nicadorii, the bodies were paraded in giant coffins all over the city and reburied with ceremonies that must be attended by any who hoped to maintain any sort of position in public life.

Down in the Chicken Market Harriet found a memorial service being held over the spot where Calinescu's murderers had lain. The trembling old peasant who sold her a cabbage said that among the mourners were "the greatest men in the world".

Who were they? she asked and was told: "Hitler, Mussolini, Count Ciano and the Emperor of Japan."

After the ceremony the site was roped off and spread each day with fresh flowers, to the inconvenience of the market traffic.

"The great day, of course," said Bella, "will be when they dig up His Nibs at Fort Jilawa. They'll wait till November, the anniversary of his death. Then, Nikko says, trouble will really begin."

The papers announced that the demand for admission to the Iron Guard was so great, the list had to be closed.

Among those who appeared in Guardist uniform was the Pringles' landlord, who was also their next-door neighbour. In the past, when he had met Harriet on the landing, he had greeted her courteously: now, in his green shirt and breeches, his moustache sternly waxed, he stared over her head and she began to fear him. He might have – almost certainly did have – a key to their flat. She remembered the mysterious disappearance of the oil-well plan. He had been one of her suspects. If he came in while they were out, he would almost certainly discover Sasha.

Once or twice, when she left the flat, she saw a man dodge out of sight on the lower flight. She spoke of this to Guy, who thought it would be some agent of the landlord. Embarrassed at having English tenants, he might be seeking an excuse to break their agreement.

She said to Despina: "Keep the front door bolted. If the landlord wants to come in, do not let him."

"No, no, *cornița*," Despina assured her, appearing to understand the whole situation. "If anyone comes, I do like this . . ." She opened the sitting-room door a crack and put her nose to it. "If it is the landlord – pouf! I do like this." She slammed the door shut. "He is a bad man," she added in explanation. "He beats his cook."

There were now four meatless days in a week, but even on the other days meat was hard to find. Despina would be away for two or three hours queueing at market stalls and often, on returning, would hold out, with a dramatic gesture, her empty basket. "In the market today, no sugar, no coffee, no meat, no fish, no eggs. Nothing, nothing."

Watching the processions, the daily pageantry amid utter confusion, it seemed to Harriet that the whole country had succumbed, without any sort of resistance, to a lunatic autocracy.

She said to Guy: "Everyone in Bucharest is trailing round after these Guardist turn-outs. Why is there no opposition to it all?"

"There's no chance of any *active* opposition," he said. "The only people with the moral fibre to oppose anything are in prison. The Communists – but not only the Communists: the Liberal Democrats, everyone and anyone likely to show a spark of revolt: they're all in prison."

"What about Maniu?"

"What can he do? Anyway, from what I've seen of him, I should not think he's much more than a showpiece: Rumania's 'Good Man'. He was the leader of the Transylvanian peasants, and Transylvania is lost. You must realise that this new dictatorship is much tougher than the old. There are not only prisons now, there are concentration camps: and there are these young men trained at Dachau, all waiting for a chance to beat someone up. Yet," Guy added, "there is opposition of a sort. A typical Rumanian opposition. Satire. It's the most difficult sort to repress." He told her how in the Doi Trandifiri, the meeting place of intellectuals, there was proof that the liberal sanity of the past survived. Deathly fearful though people were, there they were still able to laugh. They had nicknamed the Iron Guard "*le régime des pompes funèbres*" and a great many funny stories went round about Horia Sima and his visions. Sima was in conflict with Codreanu's father who declared that his son's spirit disapproved of the present leader and had appointed his father as his vicar-on-earth. The old man had to be put under house-arrest and, knowing he was in danger of assassination, he said he preferred to stay indoors as fewer accidents happened there.

"There's opposition, too," said Guy, "from a much more influential source – the German minister. He's tired of all this marching and singing '*Capitanul*'. He wants the country back at work. Several big industrial firms have had to close down because the directors are in prison and the workers are all in the Iron Guard. The financial situation is chaotic. Carol banked all the national wealth abroad in his own name. Now it's frozen. On top of that, the Guardists want to start a full-scale persecution of the Jews."

"Wouldn't the Germans encourage that?"

"No. What do they care about Rumanian racial purity. This is merely a raw material zone. Fabricius said to Sima: 'Persecutions are all very well in Germany where there are ten efficient Germans to one efficient Jew, but here there isn't one efficient Rumanian to ten efficient Jews. If we do get law and order here, we'll probably have the Germans to thank for it.' "

19

Now that he saw him every day, Sasha had become for Guy a more evident responsibility. Finding that he could not borrow or hire a gramophone, Guy brought in a mouth-organ which Sasha accepted with more excitement than he had shown over the room. "But this is spiffing," he said, gazing delightedly at the mouth-organ. "Really spiffing," and he took it at once to his room.

He kept the room tidy and made his own bed. He had pinned his drawings to the walls. The books he had borrowed from the sitting-room stood in a row on the bedside table. His possessions – a brush and comb, some pencils, paper and water-paints – were neatly set out before them. Whatever disorder might prevail in the outside world, he lived in order and was happy.

Sitting on the edge of the bed, he began to pick out a tune he had heard on the radio and which seemed to Harriet painfully applicable to their case:

> "Run rabbit, run rabbit, run, run, run,
> Don't give the farmer his fun, fun, fun . . ."

When they were alone Guy said to Harriet: "I've been speaking to David. He thinks Foxy Leverett might help us about Sasha."

"What could Foxy Leverett do?"

"Apparently he's an adept at smuggling people over frontiers. But the whole problem may be settled in a different way. Supposing, things being as they are, the Soviets decided to invade? They could get here before the Germans."

"You think the Russians would protect the son of a banker who worked for Germany and piled up a fortune in Switzerland?"

"No, but he'd be no worse off than anyone else. He could lose himself in a crowd."

Harriet was beginning to fear that the hope of losing himself in the crowd was the most they could offer Sasha.

Next morning, Bella, telephoning as was her habit, asked: "I suppose you didn't listen last night to the German Propaganda broadcast?"

"We never listen to German broadcasts."

"Neither do we." Bella paused, evidently edging her way, with tact and consciousness of tact, into revelation unwelcome to Harriet. "I don't want to worry you," she said. "But . . ."

Harriet asked, on edge: "What is it?"

"I feel I must tell you. I was rung up last night by a friend, Doamna Pavlovici – the Pavlovicis listen sometimes, just to get some real news."

"Yes?"

"The Germans read out a list of Englishmen in Bucharest whom they think are up to something. It was a warning. In fact, they said: "These men will be answerable to the Gestapo."

"Did you know any of them?"

"Well, yes, I did. There was Foxy Leverett and David Boyd – but they're all right. They must have diplomatic protection."

"Who else?"

"Inchcape and Clarence Lawson."

"And Guy?"

"Doamna Pavlovici said she heard the name Guy Pringle – that's why she rang me. But she's a bit of a feather-brain. She could have made a mistake."

Harriet, her throat constricted, did not try to reply. Bella, conscious of having shocked her listener into silence, hurried on to say: "I couldn't keep you in ignorance. You were sure to hear, anyway. I thought you could have a word with Guy. He's a bit foolhardy, you know. He goes to that Doi Trandifiri – a dangerous place, full of reds and artists. It'll be raided very soon, you'll see. And that summer school with all those Jews! I don't need to tell you . . ."

"There aren't many students left, now."

"No, I imagine not." Bella spoke as though the fact were grimly significant. There was a pause in which Harriet felt too depleted to speak. It was broken by Bella who said she had bought Nikko's release again and they had decided to spend the last weeks of summer in Sinai: "We're sick of 'Capitanul' and all the rest of it. We need a break. So I'll say 'Good-bye', my dear, just in case you're not here when we get back."

As soon as Bella had put down her receiver, Harriet telephoned Inchcape at his office. It was part of his work to listen to the

German broadcasts and he had, he admitted, heard his name, and the names of Guy and Clarence, mentioned the previous night.

"Among a lot of others," he said. "They gave a list of the engineers who were kept on in key positions on the oil fields. Yes, they did say something about the Gestapo. A lot of empty threats. Anyway, the Gestapo isn't here and I doubt if it ever will be."

"But the Guardists are," said Harriet, "And they'd be only too glad to do the Gestapo's work for it. Surely the summer school could be closed now! There aren't half a dozen students left. Guy is there every day. Almost alone. An obvious target. And it's all for nothing."

"Not for nothing. The school's a good thing. It's showing the flag. It's cocking a snook. If we closed down, it'd please them no end. They're trying to scare us. It's the old war of nerves, but I'm not playing their game. They want us to take to our heels – so that's exactly what we won't do."

Checked by this bravado, Harriet still held to the telephone, seeking in her mind some plea that would move Inchcape to reason, but Inchcape was not waiting for it. "I must go," he said. "I've other things to worry about. I've just heard Pinkrose will be landing on top of us any day now." He spoke as though the professor's arrival was an intolerable impertinence.

"But aren't you expecting him?" Harriet asked.

Inchcape gave an exasperated laugh. "To tell you the truth, what with one thing and another, I'd forgotten about the old buffer."

"He couldn't be coming at a worse time," Harriet said, intending sympathy, but Inchcape would have none of it.

"Nonsense," he said. "These internecine squabbles need not concern us. You're getting jittery, my child. Would King Michael bring his mother here if there were cause for alarm?"

Inchcape rang off before she could reply. She went to her room to dress. The heat was abating and it was possible now to wear something heavier than silk or cotton. For the first time since early spring, she put on a blue linen suit she had brought from England.

Sasha, when he saw her in it, put a hand on her sleeve, smiling, his eyes warm with an adoration he was too artless to conceal. He said: "My mother had a suit like this."

Although it was still early, Harriet walked to the University, needing to assure herself that the broadcast had not, so far, provoked trouble.

The door stood open. The porter, as usual, was nowhere to be seen. Anyone could enter. She felt furious with the man who, were he at his post, could at least give warning of attack.

She sat on the porter's bench and stared out through the peaked doorway at the glittering street. The gipsies, selling the only thing plentiful in Bucharest now, were in their usual high spirits. Their danger was as great as that of the Jews, but they knew nothing about it.

She could hear Guy's voice coming through an open door half-way down the passage. She could also hear, from somewhere distant in the street, the sound of "*Capitanul*". She had become so used to it, she would scarcely have noticed it had she not been listening for it. The Guardists were approaching the University. If any of them turned in here, she decided, she would rush to the door and shut and bolt it. She wondered if the Legation would let her have a revolver. She was becoming obsessed with the need to get Guy and Sasha through this situation unharmed. Sitting there, hypnotised by her own inactivity, she began to think of them as enclosed in a protective emanation that came of her will to save them.

She wondered how many students were in the room with Guy. She had always been somewhat irritated by the students and their claim on him. He imagined his energy was inexhaustible, but she felt that given the opportunity, they would drain him dry: and now it was for their sake that he was here at risk.

She rose and made her way silently down the passage to the lecture room. "*Capitanul*" was still wavering about in the distance. Not a great many were singing. She imagined a small posse out on some sinister mission.

The door of Guy's classroom had been propped open to create a draught.

Harriet, pressing against the wall, could see unseen through the opening. There were three students – two girls and a youth, sitting together in the front desk, their faces raised in strained attention.

Harriet moved to see Guy. Her foot slipped on the linoleum, making no more noise than a mouse. At once a frisson went through the room. The three heads turned. Guy's voice slowed.

He did not pause, but he glanced at the door. Harriet remained motionless, scarcely breathing. The lecture went on.

She tiptoed back to the bench and sat down again, satisfied, having discovered that beneath his apparent unconcern he was as alert as she was to the dangers about them.

20

THAT DAY, A FRIDAY, was the last on which the summer school opened. The following afternoon, Inchcape called on Guy to tell him that the new Minister of Information had ordered the school and the British Propaganda Bureau to close immediately.

He said: "Had to agree about the school – no choice, no choice at all! – but the Bureau is part of the Legation. I've just been to see H.E. I said: 'While the Legation remains here, we've a right to our Bureau.' I must say the old boy was pleasant enough. Indeed, he was pathetic. He seems dazed by the way things are shaping. 'All right, Inchcape,' he said. 'All right. If you want to keep your little shop open I'll see what can be done, but the school must close.' "

"Why?" Guy asked.

Inchcape shrugged. "The Minister said if the closure were not effected as from today, we would all be ordered out. No reprieve."

Guy was not satisfied. He said: "If they've relented about the Bureau, they're just as likely to relent about the school."

"No. Something's going on here. There's a rumour that a German Military Mission is on its way. The Guardist minister was adamant. They feel – not unnaturally, I suppose – that a British school is an anomaly in their midst." Inchcape's tone was rather smug but held a hint of defiance, so it occurred to Harriet that he had probably bartered the school for the Bureau: "Let me keep one open and you can close the other." Whatever the sacrifice, Inchcape must maintain an official position.

For her part, however, she was only too thankful to see the school end. She said: "So there's nothing to keep us here. We could take a holiday. We could go to Greece."

Guy, looking gloomy, said without enthusiasm: "We might get to Predeal, but no farther. I have to prepare for the new term . . ."

"But if the English Department is closed . . ."

"Nothing has been said about the Department closing," said Inchcape. "All they demanded, was the closure of the summer school."

"But surely they must mean the English Department, too. Yesterday, Guy had only three students. You can't open a department without students."

"Oh, they'll be swarming back when the term starts. They'll feel there's safety in numbers. We'll weather another winter here."

Making no attempt to argue on a point that would soon settle itself, Harriet said: "When can we go to Predeal?"

Before Guy could reply, Inchcape broke in: "Not next week. Our distinguished visitor arrives next week. This is an opportunity to make arrangements. I shall meet him at Baneasa, of course, but I'll expect my staff to be in attendance. Then we'll have to give a party; a reception. We can do nothing about that until we know the day of his arrival."

"What is the date of the Cantecuzeno Lecture?" Harriet asked.

Inchcape looked at Guy saying: "It's held every other year. You must have been here for the last one?"

"1938. The beginning of October. My first term here. The Cantecuzeno was the inaugural lecture of the term.'

"So it was," Inchcape nodded, clicked his tongue reflectively while staring at his feet, then suddenly jerked upright. "Anyway, the old buffer's reached Cairo. He may get stuck there and he may not. We must be prepared."

Early on Wednesday morning, Despina woke Guy to say Inchcape wanted him on the telephone. Inchcape shouted accusingly: "That old nitwit's coming today. You'll just have to rouse yourself and get to the airport. I can't make it."

"When is he due?"

"That's the trouble. He sent a last-minute cable saying merely: 'Wednesday a.m.' It might mean hanging round there half the day. I've got this damned reception to organise. Pauli will deliver invitations. We must have a princess or two." The imminence of the real Pinkrose seemed to have disrupted Inchcape. In the extremity of his exacerbation he became confiding: "To tell the truth, I never thought he'd get here. I thought he'd hang around in Cairo for weeks. He must have got the organisation to charter a plane. Shocking to think of such a waste of funds. And," he added, putting the question as though Guy were to blame for the contingency, "where are we going to hold this lecture, I'd like to know? Last time, we took the reception rooms over the Café Napoleon, but all that's been pulled down. The University hall is nothing like large enough. Every possible place in the town has been turned over to the Iron Guard for divisional headquarters. I suppose we could get one of the public rooms at the Athénée Palace! The acoustics are poor, but does it matter? Pinkrose is no great shakes as a lecturer. Well, get into your duds and get down there. Take Harriet. Make a bit of a show. The self-important old so-and-so will expect it."

On their way to the airport, the Pringles were to confirm a booking for Pinkrose at the Athénée Palace.

The sky that morning was filmed with cloud, an indication of the season's change. There was a breeze. For the first time since spring, it was possible to believe that the Siberian cold would return and the country, under snow, lost all colour and became like a photographic negative.

Harriet said: "Do you really think we'll spend another winter here?"

Making no pretence at optimism now, Guy shook his head. "It's impossible to say."

On Monday, with no more warning than was given by a day or two of rumours, the precursors of the German Military Mission had driven into Bucharest. They were followed on Tuesday by a German Trade Delegation. The whole parking area outside the Athénée Palace became filled with German cars and military lorries, each bearing the swastika on a red pennant. The arrivals were young officers sent to prepare the way for the senior members of the Mission.

The story was that Fabricius had demanded demobilisation in Rumania. "Send your men back into the fields," he said. "What Germany needs is food." Antonescu, aghast, replied that he had been dreaming of the day when his country would "fight shoulder to shoulder with its great ally". He finally agreed that Germany should take over the reorganisation both of Rumania's army and economy.

Guy said, as they passed through the swing-doors: "Perhaps this is an alternative to complete occupation. It may mean they will leave us alone."

At that hour of the morning, the vestibule was empty. The booking had been tentatively made by Inchcape for an indefinite day of this week and now the hotel was full of Germans. Guy went to the desk, half expecting to be refused, but the hotel maintained its traditions. It had always been favoured by the British and did not forget past favours. Guy was courteously received. A room was available for Professor Lord Pinkrose.

The airfield lay on the southern fringe of the city. The opalescent sky cast a pallor over the grass plain that stretched some forty miles to the Danube. The wind blowing off the Balkans was like a wind from the sea.

There was nothing on the field but a customs-shed. The Pringles sat on the bench before it, waiting. Since the school had been closed, Guy had been low-spirited and restless, missing employment and having nothing to take its place. He had been told he must not use the University library or any other part of the building without permission. He sometimes went to the Propaganda Bureau to read Inchcape's books and cogitate on subjects for the new term. He now took from his pockets a novel by Conrad and two books of poems by de la Mare, while Harriet read Lawrence's *The Rainbow*.

They had waited less than an hour when one of the small grey planes of the Rumanian air-line arrived from Sofia. Harriet put down her book to watch the passengers alight. Behind the usual collection of businessmen in grey suits, carrying new toffee-coloured brief-cases, came a small male figure, much wrapped up, wearing a heavy greatcoat. He descended slowly, collar up, shoulders hunched, hands in pockets, glancing cautiously about from under the brim of a trilby hat.

"Could that be Pinkrose?" she asked.

Guy adjusted his glasses and peered across the field. "Surely he wouldn't come on the ordinary plane?"

The businessmen, knowing their way about, had made straight for the customs-shed leaving the last passenger wandering, alone, on the field. Guy rose and crossed over to him. They returned together. Guy was explaining how Inchcape, busy arranging a reception in Pinkrose's honour, had been unable to come to the airfield.

Pinkrose accepted this apology with a brief nod, grunting slightly, apparently leaving further comment until more was revealed to him.

He was a rounded man, narrow-shouldered and broad-hipped, thickening down from the crown of his hat to the edge of his greatcoat. His nose, blunt and greyish, poked out between collar and hat-brim. His eyes, grey as rain-water, moved about, alert and suspicious, like the eyes of a chameleon. They paused a second on Harriet, then swivelled away to flicker over the book in her hand, the bench on which she sat, the shed behind her, the ground, the porters near-by.

Introduced to her, he made a noise behind his scarf, holding his face aside as though it would be indelicate to gaze directly at her.

The porters were carrying his baggage: several suitcases and a canvas bag weighty with books. When these were loaded on to a taxi-cab, Pinkrose drew a hand from a pocket. He was wearing a dark knitted glove, in the centre of which was a threepenny piece. He then brought out the other hand, also gloved, holding a sixpence. He looked from one to the other, uncertain which coin was appropriate. Guy settled the problem by giving each porter a hundred *lei*.

As they drove back to the centre of the town, Pinkrose sat forward on his seat, his short blunt nose turning from side to side as he watched the wooden shacks of the suburbs, and the pitted, dusty road. At the sight of the first concrete blocks, he lost interest and relaxed.

Guy began questioning him about conditions in England.

"Quite intolerable," he said, his voice – which Harriet heard for the first time – thin and distinct. He did not glance at Guy and, having pronounced on England, he was silent for some moments then suddenly said: "I was thankful to get away."

Harriet would have liked to ask about his journey but she found his aura inhibiting. It seemed to her that any question concerning his immediate person would be taken as an impertinence. Guy may have felt the same for they drove in silence until they were about to enter the square. At this point the taxi was paused by an immense Iron Guard procession which was coming from the direction of the palace.

The sight astounded Pinkrose. He shuffled forward again, staring about, not only at the marching men but at the passers-by as though expecting everyone to share his surprise. That morning no one was giving the Guardists a glance. Their processions were becoming not only a commonplace but a bore. The air, however, resounded with cheers relayed over loudspeakers fixed around the square.

Pinkrose caught his breath as the Guardists were followed by an anti-aircraft gun and two tanks, all painted with swastikas and carrying Nazi pennants.

"What *is* this?" he burst out.

Guy explained that it was an Iron Guard procession. "I think," he said, "they're celebrating the new ten-year pact between Germany and Rumania."

"Good gracious me! I thought Rumania was a neutral country."

"So it is, in theory."

The procession past, the taxi crossed the square with Pinkrose jerking his head from side to side in anticipation of further shocks. And a shock awaited all three of them. As they stepped on to the pavement a gigantic flag unrolled above their heads: a Nazi flag of scarlet, white and black. Pinkrose stared at it, his lizard mouth agape.

The Athénée Palace had, on past occasions, put out a Union Jack or a Rumanian flag of no unusual size. That morning a new gilded flag-pole had been fixed on the roof and the swastika that hung from it fell three storeys to touch the main portico.

Pinkrose demanded: "What's this building?"

"The chief hotel," said Guy.

They entered. The hall and vestibule, that earlier had been empty, were now crowded with all the morning idlers who usually filled the cafés. Little tables were being placed everywhere to accommodate them. Drawn there by hope of seeing the German officers, they tried to hid their excitement beneath a show of animated interest in each other. There were a great many women who, dressed to impress, whispered together, tense and watchful.

Hadjimoscos, Horvatz and Cici Palu, usually in the bar at this time, were seated in a row on the sofa opposite the main staircase. Like everyone else, they were drinking coffee and eating elaborate cakes made of soya flour and artificial cream.

The hotel servants, harassed by the rush of visitors, ignored Pinkrose's arrival. Unable to find anyone to bring in the luggage, Guy carried it through the swing-doors himself. Saying: "I must go and ring Inchcape," he left Harriet with Pinkrose who, still muffled up, hands in pockets, gazed about him, baffled by the atmosphere of nervous expectation in which he found himself.

Every head was turned towards the staircase. Half a dozen officers had appeared, all handsome, all elegant, one wearing an eyeglass, and were descending with constrained dignity, apparently oblivious of their audience.

Some of the women took up the attitudes of graceful indifference, but most gazed spellbound at these desirable young men who were the more piquantly desirable because they had so recently been the enemy. When the Germans passed out of sight, the women fell together in ecstatic appreciation, their eyes agleam, their sensuality heightened by the proximity of these conquerors of the world.

Pinkrose's grey cheeks became yellowish. Newly arrived from a country at war, he was so unnerved by this first sight of the opponent, that he looked directly at Harriet to ask: "They were, if I am not mistaken, Germans?"

Harriet explained their presence: "There are a great many Germans in Bucharest. You'll soon become used to them."

Guy, returning at an agitated trot, said he had been unable to telephone as the telephone boxes were all occupied by journalists sending out some story to their contacts in Switzerland. "I don't know what it is," he said: "probably something to do with the Military Mission. We'll have to wait, so let us go inside."

Pinkrose and Harriet followed him through to the vestibule. As they passed the row of telephone boxes, Galpin darted from one of them and began to push past them, unseeing, intent in his pursuit of news. Guy caught his arm, introduced him to Pinkrose, whose appearance seemed to surprise him, then asked: "Has anything happened?"

"My God, haven't you heard?" Galpin's eyes protruded at them. "Foxy Leverett was picked up dead this morning. He was lying on the pavement, not a hundred yards from the Legation. It looked as though he had fallen from a window, but the nearest house was empty; in fact, shuttered. The owner is under arrest. My hunch is, he was tossed out of a car. Anyway, however he'd got there, he'd taken a terrible beating. Dobson says he only recognised him by the red moustache."

"Who found him?"

"Labourers. Soon after daybreak. And that's not all. One of the key men in Ploesti has disappeared. Chap called McGinty. That's just come through. It's obvious the bastards are not going to be satisfied with acting as hold-up men round the Jewish offices. They want blood." He glanced aside and catching Pinkrose's intent stare, he suddenly asked: "How did this little bloke get into Bucharest?"

In a tone that invited respect, Guy said: "Professor Lord Pinkrose has come to deliver the Cantecuzino Lecture."

"The what?"

Guy explained that the lecture, given in English every other year, was part of his organisation's cultural propaganda.

Galpin threw back his head and gave a crow of laughter. "Gawd'strewth!" he said and continued on his way out of the hotel.

Pinkrose turned stiffly, looking at Guy as though explanation, if not apology, were due, but Guy was too disturbed to give either. He conducted the professor to a sofa and asked him if he would like a brandy.

Pinkrose fretfully shook his head. "I never drink spirits, but it's a long time since I had breakfast. I'd like a sandwich."

Guy ordered him sandwiches and coffee, then returned to the telephone booths. At the hint of change in the weather, the central heating had been switched on. The room was stifling and Pinkrose, after sitting fully clad for some moments, began to unbundle himself. He unwound a scarf or two, then took off his hat revealing a bald brow, high, grey and wrinkled, surrounded by a fringe of dog-brown hair. This incongruous colour caught Harriet's eye and she had to do her best to look elsewhere.

After a while the greatcoat, too, came off. In a tightly-fitting suit of dark grey herring-bone stuff, old fashioned in cut, a winged collar and narrow knitted tie, Pinkrose sat surrounded by his outdoor wear. He gave Harriet one or two rapid trial glances before he brought himself to address her again, then he asked: "What was that man saying about someone being found dead?"

"The dead man was an attaché at the Legation. We think he had something to do with the secret service."

"Ah!" Pinkrose nodded knowingly. "I believe those fellows often come to a bad end." He was sufficiently reassured to set about his sandwiches when they arrived.

Harriet, watching him, felt no reassurance at all. What had happened to Foxy, could happen to Guy – or, indeed, to any of them. And Foxy had been a likeable acquaintance. Not only that, he was the one who was "adept at smuggling people over frontiers", the one who might have helped them with Sasha. To whom could they turn now? She could not imagine that Dobson would be much practical help, and they barely knew the senior men at the Legation.

A tut from Pinkrose recalled her to her immediate responsibility. He was looking inside his sandwich. With an expression of hurt fastidiousness, he set it aside, saying: "*Not* very nice," and took a sip of coffee. He grimaced as though it were cascara. "Perhaps, after all," he said, "I will have a small sherry."

Overhearing this as he returned, much recovered, Guy said in a jocular way: "How about *ţuică*, our fiery national spirit?"

Pinkrose twitched an irritated shoulder. "No, no, certainly not. But I don't mind a sherry, if it's at all decent."

Unperturbed, Guy ordered the sherry, then sat down on Pinkrose's greatcoat, saying: "Professor Inchcape is on his way."

Moving the coat with flustered movements, acutely annoyed, Pinkrose said: "Ah!" in a tone that implied it was about time.

Guy asked him what would be the subject of his proposed lecture. Grudgingly, his head turned away, still rearranging his coat about him, Pinkrose thought he might survey the poets from Chaucer to Tennyson. Guy said: "An admirable idea," and Pinkrose raised his brows. It was becoming clear to Harriet that Guy's spontaneous friendliness towards the professor was rousing nothing but suspicious annoyance.

She was at first surprised, then she began to feel indignant – not so much with Pinkrose as with Guy, chatting enthusiastically about Pinkrose's not overbold project. She did not know whether to condemn his impercipience or to justify his innocence: and what she called innocence might, in fact, be no more than an unwillingness to admit anyone could feel animosity towards him. As he talked, Pinkrose watched him with distaste.

Looking afresh at Guy, Harriet noted that his hair was untidy, he had wine stains on his tie, his breakfast egg had dripped on to his lapel and his glasses, broken at the bridge, had been mended with adhesive tape.

She had become so used to his appearance, she had not thought to clean him up before they left.

She was thankful when Inchcape arrived to share the burden of Pinkrose's company, Catching Harriet's eye, Inchcape smiled as though he had a joke up his sleeve – not a pleasant joke – then said to Pinkrose: "So there you are!"

Pinkrose started up, a tinge of colour coming into his cheeks and affable with relief at the sight of his friend, said: "Yes, indeed! Here I am!" Smiling for the first time since his arrival, he looked like an ancient schoolboy. "And what a journey!" he added.

"We must hear all about it." Inchcape spoke as though Pinkrose were, indeed, a schoolboy and he, as ever, the headmaster. "But first I must have a drink." He turned to Guy, eyeing him as though the joke, whatever it was, was shared between them, and asked: "What have you got there? *Tuică?* All right, I'll have a *ţuică*, too." He sat down opposite Pinkrose, frowning at him with ironic humour, and asked: "Well, how *did* you get here?"

Inchcape's manner towards this old friend, who, on his invitation, had just travelled some five thousand miles, seemed to Harriet outrageous, but Pinkrose appeared to accept it. Smiling as though suddenly set at ease, he explained that he had been granted a priority flight to Malta.

"How did you manage that?" asked Inchcape.

With the glance of one who regards diplomacy as a form of conspiracy, he said: "A friend in high places. Then, believe it or not, I had to travel as a *bomb*. In the bottom of the aeroplane, you know. The pilot said to me: 'Better say your prayers. If we crash, you're a gonner.' "

"What is a 'gonner'?" Inchcape asked.

Pinkrose tittered, not taking the question seriously. "In Cairo," he said, "I met with difficulties. No one knew anything about me. I had to take the matter up with the ambassador and even then, for some reason, they would only take me as far as Athens. There, however, I discovered. to my relief, that there was a regular service to Bucharest, so here I am!"

Inchcape nodded. "So I see!" he drily said.

Although Pinkrose recounted his experiences with something near levity, it was clear that only his own determination had brought him here. He went on, rather fretfully: "England is so uncomfortable these days. And so tedious. People talk of nothing but this wretched invasion – rather overdue, I may say. We hear about it even at the high table. And life in general! So many new rules and regulations and petty restrictions! The black-out; the queueing! You, my dear Inchcape, were wise to take yourself off when you did. I cannot tell you how life has deteriorated. It couldn't be worse under the Nazis; anyway, for people like us. After all, Goering would have no quarrel with me. I've always been a good family man."

"Ah!" said Inchcape drily. "Then you won't be distressed if I tell you we may soon be under Nazi rule here."

Pinkrose tittered again. Inchcape swallowed down his *ţuică* and, his patience exhausted, said: "Let's go and eat."

Pinkrose jumped up happily. As he gathered his coat, hat and scarves, he said: "I am looking forward, I can tell you, to some good eating. Travelled friends tell me that Rumanian food is among the best in Europe."

"Their information is out of date," said Inchcape.

Pinkrose chuckled. "You always were a cod."

The dining room was empty when they entered. Three large tables in the window alcove were reserved for the officers of the *Reichswehr*. Despite the fact that there were other tables unreserved, Inchcape was seized upon as he entered and guided to an obscure corner position which he accepted with an amused shrug. Passing the menu card to Pinkrose, he said: "It's a meatless day. The steaks and roasts listed are like the paper money here, they're not backed by hard currency. But you can have any one of the three dishes at the bottom. I recommend fish pilaff?"

It was some moments before Pinkrose could be persuaded that this was not an enormous joke. "But what about caviare?" he pleaded. "Isn't that a Rumanian product?"

"It all goes to Germany."

Pinkrose's face fell. "To think," he said, "I was the envy of my colleagues . . ."

"Tonight," Inchcape told him consolingly, "you'll meet all the wit and beauty of Bucharest. I have invited several princesses noted for their hospitality. In their houses, I assure you, there are no such things as meatless days. They'll do you proud. Meanwhile, have a fish pilaff!" He looked from Guy to Harriet, grinning in appreciation of Pinkrose's discomfort, then began to discuss the mysterious death of Foxy Leverett.

"These young attachés ask for trouble," he said. "They throw their weight around, imagining they're protected against all comers. But no one's protected against a knife in the back. I'm told that Leverett was drunk at the Amalfi the other night, and he kept the table in a roar with an imitation of Horia Sima. Doesn't do, you know! One has to respect the existing régime, whatever it may happen to be. And you have to learn to live with it."

Harriet asked: "You think we can learn to live with the Iron Guard?"

"Why not? It's all a matter of personality. If you can adjust yourself, you can live with anyone or anything. It's the people who can't adjust themselves who get into trouble."

Pinkrose nodded vehemently. "I do agree. *And,* you know, once things have settled down, the world's much the same whoever's running it."

Inchcape's mood of raillery had passed. He looked at his friend with understanding. "The important thing," he said, "is to survive."

As he spoke the German officers entered. With the aplomb of conquerors they crossed the dining-room floor and seated themselves at the reserved tables.

Neither Inchcape nor Pinkrose made any comment. Apparently they had already adjusted themselves to cohabitation with the enemy.

The meal over, Inchcape suggested that Pinkrose might care to rest before the reception. "Which will be quite a 'do'," he said. "Tomorrow night I fear I'm committed to a long-standing engagement. I'm dining with a young friend who wants to tell me his troubles but," he smiled quizzically at Pinkrose, "I imagine you can entertain yourself."

Guy said: "Perhaps Professor Pinkrose would have supper with us? We could go afterwards to the Brahms concert at the Opera House."

"Splendid idea!" Inchcape said without reference to Pinkrose.

Pinkrose looked displeased but Guy, in his eagerness, noticed nothing. Jumping to his feet, he said he would go at once to book seats and Harriet watched with an infuriated compassion as, speeding off, he tripped on the edge of the dining-room carpet.

Inchcape had ordered Guy to escort Pinkrose to his flat that evening, saying: "And for goodness' sake, come early and go early. I can't stand these junkets when they drag on."

As a result the Pringles arrived too early at the Athénée Palace and had to wait twenty minutes until Pinkrose was ready. He came down the stairs in an ancient dinner-suit, too short at the wrists and ankles, its single button strained on a thread across his middle.

"I must say," he said, becoming almost jovial in anticipation, "I am looking forward to meeting these beautiful and cultivated ladies who are said to entertain so lavishly."

Guy said: "I'll introduce you to the mothers of some of my students. Doamna Blum, for instance, and Doamna Teitelbaum. They're highly cultivated and would be delighted to meet you . . ."

"No, no," Pinkrose interrupted impatiently, "I do not mean *that* sort of person. Everyone's been telling me I must meet the famous Princess Teodorescu."

Guy, rather tartly, explained that that particular princess was no longer in Bucharest. "But princesses are two a penny here. It's only a courtesy title, anyway; it means nothing. You'll probably meet half a dozen tonight."

The sky over the square was rayed with lemon and silver but the colours were smudged and the wind blowing cool, damp and smoky from the park, had a smell of autumn.

It seemed to Harriet that recently a forlorn atmosphere had come down on the city, resulting, she believed, not only from the seasonal move indoors – the evening promenade which usually went on into October was now almost dwindled to nothing – but from fear. The Jews, of course, were afraid to go out, but these days it was not only the Jews who felt, like the old Codreanu, that they would be safer indoors.

She was relieved to reach Inchcape's sitting-room where the lamps were lit in their golden shades. Inchcape had not appeared yet. Clarence, the first arrival, sat alone.

Harriet had seen nothing of him since her visit to his flat. He had gone into some sort of retreat. Guy had telephoned him several times to suggest their meeting, but Clarence had always excused himself saying he was unwell. Harriet had imagined him lying all day on his balcony, gazing out over open country, brooding on his own inadequacy, but now he looked well enough. He showed, however, no desire to talk.

When introduced to Pinkrose, he rose reluctantly and mumbled something. Pinkrose mumbled back. Neither being designed to induce loquacity in the other, they drew apart as soon as they decently could and made no attempt to speak to each other again.

Inchcape entered in high spirits. Pauli, following, held an uncorked champagne bottle, its label of origin hidden under a napkin. While this was being dispensed, Inchcape, smiling to himself, brought out his latest acquisition: a purple velvet heart supporting three china arum lilies under a glass dome. "Amusing, isn't it?" he said. "I bought it at the Lipscani market."

Pinkrose bent over it, smiling thinly, and agreed: "It has a certain macabre charm."

Watching the faces of the two elderly men, Harriet suddenly saw them similar and bound in understanding.

Inchcape promised Pinkrose: "I will take you down to the Dâmbovita. You'll be delighted by the odds and ends one can pick up there. Ikons, for instance. In my bedroom, I have quite a collection of ikons."

Time was passing. The other guests were slow in coming. The front-door bell rang at last, but the newcomers were only Dobson and David Boyd.

Dobson, usually a vivacious guest, was greatly subdued by the death of Foxy Leverett, who had been his friend. He apologised that his stay must be brief: he had only come to make the acquaintance of Lord Pinkrose.

"I left the Legation in a pretty fair flap," he said. "McGinty was found this afternoon, here in Bucharest: in a lane behind the law courts. He's in poor shape."

"You mean he's been ill-treated?" Inchcape asked.

"He's been tortured. At least, he'd been strung up by his wrists and beaten. His back was in a shocking state. I must say, H.E. has been simply tremendous about all this. He went straight to the Minister of the Interior and demanded a full enquiry into Foxy's death and this business of McGinty. He said he would not rest until the culprits were brought to justice. It was just like the great days of Palmerston and Stratford-Canning. And the Minister of the Interior wept. He's supposed to be a Guardist, but he said: 'You English are a great people. We have always loved you. Some of us believe that even now you may win the war. But what can we do? There are too many of the young men. We can't control them.' "

"But why did they pick on McGinty? What had he done?"

"Nothing. But his name was on a list . . ." Dobson paused, sipped at his drink, then, having said so much, realised he had to say more. He added: "Before the war, Britain, France and Rumania compiled a list of engineers who could be relied on to destroy the oil-wells should the Germans occupy Rumania. This list was handed to Germany by the Vichy government. Voluntarily, I may say. The men who've been kidnapped were on it."

Clarence asked sharply: "Do you mean McGinty isn't the only one?"

Dobson looked about him, flustered. "Look here," he said. "Keep all this under your hat. There's no point in starting a panic here. These men were all specialists. They knew the risk they ran. They could have left when the others went: they chose to stay."

"How many have been kidnapped?" Clarence insisted.

"Four, including McGinty. The Iron Guard imagine there's some plot to blow up the wells. They're a pack of clumsy fools. They want information. They think they can get it by beating these chaps up."

"What about the other three?" Guy asked.

"No news yet." Dobson put down his glass then, turning to Pinkrose with his official smile, made a little speech welcoming him on behalf of Sir Montagu who was "tied to his desk". "I'm afraid it's a difficult time," said Dobson smiling.

Pinkrose agreed in a surprised tone: "Things do seem a little unsettled . . ."

"A little, a little. But H.E. thinks we should hang on here as long as we can. Show them we're not defeated yet."

"I heartily agree," said Inchcape.

When Dobson had gone, David and Guy went out to talk on the terrace. Inchcape, who now seemed more resigned to Pinkrose's arrival, began asking him, pleasantly enough, about their acquaintances at Cambridge. Harriet stood around awhile, waiting to see if Clarence would speak to her. When he remained aloof, she went out to the terrace where she could hear David snuffling in delight. He was saying: "Recent events have shocked poor old Sir Montagu to the core. He was heard to say (of course, I only have Dobson's word for it): 'So young David Boyd was right. Things have come unstuck in just the way he predicted.' " David was staring modestly at his feet. He sniffed his amusement, then said with his usual tolerance: "Sporting of the old boy to admit it, don't you think? But the fact is, he still thinks that somehow or other the situation can be salvaged."

Guy said: "It could be salvaged even now – by a Russian occupation. Not that Sir Montagu would welcome that."

"No, indeed! But I'm afraid there's little hope of it. The Russians don't feel too secure. They're not likely to enlarge a frontier they may have to defend."

In the pause that followed, Harriet took the opportunity to speak of Sasha Drucker: "Now that Foxy is dead, what can we do?"

"I wouldn't worry," David said in his usual unperturbed tone. "When a Legation goes, there are always a number of committed aliens packed on to the diplomatic train. It's taken for granted. No questions asked."

"You think you could take Sasha? That would be wonderful.

But supposing we have to go before the Legation goes: what could we do with him?"

Guy took her arm. "Let's face these problems when we come to them," he said and led her back into the room.

A gloom overhung the party. No other guests had arrived. Inchcape was becoming bored and Clarence remained silent, retired into a chair. When the doorbell rang, Pinkrose watched hopefully but the new arrival was not a beautiful, hospitable princess. It was Woolley. His face was lugubrious and his conversation did nothing to lighten the atmosphere. Like Inchcape, he was inclined to blame Foxy for getting himself killed, but the ill-treatment of McGinty he took as a warning of the fate that might overhang them all. He made no mention of the other engineers who were still missing, but said:

"I don't like the smell of things. I don't like it at all. People are getting out, and I don't blame them. The Rettisons have gone. Been here three generations. Now they've moved to the Levant. It's bad for business, all this shunting and shifting. You don't know where you are from one day to the next." He brooded awhile, his long, sallow, pendulous head hanging over his glass, then he looked up and sighted his old enemy, Harriet. "My lady wife's taken herself off, as is only right and proper. His Excellency wants the ladies out of the way. He said to me only yesterday: 'If I have to evacuate the English Colony, I'm only taking young men of military age.' "

Harriet's response was sharp and quick: "If Sir Montagu thinks he can take my husband and leave me behind, he still has a lot to learn."

Woolley gave her a long, sour, threatening look. "We'll see," he said.

"Yes, we will see," Harriet vigorously agreed.

There was a silence, protracted until Pinkrose suddenly threw out his hands with the gesture of a man tried beyond all endurance. "What *is* all this, Inchcape? Evacuating the British Colony! Taking young men of military age! What *is* going on here?"

Inchcape replied in reasonable tones: "As you noted yourself, my dear fellow, things are a little unsettled. After all, there's been a revolution. You must have heard of it."

"I heard something. *The Times* mentioned that King Carol had been deposed. That's always happening in Balkan countries. No one, at any time, suggested there was any danger."

"No one suggested there was any danger!" Inchcape parted his lips and looked about him. He asked the room: "What were the London officials thinking about? Are they so wrapped up in the piddling chit-chat of administration that they are totally unaware of conditions in Eastern Europe?"

His voice rose, indignant on Pinkrose's behalf but Pinkrose was not to be diverted. "You should have warned me, Inchcape. I take this badly. I take this very badly."

"Dear me!" Inchcape, his manner changing again, now began to ridicule his friend: "Aren't we in danger everywhere these days? Weren't you in danger in England? Very *real* danger, I may say. Aren't they likely to be invaded any day? Here we have only a war of nerves. Personally, I think things will right themselves. The young King and his mother are very popular. They went out yesterday and bought cakes at Capşa's. Yes, actually went out on foot, just like our own royal family! There can't be much wrong in a country where that happens."

Pinkrose looked somewhat appeased. "Nevertheless," he said, "I was misinformed. When you wrote in the spring, you described magnificent food, a feudal atmosphere, an ancient aristocracy, opulent parties, every comfort – a return, in short, to the good old days. And what do I find, after travelling all this way mostly in a bomb-bay? No meat on the menu. And what, may I ask, has happened to the wit and beauty of Bucharest? Your reception seems sadly ill-attended?"

Inchcape opened his mouth to reply, then paused. Harriet observed him with interest, never having seen him at a loss before. He answered at last: "The English are out of favour at the moment. I believe there's a reception at the Athéneé Palace for the German officers. I fear our Rumanian guests have all gone to entertain our enemies."

"Ah!" said Pinkrose. Mollified by the humility of Inchcape's confession, he said nothing more.

Woolley, who had stood apart from this exchange, sunk into his own disgruntlement, said suddenly: "I must be off," and slapping down his glass, he went without another word.

Clarence tittered. He had been drinking steadily and the effect of it was now evident. "I hear," he said, "that since his wife's departure, Woolley's found a little Rumanian friend." Holding out his glass at arm's length, he shouted: "Hey, Pauli, a refill."

Pauli crossed to him, grinning, English drunkenness being a stock joke in Bucharest.

Pinkrose, who had also been drinking, took Inchcape aside and whispered to him.

"This way," said Inchcape briskly. He led Pinkrose from the room and a moment later, darting back alone, he addressed Guy, Harriet and Clarence with an exploding air of conspiracy: "Look here! Things being as they are, we'll never get the old buffer an audience. The thing is, to prepare him. You'll have to give a hand. Begin intimating that this is neither the time nor the place for a public lecture in English. Suggest he might be molested. Get him scared so he'll tell me he doesn't want to lecture. Understand? But do it tactfully . . ." Inchcape came to an abrupt pause as he heard steps returning. Pinkrose entered.

"Well, now," Inchcape said pleasantly, "plans for our future delectation. What about this week-end? I'm afraid I'm off to Sinai: I booked my room weeks ago. I have to have a day off before the weather breaks. But I'm sure our young friends here . . . !" He smiled invitingly on Guy, Harriet and Clarence. "What are you all up to?"

Guy responded as was expected of him. "We are going to Predeal," he said. "Perhaps Professor Pinkrose would care to come with us . . ." He glanced at Harriet for her co-operation.

She said firmly: "I am quite sure Professor Pinkrose would rather go to Sinai with Professor Inchcape."

Frowning and stirring his foot on the carpet, Inchcape said: "Why not? Why not?"

Clarence, lolling so low in his chair that his buttocks were over the edge, drawled: "I'm going away, too."

Everyone looked at him. "Right away," he said. "You hear that, Inch, you old ostrich? I'm going right away, away from your bloody organisation. Away from what you call your sphere of influence. To warmer, more colourful climes. And you can't do a thing about it!"

Inchcape paused, realising he was being told something. He said: "What did you say?" Clarence repeated most of what he had said.

Inchcape exploded: "You're leaving us? At a time like this! And without warning!"

Clarence shuffled lower, holding his glass on a level with his nose. "Not without warning," he said. "I told you weeks ago that

I was sick of hanging around here doing nothing. I only stayed to please you. You have to have your little court. You must keep up the pretence that you've a position and a staff. But I've had enough I've wired Cairo. I'm off as soon as I get my orders."

Inchcape, who had been staring severely at Clarence, now swung round and explained to Pinkrose: "Lawson was seconded to us by the British Council. If he is determined to go, we can't do anything about it. But it's a serious loss. One cannot get replacement these days."

Pinkrose nodded his sympathy and also stared severely at Clarence who was saying: "I'm no loss. Now if you were to go, Inchi-boy, it would be different. British prestige would never stand the shock."

Ignoring this, Inchcape went on talking to Pinkrose: "My feeling is, that whatever the danger, a man should not desert his post."

Clarence gave a laugh. "You're in no danger. And your post is just a joke."

At this, Inchcape swung round in a rage. "At least, I'm sticking to it. As for danger, I'd remind you that I attended Calinescu's funeral."

"The whole of Bucharest attended Calinescu's funeral."

Pinkrose, upright, alert, his cheeks aglow, glanced keenly from one to other of the contestants. For the first time since his arrival, he looked as though he were enjoying himself.

Guy went over to the pianoforte on which Inchcape's Chinese chess-set was arranged. Standing there, moving the pieces about, he appeared preoccupied but his face was sad and creased like the face of a Basanji dog, and as Clarence roused himself to press advantage, he said: "That's enough, Clarence."

"You're right, of course." Clarence stretched his arm and caught at Guy's hand. While Pinkrose goggled at this conduct Clarence said: "You're always right. You're the only one of us who can justify his existence here. The summer school may not be much, but at least it's a challenge . . ."

Guy drew his hand away. "The summer school was closed down last week."

Collapsing back into his chair, Clarence sighed deeply. "What the hell does it matter, anyway?" he mumbled.

The door opened and Pauli entered bearing two large dishes, one of rice and the other of some sort of stew. He filled plates and handed them round with lavish smiles. A local wine was served.

As they were eating, David remarked that he, too, would be away next-week-end. He was going to the Delta.

"Ha, the Delta!" said Clarence with a malign knowingness. "He says he's going to the Delta."

Pinkrose looked at Clarence in bewilderment. No one spoke until the meal ended and Inchcape rose to indicate the party was over. The gesture was not necessary. His guests were already preparing to go.

21

HARRIET NEXT EVENING was a discomfited hostess. The bones of Pinkrose's egotism remained visible despite his veil of sociability. She felt he intended they should remain visible. They represented protest. He was a guest, but an unwilling guest. He was making the barest of concessions to good manners.

That had been one of the mornings in which there was nothing in the market. "Nothing but cabbage," Despina said.

Harriet had gone to Dragomir's where there was food for those who could pay for it. The favoured customers there were no longer Rumanian males but German females: the wives of the attachés employed in vast numbers at the two big German diplomatic establishments. Strongly built and determined, living on so favourable a rate of exchange that they went shopping with bundles of thousand-*lei* notes in their hands, these women were formidable rivals whom Harriet would face only when desperate. She obtained two scrawny little chickens. She then tried to find a bottle of sherry, but sherry had disappeared from the shops. She ended up with an imitation madeira.

When offered this, Pinkrose eyed the bottle for some moments, one brow raised, before he said: "Perhaps I will try a half-glass." He sipped at it and finding it better than he had expected, expressed satisfaction by moving his bottom about on his seat. He allowed his glass to be refilled and said: "I cannot think why Professor Inchcape has put me into that hotel."

Harriet was surprised. "The Athénée Palace used to be practically an English hotel," she said. "We see it as a refuge, and the English journalists who live there almost never leave it."

"It's teeming with Germans," Pinkrose complained.

"The other hotel, the Minerva, is much worse. It's full of German diplomats. The officers of the Military Mission are only at the Athénée Palace because the Minerva had no room for them."

"Indeed!" Having made this attempt at conversation, Pinkrose retired into silence but his eyes were taking in every detail of his surroundings. Seeing them turn from the shabby upholstery to the shabby rugs, Harriet said: "We took this flat furnished. Things have received a lot of wear from different tenants."

As she spoke, he dropped his glance and his cheeks grew pink. Startled out of ill-humour, he said, pleasantly enough: "I take it the books are yours?"

She explained that the books, mostly second-hand, had been collected by Guy and brought to Rumania in sacks. He nodded his interest. Although he did not look at Harriet, he kept his attention pointedly in her direction and when Guy broke in on the talk, he looked aside in a discouraging way.

Guy had several volumes of poems by poets he had known when a student. He began taking these down to show Pinkrose signatures and inscriptions, but Pinkrose was not impressed. "These young men have a lot to learn," he said.

Guy leapt at once to the defence of the poets of his generation and while he talked, he refilled Pinkrose's glass. Too preoccupied and short-sighted to see when it was full, he went on pouring until the madeira ran from the table and dripped on to Pinkrose who tutted in exasperation. Full of apologies, Guy began to rub Pinkrose's trousers and Pinkrose, tutting again, moved his legs away.

Harriet called in Despina who, liking nothing better than to get into the room when visitors were present, spent so long mopping up round Pinkrose's feet that he said on a high note of irritation: "If we do not sup soon, we shall be late for the concert."

Supper, which he ate resignedly, was a hurried meal.

As they entered the main door of the Opera House, the Pringles were surprised by the opulence of the persons entering with them. Everyone was in evening dress, the men wearing orders, the women *décolleté* and lavishly bejewelled. Harriet began to feel something was wrong. This was not a usual Rumanian audience. The people were too large, too important-looking and they were all talking German. The vestibule was banked with flowers.

Pinkrose let out his breath in appreciation of so much splendour. "These days," he said, "we see nothing like *this* at home."

Harriet noticed that everyone who glanced once at the English party, glanced a second time in apparent disbelief. She said to Guy: "Do you think we're improperly dressed?" He ridiculed the idea and it did seem that it was they themselves, not their clothing, that gave rise to astonishment.

While they made their way to their seats, there were whisperings and a turning of heads, brought to a stop at last by the entry of the orchestra. When the musicians reached their places, they remained standing and the leader looked at the main box which jutted out at stage level. The audience, losing interest in the Pringles, also watched the box.

Harriet said to Pinkrose: "I think the King is coming." Pinkrose gave a gratified shuffle in his seat.

The door opened at the back of the box and a glimmer of shirt-front could be seen. The audience began to applaud. There entered a train of people comporting themselves with the studied graciousness of royalty, led by a large man who came to the rail and stood there. The Pringles recognised the heavy, sombre, unmistakable figure of Dr. Fabricius. The applause became clamorous. A woman in cloth of gold, his wife perhaps, made queenly movements with one hand. Fabricius bowed.

"Surely that's not the young King?" said Pinkrose.

Guy told him it was the German minister. Pinkrose's mouth fell open in disappointment but he nodded, prepared now to accept anything.

While the Legation party was entering, the box opposite had been filled by officers of the Military Mission who were escorting several resplendent women. Harriet, unable to keep from smiling, whispered to Pinkrose: "There are some of the princesses you hoped to meet."

The conductor raised his baton. The audience rose. Expecting the Rumanian national anthem, the Pringles and Pinkrose did the same. Some moments passed before the Pringles realised they were standing for *Deutschland uber Alles*. When he did so, Guy plumped back into his seat and Harriet, more slowly, followed. Pinkrose, looking embarrassed by their behaviour, remained at attention. The anthem finished, there was a pause: then came the *Horst Wessel*.

Perplexed, Guy began, for the first time, to examine his programme. He looked across at Harriet and hissed: "Gieseking."

She realised what had happened. Guy, eager and short-sighted, had bought the tickets without consulting the boards outside the theatre. This was a German propaganda concert.

When Pinkrose sat down, Harriet began to explain the mistake, but he had guessed it for himself and silenced her with a movement. "As we are here," he said, "let us enjoy the music."

The pianist had taken his seat and Beethoven's Fifth Pianoforte Concerto began.

Harriet, thankful for Pinkrose's attitude, felt as he did, but Guy was looking wretchedly unhappy. He sat through the first movement with folded arms and sunken chin, and as soon as it ended, he stood up.

Pinkrose stared at him in acute irritation. He whispered: "It's no good. I'm going."

Harriet, who had been entranced by the performance, said: "Do stay," but he pushed past her. She felt she must go with him and as she rose, Pinkrose said in alarm: "I don't want to be left here alone."

The pianist sat motionless, waiting for the interruption to end. As much amused as annoyed, the audience watched while the three English interlopers got out as quickly as they could.

In the vestibule, Guy, his face damp with sweat, apologised for having led them into the predicament and for having led them out of it. He explained: "I couldn't stand it. I kept thinking of the concentration camps."

Too angry to speak, Pinkrose turned and strutted out of the Opera House. The Pringles went after him but he managed to keep just ahead of them all the way back to the hotel.

As he was halted by the revolving door, Guy tried to apologise again but Pinkrose held up his hand. He had suffered enough. He wanted to hear no more.

PART FOUR

The Raid

22

THE TRAIN RISING INTO THE MOUNTAINS CARRIED, trapped within it, the heavy air of the city. During the week the heat had renewed itself. Bucharest was suffering the last dragging days of summer.

At Ploesti, where there was a long stop, life was at a standstill. Syrupy sunlight poured over the denuded earth and gleamed on the metal of refineries and storage bins. Oil-trains stood in the sidings, each tank bearing the name of its destination: Frankfurt, Stuttgart, Dresden, München, Hamburg, Berlin.

Inside the carriage where the Pringles sat there was no sound but an occasional grunt and the buzz of captive flies. The dark-blue plush smelt of carbon and was sticky to the touch. Granules of carbon lay among the dust on the window ledges. The other occupants of the carriage were army officers, all sprawling lax and sleepy with boredom, on their way to the frontier to guard a country that had lost almost everything it possessed.

Guy, with a rucksack of books between his knees, sat in full sunlight, pushing up his glasses as they slipped down the sweat on his nose. He was planning a course of studies.

The English journalists who had flown in to cover the abdication were still in Bucharest, detained by one outrage after another. In all, eight oil engineers had been kidnapped by the Iron Guardists. One of them had been found dead ("of a heart attack", said the newspapers) in a Ploesti back street. The rest survived, the worse for ill-treatment.

That morning the old minister who had thought it better to be united under the Russians had also been picked up dead in the Snagov woods, his hair and beard torn out and stuffed into his mouth. He had lately become a fanatical Guardist, but that had not saved him.

Galpin never left the Athénée Palace. With the aspect of a prophet who sees his worst predictions fulfilled, he said to anyone who entered the bar: "It's simply a case of 'Whose turn next?' "

They were all, it seemed to Harriet, awaiting a final collapse that might extinguish them. All, that was, except Guy. With the new term approaching, he was absorbed in preparation for it. He managed to be as busy as he had ever been, while Harriet spent more and more time with Sasha. Like people in a waiting-room, they sat on the balcony exchanging nonsense rhymes, playing paper games, telling ridiculous jokes, and giggling together as helplessly as children. There was no time to put one's mind to more serious pursuits. She knew they were on the verge of confusion, but Sasha appeared to believe their life could go on, uneventful and carefree, for ever.

She had been longing to get away from the capital, but now their week-end was come her apprehensions were heightened. Anything might happen while they were away. And what of Sasha, left in Despina's care? It had been during their last trip to Predeal that the kitten had fallen to its death. Despina, sympathising with her fears, had promised to open the door to no one. Sasha, however, had been no more concerned by her departure than the kitten had been.

He said: "We have a villa at Sinai," speaking as though it stood there empty, awaiting the family's return. "I know Predeal. Sarah went to school there. Hannah would not go – she would not leave my father."

Harriet remembered the little girl. "I could see she adored your father," she said.

Sasha nodded. "She cried all night when he married again."

"Did you mind?"

"We all minded, but Hannah most. We did not want another mother."

"You loved him very much, didn't you?"

"We all loved him." Sasha still identified his feeling with those of his family. He did not acknowledge the separation. He added: "*She* wanted to take him from us. She was beastly. Wicked."

Harriet laughed. "When I was a child I used to think my aunt was a wicked stepmother, but now I realise she was just rather stupid. She said anything that came into her head. She probably forgot it the next moment and thought I did, too."

After a long delay, the train moved out of Ploesti into foothills that were straddled by the old wooden derricks of pioneering days.

Beyond this area were alpine meadows, but soon the rocks broke through and the landscape changed into the grey shale and pines of the lower Transylvanian Alps.

When they left the stale and stifling carriage, the Pringles were startled by the glassy outside air. Scentless in its purity, it was as cold as ether on the skin. They wanted to start walking at once, but first they had to report their arrival to the police. The police officer, unshaven and grimy, reeking of garlic, pushed aside a collection of dirty coffee-cups and stamped their permits with extreme slowness, Free to stay in Predeal for no longer than a week, they carried their luggage through the long main street to the hotel.

The village, with its grey highland look, was in shadow, but the peaks above were still looped in the reddish light of the evening sun. Minute glaciers, like veins of marble, made their way down the grey rock-surfaces. Snow lay already on the upper ledges. At this height the autumn was fairly advanced. Patches of beech were golden-tawny, thrown like lion-skins among the black fur of the pines.

Predeal was both a winter and a summer resort, so out of date that the village hall announced an English film.

Harriet was slightly unnerved by the extraordinary quiet of the place. She felt they had been mad to leave the capital at such a time. If there were an invasion, they would receive no warning here. But Guy stretched his arms, throwing off the year's worries in a moment. As he breathed the light and tonic air, he said: "This is like flying out of a fog."

Their bedroom was small and bare with a stove that was lit at evening and fed with pine-logs. They were met by a scent of wood-smoke, delicate and sweet, that comforted Harriet. She began to look forward to her holiday. As soon as they had dropped their bags they went out to walk in the blue, chill air. The sky changed to turquoise. The shops lit up. The village street hung on the mountainside like a chain of light. They found the village bright enough during the day, but a wintry gloom came down after the shops shut. There was no entertainment but the cinema where the film broke down a dozen times during a showing, each break being numbered on the screen and described as an "interval". In their little ski-ing hotel there was nothing to do. Guy set out his books of verse and novels by Conrad, preparing to spend the holiday in work.

On their first morning, as he chose an armful of books to take to the public gardens, Harriet said: 'But can't we go for a walk?''

"Later," Guy promised. "Let me break the back of this first." She, he suggested, might visit the famous *confiserie*, the far-seeing owner of which had laid in vast stocks of sugar in early summer. Now people came from all the large cities to eat his cakes.

Harriet was surprised to discover how greedy this fact made her feel.

Guy took a seat in the small ornamental garden where the grass, damply green in the mild, misty sunlight, was scattered over with russet leaves. There was nothing to see here but some beds of small, brick-coloured dahlias. Harriet wandered off through a neighbouring market where the ground was heaped with apples, tomatoes and black grapes. Some of the notorious Laetzi gipsies stood about – wild, bearded, long-haired men who eyed her as though they were cannibals.

The *confiserie* was crowded. The inside tables were all taken and the counter was tightly packed about with people who had to hold their plates above their heads. Outside there were chairs vacant near the rail. Harriet soon discovered why. The beggars were at her elbow even as she sat down. There were three children, their bones hung with scraps like greasers' rags. One, with a withered leg, hopped with his hand on the shoulder of a smaller boy. The third, a girl, had lost the sight of an eye. Perhaps she had been born that way, for the eyeball remained in its socket, blankly white, like a filling of lard. The children were urged forward – not that they needed much urging – by two teen-age girls who now and then stopped their whine of "*Foame*" to titter as though this persecution of the foreign woman were too funny for words.

Harriet handed out her small change, but it was not enough to buy release. The children went on jigging and whining beside her. While waiting to be served, she watched a small green and gold beetle crawling towards a hole in the rail beside her. If it went to the right, they would get away. It went to the left and it suddenly seemed to her that their danger had become acute. Her appetite had gone. She ordered coffee. While she waited she stared out at the road and watched a peasant leading a horse and cart out of a lane opposite. The horse, its bones straining against its hide, stumbled when it reached the main road cobbles. At once the peasant flung back his whip and lashed the creature about the eyes. The blows were given with savage deliberation as though the man wanted no more than an excuse to vent a chronic rage.

She leapt to her feet with a cry, too appalled to care for the surprise of her neighbours. By the time she reached the pavement, the assault was over. Horse and peasant had turned the corner and were away down the road. She knew, if she pursued them, her Rumanian was not good enough to make her protest effective. Anyway, it would be ignored.

She gave up all thought of cakes or coffee and hurried back to the public garden. When she reached Guy, she could scarcely speak. Surprised by her agitation he said: "Whatever is the matter?"

She sat down, exhausted, and gulped back her tears. Seeing the peasant vividly, his brutish face absorbed and horribly gratified by the outlet for his violence, she said: "I can't bear this place. The peasants are loathsome. I hate them." She spoke in a convulsion of feeling, trembling as she said: "All over this country animals are suffering – and we can do nothing about it." Feeling the world too much for her, she pressed her face against Guy's shoulder.

He put his arm round her to calm her. "The peasants are brutes because they are treated like brutes. They suffer themselves. Their behaviour comes of desperation."

"It's no excuse."

"Perhaps not, but it's an explanation. One must try to understand."

"Why should one try to understand cruelty and stupidity?"

"Because even those things can be understood: and if understood, they can be cured."

He squeezed her hand, but she did not respond. He talked to distract her, but she remained withdrawn as though violated and unable to throw off the shock.

After a while he picked up his books again. "Why don't you take a proper holiday?" he said. "We're quite well off at the present rate. Wouldn't you like to take the boat to Athens?"

Her expression lightened a little. "You mean you would come with me?"

"You know I can't. Inchcape doesn't want me to leave the country. And I have to prepare for the new term. But that's no reason why you shouldn't go."

She shook her head. "When we go, we go together."

After tea, Guy felt he had done enough for the day and was

willing to take a walk. When they reached the forest, he looked in through the aisles of pines, all intent and silent as though each tree held its breath, and refused to enter. He said that within living memory it had been a haunt of bears. "Let's keep to the road. It's safer." The road carried them above the trees into the bare rock fields where the cold was keen. The sky was mottled with a little cloud and here and there a chill hung on the air like powdered glass. At first Harriet thought it was ash blown from a bonfire, then she found it was melting on her skin. She said with wonder: "It is snow." When they reached the first white pool of snow, she pressed her hand on it, leaving the intaglio of her palm and fingers. Much lighter and surer on her feet than Guy, excited by the rarefied air, she climbed at great speed until she was alone amid the silence of the topmost slopes. She heard Guy shout and, looking back, saw him standing a long way below, like an unhappy bear, defeated by the shifting rubble of the path. She sped down into his arms.

They returned to the hotel, which stood by a dimpled meadow that was covered with small flowers. Some cows had been driven on to the grass during their absence and Guy paused, unwilling to cross among them. He saw all the animals as potential enemies. He distrusted the Bucharest cab-horses and had even been frightened of Harriet's red kitten. She took his hand and led him towards the nearest cow, which lifted its head to stare at them but did not cease to chew. Watching its mouth slipping loosely from side to side, Guy said: "These beasts are probably dangerous."

Harriet laughed. "I love them," she said.

"What, these frightful creatures?"

"Not only these. All animals."

"How could you love something so totally different from yourself."

"Why not? I don't simply love myself. I think I love them because they are different. They are innocent. They are hunted, harried, slaughtered by human beings who imagine they have a God-given right to destroy whenever it's in their interest to destroy."

Guy nodded. "You want to protect them. I can understand that. But why this extraordinary love for them? It doesn't seem reasonable to me."

She did not try to explain it. Guy, she knew, believed that man's compassion for his own kind was the only true compassion to be found in this cold universe. She longed for proof of a more disinterested compassion; a supreme justice that would avenge all these tormented and helpless innocents. Trembling with her own excess of feeling, she stretched out her hand to the cow, but at the threat of her approach it moved warily backwards.

After supper, Guy lay on the bed propped with pillows and gave himself up again to his books. Harriet, drowsy from the mountain air, lay in the crook of his arm, happy in his warmth and contact. He paused in his reading to say: "You do not see much of Bella these days. Or Clarence either. You have made so few friends in Bucharest! Don't you feel the need of people?"

She said: "Not when I have you – which isn't often."

"You've quite enough of me. If you had more, you'd be bored."

She glanced up at him, realised he believed this and smiled in denial, but he was not looking at her. She closed her eyes and slept.

When they came down to breakfast on Sunday and found Dobson sitting at one of the tables, Guy gave a great cry of "Why, hello." He would, Harriet knew, have been equally delighted had the newcomer been almost anyone known to them: and it might have been someone worse than Dobson who seemed charmed by the sight of them. He had driven up late the previous night "for a breath of air", and would have only one day in Predeal. He suggested that after breakfast they should go for a walk together.

Harriet left it to Guy to make his excuses, but the invitation was too much for him. It was not only that he was a little flattered by it: he could not refuse the diversion of fresh company.

As they left the hotel, Dobson suggested they should visit a Russian church a couple of miles away, saying: "We might hear something interesting. I was enormously fortunate last time I went there. They were singing the *Cantakion* for the Dead."

Dobson spoke on a note of such breathless anticipation that Guy paused only a moment before saying: "All right." At the same time he looked at Harriet as though she might save him, but she, a little piqued, said she would like nothing better.

They went behind the village, climbing steeply among small châlets and villas. The path was dusty, slippery with flints and overhung by old chestnut trees, their leaves ochred and reddened, forming parasols of colour that set the shade aglow. The ground beneath them was stained with trodden nuts and leaves. In one garden stood a giant rowan, weighted and bronzed with berries. Many of the villas were shuttered, their gardens overgrown as though they had been unvisited all summer.

The path dwindled, the houses were left behind, and they came out on to a plateau that stretched away into remote upland hills. They walked silently on the grass that was short, greyish and set with harebells and wild scabious.

Dobson talked easily and pleasantly. Harriet found his presence in Predeal reassuring. It was true that as a diplomat, especially protected, he had less to worry about than they had, but it was unlikely he would leave Bucharest if danger were imminent. Harriet, nearly two days away from the tensions of the capital, was beginning to feel like a patient propped up for the first time after an operation; Guy asked if anything had happened since they left Bucharest.

"Well," said Dobson, "Friday, as you probably know, was the anniversary of the death of Calinescu. The Guardists spent the day marching about."

They were in sight of a hollow from which the golden domes of the Russian church rose among trees.

Abruptly changing from the subject of the slaughtered Calinescu, Dobson said: "This convent was started by a Russian princess, an abbess who came here after the revolution with a following of nuns. Queen Marie gave them the land. They collected a crowd of refugees; a lot of them are still living. Some dark tales of intrigue and murder are told about this community. What a novel they would make!"

The Pringles had known Dobson as an agreeable man who treated them and their orders to leave the country with a vague serenity. Now that he felt more was expected of him, they were experiencing the active charm of his attention and they found it delightful.

Watching him as he walked before her with his plump, incurved back, his softly drooping shoulders, his rounded backside rising and falling with each tripping step, Harriet wondered why she had once decided he would not be easy to know. Who would be easier? And here, it occurred to her, was opportunity to intercede for Sasha! Yet, she hesitated – she scarcely knew why.

She had felt an instinctive trust of Foxy Leverett. Reckless and casual though he had been, he seemed a natural liberal. Dobson,

for all his geniality, was something apart. Supposing the diplomatic code required him to betray the boy? Feeling no certainty
he would not do it, she kept silent and was fearful Guy might
speak. Guy, however, made no mention of Sasha and probably
did not give the boy a thought.

They were descending into the hollow where the atmosphere
was humid and warm and the tall feathery grasses were still soaked
with dew. Dobson led them into the shade of a vast apple orchard
where there was no sound but a ziss of wasps and the creak of
boughs bending beneath their weight of fruit. They walked
through a compost of rotted fruit.

Beyond the orchard was a flat field and a river running level
with flat banks. The church stood amid silver birch trees, the
leaves of which were yellow as satinwood. To Harriet it seemed
that not only the church, but the river reflecting the light among
birch trees, and the trees massed around the buildings in a mist of
reddish gold, all had a look of Russia. The place was not unfriendly, but it was strange. "A distant land," she thought, though
distant from what she could not have said. In this country, where-
ever they were, they were far from home.

They crossed the bridge and took the path to the convent. The
church and main buildings, of stone, were surrounded by dismal
wooden hutments, the living-quarters of the lay community. Four
women in black, heads tightly bound up in black handkerchiefs,
were approaching the church along a path, each keeping her
distance from the others. As the first of them, a very thin, old lady,
stared with interest at the visitors, her dark, wrinkled, toothless
face, eaten into by suffering, took an expression ingratiating and
cunning. She gave a half-bob at them before turning into the
church.

Guy came to a stop, frowning his discomfort, but Dobson went
on without glancing round and entered through the heavy,
wooden doors.

Harriet said: "Come on, darling, let us look inside," and led
him after Dobson. She received, however, no more than a glimpse
of the candle-lit interior where a priest, hands raised, was making
gestures over two nuns who lay on the ground before him like
little, black-clad, fallen dolls. Guy gave a gasp, then bolted, letting
the door crash behind him. The old women of the congregation
started round, the priest looked up, even the nuns stirred.

Much shocked, Harriet hurried out after him. Before she could remonstrate, he turned on her: "How could you go into that vile place where that mumbo-jumbo was going on?"

A few minutes later, Dobson came out, sauntering, his face bland, giving the impression that nothing could surprise him – but he had less to say on the way home.

Harriet walked in complete silence, knowing that Guy might, by his action, have antagonised the whole powerful world of the Legation. Guy, too, was silent, probably in reaction from the scene that had so revolted him inside the church.

They returned through a shabby area of untidy, uneven grass where flimsy châlets declared themselves to be *pensions* and private sanatoria. The road crossed a stream of clear, shallow water that purled over rusted cans and old mattresses. Harriet paused to look down and Dobson, perhaps conscious of her discomfort, leaned beside her on the parapet and said: "If you were some great lady of the eighteenth century, Lady Hester Stanhope for instance, you would be standing on the boundary line between the Austrian and Turkish empires," and as Harriet grew slightly pink at this analogy, Dobson smiled in reassuring admiration.

He joined them at their table for luncheon and tea. After tea he invited them to drive with him to Sinai.

When he brought his car out of the hotel garage, it proved to be Foxy Leverett's De Dion-Bouton. Claret-coloured, picked out in gold, with a small, square bonnet, its large body opened out like a tulip to display claret-coloured upholstery of close-buttoned leather. The brass headlamps and large tuba-like horn were beautifully polished. Dobson eyed the car with a smile of satisfaction. "I think she'll get there," he said. "She's in spanking shape."

On the road to Sinai, he was as talkative as ever. Pointing across the plateau towards some bald, ashen hills, he said: "Did you ever see such mean hills? They look as though they had something to hide, don't they? They've a bad reputation among the peasants here. I remember when Foxy and I came here to ski last winter, we thought we'd try out those hills. When we told our cook, Ileana, where we were going, she flopped down on her knees and gave an absolute howl: 'No, no, domnuli, no one ever goes there. They're bad lands.' Foxy said: 'Get up and stop being an ass.' All the time she was cutting our sandwiches, she was snivelling away. She kissed our hands as though certain she'd never see us again.

"Anyway, we drove over there and had a long climb up – they're higher than they look. The snow was magnificent. When we got to the top, Foxy said: 'It's ridiculous to say no one ever comes here. Look at all these dogs' footprints.' Then it struck us. We strapped on our skis and got down that hillside faster than we'd ever got down anything in our lives before. When we arrived back Ileana had all the cooks in the neighbourhood holding a wake for us. They screamed their heads off when they saw us. They thought we were ghosts." Dobson had been increasing speed as he talked and he now pointed with pride to the indicator. "Doing forty," he said. The car trembled with the effort.

The conversation now was all about Foxy: Foxy killing bear in the Western Carpathians, Foxy shooting duck at the Delta, Foxy taking "a record bag of ptarmigan".

Harriet burst out: "I hate all this shooting."

"So do I," Dobson cheerfully agreed, "but it's nice to keep a bit of bird in the larder. Something to peck at when you come in late."

They passed a cart-load of peasants who pointed at the De Dion, the men bawling with laughter, the women giggling behind their hands.

Laughing with them, Dobson said: "How Foxy would have loved that," and he continued a threnody on his friend – sportsman, playboy and Legation jester: "The best fellow in the world! We shared a flat in the Boulevard Carol." He went on to tell how Foxy practised revolver-shooting, using a Louis XIV clock as a target. One night he shot at the ceiling and sent a bullet into the bed of the landlord, who said: "Anyone else but you, Domnul Leverett, and I would have told him: 'This is too much.' "

The road was lined with garden restaurants. It was all very urban, but as soon as the car turned off the main road they came into a wild region of stone peaks where the rock was patched over with alpine moss and there was no vegetation but a few dwarf juniper bushes. In every hollow among the hills a small lake lay dark and motionless.

Dobson stopped the car and they went for a walk over the cinderous ground between the rocks. There was a little grass round the lakes where a few lean cows grazed. Pointing to one of them, Guy said: "Harriet says she loves these creatures."

Dobson gave his easy laugh. "She's probably quite willing to eat them," he said, and Harriet stared at her feet, conscious of her human predicament. Putting an arm round her shoulder, Guy rallied her: "Come on, tell us, why do you love them?"

Irritated that he questionned her in front of Dobson, she said defiantly: "Because they are innocent."

"And we are guilty?"

She shrugged. "Aren't we? We're human animals that maintain ourselves at the cost of our humanity."

He squeezed her shoulder. "Guilt is a disease of the mind," he said. "It's been imposed on us by those in power. The thing they want is to divide human nature against itself. That permits the minority to dominate the majority."

Dobson smiled blandly, apparently detached from the Pringles' conversation, but Harriet, certain he was listening intently, did not encourage Guy to say anything more on this subject.

They drove into Sinai as evening fell. Dobson said: "We'll snatch a bite before trying our luck," taking it for granted that the Pringles anticipated with as much pleasure as he an evening of losing money at the casino.

The casino attempted a grandeur that was thwarted by Balkan apathy and the harshness of the overhanging crags. A chill had entered the air after dark. The yellowish bulbs that lit the casino gardens, touching rocks and trees and the wavering fronds of the pampas grass, could not dispel the gloom of the failing year. The paths glistened with damp.

The large entrance hall was deserted. Such life as there was about the place had taken itself to the main salon where only one table was in use. Lit by low-hung, green-shaded globes, the gamblers sat, absorbed and silent, in the penumbra around the table.

Dobson found a seat. Guy stood behind him, watching the play, while Harriet tiptoed to the end of the table, where she paused and looked down its length at the faces intent upon the turning wheel. She thought: "What a collection of oddities!" seeing them as though they grew like distorted mushroom growths from their chairs. One man, whose shoulders were abnormally wide but who rose barely eighteen inches above the table, had a vast, formless face, like a milk jelly, glistening with ill-health. Beside him was an ancient, skeletal female, her mouth agape and askew, as though she had died without succour. One male head was abnormally large like a case of giantism. Here and there were faces, not aged and yet not young, having the immaterial look of arrested decay.

It seemed to Harriet that in this room without windows, artificially lit both by day and by night, these people, with their pallor of indoor life, existed in a self-contained world, beyond consciousness of war, change of government or threat of invasion, indeed unaware there was an outer world, like insects in a gall. They would scarcely know if the Day of Judgment were upon them. For them life's prodigiousness was diminished down to a little ball spinning in a wooden bowl.

The ball fell into a groove. A stir, almost a sigh, touched the players. It fell upon a stillness so complete she could almost feel, as they must, that did conflict exist anywhere at all, it was too remote to matter.

The croupier's rake came into the light, pushing the chips about. No one smiled, or showed concern or pleasure, but as one player, in placing his stake, accidentally touched that of another, there broke out between them a quarrel, brief but vicious, like a quarrel between the insane.

The ball was spun again. Harriet took a step forward to watch and at once the man seated before her glanced round, his face distorted with irritation at her nearness. She tiptoed on.

When she reached the other side of the table, she looked across at Dobson and realised Guy was no longer there. He had found someone to talk to in the dim, empty regions beyond the table. When she reached him, she found his companions were Inchcape and Pinkrose. He was talking with his usual animation, but in an undertone, while Inchcape, hands in pockets, head bent, listened, tilting backwards and forwards on his heels. Pinkrose stood a step apart, watching Guy with an expression that told Harriet the Gieseking concert would not be forgotten in a hurry. Inchcape looked up.

"Hah! So there you are!" Inchcape said as she approached. "Let's go and get a drink." Walking ahead, he glanced back for Harriet and as she caught up with him, said: "Have you enjoyed your break?"

"Very much. And you?"

"Don't speak of it." He dropped his voice. "I never could abide that old so-and-so."

"Then why did you invite him to Rumania?"

"Who else would have come at a time like this? How does he strike you?"

"Well . . ." Harriet evaded the question by asking: "Why, I wonder, is he so suspicious of poor Guy?"

"Him!" Inchcape snorted in amused contempt. "He'd be suspicious of the Lamb of God."

In the bar, that was large, bleak, bare and empty except for the barman, Inchcape told them he had lost chips to the value of five thousand *lei*. "That was my limit," he said. "As for Pinkrose here! Tight-fisted old curmudgeon, I couldn't get him to risk a *leu*." He turned on Pinkrose. "You're a tight-fisted old curmudgeon, eh?" He gave Pinkrose's shoulder a push. "Eh?" he insisted, staring at him with quizzical disgust as though he were a wife of whom he was more than half ashamed.

Pinkrose, sitting with his legs tightly together, his feet side by side, his little waxen hands folded on his stomach, smiled vaguely, apparently taking Inchcape's chaff as a form of admiration, which perhaps it was.

The bar was cold. The windows had been opened during the day and were still open, admitting shafts of damp, icy air. Pinkrose began to twitch. He pulled his scarfs about him, looking miserable, but before he could say anything the waiter came to them.

"I know," said Inchcape indulgently. "We'll have hot *ţuică*. We'll celebrate the coming winter. I like to hibernate. I shall devote the next six months to Henry James."

The *ţuică* was served in small teapots. Heated with sugar and peppercorns, the spirit lost its rawness and gave the impression of being much milder than it was. Pinkrose drew back, frowning, as a pot was put before him, and said: "No, really, I think not."

"Oh, drink it up," Inchcape said, with such exasperation Pinkrose poured a little into his cup and sipped at it.

"Umm!" he said, and after a moment admitted: "Pleasantly warming."

Dobson came to look for them and, as he sat down, Guy asked him: "What luck?"

"None," he cheerfully told them. "But, then, one doesn't expect to win. One plays for the fun of it. Dear me!" He stretched out his legs and rubbed a silk handkerchief over his baldness. "How one longs for the normal life! I'm not as young as I was, but I'd be overjoyed if I could close my eyes and open them to find myself enjoying a debs' dance at the Dorchester or Claridge's!" He smiled round, never doubting but that the others would take equal pleasure in such a transportation. "As it is" – he folded his handkerchief carefully and put it away – "tomorrow back to the plough." Turning to Pinkrose, he pleasantly asked: "Are you staying long?"

Pinkrose flinched as though the question were inexcusably personal. "I really cannot say," he said.

Inchcape said: "Oh, he'll soon be taking himself off." He leered at Pinkrose, repeating as though his friend were deaf: "I was just saying, you'll soon be taking yourself off."

"My goodness gracious! I've only just arrived," said Pinkrose. "A special passage had to be arranged for me; and I imagine the same will be done for my return."

"Who do you think's going to arrange it?" Inchcape asked.

Ignoring this question, Pinkrose went on: "And what about my lecture, I'd like to know? Isn't it time you fixed a date?"

"We'll have to abandon the lecture."

"Abandon the lecture? Are you serious, Inchcape? I plan to range over the development of our poetry from Chaucer to Tennyson. Central Office was of the opinion it would have considerable influence on Rumanian policy."

Inchcape laughed through his teeth. "My dear fellow, if Chaucer came here it would have no influence on Rumanian policy. If Byron came, if Oscar Wilde himself came, he could not get an audience for a public lecture on English literature."

"Are you suggesting I should return home without a word? A pretty fool I'd look! What would my colleagues say?"

"Tell them you left it too late. You should have come six months ago."

"I was not invited six months ago." Pinkrose's lips quivered. For a moment he looked as though he might burst into tears, then he suddenly smiled. "But you are, as they say, 'having me on'. My leg is being pulled, isn't it?" He glanced about in an inquiry that no one attempted to answer.

Harriet had her own inquiry: "If no one will come to the Cantecuzene Lecture, who is going to turn up to hear Guy?"

"That's different. Students are young, loyal, uncommitted, eager to learn ... But it's the look of the thing that matters. We must open."

"Is Guy expected to run the Department alone?"

"Well, if the students turn up in force, I might take a seminar for him."

There was a long silence. Harriet felt she could have said more, but the drink, warm and sweet, had begun to release her from care. If this were not the best of all possible worlds, what did it matter? Perhaps the best was yet still to come.

Dobson yawned and said he was taking a short holiday in Sofia. "I want to hear some opera," he said.

Guy turned to Harriet. "Why don't you go with him?" he suggested.

Harriet's fugitive happiness was gone. For some moments she was too embarrassed to speak, then she protested: "Darling, you are extraordinary! What makes you suppose that Dobbie would want me to go with him to Sofia?"

Dobson sat up to assure her: "I should be delighted."

"Of course he would," said Guy, who had never doubted it. He looked at Dobson and explained: "The situation here is becoming too much for her."

"I should never have thought it." Dobson smiled as though Guy were being slightly ridiculous. "As indeed he is," Harriet thought. She felt particularly annoyed that after she had, as she imagined, demolished the question of her going, it should be brought up again.

Pinkrose had finished his pot of *ţuică* and his eyelids were drooping. He nodded forward, then, rousing himself with a start, said: "I shall return to the hotel. I like an early night."

"Yes." Inchcape rose, saying briskly: "To bed. In this barbarous corner of Europe, where else is there to go?"

Outside, a wintry wind blew among the trees. Dobson, finding that Inchcape and Pinkrose were also returning to Bucharest next morning, offered them a lift. Inchcape was inclined to accept, but when Pinkrose saw the De Dion he shook his head decisively. "Oh, no! Dear me, *no*! I never could travel in an open car."

"Oh, get on, you old stick-in-the-mud!" Inchcape, irritated beyond endurance, gave Pinkrose a push that sent him teetering down the road towards the main hotel.

The drive back to Predeal was very cold. Harriet was depressed, feeling that in some ways Guy was intolerable. When they reached their room, conscious of her withdrawal, he put his arm round her and said: "Don't worry. We shall be all right."

"I'm not worrying," she replied coldly.

"You aren't sorry you came to Rumania with me?"

She shook her head, but moved out of his hold.

"Are you sorry you married me?"

He evidently needed reassurance, for when she said: "Sometimes I am," he looked very grieved. He asked: "Do you feel you needed a different sort of person?"

"Perhaps."

"Who? Clarence?"

"Good heavens, no. No, no one I have met. Perhaps no one I shall ever meet."

He asked despondently: "You mean you no longer love me?"

"I don't mean that, but I'm not sure you want to be loved very much. You want room for a lot of other people and things."

"But I have to work," he expostulated. "I have to see people, to move around. You move around, too . . ."

"Yes, there's plenty of give and take. You are quite willing for me to spend any amount of time with other people: Clarence, for instance, or Sasha. It gives you freedom and you know there's no risk. You're too good to lose."

He stared at her, hurt, looking as though this were all too much for him and she realised they were arguing on different levels. He was being practical, she emotional. She wanted to accuse him of selfishness, to point out that his desire to embrace the outside world was an infidelity and a self-indulgence, but she realised he would never understand what she meant.

"You've never mentioned before that you are discontented."

"No?" She laughed. "Truth is a luxury. We can only afford it now and then."

He laughed, too, his dejection gone in a moment. Humming to himself, happily and tunelessly, he prepared for bed.

Dobson had left before the Pringles appeared for breakfast. The cold of the previous night had presaged a change in the weather. The sky was indigo with cloud. White mist unrolled like cotton-wool down between the mountain peaks. Everything outside looked bleak and wet.

The hotel was desolating in this gloom. The central heating had been turned on that morning, but so far it had done no more than fill the air with the reek of oil and rust. In the main room the bare wooden chairs and bamboo tables were damp to the touch. A smell of dust came from the bulrushes that stood about in pots.

A drizzle began to fall. No one in Bucharest thought of rain and the Pringles had not come prepared for it. Saying: "You won't want to go for a walk today," Guy settled down to his books.

Harriet wished they had gone back with Dobson. Although she thought of their return as something like a plunge into a boiling cauldron, she looked forward to the warmth and entertainment of the capital. Besides, she was anxious about Sasha.

Watching Guy contentedly preparing a course for which there might be no students, Harriet wondered where for him reality began and ended. He could be misled by the plausible, deceived by the self-deceiving, impressed by the second-rate: all in the name of charity, of course. But was such charity truly charitable?

At one time she had been indignant when others were critical of him. Now, she realised, she was criticising him herself. Even more surprising, she could feel bored in his company.

And yet, watching him as he sat there, unsuspecting of criticism or boredom, an open-handed man of infinite good nature, her heart was touched. Reflecting on the process of involvement and disenchantment which was marriage, she thought that one entered it unsuspecting and, unsuspecting, found one was trapped in it.

23

Bucharest, when they reached it, was also wet and no longer warm. The streets were dismal. The block of flats, designed to reflect sunlight, were blotched and livid in the grey air. This was one of the days – like the day of Calinescu's funeral – that broke like a threat into the fading glow of summer.

As soon as they entered the flat, they heard the sound of Sasha playing "We're Gonna Hang Out the Washing on the Siegfried Line". Harriet realising they were back among all their old unresolved anxieties, was not only relieved but annoyed by the mouth-organ. It seemed a symbol of Sasha's unquestioning acceptance of their protection. She went in, intending to chide him for wasting time, but he looked up with so much pleasure at her return, her annoyance was forgotten.

Dear Boy [wrote Yakimov from the Pension de Seraglio],

They think I am a spy or something and they're trying to run me out on a rail. Where next? I ask myself. I'm told Bucharest is full of Nazis spending *lei* like *apa*. If one of them makes an offer for the Hispano, seize it.

Don't forget your poor old desperate Yaki.

The telephone rang. Clarence said, urgently, that he was glad they were back, for he wanted to come and see them. "Yes, do come," said Harriet, thankful to be diverted from the cheerless anticlimax of return.

Clarence, entering the flat, was clearly the bringer of important news. He frowned at the ceiling and as soon as he had accepted a drink said abruptly: "I've come to say good-bye."

Guy said, startled: "You're going so soon?"

"I'm taking the night train. I'm going on to Ankara."

Both Pringles were disconcerted by this news: Guy the more so for, whatever he might care to think, it was evident their circle was disintegrating.

Harriet said: "Why to Ankara?"

"I've to report to the British Council representative. There's some talk of an appointment in Srinagar."

"How wonderful! You almost went to Kashmir once."

"This time, perhaps, I'll get there. But I'm just as likely to end in Egypt."

"Where you would meet up with Brenda?"

Clarence did not reply but, smirking slightly, he stretched himself out in his chair and said: "Poor old Brenda! Whatever did she see in me?"

"She may have thought you needed her."

Clarence shrugged and drawled: "Who knows what I need?"

He seemed aware that he was inviting Harriet's ridicule and to be, for some reason, forearmed against it. Because of this, Harriet said cautiously: "Well, if you go to Kashmir, I envy you."

Lifting his eyelids slowly, Clarence gave her a long look, then glancing down again, said in remote, measured tones: "Sophie is coming with me."

Harriet was startled into saying: "Good heavens!" and Clarence smiled his satisfaction.

"Why, this is splendid!" cried Guy and, leaping up, he refilled the glasses for a toast. "You're getting married, of course?"

Clarence, his smile fading, shrugged again. "I suppose so. It's what she wants," and he gave Harriet a quick glance full of reproach. She thought: "He is doing this to punish himself," but Guy was full of congratulations and encouragement.

"This is the best possible thing for Sophie," he said. "She's not a bad sort of girl. Living here alone, an orphan, half-Jewish, belonging to neither community, she has never had a chance. It will make all the difference to her to get away. You'll see. She'll make a splendid wife."

Harriet had her doubts and so, it would seem, had Clarence. He did not respond to Guy's enthusiasm and, after Guy had further extolled Sophie's virtues, Clarence gloomily mumbled: "I've always wanted to help someone. Perhaps I can help her."

"You could do the world for her," Guy confidently assured him.

Clarence turned his head towards Harriet, his expression yearning and miserable as though even now she might relent and save him. But, of course, she would not. No, not she. He turned away brusquely, finished off his drink, sat upright and said: "One thing I must do before I go: I must return these shirts to the Polish store."

"You mean the shirts you gave to Guy?"

"You know I didn't give them. They weren't mine to give. I lent them. Now they must go back."

"But the store is closed. You sold all that stuff to the Rumanian army."

"The sale's still being negotiated. It takes time for these deals to go through. I'm leaving the matter in the hands of an agent. I've given an inventory and everything must be accounted for. There were some vests, too, and a Balaclava helmet."

"That ridiculous helmet!" Harriet's indignation collapsed into mirth.

As though the demand were the most reasonable in the world, Guy said: "Of course we must return the things." He looked to Harriet as the only one likely to know where they were.

Without further ado, she went into the bedroom and began searching the drawers. The vests were at the laundry. Guy had long ago lost the Balaclava helmet. She returned to the room carrying three shirts.

"All that's left," she said.

Looking grimly justified, Clarence rose to take them, but Harriet did not give them to him. Instead, she strode out to the balcony and threw them over the balustrade. "If you want them," she said, "go down and get them."

He hurried to the balcony and stared down to where the shirts were settling on the wet, grey cobbles below.

"Well, *really*!" Scandalised, he watched while several beggars converged upon the booty. The shirts were snapped up in a moment.

Clarence looked to Guy for support.

"Darling, you shouldn't have done that!" Guy said with no real belief in his power to remonstrate with Harriet.

Taking no notice of either of them, she waved encouragement to the beggars as they stared up.

Looking deeply hurt, Clarence returned to the room and threw himself back into his chair. He dug his hands into his pockets. "How could you?" He gloomed for some moments, then said: "Just when I'd brought you what you asked me for." He drew a small book from his pocket.

Alight with amusement at her own action, Harriet snatched

the book from his hand and leafed it over. She came on the photograph of Sasha.

"A passport?"

"Yes, for your young friend Drucker."

"Clarence!" Harriet threw out her arms to him and he smiled as one who deserved no less.

Standing up rather sheepishly, he explained: "It's an Hungarian passport – in the name of Gabor. Most foreigners are known to the *prefectura*, but there are so many Hungarians here, they can't keep track of them. We've put in visas for Turkey, Bulgaria and Greece. All he'll need when the time comes is an exit visa."

Realising the passport was both a parting gift and a token of truce, Harriet ran to Clarence and embraced him with a warmth to which he immediately responded. He held her overlong, saying: "You will not forget me?"

"Never, never," she cried, refusing to be serious.

Guy said: "We'll miss you."

"Soon there will be no one left," said Harriet.

Clarence picked up his scarf, preparing to depart.

"But this isn't the end," Guy said, unwilling to see him go. "We'll be at the station to see you off."

"No. I hate farewells from trains. I'd rather say good-bye now." Clarence spoke with decision and Harriet felt he did not wish them to see him possessed by Sophie. Nor, she thought, did she wish to see it.

"What's happening to your flat?" she asked.

"A new tenant comes in next week: a German consular official. I'm glad to say he's keeping on Ergie, my cook, and her family. I don't know where they'd go if they were thrown out, poor things!"

They went to the landing with him.

"We'll meet again," said Guy.

"If you have to leave here, why not come to Kashmir? We'd find a job for you." Clarence wrung Guy's hand, then caught at Harriet and pecked her nervously. She realised he was not very sober and his eyes were moist. Not waiting for the arrival of the lift, he swung away from them and ran at a furious speed down the stairs.

24

THE WEATHER WAS SLOW IN REGAINING ITSELF. The sky remained broken, twilight fell early and the air was brisk.

The new term would start early in October. Guy had heard nothing of the reopening of his department, but he was preparing for it and a day or two after Clarence left he decided to pay a visit to the University.

The visit was to be a sort of reconnoitre. He might bump into the dean or one of the professors, or he might find his students hanging about the common-room as they used to do. Anyway, there would surely be someone there who would have something to tell him.

Harriet was doubtful about this essay into forbidden territory, but Guy refused to be dissuaded. He saw the University staff as friends. He had always been popular and privileged there and was sure he would be welcome. The visit would conclude all uncertainties. When she realised he was determined to go, she said she would walk with him as far as the building and then wait for him in the Cişmigiu. When he left her at the park gate she took the main path, intending to wait at the café.

There were very few people about. A haze, silvering the sky, gave a ghostly softness to the light. The distant elevations were washes of pearly transparency.

The flower-beds now had almost nothing to show except the lank stalks of withered plants. Dahlias and chrysanthemums fell, bedraggled, across the paths. On the long and almost leafless stems of the rose-bushes there were a few roses, small and colourless, too hard pressed to look like any particular sort of rose.

The dovecots seemed to be empty. From somewhere in the distance came, dismally, the sqawks of the white peacocks.

Leaves were falling, littering the grass and sticking in wads to the damp asphalt of the paths, but beside the lake the trees were still thickly feathered, hanging over the water, drop-winged, like gorged and sleepy birds of prey.

Harriet found the café closed. She walked round to the bridge from which she could look on to the pier and see the chairs and tables stacked under tarpaulins and roped down against the coming of the winter wind. She was suddenly saddened by the sense of change in which she felt they had no part. When the café reopened, where would they be?

The lake water was pewter-dark, shirred here and there by currents of silver, and broken by the trails of the mallard ducks. Behind her the waterfall gushed bleak as a burst pipe.

Hearing a step, she turned and came face to face with Bella's husband, Nikko. He looked nonplussed by this meeting, but when she said: "Why, Nikko! How nice to see you! When did you get back?" he cried: "Harry-ott!" stumbling forward in delight that his English friends were still, in spite of all, his friends. His black eyes shone and his teeth flashed from beneath his black moustache.

"We thought on our return you would have left," he said, "but now I find you here and am so glad."

"Yes, and Guy even believes the English Department will re-open. What do you think?"

"Who can say?"

Seeing he evaded the question, Harriet changed the subject, asking: "How is Bella?"

"Very well. Our holiday has restored her. But the summer was trying for her. Usually we are all the time in the mountains. My poor Bella! She suffers that I am away so much. I get little leave, then I am recalled and she weeps. Each month it becomes more difficult. Our great ally" – he made a grimace – "demands that officers are always on the alert. For what, I ask you? But you – which way do you walk?"

Finding he was crossing the park to the rear gate, she said she would pass the time by walking with him.

They crossed the bridge together. As they went, a blur of white came into the sky where the sun hung behind the haze. The lake turned to silver. The still and humid air cut off the sound of traffic so they seemed to be moving into areas of cushioned silence.

Beyond the bridge there was a walk of lime trees, brilliantly yellow in the grey air, beneath which two German officers sauntered, in trench-coats with skirts swinging, the heels of their jackboots clicking on the paths. They gave an impression of acute boredom.

Nikko, not in uniform, eyed them, cautiously silent until he and

Harriet were well past, then he said in an undertone: "They have not yet won the war. I can tell you, Harry-ott, we are sick of the demands of the Germans. They will devour us. People are remembering the English, so honest, so dignified, so generous, and they say: 'Perhaps even now the Allies will win.' And, I say: 'Why not?' September is at an end, yet there has been no invasion. What has happened, we ask, to this talked-of invasion? The Germans put it off. They make excuses. Do not quote me, but we know already it is too late. They *cannot* invade."

Harriet turned on him in hopeful surprise. "Why not?"

"Why not?" Nikko gave her a look of astonishment. "Surely you must know why not? Already the fogs cloak your shores. The Germans cannot find their way."

"Oh!" Harriet gave a laugh of disappointment. "I'm afraid we can't rely on the fogs."

Nikko knew better. "Then why do they not invade?" he asked. After a moment, he added: "They are a strange people. I remember last time when they came here, I was a little boy. We had a German officer billeted in our home. He was not so bad, you know. It was a time of great fear, and we did for him what we could. When they retreated, taking everything they could carry, this man, leaving us, gave to my mother a great parcel – this size; very big. He said: 'This is a gift. I give you because you have been so kind.' After he was gone, she opened it and inside there was a bed-quilt. We all looked at it, thinking how nice, but my mother said: 'I have seen before such a bed-quilt. I have *already* one like this,' and she went up to the cupboard to look. What do you think? He had given to my mother her own bed-quilt! Have you ever known such a strange people?"

As Harriet laughed, Nikko said: "I have loved England; I was long ambitious to work in England. I would be interested, I need say, only in a top-hole job, for I have top-hole qualifications. I read *Punch* and *The Times* – not now, of course, for they do not arrive, but my subscription is paid. And, as you observe, my English is unerring. But the war nipped me in the bud."

Harriet laughed again. "It nipped us all in the bud," she said.

Nikko, having recalled his enthusiasm for England, now said with conviction: "I think the English Department will open again. Why not? It will open because they love Guy. He is a great man."

"Do you think so? Well, perhaps he is, in some ways . . ."

"A great man!" Nikko insisted, permitting no reservations.

"And why? Because he is himself. Many Englishmen came here to be important people – the sahibs, as they called it. They would show these foreigners how to run the world. But not Guy. He came as one of us – a chum, you might say, a human being. Only the other day as we came into Bucharest, I said to Bella: 'How I wish I had known better Guy Pringle. Now he will be gone, and I shall never know him.' "

Harriet smiled at the pattern of approval, never disclosed before and said nothing.

Sensing her doubt in his serenity, Nikko said: "Before you came, you understand, I had not much opportunity. Guy and Bella did not see eye to eye. She invited him to a cocktail, he did not turn up. She said: 'That young man is not an advertisement for England. They should not have let him come here. He is badly dressed, he cultivates Jews, he is not careful what he says. The important English do not approve him.' All this perhaps was true, yet I approved him. I said: 'Invite him again. He is always so busy . . .' "

"Much too busy," commented Harriet.

"But she would not invite him again, not until you came. You she approved."

"Oh," said Harriet, uncertain how to take this.

"But I admired Guy," Nikko went on, not feeling the subject was yet exhausted. "I admired him because he spoke to one and all and dressed so badly. He wore that old overcoat. Do you remember that old overcoat? What Englishman here would be seen dead in such a coat? No, no, they must impress us. But it is not necessary, you know. We are impressed already by the English qualities. We know here that to be English is to be honest. You do things to your own disadvantage because you know them to be right. That is remarkable, I can tell you. So we love you."

"I'm not so sure of that," said Harriet, feeling the need to introduce some sobriety into this conversation. "I often feel the Rumanians are suspicious of us, and resentful."

"A little, perhaps." Conceding the point, Nikko hurried past it: We envy you. You are a great, rich nation. We think you despise us, but we love you nevertheless. See!" He paused at a railed area of uncut grasses among which some flowers ran riot. "This is the English garden."

Harriet looked in astonishment. She had sometimes wondered

about this patch that she would not have described as a garden of any kind.

"Yes," Nikko assured her. "It is a genuine English wilderness. So you see," he nodded as though proving his point, "we have an English Bar and an English garden."

"Yes," said Harriet. They had now reached the gate and she paused before saying she must turn back.

Nikko took her hand. "Good-bye, Harry-ott. Let us, this winter, meet more often. Persuade Guy to come and have dinner with us."

She promised she would. Nikko looked pleased, as though a whole future of friendship lay ahead, but Harriet felt in their parting a note of farewell.

When she returned to the lakeside she saw Guy walking rapidly, down between the chrysanthemum beds, his expression troubled, his appearance more dishevelled than usual. When she called to him, he glanced towards her but did not smile.

"What is the matter?" she asked.

"I must see Inchcape. Will you come with me?"

As they walked together back to the main road, he described to her how, entering the University building, he had found all the doors of his department locked. Even his own study door had been locked against him. He had noticed the porter, with whom he had been a favourite, sliding out of sight as he entered. Guy, determined to speak to him, had tracked him down to the boiler-room in the basement. The old man, stammering in his embarrassment, asked: What could a poor peasant do?

"These are wicked days, *domnule!* Bad men possess our country and our friends are severed from us."

"He said that?" Harriet asked in admiration.

"Something like that," said Guy. "He said he had no keys for my rooms. They had all been taken away by the Foreign Minister."

"Have you much stuff in your office?"

"Some of my books. A lot of Inchcape's. My overcoat."

"Oh, well!" said Harriet, feeling things might have been worse.

Guy sighed, apparently stunned by a rebuff that did not surprise her in any way.

"Do you think Inchcape can do anything?" she asked.

"I don't know."

She could scarcely keep up with him as he made his way to the Propaganda Bureau. She had no wish for the department to reopen, but, remembering how, on the day of the abdication, she had found Guy waiting for the students who did not come, she felt an acute pity for him. Whatever he chose to do – and it was, after all, done from a sense of responsibility and a need to be occupied – he must be her first concern.

When they reached the main road, they became aware that something had occurred. A crowd stood opposite the English Propaganda Bureau, gazing across at it. The pavement outside it was empty of people: those who approached it, swerved away from it as though it held contagion. The trespass of the bystanders on to the road had caused a traffic hold-up. The result was an hysterical din of motor-horns.

Guy and Harriet were conscious of being watched as they crossed the road to the Bureau. The pavement when they reached it was a litter of splintered wood, glass and scraps of torn cardboard. The Bureau window had been shattered; its faded display wrecked. The model of the Dunkirk beach-head seemed to have been attacked, savagely, with hammer blows. The "Britain Beautiful" posters had been ripped down and screwed into balls. Everywhere lay remnants of the photographs of ships and soldiers.

Despite the disorder there was no sign of police or any official keeper of law and order.

Guy said: "Wait here. I'll look inside," but Harriet kept at his heels. The door stood ajar. Inchcape was alone in the downstairs office. He was sitting in the typist's chair, pressing a folded handkerchief to the corner of his mouth. He greeted the Pringles with a wry smile.

"It's all right," he said; "they barely touched me."

As he spoke, blood welled out of the corner of his mouth and trickled down his chin. Blood and serum from a wound under his hair was trickling down into his left ear. His natural pallor had taken on a greenish tinge.

"For heaven's sake," said Guy. "We must get a doctor . . ." He went to the telephone, but Inchcape detained him with a gesture.

"Believe me, it's nothing."

There was a sound of car-doors banging outside, then Galpin entered with Screwby and three other journalists from the English Bar. Galpin crossed to Inchcape, observed him keenly, flicked open a notebook, then asked: "What happened? What did they do to you?"

Inchcape regarded him with distaste. "An accidental knock or two. They came in merely to sabotage the work of the place. The attack was all over in a matter of minutes." He turned pointedly to Guy and in a changed tone said, smiling: "I rang your flat first. When I couldn't get you, I rang Dobson. He's on his way."

Galpin gave his attention to the condition of the office. "They've done a proper job." He looked at his companions and said: "My stringer here says there were these hooligans knocking the old boy about, smashing the windows, destroying things – all in broad daylight, in a crowded street. And not a soul lifted a finger. They just scurried past. Just look at them now." He flicked a hand at the audience across the road. "Piss-scared." He turned on Inchcape again and as though speaking to someone of limited intelligence he explained: "We'll want a statement. Tell us in your own words: when it happened, how it happened and who you imagine the assailants were."

Inchcape turned his head slowly and stared directly at Galpin. "I am waiting for Mr. Dobson," he explained in a style that echoed Galpin's own. "Any statement I have to make will be made when he arrives."

Disconcerted, Galpin took a step backwards, bumping into Screwby who was moving forward to say, in fulsome tones: "I must say, sir, I admire your pluck."

Inchcape's only acknowledgement of this tribute was a twist of the lips that caused him to wince. Blood welled out again.

Galpin, piqued, muttered to the others: "Well, I only hope someone's sent for a doctor. Things could be worse than they look."

"No doctor has been sent for, nor do I want one," Inchcape said and, glancing aside at Harriet, he added: "Heaven keep me out of the hands of Rumanian doctors."

Dobson arrived. Looking about him, he said: "Oh dear!" Flustered and at a loss, he stood pulling off his gloves, then suddenly became businesslike. "The fellows who did this," he asked, "were they in uniform?"

"No."

"Ah, an unofficial attack. When we protest, no one will know anything. If we persist, we may get an apology, but that will be the end of it. The authorities are powerless, of course."

Galpin said: "We're all powerless." He was showing signs of impatience. "What about that statement?" he asked.

Everyone waited. Inchcape, the centre of attention, was wiping his mouth again. After some moments, he smiled his old ironical smile and began: "I was in my office upstairs, innocently reading Miss Austen, when I heard a fracas down here. Half a dozen young men had burst in and started smashing the place up. I heard my secretary screaming. When I got down, she'd made a bolt for it – no doubt wisely: she had, in any case, begun to doubt the justice of the Allied cause."

Inchcape paused to smile to himself, apparently recalling the whole occurrence with philosophical amusement. "When I appeared," he went on, "one fellow slammed the door closed and locked it. There were seven or eight of them. Two or three gave their attention to me, the rest were absorbed in their destructive frenzy. I was hit on the head by a framed portrait of our respected Prime Minister . . ."

"Deliberately?" Galpin demanded.

"I don't know. The blow knocked me backwards into this chair. When I tried to rise, someone gripped my shoulders and held me down. One of them – the leader, I suppose – then saw fit to question me."

"What questions were you asked?" said Dobson.

"Oh, the usual. They wanted to know who was head of the British Secret Service here. I said: 'Sir Montagu.' That flummoxed them." Inchcape laughed at the recollection, but Dobson, frowning like an unhappy baby, burst out: "Really, there was no need to bring H.E. into it."

"You know they can't touch him. And if they tried, he's well protected."

Dobson seemed about to speak, then shut his mouth, silenced by the change that was coming over Inchcape's appearance. Bruises like leaden shadows were beginning to show on his brow and cheeks. His handkerchief was dark with blood. Guy offered him another, but he shook his head. "I'm all right," he said.

Galpin interrupted accusingly: "They must have knocked you about?"

Inchcape, clearly under greater strain than he would admit, caught his breath and answered with sardonic brevity: "A little perhaps."

Though he could not admit he had suffered the indignity of attack, the journalists were not deceived. One said: "I can't imagine a few accidental taps got you into this condition."

"Are you suggesting that I am lying?" Inchcape sharply asked.

"All right." Galpin snapped a band round his note-book and put it away. Buttoning his jacket, he looked round at his fellows with the air of one who has got all he wants here and has other calls on his time. "We'd better get back," he said.

They began moving off. Guy, saying he would take Inchcape home, went out to the street to find a cab. Galpin, on the pavement outside, was saying: "It's my opinion he's brought this on himself."

"In what way?" Guy asked.

He jerked a thumb at the Bureau. "He insisted, against advice, on keeping open. But there was more to it than that. I bet the lads who did this job *knew him*. Knew him too well, I mean. That's why he's keeping his mouth shut. He's always been a mean old bastard. If you ask me, the lads had something on him."

"What rubbish!" Guy said in disgust. "It was obviously a Guardist outrage."

Galpin snorted. He got into his car and as a parting shot, called out: "One has to pay for one's pleasures, you know."

Inchcape made his way to the cab with an unconvincing show of vigour. Getting into it, he stumbled and Guy had to hold him up.

At the sight of his master, Pauli gave a cry of distress and waved his arms in the air. Inchcape pushed him away with affectionate impatience, saying: "Go and make a good strong pot of tea for all of us."

While they drank it, Inchcape talked gleefully about his quick-wittedness in naming Sir Montagu as head of the Secret Service. "You should have seen their faces. They knew the old charmer was out of their reach. And having got their answer, they couldn't think of anything else to ask me."

Before the Pringles left, Inchcape said to them: "For heaven's sake, don't breathe a word of this to Pinkrose. He'd get into a panic. So promise me, not one word."

The Pringles promised.

25

Next morning, Pauli telephoned Guy to say he was worried about his master's condition. The previous evening, Inchcape, though insisting that he was perfectly well, had been unable to sleep until he had taken veronal. That morning he looked much worse and all life had gone from him. He was, in Pauli's opinion, very sick; and he was asking for Guy.

When this call came, Harriet was in the bathroom. Guy shouted to her that he would be back for luncheon and left the flat before she could ask where he was going. When she went out to the balcony, she could see him making his way rapidly across the square.

He was, in fact, unusually disturbed, and not only by his fears for Inchcape. The previous evening, in need of a drink, he had gone to the English Bar where Galpin had claimed to have "inside information" to the effect that the military mission was soon to be followed by the Gestapo. The Germans had already installed a Gauléiter, who was becoming the talk of town. He was said to be paralysed from the waist down. Though he lay in bed all day, seeing no one but his agents, he knew everything about everybody. Galpin said: "The whole German colony's piss-scared of this bastard. Even Fabricius. The Rumanians, too. They say that a deputation of Rumanian statesmen called on Fabricius last night to beg the Führer to send in an army of occupation. He said that Germany doesn't plan to occupy Rumania just yet. That's all my eye. Everything points to the fact that it's any day now."

Harriet, who had been playing a paper game with Sasha, had not accompanied Guy to the bar. When he returned, he did not tell her what he had heard there.

Unnerved by her outburst at Predeal, he had, for the first time, begun to fear for her. He had always thought of her as a pattern of courage, someone tougher than himself about whom he need not worry. Now he was beginning to realise that she had audacity without stamina. His means of living with a situation was to put its dangers behind him. Her method was to keep them in view so they might not come on her unawares. She lived in a state of preparedness that brought undue stress. He told himself he must protect her against her own temperament. He would save her from shock, even the perhaps not very great shock of seeing Inchcape in a state of collapse.

But there was more behind Guy's discomposure than that. He was suffering from shock himself. Both Inchcape and he had been named on the German radio. Both were the natural prey not only of the Iron Guard but of the Gestapo, rumoured to be on its way here.

Convinced that a testing-time was at hand, he tried to tell himself that he now knew exactly what would happen. He would be attacked without warning and struck about the face and head by thugs. He realised that in thus attempting to steady an inner nerve with certainty, he was simply imitating Harriet. And where did it bring one? To the verge of a breakdown. He could only hope that when his time came, pride would prop him up as it had propped up Inchcape. The trouble was, he had a peculiar horror of physical violence and could not foresee what his reaction would be. Even Harriet, half his size, could frighten him when she lost her temper. He flinched or cried out in the instant of being hurt. Afterwards, he would pull himself together, but that first instant stayed with him, a self-betrayal.

Whatever happened, he must save himself from Harriet's observing eye.

Pauli, opening the door for him, lifted a hand in mute dismay at what he would find. He said nothing but hurried into Inchcape's bedroom. He had feared Inchcape would be prostrate and was relieved to see him sitting up in bed, but the relief was gone as soon as Inchcape turned his head.

Noting Guy's change of expression, he said: "They haven't improved my beauty, have they?"

"It could be worse."

"How much worse?" Inchcape winced as he attempted an appearance of jocularity. Both his eyes were blackened, one of them hidden by the swollen lids. A purple bruise, spreading from under his hair, covered one side of his face. His lips protruded, and his other features, naturally pallid and fine, were so distorted that he looked, against the whiteness of the bed-linen, like a grotesque native mask.

Guy had carried for years in his mind the memory of Simon's bleeding, stupefied face – but Simon had been the victim of amateurs. Brutality had progressed since then.

Guy said: "Apart from the bruises, are you hurt at all?"

"Back aches a bit. Have a drink." Inchcape reached out towards a bottle of brandy on the table beside him, then, as though some prop had been withdrawn, he fell back among the pillows and gave a groan. He looked at Guy, gasped and said: "Don't stand there, staring. Sit down, for God's sake." He attempted his old impatience, but it was a shadow of itself.

"Let me get you a drink." Guy poured out the brandy before he sat down.

The bedroom was small, lit by a single small window that was overhung by plane leaves. On the walls were ikons so dark that to Guy they represented nothing. He wondered if it were the pervading gloom that made Inchcape look so ill.

Inchcape sipped his brandy and after a moment started to talk: "I rang H.E. this morning. I told him I was not to be coerced by these louts. I was determined to reopen the Bureau, but apparently the Bureau's been officially closed by the Rumanian authorities. Still, I'm not standing for it. I shall fight." He dug his elbows into the pillows and made another irritable effort to sit up but failed again.

Inchcape was an elderly man but one who had maintained vitality and youthfulness: now some inner power had gone from him. His neck, rising from his pyjama jacket, looked wretchedly scraggy. His whole physique seemed to have aged and weakened overnight. He said: "Dobson rang a while ago, was very pleasant, as usual. He advised me to take myself off to Turkey. I said I wouldn't dream of it. They're not going to scare me so easily."

Guy nodded his understanding. Yet with the English Department and the Bureau closed, would it not be better for Inchcape to go? He had imagined that the presence of the Legation guaranteed their safety. Well, he could no longer have any illusions about that. His work had come to nothing. He had been abused. Nothing remained but his determination to stay as long as Sir Montagu stayed.

"Still," said Guy, "there's no reason why you should not take a few weeks' leave after this."

Inchcape's one visible eye glinted at him and Guy's spirits gave a jerk. So defiance was now a sham! Inchcape wanted only to be persuaded – though, unpersuaded, his pride would probably keep him here. Suddenly Guy saw that Harriet and he might get away together unharmed; for if Inchcape went he could scarcely demand that they must stay.

"After all," said Guy, "Dobson is off to Sofia."

"That's true. Though I can't say that I approve it. And I'm told the old charmer himself recently chartered a plane and flew to Corfu. Spent a week there. A nice thing, I must say, at a time like this."

"Oh, I don't know." Guy, in fear of rousing Inchcape's obstinate opposition, found himself lapsing into clichés: "Quite a good thing to get away from a situation – enables you to get it into focus."

Latching on to Guy's extenuating tone, Inchcape permitted himself a measure of agreement. "Of course, there's more to these trips than meets the eye. There's no knowing whom Sir M. met when down there, or what was discussed. I've often thought myself I could pay a call on our agent in Beirut, I could put him wise about a few things. He's still in direct telephonic communication with London office, you know. And they should be made to realise how things are changing here. The rise in the cost of living, for instance! We can't go on indefinitely on pre-war salaries."

Guy had not heard before of this agent, but was prepared to believe in him. The organisation supplied men to the American University in Beirut. He said: "There's probably an air-service between Istanbul and Beirut."

Inchcape opened his mouth, but did not speak. There was a pause, then he nodded. It seemed to Guy that the trip was practically agreed upon. He was about to suggest that while Inchcape went to Beirut, he and Harriet could visit Athens, when he noticed Inchcape's hand trembling on the white satin counterpane. He felt stricken. Telling himself that he was harrying this aged and lonely man out of the one place in the world where he had importance, he put his hand on Inchcape's and pressed it.

At this touch, Inchcape's lips shook: a tear trickled out between his swollen lids. "We can't give in, Guy," he said. "We can't run away. We must be represented."

"We aren't running away," Guy assured him. "You are merely taking the leave that is due to you. I shall be here to represent you."

"That's true." As though he knew he had committed himself to defeat, Inchcape let his head fall back and sobbed without restraint.

Awed by this collapse of a man who had until now appeared to be inflexible. Guy realised he had always taken Inchcape at his face value, accepting him as his chief, to be obeyed and honoured. He had never doubted that much of Inchcape's temerity was based on self-deception. but it appalled him to see this temerity collapse at the moment reality broke through. But perhaps it was the indignity that had destroyed Inchcape. The whole place must seem to him contaminated by this assualt on him. No wonder he wanted to get away.

For a while Guy sat silent, at a loss before Inchcape's weeping, then, realising that initiative had now passed to him, he said: "And another thing: London office must be told that we face a final break-up here. It's only a matter of time. We should be instructed where we're to go, what we're to do when we get there. We don't want to become refugees without employment."

Inchcape nodded again. Finding a handkerchief, he dabbed gently at his eyes and nostrils. "You're quite right," he said. "It's not only advisable I should go, it's imperative. And there's no time to waste."

"None. You should go as soon as you feel equal to the journey."

"Oh, I'm all right." Inchcape gave something between a laugh and a gulp. He made another effort and this time managed to sit upright. "I'm not crippled. The sooner I get away, the sooner I'll be back. I won't take much: change of underwear, a few books, just a grip and a brief-case. I like to travel light. If there's no plane to Beirut, there should be a train of some sort. An execrable journey, I imagine, but interesting. If nothing important crops up, I might get the Orient Express on Sunday night."

"Do you think you will be well enough?"

"Nothing wrong with me. Just a few bruises." And now that matters were settled, Inchcape did seem much recovered. He threw back the coverlet, put his legs out of bed and began, in a feeble way. to feel for his slippers. Not finding them, he gave up and lowered himself back to the pillows, but he shot Guy a keen look. "You've not said a word to Pinkrose?"

"No, I haven't seen him since it happened."

"Good. He's not likely to hear in the ordinary way. He takes a pride in keeping himself to himself. When he rang up last night,

Pauli told him I was in bed with a temperature. That'll keep the old cheeser at bay. He won't risk catching anything."

"Don't you think we should let him know you're going?"

"No, definitely not. He'd get into a proper tizzy. He'd have a heart attack. Or worse, he'd insist on coming with me. I couldn't stand it." Inchcape fixed Guy, his expression piteous: "I'm not fit for it."

Guy wondered what they were to do with Pinkrose after Inchcape's departure, but, afraid to raise any problem that might impede it, he said: "Very well."

"Don't tell anyone," Inchcape said. "I'll be back before they even know I've left the country."

It was clear to Guy, as he returned home, that in sending for him Inchcape had merely sent for a persuader. Guy could not flatter himself that he had done much, but he felt pride, even a mild exultation, that by making the right gesture he had persuaded the poor old chap to take himself to safety. The resolute, he saw, were weaker than they seemed.

It occurred to him that Harriet, tackled in some such oblique manner, might be just as easily overthrown. Not that the conditions were exactly similar. Inchcape had collapsed at a first blow from reality. Harriet had never let reality out of her sight. When she said she would not leave, she saw as clearly as Guy did the dangers of staying – probably more clearly. Still, he was not discouraged. He had his own obstinacy. Once assured in his purpose, he could be as wily as the next man.

There were two weaknesses through which she might be assailed: himself and Sasha. Supposing he persuaded her to go to Athens on his behalf! Better, perhaps, persuade her to make the journey as friend and protector to Sasha.

He had long recognised her attachment to the boy without resenting it. He was glad that each could enjoy the companionship of the other. And he had no illusions about himself. He was overgregarious, busy, disinclined to suffer constraint. Were he, to accuse her of neglecting him, she had more than enough fuel for counter-accusation. If she felt the need for a friend and companion, better an innocent relationship than one that might prove less innocent. And something had to be done about Sasha. Even if he were not in danger, his life as he lived it now was hopelessly unprofitable. He had never been a brilliant pupil, but he had been a willing one. Now, in captivity, he had become idle and would not put his mind to the tasks which Guy set for him. He did not even want to read. The most he would do was play games with Harriet or cover with childish drawings the large sheets of cheap cartridge paper which she bought for him. Sometimes, at his most active, he amused himself by helping Despina in the kitchen, but that amounted chiefly to gossiping and giggling.

When Harriet had shown him the faked passport, he had looked at it blankly. When she explained: "This means you can leave Rumania," his only reaction had been dismay: "But I don't have to go, do I?"

"Not now, of course. But if we go – and we may have to – you can come with us."

Sasha's expression had revealed his fear of change, or of any sort of move even made in their company. He wanted to spend the rest of his life like a pet in a cage.

When Guy reached the sitting room he found Sasha and Despina putting the knives and forks on the table. The two were laughing together at something.

Despina, who was familiar with Harriet and motherly with Sasha, kept up the Eastern tradition that the man of the house was a minor despot. At the sight of Guy, she took herself off.

Sasha said: "Despina is so funny. She was imitating the cook from downstairs who sneaks into our kitchen and pinches our sugar. If anyone catches her at it, she whines: 'Please, please, I came only to borrow the carving knife!'."

Guy smiled, but thought that Sasha, though he spoke like a schoolboy, was, in fact, a young man. At his age many Rumanian men were married. The only hope for the boy was to be forced into an independent existence. If he and Harriet travelled together, he must be made to see himself not as the protected but the protector.

As soon as he had Harriet alone, Guy told her of Inchcape's collapse. "He's going on Sunday to Beirut."

She jerked up her head, her face brilliant with excitement. "He's going for good?"

"In theory, no: but I doubt whether he'll come back."

"So there's really nothing to keep us here, either. We can go. We can go to Athens, and Sasha can come with us. We can all go together."

Guy had to break in on her frantic delight: "No, I can't go. Not yet. I've had to promise Inchcape that I would stay. He wouldn't go otherwise. He felt he had to be represented here. And then there's Pinkrose. But look" – he seized her hands as her face dropped – "look," he coaxed her, "do something for me."

"What?"

"Go to Sofia with Dobson."

She pulled her hands from him, vexed, saying: "No, I wouldn't go to Sofia, anyway. The only place I want to go to is Greece, but I'm not going without you."

"All right, better still, go to Athens. Take Sasha with you. And I can join you there. *Listen*, darling. Be sensible. There are two reasons why you should go. I think Sasha should be got out of here in good time. If he travels on the plane with you and Dobson, he'll have your protection. They probably won't even question why he's going. He'll be treated as a privileged passenger. If there should be trouble, we can rely on Dobson to exert his influence."

"What makes you think that?"

"I do think it. I'm sure Dobson will look after you both. He'll be like a mother to you."

Neither agreeing nor disagreeing, she asked in a noncommittal tone: "And the other reason?"

"If I go to Turkey, I'll probably be sent to the Middle East. I hate those hot, sandy countries. I want to go to Greece, just as you do, and if you're there already I have the excuse of joining you."

Before she turned her face aside, he could see the idea of a mission was working on her. She bit her lip in doubt.

"And," he said, "if things settle down here, you can come back."

But she was still resistant. "This uncertainty could drag on for months. We simply haven't the money . . ."

He interrupted, urging her: "Go for a few weeks, anyway. See the head of the organisation in Athens. Tell him I want to work there. You know you can do it. If he likes you, he'll want to employ me: so when I leave here, there'll be somewhere for me to go."

It all seemed odd to Harriet, like a conversation outside reality, yet it was breaking down her resistance. Bewildered, half persuaded, she said: "If I want to come back here, they may not let me in. People are being expelled all the time."

"If you get a return visa before you go, they must let you back."

Reluctant, even at this point, to give way, she kept the argument dragging on, but in the end she found she had agreed to get a return visa. Having secured this, she could take Sasha to Athens and return alone if Guy did not join her there.

Despite something like near-intoxication from the prospect of escape, Harriet resented the fact that Guy had persuaded her to go.

Men like Woolley saw women as a "drag" in times of danger. Mrs. Woolley had been sent to England at the outbreak of war and had recently been sent somewhere else. Harriet, of a different generation, saw herself as an equal and a comrade. She was not to be packed off like that – and, yet, against her will, she had let herself be talked into going.

For Guy the day was one of modest triumph. In sending ahead Harriet, Sasha and that old self-deceiver Inchcape, he was not only safeguarding them, but clearing the decks for action in a war he had chosen to wage, the war against despotism. He believed the ultimate engagement was at hand. He could now face it alone.

26

HARRIET WOULD MAKE NO PREPARATIONS for her journey. She would not even mention their plans to Sasha. She would do nothing until she had obtained the visa that was an earnest of her return. She got a bleak and sparkless satisfaction when it seemed she probably would not obtain it at all.

She had had to queue for the exit visa, but it was given without question. For the return visa, she was directed to a compartment which contained no clerk. No one was waiting before it. She stood for some time, then inquired and was told the clerk was not in the building. He might reappear at five o'clock.

In the late afternoon she returned to the *prefectura*, but the compartment was still unattended. She demanded to see the official in charge. When he eventually came, he took her passport away and left her waiting twenty minutes before he brought it back. She could be granted a return visa only if she supplied a letter of recommendation from her Legation.

She set out for the Legation, disheartened by fatigue and indecision, and heard from a side-street the barrel-organ that played the old Rumanian tune, the name of which no one could tell her. Haunting and mysteriously simple, it reminded her of the day she had gone for a sleigh-ride up the Chaussée with Guy and Clarence. She thought of the shop-lights gilding the snow and felt an acute nostalgia for winter. She told herself she would not go. She could not leave Guy. She did not even want to leave Bucharest.

She wandered on and, crossing the square, saw Bella walking towards the Athénée Palace. The two women came face to face under the Nazi flag.

It had been a day of mild autumnal sunlight and Bella was in a new woollen suit with mink skins strung from elbow to elbow. This was their first sight of each other since her return to Bucharest. Seeing Harriet, she called out: "I was going to ring you! What do you think I got on the black market today? Just over six thousand to the pound. *And* it's rising. My dear, we're rich! I've been buying everything I could lay my hands on. After all, you never know, do you? I've just ordered a new coat – Persian lamb, of course. I picked out my own skins. *Tiny* little things! I wrote my name on the back of each so there'd be no hanky-panky. I'm getting half a dozen new suits for Nikko – best English tweed. The thing to do is to buy up what's left. *And* shoes – a dozen pairs each. Why not, I ask you? We've money to burn." Elated by her rise in fortune, she looked up and smiled at the flag and the clear pale sky beyond it. "I love this time of the year," she said. "So delicious after the fug of summer. It makes one feel so *alive*." She seemed aglitter with life, almost dancing in her new green lizard-skin shoes. Not finding Harriet very responsive, she looked at her more closely and thought to ask: "But how are you and Guy? What do you think of things?"

Harriet glanced up at the swastika. "Doesn't that disturb you?"

Bella looked up again and gave an uncertain laugh. "Does it?" she asked. "I don't know. In a way, it makes me feel safe. It's nice to be protected, even by Germans. And, you know," she gazed seriously at Harriet, a rather petulant gleam in her eye, "Rumania has been very unfairly treated. The Allies guaranteed her, then did nothing. *Nothing*. There was that plot to blow up the oil-wells, and there've always been those outside interests controlling Ploesti. Foreign engineers everywhere. No wonder we've been in an awkward position. You can't blame the Rumanians for wanting the foreigners to go."

"When they go, what will the Rumanians do?"

"Get in German experts, I suppose."

"So there will still be outside interests controlling Ploesti! Or don't Germans count as outsiders any more?"

Bella, looking sulky, tilted up her chin as though sniffing out injury. She made a movement, seemed about to go, but, held by some memory of their earlier friendship, gave Harriet a look at once annoyed and compassionate. "But what about you? Aren't you nervous, being here? I mean, it's different for little me. I've a Rumanian passport." Suddenly the thought of something restored her humour. She gave a laugh: "People think I'm a German, you know. I can get anything I want."

Harriet, fearing to enhance Bella's isolation here, had not mentioned her possible departure, but now she realised that Bella's high spirits were not a result of hysteria. She had found a means of managing her situation: she was shuffling off her own identity and taking on an aspect of the enemy.

Harriet said: "Guy wants me to go to Athens for a few weeks, but I'm having difficulty in getting a return visa."

Hooting with laughter, Bella gripped Harriet's arm. "My dear, you can get one in the twinkling of an eye. It's just a matter of going about it the right way. Put a thousand-*lei* note inside your passport. But why get a return visa? If you've any sense you'll stay there once you get there."

"I have to come back. Guy isn't supposed to leave without orders."

"Oh, I'll keep an eye on him. I'll see he doesn't get into mischief."

Bella was enjoying herself. Here she was, secure and snug, while others must take themselves into exile. She could advise from a position of vantage. "You might like me to look after some of your things," she said. "Those nice Hungarian plates, for instance. I wouldn't mind giving them a home."

"If we finally go, you can take what you like."

"Well, I must be on my way." Bella gathered her minks about her. "I've got several fittings this evening. I want to buy gloves. Look, give me a ring and tell me how you manage about the visa. I'll call and see you before you go." She hurried away with a happy "Cheerio!" and Harriet returned to the *prefectura* where she again asked to see the official in charge. When he came upon the thousand-*lei* note in her passport, he whipped it out so quickly Harriet scarcely saw it go. He stamped in the return visa.

"Doamna is intrepid," he said in English. "These times, the British who go do not wish to come back." Smirking, he handed her the passport with a little bow.

Harriet wondered how Sasha would accept the news of their going. He accepted it impassively. After all, she thought, he merely lived as his family had lived for generations: in seclusion, dreading flight, but prepared for it.

"What about Guy?" he asked.

"He'll come when he can."

She and Guy had planned to support Sasha until he could find work. He surprised her now by his immediate appraisal of what his position would be abroad. He pointed out that, once he was beyond Rumanian jurisdiction, he could draw on the fortune banked in his name in Switzerland

"I shall be very rich," he said. "If you need money, I can give it to you."

"You would have to establish your identity."

"Surely my relations would do that?"

Harriet smiled and agreed, but wondered where his relations might be.

As nothing important cropped up, Inchcape's departure was fixed for Sunday. He had only four days in which to make his arrangements, but he made them wholeheartedly. He decided to give up his flat.

On his return, he explained to Guy, he would go to a *pension*. "No good shutting one's eyes to the fact," he said. "Sooner or later, we'll have to take ourselves off, probably at a moment's notice. Better be prepared for it. Besides, one's safer in a *pension* than living on one's own."

When the Pringles called for him on Sunday evening, Pauli, opening the door, blinked at them with red-rimmed eyes. He led them through the hall filled with packing-cases and in the disordered sitting-room, where all the gold-shaded lights were lit, began to lament his quandary.

The great wish of his life, he said, was to follow the professor wherever he might go. Alas, Pauli had a wife and three children. He had been prepared to leave them but the professor, the most clement of masters, had insisted that Pauli's duty was here.

Pauli made no pretence of believing that Inchcape would return. There was too much evidence against the possibility. At the thought of their eternal separation, Pauli's eyes overflowed, his shoulders shook. He pulled out a ball of wet handkerchief and scrubbed at his face while Guy patted his shoulder, saying: "When the war is over, we shall all meet again."

"*Dupa răsboiul,*" Pauli repeated and, as though for the first time struck by the thought that the war might end, he brightened at once. Nodding, blowing his nose, saying again and again "*Dupa răsboiul,*" he hurried off to tell Inchcape that they had arrived.

Harriet said: "*Dupa răsboiul!*" thinking of the war that divided them like a sea from progress and profit in the world. The total effort of their lives might go down in the crossing of it. "And afterwards," she said, "what will be left? We may no longer be young, or even ambitious. And it may never end. We may never have a home."

Wandering about among the packing-cases, she paused at the tables and examined Inchcape's bowl of artificial fruit. There was a fig made of malachite, a purple plum, a flame-coloured persimmon. She held a pear to the light and, seeing the spangling within, said: "Do you think, if I asked him, he would give me these?"

"Of course he wouldn't." Guy was shocked at the idea and, hearing Inchcape's footsteps, he added warningly: "Put them down."

Inchcape's bruises were changing to green and violet. He looked scarcely better than he had done on the morning after the attack, but he had regained all his own sardonic swagger. He crossed over to a Chinese cabinet and took out three bottles, in each of which a little liquid remained.

"Might as well finish this," he said. "What'll you have? Brandy, gin, *tuică*?"

He had put on his overcoat and Pauli could be heard heaping up luggage in the hall, but Inchcape seemed in no hurry to go. Having poured out the drinks, he went round adjusting the shades of the lights and observing their effect. One of the ivory chessmen had toppled over. He restored it. Glancing about with satisfaction at his possessions, he said: "Pauli will pack everything beautifully. He'll put the stuff into store and keep an eye on it for me." He showed no great regret at leaving his possessions, but he was not a poor man. He could replace them.

Pauli came in to say he had found a taxi and taken the luggage down. When they left the room, he was standing by the open front door, sniffing. At the sight of Paul's grief, Inchcape's jaunty air failed and his face grew strained. He put his hands on Pauli's shoulders, seemed about to speak but moments passed before he said: "Goodbye, dear Pauli."

This was too much for Pauli, who collapsed to his knees with an agonised cry and, seizing Inchcape's hand, kissed it wildly.

Inchcape smiled again. He began edging towards the door, but Pauli shuffled after him, keeping a hold on him until they were in the outer passage. With a quick but gentle movement, Inchcape disengaged himself and sped down the stairs. Guy and Harriet followed, pursued by Pauli's heart-broken sobs.

On the long journey through the dark back-streets to the station, the three sat silent. Inchcape's head dropped, his face was sombre: then, suddenly, he looked up to say: "You haven't breathed a word to Pinkrose?"

They had not, though seeing Pinkrose sitting alone in the hotel they had felt guilty towards him. Had he approached them with any show of friendship, they would have had difficulty in maintaining the deception, but he avoided them, keeping "himself to himself".

"It would be intolerable to find the old buffer on the train," said Inchcape. He glanced at Guy. "Tomorrow, you can tell him I've been called away on urgent business. Don't tell him where I've gone. Say I'll be back, but if he wants to go himself encourage him. There's nothing he can do here. If he went to Athens, he might get a Greek boat to Alexandria."

"Where would he go from there?" Guy asked.

Inchcape chuckled. "Heaven knows. Let him organise his own return. He put plenty of pep into getting here." He smiled, reflecting on his friend, then said in a tone of the profoundest denegation: "He's not a peer, of course. Scottish title, I believe, though he's not got any sign of Scottish blood. A title like that's mere flim-flam. I wouldn't use it myself. And he inherited very little money. Even as a young man he was a queer fish. He simply came to Cambridge and never left it. It gave him all he ever wanted." Inchcape laughed to himself. "He loves to tell that old story of the don who was granted an interview with Napoleon. 'No doubt a remarkable fellow,' said the don afterwards, 'but anyone can see he's not a Cambridge man.' "

For some time after this Inchcape sat quietly shaking with amusement, perhaps at the anecdote, or perhaps at Pinkrose, but more likely, Harriet thought, at getting away and leaving Pinkrose here to fend for himself.

Three porters had to be employed to carry Inchcape's baggage to the train. Seeing Harriet watching the procession of suitcases, he explained: "I'm taking my summer clothing and a few valuables to leave in a safe place. One doesn't want to lose every stitch one's got."

The express stood in the station, but little activity surrounded it. Most of the carriages were empty. No one travelled for pleasure these days. The few passengers who stood about on the platform were lost in the echoing gloom. One group comprised the young English engineers from the telephone company. Guy, when he stopped to speak to them, learnt that they had been ordered, a few hours before, to quit the country. When they appealed to the Legation, they were advised to accept dismissal and go.

Inchcape, his sleeper secured, his luggage stowed away, stood at a corridor window. He smiled down on Guy and Harriet who, standing on the platform, uncertain whether they were expected to go or stay, could only say: "Well, have a good rest and enjoy yourself," then, after a pause: "Look after yourself."

"I'll put our case pretty forcibly when I get there," said Inchcape. "We demand a rise in pay and the right to abandon ship when we think it advisable, eh?"

There was a long pause. The atmosphere was dispirited. Perhaps it seemed to Inchcape there was something forlorn in the appearance of the two young people in front of him, for he said in a tone of self-justification: "You'll be all right. You're young."

"Does that make a difference?" Harriet asked.

"All the difference in the world. Before you're forty you never think of death: after forty you never think of anything else." He laughed, but as he gazed at them in the dingy light he seemed to Harriet pitiably aged and ill. "Besides," he said, "you'd be worse off in England."

Harriet said: "I'd rather be bombed with my own people than cut off here."

Inchcape gave a laugh. "You *think* you would."

Conversation lapsed again and Inchcape, glancing back through an open door which revealed his made-up berth, said: "Look, no point in hanging about. Dear knows when this train will take itself out. Everything's to pot these days. I feel a bit under the weather, so I'll say good-bye and get my head down." He reached out of the window and gave one hand to Harriet, the other to Guy, smiling his old sardonic smile while a single tear trickled down his discoloured, battered face: "Good-bye, good-bye. I'll be back before you have time to miss me." He pulled his hands free and, turning abruptly, entered the sleeper and shut the door.

Harriet put her hand into Guy's. As they wandered off through the cavernous dark of the station with its smells of carbon and steam, its desolating atmosphere of farewells, Harriet reflected that she herself would be gone in a day or two and Guy would be left alone.

27

RESTLESS IN UNEMPLOYMENT though he was, Guy was in no hurry to explain things to Pinkrose. He had intended to go to the Athénée Palace on Monday morning but delayed so long that luncheon was on the table and he decided to wait until evening.

As they were about to eat, the telephone rang. It was Dobson to say that Pinkrose had appeared at the Legation in a state of great alarm. That morning Galpin had seized on him in the hotel hall and insisted on telling him about the attack on Inchcape. He had gone at once to Inchcape's flat where he had been told by Pauli that his friend had left Rumania. In panic he had sped to the Legation and demanded that a plane be chartered immediately to fly him home.

"By the way," Dobson interrupted himself, "is that right? *Has* Inchcape taken himself off?"

"Yes."

"Why all this secrecy?" Dobson's tone was light, almost humorous, but there was an edge on it. Not waiting for an answer he talked rapidly on: "Well, my dear fellow, the noble lord is now your pigeon. He was over an hour here, wasting everyone's time, making ridiculous claims to special passages, etcetera. We just haven't time to cope. H.E. told him to fly to Persia or India, but he says he has no money. I suggested he might go to Athens, where he'd be out of the way of trouble and probably meet kindred spirits. Anyway, we've got him his exit visa. He's free to go whenever he likes. Meanwhile, be a good chap, keep him out of our way. Try and persuade him that, contrary to his belief, the entire Guardist movement is not, repeat *not*, directing its activities against his person." Dobson ended on a laugh, but rang off abruptly.

Guy sat down at the table, saying: "I'll go immediately after luncheon."

After luncheon he sat on. Knowing how acutely painful the coming interview would be for him, Harriet made no attempt to harry him. She was leaving next day and went into the bedroom to sort out the clothing she would take. After some minutes he followed her in, his face despondent, and said: "Perhaps you'd come with me. The fact you are still here might reassure him."

"All right, but I must first speak to Sasha."

She had bought Sasha a small cheap case to hold such clothing as Guy had given him. He wanted to take some of his drawings and, as these would have to be placed flat at the bottom of Harriet's portmanteau, she went to his room to tell him to sort them out. She found him curled like a kitten on the bed.

She had complained about the constant noise of the mouth-organ and now, his hands wrapped about it, he was playing almost without sound.

His possessions were neatly arranged on the table. The drawings were ready for her too pack.

She said: "What is that ridiculous tune you're playing?"

He took his lips from the mouth-organ to say: " 'Hey, Hey, Hey, Ionesculi'. Despina sings it."

She said, trying to speak sternly: "You know, when you get to Athens you'll have to start some serious study."

He smiled at her over the instrument, then put it back to his lips.

Though it was siesta-time when Guy and Harriet reached the hotel, the hall and vestibule were crowded. Again, as on the day of the arrival of the military mission, the hotel servants could not accommodate a half of those who had come in to drink their after-luncheon coffee.

Galpin, standing in the hall sourly surveying this assembly, told the Pringles that a rumour had gone round that a high-ranking German officer called Speidel was arriving that afternoon. "He's still young and handsome, so they say. Look as those bloody women! Like a lot of randy she-cats. And there's that bitch back again, on heat, as usual."

Princess Teodorescu had entered the hotel. She had returned to Bucharest relying, like the others of her class, on German in-fluence to protect her against the Iron Guard. It was said she had already found a lover among the young German officers, several of whom stood round her while she talked furiously, twitching her shoulders and making frenzied gestures at them. She was wearing a new leopard-skin coat. Was there any more repellent sight, Harriet wondered, than a silly, self-centred, greedy woman clad in the skin of a beast so much more splendid than herself.?

Hadjimoscos was of this party. Slipping about on his kid shoes, his plump little body that looked soft, as though stuffed with sawdust, he moved from one officer to another, talking earnestly, lifting his flat, pale Tartar face in rapture, occasionally placing his little white padded hand on a German sleeve. They were joined by a stout, flat-footed man who walked like a peregrine: a noted German financier brought here to advise on Rumania's disintegrating economy.

"But" – Galpin turned slowly and nodded towards the desk – "you've seen nothing yet. Look who's over there." The Pringles followed the direction of his gaze and saw that the scene was being closely watched by two keen, dog-faced fellows in the black uniform of the Gestapo.

"When did they arrive?" Guy blandly asked.

"No one knows. But they're not the only ones. There's dozens of them. You've heard about Wanda?"

"No," said the Pringles, feeling they should proceed to Pinkrose but willing enough to be detained.

"Ah!" Galpin jerked up his long, morose, dishonest face with an intimation of tragedy. "They've chucked her out, the bastards."

So that was another face gone from the English circle.

Pinkrose, when Guy knocked on his door, cried: "*Entrez, entrez*," in a high, agitated voice.

They found him on his knees, stuffing his clothing into his bag. He was wearing a flowered cotton kimono of a sort worn in Japan by tea-shop girls. He jerked his head round and, seeing the Pringles, seemed startled by their temerity, but he had nothing to say. He returned to his packing.

Guy attempted an explanation of Inchcape's departure. "He hopes to be back very shortly," he said.

Pinkrose appeared not to listen. Scrambling to his feet, he stripped off the kimono and pushed it in with the rest. He was wearing shirt, trousers and several woollen cardigans. He hastily got into his jacket, saying: "I'm catching the boat-train to Constanza." He went round, collecting the last of his possessions, keeping at a distance from the Pringles as though afraid they might seek to retard him. As he moved he said, breathlessly: "I take this badly, Pringle. I take it very badly. I shall not forget it. Inchcape has not heard the last of this, not by any means. His man *lied* to me. He repeatedly told me that Inchcape was ill in bed; and all the time he was plotting to slip away to safety – abandoning me, an invited guest, in a strange town where I was liable to be attacked by ruffians. Unforgiveable. I travelled several thousand miles to deliver an important lecture and . . ."

While he recounted again the details of his journey, emphasising its dangers and discomforts, he was ramming a great many small bottles and boxes into a portable medicine-chest.

"And you, Pringle," he said, giving Guy a malevolent glance, "*you* were a party to all this. I saw you in the hotel more than once. You did not choose to let me know what was going on. I had to learn from a stranger."

As Guy, listening with an air of miserable guilt, made no attempt to defend himself, Harriet broke in on Pinkrose to say: "Professor Inchcape did not want you to be alarmed. He gave definite orders that you must not be told anything until after he had gone."

Pinkrose, winding his scarves about his neck, drew his breath through his teeth, but made no other comment. A small threatening smile hung round his lips. After some moments he said: "The whole matter will be fully reported to head office. The board can judge. Meanwhile, I am forced to pay my own fare to Greece. I shall expect to be reimbursed; and I can only hope the Athens office will accord me the courtesy and consideration that has been so sadly lacking here."

The boat-train to Constanza left at half-past three. Pinkrose had barely time to catch it. That and the fact the Black Sea could be rough at this time of the year caused Guy to find his tongue. He said: "Why not wait until tomorrow? My wife is going to Athens by plane. Dobson is also going . . ."

"No, no," Pinkrose broke in impatiently, "I am looking forward to the sea journey. It will do me good." He picked up his greatcoat. As Guy stepped forward to hold it for him, he swung away with a look that suggested Guy's good-natured helpfulness was simply another indication of his duplicity.

A porter entered to collect the luggage. Pinkrose had ordered a taxicab, which now awaited him.

Harriet said: "Good-bye." Pinkrose shot her a glance, apparently not holding her culpable, and made a movement towards her which, given time, might have turned into a handshake – but he could not wait. Without a word to Guy he was gone.

The Pringles felt a sense of trespass at finding themselves alone in the room. Harriet put her arms round Guy's waist. "Darling, how can I go tomorrow and leave you here?"

"You're going to get me a job," he reminded her.

Her despondency lifted somewhat as, turning the bend in the stairs, they saw David down in the hall. He had gone "to the Delta" – whatever that might mean – when they went to Predeal and this was his first reappearance. There had been at the back of Harriet's mind a suspicion that he might not reappear at all. His covert trips at this time could too easily lead to disaster. Or he might, knowing the time was at hand here, have made his way over a frontier. But there he was, looking comfortable and confident as ever, and Harriet felt warmed by the sight of him. As Guy delightedly hurried down to greet him, David's small mouth curled at one corner in amusement at his friend's exuberance. He was about to sign the register and said: "I found, when I returned this morning, that the Minerva had given me up for lost. A member of the master race was occupying my room. My baggage had been put into the cellar. Fortunately, when I reached here, a room was just being vacated."

"Pinkrose's room, I suppose," Guy said and he described the attack on Inchcape and what he called "the flight of the professors".

Snuffling to himself at the picture of Pinkrose in the Japanese dressing-gown, David said: "I know several chaps who'd've paid to see that. Pinkrose owns one of the most magnificent houses in Cambridge, but no one ever sees inside it. He's practically a recluse. The sad thing about all this is that Inchcape is probably his only real friend."

When he heard that Clarence had also gone, David smiled indulgently. "I *liked* old Clarence," he said and gave a laugh of surprise at his own admission. He added: "I don't think any of us will be here much longer," and the Pringles, knowing he could not tell them any more, asked no questions.

As they moved together through the hall, David caught his breath, seeing for the first time the black Gestapo figures. He raised an eyebrow at Guy, but neither made any comment. They left the hotel with a sense of nothing to do but await an end. They did not want to separate.

David had to look in at the Legation and asked the Pringles to go with him.

Standing at the kerb, waiting for a *trăsură* to stop at the hotel, they watched a fleet of Guardist motor-cyclists in new leather jackets and fur caps. They passed uproariously, stern-faced and purposeful, as though on their way to an execution or an interrogation of treachery, but after circling the square at top speed, scattering the pedestrians and driving cars into the kerb, they disappeared whence they had come.

"Not a useful occupation," Harriet said, "but it must be great fun."

Waiting in the *trăsură* while David reported his return, Harriet held tightly to Guy's hand. He said to comfort her: "You heard what David said? I may be leaving here sooner than we think."

"Um." Harriet feared he might stay just too long and never leave at all; but she had ceased to plead with him, knowing he felt bound to see things to their conclusion, whatever the conclusion might be.

When David rejoined them, he said: "I have to meet someone, but not yet. Shall we drive up the Chaussée?"

The sun was low in the sky. They had put down the *trăsură* hood and they felt in their faces the keen little breeze that would sharpen through the coming weeks into the wind that brought the snow. The Chaussée had already an air of winter. The trees, parched by the fires of summer, were completely bare. The garden restaurants had packed up. The cafés had taken in awnings and parasols: some had closed down altogether. October was here and life had retired indoors.

David said: "There's a belief going round that Germany has important plans for Rumania, that she'll regain her position in the scheme of things." As he sniffed and snuffled, Guy asked: "What do you think?"

"I think the Germans will devour this place, ruthlessly. They're demanding conscripts now. Not a word about it in the papers, of course, but I'm told the Rumanian peasants are being herded into cattle-trucks and sent to train in Germany. Poor fellows, they go willingly because their officers tell them they're going to fight for England. They say: 'Tell us about these English. How do they look in the face?' "

Harriet said: "Do they actually think the Germans are British?"

"They don't think. When the times comes, they'll be told: 'This is the enemy. Fight!' and they will fight and die."

They were now in open country and could see the Snagov woods like a plum-coloured haze in the distance. The Snagov lake

reflected a brazen sky. Here and there a window flamed, but the
fields, flat and empty, had a dejected air in the rich autumnal
light.

David said: "I have to meet this fellow at the Golf Club."

"The Golf Club!"

David laughed. "It's by way of being a secret meeting. That's
why the Golf Club was chosen."

"I've never seen the Club," Harriet said.

"Come and see it now. You may not get another chance."

The Club, that stood behind a zareba of evergreens, had been
built in the twenties by prospering English business men. With
remarkable artistry they had, in this climate of extremes, reproduced the dark brick, moss-patched lawns and dank paths of a
late nineteenth-century English mansion. The front door stood
open. The house appeared to be deserted. Guy, Harriet and David
passed through to the sitting-room which, with two vast French
windows opening on to the golf course, extended across the back
of the house. It was filled with chairs covered in faded chintz.
Small tables were stacked with tattered copies of English journals.

Outside the light was changing. The sun had sunk behind trees
so the whole of the green was in shadow. A smell of cold, damp
earth entered with the air through the open glass doors. From
somewhere upstairs came the brr-brr of an unanswered telephone.

The Pringles did not ask whom David had come to meet, but
he said: "I see no cause for secrecy. This fellow who's coming is
the chairman of a new advisory committee set up in Cairo. He's
been flown here full of zeal, no doubt imagining even at this late
hour something can be done. So remote is diplomacy from reality,
H.E. still doesn't know quite what went wrong, so he's detailed
me to try and explain things." Two men had walked around the
side of the house. "There they are, now," David said and went out
to join them.

One man was Wheeler, a senior member of the Legation, whom
the Pringles had met at parties; the other was a stranger, handsome, of middle height, in early middle age, wearing a dark
greatcoat and bowler-hat and carrying a rolled umbrella.

Seeing David, who approached them confidently but with a
certain deference, being so much their junior, the two men paused.
When he joined them, they began pacing together, moving slowly
fifty yards or so in one direction, then turning and moving back

again. The grass, green after the first rain, luminous in the uncertain light, exuded a mist that obscured the distant bushes and drifted about the legs of the men as they strolled about.

Harriet remembered the period of the fall of France when she had sat day after day with other English people in the garden of the Athénée Palace which she had not entered since. Now, in another time of stress, she was in the Golf Club, which she had never visited before and would probably never visit again. She turned away from the window, saying: "What shall we do?" She felt that she and Guy were like people left in an empty world. Everything was theirs. They could do what they liked, but there was nothing to do. She began wandering about, picking up the magazines and putting them down again. At one end of the room there was a bar, shut-up and padlocked. On the walls were antlers, horns and many other second-hand trophies of the chase. There were also crossed spears and shields taken from some African tribe.

She said: "Is this what they imagined home was like?"

Guy picked up a putter which had been left in a corner and said: "Let's go outside."

They walked to the first green. Standing at an unobtrusive distance from the three in conference, Guy began to address an imaginary ball. Harriet had nothing to do but watch.

The air was full of the sissing of grasshoppers. The sun had set and twilight was beginning to sift down when the Pringles noticed the chairman, with David and Wheeler at his heels, making towards them, his expression amused. Not waiting to be introduced, he spoke to Guy with the easy affability of a man conditioned to importance: "I thought you were killing snakes."

Guy blushed slightly, laughing. "No, just killing time."

The chairman seemed delighted by this simple wit and glanced at Wheeler who, attempting to reflect the chairman's good humour, looked at Guy as though he had acquired new interest and said: "This is Guy Pringle. He was a lecturer at the University here," letting the past tense make its own comment.

"Ah!" the chairman said with a sympathetic nod.

Harriet was introduced. The chairman, whose name was Sir Brian Love, put his umbrella behind him and, leaning on it, raised his face, which was smooth, beautifully shaven and pink with good eating, and sniffed the damp and woody air of evening. "Very pleasant here," he said, imparting an atmosphere of well-being. Wheeler, a thin man, his thin mouth drooping between folded cheeks, waited, fidgeting with a car-key on a ring.

The three young people also waited, expecting dismissal, but Sir Brian seemed in no hurry to leave the Club. "Smells like England," he said. "Hot as hell in Cairo. No sign of autumn there. I doubt whether they *have* an autumn." He laughed and said to Wheeler: "Couldn't we all go somewhere and have a drink?"

Wheeler looked startled, then, worried by this suggestion, said: "There's really no time, Sir Brian. H.E. dines at seven, and as you're going back tonight . . ."

Sir Brian nodded, but still showed no inclination to move. He looked up at the dark Club windows. "Not much going on here," he said.

"Practically no members left," said Wheeler.

"Still, it's delightful after the Middle East."

"Were you in England recently, sir?" Guy asked.

"Less than a month ago. You'd find it much changed, I think. Changed for the better, I mean."

While Wheeler, with knotted brows, concentrated on the task of getting the car-key off the ring, Sir Brian talked in a leisurely way of a new sense of comradeship which he said was breaking down class-consciousness in England and drawing people together "Your secretary calls you 'Brian' and the liftman says: 'We're all in it together.' I like it. I like it very much." Once or twice, while talking, he gave a slightly mischievous side-glance at Wheeler, so the others warmed to him, feeling he was one of them and on their side against the established prejudices of the Legation.

Wheeler, not listening, gave a sigh. The key had come off the ring. He gazed at it, perplexed, then set himself the more difficult task of getting it on again.

"After the war we shall see a new world," Sir Brian said and smiled at the three young people, each of whom watched him with rapt, nostalgic gaze. "A classless world, I should like to think."

Harriet thought how odd it was to be standing in this melancholy light, listening to this important person who had flown in that afternoon and would fly out again that night – an unreal visitant to a situation that must seem unreal to him. Yet, real or not, the other men would be left to the risk of imprisonment, torture and death.

Sir Brian suddenly interrupted his talk about England to say:

"So it's all over here, eh? Geography defeated us. The dice were loaded against us. No one to blame. These things can't be helped."

His tone was conclusive: he stood upright, preparing to depart.

David moved forward. "In my opinion," he said, "this could have been helped."

"Indeed!" The chairman paused in surprise.

"We lost this country months ago through a damn-fool policy of supporting Carol at no matter what cost to the rest of the community. The better elements here refused to serve under such a rule. Maniu and the other liberals would have been with us, but we had no use for them. We kept a pack of scoundrels in power. No wonder the country was divided against itself."

"Ah!" Sir Brian was noncommittal: a just man, he was prepared to hear all sides. "And what are the facts, as you see them?"

Wheeler rubbed his brow in a despairing way.

Speaking authoritatively, all diffidence gone now, David said: "A united Rumania – a Rumania, that is, who'd won the loyalty of her minorities by treating them fairly – could have stood up to Hungarian demands. She might even have stood up to Russia. If she'd remained firm, Yugoslavia and Greece would have joined with her; perhaps Bulgaria, too. A Balkan *entente!* Not much perhaps, but not to be sneezed at. With the country solid, enjoying a reasonable internal policy, the Iron Guard could never have regained itself. It could never have risen to power in this way."

Sir Brian, hands together on his umbrella-handle as on a gun-butt, stood upright, head bowed at the neck in an attitude of mourning.

Wheeler cleared his throat, preparing to arrest this indictment, but David was not easily arrested. "And," he persisted, "there were the peasants – a formidable force, if we'd chosen to organise them. They could have been trained to revolt at any suggestion of German infiltration. And, I can tell you, the Germans don't want trouble on this front. They would not attempt to hold down an unwilling Rumania. As it is, the country has fallen to pieces, the Iron Guard is in power and the Germans have been invited to walk in at their convenience. In short, our policy has played straight into enemy hands."

Sir Brian jerked up his head. He briskly asked: "So it's now too late?"

"Too late," David agreed.

The chairman gave Wheeler a glance, no longer mischievous. He had asked for facts but clearly felt the facts were getting out of hand. Wheeler, too, was losing patience. "I really think . . ." he began.

"Dear me, yes." Sir Brian shot out his hand to David, to Guy to Harriet, concluding the discussion. "It's all been very interesting. Very interesting, indeed!" The charm was well sustained, but something had gone wrong with it. He led the way round the side of the house, the others followed. He was talking, affable again, but his affability was for Wheeler.

It was almost dark. There was no sign of light or life about the house, but the front door still stood open and through it Harriet glimpsed the white jacket of a servant whose keys clinked in his hand. He was waiting to lock up when they, the last of the British, had taken their departure.

While Wheeler opened his car-door, Sir Brian looked back at the three young people and lifted his umbrella-handle to his hat-brim before getting into the car. He did not smile. Wheeler said nothing at all but slammed the door furiously and made off. Watching the red tail-light draw away, Guy said: "We're all in it together, are we? The *bastard!*"

David remained indulgent. "The duplicity of office! And Wheeler is a prize ass. He once said to me: 'If diplomacy were as simple as it appears to the outsider, my dear Boyd, we'd never have wars at all.' "

In reaction from a sense of reprimand that touched on their youth, the three, on their way back to the town, laughed uproariously together while the wind blew coldly at them across the dark deserted *grădinăs*. They were glad to reach the lighted streets.

As they turned into the square, Harriet looked across at the large, brilliant window on the corner of the Boulevard Breteanu and saw that it was empty. The Hispano, that for two months had stood there like a monument, stood there no longer. Guy ordered the *trăsură* to stop outside the show-room and went in to inquire. He learnt that the car had been bought by a German officer who had paid the full sixty thousand *lei* without question, the rate of the Reichsmark being such that the cost of the Hispano was less than the cost in Germany of a toy. The money was being sent to Mr. Dobson at the British Legation.

Where were they going to eat? David asked. Harriet wanted to take her farewell dinner at Cina's or Capşa's. They decided to drive to Capşa's.

The main restaurants were always refurbished when they returned indoors for the winter months. There was about them all a sense of a new season that held its own excitements. After the vacancy of the streets, Capşa's interior, with its red plush and gilt and vast crystal chandeliers, seemed dazzling to the three entering, chilly, from the open *trăsură*.

Food now was not only meagre, it was often bad, as though shortage had led to hoarding and hoarding to decay. But Capsa's, much patronised by the German community, had kept a certain standard. The better cuts of meat were, of course, put aside for high-ranking Germans and their guests, but the open menu usually offered chicken or rabbit, hare in season, and even caviare of a sort. Later in the evening the place would be crowded, but now there were a good many vacant tables.

Seated by the door, accompanied by two of the young officers of the mission, were Princess Mimi and Princess Lulie. Their faces went blank at the sight of the English. As the three advanced, there was a small stir in the room. The head waiter intercepted them with a look of surprised inquiry as though it were possible they wanted something other than food.

Speaking Rumanian, David asked for a table. The head waiter replied: "*Es tut mir leid. Wir haben keinen Platz.*"

David protested in English: "But half the tables are unoccupied."

The other, from past habit, replied in the same language: "All are booked. In these times it is necessary to book."

David opened his mouth to argue, but Harriet said: "The food here is deplorable, anyway. Let's go to Cina's." She turned with the hauteur of the beset and, as she passed the princesses, she caught the eye of one of the young Germans who were watching her with sympathetic amusement.

"Well, to Cina's then," said David when they were on the pavement again.

"No," said Harriet, near tears. "We'll only be turned out again. Let us go somewhere where we're not known."

They decided on the Polişinel, a restaurant dating back to boyar days, once very fashionable, where Guy and David had often eaten when Guy was a batchelor. They found another *trăsură* and drove down to the Dâmboviţa.

The Polişinel, built when land was cheap and plentiful, surrounded a large garden site. They went to the main room which, lit by a few brownish bulbs, stretched away into acres of shadow. Only the proprietor was there, dining with his family. At the sight of the foreign visitors, he rose, delighted, and bawled importantly for the waiter. He probably thought they were Germans, but the English, thus welcomed and made to feel at home, forgot their earlier experience.

An old waiter fussed over them, placing them at a window table which overlooked the garden, then hurried to switch on more lights. He brought a large, dirty menu, hand-written in purple ink, and whispered: "*Friptură*, eh?" It was not a meatless day, but he spoke as though suggesting a forbidden pleasure and the three gratefully agreed to it.

The proprietor bawled again and in trailed a dilapidated gipsy orchestra which, seeing the quality of the company, struck up with spirit.

"Oh, Lord!" said David. "They think we're rich."

"We are by their standards," said Guy.

David pulled his chair round so his back was to the smiling players and did his best to talk above the din: "There's a story going round. Horia Sima and his boys went to the Holy Synod and demanded that Codreanu should be made a saint. The head of the Synod said: 'My son, it takes two hundred years to make a saint. When that time has elapsed, return and we will discuss it again.' "

Now that attention had been deflected from the foreigners and their wealth, David settled down happily forgetful of the music. The two men talked about Russia. Neither had visited this country to which they looked for the regeneration of the world, but the previous spring, when Soviet troops were rumoured to be massing for an invasion of Bessarabia, David had reached the Russian frontier. He had stood beside the Dniester and looked across to where there were a few cottages. The only sign of life was an old peasant woman working in her garden.

That he should tell them even as much as this of his travels in Rumania was a sign that their life here was over and his travels at an end.

"Was it possible to cross into Russia?" Harriet asked.

"No, there was no boat or bridge, no means of crossing." There was nothing but the water, grey with cold, and ruffled by the bitter wind: and beyond the water league upon league of snow-patched, yellow earth stretching into infinite distance.

Harriet told them about the Jewish frontier village which Sasha had described to her. She said: "Were all the Bessarabians as wretched as that?"

"Perhaps not," said David, "but they were wretched enough. The majority of them welcomed the Russians. The Rumanians have never learnt to rule by persuasion rather than force. They deserved to lose their minorities: not that their own people get much better treatment. The peasants have always been robbed. Why should they want to work when everything they make is taken from them? They've always been fleeced by the tax-collector or the money-lender, their own army or some other army. Now they feed the Germans. They've been kept in the position of serfs, yet, given the opportunity, I believe they would prove intelligent, creative and hard-working. In my opinion, the best thing that could happen to this country is the thing they dread most – to be overrun by Russia and forced to adopt the Soviet social structure and economy."

Guy smiled at a prospect that seemed to him too good to be true. "Will that day ever come?"

"Perhaps sooner than you think. The Rumanians imagine that with German support they can get back Bessarabia. If they try, the result could be a Russian occupation of Rumania, and perhaps of the whole of Eastern Europe."

A flower-girl came round taking from her basket small bunches of marigolds and pom-pom dahlias which she placed on the tables, then stood at a respectful distance while the diners decided to buy or not. Guy gave her what she had asked – a small sum – but she looked surprised. She had done no more than mention a point from which the bargaining might begin.

Sniffing the bitter, pungent smell of the marigolds, Harriet looked out at the garden, which was pebbled and much cluttered with stone statues. There were several old trees that had reached up beyond the surrounding buildings and now, too tall for their strength, bent and soughed in the wind. On the opposite side of the garden were the once famous *salons particuliers*, all the windows lit. In some the curtains were drawn as though the rooms were in use. In others the curtains were looped back with heavy cords so it was possible to see gilt and white walls and chandeliers with broken bulbs and lustres missing. Through the nearest window

Harriet could see a table ready laid for two and a sofa covered in green satin – a pale, water-lily green, probably very grimy. The rooms had not changed in fifty years and some people said they had not been cleaned either. Harriet was touched to see, as everything broke up about them, this seedy grandeur still limping along.

Noticing that she was not listening to their talk, Guy said: "She does not attach much importance to passing events."

Harriet laughed. "You have only to let them pass and they lose their importance."

"You may pass with them, of course," David said with a wry, sombre smile.

The food was slow in arriving. They had been served with soup. Some twenty minutes passed before the waiter placed their knives and forks, then, at last, came the *friptură*.

"In its day," David said, "this restaurant served the best steaks in Europe."

"What have we got now, do you think?" Guy asked.

David sniggered. "Apparently some *trăsură* has lost its horse."

The men remembered the spring and early summer of the previous year, when they had often come to the Polişinel garden and talked of the war that overhung them all. Diners would still be arriving at midnight and would remain until the first cream of the dawn showed through the trees. While there was one customer left, the musicians would play a series of little tunes, maudlin, banal, pretty, but, in deference to the hour, they played more and more softly, often breaking off in the middle of a phrase and starting up with something else, or just plucking a note here and there, a token of music, patiently awaiting their reward.

"How shall we reward them now?" Guy asked. He took out a thousand-*lei* note.

Harriet and David looked askance at this extravagance, but he handed it over. "For the pleasures that are past," he said.

When they reached the Pringles' flat, it was little more than eleven o'clock and David agreed to come in for a final drink. The hall was in darkness. The porter had been conscripted long ago and never replaced. They found the lift out of order.

There seemed to Harriet something odd about the house – perhaps the lack of sound. Rumanians sat up late. Usually on the stairs voices and music could be heard until the early hours of the morning; now there were no voices and no music. The three walked up from one dark landing to another, hearing nothing but their own footsteps. On the eighth floor they saw a light falling obliquely from above.

Harriet said: "It comes from our flat. Our front door is open."

They stopped and listened. The silence was complete. After some moments Guy began moving soundlessly up the last flight of stairs with David behind him. Harriet paused, unnerved by the stillness and the sight of the front door lying wide open. No sound of life came from within. Cautiously she went up a step or two so she could see past the two men in the hall. The sitting-room door stood ajar. The lights were on within.

Hearing her step on the stair, Guy whispered: "Wait." He gave a push to the sitting-room door: it fell open. Nothing moved inside.

David said: "No need to ask what's happened here."

Guy came out to tell Harriet: "We've been raided."

"Sasha and Despina? Where can they be?"

"They must be hiding somewhere."

They went through the flat, walking among a litter of papers, books, clothing and broken glass. Drawers had been emptied out, beds stripped, books thrown from shelves, pictures smashed, carpets ripped from the floor. They realised this had been done not in a frenzy of destruction but in a systematic search. The breakages and the disorder were incidental. And for what had they been searching? For something that could be hidden in a drawer or under a mattress – so not for Sasha. But perhaps it was Sasha they had found.

Anyway, there was no sign of him. His room, like the rest of the flat, was in confusion.

Guy led the way into the kitchen where the door on to the fire-escape stood open. Here drawers had been emptied, canisters of tea, coffee and dried foods had been turned out in a heap on the floor.

Harriet looked into Despina's room. It was empty. Her possessions were gone.

They went out on to the fire-escape. The well at the back of the house, on to which the kitchens opened, was usually, even at this hour, in an uproar of squabbling and shouting. Tonight all the doors, except their own door, were shut. There were no lights. The kitchens appeared to be deserted.

Harriet went up the ladder to the roof. The doors to the servants' huts were closed. Harriet pulled open that which had been used by Sasha. There was nothing inside. She called: "Sasha! Despina!" No one answered.

They returned to Sasha's room. The bed-covers were on the floor and, as Harriet piled them back on to the bed, the mouth-organ fell from among them. She handed it to Guy as proof that he had been taken, and forcibly. Under the bed-covers was the forged passport, torn in half – derisively, it seemed.

Remembering her childhood pets whose deaths had broken her heart, she said: "They'll murder him, of course."

"No," Guy said. "Why should they! I'll go to the Legation in the morning. They'll make some inquiries. Don't worry. We won't let it rest."

Harriet shook her head, unable to speak. She knew there was nothing anyone could do. The Rumanian authorities had little enough power against the Iron Guard. The British Legation had none at all. In any case, Sasha was an army deserter. His arrest was legal, and he was without rights.

David said: "I don't think we should stay here. They're quite likely to come back."

He kept watch on the landing while Harriet rapidly packed her suitcase. Guy put some shirts and underwear into his rucksack then went into the sitting-room and began picking up his books. Some of them had been trampled on and were spine-broken with the marks of heels and footprints on the pages. Recognising the savagery against which he had declared himself, he told himself: "The beast has broken in." He was thankful that Harriet was going next day. After that anything might happen.

He managed to fit a couple of dozen books into the rucksack and put six more into his pockets. He picked up a last one and put it under his arm. It contained the sonnets of Shakespeare.

Before they left the flat, they shut the back door and switched off the lights. They had no time to right the disorder. They left it as they had found it. They reached the street with a sense of having made an escape.

"I felt pretty nervous in there." David said.

"God," said Guy, "I never felt so frightened in my life before."

Harriet remained silent until they were in the square, then she said: "I can't leave tomorrow. And now there's no reason why I should."

"Oh, you must go," said Guy. "You have to find me a job. If

you stayed, you couldn't do anything. And Dobson is expecting you at the airport."

David's room contained two beds: Suddenly exhausted from shock, Harriet threw herself on one of them and was asleep in a moment. The men, too alert to sleep, sat up most of the night, talking, drinking and playing chess.

28

WHEN SHE AWOKE NEXT MORNING and remembered what had occurred, Harriet was surprised that she felt nothing. She prepared for her departure, no longer caring whether she went or stayed.

David had been called to the Legation and said good-bye to Harriet in the vestibule. As she and Guy left the hotel, they saw Galpin packing luggage into his car. Guy asked him if he were leaving.

Galpin shook his head, but said: "Something's in the wind. It's my hunch the balloon's going up."

"You think it's a matter of days?"

"It's a matter of hours. Anyway, I'm prepared. I'll give you a lift if you like."

"Harriet's off to Athens this morning. I have to stay."

"Stay? What for? A bullet in the back of the neck?"

A rare and peculiar look of obstinacy came over Guy's face. "I've a job to do," he said.

"Well." Galpin moved away, twisting himself into his raincoat as he went. "One person taking no risks is yours truly." He hurried back to the hotel.

Dobson was already on the airfield when the Pringles arrived. The morning was chilly and he was wearing an overcoat with an astrakhan collar. Having been told that Harriet would be accompanied by one of Guy's students, he asked: "Where's your young friend?"

Guy told him what had happened. The student was Sasha Drucker – no point now in hiding that fact. Guy said he intended reporting the matter to the Legation and enlisting the help of Fitzsimon who had played Troilus in his production.

Dobson listened with an expression, sympathetic but quizzical, which seemed to ask: What did Guy hope for? If the British Legation could no longer protect its own nationals, what could it do for this discredited Jewish youth who had disappeared into chaos? He said: "All over Europe there are people like Sasha

Drucker . . ." He made a gesture of despair at the measureless suffering which in their lifetime had become a commonplace.

Guy glanced at Harriet, saying: "I am sure Fitzsimon will do what he can."

Harriet looked away. Believing he was done for, she wanted to turn her back on everything to do with Sasha. She said: "I think we should take our seats."

Guy, troubled by her lack of emotion, said: "Cable me when you arrive."

"Of course." She gave her attention to the airport officials, one of whom went off with her passport. She protested and was told it would be returned to her on the plane.

When Guy put his arms round her to kiss her good-bye, her main thought was to get the parting over. Dobson took her arm, sweeping her through the last corroding moments by making light of the journey before them. "I always enjoy this little hop over the Balkans," he said.

The plane was about to leave when an official entered and, saluting her, presented her with her passport. The doors were closed, the plane slid off. As they rose, Harriet looked down and, glimpsing the solitary figure of Guy, who was watching after her, was stabbed by the thought: "I may never see him again." Immediately she wanted to return and fling herself upon him. Instead, she opened her passport and saw the word "*anulat*" stamped across her re-entry visa. She said in dismay: "They've cancelled my visa." Her indifference was shattered. Suddenly in panic at the reality of her departure, she said: "But I must come back. They can't keep me from my husband."

Dobson was reassuring: "You can get a visa in Athens. The Rumanian consul is a charming old boy. He'll do anything for a lady," and he went on to talk of the Danube, which had appeared below, a broad ribbon with river-craft and strings of oil barges black on its silver surface: "Did you know, there are maps dating back to 400 B.C. which show the Danube rising in the Pyrenees?"

"But surely it doesn't rise in the Pyrenees?"

Dobson laughed, so delighted by her ignorance that she began to feel at ease. She was grateful for his company. Before the war, when she had travelled about alone, she had enjoyed her own independence. Now she wanted to cling to Dobson as to a vestige of her normal life with Guy. She buoyed herself with the thought that she was on a mission. She had to find a job for Guy and a refuge for them both. She began to think of Bella, who would be the only English woman in Bucharest when her English friends departed. She spoke of this to Dobson, who smiled without concern and said: "I told Bella the Legation would take her out if we have to go, but she showed no interest."

"You could not expect her to leave Nikko."

"Oh, we would take Nikko, too. They both speak several languages. We could make good use of them." Dobson gave a laugh in which there was a hint of annoyance. "The truth is, she thinks she'll be a jolly sight more comfortable where she is."

Across the frontier, there was nothing to be seen but a fleece of white cloud through which the hill-tips broke, dark blue, like islands. As the morning advanced, the cloud dissolved to reveal the sun-dried Balkan uplands. Several times the plane, caught in an air-pocket, dropped steeply and there came, detailed, into view, stones, crevices and alpine flowers.

Sofia appeared amid its hills, a small town, grey beneath a grey sky. It seemed to be the destination of most of the passengers. "I wish I were staying here," said Harriet.

Dobson smiled at her absurdity. "Athens is delightful," he said. "You'll meet the most charming people." Preparing to leave her, he saw no reason at all why she should not be happy to journey on alone.

When the plane landed, Harriet walked with Dobson across the airfield to the barrier. A chauffeur awaited him and as he handed over his luggage, Harriet glanced back and saw that her suitcase had been put out on the grass. Her plane was taxi-ing across the field.

She gave a cry and said: "They're going without me."

"Surely not," Dobson said, but the plane was already rising from the ground. He spoke to the Bulgarian chauffeur who went to the customs-shed and came back with the information that the Rumanian plane had announced it would go no farther. Passengers for Athens must proceed on the German Lufthansa.

"But why?" Harriet was alarmed, remembering that Galpin had said: "When trouble starts, the air-service is the first thing to stop." She asked: "What has happened?" but there was no one who could tell her.

Dobson said: "Probably some rumour has scared them. You know what the Rumanians are like."

Harriet said: "I can't go on the Lufthansa." She was genuinely afraid. A story going round Bucharest described how some British businessmen in Turkey travelling on the Lufthansa, contrary to protocol, had been taken not to Sofia but to Vienna, where they had been arrested and interned.

Dobson smiled at her fears. "For myself, I'd feel safer on the Lufthansa than on any Rumanian plane."

"But it's forbidden."

"Only in a general way. You won't be allowed past the barrier here: you can't return to Bucharest: so you have no choice but to travel in the transport available."

The large Lufthansa stood on the airfield with a German official at the steps. Harriet felt sick at the sight of it. Stricken by her own plight, she appealed to Dobson: "Please wait with me until I go."

He said: "I'm afraid I can't. The Minister's expecting me for luncheon."

Near tears, she pleaded: "It's only about twenty minutes."

"I'm sorry." Dobson made a murmur of regret. He had lost his lightness of manner and she felt something inflexible beneath the reverence with which he said: "I cannot keep the Minister waiting."

After Dobson had been driven away, Harriet sat for a while on the bench by the shed and gazed at the German plane. Passengers were beginning to board it and she knew there was no purpose in delay. As Dobson had pointed out, she could neither stay here nor return whence she had come. She knew now what it was like to be a stateless person without a home.

Five men were filing up the steps of the plane, all, it seemed to her, inimical. Immediately in front of her was a little old man pulling on a string a toy dog, a money-box of sorts. He glanced back at her with a smile and as she noted his straggle of grey-yellow hair, his snub pink face, his wet blue eyes, she thought he looked as sinister as the rest. However, when she reached the official at the step, he produced a British passport and his aspect changed for her. Looking over his shoulder, she read that he was a retired consul called Liversage, domiciled in Sofia, born in 1865. The Germans treated the two British nationals with frigid courtesy. Harriet was thankful for the presence of this old man and his toy dog.

As they entered the plane, he stepped aside to let her choose her seat, and when she sat down, sat down beside her. He took the toy dog on his knee and, patting its worn hide, explained: "I collect for hospitals. Have collected hundreds of pounds, y'know. Thousands in fact. Been collecting for over fifty years."

The journey no longer frightened her. She asked herself, was it likely they would divert the plane in order to capture one young English woman and a man of seventy-five?

As they flew over the mountains, Mr. Liversage talked continually, pausing only to receive the answer to some question he had asked. Where was she coming from? Where going? What was she doing in this part of the world?

"Is your husband a 'varsity man?" he asked. He spoke pleasantly, but the question was clearly important to him. Her answer would place her. She wondered, would a provincial university be described as a " 'varsity"? She decided to say: "Yes," and Mr. Liversage seemed content.

Near the Bulgarian frontier, the sky began to clear. Over Macedonia, the plane suddenly emerged into brilliance, coming almost immediately into sight of the Ægean that sifted its peacock blues and greens against the golden shore of Thrace. They passed, almost at eye-level, a mountain like an inverted bucket; but before she could comment on it Mr. Liversage had talked them past it. While she looked below, seeing the Sporades fringed purple with weed, lying in shallows of jade and turquoise, Mr. Liversage talked of his life in Sofia where he had "a nice little place, nice little garden: lived very happily". But he had been advised to leave. Bulgaria, too, was threatened by the war that crept east like a grey lava to overwhelm them all.

"So here we are!" he said, his old hand with its loose, liver-spotted skin, patting the dog's rump. "Going to Athens. Probably settle down there. Bit of a lark, eh?"

Perhaps it was. Harriet smiled for the first time since she had entered the ravaged flat the night before. The memory had begun to retreat as they flew out of the Balkan world, leaving behind all intimations of autumn, returning into summer. Everything below was parched to a golden-pink. The sun, pouring in through the windows, grew steadily fiercer as the day advanced.

Throughout the journey, which lasted until evening, Mr. Liversage held his dog on his knee. He had brought a packet of sandwiches, which he shared with Harriet. Sometimes, as he talked, his hands were tensed about the dog so his knuckles shone, but his manner, matter-of-fact and cheerful, suggested it was for him an everyday occurrence to be uprooted in this way and no cause for complaint. The plane flew due south, showing no inclination to turn from its course. Indeed, Harriet realised, they were already over Athens.

"We will meet again," said Mr. Liversage as they began to descend.

Seeing the marble façades and the surrounding hills luminous in the rose-violet light of evening, she was thankful to come to rest in so beautiful a place.

29

WHEN, AFTER LUNCHEON NEXT DAY, Harriet came upon Yakimov, she felt jolted.

She had been wandering about the unfamiliar streets in a transport of release from all she had left behind. The previous evening she had gone to the cinema where the news-film had shown not the inexorable might of the German panzer divisions, but a handful of British sappers planting a mine among scrubby bushes somewhere in North Africa. At the back of her mind was the determination to return to Bucharest, but meanwhile there was the solace of this new world where to be English was to be welcome.

Yakimov, perched like a grasshopper on an old-fashioned bicycle, interrupted a dream, reminding her of the past. He leapt from the machine at the sight of her and came running downhill crying: "Dear girl! But this is wonderful! What news of the Hispano?"

"It has been sold."

"*No!*" He fetched up breathlessly beside her and began excitedly mopping his face. "Just when your poor old Yaki was asking himself where he could get a bit of the ready! What did she fetch?"

"Sixty thousand."

"*Dear girl!*" His large, pale, shallow eyes seemed to brim their sockets in delight, so she had not the heart to tell him that his sixty thousand was now worth less than ten pounds.

He was wearing his tussore suit and his Indian yellow shirt. The dark patches beneath his arm-pits had become darker and now had an edging of salt crystals. A leather strap over his shoulder held a leather satchel filled with roneoed sheets. She asked what he was doing, bicycling in the heat of the early afternoon.

"Got to get these delivered," he said: "news-sheets put out by the Information Office. Important job. They roped me in as soon as I arrived. Probably heard I'd been a war correspondent. Couldn't refuse. Had to do m'bit. Well . . ." He prepared to remount, holding the bicycle away from him as though it were not only unmanageable but vicious. "May say, you've got out just in time."

She caught his arm. "Has something happened?"

"Well, there's this rumour of a German occupation."

"But Guy is still in Bucharest."

Yakimov, one foot on the upraised pedal, blinked at her, disconcerted, then said: "I wouldn't worry, dear girl. You know what these rumours are." He gained his seat and, trembling forward, attempted his baby wave. "We'll meet again," he said. "I'm always at Zonar's."

Harriet stood in the road, looking after him. It was some minutes before all her old disquiet immersed her and she wondered how, in this strange place, where even the alphabet was unknown to her, she was to discover what was happening. Her hotel was small, staid and cheap, a resort of English residents. Someone there might be able to tell her something.

In the resident's sitting-room, four women sat, each in her separate corner. The gaunt one drinking tea could only be English, Harriet decided and, usually diffident with strangers, she addressed her now without apology or excuse: "Can you tell me, please? Is there any news about Rumania?"

The woman looked startled, then reproving of Harriet's anxious informality. There was a pause before she replied: "As a matter of fact, we have just been listening to the news. The Germans have occupied Rumania."

Clearly it was a matter of no concern to these women. Feeling that she alone knew the reality behind this announcement, Harriet burst out: "My husband is there," and she remembered how she had thought she might never see him again.

The woman, to whom she had spoken, said: "He'll be put into a prison-camp. You'll have him back after the war. My husband is dead," and having administered this rough comfort, she poured herself another cup of tea.

Harriet went to the hall and asked the clerk to direct her to the British Legation. She made her way through the deserted streets in the afternoon dazzle of salt-white walls, and found that at that hour no one was in the Legation but a Maltese porter. She told him her story, saying: "There's no knowing what the Germans may do to my husband. He's on a list of people wanted by the Gestapo." She pressed her hands over her eyes and choked in anguish, feeling an appalled remorse that she had left him without reflecting on what she might be leaving him to.

The porter, kindly and willing to help, said: "Perhaps nothing has happened at all. You know how these stories get around. I'll tell you what I'll do, I'll telephone Bucharest. I'll get through to the Legation and ask for news. I'll ask particularly about your husband."

"How long will it take?"

"An hour, perhaps two hours. Have tea at a café. Go for a walk. And when you come back, I think there will be good news."

But when she returned there was no news. The porter had been unable to contact Bucharest. "They've brought down 'the blanket'," he said, keeping up a show of optimism, but she could feel his uncertainty. This isolating "blanket" was proof that something had happened or was about to happen inside the country. He promised to try again, and again she set out to wear away time by walking first in one direction, then in another.

As evening fell, she was back at the Legation. The porter could only shake his head. "Later," he said, "I try again."

Too tired to walk farther, Harriet sat on a bench in the chancellery hall and watched people come and go. The staff had returned and the porter had duties to which to attend. No one spoke to her and she was reluctant to speak to anyone. She could do no good by pestering busy officials. If there were news, the porter would bring it to her. Some time after dark, he came out of his room and looked at her. Embarrassed now because he could do nothing for her, he said: "Better go home. Come back in the morning. Perhaps tonight we can get through."

"Is someone here at night?"

"There is always someone here."

"Then I can come back later?"

"If you wish. You might try about eleven o'clock."

Forced into the street again, she longed to confide her misery and could think only of Yakimov. Suddenly, she saw him as a friend – an old friend. Unlike the women at the hotel, he knew Guy and would sympathise with her dismay.

She ran down the hill to the city's centre. In the main road she set out to search the cafés, not knowing one from the other. Earlier in the day, people had been sitting out on the pavements, but the evening had become chilly. The chairs were empty. She went into one café after another, hurrying round them, becoming almost frenzied in her search. By the time she came on Yakimov she was trembling in a distress that was near despair.

He rose, shocked by her appearance, and said: "Dear girl, whatever is the matter?"

She tried to speak, but, fearful of bursting into tears, she could only shake her head.

"Sit down," he said. "Have a drink."

Yakimov's companion was an elderly man, heavily built, whose white hair looked whiter in contrast with the plum-dark colour of his skin. To give her time, Yakimov said genially: "Meet Mustafa Bey. Mus, dear boy, this is Mrs. Pringle from Bucharest. She doesn't really approve of poor old Yaki." He smiled at her. "What will you drink? We're having brandy, but you can get anything here. Whisky, gin, *ouzo* – whatever you like. It's all on Mus."

She chose brandy and, as she drank, regained herself sufficiently to talk. "About the German occupation of Rumania," she said, "it must be true. They've brought down a 'blanket'. You know what that means."

Mustafa Bey nodded his sombre, heavy head. "It is true," he said.

Harriet caught her breath and said: "What will happen to Guy?"

"Guy's no fool," said Yakimov. "He can look after himself, y'know."

"Our flat was raided the night before I left." Harriet saw, as she spoke, a tremor touch Yakimov's face, and she thought of the oil-well plan. The tremor betrayed him. She knew who had taken the plan, but it scarcely mattered. She had much more to worry about.

Yakimov was saying: "The Legation'll look after the dear boy. They got all sorts out of France and Italy. Dobbie's fond of Guy, and Dobbie's a good chap. He'd never abandon a pal."

Harriet said: "Dobson's in Sofia."

"No? Dear me!" No doubt thinking of his sixty thousand *lei*, Yakimov said to Mustafa Bey: "I could do with another, dear boy."

Mustafa Bey lifted a large mauve hand and signed to the waiter. More brandy was brought.

Harriet, her agitation suspended, felt very tired. She watched the clock on the wall behind Yakimov while he talked of the pleasures of Athens. Food, he said, was plentiful.

"And there are a lot of our friends here: Toby Lush, for instance."

"Is Toby Lush here?"

"Yes. In a very influential position, I'm told. So's his friend Dubedat. And a Lord Pinkrose has just arrived from Bucharest. You'll feel quite at home here when you get settled."

Harriet nodded. She thought of Guy and thought of Sasha. She wondered if, without them, she would ever feel at home anywhere in the world again. She asked how long Yakimov had been in Athens.

"Just a week." Yakimov had regained the simple grandeur of manner with which he had first assailed Bucharest society, and seemed at home himself in his new haunt which had not yet found him out.

As the hand of the clock neared eleven, she could scarcely breathe; then, suddenly unable to bear more of it, she jumped up saying: "I must get back to the Legation."

Yakimov rose with her. "I'll come with you."

She was surprised. "Please don't bother," she said. "You've been very kind, but . . . "

"Of course I shall come, dear girl. Your poor old Yaki isn't as bad as you think. Not unchivalrous, y'know, not unchivalrous." His sable-lined coat had been hanging on the chair behind him. He now draped it round his shoulders, taking on an air of rakish elegance, and said to Mustafa Bey: "I shall be back quite soon."

Mustafa Bey nodded with a leaden solemnity.

"Delightful place," said Yakimov when they were in the street. "The nicest people. Mustafa is a dear old friend. Dollie and I stayed with him when he had a house in Smyrna. Used to be a millionaire or something. Now he's on his uppers, just like your poor old Yaki."

Reminiscing about happier days, he walked with her up the hill to the Legation villa. When they reached the door, she said: "Would you go in and ask?" somehow feeling that a shock might be less shocking transmuted through another person.

Yakimov trotted in as though to show by his willingness that there was nothing to fear. She leaned against a lamp-post. The street was empty and, except for the glimmer in the chancellery, there was no sign of life. She watched the door through which Yakimov had entered. He was scarcely in when he came out again, smiling like one who bears gifts. Her spirits leapt as he said gaily:

"Just as I thought, dear girl. Everything's all right. Bucharest is quiet. It's true an army of occupation is expected, but no sign of it yet. The Legation's staying put and they say British subjects won't be molested. My guess is, you'll have the dear boy with you in a brace of shakes."

Suddenly emptied of qualms, too tired to speak, she started to weep. She wept for Sasha, for her red kitten, for Guy alone on the airfield, for the abandoned flat, the damaged books left on the floor, for war and an infinity of suffering and the turmoil of the world.

Yakimov, saying nothing, led her gently down the hill. When she started sniffling and blowing her nose, he asked where she was staying.

At the door of the hotel, he said: "A good night's rest will make all the difference."

"You've been very kind to me," Harriet said. "I wish I could do something for you in return."

He laughed in modest amazement. "Why, dear girl, look what you have done! You took Yaki in. You gave him a home. Who could do more?"

"I'm afraid that was Guy's idea."

"But you fed me. You let me stay."

She felt ashamed that what she had done, she had done so unwillingly. She said: "I see you still have your wonderful coat."

He eagerly agreed, "Yes," and, turning the front hem, revealed by the light from the hotel door the shabby sable inside. "Did I ever tell you the Czar gave it to m'poor old dad?"

"I think you did tell me once."

He lifted her hand and put his lips to it. "If you need me, you'll always find me at Zonar's." Patting her hand before dropping it he said: "Good-night, dear girl."

"Good-night."

He waved before turning away. As he went, the fallen hem of his greatcoat trailed after him along the pavement.

Friends and Heroes

To Dwye and Daphne Evans

PART ONE

The Antagonists

1

WHEN THE HOTEL PORTER RANG to say a gentleman awaited her in the hall, Harriet Pringle dropped the receiver and ran from the room without putting on her shoes.

She had sat by the telephone for two days. Her last three nights in Athens had been sleepless with anxiety and expectation. She had left her husband in Rumania, a country since occupied by the enemy. He might get away. The man in the hall could be Guy himself. Turning the corner of the stair, she saw it was only Yakimov. She went back for her shoes, but quickly. Even Yakimov might have news.

When she came down again, he was drooping like an old horse under his brim-broken panama and the sight roused her worst apprehensions. Unable to speak, she touched his arm. He lifted his sad, vague face and, seeing her, smiled.

"It's all right," he said. "The dear boy's on his way." So eager was he to reassure her that his large, grape-green eyes seemed to overflow their sockets: "Got a message. Got it on me somewhere. Must be here. Someone in Bucharest phoned the Legation. One of our chaps said to me: 'You know this Mrs. Pringle, don't you? Drop this in on her when you're passing.'" His fingers were dipping like antennae into the pockets of his shantung suit: "Bit of paper, y'know. Just a bit of paper."

He tried his breast pocket. As he lifted his long bone of an arm, she saw the violet silk of his shirt showing through the tattered shantung of his jacket, and the blue-white hairless hollow of his arm-pit showing through his tattered shirt. The pockets were so frayed, the message could have fallen out. Watching him, she scarcely dared to breathe, knowing that any show of impatience would alarm him.

Their relationship was happy enough now, but it had not always been like that. Yakimov – Prince Yakimov – had installed himself in the Pringles' flat and would not be dislodged until Bucharest became too dangerous for him. She had disliked him and he had feared her, but when they met again in Athens, they became reconciled. He was the only person here who understood her fears and his sympathy had been her only consolation.

"Ah!" he gave a gasp of satisfaction: "Here we are! Here it is! Got it safe, you see!"

She took the paper and read: "*Coming your route. See you this evening.*"

The message must have been received hours before. It was now late afternoon. Guy would already have touched down at Sofia to find, as she found, that the Rumanian plane would go no farther and he must continue on the Lufthansa. The German line had agreed to carry allied passengers over neutral territory, but she had heard of planes being diverted to Vienna so that British subjects could be seized as enemy aliens. Harriet herself had not been at risk but Guy, a man of military age, might be a different matter.

Seeing her face change, Yakimov said, abashed: "Aren't you pleased? Isn't it good news?"

She nodded. Sinking down on the hall seat, she whispered: "Wonderful," then doubled over and buried her face in her hands.

"Dear girl!"

She lifted her head, her eyes wet, and laughed: "Guy will be here at sunset."

"There you are! I told you he could look after himself."

Confused by exhaustion and relief, she remained where she was, knowing the suspense was not over yet. She had still to live until sunset.

Yakimov looked uneasily at her, then said: "Why not come out a bit? Get a breath of air. Do you good, y'know."

"Yes. Yes, I'd like to."

"Then get y'r bonnet on, dear girl."

She entered the daylight as though released after an illness. The street was in shadow but at the end she could see a dazzle of sunlight. As Yakimov turned the other way, she said, "Could we go down there?"

"There!" he seemed disconcerted: "That's Constitution

Square. Like to stroll through it? Adds a bit to the walk, though."

"But are we going anywhere in particular?"

Yakimov did not reply. They entered the square where there was a little garden, formal and dusty, with faded oranges upon orange-trees. The buildings, Yakimov said, were hotels and important offices. Some were faced with marble and some with rose-brown stucco. At the top of the square was the parliament house that had once been a palace and still had the flourish of a palace. Beside it were the public gardens, a jungle of sensitive bushy trees from which rose the feathered tops of palms. Four immense palms with silvery satin trunks stood across the garden entrance. Buildings, trees, palms, traffic, people – all were aquiver in the fluid heat of the autumn afternoon.

"Athens," Harriet thought: "The longed-for city."

Bucharest had been enclosed by Europe, but here she had reached the Mediterranean. In Bucharest, the winter was beginning. In Athens, it seemed, the summer would go on for ever.

If they could survive till evening, she and Guy would be here together. She imagined his plane where it would be now: in the empyrean, above the peacock blue and green of the Aegean. She willed it to stay on course. He had left the unhappy capital and the maniac minions of the New Order, and now she had only to wait for his safe arrival. Trying to keep her mind on this, her imagination eluded her control. She thought of those who had been left behind. She thought of Sasha.

Yakimov, acting as host and guide, was pointing out places of interest. Modestly conscious of being in a position of vantage, his manner had a touch of the grandiose.

"Nice town," he said: "Always liked it. Old stamping ground of your Yak, of course."

He had left his debts behind and none of his new friends had had time to learn about them. He had found employment. Though his clothes were past mending, they had been cleaned and pressed, and he wore them with an air that proclaimed his sumptuous past. He nodded towards an ornate corner building and said:

"The G.B."

"What happens there?"

"*Dear girl!* The G.B.'s the best hotel. The Grande Bretagne,

you know. Where Yaki used to wash his socks. Intend moving
back there when'm a bit more lush."

Turning into the main road, his steps faltered, his tall, slender
body sagged. They had covered perhaps a couple of hundred
yards but as he made his way through the crowd, he began to
grumble: "Long walk, this. Hard on your Yak. Feet not what
they used to be. Tiring place, this: uphill, downhill, hot and
dusty. Constant need for refreshment."

They had come in sight of a large café and, giving a sigh of
relief, he said: "Zonar's. Their new café. Very nice. In fact,
Yaki's favourite haunt."

Everything about the café – a corner of great glass windows,
striped awnings, outdoor chairs and tables – had a brilliant
freshness. The patrons were still dressed for summer, the
women in silks, the men in suits of silver-grey; the waiters
wore white coats and their trays and coffee pots glittered in
the sun. Behind the windows Harriet could see counters offering extravagant chocolate boxes and luscious cakes.

"It looks expensive," she said.

"Bit pricey," Yakimov agreed: "But convenient. After all,
one has to go somewhere." They crossed the side-road and
reaching the café pavement, Yakimov came to a stop: "If I'd a
bit of the ready, I'd invite you to take a little something."

So this had been his objective when they set out! Harriet
understood his form of invitation. He had delivered the message and now she was expected to make repayment. She said:
"They changed some Rumanian money for me at the hotel,
so let me buy a drink."

"Dear girl, certainly. If you feel the need of one, I'll join you
with pleasure," he sank into the nearest basket-chair and asked
impressively: "What will you take?"

Harriet said she would have tea.

"Think I'll have a drop of cognac, myself. Find it dries me
up, too much tea."

When the order came, the waiter put a chit beside his glass.
Yakimov slid it over to Harriet then, sipping his brandy, his
affability returned. He said:

"Big Russian colony here, y'know. Charming people; the
best families. And there's a Russian club with Russian food.
Delicious. One of the members said to me: 'Distinguished
name, Yakimov. Wasn't your father courier to the Czar?' "

"Was your father courier to the Czar?"

"Don't ask me, dear girl. All a long time ago. Yaki was only a young thing then. But m'old dad was part of the entourage. No doubt about that. That coat of mine, the sable-lined coat, was given him by the Czar. But perhaps I told you?"

"You've mentioned it once or twice."

" 'Spose you know m'old mum's dead?"

"No. I am sorry."

"No remittance for Yaki now. Good sort, the old mum, kind to her poor boy, but didn't leave a cent. Had an annuity. All went with her. *Bad* idea, an annuity."

He emptied his glass and looked expectantly at Harriet. She nodded and he called the waiter again.

In the past she had been resentful of Yakimov's greed, now she was indifferent to everything but the passing of time. Time was an obstacle to be overcome. She wanted nothing so much as to see the airport bus stop at the corner opposite.

"Look at that chap!" said Yakimov: "The one hung over with rugs. Turk, he is. I knew one of those in Paris once. Friend of mine, an American, bought his entire stock. Poor chap walked home without a rug on him. Caught pneumonia and died."

She smiled, knowing he was trying to entertain her, but she could not keep her mind on his chatter. She glanced about her, bewildered by her safety, unable to believe in a city so becalmed in security and comfort. Her nerves reacted still to the confusion of their last months in Rumania. As Yakimov talked, the splendid café faded from her view and she saw instead the Bucharest flat as it had been the night before she left, when the Pringles returned to find the doors open, the lights on, the beds stripped, pictures smashed, carpets ripped up and books thrown down and trampled over the floor.

She and Guy had hidden Sasha, a young Jewish deserter from the army. The louts of the Iron Guard, searching for evidence against Guy, had found the boy. Sasha was gone. That was all they knew, and probably all they would ever know.

Yakimov recalled her with a cough. His glass was empty again but at that moment the airport bus drew up and she searched in her bag to pay the bill. "I must go," she said.

"Don't go, dear girl. Plenty of time for another one. That bus waits twenty minutes or more. It's *always* there. Just one more . . . just one more," he wailed as she sped off.

Bleakly, he watched her as she crossed the road and boarded the bus. Had he known she would desert him like this, he would not have finished his cognac so quickly.

She took her seat, prepared to wait, she did not care how long. Simply to be on the bus meant another inroad upon time. It seemed to her that when the plane arrived she would have conquered anxiety altogether.

2

HARRIET'S PLANE HAD BEEN PUNCTUAL. It had swept down between the hills at a sublime moment – the moment acclaimed by Pindar – when the marble city and all its hills glowed rosy amethyst in the evening light.

Standing on the withered tufts of airfield grass, awaiting the moment as harbinger of Guy's arrival, Harriet saw the refulgence as a gift for him. But it touched perfection and began to darken; for a little while the glow remained like wine on the hills, then she was left with nothing but her own suspense. Nearly an hour passed before the Lufthansa came winking its landing-lights over Parnes.

At last it was down. She saw Guy on the steps. Short-sighted and lost in the beams of the ground lights, he knew he would never be able to find her, so stood there: a large, untidy, bespectacled man with a book in one hand and an old rucksack in the other, waiting for her to find him. She stared a moment, amazed by reality; then ran to him. When she reached him, she was weeping helplessly.

"Whatever is the matter?" he asked.

"What do you think? I was worried, of course."

"Not about me, surely," he laughed at her, frowning to hide his concern, and gave her elbow a shake: "You knew I'd be all right." In his humility, he was surprised that his danger had so affected her. Putting an arm round her, he said: "Silly," and she clung to him and led him through the shadows to the customs shed.

When the luggage came from the plane, Guy's suitcase came with it. He had been back to the flat and filled the case and rucksack full of books.

"What about your clothes?" Harriet asked.

"I've a change of underwear in the rucksack. I didn't bother about the other things. One can get clothes anywhere."

"And books," she said, but it was no time to argue: "Had anyone been to the flat?"

"No, it was just as we left it."

"And no news of Sasha?"

"No news."

When the bus stopped at the corner opposite Zonar's, Harriet pointed to the large, brilliant windows with the fringe of basket-chairs, and said: "Yakimov's here. That's his favourite haunt."

"Yaki's here! How splendid! Let's get rid of this luggage and go and find him."

"Have you any money?"

"No drachma. But you must have some?"

"Not much. And I'm dead tired."

Though impatient to gather this new world to him, Guy had to agree he, too, was tired. The fact bewildered him but on reflection, he said: "I didn't go to bed last night. That may have something to do with it."

"How did you spend the night?"

"David and I sat up playing chess. I wanted to sleep at the flat but David said it'd be a damnfool thing to do, so we went to his room."

"Did you leave him in Bucharest?"

"No. His job doesn't carry diplomatic privilege, so he was ordered to Belgrade. We travelled together as far as Sofia." Guy smiled, thinking they had parted like comrades, for they had, as David said, seen the *bouleversement* through to the end: "When we had dinner," he said, "there were German officers sitting all round us. I'm afraid we were a bit hysterical. I'd made up my mind that, come what may, I would stay on, and David was calling me the Steadfast Tin Soldier. We couldn't stop laughing. The Germans kept turning round to look at us. I think they thought we were crazy."

"If you wanted to stay in Rumania, then you were crazy."

"Oh, I don't know! I hadn't been ordered to go; but next morning the Legation got on to me and said we were all being turned out. No reprieve this time. David was just leaving for the airport, so I went with him. Young Fitzsimon promised to try to get a message to you."

"Yes, someone rang through. Yakimov brought it. You know, he's terribly important, or so he says. He's employed at the Information Office."

"Dear old Yakimov. I *do* look forward to seeing him."

In the dim light of the hotel's basement dining-room, Guy's face, usually fresh-coloured, was grey and taut. As they ate, he sighed with weariness and joy, but he had no intention of going to bed. It was early yet and there was no knowing what life might still have up its sleeve.

He said: "Let's go out and see the town."

They went to Zonar's, but Yakimov was not there. They walked around for half an hour without meeting anyone known to them – a fact that seemed to baffle Guy – then, at last, he admitted he was exhausted and ready to go back to the hotel.

At breakfast, on his first morning in Athens, Guy said: "I must see the Director and get myself a job. Have you discovered anything about him?"

"Only that he's called Gracey. Yakimov doesn't know him and I was too worried to think about anything like that."

"We'll go to the Organization," Guy said. "We'll report our arrival and ask for an interview with Gracey."

"Yes, but not this morning, our first morning here. I thought we could go and see the Parthenon."

"The Parthenon!" Guy was astonished by the suggestion but realizing the excursion was important to her, he promised: "We will go, but not today. For one thing, there wouldn't be time."

"I thought of it as a celebration of your arrival. I wanted it to be the first thing we did together."

Guy had to laugh. "Surely there's no hurry? The Parthenon's been there for two thousand years, and it'll be there tomorrow. It may even be there next week."

"So will the Organization office."

"Be reasonable, darling. I'm not on holiday. The order was that all displaced men must report to the Cairo office. I'm not supposed to be here. I took a risk in coming here, and it won't improve matters if I go off sightseeing the minute I arrive."

"No one knows you're here. We could have one morning to ourselves." Harriet argued, but faintly, knowing he was, as

usual, right. Cairo had become a limbo for Organization employees thrown out of Europe by the German advance and
Guy, hoping to avoid its workless muddle, had come here
against orders. He could justify himself only by finding employment.

Seeing her disappointment, he squeezed her hand and said:
"We will have a morning together; I promise. Just as soon as
things are fixed up. And if you want to go to the Parthenon –
well, all right, we'll go."

Harriet found that Guy had already asked the porter the
whereabouts of the Organization office and, breakfast over,
they must set out without delay. The office was in the School,
and the School was in the old district near the Museum. As the
porter had recommended, they took the tramway-car which
passed the hotel and, seated on the upper deck, they looked
down on the pavements crowded in the radiance of morning.
Sliding her fingers into Guy's hand, Harriet said: "We are here
together. Whatever happens, no one can take that from us.'

"No one will take it from us," Guy said. "We are here to
stay."

Harriet was impressed. The fact that Guy was by nature
tolerant and uncomplaining gave to his occasional demands on
circumstances a supernatural power. She was at once convinced that they would stay.

The streets in the Omonia Square area were unfashionable
and decayed, but the School – a large house that stood in a
corner site – had been restored to its nineteenth-century grandeur, and there were beds of zinnias and geraniums in the
sanded forecourt. The double front-door had elaborate brass-
work and glass panels engraved with irises. The inside stairway, carpeted in red, ran up to a main floor where there was
another door with glass panels. This was marked "Lecture
Room". Looking in through the glass, Harriet saw a man on a
platform addressing a roomful of students.

"Who do you think is lecturing in there?" she asked in a
low voice. Too short-sighted to see for himself, Guy asked:
"Who?"

"Toby Lush."

"I don't believe it."

"Yes. Toby – pipe and all."

Guy caught her arm and pulled her away from the door:

"Do you think they're both here? Toby Lush and Dubedat?" he asked.

"Probably. I remember now that Yakimov said something about Toby being in an influential position."

Guy was silent a moment before he said firmly: "That's a good thing."

"Why is it a good thing?"

"They can put in a word for me."

"But will they?"

"Why not? I helped them when they needed help."

"Yes, but when you most needed help, they bolted from Rumania and left you to manage on your own."

They were standing in a passage where the doors were marked "Director", "Chief Instructor", "Library" and "Teachers' Common Room". Before Harriet could make any further indictment of Lush and Dubedat, Guy opened the door marked "Library" and said: "We can wait in here."

A Greek girl sat at the Library desk. She welcomed them pleasantly but seemed shocked when Guy asked if he could see the Director.

"The Director is not here," she said.

"Where can we find him?" Harriet asked.

The girl dropped her gaze and shook her head as though the Director were too august a figure to be lightly discussed. "If you wait," she said to Guy, "you may be able to see Mr. Lush."

Guy said: "I would rather make an appointment to see Mr. Gracey."

"I don't think it is possible. You would have to consult Mr. Lush. But I could make an appointment for you to see Mr. Dubedat."

"Is Mr. Dubedat here now?"

"Oh, no. Not at the moment. He's very busy. He's working at home."

"I see."

Harriet murmured: "Let's go."

Guy looked nonplussed: "If we go," he said, "we'll only have to come back. As we're here, we might as well wait and see Toby."

Guy wandered off round the shelves, but Harriet remained near the door, waiting to see how Toby Lush would behave when he caught sight of them. The two men, Lush and Dube-

dat, had come to Bucharest from different occupied countries
and Guy had employed each in turn. They had become close
friends and without consulting Guy or anyone else, they had
left together, secretly, fearful of the threatened German
advance.

Harriet could hear Toby scuffing in the passage before he
entered. He blundered against the door and fell in with it, his
hair in his eyes, his arms full of books. He bumped against
Harriet, stared at her and recognized her in dismay. He looked
round suspiciously, saw Guy and dropped the books in order
to grip his pipe. He sucked on it violently, then managed to
gasp: "Well, well, well!"

Guy turned, smiling with such innocent friendliness that
Toby, restored, rushed forward and seized him by the hand.

"Miraculous," gasped Toby, his big fluffy moustache blowing in and out as he spoke. "Miraculous! And Harriet, too." He
swung round as though he had just become aware of her.
"When did you get here, you wonderful people?"

As Guy was about to reply, Toby shouted: "Into the office,"
and rushed them from the Library before they could speak
again. Inside the room marked "Chief Instructor", Toby placed
them in chairs and seated himself behind a large desk. "Now
then," he said, satisfied, and he examined them, his eyes pro-
truding with the joviality of shock.

"Who'd've thought it!" he spoke as though doubtful of their
corporeality. "So you got away, after all?"

"After all what?" Harriet asked.

Toby treated that as a joke. While he whoofed with laughter, his coarse-featured, putty-coloured face slipped about like
something too soft to hold its shape, and he clutched at his
pipe, the only stronghold in a world where anything might
happen. He was still dressed in his old leather-patched jacket,
the shapeless flannels which he called his "bags" and his heavy
brogues, but, in spite of his dress, his manner suggested that he
had become a person of consequence. The first greetings over,
he sat back importantly in his chair and said to Guy:

"So you're on your way to the mystic east, eh? The mystic
Middle East, I should say?"

"No, we want to stay here. Can you arrange for me to see
Gracey?"

"Oh!" Toby looked down at his desk. "Um." His head

dropped lower and lower while he gave thought to Guy's request, then he said in an awed tone: "Mr. Gracey's a sick man. He doesn't see anyone in the ordinary way."

"What about the *extra*-ordinary way?" Harriet asked.

Toby cocked up an eye, took his pipe from his mouth, and said solemnly: "Mr. Gracey's injured his spine."

He pushed his pipe back through his moustache and started to relight it.

"Who is doing his work while he is unwell?" Guy asked.

"Um, um, um, um." Toby, sucking and gasping, was forced to abandon one match and light another. "No one," he said at last and added, "*really*".

"Who is in charge then?"

"It's difficult to say. Mr. Gracey doesn't do any work but he likes to feel he's in control. *You* understand!"

Guy nodded. He did understand. "But," he said, "he must have a deputy. He could never run this place on his own."

"Well, no," Toby struck another match and there was a long delay while the pipe lighting went on. At last, amazingly, a thread of smoke hovered out of the bowl and, shaking out the match, he leant forward confidingly: "Fact is, when we arrived here, Mr. Gracey was in a bit of a fix. His two assistants had beetled off leaving him . . . well . . . " Toby gave Harriet a nervous glance before he completed his sentence: ". . . in the lurch."

"Why?"

"It was one of those things. I don't know the details, but you know what it's like: a misunderstanding, a few heated words. . . . Such things happen! Anyway, they took themselves off."

"How did they manage it? The Organization is a reserved occupation."

"They were transferred. One of them had influence – his father was an M.P. or something. Bit of dirty work, if you ask me. They wanted to go home but they were sent to the Far East. Mr. Gracey applied for two new assistants; the London office had no one to send. They'd had their quota. He was told he'd have to wait and keep things going with locally employed teachers. He had two or three Greeks and a Maltese chap, but no one who could give a lecture. That's how it was when we turned up."

"You saved the day in fact?" said Harriet.

"In a manner of speaking, we did just that."

Guy asked: "Who gives the lectures now?"

"Dubedat gives some. As a matter of fact . . . " Toby guffed and after a pause said with triumphant coyness: "I give the odd lecture myself."

"On what?"

"Eng. Lit. of course."

Guy seemed at a loss for comment and Harriet said: "It looks as though Gracey will be glad to have Guy."

Toby's face tautened in a wary way: "Don't know about that. Can't say." He stared down at the desk and mumbled: "Numbers've been dropping off . . . not much work for anyone these days . . . local teachers had to be sacked . . . very quiet here . . . "

Harriet broke in: "It's pretty obvious from what you say that someone's needed to pull the place together."

"That's for Mr. Gracey to decide." Toby sat up and gave Harriet a severe look. In an attempt to exclude her from the conversation, he turned in his seat and stared directly at Guy. "Mr. Gracey had this accident but he won't admit defeat. You've got to admire him. He's doing his best to run the place from his sick-bed, if you know what I mean. You can't just say to a man like that: 'You aren't up to it. You need someone to pull the place together.' Now, can you?" He frowned his emotion and Guy, touched by the appeal, nodded in sympathetic understanding. There was a long condoling pause broken by Harriet.

She wanted to know: "When can Guy see Mr. Gracey?"

Toby straightened up and put his hands on the table as though forced by Harriet's lack of tact to demonstrate his authority: "I could . . . " He hesitated and gave a last suck at his pipe before committing himself: " I could get you an interview with Dubedat."

"Are you serious?" Harriet asked.

Toby ignored her and spoke directly to Guy: "I can't say exactly *when* he can see you. It mightn't be for a day or two. He's up to his eyes. He's practically running things here, you know! But I'm sure he *will* see you." Toby nodded assuringly, then got to his feet. "Where are you staying?" He noted down the name of the hotel, then shot out a large, soft hand. "We'll keep in touch." He paused, sucked, and added: "And I'll do what I can for you. I promise."

Returning to the dusty heat of mid-morning, the Pringles walked as far as Omonia Square before either spoke, then Harriet burst out: "An interview with Dubedat! Have we come to that?"

Guy, giving a brief, shocked laugh, had to admit: "It was pretty cool."

He looked pale so Harriet did not tell him it was her belief he had created the whole situation by his indiscriminate generosity. Toby was unqualified; Dubedat's qualifications were mediocre. Neither had much ability. Guy could have managed without them and, in the end, had to manage without them. Had he not employed them, they would have been sent to Egypt and probably conscripted. As it was, they had become resentful of the fact that Guy would not let them do anything more than teach. Toby had wanted to lecture but Guy would not hear of it. Remembering the tone in which Toby had said: "I give the odd lecture myself," Harriet knew he had never forgiven Guy for standing between him and his ambition. She could see that Guy had his own methods of arousing enmity. He did not give too little, he gave too much. Those who give too much are always expected to give more, and blamed when they reach the point of refusal.

She said: "If I were you, I'd insist on seeing Gracey. And don't take 'No' for an answer."

"I'll certainly insist on seeing Gracey. I'll tell Dubedat . . . "

"Surely you won't see Dubedat? If you're wise, you'll have nothing to do with him."

"Why not? He's a pal."

"Just as Toby Lush is a pal."

"Toby is an ass, but Dubedat is different. He's no fool. He'll be much easier to deal with."

"We'll see."

Guy's faith, even his unjustified faith, had its own dynamism, and she would not weaken it. Their position was weak enough as it was. She contented herself by saying: "Toby thinks he has only discouraged us and we'll take ourselves off. He knows we haven't much money. Without money, no one can hang around a foreign capital for long."

"We'll hang around as long as we can." Guy said, and in

Stadium Street he found a bureau that gave him drachma for his Rumanian *lei*. The exchange was made reluctantly and the rate was low, but Guy was delighted to get anything at all. As soon as he had money in his pocket, he wanted to spend it. He said: "Let's go to the café you showed me: Yakimov's favourite haunt."

"Zonar's. It's not cheap."

"Never mind."

They found seats in the sun and sat amid the affluent, leisured Greeks who were reading an English newspaper with the headline: "*Seven German Submarines Sunk*." The headline filled the Pringles with wonder, for in Rumania they had come to believe, like everyone else, that the only ships sunk were British ships.

As soon as he saw the English couple, a gentle, quivering, old Greek came to Guy and held a copy of the paper before him. When Guy handed over a note, the old man neither bolted with it nor begged for more, but carefully counted the change on to the table and began to move on. When Guy pushed some of the coins back to him, he bowed and gathered them up.

Guy read his paper while Harriet watched the men moving between the chairs, selling nougat, peanuts and sponges. One of them, catching her eye, offered her an enormous melon-yellow sponge. She tilted up her chin in the Greek fashion and murmured: "Oxi." The man offered other sponges, cream, golden, fawn and brown; at each Harriet gave a smaller tilt of the chin and her "Oxi" became scarcely audible. The man did not become angry like the terrible beggars of Bucharest, but smiled, amused by her performance, and moved on. Relaxed in her chair, she felt a subsidence of tension as though some burden, carried for too long a time, was gradually losing weight. How different life would be here, in this indolent sunshine where the fate of Rumania was a minor fracas, too far away to mean anything!

Here one had only to be English to be approved. It was not only that the Greeks and the English shared a common cause, but she felt a sympathy between them. If they could stay here, she and Guy would never have reason to worry again. Wanting him to acknowledge the peace they had found, she said: "It's marvellous!"

Looking up from the paper, he turned his face to the sun and nodded.

"To feel safe!" she said. "Simply to feel safe! It's marvellous to be among people who are on your side." Having come from a country that had sold itself in fear, she was conscious of the ease of the Greeks. They had the right to be at ease; their dignity was unassailed.

When he had read the little two-page paper, he began to watch the passers-by with an eager, inquiring look, wanting to know and be known. While Harriet was content to observe people, Guy longed to communicate with them and she wished someone would appear to whom he could talk. Someone did appear: Toby Lush.

She said: "Good Heavens! Look!"

Guy looked and his face fell. Toby, getting out of a taxi, seemed anxious and, as he pushed between the people on the pavement, his movements were so discordant, he appeared deranged. Seeing the Pringles, he threw up his arms and shouted: "There you are! I thought I'd find you here!" He fell into a chair and slapped at the sweat which ran down the runnels of his face. "Must have a drink. What about you two?" He swung out his arm at a passing waiter and knocked the man's tray to the ground.

The Pringles sat suspended while Toby ordered himself an ouzo; then he said: "*Now!*" as though about to produce a solution of Guy's predicament. After a pause, he added firmly: "I've had a word with himself."

"With the Director?" Guy asked.

"No, no. With Dubedat. And he told me to tell you: 'We'll do what we can.' " Toby stared at Guy, expecting gratitude, but· Guy said nothing. Disconcerted, Toby went on: "After all, you did what you could for us."

"What do you think you can do?"

The question seemed to reassure Toby, who sagged down in his chair and got out his pipe. An air of importance came over him as he said: "The old soul thinks we might get you a spot of teaching."

"What a cheek!" said Harriet.

Toby let out his breath in a laugh and turned to Guy as though to suggest life would be easier if there were no women around. Enraged further, Harriet went on: "Guy is a member of the Organization. He was appointed in London and sent out under contract. Gracey is Director here. If Guy wants to see him, he's bound to see Guy."

"I don't think so," said Toby, speaking as one who had the upper hand. "Your hubby's got no right to be here."

"He has a right, if there's a job here. You said that Gracey had asked the London office for lecturers."

"That was a year ago. Things have changed since then. No more chaps are being sent to Europe. Europe's a write-off."

"Greece isn't a write-off."

"Not at the moment, but who knows what's going to happen? It's tricky here. Since August, it's been very tricky."

"Why? What happened in August?"

"The Italians torpedoed a Greek ship. There was a lot of feeling about it. Any day, things could go up in flames."

"Oh!" Harriet had nothing to say. This was a world in which only the ignorant could be happy.

Seeing he had deflated her, Toby gave her hand a small admonitory pat and grinned. His masculine superiority established, he drank his ouzo neat, like a man, and said: "It's like this! We'll speak to Mr. Gracey. We'll be seeing him tomorrow. Might even drop in on him tonight. Why not? Anyway, you can rely on us. We'll put in a word for you. We'll say you're a decent chap, good teacher, good mixer, reliable. One of the best, in fact."

Guy listened blank-faced to his listed virtues and at the end, said only: "We'll need some money."

"Must go into that," Toby examined the chit beside his glass and brought out a handful of small change.

"Leave that to me." Guy said.

"Oh, all right. Must get back to the School; have a busy day. Got to lecture again at twelve. Now, don't worry. Just wait till you hear from us." Toby called a taxi and was gone.

"He was sent after us," Harriet said. "He rang Dubedat and Dubedat said: 'Go after them, you damned fool. Keep them sweet. Stop them making a move on their own.' They don't want us to see Gracey, that's clear. But why?"

"Really, darling!" Guy deplored her suspicion of her fellow-men. "They're not conspirators. They *do* owe me something, and Dubedat probably saw it that way."

"They don't want us here."

"Why shouldn't they want us here?"

"For several reasons. If Gracey can get you, he might not want them. There is also the fact you know too much."

Guy laughed: "What do I know?"

"You know they bolted from Rumania in a funk."

"They lost their nerve. It could happen to anyone. They couldn't possibly think we would mention that. They know they can trust us."

"But can we trust them? I don't think we should wait to hear from them. We should find out where Gracey is and go to see him."

"Do we know anyone who knows Gracey?"

She shook her head and slid her hand into Guy's hand. "Apart from Yakimov, we have no friends."

They sat for some moments, hand in hand, reflecting upon their position, then Harriet, glancing in through the café window gave a laugh: "There is another person here who's known to us; someone, what's more, who might know Gracey."

"Who is it?"

"He's inside there, eating cakes."

Guy looked round to see a little man seated at an indoor corner table. The collar of his greatcoat was up round his ears, his trilby hat was pulled down to his eyes; his shoulders were raised as though against a draught. His hands were gloved. Using a silver fork, he was putting pieces of *mille feuille* in through his collar to his mouth. Nothing of his person was visible but a blunt, lizard-grey nose: the nose of Professor Lord Pinkrose who had also bolted from the dangers of Bucharest.

"Pinkrose," Guy said without enthusiasm.

Sent out to lecture in Rumania at a disastrous time, Pinkrose had blamed Guy, as much as anyone, for what he found there. The Pringles could hope for little from him.

Suddenly a familiar voice called: "Dear boy!" and Pinkrose was forgotten. Guy, giving a cry, jumped up and extended his arms to Yakimov, who tottered into them.

"What a glad sight!" Yakimov sang on a note of tender rapture. "*What* a glad sight! The dear boy well and safely here among us!"

They now suffered idleness. With the air growing cooler and more delicate each day, Harriet refused to sit around waiting for word from Dubedat, and said: "Let's see the sights while we have the chance."

Guy, uneasy at being taken outside the area of communication, paid a brief visit to the Museum. Next day he agreed, unwillingly, to go up to the Parthenon. Climbing the steps between the ramshackle houses of the Plaka, he could take no pleasure in their character, their coloured shutters, the scraps of gardens and the unknown trees. Several times he came to a stop and, like Lot's wife, gazed back towards the centre of the town where a message might be arriving for him. He was, whether he liked it or not, a non-combatant in the midst of war and he felt that only work could excuse his civilian status. Now even his work had been taken from him.

Unhappy for him, Harriet said: "If we don't hear from those two by tomorrow, you must go to the Legation and ask to be put into touch with Gracey. That should settle things one way or the other."

"It could settle them the worst possible way. If Gracey does not want to see me, I'd be told to take the first boat to Alexandria. We'd just have to go. As it is, Dubedat may do something for us. We have to trust him," Guy said, though there was no trust on his face.

Seeing him held against the blade of reality, forced to deduce that belief in human goodness was one thing, dependence upon it quite another, Harriet felt an acute pity for him. When he paused again, she said: "Would you rather go back?" She had brought him up here against his inclination and had lost her pleasure in the expedition because he could not share it.

He said: "No. You want to see the Parthenon. Let's get it over."

He plodded on in the growing heat. They walked without speaking round the base of the Acropolis hill and climbed up to the entrance. As they passed through the Propylaea into sight of the Parthenon, Guy stopped in amazement and gave a murmur of wonder. Harriet, with her long sight, had seen the temple clearly enough while wandering in Athens. Set on its hill, it was always surprising the eye, like a half-risen moon. Guy, myopic, saw it now for the first time.

He pulled down his glasses, trying to elongate his sight by peering through the oblique lenses, then he began making his way cautiously over the rough ground. She ran ahead, transported as though on the verge of a supernatural experience. Imagining there was some magical property in the placement of the columns against the cobalt sky, she went from one to another of them, pressing the palms of her hands upon the sun-warmed marble. From a distance the columns had a luminous whiteness; now she saw that on the seaward side they were bloomed with an apricot colour. In a state of wonder, she moved from column to column, touching each as though it were a friend. When Guy reached her, she pointed towards the haze of the Piraeus and said: "Can you see the sea?"

She watched him pull down his glasses again and was moved, remembering he had told her that when he was a little boy he dared not let his parents know that he was short-sighted because the cost of glasses would have caused a crisis in the household. At school he had not been able to see the blackboard and had been regarded as a dull boy until a perceptive master discovered what the trouble was.

"With the sea so near, we can escape," she said. "There's always a boat of some sort."

After a long look in the direction of the sea, Guy said: "I can't swim."

"You can't?"

"I didn't even see the sea until I was eighteen."

"But wasn't there a swimming-bath?"

"Yes, but it frightened me – the echo and that strange smell."

"Chlorine. A very sinister shade of yellow, that smell. I don't like it either."

They sat on the top step facing the Piraeus and the distant shadow of the Peloponnesus, and Harriet thought with dismay of the fact that Guy could not swim. There was no safety in the world. Here, on the summit of the Acropolis, she saw them shipwrecked in the Mediterranean and pondered the problem of keeping Guy afloat.

As for Guy, he sat still for four minutes then looked at his watch and said: "I think we should go back. There *might* be something."

When they reached the hotel, the porter handed Guy an envelope. Inside there was a card on which the words "At Home" were engraved. Mr. Dubedat and Mr. Lush invited Mr. and Mrs. Guy Pringle that evening to take a drink at an address in Kolonaki.

The flat occupied by Dubedat and Toby hung high on the slopes above Kolonaki Square. The Pringles, admitted by a housekeeper and left on a terrace to await their hosts, looked across the housetops and saw Hymettos. The terrace, marble-tiled, with an inlaid marble table, wrought-iron chairs and trained creepers covering the overhead lattice, impressed Harriet who, looking to where the wash of pink-cream houses broke against the pine-speckled hillside, thought that Toby and Dubedat had done very well for themselves. The district had an air of wealth without ostentation: the most expensive sort of wealth.

"Those two seem to be pretty well off," she said.

Guy said: "Shut up."

"I suppose I can say that this is where I would like to live myself?"

Toby Lush, walking silently on spongy soles, overheard her. He gulped and spluttered in gratification but, deferring to Guy's egalitarian principles, said: "Nothing too good for the working classes, eh?"

There was no democratic nonsense about Dubedat, who came out five minutes later. He had the aggressive assurance of a man who had seen bad times but had come into his own, and none too soon. He advanced on Harriet as though she were the final challenge. He swung his hand out to her, and when he spoke she noted he was trying to drop his north-country accent.

"Well," he said, "this is very pleasant." He smiled and she saw that his teeth had been scaled. His fingernails had been cleaned. The scurf had been brushed from his hair. His gestures were languid and dramatic.

Guy moved expectantly forward but Dubedat merely waved him to a chair. "Do sit down," he begged in his new social manner. His eyes and smiles were for Harriet, and Guy might have been no more than her appendage. Knowing he disliked her as much as she disliked him, Harriet supposed his belief was that if he could charm her, he could charm anyone. For Guy's sake she responded as he wished her to respond.

The housekeeper wheeled in a trolley laden with bottles and glasses. "What are we all going to drink?" Dubedat asked.

"What is there?" Harriet asked, impressed and modest.

"Oh, everything," said Dubedat.

And, indeed, there was everything.

"Shall I pour out?" Toby asked.

"*No*," said Dubedat sharply. "Go and sit down."

As he poured the drinks, there was a rattle of glass against glass. His face, with its prominent beak and tiny chin, was set as tensely as the face of a foraging rat. He became very red and at one point dropped a decanter stopper.

"Can I give a hand, old soul?" Toby solicitously asked.

"You can *not*," Dubedat fiercely replied and Toby dodged back, pretending he had received a blow.

He said: "Crumbs!" and looked at the Pringles, but there was no laughter. Both Guy and Harriet were nervous, and everyone felt the delicate nature of the occasion.

The drinks dispensed, Dubedat sat himself down briskly. "I've seen Mr. Gracey." There was a pause while he placed his glass on the table and took out a handkerchief to wipe his fingertips. The pause having taken effect, he went on: "I regret to say I've no very good news for you."

The Pringles said nothing. Dubedat frowned at Toby, who was moving about the party like an anxious old sheep-dog. "Do sit down, Lush," he said, an edge on his voice. Toby obeyed at once.

As though an impediment were out of the way, Dubedat cleared his throat and said impressively: "I've approached Mr. Gracey on your behalf. He would see you, he would like very much to see you, but he's not up to it."

"He's really ill, then?" Harriet asked.

"He had an accident. He's been unwell for some time. He has his ups and downs. At the moment he doesn't feel he can see anyone. He says you're to proceed to Cairo."

"Suppose we wait a few days ..." Guy began.

"No," Dubedat interrupted with placid severity. "He can't keep you hanging round here . . . can't accept the responsibility. He wants you to take the next boat to Alex."

"But wherever I am," Guy said reasonably, "I'll have to hang around. Egypt's full of Organization men, refugees from Europe, all waiting for jobs. The Cairo office doesn't know what to do with them. They're trying to cook up all sorts of miserable little appointments in the Delta and Upper Egypt. The work's minimal: just a waste of time. If I have to wait for work, I'd rather wait here."

"No doubt. But Mr. Gracey doesn't want you to wait. You're to proceed. It's an order, Pringle."

There was a pause, then Guy spoke with mild decision: "Mr. Gracey will have to tell me that himself. I'll stay until I see him."

Dubedat, flushed again, took on his old expression of peevish rancour. His voice grew shrill and lost its quality. "But you can't stay. You're not supposed to be here, and Mr. Gracey doesn't want you here. You're expected in Egypt. So far as the Cairo office is concerned, you're a missing person. That's why Mr. Gracey can't *let* you stay. And he's doing the right thing – yes, he's doing the right thing! You ought to know that!" Dubedat ended on the hectoring note with which he had once condemned everyone whom fortune had favoured above himself.

Guy, who had been worried by Dubedat's earlier effusion, now said with composure: "I intend to stay."

Dubedat gave an exasperated laugh. A frantic sucking noise came from Toby in the background. No one spoke for some moments; then, gathering himself together, Dubedat began to reason with Guy: "Look, there's no job for you here. What with the war and one thing and another, the School isn't what it was. Mr. Gracey hasn't been well enough to see to things. Numbers have dropped off. That's the long and the short of it. *The work just isn't there* "

"So, as Harriet said, someone is needed to get the place back on its feet."

"Mr. Gracey's in charge."

"Exactly," Guy agreed. "And I'm not prepared to leave Athens before I've seen him."

Dubedat let out his breath, suggesting that Guy's total lack of good sense was making things difficult for all of them, and said with the gesture of one throwing down a last card: "Your salary's paid in Cairo."

"I can cable the London office."

"This is Mr. Gracey's territory. The London office can only refer you to him."

"I'm not so sure of that."

Dubedat, agape between surprise and anger, shifted in his seat. It had never occurred to him that Guy, the most accommodating of men, could prove so unaccommodating. Now, as he met Guy's obstinacy for the first time, something malign came into his gaze. He put his hand into his inner pocket and brought out a letter. "I'd hoped we could discuss things in a friendly way, I didn't think I'd need to produce this. Still, here it is. Better take a dekko."

When Guy had read the letter, he passed it to Harriet. It was a typewritten statement informing anyone whom it might concern that Mr. Gracey, during the term of his disablement, appointed Mr. Dubedat as his official representative. Harriet returned it to Guy, who sat studying it in silence, his expression bland.

"So you see," Dubedat shifted about in his excitement, saying in a tone of finality: "What I say, goes. Mr. Gracey can't see you. He won't see you and he won't be responsible for you here. So if you're wise, you'll take yourself off on the first boat from the Piraeus." He snatched the letter from Guy and, folding it with shaking fingers, replaced it in his inner pocket.

Guy looked up but said nothing.

Beginning to relent a little, Dubedat leant towards him and spoke with an earnest, almost entreating, compliance. "If I were you, I'd go. Really, I would. For your own sake."

Guy still said nothing. He maintained his bland expression but it was wan, and Harriet could scarcely bear his mortification. Unassuming though he was, he was conscious of a natural authority, the authority of the upright man. He believed in people. He had always supposed that his generosity would give rise to generosity. Helping others, he would, when the need came, be helped in his turn. It was not easy for him to accept that Dubedat, a mediocrity whom he had employed out of charity, would try to run him out of Athens. And the astonishing fact was that Dubedat was in a position to do it.

There was nothing more to be said. The sun had gone down while they were talking. Watching the distant hill stained rich with the afterglow of evening, Harriet seemed to see, like something sighted from a speeding train, an enchantment they could not share. So Athens was not for them! But what was there for them in this disordered world? Where could they find a home?

Dubedat had also observed the changing light. "Oh, dear," he said, "we'll have to go. What a pity! Another night you might have stayed to supper."

Toby explained: "We've been asked to Major Cookson's.

Sort of royal command. He likes everyone to be on time."

The Pringles did not ask who Major Cookson was. It did not matter. They were not likely to receive his royal command. Guy emptied his beer and they left with scarcely another word.

The lights were coming on in the small shops and cafés in the square of Kolonaki. The central garden was dark. Pepper trees grew along the pavements, their fern-fine foliage clouding in the air like smoke. A smell of dill pickle came from the shops.

Harriet said: "*Will* you cable the London office?"

"Yes."

His decision disturbed her. Because of their insecurity, the streets seemed hostile and she began to see Cairo as a refuge. "Perhaps we'd better take the next boat," she said.

Guy said: "No," his face fixed with his resolution: "I don't want to go to Egypt. There's a job here, and I intend to stay."

Their money had almost run out. They could not afford Zonar's, so walked the length of Stadium Street and sat at a café in Omonia Square where, drinking a cheap, sweet, sleepy, black wine, Harriet thought of Yakimov and wondered how he had survived his years of beggary in foreign capitals. She, with Guy beside her, knowing the worst anyone could do was send them to Egypt, felt very near weeping.

3

THE HOTEL IN WHICH THE PRINGLES were staying had
been recommended to Harriet as the most central of the cheap
hotels. It was gloomy and uncomfortable but favoured by the
English because of its position and its extreme respectability.
Athens had been absorbing refugees since 1939 and, even before the Poles arrived, there had been a backlog of Smyrna
Greeks and White Russians seeking some sort of permanent
home. Hotel rooms were scarce; flats and houses even scarcer.

The Pringles, packed together into a single room, had been
promised a larger room should one fall vacant. When Harriet
reminded the porter of this promise, he told her that rooms
never fell vacant. People stayed at the hotel for months. Some
had made it their home. Mrs. Brett, for instance, had lived
there for over a year.

Harriet knew Mrs. Brett, a gaunt-faced Englishwoman who
eyed her accusingly whenever they met on the stair. One day,
a week after Guy's arrival, Mrs. Brett stopped her and said:
"So your husband did arrive, after all?"

As Harriet tried to edge past, Mrs. Brett stood her ground,
saying: "Perhaps you don't remember me?"

Harriet did remember her. When alone in Athens and distracted by the news from Rumania, Harriet had approached
this fellow Englishwoman and confided the fact she had left
her husband in Bucharest. Mrs. Brett had replied: "He'll be put
into a prison-camp. You'll have him back after the war. My
husband's dead."

This may have been meant as condolence, but it did not console Harriet who now wanted only to avoid the woman.

"I'd like to meet your husband," Mrs. Brett said. "Bring him
to tea on Saturday. I live here in the hotel: room 3, first floor.

Come at four o'clock," and without waiting for acceptance or refusal, she was off.

Harriet hurried to tell Guy: "That God-awful woman's invited us to tea."

"Why, how kind!" said Guy, to whom any social contact was better than no contact at all.

"But it's the woman who said you'd be put in a prison-camp."

"I'm sure she meant no harm," Guy confidently replied.

The Pringles, on the top floor of the hotel, were in a slice of room overlooking a china-bricked well and containing two single beds, end to end, a wardrobe and a dressing-table. Mrs. Brett's room, at the front, was a bed-sitting room and was crowded with an armchair and table, as well as a large bed. Mrs. Brett had hung up two paintings, one of anemones and one of lily-of-the-valley, and she had set out her china on the table beside a large chocolate cake.

Guy, delighted that someone had made them a gesture of friendship, met Mrs. Brett with such warm enthusiasm, she became excited at once and dodged around them, shouting: "Sit down. Sit down." Another visitor was in the room. This was a square-built man who was growing heavy in middle age.

"Really!" Mrs. Brett complained. "You two big men! What am I to do with you both? And," she turned to the middle-aged man with amused horror, "Alison Jay says she'll be dropping in."

"Dear me!" the man murmured.

"We'll manage. We've managed before. Mrs. Pringle can take the little chair – she's a lightweight; and I'll give Miss Jay the armchair when she comes. Now, you two! Here." She placed the two men side by side on the edge of the bed. "Sit down," she ordered them. "I don't need any help."

A hotel waiter brought in a pot of tea and while Mrs. Brett was filling cups and asking each guest several times whether he took milk and sugar, the man beside Guy spoke below the commotion. "My name is Alan Frewen."

"Didn't I introduce you?" Mrs. Brett shouted, pushing cups at her guests. "That's me all over; I never introduce anyone."

Alan Frewen, whose large head was set on massive shoulders, had a face that seemed to be made of brown rock, not carved but worn to its present shape by the action of water. His eyes, light in colour and seeming lighter in their dark setting, had a poignant expression; and as he sat on the bed edge stirring his cup of tea, his air was one of patient suffering. Having given his name, he had nothing to say but kept looking uneasily at Mrs. Brett because she was on her feet while he was sitting down.

She said to Guy: "So you're just out of Rumania? Tell us, are the Germans there or *not*?"

While Guy was answering her, Alan Frewen observed him and the large, dark face softened as though something in Guy's appearance and manner was allaying his sorrows. He leant forward to speak but Mrs. Brett did not give him a chance. She said to Guy:

"You're an Organization man, aren't you? Yes, Prince Yakimov mentioned it. I could tell you a few things about the Organization. You knew my husband, of course? You knew what they did to him here?"

As Guy said, "No," Alan Frewen gave a slight moan, anticipating a story he had heard before and dreaded hearing again.

Ignoring Frewen, Mrs. Brett stared at Guy: "I suppose you know my husband was Director of the School?"

"Was he? I didn't know."

"Aha!" said Mrs. Brett, preparing the Pringles for a grim tale. She kept them in anticipation while she handed round the cups. Alan Frewen watched her with an expression pained and fascinated. She sat down at last and began.

"My husband was Director, but he was displaced. Very meanly displaced, what's more. You must have heard of it?"

"We know very few people here," Guy said.

"It was a scandal, and there was a lot of talk. It got around much farther than Athens. My husband was a scholar, a very gifted man." She stopped and fixed Guy accusingly. "But you must have heard of him? He wrote a history of the Venetian Republic."

Guy said soothingly: "Yes, of course," and she went on:

"You know this fellow Gracey, I suppose?"

"I . . . "

"It was Gracey got him out. Gracey and that louse Cookson."

Harriet said: "We've heard of Cookson. He seems to be important here."

"He's rich, not important. Leastways, not what *I* call important. He calls himself 'Major'. He may have been in the army at some time, but I have my doubts. He lives in style at Phaleron. He's one of those people who don't need to work but want to have a finger in every pie. He wants power; wants to influence people."

"And he's a friend of Gracey?"

"Yes, Gracey's one of that set. When we first came here, Cookson asked us out to Phaleron but Percy wouldn't go. He was doing his own work *and* running the School. No time for junketing, I can tell you."

"How long ago was this?"

"Just when the war started. We knew the old Director: a fine man, a scholar, too. He retired when war broke out and offered the job to Percy. I told Percy he ought to take it. It was war work. He wasn't a young man, of course, but he had to do his bit. I think I was right."

Mrs. Brett paused and Alan Frewen stirred at his tea as though again bringing himself to the point of speech, but again Mrs. Brett thwarted him. "Well, Percy took over here and everything was going swimmingly when that Gracey turned up."

"Where did he come from?"

"Italy. He'd been living near Naples tutoring some rich little Italian boy and doing a bit of writing and so on; having a grand time, I imagine, but he knew it couldn't go on. He got nervous. He decided to come here, worse luck; then, when he got here, he wanted a job and Percy took him on as Chief Instructor. Oh, what a foolish fellow! Percy, I mean." She shook her head and clicked her tongue against the back of her teeth.

"He could scarcely have known," Alan Frewen said.

Mrs. Brett agreed as though the thought had only just occurred to her. "No, that's right, he couldn't."

"Wasn't Gracey qualified?" Guy asked.

"Too well qualified. That was the trouble. He wasn't willing to work under Percy. No, he didn't want to play second fiddle – he wanted Percy's job. He went to see Cookson and buttered him up, and said: 'You can see for yourself that Percy Brett isn't fit to run the School,' and I can tell you there's nothing Cookson likes better than to be in the middle of an intrigue. Those two began plotting and planning and telling everyone that Percy was too old and not trained for the work. And Gracey got Cookson to write to the London office . . . "

"Do you really know all this?" Alan Frewen mildly protested.

"Oh, yes." Mrs. Brett looked fiercely at him. "I've got my spies, too. And the next thing, the London office flew out an inspector to inquire into the running of the School. Just think of it! An inspector poking his nose into Percy's affairs. . . . And *then* what do you think happened?"

Mrs. Brett's voice had become shrill in tragic inquiry, and as Alan Frewen caught Harriet's eye, his pitying expression told her that Mrs. Brett's aggression covered nothing worse than unhappiness.

Sombre and weary, he dropped his gaze and Harriet, who had hoped to learn something about Gracey, began to wonder if they were listening to anything more than the fantasies of lunacy. Guy evidently thought so. His face pink with concern, he waited intently to know what happened next.

"Percy fell ill," Mrs. Brett said. "He fell ill just as the inspector arrived. Imagine what it was like for me with an inspector nosing around, and Gracey and Cookson telling him just anything they liked, and my poor Percy too ill to defend himself.

"He said to me: 'Girlie' – he always called me Girlie – 'I never thought they'd treat me like this!' He'd worked like a Trojan, you know. Unremitting, I called him. He improved the School. All Gracey did was take over a going concern and let it run down. And poor Percy! He was ill for weeks; nine, ten weeks. . . . He had typhoid." She was gasping with the effort and emotion of the story, and her voice began losing its strength. "And they got rid of him. Yes, they got rid of him. A report was sent in and then a cable came: Gracey was to take over here; Percy was to go to a temporary job at Beirut. But he never knew any of this. He died. Yes he died you know!" She looked at Guy and said hoarsely: "I blame myself." She clenched one of her ungainly hands and pressed the knuckles against her mouth, her eyes on Guy as though he alone understood what she was talking about. After some moments she dropped her hands to her lap. "He never wanted to come here. I made him. I worked it . . . yes, I worked it, really. I wrote and suggested Percy for the job, and that's why it was offered to him. We lived at Kotor, you know. I got so tired of it. Those narrow streets, that awful gulf. I felt shut in. I wanted to go to a big city. Yes, it was me. It was my fault. I brought him here, and he got typhoid."

Guy put his hand over her hand and said: "He could have got typhoid anywhere – even in England. Certainly anywhere on the Mediterranean. You've read *Death in Venice*?"

Mrs. Brett looked at him bleakly, puzzled by the question, and to distract her he began telling her the story of Mann's novella. Approaching the crisis of the plot, he paused dramatically and Mrs. Brett, thinking he had finished or ought to have finished, broke in to say: "When Gracey took over, Percy was still alive. They didn't even wait for him to die."

Harriet asked: "Is this why the two lecturers asked to be transferred?"

"You've heard about that, have you?" Mrs. Brett jerked round to look at Harriet: "I wonder who told you?"

"Dubedat and Lush mentioned it."

"*Them!*" said Mrs. Brett in disgust: "They're a pretty pair!"

"They are a pretty pair," Harriet said, and she would have said more, but was interrupted by a loud rat-tat on the door.

"Here she is! Here she is!" Mrs. Brett cried and jumping up with the alacrity of a child, she' threw open the door so it crashed against the bed: "Come in! Come in!" she shouted uproariously and a very large woman came in.

The woman's size was increased by her white silk draperies and a cape which, caught in a draught between door and window, billowed behind her like a spinnaker. Her legs were in Turkish trousers, her great breasts jutted against a jerkin from which hung a yard of fringe. As she stood filling the middle of the room, her fat swayed around her like a barrel slung from her shoulders.

"Well," she demanded. "Where do you want me to sit, Bretty?"

"The arm-chair, the arm-chair." Delighted by the arrival of this new guest, Mrs. Brett told the Pringles: "Miss Jay rules the English Colony."

"Do I?" Miss Jay complacently asked. She sank into the arm-chair and looked down at her big raffia shoes.

When she had introduced the Pringles, Mrs. Brett said: "I was just telling them how Gracey treated Percy."

"Um," said Miss Jay. "I thought I'd let you get that over before I turned up."

"I haven't finished yet." Mrs. Brett swung round on Guy: "And what do you think they did *after* Percy died?"

In an attempt to distract her, Allan Frewen said: "Could I have some more of that delicious tea?"

"When the water comes, not before," said Mrs. Brett and she continued with determined crossness: "After Percy died, I decided to give a little party . . . a little evening of remembrance. . . . "

The waiter came to the door with hot water. Mrs. Brett took the pot from him, slammed the door in his face and added firmly: "A little evening of remembrance."

Miss Jay said: "How about giving me a cup before you start again?"

Mrs. Brett attended to her guests in an exasperated way, then, the tea dispensed, faced Guy again: "You understand why I'm telling you this, don't you? I felt you ought to know something about the people who infest this lovely place. There's not only Cookson and Gracey; there's that Archie Callard, too."

Alan Frewen said: "Archie can be tiresome. He has the wrong sort of sense of humour."

"Do you think what they did to me was intended as humour?"

"I don't know." Alan Frewen looked confused. "It could have been – of a macabre kind."

"Macabre? Yes, indeed, 'macabre' is the word! What do you think they did?" Mrs. Brett turned on Guy: "When Cookson heard that I was giving my little party at the King George, he arranged to give a party himself on the same evening. A very grand party. What do you think of that? Of course they all had a hand in it: the Major, Callard and Gracey . . . "

Miss Jay said: "I really doubt whether Gracey . . . "

"Oh, I'm sure he had. Three clever fellows plotting against a poor old woman! Everyone was invited to Cookson's party

– except me, of course. It was the biggest party Cookson's ever given."

"And your party was spoilt?" Guy asked.

"I had no party. No one turned up. Some of my best friends deserted me in order to go to Phaleron. I've never spoken to them since."

"It really was most unkind," Alan Frewen murmured.

"You weren't here; you'd gone to Delphi," Mrs. Brett exonerated him. "And you . . . " she nodded to Miss Jay. "You were on Corfu." She smiled at the two who had not been in Athens to take part in her betrayal, then suddenly remembered Harriet and turned on her, asking: "What do you think of all this, eh? What do you think of the sort of people we've got here?"

Harriet, glancing aside, saw Miss Jay watching her with a keen, critical eye and knew that whatever she said would be repeated, probably with disapproval. She said: "I do not know them, and we've been living so differently. Our experiences didn't give us much time to have social worries."

"You were lucky. I'd rather have experiences," said Mrs. Brett. "We all envy you."

Looking into her weathered old face, Harriet saw there a flicker of kindness, but Miss Jay said pettishly: "Experiences! Heaven keep us from experiences."

"The Pringles have just come from Bucharest," Mrs. Brett said. "They saw the Germans come in."

"Oh, did they!" Miss Jay eyed the Pringles as though they might have brought the Germans with them. "We don't want anything of that sort here."

Alan Frewen, looking at Guy with interest, asked Guy how long he intended to stay.

Guy said: "As long as we can. But it depends on Gracey. I came here in the hope he would employ me."

"And won't he?" Frewen asked.

"It doesn't look like it. The trouble is, I can't get him to see me. They say he's too ill to see anyone."

Mrs. Brett broke in: "Whoever told you that?"

"Toby Lush and Dubedat."

"How very odd!" Alan Frewen looked at Mrs. Brett, then at Miss Jay, his face crumpled like the face of a small boy trying to smile while being caned. "I don't think there's much wrong with Gracey, do you?"

"It's him all over," Mrs. Brett said. "He can't be bothered; he doesn't want to be bothered. He leaves everything to those two louts. It's disgraceful the way the School's gone down."

Still smiling his curious smile, Alan Frewen said: "I know Colin Gracey quite well. We were at King's together. I could say a word . . . "

"I wouldn't interefere," Miss Jay interrupted with such decision that Frewen seemed to retreat. His smile disappeared and he looked so forlorn that Guy, whose hopes had been raised and then thrown down, felt it necessary to justify him.

"I suppose we must leave it to Dubedat," Guy said. "After all, he is Gracey's representative."

Mrs. Brett began to protest but Miss Jay had had enough of the conversation. Gripping her friend by the arm, she said: "I've heard about a flat that might suit you."

"*No*?" Mrs. Brett cried out in excitement; and Guy's troubles were forgotten.

"On Lycabettos. Two American girls have it at the moment. They're going on the next boat. They'll let it furnished. They're looking for someone who'll keep an eye on their bits and pieces, someone reliable. They're not asking much for it."

"Suit me down to the ground."

While Mrs. Brett discussed the flat, Alan Frewen looked at his watch and Harriet raised a brow at Guy. The three rose. Miss Jay glanced at them brightly, glad to see them go, but Mrs. Brett scarcely noticed their departure.

Frewen paused on the landing and looked at the Pringles as though he had something to say. When he said nothing, Guy decided to go down and ask at the desk if there was a message for him. They all descended the stairs together. At the bottom, a black retriever, tied to the banister post, leapt up in a furore of greeting.

At this, Frewen managed to break silence: "This is Diocletian." He untied the lead, then put on a pair of dark glasses preparatory to entering the twilit street, but he did not go. Holding his dog close, he stood with his face half obliterated by the black glass, and still could not say what he wanted to say.

Watching him, Harriet thought: "An enigmatic, secretive man."

There was nothing for Guy at the desk and as the Pringles said their good-byes, Alan Frewen said at last: "Do you know the Academy? It used to be the American Academy of Classical Studies, but the Americans went home when the war started. Now it's a pension for solitary chaps like me. I was wondering, could you find your way there one day and have tea?"

"Why, yes," Guy said.

"What about Thursday? It's a working day but I'm not very busy. I needn't get back to the office till six."

"What do you do?" Harriet asked.

"I'm the Information Officer."

"Yakimov's boss?"

"Yes, Yakimov's boss." Alan Frewen gave his smiling grimace and, the invitation safely conveyed, he let the dog pull him away.

4

Harriet was usually wakened by the early tram-car. On Thursday morning she was wakened instead by a funeral wail which rose and fell, rose and fell, and at last brought even Guy out of sleep. Lifting his face from the pillow, he said: "What on earth is that?"

By now Harriet had remembered what it was. She had heard it on news films. It was an air-raid siren.

She put on her dressing-gown and went to the landing where the window overlooked the street. The shops were beginning to open and shopkeepers had come out to their doors. Men and girls going to work had stopped to speak to each other and everyone was making gestures of inquiry or alarm. People were running down the hotel stairs. Harriet wanted to ask what was happening, but no one gave her time. As the siren note sank and faded on a sob, a batch of police came running from the direction of the square. They were bawling as they came and some had taken out their revolvers and were waving them as though revolt were imminent. In a minute all the innocent, wondering bystanders had been pushed into shops and doorways. Cars were brought to a stop and their occupants sent indoors like the rest. The police sped on, making all possible noise, and leaving the street empty behind them.

It was a fine, mild morning. Harriet pulled up the window and leant out but saw only imprisoned faces, deserted pavements, abandoned cars.

Guy, getting into an emergency rig of trousers and pullover, shouted from the room: "Is anything happening down there?"

"The police have cleared the street."

"It must be a raid."

"Let's go down and find out." Harriet spoke with the calm of an old campaigner. Conditioned to disorder, she dressed with the sense that she was returning to reality, and when they ran down the stairs to the hall, she knew what to expect. She could have described the scene before she reached it, for she had seen it before on an evening of crisis in an hotel hall in Bucharest.

But here there was someone known to her. Mrs. Brett, in a dressing-gown, her face flushed, was talking to everyone, her grey-brown pigtail whipping about as she jerked her head from side to side.

The porter was on the telephone, speaking Greek with occasional words of English, and his free hand was thumping the desk to emphasize what he said. The other guests, English, Polish, Russian and French, were chattering shrilly, while from outside there rose the high swell of the "All Clear".

Seeing the Pringles, Mrs. Brett shouted: "We're at war. We're at war." As she did so, the porter dropped the receiver on to the desk and throwing out his arms as though to embrace everyone in sight, said: "We are your allies. We fight beside you."

"Isn't that splendid!" said Mrs. Brett.

The sense of splendour possessed the hall so it seemed that in secret everyone had been longing to live actively within the war and now felt fulfilment. The Pringles, because they were English, were congratulated by people who had not given them a glance before. They heard over and over again how the Greek Prime Minister had been wakened at three in the morning by the Italian Minister who said he had brought an ultimatum. "Can't it wait till the honest light of day?" Metaxas asked; then, seeing it was a demand that Greece accept Italian occupation, he at once, without an instant's hesitation, said: "No."

"Oxi," said the porter. "He said 'Oxi'."

Mrs. Brett explained that Mussolini also wanted his triumphs. He had chosen a small country, supposing a small country was a weak country, thinking he had only to make a demand and the Greeks would submit. But Metaxas had said "No" and so, in the middle of the night, while the Athenians slept, Greece had entered the war.

"Well, well, well!" Mrs. Brett sighed, exhausted by happiness and excitement, and turning accusingly on the Pringles, said: "You see, you're not the only ones who have adventures.

Things happen here, too." She started to go upstairs, then turned and shouted: "Anything yet from Gracey?"

"Nothing, I'm afraid," said Guy.

"Well, don't go. You be like Metaxas. You stand firm. Tell him he's got to give you a job. If I were on speaking terms, I'd tell him myself."

Guy mentioned that they were going that afternoon to tea with Alan Frewen. Mrs. Brett said she, too, had been invited but Miss Jay was taking her to see the promised flat.

"You go," she urged Guy. "He'll introduce you to Gracey."

"I don't think so. He said nothing about Gracey."

"Oh, he will; Gracey's up there. He lives at the Academy. Alan'll do something – you'll see! Cookson thinks he can fix everything, but he's not the only fixer. A lot of things happen in my little room that he knows nothing about." Giving a high squawk of laughter, she shouted over her shoulder: "Oh yes, I'm a fixer, too."

The Pringles had almost exhausted their money. They had just enough to pay their hotel bill and buy steerage berths on the boat that would sail on Saturday; but, caught up in the afflatus of events, they could not face the hotel breakfast and when ready to go out, decided to take coffee in the sunlight. The streets were crowded with people exchanging felicitations as though it were the first day of holiday rather than of war. It seemed an occasion for rejoicing until the Pringles met Yakimov, who was wheeling his bicycle uphill, a look of gloom lengthening his lofty camel face.

In the past he had gone through every crisis with the optimism of the uninformed. Now, working in the Information Office, nothing was hidden from him.

"Greeks won't last ten days," he said.

"Is it as bad at that?" Guy asked.

"Worse. No army. No air-force. Only one ship to speak of. And the I-ties say they'll bomb us flat. What's going to happen to us, I'd like to know? They starve you in these prison-camps."

"Surely we'll be evacuated?" Harriet said.

"Don't know. Can't say. All depends."

Having reached the level of University Street, he ran his bicycle along, leapt at it, somehow landed on the saddle and, high perched in precarious dignity, he weaved away.

The Pringles, knowing Yakimov, could not rely on anything

he said. They bought the English newspaper, which took an inspiriting view of the new front and made much of the fact the British had promised aid.

Harriet said: "Whatever happens, I want to stay. Don't you?" She felt confident of his answer and was dismayed when he replied: "I want to stay more than ever, but . . . "

"But what?"

"I can't work for a man like Gracey."

She realized the trouble was Mrs. Brett. When, after the tea-party, she had asked Guy what he thought of Mrs. Brett's stories, he would not discuss them. Caught up in a conflict between his desire to remain here and the fact he could remain only by Gracey's favour, he had to reflect upon them.

"So you believe all she said?" said Harriet.

"I can't imagine she invented it."

"There might be a basis of truth, but I felt she was pretty dotty. I'm sure if we knew the whole of it, we'd find it was quite different."

"I don't know. She may have exaggerated, but the others didn't defend Gracey. He seems to be quite despicable." Guy looked angry and defiant at the very thought of Gracey and Harriet knew that in this mood he would make no attempt to win him. Guy's persuasive force could function only with people for whom he had respect. He was incapable of dissimulation. Once he had accepted the dictates of his morality, he could be inflexible. If he despised Gracey, or had cause to doubt his own personal probity in the matter, their cause was as good as lost.

She began to fear they would be on the Egyptian boat when it sailed in two days' time.

By midday the first plaudits of war were over. By the time the Pringles set out to find the Academy, there had been news of a raid on the factories at Eleusis, and a rumour that Patras had been bombed. Athens, so far untouched, was sunken into the somnolence of afternoon.

Following the directions given by the hotel porter, the Pringles took the main road towards Kifissia. They were alone on the long, wide, sun-white pavement when a convoy of lorries, full of conscripts, passed on their way to the station. As the Pringles waved and shouted "Good luck", the young men, recognizing them as English, shouted back "Zito the British navy" and "Zito Hellas" and, as Harriet called out to them, one of the young men bent down and caught her hands and said in English: "We are friends." Gazing into his dark ardent eyes, she was transported by the glory of war and threw herself on Guy, crying: "It's wonderful!"

Guy hurried her along, saying: "Don't be silly. They may all be dead in a week."

"I don't want to go to Egypt," she said, but Guy refused to discuss it.

The Academy came into view: a large Italianate building painted ochre and white and set in grounds that had been dried to an even buff colour by the long summer heat.

Alan Frewen was waiting for them in the common-room. He hurried towards them, his dog at his heels, his manner stimulated by the day's events, saying: "I'm glad you're early, I may get called back, but probably not. At the moment the Information Service is little more than a joke, but if the Greeks make any sort of a stand, then we'll have to pull up our socks."

"Can the Greeks make a stand?" Guy asked. "Have they anything to make a stand with?"

"Not much, but they have valour; and that's kept them going through worse times than these."

While Alan talked, Harriet glanced about her. Agitated by the fact she was in Gracey's ambiance, she wanted to see the other occupants of the vast room who, seated on the faded armchairs and sofas, gave a sense of being intimately unrelated in the manner of people who exist together and live apart. The room itself had been bleached like the garden, by the fervour of the light. Even the books in the pitch-pine bookcases were all one colour, and the busts that looked down from the bookcase tops were filmed with dust and as sallow as the rest. She made a move towards one of them but Alan stopped her, saying: "All locked. We are in the Academy, but not of it. The students left their *materiel* behind but we, of course, must not touch."

He led them out to the terrace where seats and deck-chairs, blanched like everything else, were splintering in the sun. Stone steps led down to a garden where nothing remained of the flower-beds but a tangle of dry sticks. The lawn beyond, brick-baked and cracked in the kiln of summer, was an acre of clay tufted over with pinkish grass. The tennis courts were screened behind olives, pines and citrus trees. The wind that played over the terrace was full of a gummy scent, unique and provocative, that came from the pines, and from the foliage that had dried and fallen into powder.

"That is the smell of Greece," Harriet said.

Alan Frewen nodded slowly: "I suppose it is."

"Can we have tea out here?"

"I am afraid it is not allowed. Miss Dunne – who decides things here – says it makes too much work for the girls. The girls say they don't mind, but Miss Dunne says 'No'." A bell rang and they went inside and sat near the french windows. A plate of cakes came in with Alan's tea-tray and he said: "I'm glad you're here to help me eat these. When I heard the last boat had gone, I was afraid you might be on it."

"The last boat? Do you mean the boat that was going on Saturday?"

"Yes. There won't be another. The Egyptians won't risk their ships, and who can blame them? The boat went this morning and the shipping clerks closed the office and went with her. I'm told that a few wide-awake people managed to get on board, though I don't know who could have warned them."

Guy said: "Surely there are Greek boats?"

"No. Anyway, not for civilians. Greece is on a war-time basis now."

"And no air-service?"

"There never was an air-service to Egypt."

Looking at Guy, Harriet laughed and said: "Freedom is the recognition of necessity."

"What about Salonika?" Guy persisted. "There must be a train to Istanbul?"

"That's a war zone, or soon will be. Anyway, there's an order out: foreigners are not allowed to leave Athens. You might be refused an exeat to Salonika."

"Is that likely?"

"Anything's likely here during an emergency. Greek officials are very suspicious."

"So we can't get away? In fact, no one can get away?"

"There may be an evacuation boat of some sort. The Lega-

tion think they ought to send away the English women with
children. I don't know. Nothing's been arranged yet. If Mrs.
Pringle wants to go, I could probably get her a passage."

Harriet said: "I'm staying here, if I can."

"That's the spirit. Anyway, what's this talk of trains to Istanbul? I thought you both wanted to stay?"

"It's Mrs. Brett's stories. Guy doesn't like the idea of working for Gracey now."

"Oh!" Alan Frewen rubbed the toe of his shoe up and down
the dog's spine and smiled in apparent pain as the dog
stretched in pleasure.. He reflected for some moments, then
said: "Mrs. B.'s obsessional. She's always telling stories about
the Cookson set. I think Brett was treated meanly, but he
was an old fuddy-duddy; quite incapable of running the
School. All the work was done by the two lecturers, who
liked him. They left when Gracey took over, as I think you
know."

Harriet said: "What about the business of the memorial
party?"

"It was unkind, but she provoked it. She has been inexcusably rude to Cookson at different times. She practically accused him of murdering her husband. She's a bit hysterical.
You saw it yourself."

"If you'd been here, would you have gone to Cookson's
party?"

Frewen raised his eyebrows slightly at Harriet's question, but
smiled again: "I might, you know. It would have been a difficult choice. Cookson's parties are rather grand."

Guy said with conviction: "I am sure you would not have
gone. No decent person would treat a lonely, ageing woman in
that way."

Frewen's smile faded. He gave Guy a long, quizzical look,
but before he could say anything a middle-aged woman in
shorts, tennis racquet under arm, came in through the french
windows. Lumpish, bespectacled, with untidy fox-red hair, she
was hot and damp and breathing heavily. She acknowledged
one or two of the men with sidelong grimaces, then, catching
sight of the strangers, she rolled up her eyes in appalled self-
consciousness and sped from the room.

"Who?" Harriet whispered.

"That's Miss Dunne, the terrible sportsgirl."

"Is she at the Legation? What does she do?"

"Oh, something so very hush-hush, I'm told she's led to it blindfolded. But I wouldn't know, and I wouldn't dare to ask. She's the genuine thing, sent out by the Foreign Office. Most of us are only temporary, so she's a cut above the rest."

Harriet said under her breath: "Pinkrose." Guy looked up quickly. They watched as Pinkrose came across the room with a cake carton in his hand. He sat down, placed the carton very carefully on his table and opened it. When his tea arrived, he took out three ornamental cakes, disposed them on a plate and studied them. He chose one, transferred it to a smaller plate, then, on reflection, returned it to the big plate and studied the three again.

Harriet asked Alan Frewen: "Do you know him?"

"Indeed I do. He's by way of being a colleague of mine."

"You mean he's found a job already?"

"Yes, though job is no name to call it by. He got into the Information Office somehow. I gave him a desk in the News Room and he potters about. That enables him to live here. He told them at the Legation he couldn't afford an hotel."

"You're joking?"

"I'm not. He could have gone back to England. There was a ship going from Alex round the Cape, but he wouldn't risk it. He said he had a delicate constitution and would be less of a burden to others in a comfortable climate."

"He may be regretting that now."

"If he is, it's not affecting his appetite."

After tea they strolled with the dog about the garden and coming back through the lemon trees that shaded the drive, Alan said diffidently: "I mentioned to Gracey that you would be here this afternoon. He suggested you might go and see him about six. Of course, if you don't want to, I can make your excuses."

Guy grew red and after a moment said: "This is very kind of you."

"Oh, no. I made the merest mention, I assure you. It was his idea."

"I will go, of course. I'm very grateful."

"I'll take you up to Gracey's room, but I can't stay. I'm due back at the office."

Gracey's door was at the end of the long, broad, upstairs

passage. Alan knocked. The voice that called him to enter was firm, musical and beautifully pitched.

The room inside was a corner room with windows overlooking the gardens to north and east. Between the two windows Gracey was stretched out on a long chair, a table nearby and a circle of chairs about him.

He welcomed them on a high note: "Ah, *do* come in! Do sit down! How nice to meet you two young people at last! Alan, be a good chap; pour us some sherry! It's on the chest-of-drawers."

When he had handed round the glasses, Frewen said he would have to go.

"So soon?" Gracey sounded very disappointed. "Are you so terribly busy?"

"Not busy at all, I'm afraid. I wish we were. The situation demands action, and we don't know what to do. Still, one must put up a show. I feel I ought to get back."

Gracey protracted the good-byes as though he could not bear to part with Alan; then, the parting over, he leant earnestly towards Guy: "You must tell me all about your escape from Bucharest. I want to know every detail."

He spoke as though their safe arrival had been a profound relief to him and the bewildered Pringles did not know what to say. Their "escape" was over and done with, the "details" were losing importance. No one could tell what was happening in Rumania now. A door had shut behind them and they had other things to worry about.

Awkward in his distrust of Gracey, Guy did his best to give an account of the Rumanian break-up, while Harriet observed the man who had been, they were told, too ill to see them. His long, graceful body lay in an attitude of invalidism, but the impression he gave was of perfect health, almost of perfect youth. There was, she felt, something almost shocking about his fair, handsome head. It was some minutes before the effect began to crumble. There were lines about his eyes, his cheeks were too full for the structure of his face and his hair was blanched not by sun, but by age. He must be forty or more; perhaps even fifty. She began to see him as mummified. He might be immensely old; someone in whom the process of ageing was almost, but not quite arrested. As he gazed at Guy and listened, the smile became congealed on his face.

Guy's constraint was making things difficult. Even if he had not heard Mrs. Brett's stories, he would not have been at his best. He was a man whose charm and vitality were most evident when he was himself the giver. Now, dependent upon Gracey's bounty, his spirit shrank.

Gracey let him struggle on a little longer, then asked: "You knew Lord Pinkrose, of course?"

"Yes."

"He may look in this evening, I'm sure he'll be delighted to see you. My friends are so kind. Major Cookson has been particularly kind. They all come to cheer me up after supper. Sometimes there's quite a crowd here."

Gracey sipped at his sherry, then, as though the moment had come, he asked, laying the question like a trap: "What exactly were you doing in Bucharest?"

Guy looked surprised, but answered mildly: "I assisted Professor Inchcape who was in charge of the English Department. When war started, he became Director of Propaganda for the Balkans and I ran the department. It was rather reduced, of course."

"Of course. And our friend Dubedat? What part did he play in all this?" Gracey was again leaning towards Guy and his smile encouraged confidences.

Guy answered stiffly: "Surely Dubedat told you what he did?"

Gracey lay back, not answering the question but apparently reflecting upon it, then said: "I am grateful to Dubedat; and to Lush, too, for that matter. They've proved invaluable. When I had my accident, they took over and thus enabled me to recoup in peace and quiet. You may have heard there had been a little trouble here? Two lecturers left. They had been fond of Brett. He was hopeless as Director, but a nice enough old fellow and his men resented me. So off they went and I was left to cope alone. The London office couldn't replace them. When Dubedat and friend turned up, I didn't inquire too closely into their teaching experience being thankful to get them."

Gracey's tone implied that he was inquiring now. He looked expectantly at Guy, but Guy merely said: "I understand."

His tone a little sharper, Gracey said: "I've never regretted the association; I've only wondered why you let them go."

"They chose to go," Guy said.

"Ah?" Gracey regarded Guy with a warm interest. "I gather there had been jealousy. Dubedat and Lush are active fellows; apt, perhaps, to take too much upon themselves. After all, they were not officially appointed. Someone may have wanted them out of the way? Most likely Professor Inchcape?"

Guy said: "Professor Inchcape barely knew them. They were employed by me."

Still holding Guy with his warm, smiling regard, Gracey said: "Anyway, the story seems to be: they received the usual order to leave the country and no one made a move on their behalf. They were just let go."

"They told you that?"

Gracey looked perplexed. "Someone told me. It's so long ago: I've quite forgotten the details."

"May I ask," Guy asked, "did Dubedat mention that I came to Athens in the hope that the Organization could use me here?"

"Yes. Oh, yes, Dubedat let me know you were keen to stay." Gracey sat up and stared, as though entranced, from the window to where the sun had dropped down behind the olive trees and the light came broken through the small grey-silver leaves. "I have no wish to criticize," he said. "You were answerable to your professor, of course; no doubt he approved. But don't you think there was a lack of – what? *Seriousness,* shall we say? . . . Well, to put it another way: wasn't it a tiny, a very tiny, bit frivolous to put on a theatre production during the blackest days of the fall of France?"

Guy, startled by this criticism, flushed and began to say: "No, I—" But Gracey went on: "*And* when your students needed elementary English in order to get to English-speaking countries?"

"I suppose Dubedat told you that he took a part in the play?" Harriet said.

Guy moved a hand to silence her. Dubedat's part in the play was a point beside the point, and one he would not make. Willing to do more work than most, conscious of his own integrity, he had, over the years, become unused to criticism and tended to see himself as above it. But he was ready to accept the justice of Gracey's criticism and said only: "Am I to take it that this is why you do not choose to employ me?"

"Good gracious me, no," Gracey laughed. "That is merely a private opinion. The question of your employment doesn't rest with me any longer. I'm *hors de combat*. I've delegated authority, and, I may say, I'm preparing to leave Greece. A friend, a very generous friend, feels I must have proper treatment. He has offered to send me to the Lebanon where there is an excellent clinic."

Harriet said: "Mr. Frewen says there are no ships. The Egyptian line has come to a stop."

"That won't affect me. I'm hoping to get a priority flight, but it's all hush-hush, of course."

"So Dubedat is in charge?" said Guy.

"Someone has to be," Gracey said. "But I cannot say who will take over when I'm gone. There are several candidates for the post."

"I suppose the London office knows . . . "

"Oh, dear me, yes. Cables have gone forth and back. It all takes so long nowadays."

"Is there any likelihood of Dubedat being appointed?"

"Dubedat's name had been mentioned, but it does not rest with me. The London office will make the appointment."

Guy stared into his glass, his eyebrows raised, his lips slightly pursed. He had had his interview with Gracey; he now had no cause for suspicion or complaint. He looked towards Harriet and put down his glass, preparing to go. He said: "If there's no transport, we'll have to stay in Athens – anyway for the time being. I don't suppose you want me to be around doing nothing?"

"Oh!" Gracey made a gesture that suggested the matter was too trivial to be discussed further. "Argue it out with Dubedat. He's in charge of the School now. If you don't try to high-hat him, you'll find him quite helpful. Go and be nice to him."

The Pringles started to rise.

"Stay a while. Have another drink."

The command was cordial, but it was a command. Guy and Harriet settled back in their seats unwillingly, but not without hope. They had nowhere else to go. They might as well stay and perhaps, by staying, something could be gained.

Gracey now lay back as though the interview had wearied him. The Pringles, despondent, were not much company and they felt he was waiting in the hope of better.

Harriet said: "This is a pleasant room."

Gracey looked at it doubtfully: "Rather comfortless, wouldn't you say? A student's room. This was a hostel for the young, of course. So cold in winter. And the cooking's dreadful."

Gracey's complaints went on while Harriet looked round the vast, bare room in envy. The sun was low and the windows were in shadow, but outside the sunlight still trickled, like an amber cordial, beneath the olive trees. The distant glow was refracted into the room so the twilight about them was as tawny as the glitter in apatite.

This, she thought, was the room for her. The unpolished floorboards, the dusty herbal scent and the space, made more spacious by the vistas of garden, seemed familiar. For a moment she knew where she had encountered it before, then the knowledge was gone. As she pursued it through memories of childhood books, a noise recalled her.

Someone opened the door. Gracey, revivified at once, sat up and cried: "Archie, what a joy!"

A young man entered the room with a shy aloof smile, sidling in as though he knew himself more than welcome and wanted to counter the fact by apparent diffidence.

Gracey said to Harriet: "This is Archie Callard," then, seeing there was a second visitor following the first, added in a tone of anti-climax: "And this is Ben Phipps."

Both men noted the Pringles as they might note people whom they had heard discussed. Ben Phipps stared with frank curiosity, but Callard gave no more than an appraising glance hidden at once in a show of indifference.

"Where is the Major?" Gracey eagerly asked.

Callard murmured in an off-hand way: "Gone to a party. He'll come later."

It was clear to the Pringles that they had been detained on view for Gracey's friend. Once introduced, they could take a back seat and they were in no mood to do much else. Guy, usually stimulated by new acquaintances, sat silent, his glass held like a mask at the level of his lips. Harriet tried to accept the situation by detaching herself from it and watching the company as she would watch a play.

At first sight she could see no more reason for Callard's welcome than Phipps's lack of it. Callard was the better looking, of course, but Phipps had vitality and a readiness to please. When asked to pour drinks "like a good fellow", he went at the task with a will. Perhaps he was over-ready. If that were a fault, it was not one of which Callard was guilty. He threw himself at full length on one of the two beds and when Gracey questioned him further about the Major's whereabouts, did not trouble to reply.

Phipps gave the answers, only too eager to be heard. When the drinks had been handed round, he placed himself in the middle of the room, somehow extruding his personality, prepared to talk.

Addressing him as someone who knew, Gracey asked: "What's the news from the front? Is anything happening up there?"

Phipps, short, thick-boned, with mongrel features and a black bristle of hair, sat forward on his strong, thick haunches and said in a decided voice: "Not much news. Town's full of rumours, but no one knows anything."

Archie Callard, muffled by the pillow, said: "The Italians'll be here tomorrow – and that's no rumour."

Gracey jerked his head round and said reproachfully: "That's not funny, Archie."

"It's not meant to be funny. They crossed the frontier at six a.m. They're making for Athens. What's to stop them coming straight down?"

Gracey turned in appeal to Phipps: "Surely there'll be some resistance? Metaxas said they would resist."

Phipps, staring at his host, had an air of obliging good humour that came from the fact his gaze was neutralized by a pair of very thick, black-rimmed glasses. Harriet, viewing him from the side, could see, behind the pebbled lens, an observant eye that was black and hard as coal.

"Oh, they'll resist, all right," said Phipps. "Submission is all against the Greek tradition. They're a defiant people and they'll resist to the end, but . . . " Having started out with the intention of reassuring Gracey, he was now led by his informed volubility into a far from reassuring truth. "They've got no arms. Old Musso's been preparing for months, but the Government here's done damn all. They saw the war coming and they just sat back and let it come. Half of them are pro-German, of course. They want things over quickly. They want a Greek collapse and an Axis victory . . . "

Guy, his attention caught by this criticism of the Metaxas Government, watched him with an intent interest, but Gracey, more mindful of the particular than the general, moved uneasily in his chair and at last broke in to protest:

"Really, Ben! You're trying to frighten me. You both are. I know you're just being naughty, but it's too bad. I'm an invalid. I'm in great pain when I walk. I couldn't get any distance without help. If the Italians march in, you can take to your heels. But what can I do?"

Phipps gave a guff of laughter. "We're all in the same boat," he said. "If there's a ship of some sort, we'll see you get away all right. If there isn't, none of us'll get far. The Italians will blow up the Corinth Canal bridge and here we'll be – *stuck!*"

"Why worry?" Callard sat up, laughing. With auburn hair too long, mouth too full, eyes too large, he looked spoilt and entrancing, and conscious of being both. "The Italians are charming and they've always been very nice to me."

"I don't doubt," Gracey said in a petulant tone. "But times have changed. They're Fascists now, and they're the enemy. They're not going to be very nice to a crowd of civilian prisoners." The reality of war, touching him for the first time, was shattering his urbanity. He frowned at Ben Phipps, who may have been aware of his fears but too roused by the situation to be impeded by them.

"I must say," said Phipps, "I like the idea of Metaxas coming down to see Grazzi in a bath-robe. It was about three-thirty. The ultimatum gave the Greeks about two and a half hours to hand over lock, stock and barrel. Metaxas said: 'I couldn't hand over my house in that time, much less my country.' I've never had much use for him but I must admit he's put up a good show this time."

"Yes, but what am I to do?" Gracey asked impatiently. "I've got to get to Beirut for treatment."

The boasted "priority flight" forgotten, he was twitching with so much nervous misery that Harriet could not but feel sorry for him. She said: "I've heard there's to be an evacuation boat. It's for women and children but I'm sure . . . "

"Women, children and invalids," Archie Callard interrupted. "Don't worry, Colin. The Major will get you safely away. He'll fix it."

Gracey subsided and his smile returned. "One certainly can rely on the Major." As a tap came on the door, he added happily: "And here's the man himself. *Entrez, Entrez.*"

Pinkrose entered.

"Oh, it's Lord Pinkrose." Gracey greeted him without enthusiasm.

Pinkrose did not notice how he was greeted. Trotting across the room, he nodded to Callard and Phipps, ignored the Pringles, and began at once: "I'm worried, Gracey; I'm extremely worried. We're at war – but perhaps you know? You do? Well, I went up to the Legation to ask about my repatriation. I could have spoken to Frewen, but I thought it better to deal with the higher powers."

"Who did you see?" Gracey asked.

"Young Bird."

"Good God!" Archie Callard sobbed his laughter into the pillow. "Is that your idea of higher power?"

"What did they say?" Gracey asked.

"Not very much. Not very much. No, not very much. There may be a boat."

Gracey seemed displeased that Pinkrose knew about the boat and said reprovingly: "If there's a boat, it'll be for women and children, not for *men*. You can't force your way on. It would never do."

"Indeed?" Pinkrose gave Gracey a look of startled annoyance while Gracey faced him indignantly. The two men eyed one another in a fury of self-concern.

The light had almost faded. In the spectral glimmer of late dusk, Gracey's desiccated youth looked deathly while Pinkrose's cheeks were as grey and withered as lizard skin. Seeing Pinkrose glaring like a wraith in the gloom of hell, Gracey pulled himself together and said with strained amiability:

"Be a good fellow, Ben, and switch on the lights."

As the light restored him, Gracey leant back and said: "*I* may *have* to go on the boat; but, given the choice, I would not dream of it. The Mediterranean is full of enemy shipping: submarines, U-boats, mines, and so on. It's a perilous sea."

"Oh!" said Pinkrose, faltering.

Archie Callard, who was sitting up in amusement, agreed. "I wouldn't dream of it either. Any British ship is 'fair game' on the Med., and there'll be no convoy. The navy can't spare a cruiser."

"Oh!" said Pinkrose again and he looked about with fearful eyes.

He was about to speak when another tap came on the door and Gracey brought him to a stop by saying joyfully: "The Major, at last!"

They all watched as the door crept open and a hand, pushed through, waved at them. A head appeared. Smiling widely, Major Cookson inquired in a small, comic voice: "May I come in?"

"Come in, come in; bless you," Gracey cried.

The Major was carrying several prettily wrapped parcels which he brought across and dropped on Gracey's table. "A few goodies," he said, then stepped back to examine the invalid with an admiring affection. "How are we today?"

Querulous in a playful way, Gracey said: "Those tiresome Italians! Such a worry."

"Not for you. *You're* not to worry. Leave that to your friends."

Middle-aged, of middle height, with a neat unremarkable face and bleared blue eyes, the Major held himself tightly together, hands clasped at the bottom edge of a neat, dark, closely buttoned jacket. When he sat, he sat with a concise movement and, unclasping a hand which held a tightly rolled handkerchief, dabbed at his nostrils.

Archie Callard jumped up from the bed with a sudden show of energy and, coming to the table, began to sniff at the parcels and put his nose into bags.

"Naughty!" The Major gave him a surprisingly sharp slap and he jumped aside like a ballet dancer. Gracey giggled helplessly.

There was a sense of union between the three who seemed to be hinting at a game that was not played in public. Pinkrose watched perplexed but it was Ben Phipps who seemed to be the real outsider here.

Gracey wanted to have news of the party at which the Major had been detained. While he talked with Cookson and Callard, Phipps made several attempts to join in and each time was ignored. On edge at this treatment, he pushed himself to the fore, talking too much and too loudly, and the others looked at him in exasperation.

Discomforted by his behaviour, Harriet saw that the over-

cultivated voice and over-large glasses were blazonry intended
to disguise his own plainness of person. She suspected that he
rode a rough sea of moneyless uncertainty and was a man
who would always demand from life more than life was likely
to give.

The Major began opening the parcels, saying: "I thought as
I could not get here until supper time, it would be nice if we
all took a little bite together."

"What a charming idea!" Gracey said.

He had not troubled to introduce the Pringles to Cookson
and they knew they were now required to take themselves
off. As they got to their feet, Gracey sped them with a smile.

"Do come again some time," he said.

The parcels were being opened before they left the room.

Down in the hall the supper bell rang. The Academy food
might be indifferent, the lights cheerless, the rooms under-
furnished, but Harriet longed to be sheltered here, one of a
community, fed, companioned and protected.

The streets were unlit. The authorities had imposed a
blackout. The Pringles clung together in the darkness of the
unfamiliar district where pavements were uneven and areas
unrailed. Guy, quite blind under these conditions, fell over
some steps and groaned with pain.

Savagely, Harriet said: "Bloody Dubedat!" and Guy had to
laugh: "You can't blame him for the black-out."

"No, but I blame him for a lot of other things. I'd like to
know what he told Gracey about you."

"So would I; but what does it matter? Dubedat wanted to
do something more than teach. He asked me if he could give an
occasional lecture. I refused. I must have hurt his pride."

Harriet, feeling for the first time that she had had enough of
Guy's forbearance, said: "Dubedat is nothing but a conceited
nonentity. The pity is that you ever employed him at all. I hope
you don't intend to ask him for any favours."

"No. We'll wait and see who gets Gracey's job."

"Could the London office appoint Dubedat? Is it possible?"

"Anything's possible. All they know is what Gracey cares to
tell them. He said there were several candidates. The choice
will really be Gracey's choice because they will choose the
person he recommends. It's as simple at that."

"He couldn't recommend Dubedat."

"He could recommend worse . . . I suppose."

"I doubt it. But we'll see. Meanwhile, what are we going to do about money?"

"Don't worry. The Organization won't let us starve."

"You'll speak to Gracey?"

"No. I'll cable the Cairo office."

"You might have done that days ago."

"If I had, we'd've been ordered to Cairo. Now we're stranded here. They'll have to let me have my salary."

She was suddenly exhilarated. Their hopeless and money-less condition had filled her with fear, but suddenly her fear was gone. She threw her arms round Guy, feeling that his human presence was a solution of all life's difficulties, and said: "What would I do without you?"

Perhaps he was not as confident as he wished her to think, for he returned her embrace as though lost himself in the darkness of this city that had nothing to offer him. They stood for some minutes wrapped together, each thankful for the other, and then guided each other down through the main square to the hotel. There they went to supper in the basement, the only place where they could get a meal without making an immediate payment.

5

THE YOUNG MEN WERE DISAPPEARING from the city. The porter left the Pringles' hotel, first saying an emotional farewell to everyone, and his place was taken by an old man moustached like the great Venizelos.

Each day lorry-loads of conscripts were driven through the streets to the station and the girls threw flowers to them. Farmers came into Athens leading horses that were needed for the army. But there was no sight of the Italians.

Mussolini had told Hitler that he would take Greece in ten days, just as the Germans had taken France. At the end of the ten days his troops were still on the Kalamas River, at the spot where they had found the Greeks waiting for them.

The Italian radio complained of their reception. It said that the Duce had offered to occupy Greece in a friendly, protective spirit and had not been prepared for this resistance. It would take the Italians a day or two to get over the shock.

The Italian Minister had not left Athens and was pained when he found his telephone had been cut off. He rang Metaxas to ask why he was being treated in such a fashion. Greece and Italy were not at war.

"Sir," Metaxas replied, "this is no time for philological discussion," and he put down his receiver.

The war was, in its way, comic, but no one imagined it would remain comic for long. The Italians had behind them the weight of Axis armour. Beneath all the humour was the fear that the Greek line would break suddenly and the enemy arrive overnight.

An order had gone out from the Legation that British subjects must be prepared to leave Greece at an hour's notice. Each person could take a suitcase, and the suitcase should be kept ready packed. When Guy presented himself at the Legation and asked for his salary to be diverted from Cairo, he saw a junior secretary who said: "If that's how you want it, I'll pop a note in the jolly old bag; but my guess is: while the transfer is winging its way here, you'll be off to where it came from. Do you want to take the risk? Righteo, then! You know the drill? You chaps draw from Legation funds. If you like, you can have a small advance to settle your hotel bill."

The bill was settled, to Harriet's relief, but there would be no money to spend until the transfer arrived.

The Pringles heard nothing more from Gracey. No word came from Dubedat, but a few days after their visit to the Academy, the porter rang to say a visitor was on his way up.

Harriet opened the door. Toby Lush, outside, said with ponderous gravity: "I'd like a word with himself."

Guy was sorting out his books. Greeting him with unusual sobriety, Toby sat on the edge of the bed and contemplated his pipe. The Pringles waited. He spoke at last:

"We hear you went and saw Mr. Gracey?"

Guy said: "Yes."

"Well, it's like this . . . " Toby stuck the empty pipe into his mouth and sucked it thoughtfully. "When we came here, the old soul and me, we had to find work. After all, we had to *eat*. So when we met Mr. Gracey, we laid it on thick. Anyone would under the circumstances."

"What did you tell him, exactly?"

"Oh, this and that. We said we'd done a spot of lecturing up in Bucharest . . . a few other things. You don't want the gory details, do you? Just a bit of hornswoggle. *You* understand. But the thing is, the old soul's moidered; hopes you didn't give us away."

"I didn't give anything away."

"That's all right then. But . . . " an expression of inquisitorial cunning came over Toby's features and he pointed the pipe stem at Guy: "Supposing Mr. Gracey asks you direct what we did?"

Formal with annoyance, Guy replied: "I would tell him I do not discuss my friends' affairs."

"Oh, good enough! Good enough!" Toby whoofed with relief: "And you didn't mention we'd done a bolt?"

"Certainly not."

"Fine. Splendid. I said you wouldn't." Much heartened, Toby leant back against the wall and, taking out his tobacco and matches, prepared himself for a chat.

Harriet was having none of this. "Now," she said, "I'd like to ask you something. What did *you* tell Gracey? Did you say that Guy wasted his time producing *Troilus and Cressida?*"

Toby jerked up with a pained frown. "Me? I never did."

"What about Dubedat?"

Toby sat up. Scrambling his equipment together with agitated hands, he said: "How do I know? He sees Mr. Gracey in private. He doesn't tell me everything." He got to his feet. "Have to scarper. The old soul's a bit carked. I'll let him know you didn't sneak. He'll appreciate it."

"He ought to."

Toby made off with the gait of a guilty fox. When he had gone, Harriet said to Guy: "Dubedat means to be Director. He's afraid you might have queered his pitch."

"It certainly looks like it," Guy was forced to agree. Pale and unhappy, he returned to his books, wanting to hear no more. Harriet pitied his disillusionment, but had no patience with it. Reality was not to be altered by an inability to recognize fact.

She had remained with Guy, imprisoned in the room, but now, uplifted by a sense of being the stronger of the two, she said: "Come on, let's go for a walk."

He did not move. "You go. I don't want to go."

"But what will you do, shut up here alone?"

"Work."

"Have you any work?"

"I'm getting quotations for a lecture on Coleridge."

"Surely you could do that any time? You might not lecture again for months."

He shook his head. Bent over his books, he whistled softly to himself: a sign of stress. Harriet stood at the door, longing to go out, not knowing what to say. During past crises – the fall of France, the final break-up in Bucharest – he had found escape, first by producing *Troilus and Cressida*, then by organizing a summer school. Throwing himself into one occupation or another, he had managed to keep anxiety on the periphery of consciousness; now, without employment, without friends, without money, he was trying to follow his old escape pattern. But there was no route open to him. All he could do was sit here in this dark, narrow room and try to lose himself in work.

"Wouldn't you be better at the School library?" she asked.

"I'd rather not go there."

One afternoon, while wandering about alone, Harriet met Yakimov and, strolling with him up University Street, took the opportunity to ask about some of the people they had seen in Athens.

"Who is Major Cookson?"

Yakimov answered at once. "Very important and distinguished."

"Yes, but what does he *do*?"

That was more difficult. "*Do*, dear girl?" Yakimov pondered the question heavily, then brightened: "Believe . . . indeed, have inside information to the effect: he's something big in the S.S."

"Good heavens, the German S.S.?"

"No. The Secret Service."

As there was little point in pursuing that fantasy, Harriet went on to inquire about Callard and Phipps. Sighing at being forced into intellectual activity, Yakimov dismissed them as "both very distinguished".

"What about Mrs. Brett and Miss Jay?" Harriet persisted.

"Don't ask me, dear girl. Town's full of those old tits."

"Yes, but what are they all *doing* here?"

"Nothing much. They live here."

The English who lived in Bucharest had gone there to work. The English in Athens were clearly of a different order. Encountering for the first time people who lived abroad unoccupied, she was amazed by their inactivity and, learning nothing from Yakimov, decided to take her curiosity to Alan Frewen. He had asked them if they would go with him on Sunday morning when he exercised Diocletian in the National Gardens.

He called for them as agreed and Guy said to Harriet, as he had said before: "You go."

She pleaded: "Do come darling. He doesn't want me alone. Why not bring your work and sit in the gardens while we walk round!"

Resolute in his revolt against circumstances, Guy said: "No, I'm all right here. Go on down. Alan'll love having you to himself."

Harriet could not believe it. She descended diffidently to the hall where Alan waited, his face so obscured by his glasses it was impossible to tell how he felt. He was as shy as she was and they said nothing until they reached the square.

He was limping and several times when the dog pulled on the lead, he had difficulty in keeping his footing. He apologized, explaining that he had had an attack of gout.

"I had to stay home for a couple of days," he said. "Not that it mattered. Things are still slack at the office. There's not much to do except get out the News Sheet."

"What does Yakimov do?" she asked.

"Oh, his job is to deliver it."

"Is that all?"

Alan gave a laugh and did not reply.

There had been a shower of rain, the first of the autumn. It had scarcely moistened the ground but the sky, broken with mauve and blue clouds, had taken on the fresh expectancy of spring. Harriet longed for Guy to be with them, not only to ease their constraint but to enjoy, as she enjoyed, the changing season.

She suddenly burst out: "Guy's very unhappy. What can we do for him?"

"You had no luck with Gracey, then?"

"None at all. He said he had delegated his authority. He suggested Guy go and ask Dubedat for work."

Alan stared down frowning, considering what she had said, then started to speak with some force: "I really feel this can't go on. The school's becoming a laughing-stock. There are all sorts of stories going round about the lectures. Apparently Lush suggested that Dante and Milton might have met in the streets of Florence. When one of the students pointed out that there was about three hundred years between them, Lush said: 'Crumbs! Have I made a clanger?' Cookson's protected the lot of them for some time, but there've been complaints. I know Mrs. Brett has written home. I'm sure a responsible person will be appointed when Gracey goes. My advice is: wait."

"Guy would agree, but I'm afraid he finds it a strain."

"I know. I know," Alan nodded his sympathy, and after this she felt there was harmony between them.

It occurred to her that Alan was the first friend she and Guy

had made on equal terms. In Bucharest the people she knew
had been the people known to Guy before his marriage and she
imagined herself accepted because she was Guy's wife, a state
of affairs the more disjunctive because she was unused to being
a wife. It had seemed to her then that she had left behind not
only her own friends but her individuality. Now she began to
feel the absurdity of this. Why, after all, should Alan Frewen
not be as content with her as he would be with Guy?

They passed the Washingtonia Robusta palms that stood
with their great silvery satin trunks across the entrance to the
gardens. Inside, the sandy walks curved and flowed beneath
sprays of small, tremulous leaves. The sun came and went.
Moving soundlessly, they entered a tropical dampness filled
with the scents of earth. Alan released Diocletian, who was
off at once prospecting beneath the bushy trees that sifted the
sun on to the dark, soft, powdery ground. The paths were all
much alike. The foliage was all light, a peppering of dry, rustling greenery that dappled the sand with light and shade. Then
a vista opened. There was a drive lined with greyish, rubbery
trees.

"Judas trees," Alan said. "You must see them in the spring."

"Is that when they flower?"

"They flower for Easter."

And where would they be at Easter? Alan had said "Wait",
but he said nothing more. And what could he say? By coming
here, Guy and she had created their own problem, and they
must solve it for themselves.

She had thought they need only reach a friendly country and
their lives could begin; but here they were, and their lives
were still in abeyance. In Bucharest they had had employment and a home. They had had Sasha. Guy might find employment here, they might even find a home but Sasha, she
feared, was lost for ever. Even his memory was disappearing
into the past. For the last week or more she had not given him
a thought, though there always remained, like a shadow on her
mind, the hollow darkness into which he had disappeared. He
was dead, she supposed, like her loved red kitten that had
fallen from the balcony of the flat. If one could not bear the
memory of the dead, then they must be shut out of memory.
There was no other action anyone could take against the
bafflement of grief.

She was recalled from her thoughts by the squawks of water-birds and the cries of children. They were walking through a coppice where the air was jaundiced with the weedy, muddy smell of lake water.

Alan said: "Where's Diocletian? I'd better put him on the lead."

He held the dog close as they emerged from under the trees and came to a sunlit clearing where small iron seats stood round the sandy lake edge. The lake was small. A bridge spanned the water that now, in the last days of the dry season, was scarcely water at all, but a glossy, greenish film in which ducks, geese and swans were squelching about. The children were feeding the birds and the birds, snatching and quarrelling, were making all the noise in the world.

Limping towards a couple of vacant chairs, Alan said he must sit down. He lowered his large backside on to the little iron seat and with a sigh let his bulk settle down. When they were both seated, an attendant came and stood at a distance, respectfully awaiting the sum that was payable in fee. When Alan handed over the money, the old man counted back some coins so small they now bought nothing but the right to sit for a while beside the lake. Alan talked in Greek with the attendant and afterwards told Harriet they had been discussing the war. The old man said he had two sons at the front but he was not at all disturbed because the English had promised to aid the Greeks and everyone said the English were the strongest people in the world.

"He knows me," Alan said. "I come here often to read Cavafy. I suppose you know Cavafy? No? I'll translate 'The Barbarians' for you one day. It fits our times."

"Are the English going to send aid?"

"I wish I knew. They haven't much to send. I've heard the Greeks aren't interested in half-measures and I don't think we could rise to a full-scale campaign."

There was not much to be said about the war and when they had said it all, they sat for a long time in the sunlight while Harriet considered how she might put to him the questions that Yakimov could not answer. She at last overcame her own reticence and asked:

"Have you known Cookson long?"

"I've been seeing him on and off, over the years."

"You've lived here a long time, then? Before the war, were you one of these people who live abroad and do nothing?"

Alan laughed at her disapproving tone and said: "Indeed I was not. I had to earn my living. I came here as a photographer. I had a studio on Lycabettos and I went to stay in places like Mycenae, Nauplia, Delphi and Olympus. When I settled in a place, I'd try to absorb it and then record it. I wrote a few introductory pieces to albums of photographs, nothing much, the pictures were the thing. I'd like to record the whole of Greece."

"And when you have, what will you do?"

"Begin at the beginning again."

"And Diocletian goes with you?"

"Of course. Diocletian is a Grecophil like me. I brought him from England when I was last there, five years ago – partly for his own sake and partly so I need not go back." When he saw her look of inquiry, he smiled. "If I took him back he would have to go into quarantine. We would be separated for six months, which is unthinkable. He is my safeguard. When my relatives write reproachful letters, I reply: 'I would love to come and see you, but there is the problem of Diocletian.'"

"But supposing you have to leave? I mean, if we all have to leave? What will you do?"

"Let us consider that when the time comes."

She took the chance to return to Cookson. "He seems to be very influential," she said.

"He is, I suppose. He's lived here a long time and knows a great many influential people. He's liked. He's rather a charming old thing; he has this house at Phaleron – by the sea, very pleasant in summer. He's hospitable. His parties are famous and no one wants to be left out."

"Is he married?"

"He was once, I think."

"And now?"

Alan laughed. "Now? I really can't say. He invited me once to 'a ra-ther small and ra-ther curious party'. I'm afraid I left early; I could see it was going to get curiouser and curiouser."

"He seems to have been extremely kind to Gracey."

"Yes, they're great friends. Gracey played up to him. They all play up to him. That's all that's necessary."

"I wish Guy could do that," Harriet said. "But he never plays up to the right people."

"I imagine that's the nice thing about him?"

"Perhaps, but I don't suppose it will get us anywhere."

Alan laughed and when he said nothing, she went on to ask about Gracey. Was he really an invalid?

"Who can say? He certainly slipped on Pendeli and hurt his back. A good many people have done that but I've never known anyone before who had to spend months lying in a chair. Still, he seems determined to get to the Lebanon clinic for a cure."

"My belief is, he's tired of the whole game."

"Really?" Alan looked round, his face alive with amused interest: "You mean the injury? You think it's a game, do you?"

"Yes. Mrs. Brett says he's bone lazy. I'm sure he never wanted to run the School, he wanted to be an elegant figurehead; but the lecturers went off leaving the place on his hands. He must have been thankful when Toby and Dubedat turned up; and the accident was a godsend. It excused his idleness, but now the pretence has been going on too long. He's stuck with it till he can get away."

"You may be right." Alan edged himself off the seat and managed to stand up. Rejecting Gracey as an enigma of little importance, he said: "It looks as though we're in for another shower."

The sun had gone in. The grown-ups were calling the children from the lake and a few drops of rain made small moon-craters around the fluttering water-birds.

Walking back under the trees, Alan stared ahead and did not speak. Unless stimulated by questions, he seemed to feel no need for conversation and Harriet wondered why a man so withdrawn and silent should seek out company at all. As there was little else to be said, she might as well continue to ask her questions. What about Archie Callard? He was, of course, a friend of the Major, but was he anything more than that?

"He's a clever young man," Alan said. "No fool I assure you, but he's handicapped by having a rich father. He is not forced to work but is always complaining that he doesn't get enough to spend. He occasionally starts out on some project that he hopes will bring in money. He went to Lemnos to look for a labyrinth that probably never existed. Recently he's been staying on Patmos with some idea of writing a life of St. John. Of course he gets bored, and back he comes and that, for the moment, is that."

"And Ben Phipps? I shouldn't have thought he had a rich father."

"Indeed he hasn't. He's been working here as a journalist and he's published a few things. I haven't read any, but I believe he has some reputation."

"What's he doing in that set?"

"Hanging on hopefully."

"But what is he likely to get?"

"Preferment. He's sick of scraping a living with his bits of journalism. He'd like an easy, steady, well-paid job; a job that would place him right in the front of the social picture."

"You mean: Gracey's job?"

"That would do as well as another."

"I see. If he got it, do you think he'd employ Guy?"

"He very well might. I know he doesn't think much of Rosencrantz and Guildenstern."

"Lush and Dubedat? The betrayers who served the king. What rewards, I wonder, for those who have served Gracey?"

"We'll know soon enough."

They were now back at Harriet's hotel and as she paused, Alan said: "I'm meeting Yakimov at Zonar's. Won't you join us?"

She said: "I'd love to. I'll see if I can get Guy out," and she ran upstairs to persuade him.

She half-expected to find him gone, for restless, gregarious, eager to entertain and influence, he was not one to spend two hours alone in their little room, yet he was still there lying on the bed, propped up with pillows, his glasses pushed to his brow, a pencil stuck in his hair and books all around him.

She scolded him: "You've been here long enough. You need a drink. Come on."

"I'd rather not."

"What's the matter with you, for heaven's sake? Are you ill?"

"No," he pulled down the glasses in order to see her. "We haven't any money."

"Let Yakimov buy you a drink. You bought him plenty when he was hard up."

"I can't go to cafés in the hope someone else will pay for me."

"Do come. I'll pay for you."

"No, don't worry about me."

"Then come down to the dining-room and have something to eat."

He followed her and took his meal without saying much. She had hoped that, alone here, dependent upon each other, they would be closer than they had ever been. Now it seemed to her she had been nearer to him when he was not here; nearest, probably, when she had imagined him in the Lufthansa above the Aegean. He had only to arrive to take a step away from her.

He was not to be shut up in intimacy. The world was his chief relationship and she wondered whether he really understood any other. His quarrel now was not with her, but with defaulting humanity and he was in retreat from it. And here they were with leisure and freedom – things they had not had before in the year of marriage – and Guy was closeted with his dilemma while she went for walks with a stranger.

6

NEXT MORNING, CALLED TO THE TELEPHONE while at breakfast, Guy returned transformed. He took the dining-room steps at a run, his face alight, his whole person animated, and called to Harriet: "Hurry up. We're going to the Legation."

"Really? Why?"

"The Cairo office has approved my presence here. Apparently they've got all the chaps they can deal with in Egypt. They don't want any more. The Legation say I can have some money."

Harriet walked up with him and waited in the Chancellory while Guy saw the accountant and was permitted to draw on Legation funds. She could hear his voice raised happily in the office and when he came out he was pushing his drachma notes into an old two-penny cash-book which he kept in his breast pocket. He expressed by his action his indifference to money but he was not, Harriet now knew, indifferent to the lack of it.

"And what do you think?" he said: "Our old friend Dobbie Dobson is being sent here from Bucharest. We'll have a friend at Court."

"Will we?" Harriet doubtfully asked.

"Of course." Guy was confident of it and walking downhill to the main road, he said: "I like Dobson. I do like Dobson. He's so unaffected and amiable."

Guy, too, was unaffected and amiable which, considering the poverty in which he had grown up, was a more surprising thing. He had seemed to Harriet to have a unique attitude to life, an attitude that was a product of confidence and simplicity, but she had seen that the simplicity was not as unified as it seemed, the confidence could be shaken. Moneyless, he had remained under cover and now, emerging, he emerged for her in a slightly different guise.

She said: "I'm never quite sure with you where showmanship ends and reality begins."

"Don't bother about that," he said. "Where do you want to eat tonight?"

"Anywhere but the hotel crypt."

"Let's ask Frewen to supper. He'll say where we should go."

At midday they found Alan at Zonar's, in his usual place. When he received their invitation, he grew red and his face strained into its painful smile with a gratitude that was almost emotional. They could see how deeply he wished for friends. And how odd, Harriet thought, that he had so few and, after all his years in Greece, should be dependent upon newcomers like Yakimov and the Pringles. Was it that he approached people, instigated friendship, but could go no further? She could imagine him with many acquaintances but known by none of them.

He suggested that they go a taverna where they might see some Greek dancing. He knew one beyond the Roman agora and that evening called for them in a taxi. He handed Harriet a bunch of little mauve-pink flowers.

She said: "Cyclamen, already!"

"Yes, they begin early. In fact, things here begin almost before they stop."

"Do you mean the winter stops before it starts?"

"Alas, no. The winter can be bitter, and it's likely to come down on us any day now. The weather's broken in the mountains. Reports from the front say 'torrents of rain'. I only hope the Italians and their heavy gear get stuck in the mud."

They were put down in a wide, dark road where the wind blew cold. Alan led them between black-out curtains into a small taverna where there was only the proprietor, sitting as though he despaired of custom. At the sight of Alan, he leapt up and began offering them a choice of tables set round an open space. The space was for dancing, but there was no one to dance.

When they sat down, he stood for some time talking to Alan, his voice full of sorrow, his hands tragically raised, so the Pringles were prepared for unhappy news long before Alan was free to interpret it. The proprietor had two sons who, being themselves skilled dancers, had drawn in rival performers from the neighbourhood. But now his sons and all the other young men had gone to the war and here he was, alone. But even if the boys were home, there would be no dancing, for the Greeks had given up dancing. No one would dance while friends and brothers and lovers were at the war. No, no one would dance again until every single enemy had been driven from the soil of Greece. Still, the taverna was open and the proprietor was happy to see Alan and Alan's companions. When introduced to Guy and Harriet, he shook each by the hand and said there was some ewe cooked with tomatoes and onions, and, pray heavens, there always would be good wine, both white and black.

He went to the kitchen and Alan apologized for the gloom and quiet. Seeing him crestfallen, Harriet began asking him about the boys who used to dance here. How did they dance? Where did they learn?

Stimulated at once, Alan began to talk, saying: "Oh, all the Greek boys can dance. Dancing is a natural form of self-expression here. If there's music, someone runs on to the floor and stretches out his hand, and someone else joins him and the dance begins. And then there's the *Zebeikiko*! The dance they do with their arms round each other's shoulders. First there may be only two or three, then another joins and another; and the women clap and . . . oh dear me! The whole place seems to be thudding with excitement. It stirs the blood, I can tell you."

"I would love to see it."

"Perhaps you will. The war won't go on for ever."

When the wine was brought, Alan invited the proprietor to drink to a speedy victory. The old man held up his glass, saying: "Niki, niki, niki," then told them the Italians would be on their knees before the month was out. He had no doubt of it.

When he left them, the room was silent except for the purr of the lamps that hung just below the prints pinned on the walls. One print showed the Virgin done in the Byzantine manner; another was a coloured war-poster in which the women of Epirus, barefooted, their skirts girded above their knees, were helping their men haul the guns up the mountainside.

After he had brought in the food, the proprietor retired tactfully and sat at his own table, apparently preoccupied until Alan called to him: "Where are all the customers?"

The proprietor sprang up again to reply. He explained that in these times people were not inclined to go out. They would not seek merriment while their young men were fighting and losing their lives.

When the man returned to his seat, Alan gazed after him with a reminiscent tenderness and Harriet said: "You love Greece, don't you?"

"Yes. I love the country and I love the people. They have a wonderful vitality and friendliness. They want to be liked, of course; but that does not detract from their individuality and independence. Have you ever heard about the Greek carpenter who was asked to make six dining-room chairs?"

"No. Tell us."

"The customer wanted them all alike and the carpenter named an extremely high figure. 'Out of the question,' said the customer. 'Well,' said the carpenter, 'if I can make them all different, I'd do them for half that price.' "

Alan talked for some time about the Greeks and the countryside: "an idyllic, unspoilt countryside". Guy, interested in more practical aspects of Greek life, here broke in to ask if by "unspoilt" Alan did not mean undeveloped, and by "idyllic", simply conditions that had not changed since the days of the Ottoman Empire. How was it possible to enjoy the beauty of a country when the inhabitants lived in privation and misery?

Alan was startled by Guy's implied criticism. His great sombre face grew dark and he seemed incapable of speech. After some moments he said, as though his vanity had been touched:

"I've seen a great deal of the country. I have not noticed that the people are unhappy."

There was a defensive irritation in his tone and Harriet would, if she could, have stopped the subject at once, but Guy was not easily checked. Certain that Alan, a humane and intelligent man, could be made to share his opinions, he asked with expectant interest:

"But are they happy? Can people be happy under a dictatorship?"

"A dictatorship!" Alan started in surprise, then laughed. "You *could* call it a dictatorship, but a very benevolent one. I suppose you've been talking to members of the K.K.E.? What would they have done if they'd got power? Before Metaxas took over there'd been an attempt to impose a modern political system on what was virtually a primitive society. The result was chaos. In the old days there'd been the usual semi-oriental graft but as soon as there was a measure of democratic freedom, graft ran riot. The only thing Metaxas could do was suspend the system. The experiment was brought to a stop. A temporary stop, of course."

"When do you think it will start again?"

"When the country's fit to govern itself."

"And when will that be? What's being done to bring Greece into line with more advanced countries? I mean, of course, industrially advanced countries?"

"Nothing, I hope." Alan spoke with a tartness that surprised both Guy and Harriet. "Greece is all right as it is. Metaxas is not personally ambitious. He's a sort of paternal despot, like the despots of the classical world; and, all things considered, I think he's doing very well."

Guy, assessing and criticizing Alan's limitations, said: "You prefer the peasants to remain in picturesque poverty, I suppose?"

"I prefer that they remain as they are: courteous, generous, honourable and courageous. Athens is not what it was, I admit. There used to be a time when any stranger in the city was treated as a guest. As more and more strangers came here, naturally that couldn't go on; yet something remains. The great tradition of *philoxenia* – of friendship towards a stranger – still exists in the country and on the islands. It exists here, in a little café like this!" Alan's voice sank with emotion; he had to pause a moment before he could say:

"A noble people! Why should anyone wish to change them?"

Guy nodded appreciatively. "A noble people, yes. They deserve something better than subsistence at starvation level.

"Man does not live by bread alone. You young radicals want to turn the world into a mass-producing factory, and you expect to do it overnight. You make no allowance for the fact different countries are at different stages of development."

"It's not only a question of development, but a question of freedom; especially freedom of thought. There are political prisoners in Greece. Isn't that true?"

"I'm sure I don't know. There may be, but if people are

intent on making a nuisance of themselves, then prison is the best place for them."

"They're intent on improving the conditions of their fellow men."

"Aren't we all?" said Alan, with the asperity of a docile man attacked through his ideals. He took his dark glasses out and sat fingering them.

Seeing that his hands were trembling, Harriet said: "Darling, let's talk of something else," but Guy was absorbed in his own subject. As he spoke at length of good schools, clinics, ante-natal care, child-welfare centres, collective farms and industries communally owned, Alan's face grew more and more sombre. At last he broke in, protesting:

"You come from an industrial area. You can only see progress in terms of industry. Greece has never been an industrial country and I hope it never will be."

"Can Greece support its people without industry?"

Without attempting to answer, Alan said: "I love Greece. I love the Greeks. I do not want to see any change here."

"You speak like a tourist. A country *must* support its populace."

"It does support them. No one dies of starvation."

"How do you know? Starvation can be a slow process. How many Greeks have to emigrate each year?"

There was a sense of deadlock at the table. Alan put his glasses down, stared at them, then gave a laugh. "You'll have to have a talk with Ben Phipps," he said. "I think you'd see eye to eye."

"Really?" Harriet asked in surprise.

"Oh, yes. Ben prides himself on being a progressive."

"Surely Cookson wouldn't approve of that?"

"He's not taken seriously at Phaleron. It's fashionable to be left wing these days, as you know. Phipps is accepted as a sort of court jester. He can believe what he likes so long as he doesn't try to change anything."

"I'd like to meet him again," Guy said.

"I think it can be arranged."

"Let's have another bottle."

Alan had lost possibility for Guy, but unaware of this, he looked like a boy let out of school and returned to the beauties of Greece, talking at length about his travels on the mainland

and to the islands. Guy, sitting back out of the conversation, attended with a smiling interest, viewing him no more seriously than Cookson viewed Phipps.

When they left, the proprietor took their hands and held to them as though he could scarcely bear to be left alone again in the empty silence that had once been alive with music and dancing youths.

There was little traffic outside and no hope of a taxi. Alan, walking ahead, led them through the narrow streets to the Plaka Square which they reached as the air-raid warning sounded. Police regulations required everyone to go under cover during an alert, but the raids, that came every day, were over the Piraeus, and Athenians avoided the regulation if they could. Alan suggested they should sit on the chairs outside the café in the square. They could hurry inside if the police appeared.

The moon, that shone fitfully through drifting cloud, touched the old houses and trees, and the plaque that said Byron had lived somewhere near. The strands of the pepper trees in the central garden moved like seaweed in the wind. It was too cold now to sit out after dark, but the outdoor chill was preferable to the hot, smoky air behind the curtain of the little café.

The café owner, hearing voices outside, looked through the curtains and asked if they would like coffee. Alan explained that they were only waiting for the raid to end. The owner said they might wait a long time and he invited them to take coffee as his guests. The coffee, hot and sweet, came in little cups, and the waiter left the curtain open slightly as a gesture of welcome while someone with a concertina inside began to play "Tipperary" in their honour. They drank down their coffee and ordered some more. The moon disappeared behind cloud and there was darkness except for the crack of light between the café curtains.

Alan said: " 'They are daring beyond their power and they risk beyond reason and they never lose hope in suffering.' "

"Thucydides?" asked Guy. Alan nodded and Harriet begged him: "Repeat some of your translations of Cavafy."

He reflected for a while then began: "Why are we waiting, gathered in the market place? It's the barbarians who are coming today . . . " He stopped. "It is a long poem; too long."

"We have nothing to do but listen," said Harriet, and she suddenly realized how happy she was here with Guy, come out of his seclusion to be a companion of this freedom that, having neither past nor future, was a lacuna in time; a gift of leisure that need only be accepted and enjoyed.

Alan was about to start his recitation again when the all clear sounded. "Another time," he said. "Now I must go back and feed my poor Diocletian."

7

ALAN HAD ASKED HARRIET if she would join him again
when he went to the greens and, being told there was a visitor
in the hall, she said to Guy: "Won't you come, too?"

Guy, restored to all his old desire for contact with life,
said: "I'd like to come," but running down the stairs, he
stopped and whispered: "I don't want to see him."

"Who?"

"It's Toby Lush again."

Guy's expression, injured and apprehensive, roused her to
fury. "I'll deal with him," she said. "You stay there."

Toby, in his leather-bound jacket, with his wrack of moustache and hair in eyes, looked like some harmless old sheep-
dog. He grinned at Harriet as though he had come on a
pleasing errand and seemed startled by her tone when she
asked:

"What do *you* want?"

"The old lad. Is he about?"

"No."

"When can I see him? It's urgent."

"You can't see him. You can leave a message."

"No. Have orders to see Guy in person."

"He refuses to see you. If you have anything to say, you can
say it to me."

Toby spluttered and shifted his feet, but in the end had to
speak. "There's going to be an evacuation ship. It's all arranged. Dubedat told me to tell you he's wangled berths on it
for the pair of you."

"Has he? Why?"

"It's your chance, don't you see? There's nothing here for
you: no job, no money, nowhere to live, and now the Italians
invading. You're jolly lucky to be getting away."

"And is Gracey going?"

"Yes, we're losing him, sad to say."

"And you and Dubedat?"

"No, we'd go if we could, but we've got to hold the fort. The ship's not for us chaps. The old soul used his influence and they stretched a point because he said you're stranded." Laughing nervously, his moustache stirring, damp, beneath his nose, Toby added; "I'd rather go than stay."

"You surprise me. The news is unusually good. I've been told the Italians are putting up no fight at all. There's a whole division trapped in a gorge of the Pindus mountains and they're not even trying to fight their way out."

"Oh, you can't believe those stories. The Greeks'll say anything. The I-ties may be stopped for the moment, but they're bound to break through. They've got tanks, lorries, big guns, the lot. Once the break comes, they'll be down here in a brace of shakes. We don't want to stay here, but we've got a job to do."

"You had a job to do in Bucharest, but you bolted just the same."

"Oh, I say!" Toby had been searching his pockets and now, finding a match, he began digging about in the bowl of his pipe. "Play fair!" he said. "The old soul's put himself out for you. And you're lucky to be going."

"But we're not going."

Toby's eyes bulged at her. "You are, you know. It's orders. You saw that letter. Dubedat's boss here now and if Guy's sensible he won't make trouble. If he reports for work in Cairo, we'll stay mum. Not a word about his coming here against orders. The old soul promises. Now be sensible. It's the only boat. The last boat. So hand over your passports and we'll do the necessary."

Harriet repeated: "We're not going," and went upstairs while Toby shouted: "We'll ring the Cairo office. We'll complain . . . "

Guy had gone to the room where Harriet found him sprawled on the bed, a book in his hand, an air of detachment hiding his anticipation of a new betrayal.

"We're ordered on to the evacuation boat. Dubedat's command."

"Is that all?" Guy laughed and dropped the book.

"It's the last boat. If we don't go, we're stuck."

"We couldn't be stuck in a better place."

8

THE NIGHT BEFORE THE SHIP SAILED, Cookson gave a farewell party for Gracey. Yakimov was among the invited.

"Who was there?" Harriet asked him next day.

"Everyone," said Yakimov.

Harriet felt excluded because she had imagined herself and Guy to be part of English life here; now it seemed they were not. But when the ship had sailed a different atmosphere began to prevail. Uncertain who had gone and who had not, the survivors met one another with congratulations and, like veterans left behind to stem an enemy advance, they felt a new warmth towards one another.

At the same time, the situation had changed. The ship had no sooner gone than the streets were jubilant with the news that the Alpini Division trapped in the Pindus had surrendered to a man. The Greeks had taken five thousand prisoners. People said to one another: "Even Musso can't make the I-ties fight." The Greeks, who had fought but imagined the fight was hopeless, now began to see the enemy as a pantomime giant that collapses when the hero strikes a blow.

On top of all this excitement, British airmen began to arrive at Tatoi and Eleusis and appeared in the streets just when the Greeks were buoyant with triumph and hope.

Guy and Harriet, invited to Zonar's by Alan, saw the young Englishmen, pink-faced, and sheepish, pursued and cheered by admirers in every street. Walking up to the café, they met a crowd running down the road with a bearded English pilot on their shoulders. As he was carried towards Hermes Street, the Greeks shouted the evzone challenge of "Aera! Aera!" and the pilot, his arms in the air, shouted back: "Yo-ho-ho and a bottle of rum."

A woman on the pavement told everyone that that was the very pilot who had shot down an Italian bomber over the

Piraeus. The statement was accepted as fact and there was applause among the Greeks seated outside Zonar's. When the Pringles joined Alan, a man nearby, hearing them speak English, asked: 'What is the 'yo-ho-ho and a bottle of rum'?'"

"It is an old English battle-cry," Alan replied and as his words were repeated around, the applause renewed itself.

The pilot was now out of sight, but before enthusiasm could die down, a lorry-load of Greek soldiers stopped on the corner. The men were perched on bales of blankets and heavy clothing donated by the Athenians who were giving all they could give to the troops now fighting in rain and sleet. At the sight of the lorry, people went out to seize the soldiers by their hands. Harriet, carried away by the ferment, lifted Alan's glass and ran with it to the road, where she held it up to the men. One of them, smiling, took it and put it to his lips, but before he could drink, the lorry drove off taking both man and glass.

Harriet said: "I'm sorry."

"You could have done nothing more fitting," Alan assured her. "The Greeks love gestures of that sort," and added: "As this is our first meeting since the ship sailed, let's drink to the fact you've stayed in spite of everything. And, I think, wisely. It's my belief we'll see the weak overcome the strong, the victims overcome the despoilers."

They drank and Harriet said: "Now, I suppose, Dubedat really is in charge?"

"No," said Alan. "There was an interesting little incident at the party. With everyone watching, Gracey required Dubedat to return the letter that appointed him Acting-Director, having decided the School should close until a new Director be appointed."

"Still, Dubedat might be appointed Director."

"He might. Who can say? And here's another contender for the title. Guy said he would like to meet him again."

Ben Phipps, crossing University Street, had lost his cheerful air but, seeing Alan, he waved and hurried to the table. He looked over the company with an alert gaiety, but the disguise was carelessly assumed and the man himself seemed to be a long way behind his manner.

He said: " 'Fraid I can't stay long. I'm dining at Phaleron and I've had trouble with the car. Had to leave it at Psychico."

"I suppose you'll have time for a drink," Alan said with an

ironical sharpness that caused Phipps to try to connect with his genial mask. "Hey," he said, "don't get shirty. I'm none too bright. I've still got a bit of a hangover as a result of the great Farewell."

The two men were talking about Cookson's party when Mrs. Brett passed on her way into the café with her friend Miss Jay. She stopped to say she had just moved from the hotel.

"I've a flat of my own now. I'll be giving parties, you wait and see! Splendid parties. You'll come, won't you?" she demanded of Alan, then jerked her head round to the Pringles: "And you two?" She ignored Ben Phipps, who gazed over her head as though she were unknown to him. When she had finished describing the wonders of the new flat, she gave him a venomous glance and said: "So we've got rid of Gracey! I hear there were great rejoicings down at Phaleron! Obviously I wasn't the only one glad to see the back of him."

Taking this to himself, Phipps now turned to Miss Jay and asked smoothly: "How did you enjoy the Major's party? I saw you having a good tuck-in at the buffet."

For answer, Miss Jay and her white spinnaker swept ahead into the café, but Mrs. Brett stood her ground and, stimulated by the presence of an enemy, talked with more than her usual excitement. "What about Lord Pinkrose?" she asked. "I hope he didn't go?"

Alan, standing unsteadily on his gouty foot, smiled in pain and embarrassment. "No, he didn't go. He was a doubtful starter right up to the last, then he decided to stay in Athens. I think the news from the front was a deciding factor."

"Good for him." Mrs. Brett spoke as though Pinkrose had shown some unusual courage in staying. "I'm told he's in the running for the Directorship, and I hope he gets it. A scholar and a gentleman, that's what's needed here. There aren't many of them. It'll be a nice change to get one."

She went at last and as the other men sat down, Phipps sank as though winded into his chair. His voice had grown weak. "I didn't know Pinkrose was a candidate?"

"He is, indeed."

"A *likely* candidate?"

"Who knows? But he certainly courted Gracey. I was always seeing him slipping into the room with little gifts: a bottle of sherry, chocolates, a few flowers . . . "

"Good heavens," said Harriet.

Alan laughed. "I shall never forget the sight of Pinkrose, smirking like a lover, with two tuberoses in his hand."

Ben Phipps did not laugh, but looked at his watch.

Alan said: "I really asked you along because Pringle here would like to meet some of your young Greek friends: the left-wing group."

"Oh?" Ben Phipps did not look at Guy. His black eye-dots dodged about behind his glasses as he said, with a glance at Alan: "I don't see much of them nowadays."

Eager for information, Guy asked: "I suppose they're mostly students?"

"Mostly, yes," Phipps said. "The older chaps'll be in the army now." There was a pause while Guy looked expectant and Phipps, forced to make some concession, lifted a brow at Alan. He said: "You could take him to Aleko's. They're always there. Introduce him to Spiro, the fellow behind the bar; he'll put him in touch."

"I could, I suppose," Alan reluctantly agreed.

Phipps looked at Guy for the first time and said by way of explanation: "I haven't been there for some time," then seeing a bus draw up, he jumped to his feet saying: "My bus. Good-bye for now," and hastened to catch it.

Looking after him, Alan said: "The Major usually sends his Delahaye in for favoured friends. I think poor Ben has reason to be nervous. And he seems to be shuffling off his left-wing affiliations."

Turning on Guy, Harriet said suddenly: "Why shouldn't you be Director?"

He looked at her in astonishment, then laughed as though she had made a joke.

"Well, why not? You're the only member of the Organization left in Athens. Pinkrose is a Cambridge don. He has no knowledge of Organization work."

"Darling, it's out of the question." Guy spoke firmly, hoping to crush the suggestion at its inception.

"But why?"

He explained impatiently: "I have not had the experience to be a Director. I was appointed as a junior lecturer. If I can get a lectureship here, I'll be doing very well."

"You've had more experience than Phipps or Dubedat."

"If either were appointed – and I'm pretty sure neither will be – it would be a piece of disgraceful log-rolling. I'm having no part in it. I'm certainly not using this situation to get more than my due." Turning away from her, Guy spoke to Alan: "I'd like to go to that place Phipps mentioned."

"Aleko's? We might go later, but . . ." Alan looked for the waiter.

Twilight was falling; a cold wind had sprung up and people were leaving the outdoor tables. Alan said: "I was hoping you'd take supper with me?" When Harriet smiled her agreement, he asked: "Is there any place you would like to go?"

"Could we go to the Russian Club?"

Alan laughed. This, apparently, was a modest request and he said: "I'm sure we can. It's called a club but no one is ever turned away."

The club, a single room, had been decorated early in the 'twenties and never redecorated. As they entered, Alan said: "We might see Yakimov," and they saw him at once, seated at a small table, a plate of pancakes in front of him.

He lifted an eye and murmured affectionately: "Dear girl! Dear boys! Lovely to see you," but he did not really want to see them. While they stood beside him, he spread red caviare between the pancakes then gazed at the great sandwich with an absorbed and dedicated smile before pouring over it a jugful of sour cream.

"You're doing yourself proud," Alan said.

"A little celebration!" Yakimov explained. "Sold m'car, m'dear old Hispano-Suiza. German officer bought it in Bucharest. Thought I'd never get the money, but m'old friend Dobson brought me down a bundle of notes. Your Yak's in funds, for once. Small funds, of course. Just a bit of Ready. Have to make it last a long time." He waited for them to move on. In funds, he had no need of friends. When he could buy his own food, he ate well and ate alone.

Alan and the Pringles sat in a bay window, looking out at the Acropolis fading into the last shadowy purple of twilight. They, too, had pancakes with red caviare and cream, and Harriet said: "Delicious."

Guy was tolerant of the Russian Club. He was also tolerant of Alan Frewen. He could accept the fact that some of his friends were what he called "a-political" just as some might be colour-blind. He would not blame Alan for his disability, but his slightly distracted manner made it clear that his mind was elsewhere. Harriet knew he was simply marking time until he could get to Aleko's and meet those who thought as he did, but Alan had forgotten Aleko's. Having invited them here, he was relaxed happily in his chair and wanted to make much of the meal. He looked as though he were settled there for the evening.

Guy, on edge to be gone, took it all patiently. Harriet took it with pleasure. Something about the place stirred an old, buried dream of security, a dream she had despised when she went to earn her living with the other unconventional young in London. Then she would have repudiated with derision the idea of an orderly married life. She married for adventure.

In Bucharest once she had been amused when Yakimov said: "We're in a nice little backwater here. We should get through the war here very comfortably," for she and Guy had set out expecting danger and not unprepared to die. Now after the perturbed months, the subterfuges and the long uncertainty, she knew she would be thankful to find a refuge anywhere. But the uncertainty was not over yet.

She said: "*Are* the Italians going to break through?"

"Why?" Alan laughed. "Do you want them to break through?"

"No, but if we're going to spend the winter here, we'll have to get some heavy clothing. I left all mine in Bucharest and Guy brought nothing but books."

"You'll certainly need a coat of some sort."

Guy said: "Harriet can get a coat if she wants one, but I never feel the cold."

"*And*," said Harriet, "we'll have to find somewhere to live."

"Nonsense," Guy said: "The hotel's cheap and convenient." He would not waste time discussing clothes and homes; the important thing was to get the meal over. As Alan lifted the menu again, he said: "I don't want anything more. If we're going to Aleko's, I think we ought to go."

Still resistant, Alan looked at Harriet: "How would you like some baklava? I'm sure you would. I must say, I'd like some myself."

Guy smiled while they ate their baklava, but Harriet, aware of his hidden longing to be gone, could not enjoy it. When

Alan suggested coffee, she said: "Perhaps we ought to go. It's getting late."

"Oh, very well." Alan eased himself up, groaning, and as he balanced on his feet, he gave a slow, dejected salute to the sideboard on which the coffee cona stood. Seeing the disappointment beneath the humour, Harriet, who had felt the need to indulge Guy, now felt resentful of his impatience to be elsewhere. She decided she would not go to Aleko's. Bored by politics, she was becoming less willing to accept Guy's chosen companions in order to gain Guy's company.

Yakimov had also finished supper. Lounging in an old basket-chair, over which he had spread his sable-lined great-coat, he was sipping a glass of Kümmel.

"Whither away?" he asked, more alive to their departure than he had been to their arrival.

Alan said: "We're going to Aleko's."

"Indeed, dear boy! And where is that?"

"Behind Omonia Square. A little café, patronized by progressives. Like to come?"

"Think not. Not quite *simpatico*. Not quite the place for your poor old Yak."

They had to walk to Constitution Square in search of a taxi and, as he limped along, Alan suggested more than once that Aleko's might be left for another night. Guy would not hear of it. Seeing a taxi pass the top of the square, he pursued and caught it and brought it back.

Giving him no time to over-persuade her, Harriet now said: "I won't come. I'm going back to the hotel to bed."

"Just as you like. I won't be late." Guy, bouncing to be off, caught Alan's arm and pulled him into the taxi before he, too, could excuse himself; then, slamming the door shut, he shouted: "Aleko's. Omonia Square."

Watching the taxi drive off, Harriet marvelled at Guy's vigour and determination in the pursuit of his political interests. Why could he not bring as much to the furtherance of his own career. He was eager – too eager, she sometimes thought – to give, to assist, to sympathize, to work for others, but he had little ambition for himself.

When she first met him, she had imagined he needed nothing but opportunity; now she began to suspect he did not want opportunity. He did not want to be drawn into rivalry.

He wanted amusement. He also wanted his own way, and, to get it, could be as selfish as the next man. But he was always justified. Yes, he was always justified. If he had no other justification, he could always fall back on some morality of his own.

She walked despondently back to the hotel, beginning to fear that he was a man who in the end would achieve little. He would simply waste himself.

PART TWO

The Victors

9

ONE EVENING, IN THE STEEL-BLUE CHILL of the November twilight, the church bells began to ring. They had been silent for nearly a month. No bell in Greece would sound while one single foreign invader remained on Greek soil. Now the whole of Athens was vibrant with bells. People came running into the streets, crying aloud in their joy, and when Harriet went out to the landing, she heard the chambermaids shouting to one another from floor to floor.

The Italians had been driven back. The Greeks had crossed the Albanian frontier. Greek guns were trained on the Albanian town of Koritza and Greek shells were falling in the streets. All that had happened, but the bells had not rung. What could have caused them to ring now?

Harriet threw up the landing window and looked out in search of an answer. One of the chambermaids, seeing her there, shouted to her in Greek. When Harriet shook her head to show she did not understand, the girl lifted a hand and slapped it down on the window-sill: "Koritza," she shouted. "Koritza."

So Koritza had fallen. It was a victory. The first Greek victory of the war. As Harriet laughed and clapped her hands, the girl caught her about the waist and swung her round in a near hysteria of delight.

Outside it was almost dark but the black-out was forgotten. The Italians were much too busy now to take advantage of a few lighted windows. Someone began speaking on the wireless. The voice, rapid, emotional, pitched in triumph, began coming from all the lighted windows and doorways, and people in the streets cheered whenever the word "Koritza" was spoken. Another voice came very loud from the square, speaking over an uproar of shouting, music, applause, with the bells pealing above it all. Harriet could not bear to stay in, but was afraid to go out for fear that Guy would return for her.

The winter was setting in. There were still bright days, but mostly the sky was white with cold and a wind, high, sharp and gritty, swept the dust along the pavements. The night before it had poured with rain. When Harriet went to the gardens she saw the palm fronds blown from side to side like shocks of hair. The paths, that a week before had been warm and quiet, were now draughty channels, so cold that she realized if she did not get a coat, she would soon have to stay indoors.

Having left Guy with his books, contemplating a lecture on Ben Jonson, she hurried back to get him out to the shops and found him gone. He had left no message. She knew he had gone to Aleko's.

Guy had taken her there once but the visit had depressed her. She liked the Greek boys but was shy with them – being so constituted she could cope with only one or two people at a time; but Guy, she saw, was having the time of his life. He was an adolescent among adolescents, and they were all elevated by the belief that, together, they would reform the world. She was made uneasy by their faith in certain political leaders, their condemnation of others, the atmosphere of conspiracy and her own guilty self-doubt. She was an individual and as such had no hope of reforming the world. The stories that inspired them – stories of injustice and misery – merely roused in her a sense of personal failure.

"But you must sacrifice your individuality," Guy told her. "It's nothing but egoism. You must unite with other right-thinking, self-abnegating people – then you can achieve anything."

The idea filled her with gloom.

Guy, who was learning demotic Greek, could already discuss abstract ideas with the students in their own language. He amazed them.

One of the boys said to Harriet: "He is wonderful – so warm, cordial and un-English! We have elected him an honorary Greek." As an honorary Greek, admired and made much of, Guy was at Aleko's all the time.

Harriet, out of it and a little jealous, refused to go to the café again. Guy told her she was "a-political". Alan Frewen had been similarly condemned. He was, Guy said, the sort of man who thinks the best government is the one that causes him least inconvenience. So much for Alan; but Alan, unaware that his epitaph had been spoken, continued to invite them as though he saw himself the friend of both.

When the telephone rang in the bedroom, it was Alan, calling from his office: "I've heard that Athens is *en fête*. No night for cold mutton at the Academy. How about coming to Babayannis? If there's anything to celebrate, that's where everyone goes."

"I'm worried about Guy," Harriet said. "I think he must be at Aleko's."

"I'll call with a taxi. We'll roust out the old bolshie on the way."

When she joined Alan in the taxi, he told the driver to go through the Plaka. "I want you to see something," he said to Harriet. They turned into the square where the loudspeaker was singing out: "Anathema, anathema . . ." The curse, of course, was on those who said that love is sweet: "I've tried it," said the song. "And found it poison." But the curse was also on those who had imagined Greece was there for the taking. The Italians had tried it and they, too, had found it poison.

As they went through the narrow Plaka streets, the Parthenon appeared. It was flood-lit, a temple of white fire hanging upon the blackness of the sky.

Harriet, catching her breath, said: "I've never seen anything more beautiful."

"Is there anything more beautiful to be seen?" Alan asked.

In the Plaka Square, where they had sat during the raid, the café had pulled aside its black-out curtains. The light, streaming greenish pale through the bleared window, lit the men dancing in the road.

"It's the *Zebeikiko*," Harriet cried, wildly exhilarated by all the rejoicings.

Alan, amused that she had remembered the name, told the taximan to stop and they watched the dancers, arms about one another's shoulders, moving through the light, beneath the pepper trees. The music changed. A man standing on a chair against the window took a leap into the middle of the road. He shouted. The others shouted back. Someone threw him a handkerchief and he stood poised, holding the handkerchief by one corner at arm's length. Another man ran out to take the opposite corner. Both men were grey-haired, with the dark, lined faces of out-door labourers, but they danced like youths.

The city was intoxicated. In the narrow streets the taxi crawled through a mass of moving shadows. There were mouth-organs and accordions; and between great outbursts of laughter people sang popular songs to which they fitted new words about the behaviour of Mussolini and his ridiculous army.

When they reached Aleko's, Harriet sent Alan in, saying: "If we both go, Guy will only persuade us to stay."

Alan stayed inside for several minutes, then came out and said with a shrug: "He says he'll join us at Babayannis'."

Bitterly disappointed, Harriet said: "But I want him to come with us. I want him to see everything. I want him to enjoy it, too."

Alan climbed with a sigh back into the taxi. "You must accept him as he is," he said. "After all, his virtues far outweigh his faults."

At the taverna called Babayannis', the curtains had been looped back and the smell of cooking came out like a welcome. The entrance light had been dimmed but there was enough to show the big stone-flagged hallway where there was a range on which the food was displayed in copper pots. The chef in attendance knew Alan. He spoke in English and said he had once worked in Soho. He was sad there was so little to offer the English guests but, as was fitting, the best of the meat went to the fighting-men and restaurants had to take what they could get.

Looking down into the brown cream of the moussaka, the red-brown stews with pimentos, tomatoes, aubergines and little white onions, Harriet said: "Don't worry. This is good enough for me."

The inner room was crowded. The lights were not very bright but the whole taverna seemed a-dazzle with vivacious life. Almost as soon as Alan and Harriet were seated, Costa, the singer, came out to sing. He was laughing as he appeared and went on laughing as though he could not repress his high spirits. At once, responding to his gaiety, the audience began a frantic clapping and shouting, demanding songs they had not heard since the invasion began. In the past, the songs had been sad, telling of the need to fight and die, of lovers separated and loved ones who would not return. But all that, they seemed to think, was over and done with. Now they need do nothing but rejoice.

In the midst of this uproar, Costa stood laughing, turning from side to side, his teeth brilliant in his long, dark, folded face; then he held up a hand and the noise died out. People sat intently silent, scarcely breathing for fear of missing a word.

He said: "The invaders have fled. But there are still Italians on our soil; a great many Italians, several thousand. However, they are all prisoners."

In the furore that followed, people wept with joy and leapt up, laughing while the tears streamed down their cheeks. Costa asked: "What shall I sing?" and sang "Yalo, yalo" and "Down by the seaside" and every other song for which they asked. There could be no doubt of it: the mourning days were over and people were free to live again.

Harriet murmured several times: "If only Guy were here!"

Alan's face crumpled into its tragic smile: "Don't worry," he said. "Costa will sing again later."

When the singer retired, people who had waited at the entrance began to move in to their tables. Among them Harriet saw Dobson who had been Cultural Attaché in Bucharest and was now in Athens. She did not share Guy's faith in Dobson's essential good-nature but as soon as he caught sight of her, he captivated her at once.

He seized her shoulder with affectionate familiarity: "What fun!" he said. "We're all here together. How naughty, you two, choosing Greece instead of the heat, dirt, flies, disease and all the other delights of the Middle East! But who cares? Not the London office, I'm sure." He rubbed his hand happily over his baby-soft puffs of hair and rocked his soft, plump body to and fro. "You're well out of Bucharest. Not much 'Paris-of-the-East' these days. *And* what do you think has happened on top of everything else? The most terrible earthquake. You know that block you lived in, the Blocul Cazacul? It collapsed in a heap. Went down like a dropped towel with all the tenants buried beneath it."

Harriet stared at him, shocked by this resolution of their year in Bucharest, then said: "I hope our landlord went down with it."

Dobson opened his blue baby eyes and laughed as though she had been extremely witty. "I expect he did. I expect he did," he said in delight as he moved off.

Harriet laughed too. Bucharest had become a shadow and its devastation had little reality for her, but as she put the past back where it belonged, she suddenly saw Sasha dead among the ruins. For a second she caught his exact image, then it was gone. Sasha, too, had become a shadow. As she searched for his face in her mind, she found herself looking into another face. A young man was watching her. When their eyes met, he turned his head away. His action was self-conscious. He looked young enough to be a schoolboy but he was wearing the uniform of an English second-lieutenant. She noticed that the men with whom he sat were Cookson, Archie Callard and Ben Phipps.

"Who is the English officer at Cookson's table?" she whispered to Alan.

"English officer? Oh yes, Charles Warden. He's just come here from Crete."

"But I thought the Greeks wouldn't have British troops on the mainland?"

"He's in the Military Attaché's office. You know we're going to have a Military Mission? Well, I think he's being groomed to act as liaison officer."

Harriet observed the young officer for a moment and said: "He's very good-looking."

"Is he?" Alan gave him a wry, dismissive glance and said: "Yes, I suppose he is."

Sasha had not been good-looking, but he had had a gentle face like that of a tamed and sensitive animal. There was nothing gentle about Charles Warden. He had been caught looking at her once and would not be caught again. He looked away from her and his profile, raised with something like arrogance, suggested a difficult and dangerous nature. Alan had shown that he did not like Warden, and he was probably right.

"Not a pleasant young man," she thought.

When they were served with wine, Harriet caught Dobson's smiling eye and said to Alan: "Do you think we might move to the Academy? Perhaps Dobson could put in a word for us."

"You'd hate the place," Alan said. "It's like a dreadful girls' school. That bossy red-headed virgin Dunne won't even let poor old Diocletian sleep on the chairs."

Sitting among the hilarious Greeks, Harriet did not want to hear about Miss Dunne, but Alan had started a long story about Miss Dunne's taking all the hot water for a bath then blaming him when he used what remained because she wanted to wash her stockings.

Harriet laughed but Alan did not laugh. She could see how intolerable it was for him, after his year of solitary freedom, to live a sort of conventional life beneath a female tyrant, but his complaints did not discourage her. She remembered Gracey's spacious, shabby room and could imagine their days there, planned, coherent and beautiful. She had had enough of disorder and had seen that in war there was anxiety instead of expectation, exhaustion instead of profit, and one burnt one's emotions to extract from life nothing but the waste products: insecurity and fear.

She said: "For a while, I'd love to live in an ordered community. You can have too much of confusion. In no time, you begin to think that war is real and life is not."

"Or that war is life?"

She nodded. "I couldn't believe in the peace-time society here. It was almost a relief when the air-raid siren sounded. I felt at once that I knew my way around."

Alan laughed and some minutes later asked her: "Would you take a job, if there was one?"

"I certainly would."

"We'll have to expand when the Mission arrives. Nothing definite yet, but I may be able to offer you something. We'll see. Ah!" On a rising note of satisfaction Alan added: "Here's our man at last."

Guy, making his way round the restaurant, was not alone. He was talking boisterously and his voice told Harriet that he had had more than enough to drink. He was followed by a train of young men in air-force uniform, among them the bearded pilot whom they had seen carried shoulder high past Zonar's.

The procession arrested the whole room. Even Cookson's party paused to gaze. Guy, leading his prize in, waved to Dobson and Dobson, not over-sober himself, stood up and embraced Guy fervently.

"Welcome," said Alan. "Welcome."

Guy's introductions were wordy but vague, for he had found the airmen wandering aimlessly through the narrow lane of the Plaka and did not know what they were called.

The waiter, flustered and important because the British aircrew had come to his table, seized chairs wherever he could find them and seated the men down with a proprietary firmness. He insisted that the pilot sit on one side of Harriet and the rear-gunner on the other. As this was being arranged, she glanced over at Charles Warden and found him watching her. He gave her a smile of quizzical inquiry, but now it was her turn to look away, and with an expression that told him she had enough young men and could manage very well without him.

She wanted to know what the pilot was called.

"Surprise," he said. Surprise what? Nothing – just Surprise. But he must have another name? He shook his head, smiling. If he had, he had forgotten it.

"Why are you called Surprise?"

He laughed, not telling. Sprawled in his chair, his eyes half-closed in sleepy amusement, he treated her questions as a joke. He seemed not to know the answer to anything. He simply laughed.

Harriet turned to the rear-gunner, an older man, who said he was called Zipper Cohen. She asked: "Tell me why he's called Surprise."

Cohen said: "When the Group Captain saw him, he was so surprised he fell off his chair."

"Why?"

"Because he was wearing a beard."

"They're not worn in the air force, are they? How can he get away with it?"

"He can get away with anything."

The navigator, Chew Buckle, was a small, thin, sharp-nosed boy who, in normal times, would probably be morose and unsociable. He still had nothing to say, but he laughed without ceasing.

Guy was drunk enough but the airmen were more drunk and evaded any sort of serious topic as a blind man evades obstacles. Only Zipper Cohen was ready to talk. He took out a cigarette-case, opened it and, showing Harriet a photograph tucked into the lid, watched her keenly as she looked at the face of a young woman holding a child.

"My wife and little girl," he said. He seemed the only one whose feet were on earth and when Harriet handed back the cigarette-case, he sat staring at the picture which attached him to the real world. But this incident did not last long. In a moment he shut the case, put it away and began asking what was wrong with the girls in this place. Harriet was the only girl who had given him a smile since he got here.

"The Greek girls won't look at us," he complained.

"It's their way of being loyal to their men at the front."

Zipper gave a howl of laughter. "I hope my old woman's being as loyal as that."

Alan, drawn into the rantipole merriment of the young men, tried to talk to Chew Buckle who sat beside him. Why were they stationed so far behind the lines? he asked.

Chew Buckle giggled. He was a man used by events but not involved with them. When asked a direct question, he knew something was expected of him, but could scarcely tell what.

The war had plucked him out of his own nature but given him nothing to take its place. He giggled and shook his head and giggled.

Zipper explained that the Greeks, fearful of provoking the Axis, kept them well behind the lines with some idea that the Germans would not notice them. "We just about managed to get to Albania and back. When we landed last night, there wasn't a pint in the tank."

"Suppose you're forced down?" asked Alan.

Zipper laughed. "It's a friendly country. Not like Hellfire Pass."

The mention of Hellfire renewed the laughter and Chew Buckle, speaking in a deep, harsh voice, said: "They cut y'r bollocks off there." The others collapsed.

It was some time before the three civilians could discover that, if the Arabs of Hellfire Pass caught a pilot, they held him to ransom and, as proof of his existence, sent his expendable parts to Bomber Command.

When Costa came out to sing again, the enjoyment had a second focal point, and Costa, acknowledging applause, waved at the aircrew to show they were as much part of the entertainment as he was. Glasses of wine were sent over to the young men and, as a special honour, apples were sliced and put into the glasses. More bottles were ordered by Guy and Alan so these compliments could be repaid, and glasses passed to and fro, and were sent to Costa, then to the proprietor and the waiters, and soon the tables all around were covered with glasses, some empty, some half full and some waiting to be drunk. The restaurant swayed with drink, and the air quivered with admiration, affection and the triumph of the day.

Suddenly one of the waiters, a middle-aged man as thin as a whippet, ran into the middle of the floor, and began to dance, and the audience clapped in time for him. Cookson and his friends watched, not clapping but indulgently approving.

Guy was in a jubilant state. He suffered from his own frustrated energy and the challenge of other men's activity, but now it seemed nothing could daunt him. A sort of electricity went out from him and infected the neighbouring tables, and even the airmen began to talk. They told, in terms of riotous humour, how they were sent out every morning over Valona at exactly the same time. It was intended as a double bluff. The Italians were expected to think such tactics impossible and so be unprepared.

"But the bastards are expecting us every time," shouted Zipper Cohen, and Surprise, shaking in his chair, said: "Thank God for the Greek air force. They'll fly anything. They go up on tea-trays tied with string."

The wine was as much for Guy as for the air-crew. Among the Greeks he was an honorary Greek, among the fighting-men, he was an honorary fighting man. Aware that she could not, for the life of her, attract so much enthusiasm, Harriet was moved with pride in him.

Now there were six men out dancing and the clapping had settled into a rhythmic accompaniment that filled the room. Unfortunately, while things were at their height, Major Cookson felt he must take his party away. He said to those around that it was all very pleasurable but, alas, he had invited friends to drop in after dinner and must be at Phaleron to greet them. Those with him rose, but not very willingly. Harriet felt Charles Warden look at her as he went, but she kept her eyes on Zipper Cohen.

The departure of Cookson brought the dancing to a stop.

In the silence that came down, Chew Buckle threw back his head and sang to the tune of "Clementine":

> "In a Blenheim, o'er Valona,
> Every morning, just at nine;
> Same old crew and same old aircraft,
> Same old target, same old time.
> 'Bomb the runway,' says Group Captain,
> 'And make every one a hit.'
> If you do, you'll go to heaven;
> If you don't, you're in the . . . whatd'ycallit . . .?"

Amidst the applause, Buckle climbed slowly and deliberately up on his chair, then to the table where he bowed on every side before sinking down, as slowly as he had risen, and going to sleep among the bottles.

Alan said it was time to get the boys back to Tatoi. He went out to order a taxi while Guy roused Chew Buckle and got them moving. As they left the room, Dobson called to the Pringles:

"Hey, you two! There's a special film show. You've got to come. It's in aid of the Greek war effort. After the show, we're holding a reception."

Guy looked at Harriet and said: "Would you like to go?"

"I'd love to go," she said.

"Then you shall." In elated mood, he flung an arm round her shoulder and said: "You know if you want to go, you've only got to say so. Whatever you want to do, you've only got to let me know. You know that, don't you?" He spoke so convincingly, that Harriet could only reply: "Darling, yes, of course."

10

EVERY DAY NOW THERE WAS something to celebrate. There might not be a decisive victory like Koritza, but there was always an advance and always stories of Greek prowess and heroism. People queued to give food and clothing to the men who, having quelled the invaders, were now driving them into the sea.

The snow was falling in the Pindus mountains. As it blocked the passes and disguised the hazards of the wild, roadless regions, the retreating Italians abandoned their guns and heavy armaments. It was said the mere sight of an unarmed Greek would put a whole Italian division to flight. Posters showed the Greeks in pursuit, with nothing to abandon, leaping like chamois from crag to crag. The Italian radio called them savages who not only pitched their enemies over precipices but threw after them the splendid equipment which the Italian people had bought at such sacrifice to themselves.

While it snowed in Albania, it rained in Athens. The wind blew cold. The houses were unheated. People went to cafés and crowding for warmth behind the black-out curtains, told one another if it were not victory by Christmas, it would be victory by spring.

Guy could be idle no more. He went to Aleko's and announced his intention of starting an English class. Would any student lend a living-room in his house? The boys, made exuberant by his exuberance, all offered living-rooms.

When Guy turned up for the first class, expecting perhaps a dozen pupils, he found the room packed to the door with young people who acclaimed him not merely as a teacher but as a representative of Britain. Some of them had attended the School before it closed, but the majority knew only a little English. They felt if they were too young to fight, they could

at least learn the language of their great ally. Guy, greatly
stimulated by their response, began to plan a course of study.
He would divide up the students into grades and hold a class
every night. But where? The householder, a widow, treating
the invasion of her living-room as a joke, said: "Tonight, yes.
Very good. Other nights, some other place. Yes?" The classes
were moved from house to house, but no room was large
enough and everyone hoped that soon some permanent meeting-place would be found.

Guy, pressed by obligations, was now in the condition he
most enjoyed. He wanted to do more and more. One night,
coming back to the hotel-room, he told Harriet that the
students were eager to do a Shakespeare play. He was thinking of producing *Othello* or *Macbeth*.

"But then I'll never see you at all," Harriet said in dismay.

"Darling, I have to work. You wouldn't have me hanging
around doing nothing while other men are fighting?"

"No, but I can't spend my life doing nothing, either; and
certainly not in this miserable little room."

"You can always go to a café."

"Alone?"

"Alan would be glad to have you with him." Guy had
relegated Alan to the position of Harriet's friend.

"I don't always want to be with Alan. Besides, people talk."

"Good heavens, what does that matter?"

"I'm sure if you spoke to Dobson, he could get us into the
Academy. We might even have Gracey's room."

Eventually persuaded, Guy approached Dobson, but his approach was not successful. Dobson explained – "quite nicely",
Guy said – that the rooms had to be kept in case Foreign Office
employees turned up.

"Fact is," Dobson had said: "Gracey had no right to be
there. Don't know how he worked it, but I suspect the Major's
influence. Anyway, if he'd stayed on, he'd've been told to find
'alternative accommo', so you can see it's a case of 'no can
do'."

"And that's that," Guy said to Harriet, glad that his onerous
task was over.

Harriet had to accept it: the Academy was not for them.
She said: "At least he's sent us tickets for the film-show."

"What film-show?"

"The one he told us about. A new English film has been flown out. It'll be the first new film we've seen since Paris fell." She handed him the tickets that would admit them to a showing of a film called *Pygmalion*. Guy handed them back.

"Sorry. Can't manage it. That's the evening I promised to address a gathering of students on the state of left-wing politics in England."

"But you promised to take me. You said when we were at Babayannis' that we would go."

"I'm afraid I forgot. Anyway, the meeting's much more important. I can't let the students down."

"But you can let me down?"

"Don't be silly. What does a film-show matter?"

"But I've been looking forward to it. I haven't seen a new English film for months."

"You can get someone else to take you. Give my ticket to Alan."

"He doesn't need your ticket. He's going with Greek friends."

"Then ask Dobson to take you."

"I wouldn't dream of asking Dobson to take me."

"It's only a cinema. Why not go by yourself?"

"There's a reception as well; and I won't go by myself. I should hate it by myself. You ought to understand that. You promised to take me, and I want you to take me. I've been looking forward. So you must ask the students to change the day of the meeting."

"I can't do that. I can't put them off. It's not possible. If you break an appointment with English people, you can explain. But it's different with foreigners. They would think there was more to it. They wouldn't understand."

"You expect me to understand?"

"Of course."

To Guy, the discussion had been light and Harriet's disappointment was of so little moment that he scarcely paused to consider it. To her it was shattering. She could not believe it. She was certain that when Guy had reflected upon it all, he would arrange to change the day of the meeting and, this accomplished, would present the change to her as a token of their importance to each other; but he did nothing of the kind.

The days passed. She began to wonder whether he had given the film-show another thought. He had not; and he was surprised when, at the last minute, she mentioned it again.

"But we have discussed all this," he said. "I told you I had to go to the meeting. There was no question of putting it off. If it's a choice of a film-show or a political meeting, naturally the meeting must come first."

To Harriet it seemed a choice between much more than that. She said: "You promised to take me."

"I told you to get someone else to take you."

"Wherever I go, I have to get someone else to take me. Why? Being married to you is much the same as not being married at all. You ought to understand my feelings. I want you to take me; just to show you understand. You're my husband."

"My husband!" he echoed her. "The trouble is, you cling too much to things. You cried your eyes out when that kitten died. You couldn't have made more fuss if it'd been a baby."

"Well, it wasn't a baby."

Ignoring this, he went on: "*My* husband! *My* kitten! You promised *me*. What an attitude!" His face shut off in a mask of obstinacy, he began collecting his books together, eager to get away before she spoke again.

She did not try to speak again. Instead, she told herself that the meeting was important to him not because of his political ideals, but because it would accord him what he wanted most: attention. He was simply longing to be on view again. Lecturing or teaching, producing plays or giving advice to students, he was what he most wanted to be – the centre of attention. That meant more to him than she did.

As he made off, his face blank with purpose, she felt angry, but more than that, she felt abandoned. She sat for a long time on the bed, stunned and yet acutely lonely. The mention of the kitten had renewed in her a sense of loss. She had lost the kitten, she had lost Sasha, she had lost faith in Guy. Collapsing suddenly, she lay on the bed and wept helplessly.

She might have asked someone to take her to the reception but to do so, she felt, would be a public admission that Guy had failed her. She imagined herself being taken out of charity, an object of pity, a creature wronged and humiliated. If she went alone, it would be the same. Guy, in the past, had laughed at what he called the female "zenana-complex", no intelligent woman could possibly be restricted by such feelings. Yet something in her upbringing put an absolute check on the possibility of going alone.

It was an evening of full moon. With nothing else to do, she went out, and, drawn to the occasion, made her way up through Kolonaki past the hall where the film was to be shown. She may have hoped that someone she knew would see her and persuade her in; but she walked so quickly and purposefully that anyone who did see her would have supposed she was hurrying to another engagement.

And someone did see her. Charles Warden was standing outside the hall and as she gave a glance, fleet and longing, at the open door, she saw his face white in the white light of the moon. Safely past, hidden by shadow, she looked back. He was watching after her, regretfully; and she went regretfully on.

Energetic in unhappiness, she made her way uphill until she reached the final peak of the town where the old houses, crowded together among trees and shrubs, made a little village on their own. It was here that Alan had had his Athens studio. A path ran away into the rough, open ground of the hilltop. Following it, she found herself in a deserted waste-land, passing further and further out of human existence; the moon her only companion. Hanging oddly near, just above her shoulder, the great white uncommunicating face, blank in a blank grey-azure sky, increased her sense of solitude.

Athens, stretched below, was a map of silver. As she rounded the hill and came in sight of the Piraeus, the air-raid sirens began. At this height their hysterical rise and fall was faint and seemed not to relate to the city that in the blue-white light might have been a toy city, an object of crystal and moonstone.

From habit, she looked for shelter. Ahead there was a hut where refreshments were sold in summer. Standing against it, she watched the bombers coming in from the sea. The guns opened up but the aircraft came on, untouched. One bomber dropped a star of light that hung, incongruous and theatrical, in the moon-hazed distance. Apart from the distant thud-thud of the guns, the whole spectacle appeared to be in dumb-show until an explosion startled the air. A fire sprang up.

All the time the white, unharming city lay like a victim, bound and gagged, unable to strike back. The raid was brief. In a moment the raiders had turned. They flashed in the moonlight and were gone. The fire burnt steadily, the only thing alive among the white toy houses.

The all-clear did not sound and at last, bored and cold, she started to walk again. The path brought her to the top terrace of houses. The releasing blast of the all-clear rose as she made her way down to University Street. After the empty hill-top even Toby Lush, when she met him, seemed a friend. She told him where she had been and he spluttered and guffed and said: "Crumbs! I wouldn't do that walk alone at night for a lot of money."

"But surely it's not dangerous?"

"Don't know about that. There're bad types in most cities. I'm told it's not safe to go on the Areopagus after dark."

"Oh dear!" She was unnerved at having taken a risk from ignorance and, remembering the cinderous hill-brow in the ghastly light, it seemed to her there had been menace everywhere. She went back to the hotel, amazed at having survived the longest and loneliest walk of her life.

11

THE BELLS RANG AGAIN FOR THE capture of Muskopolje. They rang again for Konispolis. And on the first day of December, while the rain teemed down on Athens, they rang for the great victory of Pogradets. This battle, that lasted seven days, was fought in a snowstorm. The old porter, who waited in the hall with the news, enacted for the Pringles and other foreigners the drama of the encounter. He stumbled about to show how the Italians had been blinded by snow then, drawing himself up, eyes fixed, expression stern, he showed how the Greeks had been granted miraculous penetration of vision by Our Lady of Tenos.

"Why Our Lady of Tenos?" someone asked.

Because, explained the porter, his wife, who came from Tenos, had sent their son a Tenos medallion only two days before the battle began.

Now victory followed victory. When the bells started up, strangers laughed and shouted to each other: "What, another one!" The Athenians danced in the streets. Elderly men danced like boys and the women on the pavements clapped their hands. People said the Greeks had taken prisoner half of Mussolini's army. As for the war materials captured, they could challenge the world with it.

When someone came into a café and shouted a name that no one had heard before, there was no need to ask what it was. It was a victory. In no time it was familiar. Everyone repeated it: it was the most repeated name in Athens. Then, overnight, it became yesterday's victory, and another name took its place.

After Pogrodets, there came the capture of Mt. Oztrovitz; then Premeti, Santa Quaranta, Argyrokastro and Delvino. The evzoni captured the heights of Ochrida in a snowstorm. The attack lasted four hours and the Greek women, who had followed their men, climbed barefooted up the mountainside to take them food and ammunition.

For every victory the bells rang. People asked gleefully: "What now?" The Greeks had captured a little town that no one could find on the map. Then came a halt. The Greeks had advanced along the whole Albanian frontier and, unprepared for such success, they were outdistancing their supply lines. This was a breakthrough on a grand scale. They must treat it seriously.

On the morning when news came of the capture of Santa Quaranta – an important capture for the Greeks needed a port at which to unload supplies – Guy returned early for luncheon. He had heard, quite casually, from a student, that the new Director had been appointed. The School was to re-open. The students, weary of tramping around from one house to another, sent one of their number to tell Guy: "We have been grateful, sir, but now we must work at the School. There is no longer a room for teaching in any house. Our parents order us to enrol where there is space to learn."

"And who is the Director?" Harriet asked. "Not Dubedat?"

"No."

"Pinkrose?"

"No."

"So it's Ben Phipps?"

"No."

"There's no one else."

"Archie Callard."

Electrified, Harriet said: "But this is much better than we expected. We had nothing to gain from Dubedat and Pinkrose, but with Archie Callard, there's no knowing. He might do something for you."

"Yes."

They went to the hotel dining-room that nowadays, with food becoming scarce, was no worse than anywhere else. Guy behaved as though nothing singular had happened but there was something distraught in his appearance and he could not keep his mind on the meal.

Harriet said: "When do you suppose Callard heard?"

"Yesterday, I should think."

"Then he may still contact you."

"Oh yes, I'm not worrying."

"If he doesn't, what will you do?"

"I don't know. I haven't thought."

"You have every right to contact him. He's now your Director."

"Yes," Guy said doubtfully, disturbed by the possibility of having just such a move forced on him. Harriet, observing his timidity when it was a question of fighting his own battle, thought how little they had known each other when they married, hurriedly, under the shadow of war. The shadow, of course, had been there for years; but during the warm, dusty summer days when they first met, it had been the shadow of an avalanche about to drop. Having nowhere else to turn, people turned to each other. Guy had seemed all confidence. Had he grown up under the protection of wealth, he could not have displayed more insouciance, good-humour and generous responsibility towards life. Offering himself, he seemed to offer the protection of human warmth, good sense and reliability. And, in a sense, those qualities were his, but in another sense, he was a complex of unexpected follies, fears and irresolutions.

She said: "He *must* appoint you Chief Instructor. There's no one else capable of doing the job. Pinkrose or Ben Phipps might have done as Director; but when it comes to teaching, who is there?"

"Dubedat."

"Don't be ridiculous, darling."

The only heat in the hotel came from the oil-stove in the restaurant. The tables were set round it and guests were slow to take themselves up to their rooms. The Pringles were still sitting over their little cups of grey, washy coffee when the porter came down with a hand-delivered letter. He gave it to Guy, who, opening it, laughed and said casually: "It's from Callard. An invitation to tea at Phaleron where he's staying with Cookson. You're to come, too."

"But this is wonderful, darling."

"Perhaps. We don't know what he wants."

"Oh yes, we do. He's got the directorship; now he wants someone to do the work."

"Come on. I'll buy you some real coffee at the Braziliana."

In the little bar, that was so small there was nowhere to sit, people stood elbow to elbow drinking the strong, black coffee that was rare enough at the best of times but was now a luxury. Looking between the crowded faces, Harriet saw Ben Phipps. Thrust into a corner beside the door, he stood by himself, staring into the street with an air of bitter dejection. Could the directorship have meant so much to him?

If she had liked him better, she would have pointed him out to Guy and Guy, of course, would have hurried over to console him. As it was, Guy was too short-sighted to see him and she too nervous to give him a second thought.

It was a sepia day. When the bus left them on the front at Phaleron, they saw a yellowish sea indolently spreading its frills of foam like a bored bridge player displaying a useless hand. The shore was as empty as an arctic shore, and almost as cold. The esplanade, stretching into the remote distance, was grey and bare, but there were palms.

"The Mediterranean," said Harriet.

Guy adjusted his glasses to look at it: "Not exactly the sea of dreams," he said, but that afternoon they had something else to think about.

Passing the villas where no one seemed to be at home, he hummed to express confidence in the interview ahead, and walked too quickly. Harriet, trotting beside him, kept up without comment. They hurried to meet the moment when their equivocal position would be resolved at last.

Cookson's villa was easily found. It was the largest of the seaside villas and its name, "Porphyry Pillars", was written in roman letters. The villa was of white marble. The pillars – mentioned in Baedeker, Alan had said – were not at their best in this light.

Harriet whispered: "They look like corned beef," and Guy frowned her to silence.

A butler admitted them to a circular hall where there were more pillars, not porphyry but white marble, and on to an immense drawing-room filled with Corfu furniture and hung with amber satin.

Out of the prevailing glimmer of gold, the Major rose and shifted his rolled handkerchief so he might extend a hand.

"How delightful to meet you again," he said, though they

had scarcely met before. He placed Harriet on an amber satin
sofa as in a position of honour and apologized to Guy: "So
sorry Archie isn't here. He had a luncheon appointment in
Athens and.hasn't got back yet."

Guy blamed himself for being early, but the Major protested: "Oh, no, it's Archie who is late. Such a naughty boy!
A little fey, I'm afraid. But never mind. For a tiny while I have
you to myself, so you must tell me about Bucharest. I was
there once and met dozens of princes and princesses; all delightful, needless to say. I hope no harm will come to them.
What a débâcle! How *do* you account for it?"

Guy talked more readily to Cookson than he had talked to
Gracey. As he analysed the Rumanian catastrophe, Cookson
gave exclamations of wonder and horror, then insisted on
being told how the Pringles managed to make their escape.
"And you," he asked Harriet with deep concern, "weren't you
most terribly worried by it all? Even, perhaps, a little frightened? And when you left, were you very, *very* sad?"

The Major, looking from Harriet to Guy, from Guy to Harriet, exuded so attentive a sympathy that Harriet was completely won by him. His attitude was that of a courteous and
benevolent host welcoming newcomers into the circle of his
friends. And how privileged, these friends! She could well
understand why, in the social contest, poor Mrs. Brett had
scarcely made a showing.

But Guy was less easily beguiled and less ready to desert
Mrs. Brett. Though he responded to the Major – being quite
incapable of not responding – it was not his usual whole-
hearted response to a show of friendship. Once or twice when
there was some noise in the house, he glanced round, hoping
for Archie Callard's arrival. The Major, apparently unaware
of such moments of inattention, said: "Do tell me ..." asking
one question and another, doing his best to distract them
from their unease. But too much depended on the interview
ahead. The atmosphere was amiable but Guy's thoughts
wandered and the Major murmured, "Where *can* Archie be?"

At last the door opened and Callard appeared. Though the
light was failing, the Pringles saw from his face that he had
forgotten them. He was not alone. Charles Warden was with
him.

Harriet and Warden exchanged a startled glance, and Harriet felt her temperature fall. It was as though some trick had been played upon the pair of them.

Callard had dropped his old air of jocular indifference to life and, conscious of responsibility, was sober and constrained. "How kind of you to come," he said. "You do all know each other, don't you?"

Accepting this as introduction, Harriet and Warden bowed distantly to each other and waited to see what would happen next.

The Major, who seemed flustered by Callard's new importance, rose and said:

"Archie dear, I think I'll take Mrs. Pringle and Charles into the garden while you have your little talk. There's just light enough to see our way around. Now, don't be long. I'm sure we're all dying for our tea."

He opened the french windows and led the young people outside. Harriet went with some excitement but, looking back as the door closed, she saw Guy inside, his face creased with strain. Guilty at having gone so willingly, she hurried ahead to join the Major, behaving as though he and she were the only people in the garden. He conducted her round the beds, describing the flowers that would appear after the spring rains, and though there was not much to admire, she exclaimed over everything. Flattered by her vivacious interest, he said: "You must see it in April: but, of course, I hope you'll come many times before that."

The lawn was set with citrus trees that stood about in solitary poses like dancers waiting to open a ballet. Harriet kept her back turned to Charles Warden but, pausing to examine some small green lemons, she glanced round in spite of herself and saw him watching her behaviour with an ironical smile. She was gone at once. Catching up with the Major, she defiantly renewed her enthusiasm.

As they rounded the house and came in sight of the sea, the clouds were split by streaks of cherry pink. The sun was setting in a refulgence hidden from human eye. For an instant, the garden was touched with an autumnal glow, then the clouds closed and there was nothing but the wintry twilight.

"Yes," said the Major regretfully, "we must go in; but you will come again, won't you? You *really* will? I give a few little parties during the winter, just to help me pass the gloomy weeks. There's always a shortage of pretty girls – I mean, of course, pretty English girls. Plenty of lovely Greeks, and how lovely they can be! Still, English girls are a thing apart: so slender, so pink and white, so *natural*! Do promise you will come?"

Smiling modestly, Harriet promised.

The chandeliers had been lit inside the golden drawing-room. The Major tinkled on the glass, at the same time opening the door and saying: "May we join you?"

"Yes, of course," said Callard, as though he could not understand what they were doing out there.

Apparently the talk inside the room had finished some time before. Harriet had entered in high spirits but, meeting Guy's eye, she lost her buoyancy. He gave her a warning glance, then stared down heavily at the floor. Now, she only wanted to leave this treacherous company, but the Major was saying: "Come along. You've got your business over, so let's have a jolly tea."

The dining-room was on the other side of the hall. Tea was served on a table with rococo gilt legs and a surface of coloured marbles. The marbles formed a composition of fruits and game entitled in letters of gold: "The Pleasures of Plenty". Placed on the centre of the picture was a plate of very small cakes. The Major said:

"Dear me, look at them! As cakes increase in price, they decrease in size. One day, I fear, they'll vanish altogether."

As though he found these remarks frivolous or vulgar, Archie Callard said: "Then you won't have to pay for them."

The Major laughed, knowing himself reproved, and went on in a pleading tone: "But, Archie, such absurd little cakes! Do look at this one! Who would have the heart to eat it? Really, I'm ashamed, but . . ." He turned to Harriet: "It's not easy to get any these days, even at the Xenia. Don't you find shopping *terribly* difficult?"

"We live in an hotel," she said.

"How wise! But not, I hope, at the G.B.? I hear the Military Mission has taken possession of our darling G.B. and all our friends have been turned out. So sad to be turned out of one's suite at a time like this! Dear knows where they've all gone. And no more cocktail parties in that pretty lounge! Not that there have been many since the evacuation ship took the ladies away. Still," he added quickly: "We mustn't complain. Others have come in their place."

"Really!" said Archie Callard, "you seem to suggest that the ship took the rightful occupants of Athens and left behind nothing but wartime flotsam."

"Archie, that's quite enough!"

Delighted at having shocked the Major, Callard gave his attention to Charles Warden. He wanted to know *all* about the Mission. What was its function? How many officers were there? What position would Charles himself hold?

Speaking stiffly and briefly, the young man said he knew nothing. The Mission had only just arrived.

There was, Harriet thought, a hint of self-importance in his tone and she condemned him not only as an unpleasant young man but as one who took himself too seriously.

The telephone rang somewhere in the house. A servant came to say that Mr. Callard was wanted.

Archie Callard, tilting his head back with a fretful air, asked who was on the line. When told the British Legation, he said: "Oh, dear!" The Major sighed as though to say that this was what life was like these days.

When Callard went off, the others waited in silence. Glancing at Charles Warden, Harriet found his gaze fixed on her and she turned her head away. He said to Cookson: "I'm afraid I must get back to the office."

"But *you* don't have to go, do you?" the Major smiled on Guy and Harriet. "*Please* stay and have a glass of sherry!"

Before they could reply, Archie Callard returned with a rapid step, his manner dramatically changed. Both his fraudulent gravity and his irony were gone. Now he was not playing a part. With face fixed in the hauteur of rage, he ignored the guests and demanded of Cookson: "Did you know Bedlington was in Cairo?"

"Bedlington in Cairo? No, no. I didn't." Bewildered and alarmed, the Major dabbed at his nostrils. "But what of it? What has happened?"

"You should have known."

"Perhaps I should, but no one told me. People are too busy to keep me posted and, living down here, I'm a bit out of things. Why are you so annoyed? What's the matter?"

"I'll tell you later." Callard made off again, slamming the door as he went.

"What can it be?" said the unhappy Major. "Archie's such a temperamental boy! It's probably something quite trivial."

The invitation to sherry was not repeated. The Major's anxiety was such he scarcely noticed that the guests left together.

A staff car was waiting outside for Charles Warden and he offered the Pringles a lift. Heartened by this kindness, Guy rapidly regained his spirits and as they drove up the dark Piraeus road, was voluble about an entertainment which he planned to put on for the airmen at Tatoi. He may only just have thought of it – certainly Harriet had heard nothing about it – but now as he talked, the idea developed and inspired him. The Phaleron interview was forgotten. If he had been depressed, he was depressed no longer; and Harriet marvelled at his powers of recuperation.

If he had been offered nothing, if his future was (as she feared) vacant, he was already filling the vacancy with projects. The entertainment at Tatoi was only one thing. He discussed the possibility of producing *Othello* or *Macbeth*. And why should he not restage *Troilus and Cressida*?

Was there ever any need to pity him! He was never, as she too often was, disabled by disappointment. He simply turned his back on it.

Harriet noticed that Charles Warden laughed with Guy, not at him. Listening to Guy's schemes, he murmured as though Guy and Guy's vitality were things he had seldom, if ever, encountered before. She realized now that his restraint when replying to Callard had shown not self-importance but a disapproval of Callard's insolent wit. She had to admit the young man was by no means as unpleasant as she had wished to believe.

The car stopped outside the main entrance to the Grande Bretagne.

"Let's meet again soon," said Guy.

"Yes, we must," Charles Warden agreed.

Walking back to their hotel, Guy could talk of nothing but this new friendship until Harriet broke in: "Darling, tell me what Callard had to offer."

"Oh!" Guy did not want any intrusion upon his felicity. In

an offhand way, as though the whole matter were of no consequence, he said: "Not much. In fact, he wasn't able to promise anything."

"But he must have had some reason for sending for you?"

"He wanted to see me, that's all."

"Didn't he tell you anything?"

"Well, yes. He told me ... he felt he ought to tell me personally – which was, after all, very decent of him – that he had been forced to make Dubedat his Chief Instructor. He had no choice. Gracey made him promise."

"I see." For some minutes her disappointment was such she could not say anything more.

Guy talked on, doing all he could to justify Callard. Knowing that what he said was a measure of his own disappointment, Harriet listened and grew angry for his sake. She said at the end:

"So Archie Callard was appointed on the understanding that he rewarded Dubedat for Dubedat's services to Gracey?"

"It looks like that. I will say Callard was rather apologetic. He said: 'I'm sorry about this. I hope you won't refuse to work under Dubedat?' "

"He expects you to work under Dubedat? He must be mad."

"He said there would be work, but not immediately. He hopes to fit me in when things get under way. I must say, I rather liked Callard. He's not at all a bad chap."

"Perhaps he isn't. But here you are, the best English instructor in the place, expected to hang around in the hope that Dubedat will offer you a few hours' teaching. It's monstrous!"

"I came here against orders. I'll have to take any work I can get."

"What's this about Lord Bedlington being in Cairo? Couldn't you write to him or cable him? You have a London appointment. You've a right to state your case."

"Perhaps, but what good would it do? Bedlington knows nothing about me. Gracey, Callard and, I suppose, Cookson have all backed Dubedat. There's no one to back me. I'm merely an interloper here. The fact that I was appointed in London doesn't give me a divine right to a plum job. I could make trouble – but if I do that and gain nothing by it, I'm in wrong with the Organization for the rest of my career." Guy put his arm round Harriet's disconsolate shoulder and squeezed it: "Don't worry. Dubedat's got the job and good luck to him. We'll work together all right."

"You *won't* work together. You'll do the work, and Dubedat will throw his weight around."

Guy's tolerance of the situation annoyed Harriet more than the situation itself. He had achieved education and now, she suspected, his ambition had come to a stop. In his spiritual indolence, he would be the prey of those with more ambition; and he would not worry. It was, after all, easier to be used than to use.

She asked bitterly: "Will it be like this all our lives?"

"Like what?"

"You doing the work while other people get the importance."

"For heaven's sake, darling, what do you want? Would you prefer that I became an administrator: a smart Alec battening on other men's talents?"

"Why not, if there's more money in it? Why should you be paid less for your talents than other men are for the lack of them? Why do you encourage such a situation?"

"I don't. It's the nature of things under this social system. When we have a people's government, we'll change all that."

"I wonder."

They had reached the hotel. Her hands were clenched and Guy, picking them up and folding them into his own hands, smiled into her small, pale, angry face, saying, as he had said many times before: " 'Oh, stand between her and her fighting soul.' "

"Someone has to fight," she said. Repeating a remark she had heard as a child, she added: "If you don't fight, they'll trample you into the ground."

Guy laughed at her: "Who are 'they'?"

"People. Life. The world."

"You don't really believe that?"

She did not reply. She was more hurt for him than he was for himself. She had imagined because he was amiable, he must be fortunate, and now she saw others, neither able nor amiable, put in front of him. She felt cheated but tried to reconcile herself to things. "I suppose we are lucky to be here; and we're lucky to be together. If you're prepared to work under Dubedat, well, there's no more to be said."

"I'm prepared to work. It doesn't matter whom I work under. I'm lucky to be employed. My father was unemployed half his life and I saw what it did to him. We've nothing to complain of. Other men are fighting and getting killed for people like us."

"Yes," she said and embraced him because he was with her and alive.

An announcement in the English newspaper stated that the School would open under the Directorship of Mr. Archibald Callard. Mr. Dubedat was to be Chief Instructor and Mr. Lush would assist him. But, for some reason, there was a delay.

The students returned to the School and waited about in the library and the lecture-room but Mr. Callard, Mr. Dubedat and Mr. Lush did not appear. The librarian-secretary said they were not in the building. There was no one to enrol students. The offices were locked and remained locked for the next couple of weeks.

12

It was a dull December. The Greek advance had come to a stop. The papers explained that this was a necessary remission: the supply line must be strengthened, supplies brought up and forces rearranged. There was no cause to be downcast. But the victories, the bell-ringing, the dancing, the comradeship of triumph – these things were missing, and the city became limp in anti-climax. Even the spectacle of the Italian prisoners did little to distract people in a hard winter when it was as cold indoors as out and food was disappearing from the shops.

The prisoners were marshalled through the main streets: a straggle of men in tattered uniforms, hatless, heads bent so that the rain could drip from their hair. They were defeated men yet in every batch there were some who seemed untroubled by their plight, or who glanced at the bystanders with furtive and conciliatory smiles, or gave the impression that the whole thing was a farce.

"Where are they going?" people asked, fearful that there would be more mouths to feed, but the prisoners were not to stay in Greece. They were taken to the Piraeus and shipped to camps in the western desert.

No wonder there were some who smiled. They would eat better than the Greeks and a camp in the sun was more comfortable than the Albanian mountains where men bivouacked waist deep in the snow.

At the canteen started for British servicemen, Guy washed dishes and Harriet worked as a waitress. The men were mostly airmen, but a few sappers and members of the R.A.S.C. had arrived. Food and fuel were supplied by the Naafi and the civilians were thankful these winter nights not only for occupation, but for warmth.

The wives of the English diplomats organized the work and agreed among themselves that the food should be for the servicemen and only for them. They were honour bound not to touch a mouthful themselves. In the first throes of unaccustomed hunger, the women fried bacon, sausages, eggs and tomatoes and served men who accepted their plates casually and took it for granted that the civilians ate as much as they did.

One night, Harriet, carrying two fried sausages to a table, nearly burst into tears. A soldier, observing her with an experienced eye, said: "You look fair clemmed. Don't she look clemmed?" he asked his friends: "Ev'nt seen no one so clemmed since my old man mowed a grass-pitch for a tanner and lost his sick benefit."

Harriet laughed, but the men were concerned for her and asked: "You get your grub here, don't you?"

She explained the rules of the canteen and the first man said: "That's fair silly. There's lashings more where this comes from. Here," he pushed his plate at her, "have a good tuck-in."

She laughed again and shook her head and made off for fear she might succumb. The rule had been made and no one had the courage to break it, least of all Harriet who was shy among the diplomatic set.

A few nights later the same group of sappers arrived with a parcel which they put into Harriet's arms: "We won it," they said. "It's for you."

When she opened it in the kitchen, she found a leg of Canterbury lamb. The other women looked at it with some disapproval, and Harriet explained: "They won it."

Only Mrs. Brett, on duty at the gas-stove, had anything to say: "And I expect they did," she said. "There's always a raffle or a draw or some game of that sort going on in these camps." Eyeing the meat, she remarked confidentially to Harriet: "That's a nice piece of lamb."

"Yes, but what can I do with it?"

"Not much use to you, is it? Where could you cook it? I should have been the one to get it."

Presented with the meat, Mrs. Brett parcelled it up in a businesslike way and put it with her outdoor clothing. When she came back, she nudged against Harriet and said with fiercely threatening sympathy: "So that Archie Callard's the new Director? What's he going to do for Guy?"

"Very little. He says he promised Gracey he'd put Dubedat in charge."

"It's sickening." Mrs. Brett stared for some moments at Harriet, then seemed to come to a decision: "You want to get away from the hotel, don't you? Well, I know a Greek couple who are thinking of letting their villa. It's not much of a place, mind you, but you've got to be glad of anything these days."

When Harriet began to thank her, Mrs. Brett interrupted sternly: "Don't thank me. You gave me the joint, didn't you? You go and see about the villa before someone else gets wind of it."

The villa was on the outskirts, between the Piraeus and Phaleron roads, and so likely to be cheap. Guy let himself be taken to see it but would make no comment on the two rooms and their bare functional furniture. The hotel was enough for him. Before he married he had lived for months at a time with no room of any sort, keeping his possessions in a rucksack and sleeping in the houses of friends, often on the floor. He resisted the extravagance of the villa, but resisted more the bus or metro journeys in which it would involve him.

The owner of the villa, Kyrios Dhiamandopoulos, was an artist – *très moderne*, said his wife – and had designed the villa himself. Kyria Dhiamandopoulou went up on to the roof-terrace and left the Pringles alone to make their decision.

"Can we take it?" Harriet asked.

"Do you really want to take it?"

"It's the best we're likely to get."

"Why not stay where we are?"

"Because we can have a house of our own. A home. In fact, our first home."

"Our first home? What about the flat in Bucharest?"

"That was different. A house is a home, a flat isn't."

"Why?"

"A house is good for the soul." She was excited by the thought of their own house, even this house, and Guy said: "Very well; take it." He accepted Harriet's eccentricities as symptoms of immaturity. He usually ignored them but this was one he felt he must indulge.

13

As Christmas approached Guy said: "I've been un-employed for three months. I'm beginning to deteriorate." All unemployment, even unemployment with pay, seemed to him a rebuttal of a basic human right. In desperation, he called at the School library, hoping the sight of him would remind Archie Callard of his need for work. But Archie Callard was not at the School. The secretaries said they had never seen Mr. Callard. The students had given up and gone away. The librarian, won to sympathy by Guy's mildness of manner, ad-mitted that it was "all very odd". In fact, if things went on like this, there would be *un scandale*.

When another letter came for Guy, it was not from Archie Callard or Dubedat but from Professor Lord Pinkrose. Pink-rose, describing himself as Director of the English School, sum-moned Guy to appear at the Academy. Harriet telephoned Alan and asked: "What has happened now?"

He said: "All I know is: Archie's out and Pinkrose is in. As to how it happened, I'd be glad if you could tell me."

The Pringles were not cheered by the change. Archie had shown some goodwill but they could expect nothing from Pinkrose who, whenever he met them, behaved as though they did not exist.

They walked up to the Academy between the rain showers. As the Academy building appeared, flashing its ochre colour beneath the heavy sky, they saw a Greek soldier moving pain-fully towards them. His left foot was bandaged but fitted into an unlaced boot, the right was too heavily bandaged to wear anything. He had a crutch under his right arm and paused every few yards to rest with his free hand against the wall.

Everyone had heard of the glory of the Greek advance, but it was not all glory. The truth was coming out now. There were

terrible stories of the suffering that had been caused by un-
preparedness. Many of the men had been crippled by long
marches in boots that did not fit, while others, who had no
boots at all, fought barefoot in the snow. Struggling through
the mountain blizzards, they were soaked for days. Their ragged uniforms froze upon them. Their hands and feet became
frost-bitten and infected for lack of sulpha drugs. Their
wounds were neglected. There were thousands of cases of
gangrene and thousands of amputations.

The Pringles, as they approached the soldier, gazed at him
with awe and compassion. He met their pity with indifference.
His gaunt face was morose with pain. He was intent on nothing
but making the next move.

On the other side of the road there was a hospital. Other
wounded were making their way round the tarmac quadrangle.

As they looked across, Guy raged against the pro-German
ministers who, knowing the war would come, had prevented
the stock-piling of medical supplies, but Harriet said nothing,
knowing if she tried to speak she would burst into tears.

The Academy door stood ajar. They went through to the
common-room where the air was dank with cold. There was
no one to meet them. At that hour the inmates were at work
and the whole building was silent. Not knowing what else to
do, they sat down to wait. Pinkrose must have been watching
for them. He let them linger in suspense for ten minutes, then
they heard the trip of his little feet coming down the stairs and
along the tiled passage.

"Ah, there you are!" he said. His tone surprised them. It was
not a friendly tone but it suggested he might have something
to offer.

Guy stood up. Pinkrose gave him a rapid, oblique glance
then gazed at the empty fireplace. He was wearing his greatcoat and scarves and though he had no hat, his flattened dog-
brown hair showed a ring where his hat had been.

He took a letter from his coat pocket and slowly unfolded
it, saying: "I sent for you ... Yes, I sent for you. Lord Bedlington ... by the way, are you known to him?"

Guy said: "No."

"Well, strangely enough ... he's chosen you to be Chief
Instructor. You're to be appointed. It's a definite order. I could
say, you've already *been* appointed. It's in this letter here. You

may read it, if you wish. Yes, yes, if you wish, you may read it." He pushed the letter at Guy as though disclaiming any part in it.

Embarrassed by his discourtesy, Guy said: "May I ask what has happened? I was recently called out to Phaleron to see Mr. Callard."

"I know you were. Yes, I know you were. Mr. Callard heard from the Cairo office that he was to be Director, but the appointment was not confirmed. No, it was not confirmed. In fact, it was rescinded. Mr. Callard's announcement was premature *and* a trifle unwise, I think. Lord Bedlington decided that the position called for an older man. *I* am to be Director and have asked Mr. Callard to act as Social Secretary, a position more suited to his particular gifts."

Guy extruded unspoken inquiry as to how this had come about. Pinkrose, after a reflective pause, chose to explain: "I contacted Lord Bedlington ... I made it my business to contact him. We were at Cambridge together. He was unaware that I was in Athens. I fear that Mr. Gracey had failed ... had failed to mention me. An oversight, I have no doubt. Never mind, the matter has been put right; and in accordance with Bedlington's wishes, I am appointing you Chief Instructor."

"May I ask if you were kind enough to recommend me?"

"No. No, I can't say that I did. I recommended no one. You are Lord Bedlington's choice."

"And what about Dubedat and Toby Lush? Am I to employ them?"

Pinkrose gave no sign that he had ever heard of Dubedat and Lush. "You may employ whom you please," he said.

"When will the school reopen?"

"I suggest the first of January. Yes, the first of January will be an excellent date."

"And may I start enrolments?"

"You may do what you like." Pinkrose walked out of the room without a good-day and Guy and Harriet were left to find their way out. They took the steps down to the garden where the new green was pushing through the straw tangle of dead plants. Once they were safely away from the house, Harriet said: "That was interesting. It looks as though Pinkrose, when pushed, is tougher than we thought."

Grinning in exultation, Guy said: "We know how he got his job; but heaven knows how I got mine."

"You've got it. That's all that matters." Harriet was as exultant as he: "In spite of your follies, luck is on your side."

14

Two days before Christmas, the bells started up again. The Greeks on the Albanian coast road had taken Himarra. So the advance continued and the hope of a conclusive victory lightened the winter. Everyone was certain that in a few weeks, in a month or less, the enemy would be asking for terms. The war was as good as over.

Still, it was a sparse Christmas. There was little enough for sale in the shops that did their best, decking the windows with palm and bay in honour of the Greek heroes, and olive for the expected peace.

There were candles and ribbons – blue and white ribbons, and red, white and blue ribbons – and, for the short space of twilight, the shops were allowed to shine for the festival. Everyone came out to see the brilliance of the streets, but when darkness was complete, the black-out came down and those who could afford it crowded into the cafés. The others went home.

Harriet went shopping to celebrate another victory: the conquest of a city that was on no map but their own. Guy was employed. They had found a home. They could remain where they most wanted to be. She bought Guy a length of raw silk to be made into a summer jacket, one of the last silk lengths left in a shop which had been opened by an Englishwoman to encourage the arts of Greece. The woman had gone back to England, and no one had time now to weave silk or make goat-skin rugs or pottery jars for honey.

The Pringles were asked to two Christmas parties, one to be given by Mrs. Brett and one by Major Cookson. The Major's invitation came in first but Guy thought they should accept Mrs. Brett's. "We owe it to her," he said. "She would never forgive us if we went to Cookson."

"Why do we owe it to her?" asked Harriet, who was drawn to the idea of the Phaleron party.

"She's been so badly treated."

"She probably deserved it. I would much rather go to Cookson's."

"It's out of the question. She'd be deeply hurt."

In the end Harriet was over-ridden, as she always seemed to be, and the argument came to an end.

On Christmas Day the sky was overcast. The parties did not begin until 8 o'clock and they had to get through the day that was a sad and empty day of the homeless.

When they went out to walk in the shuttered streets, the Pringles met Alan Frewen who was wandering about with his dog. He joined them and they went together towards Zonar's where Ben Phipps sat staring into vacancy. At the sight of them, he jumped up, asking eagerly: "Where are you off to?" They did not know.

University Street stretched away, long, straight and harshly grey, with only one figure in sight – Yakimov, his tall, fragile body stooped beneath the weight of his fur-lined coat. Seeing four persons known to him, he began to hurry, several times tripping over his fallen hem, and came to them smiling a smile of great sweetness, and singing out:

"How heartwarming to see your nice familiar faces! What can one do on this day of comfort and joy? Where, oh where, can poor Yaki get a bite to eat?"

Alan said he had promised to give Diocletian a Christmas present of a real walk. Why should they not take the bus down to the sea-front and stroll along the beach?

Yakimov looked discouraged by this suggestion but when the others moved towards the bus stop, he followed with a sigh.

They were alone on the shore. The air was moist but there was no wind, and the cold, instead of blowing into their faces, seeped down from the yellowish folds of cloud above their heads.

The sea was fixed like a jelly in bands of sombre colour: neutral at the edge, a heavy violet in mid-distance, indigo where it touched the horizon.

In the jaundiced light the esplanade was grey but the pink and yellow houses shone with an unnatural clarity, while the

Major's villa was as white as a skull within a circlet of palms and fur-dark pines.

The dog, released, had taken off like a projectile and now dashed back and forwards, sending up flurries of sand and barking its joy in freedom. Alan, chiding it with a doting smile, made matters worse by throwing stones for it.

Ben Phipps, who on the bus had been silent as though unsure of his welcome in this company, frowned as the dog chased about him. When the uproar tailed off, he said: "I heard a bit of news yesterday evening."

"Good news, I hope," Guy said.

"Not very. It might even be bloody bad news."

That put a stop to Alan's activity and when everyone was attending him, Phipps went on: "One of our chaps, out on a reccy over the Bulgarian front, thought he saw something in the snow. Something fishy. He dropped down to have a dekko and nearly had kittens. What d'you think? Jerry's got a mass of stuff there – tanks, guns, lorries, every sort of heavy armament. All camouflaged. *White*."

"You mean it hadn't been there long?" Harriet said. "But it could have been painted on the spot."

Phipps gave her a look, surprised by her grasp of his point and not over-pleased by it. "Unlikely," he said. "That sort of stuff isn't painted, it's sprayed. A factory job."

"Couldn't it be sprayed on the spot?"

"Perhaps it could." A repository of information in Athens, he seemed more annoyed than not by the fact Harriet's suggestions made sense.

"Where did you hear all this?" Alan wanted to know.

"In the mess at Tatoi. I've been doing a piece on British intervention in Greece. It may be hush-hush but when I was there the place was buzzing with it. The pilot had just come in. No one had had time to clamp down on his report and the chaps were talking."

"You think the Germans are preparing an invasion?"

"Your guess is as good as mine. You might even say it's as good as D'Albiac's. No one knows anything. But you'd better keep it under your hat." Feeling he may have said too much, Ben Phipps looked sternly at the Pringles and turned to warn Yakimov, but Yakimov was dawdling far behind.

The party, oppressed by the day, became more oppressed as they contemplated the possibility of a German move. And how possible it now seemed! Why should the stronger partner of the Axis stand by inactive while the weaker suffered ignominious defeat? Yet who could bear to think the Greeks had suffered in vain?

Guy said: "The Bulgarian roads are the worst in Europe. There's only one bridge over the Danube. How could all this heavy stuff get to the frontier? Don't you think it's some cock-and-bull story?"

"Well . . ." Having blown up his sensation, Ben Phipps saw fit to deflate it: "The pilot saw something all right, but perhaps it wasn't what it seemed. It could have been a sham – something set up to scare the Greeks or, for that matter, the Jugs. There's this tricky situation in Yugoslavia: Peter and Paul. Which one's going to fly away? The pro-German faction's behind the Regent; the others are behind the King. If Paul's allowed a free hand, then the Germans'll let things ride. Their troops are spread thin enough as it is. They don't want to hold down more unproductive territory."

Alan murmured his agreement. It was not much of a hope, but these days they existed off just such a hope as this one. And there was the persisting human belief that nothing could be as sinister as it seemed. They began to rise out of their consternation and as they did so, found that Yakimov, hurrying to catch them up, had caught a sentence or two of Phipps' talk.

"What's this, dear boy? The Nasties coming here?"

Looking into Yakimov's great, frightened eyes, Ben Phipps could only laugh: "I didn't say so."

"But if they do: what'll happen to us?"

"What, indeed!"

Harriet said: "We have the sea. It makes me feel safe."

"This great ridiculous mass of useless water!" Ben Phipps peered at it: "I'd feel a lot safer if it weren't there."

Guy said: "I'm inclined to agree," and the two men laughed as though they shared a joke.

Phipps' manner towards Guy suggested understanding and incipient intimacy while Guy, aware of the interest they held in common, behaved as though their concurrence were only a matter of time. Harriet was disturbed, feeling that the atmosphere between them was like the onset of a love-affair. She became more critical of Phipps, suspecting he was the sort of man who, though sexually normal, prefers his own sex. He disliked her and probably disliked women. He had about him the reek of the trouble-maker, the natural enemy of married life; the sort of man who observes, or seems to observe, the conventions while leading husbands astray and undermining the authority of wives.

She walked between them but when they reached the point at Edam, they turned and Phipps placed himself beside Guy, saying: "I heard you'd been appointed Chief Instructor, and I was jolly glad. I never had any use for that twit Dubedat. And what about Callard? I bet he's had some little *douceur* slipped into his hand?"

"He's to be Social Secretary."

"Social Secretary!" Phipps's tone was hollow with disgust. "The rest of us work our balls off for a living while he lies around at Phaleron and gets paid for it."

Guy laughed. This exchange confirmed the understanding between them. Their unfortunate introduction at Zonar's was forgotten and Guy's manner lost a last hint of restraint.

Phipps became confidential: "I won't pretend I wasn't after the directorship. I *was*. I need something more than free-lance journalism to keep me going, but it was Gracey who led me to believe I might get it. He humbugged me. And Pinkrose and Dubedat. We were all after it, *you* know that. He had us all running errands and taking him gifts and circling round him like planets round the sun. If he spoke we listened openmouthed. We were all waiting for the crown to drop from his nerveless fingers; each one thought he'd get it when it fell."

"Did you know Callard was in the running?"

"No. That was a secret between Archie and Colin Gracey. *And* the Major, of course. The rest of us poor mutts were just led up the garden. I have a reputation – you may have heard that I scribble a bit. I had a book published by the Left Book Club. I'm not unknown. I got friends at home to do a bit of lobbying. Then, if you please, word comes from Cairo that Archie's got the job. Gracey had fooled me. I was mad. In fact, I was hopping mad."

"But why did Gracey choose Callard?"

"A matter of friendship. Gracey liked to move in the right circles."

"And had Callard any sort of qualifications?"

"He'd a degree of sorts; third in History or something. It's quite fashionable to get a third, of course. One of his Oxford admirers described him as 'frittering away an intellectual fortune'. The fortune, if it exists, is kept well under lock and key. I've seen nothing of it. Have you?" Phipps spoke in a tone of breathless inquiry as though a sense of injustice were at last bursting free. "I could do the job better; you could do the job better; even Dubedat could do it better. Yet it was simply handed to Callard as though he had some natural right to it."

Guy nodded in understanding of Phipps's indignation. "He probably thought he had a natural right to it," Guy said. "A class right. There's a certain sort of rich, privileged young man who imagines he is born to be in the front rank of every-thing; even the arts. If he chooses to write or paint, he must be a genius. There are some who feel quite a sense of grievance when proved wrong. Really, believe it or not, there were those who felt it monstrous that D. H. Lawrence, a miner's son, should have so much talent. Some of them remain dilettante, believing that if they chose to apply their talents, they'd be remarkable; but they don't choose."

Ben Phipps's laughter stopped him in his tracks. He threw back his head, shouting: "You're right. That's Archie: a genius by right of birth who has chosen to be a dilettante. The great 'might have been'." Phipps's laughter came to an abrupt stop. He said: "I can tell you this: if his appointment had been con-firmed, I intended to institute an inquiry."

"I think Pinkrose did institute an inquiry."

"Did he? Good for him. Still, I can't see him making a go as director here. He's too narrow, too much the don. It's a posi-tion for a younger man. I should have got it."

"I think so, too," Guy spoke a firm declaration of faith in Phipps and Harriet, looking at Phipps, said:

"You'd better not pass that on to Pinkrose."

"What do you think I am?" Phipps stared angrily at her and she stared back, offering no conciliation. If Guy chose to make a declaration of faith, she was just as ready to make a declar-ation of war. Phipps turned his back on her and said to Guy: "Pinkrose's own appointment was a bit of a wangle, I bet? How did he fix it?"

"He's a friend of Lord Bedlington. They knew one another at Cambridge."

"Hah!" said Phipps, needing to be told no more, and the two walked just a little quicker, drawing ahead and dropping their voices in a privacy of agreement. Catching a word here and there, Harriet knew they were discussing in an atmosphere of scandalized conspiracy, the suppression in different countries of the left wing opposition, which was for both of them the suppression of desirable life.

"Look at them!" Harriet said to Alan. "They're like a couple of schoolgirls discovering sex."

Alan smiled. Sensing her jealousy but refusing to become involved with it, he started hunting for flat stones which he sent skimming over the sea for the entertainment of Diocletian. As the dog ran about, Harriet saw that its vertebra was visible and its haunches stood out from its skin, but, galvanized by the game, it tore about the beach, splashing in and out of the water, and panting in anticipation whenever Alan felt need for a rest.

Yakimov said confidentially to Harriet: "I expect, dear girl, you're feeling a trifle peckish. I know I am. Where are we going to eat? We ought to give our mind to the problem, don't you think?"

"Yes, I think we should."

They had hoped to eat in one of the sea-side restaurants, which before the war had been noted for their crayfish and mullet, but now they were all shut, not from a shortage of fish but a shortage of fishermen.

She said: "We could try the Piraeus. There must be some sort of eating place for the men employed about the harbour."

"You think that's the best we can do?" Yakimov looked glum. "I know, dear girl, one mustn't complain. Not the done thing. Must think of the fighting men; but it comes a bit rough on your poor old Yak. I'm doing an important job, too. I need nourishment. Don't get paid much, but it's regular. For the first time in years your Yak can lay his hands on the Ready, and he can't get a decent meal for love nor money."

"It's hard," Harriet agreed: "But, remember, you're going to the Major's party."

"Oh yes. Get a bite there all right." He turned to Alan: "What about you, dear boy?"

Alan, like the Pringles, had been invited to both parties. He had, he said, decided to support Mrs. Brett.

Harriet looked to where Guy and Phipps walked with their heads together: "Why don't we ditch Mrs. Brett?" she said.

Alan said, shocked: "No. No, we couldn't do that."

The rain began to fall in a gentle film, chilling their faces like powdered ice. Someone was coming towards them along the esplanade: a man with a fish basket, the first human being they had met since they left the bus. They were all hungry with a hunger that had not yet touched starvation but caused an habitual unease. As the man approached, Harriet, though talking of something else, watched him in expectation, certain he was there on their behalf. He had fish in the basket and would open his restaurant for no purpose but to feed them. Impelled by her faith, or so it seemed, he made for a wooden cabin, unlocked the padlock and went inside.

Alan grunted as though he had shared Harriet's dream, and said: "It looks as though we may get something after all."

The cabin, of clinker board, was built out to form a verandah over the shore. A stairway led up from the beach.

Recalled by the same excitement that possessed the others, Ben Phipps and Guy went up the stair and knocked on the door. Alan, Harriet and Yakimov watched hopefully from below. The man came out, surprised to have custom, but when Phipps explained their need, he smiled and said he had come from Tourkolimano where he had been able to buy some red mullet. He waved them to the verandah tables, for the cabin itself was nothing but a cook-house.

The verandah had a roof and there were rush-screens at either end so that the party would be protected from the rain if not from cold.

As the smell of frying mullet came from the kitchen, Yakimov hunched his shoulders and clasped his hands to his breast as though in prayer. The others swallowed down their impatience and stared out at the sea that had lost its violet and green. The band of indigo still lay along the horizon but the rest was a glaucous yellow pocked by rain-drops. The rain, gathering strength, bounced on the glossy sand and hit the roof above their heads. Diocletian had remained on the shore, but soon had had enough of it and came up in search of his master. Finding Alan, he shook himself violently then eagerly sniffed the air. "Lie down," said Alan and he lay, head on paws, but with eyes restless, on edge with hunger like the rest of them.

The talk had lapsed. Harriet asked Yakimov if he could still get *blinis* at the Russian Club. He sighed: "*Hélas!* No caviare, no cream, no *blinis*. But sometimes they have octopus. Do you like octopus?"

"Not much." She had an innate horror of eight-legged creatures, but was glad enough to eat anything for now not only the flesh of beasts, but the hearts, kidneys and livers went to the army, and the civilians ate the intestines. Grey, slippery and bound up like shoelaces, these had brought about an epidemic of dysentry.

The mullet was ready. The proprietor hurried out to set the table and Alan asked if he had anything to spare for the dog. The man bent down and ruffled Diocletian about the ears then, shaking his head in compassion, he described the dog's condition with sad gestures. When he brought out the mullet, he placed three squid before the dog. Diocletian opened his mouth and they were gone. The company watched open-eyed, but they had been small squid and the fish also were small. They disappeared as quickly as the squid. Guy said: "We've had our Christmas dinner, after all."

"I wish we could have it again," said Yakimov. "D'you think he'd fry a few more?"

"We have had our share."

The man came out and said he was leaving but the guests were to remain seated until the rain grew less. He refused payment for the squid which were a present for the dog, and charged very little for the mullet. After they had settled their bill, he remained for a while talking to Alan with so much vitality and laughter that Harriet and Yakimov, who knew no Greek, thought he was telling some entertaining story. When he had shaken hands with them all and gone off, still carrying his fish basket, Alan said: "He said he didn't intend opening today. He went to Tourkolimano at dawn and waited all morning to get the fish. It was for his own family. He came here merely to get his knife, but seeing we were English, he could not refuse us."

"So we've eaten his food?" said Harriet.

Phipps said: "I expect he's got more in the basket."

Guy, overwhelmed, praised the generosity of the Greeks

and their tradition of hospitality. He talked for a long time
and at the end Harriet said: "And they are poor. If you are
really poor, you can't refuse to sell anything."

"He did not sell Diocletian's food. It was a gift."

"Yes, if you are poor you sell things or you give them away.
What you cannot do is keep them."

Guy regarded her with quizzical wonder before he said:
"Why aren't you a Progressive? You recognize the truth yet
don't subscribe to it."

"I disagree. Truth is more complex than politics."

Guy looked to Ben Phipps but Ben was not taking on
Harriet. Instead, he bawled out:

> "A petty bourgeois philistine,
> He didn't know the party line.
> Although his sentiments were right,
> He was a bloomin' Trotskyite.
> Despite great mental perturbation,
> Persistent left-wing deviation
> Dogged his foot-steps till at last,
> Discouraged by his awful past
> And taking it too much to heart, he
> Went and joined the Labour Party.
> The morale of this tale is when in
> Doubt consult the works of Lenin."

Thinking he was having a sly dig at her, Harriet was not
much pleased by this song, but Guy was delighted. Phipps,
encouraged, passed into a gay, satirical mood and began to
entertain the company. He lifted the edge of Yakimov's coat
and after examining the lining, whistled and said: "Sable, by
Jove! Always thought it was rabbit."

In no way offended, Yakimov smiled and said: "Fine coat.
Once belonged to the Czar. Czar give it to m'poor old dad."

"Thought you were English?"

"Certainly I am. Typical Englishman, you might say. Mother
Irish."

"And your father?"

"Russian. White Russian, of course."

"So you're against the present lot? The Soviets?"

A wary look came over Yakimov's face. "Don't know about
that, dear boy. Lot to be said for both lots."

Phipps stared at Yakimov with mock severity then said: "This story about you doing undercover work? I suppose there's no truth in it?"

Gratified by Phipps's interest, Yakimov murmured: "Not in a position to say."

"Um. Well, if I were you, I'd issue a denial."

"Really, dear boy? Why?"

"I just would, that's all. British Intelligence isn't popular here. The Italians took exception to their activities. It's my belief, if those goofs had kept out, there'd've been no attack."

Yakimov's eyes grew moist with disquiet. He said: "Wish you'd elucidate, dear boy," but Phipps merely nodded with the threatening air of one who knows much but will say nothing. Yakimov sniffed with fear.

"Don't tease him," said Alan.

Bored and dispirited, they watched the rain plop heavily into the sand and the sea, jaundiced and viscous, move an inch forward and inch back. With the same viscous and inane slowness the afternoon crawled by. Cold and bored, they remained on the rickety verandah chairs because there was nothing else to do, nowhere to go. Yakimov said suddenly: "Athens, the Edinburgh of the south!"

It was so long since he had roused himself sufficiently to exercise his wit that the others looked at him in astonishment. He smiled and subsided and for a long time no one spoke.

Alan broke the silence to say that his friend Vourakis had told him a curious thing. The Greek people were saying that someone had run to Athens with the news of the victory of Koritza and, crying "Nenikiamen", had fallen down dead.

"I've heard that before," said Ben Phipps.

"We've all heard it before," said Alan. "After the victory of Marathon the runner Phidipides ran with the news to Athens and, crying 'Nenikiamen', fell dead."

"It is possible," Guy said, "that the Marathon story had no more truth than the Koritza story."

"It is possible," Alan nodded. "But it is not a question of truth. This war, like other wars, is collecting its legends."

The rain drummed on the slats above their heads, its rhythm breaking every few minutes when an overflow pipe released a gush of water. At last the fall slackened. The light was failing and they had to get to their feet and go.

As they reached the bus stop, a car came hooting behind them.

The car, a Delahaye, slowed down by the kerb and a head covered with wild, straw-coloured hair, shouted: "Hello, there!"

The car stopped and Toby Lush jumped out. "What brings you all to Phaleron?" He ran at Guy, slipping on the wet road, almost falling headlong in his eagerness to clinch the meeting. "What a bit of luck, meeting you! Come on. Get in. Room for everyone."

Yakimov and Ben Phipps, needing no second invitation, got themselves into the back seat, but Guy, though he found it impossible to snub Toby, had no wish to be driven by him.

Alan said: "There isn't room for the dog. I'll take the bus." He limped off, and Guy looked after him.

"Get in. Get in." Toby seized Guy's arm and manoeuvred him into the front seat. "Three in front," he shouted, then caught Harriet's elbow: "Come along now. In there beside Guy."

He was more than usually excited and, when under way, told them he had been helping to prepare the villa for the Major's party. "They're laying out the buffet. Gosh! Wait till you've had a dekko! You're all coming, aren't you?" He was hilarious as though he had won a prize which, in a way, he had. The prize was Guy, and Toby had not captured him without reason.

"Jolly glad you got that job," he said. "No one better fitted for it. *Jolly* glad. We're both jolly glad. I don't mean the old soul wasn't put out. He was a bit, you know! Stands to reason; but what he said was: 'If it's not to be me then I'm glad it's old Pringle.' "

Guy gave an ironical: "Oh!" but it was an amused and good-natured irony, and Toby, encouraged, went on: "You're opening in the new year aren't you? You'll be needing teachers? Well, what I wanted to say is: you can rely on the pair of us. We'll help you out." His tone of open-hearted friendliness suggested that all was forgotten and forgiven.

Guy said "Oh!" again and laughed. Harriet thought it likely enough that Dubedat and Toby Lush, when the School reopened, would be installed there as senior teachers.

"Perhaps you think we behaved like a couple of Bs," Toby

said. "Well, we didn't. I'd like you to know that. We'd've done what we could for you but Gracey was dead against you. So we couldn't do a thing."

"Even though Dubedat was in charge?" Harriet asked.

"That was all my eye." Toby blew out his moustache in disgust: "The old soul was hamstrung. He daren't make a move without consulting Gracey."

"And why was Gracey dead against Guy? Because somebody told him that Guy neglected his work in order to produce a play?"

"Look here!" Toby Lush exploded in an injured way. "We told him the play was a smash hit. We said H.E. was in the royal box and every seat was sold. It was Gracey who disapproved — and I can tell you why! He was jealous. He couldn't bear someone to do something he hadn't done himself."

"Couldn't he produce a play?" Guy asked.

"He'd be terrified to take the risk. Suppose it didn't succeed! Besides, he was too damned lazy."

"Why didn't you tell us this before?" Harriet asked.

"There's such a thing as loyalty."

"Then why mention it now?"

"Oh, I say!" Toby now was both injured and indignant. "You can't blame us. Look how the old soul's been treated. He worked like a black doing Gracey's job for him and what's he got to show? We're loyal. We're loyal all right but . . . "

"You weren't loyal to Guy." Harriet broke in but Guy had had enough enmity and he talked her down, assuring Toby that both he and Dubedat would get all the work they wanted when the School re-opened.

When he dropped Guy and Harriet at their hotel, Toby shot out his hand in a large liberal gesture that bestrode all the disagreements of the past. "See you tonight," he said.

Guy explained that they could not go to the Major's party because they had committed themselves to Mrs. Brett.

"Why not go to both?" said Toby and as Ben Phipps and Yakimov joined in persuading him, Guy said: "I suppose we could."

"Right. I'll pick you up," Toby said, gasping with importance. " 'Fraid I won't be able to take you to old Ma Brett's. This is the Major's car. Got the loan of it to run a few errands for him. See you later, then."

Guy was surprised that Harriet showed no particular pleasure at this change of plan.

"You're not going to please me," she said. "You're going to
please Toby Lush and horrid little Phipps."

He had to laugh: "Darling," he pleaded: "Don't be so un-
reasonable.'

When Toby returned for the Pringles, Dubedat was sitting
in the front seat. Guy, to reassure him, greeted him affably,
but Dubedat sat with his shoulders hunched and did not even
grunt. He had renounced his fine social manner and was as
sullen as he had ever been. He made no attempt to talk in the
car and the Pringles, when they came into the lighted hall at
Phaleron, saw his face set again in lines of discontent. Toby,
who had been chatting happily with Guy, wanted to stay with
the Pringles but Dubedat was having none of that. Calling
Toby to heel, he marched him off to another room and Harriet
said: "You didn't get much change out of that one."

"I certainly didn't. I'm afraid he thinks I've somehow done
him out of a job."

"He probably thought it was his by rights. He thinks everything is his by rights. If he doesn't get it, he's been done out of
it. That accounts for his resentful expression."

Guy laughed and squeezed her arm. "You're a terrible
girl!" he said.

The Pringles were early but the rooms were already
crowded. Yakimov came pushing through to them with a
dejected air. "Nice state of affairs," he complained. "First
here, I was. First on the green, and the butler said no one's to
touch a sliver till the Major gives the word. He's standing
guard over the grub. Not like the Major at all. If we wait for
the whole mob to arrive, there won't be enough to go round." He
had left the dining-room in disgust but could not stay away for
long. "Come and have a look," he said to Harriet. "Must say,
it's a splendid spread."

Guy had found Ben Phipps, so Harriet went willingly to the
dining-room where the hungry guests, packed about the buffet,
were doing their best to hide their hunger.

Yakimov, crushed against Harriet, whispered: "Most of them
were here on the dot. Usually it's a case of first come, first
served, but last time they'd wolfed the lot in the first fifteen
minutes. S'pose there've been complaints. I recommend stand-

ing here beside the plates. Soon as we get the nod, grab one and lay about you."

"Where does it all come from?" Harriet asked in wonder.

"Mustn't ask that, dear girl. Eat and be thankful. My God, look at that! _Cream._"

As more people came in, those at the centre were so pressed against the buffet they could scarcely keep their feet.

Trembling in an agony of anticipation, Yakimov said to the butler: "Dear boy, there'll be a riot soon." The butler began to look for the Major.

Harriet noticed Guy beckoning her to join him in the doorway. As she moved, Yakimov said: "Don't go. Don't go. They're just about to give the word."

"I'll come straight back."

Guy gripped her wrist and said in fierce indignation: "Who do you think is here?"

"I've no idea."

"The Japanese consul."

"How do you know?"

"Ben pointed him out."

Ben Phipps, standing behind Guy, looking more amused than indignant, said: "Last Christmas the Major invited the German minister, an old pal of his. He went round saying 'What's a war between friends?' The British diplomats were furious and Cookson got his knuckles rapped."

Pulling Harriet from the room, Guy said: "Come on. We're going."

"Not yet. Let's eat first. And we haven't seen anything." She looked round at the sumptuous dresses of the rich Greek women, the hot-house flowers, the laurel swags decorating the marble pillars and said: "I don't want to go yet." As she spoke, she saw Charles Warden. He was looking at her and, catching her eye, took a step towards her. Impulsively, she moved away from Guy, who held to her, saying: "Get your coat. I'm not staying here."

"But we're not at war with Japan."

"I won't remain in the room with the representative of a Fascist Government. Besides, we're due at Mrs. Brett's."

Ben Phipps was looking the other way. Before Harriet could say more, Guy led her firmly to the alcove where she had left her coat. The Major, still welcoming the incoming guests, looked perplexed by the departure of the Pringles. "Surely you are not going so soon?" he protested.

"I am afraid we must," said Guy. "Mrs. Brett has invited us to supper."

"Oh!" The Major caught his breath in a snigger at the mention of Mrs. Brett, but it was a peevish snigger. He could not bear that anyone, not even young people like Guy and Harriet, should leave his party to go to another.

They had scarcely entered the house when they were outside it again. Harriet, feeling as peevish as the Major, said: "Mr. Facing-both-ways stayed on."

"*Who?*"

"Your friend Phipps."

"You're always wrong about people."

"I don't think so. I never liked Dubedat and I was right. I was doubtful of Toby Lush ..."

"You're doubtful of everyone."

"Well, you do pick up with the most doubtful sort of people."

Guy made no reply to this but, keeping his hold on her, hurried her to the bus stop where a bus was preparing to depart. The bus carried them away but Harriet's thoughts remained with the radiant dresses, the splendid villa – and with Charles Warden.

Mrs. Brett's flat on the slopes of Lycabettos was equipped with two small electric fires. Electric fires had become valuable possessions, not to be bought at any price now. The guests, delighted to find the rooms warm, were still discussing the fires when the Pringles arrived.

Mrs. Brett was shouting in self-congratulation: "Aren't I lucky! Yes, aren't I lucky! The girls left them behind. I opened a cupboard and there they were. I thought: 'What sensible girls to spend their pennies on things like this instead of silly fripperies.'"

Spreading her large-boned hands in front of one of the fires, she was shaking all over and nearly deranged at being the centre of so much attention. When the Pringles tried to speak to her, she pushed them aside and went to the kitchen where something was cooking.

The room was full of middle-aged and elderly guests, mostly

women who had remained in Athens because they had no reason to go anywhere else. Harriet, seeing no one she knew, thought: "If we hadn't come, we would not have been missed." They remained unwelcomed until Mrs. Brett returned to the room. Becoming aware of them, she seized hold of Guy as though his arrival were a long-awaited event. "Attention," she called. "Attention. Now! I want you all to meet the new Chief Instructor at the English School: Mr. Guy Pringle." This announcement was made with such impressement that there was a flutter of clapping before anyone had time to reflect and ask what it was all about. Mrs. Brett, hand raised, stood for some moments rejoicing in their bewilderment, then decided to enlighten them. She said:

"You all saw the announcement that Archie Callard was to be the new Director at the School! Perhaps you don't all know that he isn't the new Director after all? The appointment wasn't confirmed. No. Lord Bedlington decided that Lord Pinkrose was better fitted to take charge in an important cultural centre like this, and I'm sure you all agree with him. Lord Pinkrose is *somebody*, not like ... well, naming no names. Anyway, Lord Pinkrose was told to appoint Guy Pringle here as Chief Instructor; and do you know why?" She grinned at the circle of blank faces, then turned on Guy: "Do you know why?" Guy shook his head.

"Does Lord Pinkrose know why?"

"I don't think he does," Guy said.

"I'll tell you why. I'll tell you all why. I had a hand in it. Oh, yes, I had. My Percy had friends in high places. We knew a lot of people. The poor old widow's still got influence. We knew Lord Bedlington years ago when he was just young Bobby Fisher, travelling around, and he used to stay with us at Kotor. He's just been made Chairman of the Organization, and when I heard he was in Cairo, I sent him a letter. It was a strong letter, I can tell you. I let him know what's been going on here. I let him know about Gracey and Callard and Cookson. I said we were all disgusted at the way the School had gone down; and I said things would be no better under Callard. I said Callard couldn't run a whelk-stall. Yes, I said that. I don't mince matters. And I said there was this nice young chap here, this Guy Pringle, and he was being discriminated against. I opened Bobby Fisher's eyes, I can tell you. And the

long and the short of it is, our friend Guy Pringle's got the
job he deserves." She lifted her hands above her head and
applauded herself.

"What an *éclaircissement!*" said Miss Jay acidly. "Just like
the last act of a pantomime." But whatever doubts she raised
were dispelled by Guy who flung his arms round Mrs. Brett
saying: "Thank you. Thank you. You're a great woman!" He
kissed her resolutely on either cheek.

Flushed, bright-eyed, gasping from her oration, Mrs. Brett,
not a little drunk, danced up and down in his arms, snapping
her fingers to right and left, and shouting: "That for Gracey;
and that for Callard! And that for the hidden hand of Phaleron! You can go and tell Cookson there's life in the old girl
yet!"

If she had caused embarrassment, Guy's spontaneous and
artless good nature had won the guests and the embarrassment went down in laughter. Everyone, even Miss Jay, joined
Mrs. Brett as she banged her hands together. Harriet, observant in the background watched the room converge round
Guy while he looked to her, smiling, and held out his hand.
He might have said: "You see how right I was to come here,"
but he said nothing. He merely wanted to include her in the
fun.

The rumpus subsided when Mrs. Brett shouted: "The hot-
pot! The hot-pot!' and ran back to the kitchen.

"About time," said Miss Jay whose heavy cream wool dress
with all its fringes hung lank upon her.

The lean times were telling on Miss Jay and her monstrous
face had drooped into the sad, dew-lapped muzzle of a blood-
hound. It was not only her flesh that had collapsed. Her
malicious self-assertion had lost its force and her remarks
made no impact at all.

Harriet knew now she could, if she wished, say anything she
liked about English society in Athens. Miss Jay counted for
little. Local society had shrunk like a balloon losing air and
Miss Jay had shrunk with it. Harriet was free to speak as she
pleased.

During the excitement of Mrs. Brett's speech, she had
noticed Alan Frewen among the guests. Moving over to him.
she asked: "Is Miss Jay a rich woman?"

Amused by this direct question, Alan said: "I believe she

has a modest competence, as Miss Austen would say."

"A modest competence" seemed to disclose Miss Jay. Harriet saw her with her modest competence, tackling the world and getting it under control; but the world had changed about her and now, an obsolete fortress, with weapons all out of date, there was not much due to her but pity.

Alan suggested that Harriet meet the painter Papazoglou who, young and bearded, in a private's uniform, was spread against the wall as though he would, if he could, sink through it and out of sight. Alan said that as everyone was doing something to enhance the Greek cause, Mrs. Brett had proclaimed herself a patron of the arts and had placed the young man's canvases round the room, calling attention to them with such vehemence that several people present were still under the impression she had painted them herself.

Papazoglou spoke no English so Harriet went round peering into the little paintings of red earth, dark foliage and figures scattered among the pillars and capitals of fallen temples. Much moved, she came back and said to Alan: "What can I do? Isn't there any work for me?"

"We've been given an office in the Grande Bretagne," he told her. "Now that we have more room, I'll find you a job."

A scent of stewed meat drifted out from the kitchen where Mrs. Brett had been unpacking a case of borrowed plates. She came out shouting: "Supper's ready," then explained how she had hired a taxi the day before and gone to Kifissia, having heard that a small landowner, taking advantage of the high prices, was killing off his goats for the festival. She could not find the landowner but she had been passed from one person to another and in the end had managed to buy a whole leg of kid. "And what do you think I've made? A real Lancashire hot-pot. I come from Lancashire, you know ..."

While Mrs. Brett talked, the smell of the hot-pot grew richer until Miss Jay broke in with: "Cut it short, Bretty. I'll help you dish up."

Miss Jay's expression was avid as she spooned out the hot-pot. The plates were quickly emptied and Mrs. Brett went round urging everyone to eat, saying: "Who's for second helpings? Plenty more in the pot."

Miss Jay was catching the last of the gravy in the spoon when a ring came at the front-door. Three women who had been detained at the bandage-rolling circle, walked in bright-faced, cold, hungry and ready to eat.

"I forgot all about you," Mrs. Brett said, "But never mind! There are some jolly nice buns for afters."

Guy, appreciative of everything, handed back his plate with the remark that the hot-pot had been the best he had ever eaten.

The hungry ladies, taking it in good part, munched their buns and made jokes about not getting Mrs. Brett's goat.

"Wasn't that a good party!" Guy's voice rang through the empty darkness of the streets as they went home: "You wouldn't have enjoyed the Major's half so much."

Blind in the black-out, he clung to Harriet as they slipped on and off the narrow pavement, and slid over the wet and treacherous gutter stones: "Isn't Mrs. Brett magnificent? Thanks to her, I have the job in the place where I most want to be."

Harriet pressed Guy's arm, happy to rejoice with him, and said: "Alan thinks the war might end this year."

"It might, I suppose. The Germans have most of Europe. We are alone. We may be forced into some sort of truce."

"But *could* the war end that way?"

"No; and don't let us deceive ourselves. It wouldn't be the end. There would be an interval of shame and misery, then we would have to return to the fight."

"In fact, the real enemy is untouched. The real war hasn't even begun."

"It could last another twenty years," said Guy.

The excitement of the party was wearing off. The warmth of the wine was passing from them and as they turned into the wet wind blast of the main street, they held to each other. knowing they might never see the end of hostility and confusion. The war could devour their lives.

Next day Yakimov was full of the fact that by leaving the Major's party, the Pringles had missed "no end of a dust up". Everyone was talking about it. Late in the evening, Phipps, described by Yakimov as a "a trifle oiled", had attacked the Major for supporting Archie Callard's appointment and deceiving Phipps himself about his chances.

"Callard's never done a day's work in his life," he told Cookson and an attentive company. "What good did you think he'd be as Director? He'd've been a figurehead and a poor one, at that! He's a playboy and a poseur with nothing but his neuroses to recommend him."

"And so on and so on," said Yakimov, aghast and delighted by such plain speaking.

Callard, listening, had put up a show of indifference, but the Major had been much upset. He had sniffed and dabbed his nose and tried to hush Phipps, but in the end he had turned and "told Ben P. a thing or two". He had said that Gracey. when asked for his opinion, had cabled the London office to say that Phipps, as a result of his politics, his past association with undesirable persons and his generally facetious attitude towards the reigning authorities, was totally unsuited to be in any sort of authoritative position.

Having revealed this, the Major, in a state near hysteria, had shouted shrilly: "And I agree. I agree. I agree."

"Then you know what you can do," Phipps had told him and raging out of the house, had crashed the front door so violently the glass had fallen out and broken in pieces all over the hall.

Guy said: "We were fortunate to miss that." An opinion Harriet did not share.

PART THREE

The Romantics

15

In the New Year, when the move to the villa was imminent, Guy was too busy even to discuss it. He had returned to work like a reformed drunkard returning to the bottle. He was exuberantly busy.

Some mornings he would not wait for breakfast. When Harriet asked what he did all day, he said he was arranging schedules, laying out lecture courses, enrolling students and reorganizing the library. And what on earth kept him so late at the School each night? He interviewed students and advised which course of study was more suitable for each. Soon he would be even more busy, for he was about to rehearse the entertainment he had promised the airmen at Tatoi.

"Is that still going on?"

"Certainly."

"There seems to be no end to it."

"Of course there's no end to it," Guy cheerfully replied. "That's what teaching is."

When she asked if he would help move their stuff to the villa, he could only laugh.

"Lunch time, or evening, would do," Harriet said.

"Darling, it's impossible."

She took the baggage in a taxi. The taxi could not get down the narrow lane to the villa. Kyria Dhiamandopoulou, seeing her carrying the cases to the door, asked playfully: "Where is that nice Mr. Pringle?"

"Working."

"Ah, the poor man!"

Kyria Dhiamandopoulou was ready to leave but had to wait for her husband who had driven into Athens on some piece of business. She was a small, handsome woman who, in spite of the food shortage, had managed to stay plump. When they first met, she had been off-hand and seemed harassed; now, on the point of departure, she was in high spirits.

She insisted that Harriet must come up to the roof where the mid-day sun was warm. "See how nice," she said. "In spring you will see it is very nice." A marble table was set beneath a pergola over which a plant had been trained. Kyria Dhiamandopoulou touched the branches that flaked like an old cigar. "My pretty plant," she sighed. "How sad that I must leave it! Here, here, sit here! It is not so cold, I think? We will take coffee till my husband come."

She sped off to fetch a tray with cups like egg-cups and a brass beaker of Turkish coffee. While they sipped at the little cups of sweet, black coffee, she pointed out the distant Piraeus road and the rocky hill that protected the roof from the sea wind. "On the other side there is a river. Now not much, but when there is more rain there will be more river. It is the Ilissus. You have heard of it? No? The classical writers speak of it. It is a classical site, you know. Before the invasion, they were building here, but now they have stopped. It is quiet like the country," she sighed again. "How sad that we must leave!"

"But why are you leaving?" Harriet asked.

Kyria Dhiamandopoulou gave her a searching glance before deciding to let her know the truth.

"I dream true "

"Do you?"

"I will tell you. You know, *par exemple*, that old woman who begs in Stadiou? In black, with fingers bound in such a way?"

Harriet nodded. "I'm frightened of her. They say she's a leper, but I suppose she can't be?"

"I don't know, but I don't like. Now, I'll tell you. I had a dream. I dreamt she came running at me in Stadiou. I ran from her ... I ran to a shop, a pharmacy; she ran after me. I scream, she scream. What horror! She has turned crazy. Well, next day, I forgot. One forgets, you know! I went to Stadiou and there was the woman and when she saw me, she rush at me ... 'My dream!' I cry and I run to a shop. It is a pharmacy – the same pharmacy, mind you! The people inside, alarmed that I scream – the same! The very same! 'Help me, she's mad!' I cry and someone slams the door. The proprietor telephones the police. I sit in a chair and shake my body. It was unspeakable!"

"Yes, indeed! But surely you are not leaving because of that!"

"No. That was one dream only. I have many. Some I forget, some I remember. I dreamt the Germans came here."

"You mean to this house?"

"Yes, to this house. When I wake, I say to my husband: 'Now is the time to leave. I have a brother in Sparta. We will go to him.'"

"Are you sure they were Germans? They might have been Italians."

"They were Germans. I saw the little swastika. They came down the lane. They struck upon the door."

"Then what happened?"

"I saw no more."

"But Greece is not at war with Germany."

"That is true. Still, we go to Sparta."

"If the Germans come here, won't they go to Sparta?"

"I have no indication."

Harriet, easily touched by the supernatural, was dismayed by Kyria Dhiamandopoulou's dream, but Kyria Dhiamandopoulou, mistaking her fearful immobility for phlegm, said: "You English have strong nerfs!"

Before Harriet could disclaim this compliment, a hooting came from the unmade road at the top of the lane and Kyria Dhiamandopoulou leapt up delightedly, crying: "My husband. Now we can go," and she ran down to join Kyrios Dhiamandopoulos who had already started loading up the car.

Joining in the bustle and laughter of the departure, Harriet forgot the dream, but then, all in a moment, the Dhiamandopoulaioi were gone and she was alone in the unfamiliar silence.

When she had unpacked the clothing, she went out to look at the Ilissus. The lane led over the hill through the damp, grey clay from which flints protruded like bones. On the other side a trickle of water made its way between high clay banks overhung by a wood of wind-bent pines. It looked a sad little river to have engaged the classical writers and survived so long. Half-built houses stood about amid heaps of cement and sand, but the district seemed deserted.

The memory of Kyria Dhiamandopoulou's dream came down on her and she knew she had made a mistake. She had brought Guy here against his will. They had no telephone.

They were too far away from things. They would be forgotten and one day wake to find the Germans knocking at the door.

Cold with fear, she went back to the villa and found Guy in the living-room. Gleefully, she cried: "How wonderful. But why are you here?"

She ran at him and flung her arms round him but he was unresponsive. He had been unpacking his books and had a book in his hand. He stared at it with his lower lip thrust out.

"What's the matter?"

He did not answer for a minute, then said: "They've closed down the School?"

"Who? Who did it? Cookson?"

"Cookson? Don't be silly. The authorities did it. They didn't realize we intended opening again. When they found we were enrolling students, they ordered an immediate closure."

"But why?"

"Oh, the old fear of provoking the Germans. I suppose British cultural activities could be regarded as provocation!"

"I'm sorry," she held to him but in his despondency he simply waited for her to release him. When she dropped her arms, he returned to his books.

"What will you do?"

"Oh," he reflected, then began to rouse himself: "I'll find plenty to do. I'm organizing this air-force revue, for one thing. Now I can start rehearsals at once." As he arranged his books, he became cheerful and said: "Coming here wasn't such a bad idea, after all."

"You think so? You really think so?" She was relieved, for in the twilight the villa, bare, functional and very cold, had seemed worse than a mistake; it had seemed a disaster.

"Oh yes. It's splendid having a bathroom and kitchen, and two rooms of our own. We can give a party."

"Yes, we can."

She had not intended telling Kyria Dhiamandopoulou's dream but could not suppress it.

Guy said: "Surely you don't believe her?"

"You mean, you think she made it all up? Why should she?"

"People will say anything to appear interesting."

Unable to accept this, Harriet said: "You think there's nothing in the world that can't be explained in material terms?"

"Well, don't you?"

"I don't," she laughed at him. "The trouble is, you're afraid of what you can't understand so you say it doesn't exist."

As they worked together, putting their possessions straight, Harriet felt a sense of holiday and said: "Let's do something tonight! Let's go and eat at Babayannis'!"

He said: "Well!" In the face of her excitement, he could not disagree at once but she saw there was an impediment. It turned out that he had arranged to go to Tatoi. Ben Phipps was driving him out and they had been invited to drinks in the Officers' Mess.

"We've got to discuss arrangements for the revue," he said.

Inclined, unreasonably, to blame Phipps for Guy's engagement, she said crossly: "I don't know what you see in him. He's taken up with you simply because he's fallen out with Cookson."

"Don't you want me to have a friend?"

"Not that friend. Surely you could find someone better. What about Alan Frewen?"

"Alan? He's a nice enough fellow, but he's a hopeless reactionary."

"You mean he doesn't agree with you? At least, he's honest. He's not a crook like Phipps "

"Ben is a bit of a crook, I suppose," Guy laughed. "But he's amusing and intelligent. In a small society like this, if you're over-critical of the people you know, you'll soon find you don't know anyone."

"Then why were you so critical of Cookson?"

"That Fascist! Whatever you may say about Ben, he has always been a progressive. He has the right ideas."

"Would he go to the stake for them?"

"Who knows? Worse men than Ben Phipps have gone to the stake for worse ideas."

"You think the occasion makes the man?"

"Sometimes the man makes the occasion."

She said bitterly: "I'm surprised you bothered to come home at all."

"You said you wanted me to help you move in."

"Well, don't let me keep you now."

Untroubled, he agreed that it was time for him to get the bus into Athens.

Late that night Harriet, tensed by the unfamiliar noiseless-
ness outside, lay awake and listened for him.

Some time after midnight he came down the lane singing
contentedly:

> "If your engine cuts out over Hellfire Pass
>   You can stick your twin Browning guns right up your
>   arse."

He had been privileged to see a squadron set out on a raid
over the Dodecanese ports. Ben Phipps had gone home to
write a "think piece" based on this experience and Guy would
show his appreciation, too, by putting on the best entertainment the Royal Air Force had ever seen.

Early next morning the Pringles were awakened by the
sound of someone moving about in the villa. They found an
old woman like a skeleton bird, with body bound up in a black
cotton dress, head bound in a black handkerchief, setting the
table for breakfast. At the sight of the Pringles, she stood grinning, her mouth open so they saw she did not possess a single
tooth. She pointed to her breastbone and said: "Anastea."

Guy did his best to question her in Greek. The master and
mistress had forgotten to tell her they were leaving, but she
was not much concerned. One employer had gone, another
had come. She said that in the mornings she did the housework
and shopping; in the evening she came in to cook a meal. Guy
said: "Let her stay. We can afford her." Harriet was doubtful,
but said: "We could afford her if I got a job."

While the Pringles conversed in their strange foreign tongue,
Anastea stood with hands modestly clasped before her, confident that the great ones of the world would provide for her.
When Guy nodded, she grinned again and continued her
work without more ado.

16

THE INFORMATION OFFICE, which had once been an unimportant appendage of the Legation, now had independent
status within the domain of the Military Mission. Harriet found
"Information Office (Billiard Room)" signposted right through
the Grande Bretagne but when she came to the Billiard Room,
which was at the rear of the hotel, she saw it could have been
reached directly by the side entrance. There was no sound
behind the Billiard Room door. She imagined Alan Frewen
and Yakimov at work there, but when she opened the door
she met the stare of two elderly women whom she had never
seen before.

The women sat opposite each other at desks placed back to
back in a greyish fog of light that fell through a ceiling-dome.
There was no other light. The room, with its dark panelling,
stretched away into shadow. From where Harriet stood at the
door the two old corpse-white faces looked identical, but when
she reached them, Harriet saw that one, who looked the elder,
was bemused, while the younger had the awareness of a guard-
ian cockatrice.

"Yes, what is it?" the younger demanded.

"I'm looking for Mr. Frewen."

"Not here."

"Prince Yakimov?"

"No."

Both women were paused in their work. The elder hung
over a typewriter, her bulbous puce-purple lips wet, tremulous
and agape; the brown of her eye had faded until nothing remained but a blur of sepia, lacking comprehension; but the
younger sister – they could only be sisters – still had a dark,
sharp gaze which she centred on Harriet's chest.

"When will Mr. Frewen be back?" Harriet asked.

The younger sister seemed to quiver with rage. "I really can't
tell you," she said, her quivering sending out such a dispelling

force Harriet felt as though she were being thrust out of the room. The women suspected her purpose in coming to the office and would tell her nothing. Defeated, she moved away and as she did so, the elder dropped her head over her machine and began to strike the keys slowly, producing a measured thump like a passing bell.

Alan and Yakimov were often at Zonar's. When Harriet went there, she found only Yakimov. He was inside and had just been served with some unusual shell-fish which were set out on a silver dish with quarters of lemon and triangles of thin brown bread. When she approached, he looked flustered as though he might have to share this elegant meal, and said: "Nearly fainted this morning. Lack of nourishment, y'know All right for you young people, but poor Yaki is feeling his years. Like to try one."

"Oh, no, thank you. I'm looking for Alan Frewen."

"Gone back to feed his dog."

"When can I find him in his office?"

"Not before five. The dear boy seems upset. If you ask me, Lord Pinkrose upset him. The School's been closed down – 'spose you know? – so Lord P.s' landed back on us."

"And Alan doesn't want him?"

"Don't quote me, dear girl. Alan's a discreet chap; soul of discretion, you might say. And I've nothing against Lord P. Very distinguished man, doing important work . . ."

"What sort of important work?"

"*Secret* work, dear girl. And he has influential friends. This morning he said there was need here for a Director of Propaganda, so he's cabled a friend in Cairo – an extremely influential friend . . ."

"Lord Bedlington?"

"Could be. Bedlington! Sounds familiar. Anyway, it looks as though Lord P.'ll be promoted. Sad for Alan. He didn't say a thing, not a thing, but I thought he looked a trifle huffed."

"Understandably," said Harriet.

"Ummm." Fearful of committing himself, Yakimov made a neutral murmur. In recognition of Harriet's presence, he had lifted himself a few inches out of his chair but now cried out piteously: "*Do* sit down. I'd offer you an ouzo but I'm not even sure I can pay for this little lot."

Harriet sat and Yakimov relaxed into his chair and squeezed

lemon over the shell-fish. "Why don't you order some? Give yourself a treat?"

Harriet, convinced she had only to eat a single shell-fish to be laid out with typhoid, asked: "What are they?"

"Sea-urchins. Used to get them along the front at Naples. Quite a delicacy. I suggested them to the head waiter here and he said: 'People wouldn't eat them.' I said: 'Good heavens, dear boy, when you think what people *do* eat these days.' " Tackling the urchins with avidity, he spoke between sucks and gulps. "Try them; try them," he urged her, but Harriet, who feared strange meats, ordered a cheese sandwich.

"Who are those women in the Billiard Room?" she asked.

"The Twocurrys. Gladys and Mabel. Mabel's the batty one. Just a pair of old trouts."

"What do they do?"

"Unsolved mystery, dear girl."

"Alan thought he could give me a job in the office."

"Why not?" Yakimov, having downed the urchins as rapidly as Diocletian had downed the squid, mopped the remaining juices with the corners of bread. "Excellent idea!"

"But I wouldn't want to work for Pinkrose."

"War on, dear girl," Yakimov dismissed her qualms in a lofty way. "Can't pick and choose who you'll work for, y'know. Look at me. Must do one's bit."

Having eaten, he sat for a while with eyelids drooping, then slipped down inside his great-coat. "Time for beddy-byes," he said and began to doze.

Harriet, uncertain whether to remain or go, looked round for the waiter and saw Charles Warden descending from the balcony restaurant. He was looking in a speculative way in her direction and came straight to Yakimov's side. Yakimov opened an eye and Charles Warden said: "I have a permit to visit the Parthenon. Why don't you come with me?" He turned to include Harriet: "Both of you," he added.

Roused out of sleep, Yakimov sighed: "Not me, dear boy. Your Yak's not fit ... overwork and underfeeding ... the years tell ..." He resettled himself and slept again.

Charles Warden looked to Harriet with a smile that seemed a challenge and she got to her feet.

They walked without a word through the Plaka. While each waited for the other to speak first, Harriet observed him from the corner of her eye, seeing his firm and regular profile lifted slightly, as though he were preoccupied with some solemn matter; but she was aware of his awareness. She wanted to say something that would startle him out of his caution, but could think of nothing.

She noticed as they went through the narrow, confusing streets, that he led her with unhesitating directness to the steps that climbed the Acropolis hill. On the way up, he asked abruptly: "Where do you live in Athens?"

"Beside the Ilissus. It's a classical site."

This remark amused him and he said: "The Ilissus runs right through Athens."

"It doesn't!"

"I assure you. Most of it's underground, of course."

"We are a long way out. Half-way to the Piraeus. A rather deserted area, but not so deserted as I thought at first. You can see a few little houses on the other side of the river and, of course, people live near the Piraeus Road. They're quite friendly; they recognize us because we employ Anastea. I like it better now. It's a home of sorts."

He said: "I'd be quite happy to have a home of any sort." He told her he had stayed, when he first came, at the Grande Bretagne, but had been crowded out when the Mission arrived. They had had to find him a room at the Corinthian.

"That's nothing to complain about." From nervousness, she spoke rather sharply and he looked disconcerted, supposing she intended some reflection on young military men who manage to get themselves billeted in the best hotels. He stared into the distance, and she knew they would return to their difficult silence if she could not think of something to say. She said: "You seem to know Athens quite well."

"I was here before the war."

"Did you know Cookson then?"

"He was a friend of my people. I was staying with him when the war started."

"It must be pleasant there in summer?"

"Yes, but we had the war hanging over us."

"I know. And it was a beautiful summer. Were you on holiday?"

"Not altogether. I came to learn demotic."

"You did languages?"

"Classics."

"You've got a classics degree?"

"No. I hadn't time. I'll go back after the war."

She realized he must be two, even three, years younger than she, and not much older than Sasha. His youth had an untouched brilliance like something newly minted. She felt he had done nothing; experienced nothing. The whole of his life lay ahead. To keep him talking, she said: "I suppose you were posted here because you speak Greek?"

"Yes." He gave a laugh. She wondered if he found her questions inapposite or naïve? He looked at her, smiling, expectant of more, but she refused to say more.

Walking round the base of the Acropolis, they were conscious of tension that could, in a moment, spark into misunderstanding.

Since Harriet had last climbed up, a change had come over the rocky flank of the hill. The first rains had been enough to bring the earth to life. Every patch of ground was becoming overlaid with a nap of tiny shoots, so tender that to tread on them was to destroy them.

Seen from this height the green spreading over the Areopagus seemed not a composite of yellow and blue but a primary colour, lucid and elemental.

When they turned the corner and came in sight of the sea, Harriet was struck by the immense structure of cumulus cloud rising out of the Peloponnese. The sky visible between the Plaka roofs had shown only a meaningless patching of grey and white. At this height, the cloud capes of pearl and slate and thunderous purple could be seen swelling upwards like a cosmic explosion, while to the east a luminous undercloud, floating out like a detached lining, lay peach-golden against the blue.

Observing this spectacle, yet oddly removed from it, Harriet felt she should stop and appreciate it; but Charles went on, behaving as though he were rather more displeased than not by such a distraction. Indeed, when they reached the Beulé gate, he bounded up the stones ahead of her as though enraged by the whole outing.

The evzone sentry examined Charles' permit, then looked Harriet over approvingly. When he returned the permit, he presented arms with as much exertion and clatter as his equipment allowed.

This performance broke down Harriet's nervous restraint. Laughing, she asked: "Are you entitled to a salute like that?"

Charles flushed, then burst into laughter himself: "They lay it on a bit if you're with a girl," he said.

She was enchanted. Detached from limiting reality, lifted into a realm of poetic concepts, she saw Charles not as an ordinary young man – she had, after all, known dozens of ordinary young men, some of whom had been quite as handsome as he – but a man-at-arms to whom was due both deference and privilege. She was her own symbol – the girl whose presence heightened and complimented the myth. Enchanted, she was almost immediately disenchanted; was, indeed, amazed at finding herself dazzled by the cantrips of war. She was against war and its trappings. She was thankful to be married to a man who, whether he liked it or not, was exempt from service. She was not to be taken in by the game of destruction – a game in which Charles Warden was a very unimportant figure. Giving him a sidelong glance, she was prepared to ridicule him; instead, as she found his eyes on her, she felt warmed and excited, and the air about them was filled with promise.

They had the plateau to themselves. The wind blew fresh. singing between the columns, and the distances, sharpened by winter, were deeply coloured. The paving inside the Parthenon was brilliant. Again and again during the last weeks the slabs had been washed by rain and dried by wind until now the whole great floor, reflecting the gold and blue and silver of the sky, seemed to be made of mother-of-pearl.

Harriet wandered about, amazed by the lustre of the marble which held, in its hollows, small pools of rain left by the morning showers, and when she returned to Charles she said: "If you hadn't brought me, I would never have known it could be like this."

He was pleased by her pleasure, and for the first time she saw his simplicity. She had thought him vain and critical, and now she thought he was not only young but artless, almost as artless as Sasha. They moved around the Acropolis contained in a contentment like a crystal, that both excluded and burnished the outside world. Harriet exclaimed about everything. The view that in autumn had been flattened by dust and sun, now fell back to the remotest rises of the Argolid with the hills blue-black and violet, the gulf waters an ashy blue and stained with shadows as with ink.

She said: "Why must they close the Acropolis to visitors?"

Charles did not know. In the seventeenth century the Parthenon had been hit by a Venetian cannon ball and he thought perhaps the Greeks feared more destruction.

She spoke of the golden patina on the columns and asked why he supposed it was darkest on the seaward side. She watched him while he examined the marble. His expression grave and inquiring, he placed his hand on the surface as though he could divine by touch the nature of the marble's disorder. His hand was square, the fingers no longer than the palm, an intelligent and practical, but not a visionary, hand. Her dislike had changed – and changed suddenly – to a sense of affinity. She was amazed and worried as though by something supernatural.

With his hand starred out on the column, he said he thought the salt wind had drawn some mineral from the marble. "Iron, I should think. It's a sort of rust, in fact. The marble has been oxidized by time."

She watched him, not really listening. When he turned and found her eyes fixed so intently on him, he smiled in surprise; and she saw how this sudden, unselfconscious smile transformed his face. As they looked at each other, a voice said: "Love me."

Harriet did not know whether he had spoken or whether the words had formed themselves in her mind, but there they were, hanging on the air between them, and conscious of them, they were moved and disquieted.

She said: "I must get back. I'm seeing Alan Frewen at five."

"I must go, too."

They returned as they had come, without speaking, but now their silence was luminous and unnervingly fragile. A sentence could corroborate their expectations, if it were the right sentence. Neither would take the risk of speaking; anyway, not then, not at that moment.

As they approached the centre of the town, Harriet felt this suspended anticipation more than she could bear. In Hermes Street, fearing to be caught in further, she planned her escape. She would buy – what? She thought of writing-paper, but before they reached the stationer's shop, she felt the vibration that preceded the air-raid warning. She stopped. Charles paused in inquiry. They were held an instant as though the tremor were some tangible assertion of their nervousness, then the sirens broke out.

She said: "I'm supposed to take cover."

Charles, though exempt from the order, caught her arm and looked round for shelter. The street was clearing. They followed the others into the basement of an office block that had been left unfinished when war began. They went down a flight of steps and through a swing door. On the other side, they were in darkness.

Though they could see nothing, they could feel the breathing presence of people and, uncertain what was ahead, came to a stop just inside the door. As a precaution against panic, it was forbidden to speak during a raid, but the whole shelter was alive with small noises, as though the floor ran with mice. The traffic had been stopped and the city was still. The noise, when it came, was shocking. One explosion followed another, each uproarious so it seemed that bombs were bursting overhead. The concrete shuddered and a moan of terror passed over the crowded basement. Harriet felt a movement and, afraid of a possible stampede, she put out her hand and met Charles's hand outstretched to touch her.

He whispered: "It's nothing. Only the guns on Lycabettos."

"Are there guns on Lycabettos?"

"Yes, there's a new anti-aircraft emplacement."

The raid was a long one. The air grew hot. Whenever the Lycabettos guns opened up, the same curious moan filled the shelter and fear, like a breeze, passed over it, rustling the crowd. As Harriet pressed against the door, it opened an inch and, seeing the twilight outside, she whispered: "Couldn't we stand out there?" They slipped quietly out.

Two other people were on the basement stair: a woman and a small boy. The woman, not young, was seated with the boy on her knee. She was pressing the child's cheek to her bosom and her own cheek rested on the crown of his head. Her eyes were shut and she did not open them when Harriet and Charles came out. Aware of nothing but the child, she enfolded him with fervent tenderness, as though trying to protect him with her whole body.

Not wishing to intrude on their intimacy, Harriet turned away, but her gaze was drawn back to them. Transported by the sight of these two human creatures wrapped in love, she caught her breath and her eyes filled with tears.

She had forgotten Charles. When he said: "What is the matter?" his lightly quizzical tone affronted her. She said: "Nothing." He put a hand to her elbow, she moved away, but the all clear was sounding and they were free to leave.

Outside in the street, he said again: "What's the matter?" and added with an embarrassed attempt at sympathy: "Aren't you happy?"

"I don't know. I haven't thought about it. Is one required to be happy?"

"I didn't mean that. 'Happy' isn't the word. I don't know what I meant."

She knew what he meant but said nothing.

"Guy is a wonderful person," he said at last. "Don't you feel you're lucky to be married to him?"

"You scarcely know him."

"I know people who know him. Everyone seems to know him, and speak highly of him. Eleko Vourakis said: 'Guy Pringle will do anything to help anyone.'"

"Yes, he will. That's true."

Not enlightened by her agreement, Charles gave a laugh – the brief, exasperated laugh of a man who suspects he is being swindled. It occurred to her that her first impression of him had had some justification. Whatever he might be, he was not simple. She was relieved when they reached the Grande Bretagne.

"Are you seeing Frewen now?" he asked.

"Yes. I may get a job in the Information Office."

"Then you'll be next door to me."

"It's not settled yet."

"Have tea with me tomorrow?"

"Not tomorrow."

"Then, when?"

"Thursday is possible. I'll have to see what Guy is doing."

He opened the hotel door and as the interior light fell on his face, she saw he was chagrined. "Perhaps you'll let me know," he said.

"Yes, I'll let you know." She went off, scarcely knowing why she felt elated, and made her way back to the Billiard Room. This time the Misses Twocurry did not give her a look. The desks were overhung by two green-shaded bulbs pulled down so low there was nothing to be seen but the desk-tops and the outline of the women. Harriet asked for Mr. Frewen and, as though too occupied to speak, the younger waved her towards a door.

Alan and Yakimov were in a room marked News Room. Filled with elegant little escritoires and gilt, tapestry-seated chairs, it had once been the hotel writing room. Every piece of furniture was hung with news-sheets Roneoed over with blocks of information that had either been marked as important or heavily crossed out.

Alan was seated behind a massive desk that might have come from the manager's office. He was working on the sheets with a charcoal pencil, scoring out or underlining information, then handing them to Yakimov who sat, with negligent humility, in front of the desk. Although, as a military establishment, the hotel was heated, Yakimov still had his coat about him. At the sight of Harriet, he struggled to his feet, delighted that she should not only see him working but interrupt his work.

Alan was less sociable. He seemed ill at ease in the position of employer, but he was prepared for her arrival. He had books, maps, depositions and newspaper cuttings stacked ready, and started at once to explain how she must correlate the material in order to make a handbook for the troops who were preparing to invade Dodecanese. He was in the midst of this when Miss Gladys Twocurry entered and started to sort the letters in a tray. Alan stopped speaking and when Harriet began to question him, he lifted a hand to silence her. When at last it became evident that Miss Twocurry would hear nothing, she took herself off.

Alan made no comment on this sally but said to Harriet: "I had hoped to put you in here with Yakimov, but apparently we are to have a Director of Propaganda."

"Lord Pinkrose?"

"Yes. The Legation says his appointment is imminent. He has decided he must have my office, so I've had to move in here. There'll be more space for you in the outer office. Don't let anyone quiz you about your work. Simply say you're not allowed to discuss it."

He gathered up Harriet's impedimenta and led her back to the Billiard Room where he switched on a central light, disclosing a confusion usually hidden beneath the gloom of day or the shadows of night.

As though scandalized by this, Miss Gladys Twocurry clicked her tongue.

Alan passed her without a glance. The billiard tables, with their stout legs and little crocheted ball-traps, had been pushed against the walls and covered with dust-sheets. The sheets, intended to protect the baize, had fallen awry. Unfiled papers were heaped on the green surface which was growing grey with dust. Beside the billiard tables there were dining tables, bureaux, military trestle-tables and card tables; and every surface was covered with letters, reports, news sheets, newspapers, maps and posters, all thrown pell-mell together and growing écru with age. An open bureau was filled with rolls of cartridge paper, made brittle by the summer heat, and as Alan swept them to the floor, they cracked like crockery and Miss Gladys clicked again, more loudly.

Alan said: "You can work here. If you need anything, let me know." He left the room.

Harriet, arranging her books and papers, was conscious of the Twocurrys behind her. Miss Mabel's typewriter was still Miss Gladys seemed not to breathe. Then, suddenly, Miss Gladys crossed the room and her personal smell, a smell like old mutton fat, filled the neighbourhood of Harriet's desk. She was peering down at a copy of the *Mediterranean Pilot* which Harriet had opened on the table.

She asked severely: "What are you doing here?"

"I'm working. I've been employed."

"Indeed! And what are you working at, may I ask?"

"I'm afraid I can't tell you."

"*Indeed!*" Miss Gladys's head quivered with indignation. "Who employed you? Lord Pinkrose?"

"I was taken on by Mr. Frewen."

"Ah!" Miss Gladys seemed to think she had uncovered a fault and, turning, went purposefully from the room.

Harriet waited apprehensively, knowing her apprehensions were absurd. If Pinkrose disapproved her, he could do no more than dismiss her. As he was not yet Director of Propaganda, he could not, as yet, do even that.

The door opened again. She could hear Pinkrose's grunts and coughs and, glancing over her shoulder, she saw he had stopped at a safe distance from her and was viewing her as though to confirm whatever Miss Gladys had said.

"Good evening, Lord Pinkrose," Harriet said.

He coughed and muttered: "Yes, yes," then went to a bookcase where he took down a book, opened it, fluttered the pages, clapped it to and returned it. He muttered several time: "Yes, yes," while Miss Gladys stood by hopefully and watched. Harriet returned to her work. Having dealt with several other books, Pinkrose left the bookcase and began rustling among the papers, several times saying: "Yes, yes," in an urgent tone, then suddenly he sped away. Miss Gladys let out her breath in an aggravated way. For the first time it occurred to Harriet that Pinkrose was as nervous of her as she was of him.

Next morning, soon after she arrived in the office, a military messenger rapped the door and came in with a note.

"Bring it over here," Miss Gladys pointed imperiously to a spot on the floor beside her.

The messenger said: "It's for Mrs. Pringle."

Harriet took the note and read: "Will you have lunch today?" There was no signature. In the space for a reply, she wrote "Yes" and handed back the paper. Miss Mabel thumped on unawares, but Miss Gladys watched with the incredulity of one who wonders how far insolence can go.

Charles Warden was at the side entrance, standing casually as though he had merely paused to reflect and would, in a moment, move away. When Harriet said: "Hello," he appeared surprised and she said: "Someone invited me to lunch. I thought it might be you."

"You weren't sure? It could be someone else?"

"I do know other people."

"Of course," he agreed but his serious, speculative expression seemed critical of the fact. She laughed and his manner changed. He seemed to laugh at himself, and asked: "Where shall we go? Zonar's?"

She said: "Yes," but she did not want to go to Zonar's. It was the restaurant where Alan ate at mid-day, usually taking Yakimov with him. Ben Phipps also went there. Because of Charles's good-looks and the current of understanding between them, she knew their friendship could be misunderstood.

There was disloyalty to Guy in inviting such misunderstanding. But this was not easy to explain. Also, Guy had said he cared nothing for the suspicions of others, so why should she hesitate and shift and evade, and have guilt imposed upon her?

When Zonar's came into view, it was Charles who hesitated: "Do you want to go there?" he said. "We'll probably run into people we know. Let's go to the Xenia! The food's still tolerable there."

"Yes, I'd like to see the Xenia."

No one known to Guy ever went there. Harriet was stimulated by the thought of this expensive restaurant and when she found it dingy, the walls decorated in shades of brown with peacocks and women in ancient Egyptian poses, and hung with lamps of Lalique glass, she was disappointed.

The tables not already taken were reserved and Charles had to wait while the Head Waiter, unwilling to turn away an English officer, consulted his list and decided what could be done for them. In the end an extra table was set up close to the curtain that separated the restaurant from the famous Xenia *confiserie* where Major Cookson had bought his very small cakes.

Harriet said: "This place is a relic of the 'twenties."

"The wine is good," Charles said defensively.

Most of those present were businessmen but there were some officers, Greeks on leave or Englishmen from the Mission. The atmosphere was dull and though the wine was, as Charles said, good, the food, which imitated French food, seemed to Harriet much worse than the taverna stews.

To avoid Charles's fixed regard, Harriet watched the comings and goings on the other side of the coffee-coloured chiffon curtains. The people who entered the shop, some furtively, some with nonchalance or aggressive rapidity, chose cakes which were handed to them on a plate with a little fork. However chosen, the cakes would be devoured with the greed of chronic deprivation. Harriet, brought to a state of nervous nausea by Charles's proximity, had no appetite herself and she began to wonder what she was doing, fomenting a situation that reduced her to such a state.

She sat with a hand on the table and, feeling a touch, found Charles had stretched out his little finger and was pulling his fingernail along the edge of her palm.

"Tell me why you were crying yesterday."

"I don't know. Not for any reason, really. I suppose I was frightened."

"Of the raid? You know Athens hasn't been bombed."

"The guns startled me."

He gave his laugh, the laugh of a swindled man, that she now began to see was characteristic of him. He would not even pretend to accept her explanation. Her original dislike was roused again and she began to wish herself away. Once away, she would see no more of him.

An apathetic sense of failure came down between them. Charles looked sullen. She felt he was reproaching her for attracting him, then telling him nothing. He fixed her with his cold light-coloured eyes and asked: "How long have you been married?"

"We married just before the war. Guy was home on leave."

"Had you known one another long?"

"Only a few weeks."

"You married in haste?"

The questions were asked mockingly, almost derisively, and she gave her answers with the intention of annoying him: "Not really. I felt I had known him all my life."

"But did you? Did you know him?"

"Yes, in a way."

"But not in every way?"

Knowing he was taking revenge for her refusal to confide in him, she felt her own power and answered composedly: "Not in every way. There are always things to be discovered about every human being."

"But you still think him wonderful?"

"Yes. Too wonderful, perhaps. He imagines he can do everything for everyone."

"But not for you?"

"He sees me as part of himself. He feels he does not need to do things for me."

"Are you satisfied with that state of affairs?"

People waiting for tables were queuing on the other side of the curtain and this gave her excuse to say: "Don't you think we should go?"

"You've hardly eaten anything."

"I'm not very hungry."

Outside, in the bright, brief light of afternoon, with two hours of freedom before them, Charles asked: "What would you like to do now?"

The question was a testing-point and, from his tone, she saw he expected her to refer the question back to him. She said casually: "I've never been to the Lycabettos church. Let's go up there."

"If you want to."

He did not hide his resentment. Though he turned towards the hill, he made no pretence of interest in the excursion. She felt the distance between them and a bleak relief in not caring. The relationship would go no further.

She asked him about the possibility of a German attack. He gave an offhand answer: a German attack was "on the cards". It had been from the first.

She said: "There is a rumour that the Germans are piling up armaments on the frontier."

"That rumour's always going round."

"If there is no attack, what do you think will happen? Can the Greeks win?"

"I don't know. I doubt it. Greek ammunition is running out. They say present supplies won't last two months."

"But surely we can send them ammunition?"

"It would be no use. The Greek firearms were bought from Krupps. Our ammunition doesn't fit."

"Can't we send both guns and ammunition?"

He answered with laconic grimaces, speaking, she knew, out of an inner grimness, conceding her nothing: "We haven't the guns to send. In Cairo our own men are wandering about doing nothing because we have no arms to give them. But even if we had all the rifles in the world, there'd still be the problem of transport."

"We can't spare the ships?"

"Our losses have been pretty heavy, you know!"

She gave him a sidelong glance and saw him sternly detached from her. She wondered if he were trying to frighten her and said appealingly: "Things can't be as bad as that? Are you suggesting we might even lose the war?"

He gave his ironical laugh: "Oh, I imagine we'll pull through somehow. We always do."

The climb was a long one. The road ended at the terrace where the Patersons had their flat. Above that the path was rough. By the time they reached the church the sun was only just above the horizon and the whitewashed walls were tawny with the winter sunset. A chilly wind swept across the courtyard of the church. The place was deserted except for a boy who sold lemonade, and he was packing up his stall. Charles stood with an unforthcoming patience while Harriet leant against the wall and looked over the great sea of houses that ran into shadow against the new green of Hymettos. She turned and asked Charles if he had been before to the church.

He stared away from her. She thought he would not reply, but after a moment he said he had been here at Easter when the Greeks made it a place of pilgrimage, carrying candles that could be seen from the distance like two lines of light, one passing up, the other down, the hill.

"I suppose you saw the processions? The burial of Christ and the great resurrection procession on Easter Sunday?"

"Of course."

"Will they hold them this year, do you think?"

"They may, if things are going well." He answered unwillingly as though she were forcing him to give her information but when her questions stopped, he said: "The evzones are in Albania. The processions wouldn't be much without them. On Easter Sunday they wear their full regalia. You know – fustanella and tasselled caps and slippers with pompoms," he suddenly laughed. "The processions end up in the square ... the girls on the hotel terrace had those sparkler things and they were shaking them down on the men's skirts, trying to set them on fire ... "

She smiled and put out her hand to him: "If they hold the processions this year, we might see them together."

He took her hand but there was still something wrong. Staring down at the ground, he said: "This is only a temporary posting. I probably won't be here at Easter. You do realize that, don't you?"

"No, I didn't realize ... "

She moved away from the wall. The view had become meaningless. She noticed how cold the wind was; and the sun had almost set. They began walking down the steps.

While she had contemplated a long, developing relationship, he had, she now saw, been obsessed by the knowledge that their time was short. She had had an illusion of leisurely intimacy, imagining them trapped together here, likely to share the same fate. It had all been fantasy. Whatever their fate would be, he would not share it. Guy and she might not save themselves, but they were free to try.

He was a different order of being. His function was not to preserve his own life but protect the lives of others. In this present situation, he might run no greater risk than she herself; he was not more likely to lose his life – and yet, against reason, glancing sideways in the twilight, she saw him poetic, transfigured, like one of those sacrificial youths of the last war whose portraits had haunted her childhood. With his unmarred, ideal looks, he was not intended for life. It was not his part to survive. She was required to live but he was a romantic figure, marked down for death.

And the relationship was urgent.

It was not quite dark when they reached the bottom of the road. Lights were on in the shops but the black-out curtains had not been pulled across. They passed a small grocery-shop with empty shelves. From habit she looked in, just in case there was something for sale. She saw nothing but a jar of pickled cucumbers.

As they crossed the road to the Grande Bretagne, Charles said: "Will you meet me again later? We could have supper at the Corinthian."

The request was peremptory, almost a command, but she had to resist: "I'm going to Guy's rehearsal."

"Do you have to go?"

"I promised him."

"I see."

They had reached the main entrance of the hotel and he was about to enter without speaking again.

She said: "Will you come to lunch on Sunday."

"Where?"

"At our house. The villa beside the Ilissus."

"I will if I can." He turned to go then paused and added more graciously: "I would like to come."

"Yes. Do." She spoke with enticing sweetness and he smiled and said: "Then of course I will."

17

GUY'S POSITION HAD NOT become wholly void. He had visited the Greek officials and persuaded them to return the keys of the School. As a result of his earnest and energetic appeal, they agreed that the library might remain open and the School premises be used as a club. He was now rehearsing the entertainment for the airmen at Tatoi and rehearsals were held in the Lecture Room.

Pinkrose did not object to this because he knew nothing about it. His appointment as Director of Propaganda had been confirmed. When Guy asked him to approve some action taken to restore the function of the School, Pinkrose said he was much too busy to be worried by matters of that sort. Guy could do what he liked.

Pinkrose came to the Information Office several days a week and shut himself into the room that had once been Alan's office.

"What does he do?" Harriet asked.

"He's writing a lecture," Alan solemnly replied: "His subject is 'Byron: the Poet-Champion of Greece'."

"When will he deliver it?"

"That remains to be seen."

The Tatoi entertainment was progressing. The theme song had been written by Guy himself and when he was home, which was not often, he sang it around the house until Harriet begged him to stop.

"Was I singing?" he would ask in apology. "I didn't realize," and in a moment would sing again:

"There's fun and frolic, jokes and sketches, too.
You'll find them all together in the R.A.F. revue."

On the morning of Harriet's luncheon with Charles, Guy

had mentioned that the chief item of the revue, a play called *Maria Marten*, would be given its first run through that evening.

"You can come and see it," he said. "You might even join the chorus."

The invitation surprised her. In the past Guy had discouraged her from attending rehearsals. He had put her out of his production of *Troilus and Cressida* – a fact she had not forgiven – and when she protested, told her they could not work together. The trouble was, she did not take him seriously enough.

She said now: "Do you really want me to come? Don't you find me a nonconforming reality in your world of make-believe?"

Untouched by mockery, he said: "The revue's different. It's not like a serious production. In fact, it's just a joke. Why not come along this evening?"

"I might." Remembering her past rejection, she would not commit herself, yet later in the day she said to Charles: "I am going to Guy's rehearsal."

There had, she decided, been a promise; and she set out, resolute, after supper, keeping her promise as a gesture of fidelity. When she reached the School, she could hear the rehearsal from the street. The chorus seemed to come from a hundred voices:

"There's fun and frolic, jokes and sketches, too.
   You'll find them all together in the R.A.F. revue."

Looking in through the glazed doors, she saw a hundred mouths opening and shutting. Or what seemed like a hundred.

She knew perhaps ten people in Athens. Guy knew more, of course. She could not keep up with his gregariousness. Though she took it for granted, she wondered: Where did he find all these people? Peering in cautiously, she realized that among them were almost all the women who had been at Mrs. Brett's party. Confused by the number of Mrs. Brett's guests, she had not tried to separate and identify them, but for Guy each had been an individual and, individually contacted, they had come here to help him; now they were singing, whether they could sing or not.

She saw Mrs. Brett bawling away. And at the piano there was – of all people! – Miss Jay.

The chorus of pretty girls – students mostly, with one or two of the younger Legation typists – stood in line down the middle of the room. Behind stood an equal number of personable young males. They produced only a part of the uproar. Everyone was required to join in while Guy, acting as conductor, was inspiring, exhorting, giving himself and demanding that everyone else give, too.

"Come on: *give!*" he shouted, refusing any sort of compromise, requiring from them all the volume, vitality and abandon of which they were capable.

The only ones exempt from duty were the cast of *Maria Marten* – Yakimov, Alan Frewen and Benn Phipps who sat "saving their voices" in a row along the wall.

Those who knew Harriet were too engrossed to notice her. Entering unseen, she sat beside Ben Phipps who, with hands in pockets and feet thrust out before him, watched the proceedings with a sardonic grin.

The song ended. Guy was far from satisfied. He scrubbed his handkerchief over his face and told the boys and girls of the chorus they would have to work. The others must work, too. They might be non-appearers, mere enhancers, but only their best was good enough. Now! He stuffed the handkerchief away, and signalled Miss Jay. The song broke out again.

Guy had thrown off his jacket. Singing at the top of his voice, he stripped off his tie and undid his collar button. He rolled up his sleeves but as he waved his arms in the air, his sleeves unrolled themselves and the cuffs flew around his head.

"Once more," he demanded even before the chorus had panted to an end. "What we want is spirit. Give it more spirit. This is for the chaps at Tatoi. Come on now, they don't get much fun out there. Put your heart and soul into it."

Watching him urging the performers with the force of his personality, Harriet wondered: "How did I come to marry someone so different from myself?"

But she had married him; and perhaps, unawares, it was his difference she had married.

Though she had no wish to know many people, could not endure for long the strain of company, she could take pride in his wide circle; even satisfaction, feeling that she lived, if only at second-hand. But to live at second-hand was to live at a distance. By withdrawing from Guy's exhausting enterprise, she withdrew from Guy. The activity was the man. If she were not willing to be dragged at his elbow then, she feared, she must watch him pass like a whirlwind and the day might come when she must wave good-bye.

The chorus sang the song again and again until at last, scarcely able to keep on their feet, the young people were dismissed and Guy, unwearied, called for the cast of *Maria Marten*. Looking round, he saw Harriet and waved, but he had no time to speak. Ben, Alan and Yakimov were already on their feet.

The rehearsal over, Guy walked in the midst of a noisy group to Omonia Square. The girls had to return home early and the male students were deputed to see them safely back. But that was not the end of the evening for Guy. He insisted that everyone else must come and have a drink.

Mrs. Brett and her friends, intoxicated by all the commotion, let themselves be led to Aleko's, a café that at any other time they would fear to enter. When they were packed together in the plain little room behind the black-out curtains, Mrs. Brett was as boisterous as she had been at her own party. Catching sight of Harriet for the first time, she gripped her wrist and shouted: "You're a lucky girl!"

Harriet smiled: "I suppose I am."

"My, what a lucky girl you are." She looked about her shouting above the noise. "Isn't she a lucky girl!" confident she spoke for all present.

As no doubt she did. Harriet, becalmed against the wall, saw Guy at the centre of the group shining and jubilant. She knew then the thing he loved most was the fatuous good-fellowship of crowds. Of course she had suspected it before. On the train to Bucharest, she had watched him surrounded by admiring Rumanian women, his face alight as though with wine, his arms extended to embrace them all. To someone so enamoured of the general, could the particular ever really mean anything?

Looking her way and meeting her speculative gaze, he thrust out his arm and drew her into the mêlée. "What did you think of *Maria Marten*?" he asked.

"Very funny. The men will love it."

"They will, won't they?" Had he been engineering some great work that would last for all time, he could not have been more gratified. He would not let her go. Holding her to him, his arm about her shoulder, he coaxed her into the talk as though she were a shy child.

But she was not a child, and she was only shy when forced, as she now was, into a confusion of people whom she scarcely knew. He was eager that she should share his joy in the company; while she, doing her best to smile, was eager only to escape it. Forcibly held in the centre of uproar, she bore the situation as long as she could, then managed to get away. He glanced after her, a little puzzled, a little grieved, wondering what more she could want. But the problem did not hang long on the air. Distracted by some question put to him about the production, he was caught again into a hurly-burly of suggestion and counter-suggestion, of public extrinsicality so pressing and time-absorbing that the problem of living had to be put on one side until tomorrow, or the day after or, indeed, until death should come and fetch him.

18

WHEN HARRIET MENTIONED TO GUY that she had invited Charles Warden to luncheon, he said: "Good! But I won't be around long."

"I thought you would like to see him again."

"I would, of course; but I'll be rehearsing all afternoon."

Harriet also invited Alan Frewen. Hearing there were to be two guests, Anastea threw up her hands and asked what were they to eat? Her husband, who was a night-watchman, could sometimes, by joining a queue early in the morning, obtain food for the Pringles as well as for his family. But it was becoming more difficult; he might queue for three hours and at the end get nothing. Seeing the old woman distraught by the problem, Harriet promised to find something herself in Athens.

The villa, a flimsy summer structure, was very cold now. There was no oil for the heaters and on a fine day it was warmer outside than in. Sunday was bright and gusty. When Alan walked out to the villa with his dog, the Pringles took him up to the sheltered roof-terrace to drink ouzo. Harriet, looking towards the Piraeus road on which she expected the staff car to appear, said: "Charles Warden is coming."

"Is he?"

"You do like him, don't you? You must have known him before the war?"

"I did know him slightly. Rather a spoilt boy, don't you think?"

"I wouldn't say so."

This reply daunted Alan who, made to feel that he had shown discourtesy towards a fellow guest, bent down and spent some time adjusting Diocletian's collar.

A military car passed on the Piraeus road. Harriet watched

it, unable to believe it had not gone by in error, but it did not come back. Guy looked at his watch and said his rehearsal was called for half past two. Harriet said: "I think we had better eat."

"What about young Warden?"

"We can't wait all day for him."

Harriet had found nothing in Athens but potatoes which she told Anastea to bake. When they came to the table, they were mashed and served like an immense white pudding.

Alan laughed at Harriet's apologies: "Potatoes in any form are a luxury to me. All we get at the Academy these days is salad made of marguerite leaves?"

"*Can* one eat marguerite leaves?"

"If they aren't marguerite leaves, I don't know what they are."

When they had each taken a share of the potatoes, Harriet put the plate down for Diocletian. As the last vestige of potato was swept up by the dog's tongue, Anastea came from the kitchen and gave a cry. Usually so meek and accepting of her employers' peculiarities, she made a threatening movement at the dog, her face taut with anger. Alan paled and caught his breath.

Harriet had forgotten Anastea. She said: "What can we give her?" but there was no answer to that question.

Guy put his hand in his pocket: "I'll give her some money."

"What good is money? She wants food."

Anastea herself said nothing. Having made her gesture, she took the dishes and went.

This incident hastened Guy's departure; and Alan and Harriet went for a walk. They crossed the Ilissus and strolled through the sparse little pinewood where the trees had been dwarfed and distorted by the wind from the sea. Beneath the trees, the spikes of green were already shaping themselves into the foliage of future flowers. January was nearing its end and the light on the puddles on the glossy banks of wet clay had a new brilliance. Harriet said she could smell leaves in the wind. Alan said he could smell nothing but the brewery on the Piraeus road.

Harriet was contemplating a changed attitude to life. What she needed was independence of mind. She would turn her back on emotional involvements and seek, instead, the compensating interest of work and society. Charles was as good as forgotten; but when she returned to the villa, she asked Anastea if anyone had called in her absence.

"*Kaneis, kaneis,*" Anastea replied.

And that, Harriet decided, was that.

19

Sorry about yesterday. Lunch today?
Harriet answered: *No.*

The military messenger was back within ten minutes. The second message read: *Forgive and say yes!* Again Harriet replied: *No.* A third message came: *Dinner and explanations?* Harriet scribbled across it: *Impossible.*

Miss Gladys Twocurry said: "We can't have this young man coming in and out of here with his noisy boots. He's upsetting my sister."

"It's an essential part of my work," Harriet replied.

"If it goes on," Miss Gladys threatened, "I'll complain to Lord Pinkrose," but the messenger did not come back.

Miss Gladys also had a typewriter, a newer and finer machine than that provided for Miss Mabel. It stood on a billiard table and twice a week it was carried over to her desk by the Greek office boy. She used it to cut the stencil for the bi-weekly news-sheet, which Yakimov delivered on his bicycle. The stencil cutting, her chief employment, was treated as the most important activity in the office. The duplicator stood in a corner and when not in use was covered with a sheet. The Greek boy would uncover it and spread the ink from the tube. Then tutting, sighing, breathing loudly, Miss Gladys fitted on the stencil. This done at last, the office boy turned the handle and kept the copies neatly stacked. When twenty were ready, they were handed to Miss Mabel, who folded them and put them into envelopes. The envelopes then went to Miss Gladys, who addressed them from a list in a bold, schoolgirlish hand. When the addressed envelopes began to pile up, Yakimov would receive his call from the boy and appear ready-coated, bicycle-clips in place.

Everyone concerned treated the production and delivery of

the News-Letter as a supremely exacting operation. If a query arose, it was discussed in whispers.

Yakimov, packing the letters into his satchel, would also speak in whispers; and setting out on his delivery round, he went with strained and serious face.

The last letter run off, folded, placed in an envelope, addressed and delivered, everyone was exhausted, but the most exhausted was Yakimov who, safely back in his office, would collapse into his chair and seem, like the runner Phidipides, about to die from his efforts.

Altogether some four or five hundred envelopes were sent out, some to Greeks but most to English residents in and about Athens. Harriet had been surprised to realize how many British subjects remained, and how much ground Yakimov had to cover on his bicycle. Letters, tied up in batches, were marked not only for the city centre, but for Kifissia, Phychiko, Patissia, Kalamaki, Phaleron and Piraeus.

The first time she had seen them prepared for delivery, she tried to break down Miss Gladys's hostility by saying: "I never knew poor Yaki worked so hard."

"Poor Yaki!" Miss Gladys caught her breath in horror. "Are you referring to Prince Yakimov?"

Harriet did not improve matters by laughing. She might treat Yakimov as a joke, but he was no joke for the Twocurrys. Her casual manner towards a man of title marked her for them as one who had too high an opinion of herself. Several times in the office Miss Gladys often began remarks with "I never presume" or "I know my station", and she saw her station increased by the fact she worked with a lord and a prince.

The Twocurrys were not alone in respecting Yakimov's title. Several among the remaining English were delighted to have a prince drink himself senseless at their parties.

Alan told Harriet that soon after Yakimov arrived he was seen standing on the balcony of a flat where a party was in progress. Singing mournfully to himself, he displayed the organ, the secondary function of which is the relief of the bladder, and sent a crystal trajectory through the moonlight down on to the heads of people drinking coffee at an outdoor café below.

Alan told the story with tolerant affection. In Rumania,

where there were too many princes, most of them poor, it would have been told with venom and indignation. His situation there had become such he would, had Guy not given him refuge, have died, as the beggars died, of starvation and cold. In those days he used to speak contemptuously of Greek cooking, yet it was here in Greece that he had regained himself and found friendship.

Harriet, who saw him often, could not imagine why she had ever disliked him. He had become not only a friend, but an old friend. They shared memories that gave them the ease of near relationship.

When Alan and Yakimov went to Zonar's or Yannaki's, they would take Harriet with them. "Do come, dear girl, we'd love to have you," Yakimov would say as though it were he and not Alan who dispensed hospitality.

Yakimov did not buy drinks for his companions. The habit perhaps had been lost during his days of penury, but once in a while, when the glasses were empty, he would become restless as though, given time and money enough, it might return. It never did. Alan would say: "How about another?" and Yakimov would remain poised for a second, then ask in hearty relief: "Why not?"

Yakimov would contribute a joke, his own joke; but once conceived, it had to do long service. The joke of the moment, derived from his contact with the decoding office, was one that called for careful timing. He had to wait until a second order was given then, the waiter having come and gone, he would say with satisfaction: "Three corrupt groups asking for a repeat."

When at last Alan said, "Need we repeat it again?" Yakimov murmured sadly, " 'M growing old; losing m'*esprit*. Poor old Yaki," and the joke went on as before.

Alan and Yakimov would discuss *Maria Marten* and the gossip of the rehearsals, and Harriet learnt more from them than she ever learnt from Guy.

It was Yakimov who mentioned that Dubedat and Toby Lush had approached Guy and asked if they might take part in the revue. Guy had made no promises and later the two found the rehearsals were proceeding without them.

"Bit of a jolt for them," said Yakimov. "Am told Dubedat was ruffled. Trifle put out, you know. Goes round telling

people if it weren't for him that show we did in Bucharest –
what *was* it called, dear girl? – would have been a fair foozle.
Says that only his performance saved the day. Told the Major
that. Bit unfair to the rest of us, don't you think? Or wouldn t
you say so?" Yakimov gazed anxiously at Harriet, who, assuring him that in her opinion it was *his* performance that carried
the production to the heights, said: "You were Pandarus to the
life."

Much gratified, Yakimov said: "Had to work very hard.
Guy kept me at it." He reflected for some minutes then a look
of pique crumpled his face. "But what came of it? Nothing.
When it was all over, your Yak was forgotten."

"Nonsense."

"Yes, forgotten," Yakimov insisted bleakly. "Dear fellow,
Guy. Best in the world. Salt of the earth, but a trifle careless.
Doesn't understand how a poor Yak feels."

Harriet was startled by this criticism – she had imagined she
was the only one who criticized Guy – and the more startled
that it should come from Yakimov. Yakimov, picked up when
hungry and homeless, had been lodged by them for seven
months and she felt angry that he should dare to criticize
Guy, and criticize him in front of Alan.

Yet, startled and angry as she was, she realized he had
spoken out of a genuine sense of injury. Guy had made much
of him, then, the play over, had abandoned him. Guy imagined
he was all things to all men, but did he really know anything
about any man? Did he know anything about her? She doubted
it. She, too, was beginning to accumulate a sense of injury.

Yakimov had suffered from coming too close to Guy. Guy
was, she suspected, resentful of those near enough to hamper
his freedom. It occurred to her that he might resent her. Why,
for instance, had he not told her himself that Lush and Dubedat had asked for a part in the revue and been rejected? He
may have forgotten to tell her, but more likely he had not
chosen to tell her. He would not admit that he felt about them
as she did. He would rather protect them against her judgement.

She felt his attitude betrayed the concept of mutual defence
which existed in marriage.

But perhaps it existed only for her. It would be impossible
to persuade Guy that he betrayed a concept that did not exist

for him. He would condemn it as egoism. He might have his own ideas about marriage, but she doubted it. Having married her, he simply ceased to see her as another person. She had once accused him of considering her feelings less than those of anyone else with whom they came into contact. Surprised, he had said: "But you are myself. I don't need to consider your feelings."

In Bucharest, where he continued his classes for Jewish students in spite of Fascist demonstrations, he said: "They need me. They have no one else. I must give them moral support," yet he seemed unable to understand that, living as they did, she, too, needed "moral support". As she met every crisis alone, it seemed to her she had been transported to a hostile world, then left to fend for herself.

Here, if she had nothing else, she had her work and the friendship of Alan and Yakimov. Alan, seeing her daily, had become more easy company. He would talk freely enough, though he had areas of constraint. One of these was Pinkrose and everything to do with Pinkrose.

When Harriet asked, "Does he object to my being in the office?" Alan shrugged and would not reply. Pinkrose had imposed himself on the office. Useless though he was, he had become Alan's superior and must not be discussed. Still, he could be mentioned in relation to the Twocurrys.

Alan said: "Gladys appointed herself chief toady to Pinkrose the minute she set eyes on him. I suspect she's a bit infatuated with him."

Harriet wanted to know how the Twocurrys ever achieved their position in the Information Office. Alan told her:

"We started the office on a shoestring. I had to take any help I could get. Later we got a grant and I could have had a real secretary: one of the delightful English-speaking Greek girls. Instead I kept on old Gladys and Mabel. They needed the money. I just hadn't the heart to chuck them out; and now I've got Gladys spying on everything I do and at the slightest upset rushing off to complain to Pinkrose. The moral of this story is: never let your heart get the better of your sense."

"You could get rid of her now."

"Oh, Pinkrose would never let her go. He described her the other day as 'invaluable'."

"I suppose they aren't paid much?"

"Not much, no. They scarcely get a whole salary between them; but then, they scarcely do a whole job. Mabel, in my opinion, is more nuisance than she's worth."

The letters sent in to be typed by Miss Mabel were written very carefully in letters an inch high. Her speech, which Harriet heard seldom and always found distressing, was understood only by Miss Gladys. She never moved unaided from her chair. If she had to visit the cloakroom, she put up a panic-stricken babble until Miss Gladys led her away. When the time came for their departure, Miss Gladys would first put on her own coat and hat then grip her sister by the upper arm and get her out of the chair. While Miss Mabel mumbled and moaned, demanded and protested, Miss Gladys fitted her into her outdoor clothing. Both wore hats of sunburnt straw. Miss Gladys's coat was bottle green and Miss Mabel's coat was of a plum colour reduced in its exposed places to shades of caustic pink. Miss Mabel, who was delicate, was not allowed out without a tippet of ginger-brown fur.

When they left the office, where did they go? How did they live? How did women like the Twocurrys come to be in Athens at all? Alan said they had been the daughters of an artist, a romantic widower, who had saved up to bring himself and his little girls to Greece. They had found two rooms in the Plaka and the father, while alive, made a living by drawing Athenian scenes which he sold to tourists. That had been way back in the '80s and the sisters still lived on in the Plaka rooms. Before the war Miss Gladys had worked at the Archaeological School piecing together broken pots. She had taken Miss Mabel with her every day and, said Alan, "the Head, not knowing what on earth to do with her, shut Mabel up with a typewriter. Weeks later, mysterious sounds were heard through the door ... thump-thump-thump. *She had taught herself to type.* When the war started, the Archaeological School closed down and the Twocurrys were thrown upon the world. I seized them as they fell. And now," Alan gave his painful grin, "you know their whole history."

"So the office is all their life."

"I doubt whether they have any other."

Harriet doubted whether she herself had any other. But it was a life of sorts. Her position in the office, though minor, was recognized. She was even invited to a party by the Greek

Minister of Information. Delighted by this courtesy, she wanted to share it and hurried to ask Alan if she might take Guy with her. Alan telephoned the Ministry and a new card was delivered addressed to Kyrios and Kyria Pringle, but Guy, when he saw it, said he could not accept. His revue was to be staged at Tatoi during the first week in February and rehearsals were now so intensive, he had no time for parties. In the end, it did not matter. Metaxas, whom the war had changed from a dictator to a hero, died at the end of January from diabetes, heart failure and overwork. The party had to be cancelled.

20

THE REVUE, LIKE THE WAR, WENT ON. Death was incidental to the times and the needs of the fighting men were deemed to be the major consideration. During the last week of rehearsals Guy disappeared from Harriet's view and the only daylight glimpse she had of him was at the funeral of an English pilot which they attended in the English church. He then had a look of frenzied incorporeity that came of not sleeping or eating or bating effort for three days at a time. In the few minutes that they spent together after the funeral ceremony, she protested that Guy was over-doing it. The revue, after all, was, as he had said, a joke. The audience of airmen would not be overcritical. But Guy could not do less than his utmost. He was just off to Tatoi for the dress rehearsal and would probably not manage to get home that night. Where would he sleep? Well, if he slept at all, he would probably doss down on the floor at the house of one of the Greek students who lived near the airfield. He had not returned to his adolescence; he had, she decided, never left it.

All evening she imagined him, exhorting the chorus and standing behind the stage, singing and shaking his hands in the air, possessed by a will to electrify the show and sweep it to the heights. When she went to bed in the silence of their empty suburb, she could imagine the day when Guy would be too busy ever to come home at all. They might meet occasionally for an instant or two, but he would disappear from her life. He would have no part in it. He would simply have no time for anything that was important to her.

Next evening, staff cars took the players and their friends to Tatoi, where the main hangar had been rigged out as a theatre. The wind, sweeping over the dark reaches of the airfield, was wet with sleet. The women were not dressed against the dank and icy chill inside the hangar and the officer-in-charge, noticing that the visitors were shivering, sent to the store and fitted them all out with fur-lined flying jackets.

The curtain went up and the boys and girls, feverish from their all-night effort, burst into uproarious song:

"There's fun and frolic, jokes and sketches, too.
You'll find them all together in the R.A.F. revue."

Just as Harriet had imagined, Guy's hands could be seen waving wildly behind the two lines of the chorus.

The concert-party jokes were applauded with good-natured resignation. In spite of all the work, the first half of the show was neither better nor worse than most shows of its kind. It was *Maria Marten* that turned the entertainment into a triumph.

Maria, played by Yakimov, was met with unbelieving silence. Wearing false eyelashes, a blond wig, a print dress and sun-bonnet, he looked like a wolf disguised as Red Riding Hood's grandmother, but a wolf imitating outrageous, salacious girlhood. When he tripped to the footlights, put forefinger to chin and curtsied, a howl rose from the back of the hangar. The men, who had respectfully applauded the real women, were released into a furore of bawdry by the travesty of femininity. Yakimov acknowledged the shouts and whistles by fluttering his eye-lashes. The howls were renewed. A full three minutes passed before anyone could speak.

Alan, a monstrous and sombre mother-figure, opened the play, saying: "You have not been well of late, Maria dear! What ails thee, child?" to which Maria, in a light epicene voice, coyly replied: "Something strange has happened to me, mother dear." This produced a stampede over which could be heard cries of "Watch it, girl", "Up them stairs", and "Meet me behind the hangar and I'll see what I can do".

The text, concocted by the players themselves, had been bawdy enough in its original, but under the stimulus of rehearsals, much more had been added. While Yakimov held the stage, there was a cross-talk of ribaldry between actors and audience. Maria's violent death brought a sense of loss to both.

Her burial by William Corder, played by Ben Phipps, was followed in tense silence. Phipps made heavy weather of digging the grave but filling it in, he said: "This is easier work than the other," and the tension lifted. Someone shouted:

"Don't forget to camouflage it," and uproar broke out again. The villain, peering villainously through his spectacles, found he had lost his pistol. Then a terrible realization came: he had buried it with the body. The audience groaned. Someone asked: "Did you sign for it, chum?" Corder, lacking courage to reopen the grave, sloped off.

In the next act Corder, splendidly attired in a frock coat, his top-hat balanced on his arm, stood posed beside a potted palm. "Well, here I am in London, and all is well," he told the audience; but it was not well for long. Guy, stating that he was a Bow Street Runner, visited Corder and extended evidence of guilt: the pistol found in the grave. Corder repudiated it. In a rich voice of doom Guy declared: "Here are your initials on the butt: W.C." The rest was lost in catcalls. Corder, on the gallows, the rope about his neck, was permitted to make a last defiant speech. Not a sound came from the audience. Purged of pity and terror, it had shouted itself mute.

A party was given for the visitors in the officers' mess. Harriet had seen Charles Warden in one of the front seats. Not knowing whether he had joined the party or not, she kept her back to the room, feeling his presence behind her while she listened to Mrs. Brett. Mrs. Brett, having gathered Surprise and the other pilots about her, wished to make evident how much she knew of their flying conditions. "It's disgraceful the way they won't let you have an airstrip near the frontier. That long haul – 200 miles, isn't it? – and all that snow and heavy cloud! No wonder the squadron's falling below strength."

Surprise gave his carefree laugh: "Is it falling below strength?"

"Oh, yes," Mrs. Brett assured him. "And I'm told there's a shortage of spare parts. *Is* there a shortage of spare parts?"

"We manage."

"Perhaps you do, but it's a serious situation." Mrs. Brett ducked her head in disgust but Surprise, an aristocrat of war from whom nothing could be demanded but his life, laughed again.

There was a touch on Harriet's arm. Prepared for it, she turned and faced Charles with a sociable smile. "How did you enjoy *Maria Marten*?" she asked.

"Well ... it was very funny. I've never seen anything quite like it before."

"Not even at school?"

"Certainly not at school. I want to apologize – I could not come to luncheon that Sunday. Something kept me. I would have telephoned but the exchange could not find your number."

"We have no number."

"I had to stand by, I'm afraid. Someone flew in from Cairo H.Q."

"Someone important?"

"Very important."

"I suppose I mustn't ask who?"

"I'd better not say; though I imagine everyone'll know soon enough."

"Is something happening?"

"It looks like it. Will you meet me tomorrow?"

"You mean you'll tell me then?"

"I can't." He was annoyed by her flippancy and said: "I may not be here much longer."

"Where will you go? Back to Cairo?"

"No. Will you have lunch tomorrow?"

"I don't think I can."

"The day after, then?"

"I would rather not."

As he began to argue, she slipped past him and went to Guy who, relaxed and genial, was entertaining the senior officers with a description of the *Maria Marten* rehearsals. He put an arm round her shoulder and introduced her with pride: "My wife."

She looked back to where she had left Charles, but he was not there. She could not see him anywhere in the room. Her spirits dropped. The party had lost its buoyancy. She felt it was time to go home.

When Toby Lush entered the Billiard Room, Miss Gladys tittered flirtatiously: "Why, Mr. Lush, this is an honour! An honour indeed! We don't get you in often, do we?"

Toby spluttered and sniggered, doing his best to respond in kind, but the sight of Harriet quite unmanned him and Miss Gladys had to ask: "Are you wanting his lordship?"

"Um, um, um," Toby seemed not to know what he wanted. To gain time, he champed on his pipe, but the question had to be answered and he mumbled: "Perhaps he'd give me a minute – if he's not too busy, that is."

"Sit down, do. I'll see how things are in the inner office."

Miss Gladys went off and Toby sat on the edge of Harriet's desk: "Didn't know you worked here. Employed by old Pinkers, eh?"

"No. Alan Frewen."

"Ah!"

Harriet had not spoken to Toby or Dubedat since the School closed, but had heard they were working for Cookson and had seen them driving round Athens in the Delahaye.

She asked if they had given up their flat.

"It gave us up. The old soul rented it from Archie Callard. Archie wanted it back, worse luck, but now he's got it, he doesn't live in it. He's always at Phaleron. But he's sick of Athens. He says he wants to do something big . . . go to Cairo, get into the war, join the Long Range Desert Group. The Major's working on it."

"What can the Major do?"

"*The Major!* He can do anything."

"But he can't produce transport where there isn't any."

"Don't you be so sure. Planes come here from Cairo. If someone very important wanted to go back on one, he could wangle it."

"Is Archie Callard as important as that?"

"No, but the Major is. And there's no knowing what Archie may do! He's talking of starting a private army."

"Are there private armies these days?"

"'Course there are. Plenty of them."

"I hear you're employed by the Major?"

"We help a bit. There's not much staff at Phaleron. The chauffeur's gone, so I have taken over. The Major's very decent. He's given us the flat over the garage."

"What does Dubedat do?"

"Helps around." Toby lowered his voice as though disclosing something shameful: "The old soul does a bit of gardening, cleans silver, makes the beds. The other day the butler told him to wash the hall tiles. Bit of a come-down, eh? Man like that washing tiles! If he'd had his rights, he'd have been Director. Can't get over it. Disgraceful, the way the old soul's been treated!"

Bleak and brooding, Toby stared at the floor until Miss Gladys reappeared. "Come along," she said, and rising and projecting himself in one movement, Toby nearly went down on his face.

Alan had always described the food at the Academy as "execrable", but the Sunday on which he invited the Pringles to luncheon promised to be a special occasion. He would not explain further, having no wish to raise hopes that might not be fulfilled.

Walking between showers up the wide, grey, windy Vasilissis Sofias, Guy talked exuberantly about a new production of the revue that was to be bigger, funnier, and better dressed, and staged in Athens on behalf of the Greek war effort. The times were gloomy but once again Guy had escaped from them.

There were no victories now. The bells had ceased to ring. The Athenians, living under conditions that resembled those of a protracted siege, were bored with the present and saw little to cheer them in the future. The Greeks were bogged down in the mountains. They had come to a stop on the Albanian coast. Some said they had given up hope of taking Valona. The men were exhausted. There was no food. Ammunition was running out.

Turning off towards the Academy, Harriet looked into the forecourt of the military hospital and saw the wounded still dragging round the wet asphalt square.

Guy said: "We'll have to improve our theme song. I don't think its bad, mind you, but we can't keep singing the same thing."

"I suppose not."

February, that in other years held intimations of spring, this year prolonged the bitter weather. Suffering to a point beyond endurance, the men in the mountain snows complained that supplies were not coming to the front. The Athenians, illfed, chilled to the bone, had no supplies to send.

Harriet said: "They'll have to accept a truce."

"What?"

"Look at those men. How can the Greeks go on like this?"

Guy looked, his face contracting, and after a long pause said: "The British may be joining in."

"Nobody seems to want them."

The rumour that British troops were already on their way had caused as much alarm as rejoicing, for people feared they would do no more than expedite a German attack.

"Still," said Guy, "anything is better than this sort of stale-mate."

It was colder inside the Academy than out. A small wood fire had been lit in the common room but the damp hung like mist in the air. Most of the chairs were taken and the talk carried a surprising intonation of cheer. Alan had a bottle of ouzo on his table and he started filling the glasses as soon as he saw Guy and Harriet cross the room.

"So it *is* a special occasion!" Harriet said.

"It is," Alan agreed; and when they were seated and warmed by the ouzo, he told them that one of the inmates, a man called Tennant, had been promised a piece of beef by an officer on a visiting cruiser. "The promise," said Alan, "led to some slight disagreement. Miss Dunne, as usual, tried to boss the show. Before the beef had even arrived, she stuck a notice on the board saying that this Sunday guests would not be allowed. I appealed to Tennant who, after all, should be the one to decide. He said: 'Ask whomsoever you like. The beef may not materialize. And if it does, it'll probably be bitched by that God-awful cook.' "

Miss Dunne, defeated, sat beside the fire, her gaze on a book, apparently aloof from the famished anticipation that stirred the rest of the room.

Above the general animation Pinkrose's voice, precise and scholarly, carried clearly from some distant corner. He, also, had a visitor, to whom he was describing the intention and content of his lecture on Byron.

Wondering if the visitor could be Miss Gladys Twocurry, Harriet said: "Do you think the younger Miss Twocurry has intentions towards Pinkrose?"

Alan nodded gravely: "I'm sure of it. And, you must agree, she would make a very toothsome Lady Pinkrose."

Listening for the luncheon bell, they listened perforce to the Pinkrose monologue which persisted until it had silenced all about it. At last the bell sounded and a sigh went over the room. The inmates did their best to leave in good order, letting the women go ahead. When Miss Dunne saw she was not the only one of her sex, she hastened to be the first from the room. Harriet now had a sight of Pinkrose's guest. It was Charles Warden.

The main meals at the Academy were taken round a table,

as they had been when the diners were students with a common interest and lived as a family. Alan had said: "I'm afraid our table talk wouldn't be out of place in a Trappist refectory. Sometimes someone makes a mention of work but not, of course, when visitors are present. You are liable to meet with complete silence."

The meal was served. Everyone – Diocletian not forgotten – received a slice of beef, overcooked and dry, but still beef; and the diners gave a few appreciative "hahs" and "hums". One man even went so far as to say: "*I say!*" Pinkrose, respecting the traditional taciturnity, talked below his breath. Charles, attentive, kept his eyes lowered.

A salad came with the meat. Harriet examined the coarse, dark leaves and said: "They could be marguerite leaves." Alan handed her oil and vinegar. "Put on plenty," he advised. "It's only the olive oil that keeps us alive," and Miss Dunne, sitting opposite, raised her brows.

Guy, not easily subdued, asked his neighbour if there were anything in the story that the British were about to intervene on the Greek front.

Stunned by the question, the man caught his breath and whispered: "I shouldn't think so."

"No? I've heard that British troops are already disembarking on Lemnos."

Miss Dunne, usually pink, grew pinker; then, unable to restrain herself, burst out: "If you've heard that, you've no right to repeat it."

"It's being pretty widely repeated," Alan said, and tried to divert Guy by suggesting to him that Naxos would be a more likely half-way house for troops bound for the Piraeus.

"But are they bound for the Piraeus?" Guy asked. "They may go to Salonika."

Miss Dunne, appalled by this discussion, gasped and goggled as though suffering strangulation; and Guy, observing her discomfort, leant towards her and asked with friendly interest: "What is it you do at the Legation?"

Her answer was immediate: "I'm not in the habit of discussing my work."

Even for Guy, Harriet thought, that should be enough; but far from it. Challenged by her awkwardness and vanity, he cajoled her as though she were a difficult student, telling her about the revue. There was to be a repeat performance and he suggested she might take part.

While he was talking, Miss Dunne wriggled so much her chair worked backwards until she was two foot or more from the table. When he paused for a reply, she gave her head a violent shake. Those nearby watched his tactics with apprehensive delight.

The revue dismissed, Guy said he was a tennis player himself. Would Miss Dunne be willing to give him a game?

At this, Miss Dunne's colour darkened and spread up among the roots of her red hair and down the front of her emerald green dress. At the same time a knowing smirk spread over her large carmine face. She said archly: "I'll think about it."

Harriet, turning a glance of appeal on Alan, caught Charles's eye. He gave her a sympathetic grin, and she grinned back. At this exchange, life lost its threatening desolation and the air grew bright.

Alan said he had arranged for their coffee to be sent to his room. Harriet, taken unwillingly upstairs, felt she was being taken from the one person she wished to see.

Alan's room, which had only one window, was smaller than that which had been occupied by Gracey. When the door shut, Harriet turned on Guy:

"That idiotic woman thought you were making advances to her."

"Darling, really! You are being ridiculous." He looked to Alan for support but Alan was inclined to side with Harriet.

"I admired your campaign," he said. "I really think you won Miss Dunne's heart. No small achievement. But, then, it would take a ruthless misanthrope to hold out against so simple and beneficent an approach to one's fellow men."

Alan had recently collected some photographs, taken during his wanderings in Greece, which he had kept in store. Now, lifting the large prints one by one from the portfolios, he studied each tenderly and nostalgically before passing it to Harriet or Guy.

He was so pleased to have his friends share the sights he had seen, Harriet was touched and did her best to put Charles from her mind. Gazing into his pictures of rocky islands, olive trees, classical temples outlined against the sea, and chalk-white churches and houses taken at mid-day when the shadowed walls shimmered with reflected light, she said: "We wanted to come here. This is the country where we most wanted to be, but we have seen nothing. We might as well be in prison."

On an impulse, Alan said: "I shall never leave Greece."

"But if the Italians come, how can you stay?"

"I could hide out on the islands. I speak the language. I have friends everywhere. People would shelter me. Yes, I'm sure they would shelter me."

Watching Alan as he spoke, Harriet saw him a ponderous man, quiet, sardonic yet gentle, patient and long-suffering. She had thought he loved only Greece and his dog, but now she saw that to him Greece was not only a love, it was sanctuary. But she could not suppose his plan to remain in hiding here was more than romantic fantasy. There had been English-women in Bucharest, ex-governesses, without friends or money outside Rumania, who were determined to stay but, in the end, they had left with the rest.

While Alan was talking, she heard Pinkrose's voice raised in the garden and, moving as though aimlessly, she went to the window. Pinkrose, muffled to the eyes, was standing on the carriage-way saying good-bye to Charles. She watched Charles as he saluted and turned and walked off towards the back garden gate. The lemon trees hid him from sight but she re-mained by the window, looking in the direction he had gone.

Guy and Alan were still intent on the photographs, with Alan giving a disquisition upon his photographic technique. Harriet knew Guy did not understand a word and it seemed to her that nothing Alan said had any relation to life. Nothing in the room had any relation to life. She could scarcely con-tain her impatience to follow Charles out of the garden and down to the town centre where at that moment he was prob-ably wondering what had become of her.

Alan, transported by Guy's admiration for his work, dusted and opened more portfolios, and said with the emotion of a lonely man: "You will stay to tea, won't you?"

Guy had had other plans for the afternoon, but the appeal was too much for him.

"We would like to stay," he said.

21

HARRIET WAS CERTAIN SHE WOULD hear from Charles next morning. She suffered, as he had suffered, a feverish sense of urgency; but the messenger did not arrive. As the morning passed without a sign, her excitement died down. She had been mistaken. It had all been a mistake. There was nothing to hope for.

When she left the office at mid-day, Charles was passing the door. He gave her a sidelong smile but hurried on, too busy to stop. He did not look round. His long, quick strides took him down the square to the Corinthian. He disappeared inside.

Crestfallen, she, too, went down the square, but slowly, with no object in view. As she approached the Corinthian, Charles came out again. He stood at the top of the hotel steps, a cable-gram in his hand. Seeing her, he came pelting down as though it were all some sort of game, and lightly asked: "Where are you going to eat?"

"I haven't decided yet."

She felt he expected something from her, but she did not know what. Irritated by the incident, she made to walk on and his face contracted with an odd, almost bitter, dismay: "Don't go."

"I thought you were busy."

"Not now. I had to pick up this cable. It could have been important."

"But it wasn't?"

"Not very. Anyway, not so important it can't wait."

At a loss, she said: "I expected to hear from you."

"You turned me down at Tatoi. It rests with you now."

"Does it?" she laughed and in her surprise examined him as though she had taken a step away from him. Behind his in-culcated good manners, she had been aware of his demanding arrogance – the quality that had caused Alan to describe him as " a spoilt little boy". Now it was subdued. Perhaps he was being cautious, but he gave an impression of humility. His fixed, entreating gaze brought Sasha to her mind, and, stretching out her hand, she smiled and said: "Then come and have lunch with me."

In the second stage of their relationship, it seemed to Harriet she had no aim or purpose beyond seeing Charles; but she was not obsessed out of all reason. She knew the same compelling intention had once been directed on to Guy. Directed and deflected. Had Charles asked her, she would have said she had found her marriage hoplessly intractable. "Don't blame me. It's all too difficult." Charles asked her nothing. Apparently he had decided that explanations also rested with her. Unasked, she gave no answers. She had her own sort of loyalty.

The rain came and went. On wet afternoons they would take tea at the Corinthian. When it was fine, they walked about Athens, sensing the spring in the electric freshness of the air.

A haze of green was coming over the trees at the top of Constitution Square. During the weeks of winter Alan, unwilling to go far, had exercised his dog about the area of the Academy, and now that the weather was improving, he was aware of Harriet's withdrawal and would make no claim on her. If she cared to join him at his mid-day session with Yakimov, then she was welcome, but he did not ask her to come for walks in the gardens. Once or twice when he met Harriet with Charles in the street, he glanced away, preferring to remain unaware of her new relationship.

Unreasonably, she felt deprived by Alan's bashfulness. When she noticed the gardens coming to life again, she told Charles they must go in and visit the water-birds.

"Which water-birds?" he asked.

"Those on the pond in the middle of the gardens."

"Oh!" He smiled, but made no other comment.

As they passed the palms that stood sentinel at the gate, she said: "In this country even the trees are required to imitate columns "

"Don't you think the first columns were meant to imitate trees?"

"I suppose they were. How clever you are! When you've taken your degree, will you become an archaeologist?"

"I don't think so."

"What will you do?"

"I've really no idea."

His vagueness perplexed her. Every other young man known to her had seen the future as a struggle for life, and had prepared his means of livelihood long before he reached the age of twenty. If Charles were unconcerned in this, then his background must be very different from hers. There was something unfamiliar in him – the unfamiliarity of the rich, the more than rich; but she would not question him. He did not ask her about her family and upbringing, and did not speak of his own.

Their sense of likeness astonished them. It resembled magic. They felt themselves held in a spellbound condition which they feared to injure. Although she could not pin down any overt point of resemblance, Harriet at times imagined he was the person most like her in the world, her mirror image.

Fearful that some revelation should break this enchantment, they instinctively suppressed their disparities. Their conversations were sporadic and strained; and often they would walk round the gardens without a word.

In spite of the war, the cold, the shortage of food and hope, the spring was beginning again with small red shoots on the wistaria and buds on the apricot trees. Threads of green, rising from seeds that had lain all the previous summer invisible, like dust among the dust, were already putting out minute leaves, each of its own pattern. Harriet listened for the noise of children and birds, but there was no noise. As they advanced under the trees, the quiet grew more dense.

"Are you sure this is the place?" she asked.

He nodded and before she could speak again, they came out to the clearing. It was the same pond, filled by the winter rain. The sun broke through and dappled the water. On the sandy verge the iron chairs stood tilted to right and left. All the properties were there, but it was a stage without life. There were no children, no birds, no grown-ups, no old man to collect the small coins. The water was still. The air silent.

"Where are they all? What has happened to the birds?"

He gave his brief derisive laugh: "What do you think?"

She wondered if her dismay had amused him, but he did not look amused. His smile was almost vindictive, as though she had hurt him and now was hurt in her turn. She said nothing. She shut herself off in silence, refusing to betray any emotion at all. They passed through the thicket to the formal gardens of the Zappion. The sunlight was cold; the low-cut shrubs offered no protection from the wind. Clouds, black with snow, were coming up out of the sea. At the end of the garden the monstrous columns of the temple of Olympian Zeus flashed against the heavy sky.

Harriet came to a stop and said: "I won't go any further. I should get back. I have some work to do."

Contrite, Charles said: "Come and have tea with me first," speaking as though this suggestion would put everything right.

"No. I'd better go to the office." Harriet turned and walked back with her mind made up.

In sight of the Grande Bretagne, Charles said: "Must you go in?"

"Yes."

"Do come and have tea!"

She did not reply, but when they reached the office entrance, she walked on with him to his hotel.

The Corinthian was still new enough to look opulent. Its modernity had remained modern because no one had time these days to outdate it. The foyer, with its plum-red carpet and heavy, square-cut chairs, had strips of neon secreted behind the cornices. The main light came from the showcases, emptied now of everything except jewellery, which no one felt inclined to buy.

Though crowded with refugees and service-men, the hotel maintained such standards as it could, and was one of the few places where young Greek women might meet unchaperoned.

Several Greek girls sat at the walnut tables, some with fiancés on leave from the front. Harriet, following Charles through the plum-red gloom, noticed Archie Callard taking tea with Cookson. She caught Callard's glance, saw him look at Charles, then turn and murmur to Cookson who, staring pointedly in a different direction, grimaced with unreal amusement.

Seated beside Charles, she asked him: "Do you see much of Cookson?"

"I see him occasionally. He sometimes gives me supper."

"Has he ever invited you to one of his small and rather curious parties?"

"No. Does he give small curious parties? What happens at them? How are they curious?"

She was paused by the innocence of Charles's inquiry and, not attempting to answer, asked instead: "How do you come to know Pinkrose?"

A slow and quizzical smile spread over Charles's face. "He was my tutor. Surely you don't imagine I go to curious parties with Pinkrose!"

She blushed and did not reply, but after a moment said: "If you dislike me so much, why do you want to see me?"

His smile went at once. A concerned and wondering expression took its place. He moved towards her and was about to speak when Guy's voice came in an anguished cry across the foyer: "Darling!"

Charles started away. Guy, his glasses askew, his hair ruffled by the wind, his arms stretched round an untidy mass of papers, was hastening towards them, his whole natural disorder exaggerated by the heedlessness of misery. Something was wrong. Imagining he had sought her out to accuse her, Harriet sat motionless; but it was nothing like that. Reaching the table, he let the books and papers drop in a heap and said: "What do you think has happened?"

She shook her head.

"Pinkrose has stopped the show."

"What show?"

"Why, the revue, of course. The show we did at Tatoi. He forbids a second performance."

"I don't understand..."

"He says it's indecent. We were rehearsing at the School when the boy from the Information Office brought a letter. He said he had received complaints about the revue and could not let the School be used for rehearsals. Also, he could not let Alan Frewen, Yakimov or me take any further part in it. As though it could go on without us!"

Harriet pulled herself out of her confusion and said: "The trouble must be *Maria Marten*. Couldn't you leave it out?"

"But *Maria Marten*'s the chief attraction. Everyone's talking about it. Everyone wants to see it. Yakimov's performance was the success of the show. We've already sold most of the tickets."

"I am sorry." Harriet wished she could say more, but Guy had taken himself and his activities so far beyond her ambience, she could only wonder why he had brought his anxiety to her. She glanced up at Charles who had risen and now stood looking troubled, until Guy, as though seeing him for the first time, said: "Hello."

Charles said: "Won't you have some tea?"

"Yes. I'd like some."

Guy pulled up a chair and took over the conversation, unaware that they could have any topic of interest other than the revue and the calamitous ban Pinkrose had placed on it.

Harriet suggested that the Air Commodore at Tatoi be asked to reason with Pinkrose.

Charles said: "The Blenheims have moved forward."

Guy nodded: "Ben says he'll try to contact the C.O., but that'll take time."

Harriet said: "We now know why Toby Lush came in to see Pinkrose."

"*He* wouldn't complain, surely?"

"Someone complained. Yakimov says Dubedat was indignant at being left out of the revue. I bet he went snivelling to Cookson; then Toby Lush was sent in to complain to Pinkrose."

"You think that?"

"Yes I do."

"You could be right," Guy said and looked dashed, as he usually did when Harriet revealed the prosaic wiring that lay behind the star-bursting excitements of life. Charles, too, looked dashed, but for another reason, and Harriet tried to distract him with an appeal:

"You saw *Maria Marten*. It is only a joke. You know Pinkrose. Can't you persuade him to be reasonable?"

As she spoke, she saw on Charles's face the resentment of a deprived child. He said: "I don't think he'd be influenced by me," and looked away. He would have to return to the office.

Harriet, though she was due back herself, let him go and delayed her own departure as a gesture of sympathy with Guy. "How did you know where to find me?" she asked.

"Ben Phipps saw you come in here."

Did he, indeed! She looked over to where Cookson and Callard had been sitting and was thankful to see they had gone. She suddenly felt impatient of Guy's quandary, knowing he was more than able to meet this situation without her aid.

She said she had to go to work. To her surprise he said he would meet her at seven o'clock. They could go home together. She had expected to see Charles, who had made a tentative suggestion, not confirmed, that they should hear the singer at the Pomegranate. If Guy wanted, for once, to go home, she could do nothing but agree.

The following morning carried an atmosphere of moment. Pinkrose and Alan Frewen, summoned to the Legation, went off in separate taxis. The News-Sheet, in preparation, carried nothing more immediate than raids on Cologne and a "brush" in Libya. No one knew what was happening, but Yakimov and Miss Gladys gumshoed about the Billiard Room, conversing in choked whispers as though they were being stifled beneath a blanket of secrecy.

At mid-day, when she found Charles waiting for her, Harriet gave him no opportunity to sulk. Seizing on him, she asked excitedly: "What is going on?"

"Well ... *something*." He tried to maintain reserve but he, too, was stirred by events. "It looks as though our chaps will be here in a day or two."

"Does that mean you'll leave Athens?"

"I don't know. Not immediately, anyway. Come to the hotel for lunch. I'm supposed to remain on tap."

When they reached the Corinthian, they were disconcerted to find Guy and Ben Phipps seated in the sunlight at one of the outdoor tables. Guy jumped up as if he had been waiting for them, and Ben Phipps, with unusual cordiality, pulled Harriet down to the seat beside him and asked her what she would drink.

The invitation did not include Charles who stood by the table, uncertain whether he had lost her or not. Ben Phipps grinned up at him. "Well, you're a right lot of bastards! You've done for us this time."

"Have we?"

"What do *you* think? Hitler's waiting to go into Bulgaria.

We've only to move and he'll be on top of us in a brace of shakes."

Trying to look knowledgeable but uncommunicative, Charles said, "It's on the cards that they'll move first."

"Maybe; and then what'll you do? The last offer was a force 'not large but deadly'. So bloody deadly, in fact, it couldn't frighten pussy. No wonder it was turned down. But how can you improve on it? What have you got?"

Charles maintained an impassive air, but he was too young and inexperienced to stand up to Phipps. He could not pretend to know anything Phipps did not know. Disconcerted, he said: "There must be men available now Benghazi is in our hands."

"A few units. What about supplies?"

Charles made an uneasy move away from the argument. "The top brass know what they're doing."

"If you think that, you're cuckoo."

Charles gave Harriet a cold and angry smile, then ran up the steps into the hotel.

"Thank God we've got rid of that toffee-nosed bastard," Ben Phipps grinned connivingly at Guy, but Guy did not look happy. He picked up one of Harriet's hands and caressed it with his thumb as though to erase memory of Phipps's brash and pointless attack on Charles. Harriet had lost weight and her hands, normally thin, now looked too delicate for use. "Little monkey's paws," he said.

Harriet watched the hotel door. The last time she had seen Charles disappear in that way, he had come out again almost immediately. This time he did not come out. Her impulse was to follow, to exonerate herself, but of course she could not do that.

Guy also knew she could not do that. He gave her hand a benedictory squeeze and dropped it. Charles had been routed and the two men were free to return to matters that interested them.

Harriet guessed that Phipps was behind all this. She had no doubt that it was he, with his sharp and suspicious awareness, who had seen her about with Charles and advised Guy to take action. It would be Guy's idea to recall her with a claim on her sympathy; Phipps had evidently enjoyed himself and yet – why was he concerning himself in Guy's affairs? Not out of love for Guy. There was something in his manner that caused her to relate his behaviour to himself. He had to have controlling power somewhere. Ousted from the Phaleron circle, he had taken over Guy and he wanted no distracting gesture from Harriet.

If he could not keep his friends away from their wives, he could at least control the wives and put a stop to what he called "attention-getting ploys". She was certain he had never considered her as a separate personality who might have just cause for revolt. She was a tiresome attachment that must be pushed into the background and kept there.

Catching her fractious eye, Guy said: "I think we'd better find Harriet some food."

Phipps rose, zealous on her behalf: "Shall we try Zonar's?" He and Guy, unnaturally attentive as though she were near mental or physical collapse, walked her round to Zonar's where Ben Phipps had a talk in Greek with one of the waiters. The waiter went off to see what he could do and returned with the promise of an omelette. The men were delighted. Seeing her served with a small, lemon-coloured omelette, they seemed to think they had solved all Harriet's problems and removed her last cause for complaint. Ceasing to worry about her, they returned to a more crying need: the need to reform the world.

Although Guy had had to agree that Phipps was "a bit of a crook", he respected him as one of the "politically educated". In a wider society Guy would have been entertained by him, but would not have chosen to associate with him. Here in Athens, each felt fortunate in finding anyone who shared his radical preoccupations. However much a crook Ben might be, Guy felt that he had more to offer the world than some fellow like Alan Frewen who merely wanted to lead a quiet life.

Ten years Guy's senior and an established left-wing figure, Phipps was adept at ferreting out the authors of misrule and was ready at any time to talk about the mysterious forces that had brought the world to its present pass. Some of these – such as the Zoippus Bank, the Bund and certain Wall Street Jews who had financed Hitler in the hope of forcing the whole Jewish race to move to Palestine – were new to Guy. Phipps sometimes said he had uncovered them by personal investigation. He could prove (Harriet had heard him do it more than once) that were it not for the machinations of bankers, big business, financiers, shareholders in steel and certain *intrigants* of the allied powers who were still, through the medium of the Vatican, in unnatural conclave with German cartels, Hitler would never have come to power, there would have been no *casus belli* and no war. It seemed to Harriet that for Phipps this contention had become a gospel to which life itself was simply a contributing factor. Referred to, it answered all questions. It might have some sort of basis in truth, but a basis on which Phipps had built his own fantasy; and political fantasy bored her even more than politics.

When she had eaten the omelette, she became restless and thought of going for a walk. Guy put his hand over hers and held to her, saying: "Listen to Ben."

Ben, alerted by Guy, turned his gaze on her but could not keep it fixed anywhere for long. In ordinary exchanges he kept up an attitude of confident repose but when excited by his own disclosures, his pupils dodged about, black and small as currants behind his heavy lenses.

Harriet seized on a moment's silence to inquire about the revue. Guy said that Alan Frewen had undertaken to speak to Pinkrose. Harriet attempted another question but Guy motioned her not to interrupt Phipps. At last Phipps reached his usual conclusion and paused to let Guy expose his own belief that had the forces that brought about the war used their wealth and energy to further the concepts of Marx, the earthly paradise would be well established by now.

Both Guy and Ben Phipps were proud of their inflexible materialism yet, Harriet decided, Phipps had a mystic's insight into the workings of high finance, while Guy read *Das Kapital* as the padre might read his Bible. Seeing them hold to political mysteries as other men held to God, she told herself they were a pair of hopeless romantics. Their conversation did not relate to reality. She was bored. Ben Phipps bored her. Guy and Phipps together bored her. Would the day come when it was Guy who bored her?

She remembered when she had wanted him to take over her life. That phase did not last long. She had soon decided that Guy might be better read and better informed, but, so far as life was concerned, her own judgement served her better than his. Guy had a moral strength but it resembled one of those vast Victorian feats of engineering: impressive but out of place in the modern world. He had a will to believe in others but the belief survived only because he evaded fact. Life as he saw it could not support itself; it had to be subsidized by fantasy. He was a materialist without being a realist; and that, she thought, gave him the worst of both worlds.

Ben Phipps' talk came to a stop when he noticed the time. He had to return to write up events. Guy, speaking as one conscious of new responsibilities, offered to take Harriet that evening to the cellar café, Elatos, and asked: "How about you, Ben?" Ben said: "I'll join you but, things being as they are, I'll have to keep near to a telephone."

It seemed that Guy did intend to take over her life. But too late. Much too late. And Phipps came with them wherever they went.

"Darling," she said. "I don't know how you can stand so much of him."

Guy was astonished. "He's a most lively, stimulating companion."

"Well, I don't want to listen to him. Especially now, when things are happening here."

"If more people had listened to him, none of this need have happened at all."

"How can you be so ridiculous!" She was beginning to fear she had married a man whom she could not take seriously.

"Besides," Guy added with reason: "Ben knows what's going on here. He knows more than most people. He told me that British troops were disembarking on Lemnos, and he was right. Now he's found out they're moving to the mainland. I don't suppose even your friend Frewen could have told you that."

"He could, I don't doubt; but he didn't. I imagine it's inside information."

"Well, if you want inside information, you'd better stick to Ben."

Important visitors arrived in Athens. The Parthenon was opened to them and Ben Phipps, intending to report the occasion, obtained tickets and took the Pringles with him. The British Foreign Secretary stood at the Beulé Gate and smiled at Harriet as she passed. Harriet, smiling back at the youthful, handsome, familiar face, was transported as though some part of England itself had come to be with them here in their isolation.

Ben Phipps kept silent till they were upon the plateau, then he grinned round to Guy, his eyes sparkling with ironical glee, his whole square, heavy body twitching in his eagerness to shatter the moment's awe. He began to say: "I bet . . ." and Harriet said: "Shut up."

"Your wife's a bloody Conservative," he complained.

"Oh no," Guy put an arm round her shoulder, "she's merely a romantic."

"Same thing."

"I wouldn't say so. Romantics are relatively harmless."

Harriet moved from under Guy's restraining arm and made her way among the officers and officials who stood about on the hilltop in the last of the afternoon sunlight. Charles was not among them. She ran up the Parthenon steps and stood between the columns, watching Guy and Phipps crossing the rough ground; Phipps, in brown greatcoat, rocking heavy-footed on the stones, like a stout brown bear.

They decided to go to the Museum. As they walked inside the Parthenon, Charles, with two other officers, climbed the steps at the eastern end and came towards them. He saw Harriet. He looked at her companions and looked away. He smiled to himself. Neither Guy nor Ben Phipps noticed him. At the steps she managed to glance back, but he was already out of sight.

Not much was left in the Museum but enough to detain them. Harriet stood for a long time gazing at the archaic horses with their gentle curving necks, and thought: "It doesn't matter. It was an impossible situation." Now, thank goodness, it was over.

When they came out the sun was sinking and the important visitors had gone. The last of the officers were wandering, shadowy in the later light, towards the gate. Outside the gate Alan Frewen was making his way cautiously down the rocky slope to the road and Ben Phipps asked: "What's the great man doing here?"

Alan laughed: "I expect you know as well as I do."

"Would he stand for an interview?"

"He might."

"Where's he now?"

"Probably half-way to Cyprus."

"Thanks for telling me. Come on, I'll give you a lift back."

When Ben dropped Harriet and Alan at the office, Guy

arranged to pick her up again at seven o'clock. He and Ben were taking her to supper at Babayannis'.

Even octopus was scarce now. At Babayannis' the menu offered lung stew and the laced up intestines that had given Harriet a chronic stomach disorder.

Guy said: "What does it matter? There's plenty of wine!!"

Both men preferred drink to food; but Harriet would rather eat than drink. Made irritable by hunger, she felt she had been imprisoned long enough by Phipps and Guy; and she was further irritated by Guy's folly. Everything said seemed to confirm it. In the past she had complained because she did not have enough of Guy's company. Now she had too much.

Hacking away at the grey, slippery intestines, she heard Phipps repeat again Hemingway's reply to Fitzgerald's observation: "The rich are different from us."

"He said," said Phipps gleefully, " 'Yes, they have more money.' "

She fixed Phipps in a rage and said: "I suppose you agree with Hemingway?"

"Don't you?"

"I don't. I think his answer exposes both Hemingway and his limitations. He simply didn't know what Fitzgerald meant."

"Indeed!" Ben Phipps smiled indulgently: "And what did he mean?"

"He meant that the rich have an attitude of mind which only money can buy."

"I can't say I've noticed it."

"You should have noticed it. You hung around Cookson long enough."

"Cookson amused me."

"And you amused Cookson. I'm told you were the Phaleron court jester."

"I certainly laughed at him and his money."

"That was one way of defending yourself."

"Defending myself?"

"Surely you know laughter is a defence? We laugh at the things we fear most."

"She's joking," Guy said, but Ben Phipps knew she was not joking. He lost his indulgent air. His expression hardened and she saw him control, but only just control, the impulse to insult her.

He disliked her as much as she disliked him, so why should she waste her life here, acting as audience to a man she despised? As for Guy, sitting there uneasily smiling, he seemed at that moment merely a gaoler who hemmed her in with people who did not interest her and talk that bored her. She had found no release in marriage. It had forced her further back into the prison of herself. Acutely conscious now of the passing of time, she felt she was not living but was being fobbed off with an imitation of life.

As the evening went on, Phipps returned, inevitably, to the sources of the world's mishap and Harriet, listening, reached a point of conscious revolt. At the mention of the mysterious Zoippus Bank, she broke in on him: "There is no Zoippus Bank. There never was and never will be a Zoippus Bank. I'm quite sure no Jew ever financed Hitler. I know the Vatican was never involved with Krupps and Wall Street and Bethlehem Steel . . ."

"You know fuck all," said Ben Phipps.

Harriet met the hatred of his small eyes, and said with hatred: "You *ugly* little man!"

His mouth fell open. She could see that she had hurt him.

Guy was hurt, too. In shocked remonstrance he said: "Darling!"

She jumped up, near tears, and hurried through the crowded restaurant. Guy caught her as she was leaving the front hall. He said: "Come back."

"No." She turned on him, raging: "Why do you drag me round to listen to Ben Phipps. You know I can't bear him."

"But he's my friend."

"Charles Warden was my friend."

"That was different . . ."

"I don't think so. You want Phipps's company; I prefer Charles."

"But you don't need Charles. You have me."

Harriet did not reply to that.

Pained and puzzled, Guy reasoned with her: "Why do you dislike Ben? He's much more amusing than the people you *do* like. I find Alan Frewen a dull dog; and as for Charles Warden! He's a pleasant enough fellow, but he takes himself too seriously. He's quite immature." Guy looked to her for agreement and when she did not agree, said: "But he's good-looking. I suppose that means something to you?"

"He is good-looking, it's true; but that has nothing to do with it. In fact, when I first saw him, I thought he had a vain, unpleasant face."

"You don't think so now?"

"No."

Guy lowered his head, frowning to hide his distress, and asked: "Do you want to leave me?"

"Good heavens, no; there's no suggestion of such a thing."

Guy's head dropped lower. Miserably embarrassed, he said: "I suppose you want to have an affair with him?"

"Really!" Harriet was appalled at such a question. An unanswerable question at that! "It's out of the question. As though one could, anyway – life being what it is! The impermanence of things; and the fact one has no time, no opportunity! But there never was any question . . . It was simply that I was lonely."

"You're not lonely now. You're always out with Ben and me."

"Ben bores me."

"Darling, you know I don't want to deprive you of anything."

"What is there to deprive me of? Charles isn't here for long. It's just that I would like to see him."

"Very well. But come back to the table. Be nice to Ben. He knows he's ugly. No need to rub it in. Tell him you're sorry, there's a good girl?"

"I am sorry. I didn't want to hurt him."

"Come along, then." Guy took her hand and led her back into the restaurant.

22

THE RAIDS WERE MORE FREQUENT NOW: a sign, Ben Phipps said, of impending events. Some mornings it was scarcely possible to get into Athens between the alerts. On one of these mornings, walking from the metro station at Monastiraki, Harriet came upon two British tanks. They had stopped just inside Hermes Street and the men were standing together in the road.

There had been snow during the night. The pavements were wet; the light, coming from the dark, wet sky had the blue fluorescence of snow-light, yet a tree overhanging a garden wall was in full blossom.

Harriet was not the only one who stopped to look at the tanks. Some of the people seemed mystified by their sand-coloured camouflage and the insignia of camels and palms. To Harriet they were familiar, but in a recondite, disturbing way as though they belonged to some life she had lived long ago. The young Englishmen also came out of the past. They all looked alike: not tall, as she remembered the English, but strongly built, with sun-reddened faces and hair bleached blond. When they became aware of her, they stopped talking. They looked at her, rapt, and she looked back, each remembering the world from which they had come, too shy to speak.

She made off suddenly. In the office the atmosphere was emotional and even Miss Gladys was moved to speech. To Harriet and to anyone who entered, she said: "Our lads are arriving. Our lads are arriving. Isn't it great! I was in the know, of course. Oh yes, I've known all along. Lord Pinkrose let something drop, but not accidentally. Oh, no, not accidentally! He often says something to show that he trusts me."

Ben Phipps, when he came in, did not wait to hear the whole of this speech but hurried through to the News Room, leaving all the doors open so, noisy and voluble, he could be heard shouting: "We've had it now. We've issued a direct challenge to the Boche."

He had just come from the Piraeus where he said troops were disembarking and supplies were being off-loaded on to the very steps of the German consulate.

"Does the Legation know this?" Alan asked.

"I telephoned them, but what can they do? The Greeks aren't at war with the Germans; at least, not yet. And there the stuff is, for all to see. The Italians are bombing it and the German Military Attaché is making notes. When I arrived, he was counting the guns. He gave me a nod and said: '*Wie gewöhnlich – zu wenig und zu spät!*' "

"Is this true?" Alan asked.

"It would be damned funny if it were."

"I mean, is it true the Germans are watching the disembarkation?"

"It certainly is. Go and see for yourself."

Alan put his hand to the telephone, paused and took it away again.

"Nothing to be done," Phipps said. "The usual army cock-up. But what does it matter? We don't stand a chance."

"I'm not so sure," Alan said. "It's amazing what we can do in a tight corner. But whatever happens, it's better to suffer with the Greeks than leave them to struggle on alone."

In the exhilaration of expectation and preparation for action that might, after all, succeed, Harriet felt justified in contacting Charles. She wrote: "I want to see you. Meet me at one o'clock," and gave the note to a military messenger in the hall.

Charles, waiting, unsmiling, at the side entrance, met her with a strained and guarded look of inquiry.

Fearing she had behaved unwisely, she said: "I am going to the Plaka. Will you come with me?"

He did not reply but followed her through the crowds that were out to see the British lorries and guns coming into the town. "This is exciting, isn't it?" she said.

"I suppose it is exciting for you."

"But not for you?"

"To me, it means I won't be here much longer."

They came into the square where Byron had lived. Tables and chairs had been placed outside the little café but no one could sit in the bitter wind that cut the tender, drifting branches of the pepper trees. Having come so far, Charles suddenly asked: "Where are you going?"

"To the dressmaker. I hoped you'd translate for me; my Greek isn't very good."

He grew pale and stared at her in resentful accusation: "Is that why you wanted to see me? You simply wanted to make use of me?"

"No." She was wounded by his reaction. She had supposed he would see the request as a gesture of intimacy, would know at once that it was an excuse for summoning him: "Don't you want to do something for me?"

His expression did not change. For some minutes he was silent as though he could not bring himself to speak, then burst out: "Where is this dressmaker?"

"Here. But it doesn't matter. Let's go to Zonar's and see if we can get a sandwich."

He neither agreed nor disagreed but turned when she turned and walked back with her towards University Street. Because she had been misunderstood, she did not try to speak but, glancing once or twice at his severe profile, she wondered what attached her to this cold, distant and angry stranger. This of course was the moment to break away, and yet the attraction remained. Even seeing him detached and unaccountable, she still had no real will to leave him.

Half a dozen Australian lorries had parked on Zonar's corner and the men had climbed down. Some were drinking with newly made Greek friends: others were lurching about between the outdoor tables, occasionally knocking down a chair, but still sober and reasonable enough. The Greeks seemed delighted with them but Charles came to a stop and, shaken out of his sulks, said: "We'd better not go there."

"Why ever not?"

"It's out of bounds to other ranks, which makes things awkward for me. But, worse than that, they're drinking, so there's likely to be trouble. I don't want you mixed up in it."

"Really! How ridiculous!"

He caught her arm and led her away protesting. Laughing at him and refusing any longer to be restrained by his ill-humour, she said: "If you won't go there, we'll go to the dressmaker!"

She walked him back to the Plaka where a young Greek woman was making her two summer dresses. Charles translated her instructions with a poor grace, then said: "I'll wait for you outside." She half expected when she left to find he had gone, but he stood in the lane beside a flower-shop. He had been buying violets and, seeing her, he held the bunch out to her. She took it and put it to her mouth.

She spoke through the sweetness of the petals: "We mustn't quarrel. There isn't time."

"No, there certainly isn't." Giving his ironical laugh, he asked: "Now where do you want to go?"

"I don't mind where we go, but don't be cross."

"We might get something to eat. It's too late for luncheon but, if we go to the Corinthian, I know one of the waiters. He'll find something for us."

Racing back to the square, dodging the crowds on the pavements, Charles held to her, pulling her along, caught up in the inspirited air of the city centre where so much was happening. They were both elated as the enchantment of their companionship renewed itself.

How much longer was he likely to stay in Athens? He did not know. The Mission was to be absorbed into the Expeditionary Force, but he still had his work at the Military Attaché's office and would remain until his detachment arrived. That could be within a few days, or not for two or three weeks. No one seemed to know when the different units would turn up. Hurriedly organized, its contingents mixed and withdrawn from different sectors, the campaign was in some confusion.

One thing only was certain – there was no certainty and very little time.

The lorries, crowding in now from the Piraeus, were trying to find their way to camps outside Athens. Several, having gone astray, had made their way into Stadium Street and one after another stopped to get directions from Charles. Each time, as the Englishmen talked, a little crowd gathered to watch. A girl threw a bunch of cyclamen up to the men who leant over the lorry side. At this the men began to call to the passers-by and more flowers were thrown, and a fête-day atmosphere came into the streets. Suddenly everyone was throwing flowers to the men and calling a welcome in Greek and English. All in a moment, it seemed, fear had broken down. British intervention might indeed mean that Greece was lost, but these men were guests in the country and must be treated as such.

Then the men, who had been bewildered by the suspicion, the unexpected winter weather, the fact the girls would not look at them, were reassured and began good-naturedly to respond.

Amidst all the shouting and waving and throwing of flowers, Harriet held on to Charles and said: "It's fun not to be alone."

Charles smiled down on her, in quizzical disbelief: "But are you ever alone?" he asked.

"Quite often. Guy is always busy on something. He's ..." She was about to say "He's too busy to live," but checked herself. It was, after all, a question of what one meant by living. She said instead: "He has his own interests."

"Interests that you don't share?"

"Often they're interests I can't share. These productions, for instance: he enjoys putting them on but he prefers not to have me there. It's quite understandable, of course. The production is his world; he's the dominating influence – and he feels I don't take him seriously. When I'm there, I spoil it for him. And he does much too much. In Bucharest, when he staged *Troilus and Cressida*, he worked on it day and night. The Germans were advancing into Paris at the time. I never saw him. He simply disappeared."

"What did you do? Were you alone?"

"Usually, yes."

Charles watched her gravely, awaiting some conclusive revelation satisfactory to himself, but she said no more. After a moment he encouraged her: "You must have been lonely, in a strange country at a time like that?"

"Yes."

"You married a stranger, and went to live among strangers. What did you expect?"

"Nothing. We did not expect to survive. It's our survival that's thrown us out. However, as a potential, Guy seemed remarkable. Now I'm not so sure about him. As a potential, he probably is remarkable, but all he does is dissipate himself. And why? Do you think he's afraid to put himself to the test."

Charles did not know the answer to this question, but said: "He seems confident enough."

"Guy's confidence really comes from a lack of contact with reality. He's stuck in unreality. He's afraid to come out."

Trying himself to gain more contact with reality, Charles asked: "What's he doing at the moment?"

"Rehearsing the revue again. They've all decided to defy Pinkrose, and the padre's letting them use the church hall. He's probably over there now."

In this she was wrong, as she soon discovered. They passed a café. The day had brightened and sitting outside in the sun was Guy with a British army officer. "See who's here," he called out to her.

Harriet had already seen who was there. The officer was Clarence Lawson, one of their Bucharest friends, now dressed up as a lieutenant-colonel. Grinning, Clarence rose up, tall and thinner than ever, keeping his long, narrow head on one side as though seeking to efface himself. In fact, Harriet knew, he was not only aware but disapproving. He had given her a swift, appraising glance, and she saw him sum up the situation.

Clarence was not successful with women but he was a man whose life was lived in acute consciousness of the opposite sex, passing from love to love, preferring an unhappy passion to no passion at all.

She said: "Why, hello!" hoping by her tone of hearty interest to distract him from the intimacy he observed between her and Charles. She held out her hand. He took it, but his eyes were on the hand that held the violets.

She rallied him on the rank he had reached since they last saw him. His grin became rueful and he mumbled:

"Doesn't mean much."

Guy said gleefully: "You could not have come past at a better time. Clarence is only here for a few hours. He's just arrived. I was on my way to the rehearsal when I bumped into him. Wasn't it an amazing bit of luck? Here." Guy pulled up two chairs. "Sit down, both of you. What will you have? Coffee?"

"We haven't eaten yet."

"You won't get anything now, but they might make a sandwich."

Harriet, glancing at Charles, saw his face shut against her. He did not meet her eyes but spoke to Guy as though she were not present.

"I'm afraid I can't stay. There's a lot going on at the

moment. I ought to be at the office." Giving no one a chance to detain him, he turned abruptly and crossed the road.

Watching him as he went, Harriet's sense of loss was so acute, she could not keep quiet: "I must go after him. I can't let him go like that. I must explain . . ."

"Of course," Guy said, voice and face expressionless: "If you feel . . ."

"Yes. I do. I'll come back. I won't be long." She sped off and managed to catch sight of Charles among the crowd on the opposite pavement. He went into a shop that sold newspapers and cigarettes. She slowed to regain her breath and reaching him, was able to speak calmly: "Charles, I'm sorry."

He swung round, startled to see her there beside him.

"Clarence is here for so short a time. I'll have to stay with them. I've no choice."

"Part of your past, I presume?"

"No. At least, not as you mean it. Why do you say that?"

"He looked pretty sick when he saw I was with you."

"He's only a friend; as much Guy's friend as mine."

"You'll be saying that about me one day."

She laughed and slid her fingers into his hand. He was still annoyed but let her hand rest with his. She said: "I'll see you tomorrow?"

"Will you have luncheon with me?"

"Yes."

She made to pull her fingers away; he held to them a moment, then let them go. The meeting arranged, they could part with composure. Harriet went back to join Guy and Clarence. Clarence was restrained, making his disapproval evident and she tried to rally him: "I thought you were a conscientious objector?" she said.

"I still am a conscientious objector."

"But you've joined the army."

"Well . . . in a manner of speaking, yes." Clarence, lolling as he used to loll, hiding his discomfort beneath an appearance of ease and indifference, would not respond to her raillery. Despite his disapproval, he was, as he always had been, on the defensive.

"Are you in the army or aren't you?"

Clarence shrugged, leaving it to Guy to explain that Clarence was not a real lieutenant-colonel. He merely belonged to a para-military organization intended to protect British business interests in the war zones. He was on his way to Salonika to keep an eye on the tobacco combines.

"Really! What a shocking come-down! Just an agent of the Bund, Wall Street and Zoippus Bank! He'd better not meet Ben Phipps."

Clarence shrugged again, refusing to protect himself; and Harriet went on to ask what he had done since leaving Bucharest in the company of Sophie, the half-Jewish Rumanian girl who had once hoped to marry Guy. He had been on his way to Ankara to take up a British Council appointment but Sophie had deflected him. She had decided that Ankara was not for her. When they left the express at Istanbul, she demanded that they take the boat to Haifa and from there make their way to Cairo.

"So that's where you ended up?"

"Yep."

"What about the Council? Couldn't they hold you?"

"No. I was only on contract. They let me go."

"And now you're a colonel! That's pretty quick promotion."

"Yep. Lieutenant one day: major by the end of the week: lieutenant-colonel the week after. That's what it's like." He snuffed down his nose in self-contempt. "The office in Cairo is full of bogus half-colonels like me."

"And what about Sophie?"

"She's all right."

"Did you get married?"

"Yep."

"Good for Sophie. And now she's the wife of a lieutenant-colonel! I bet she likes that?"

Clarence hung his head and did not reply.

Taking this for a happy conversation, Guy decided he could safely go. He handed Clarence over to Harriet, saying he had been due at his rehearsal at 2.30 and he could not keep the cast waiting any longer. "I'll be back at seven," he said. "I'll meet you here. Think where you'd like to go for supper. Anyway we'll spend the evening together," and, gathering together his papers and books, he was gone.

"Guy hasn't changed much," Clarence said.

"Did you expect him to change?"

Harriet put the violets on the table in front of her and

Clarence frowned on them. "Guy's a great man," he said. "Well ... yes."

They had had this conversation before and Harriet could think of nothing new to say. She had seen a great deal of Clarence, who in Bucharest had been her companion when, as usually happened, Guy was not to be found. She had accepted his generosity and given him nothing, but her chief emotion at the sight of him was irritation. Clarence, it seemed, was born to suffer. He wanted to suffer. If she had not ill-treated him, someone else would. But Clarence could take his revenge. He encouraged confidence and often gave sympathy, but was just as liable to snap back with: "Don't complain to me. *You* married him," or: "If you didn't let him play on your weakness, he wouldn't impose these lame dogs on you."

Now she was cautious. With the vindictiveness of the weak, he was likely to repay her behaviour with Charles; and given any opportunity, he would sink her with some appalling truth.

"A great man," Clarence repeated firmly. "He's not self-seeking. He's generous. He's a *big* person."

"Yes," said Harriet.

"You're jolly lucky to be married to him."

"I suppose I am ... in a way."

"What do you mean: 'in a way'? You're damned lucky!"

Harriet let it pass. The café produced a sandwich for her. As the sun passed off the outdoor tables, the cold returned. Though the damp breeze smelled of spring, and almonds and apricots were in bloom, an icy tang came into the air at twilight. The nights were cold enough for snow.

She left earlier than she need to go to the office. When she returned, Clarence had moved inside. He had been drinking cognac and his gloom had lifted. He now accorded her his old romantic admiration.

At eight o'clock Ben Phipps, on his way to the Stefani Agency, entered and came to the table, doing a favour but not willingly. He had a message from Guy and his delivery was off-hand: "He says he'll have to rehearse the chorus again. But you're to go to the Pomegranate and he'll join you there."

"Why the Pomegranate?"

"Don't ask me. That's what he said."

"How long will he be, do you think?"

"God knows. You know what he's like."

Clarence asked Phipps to join them for a drink, but Phipps, humorously patronizing, somehow implying that to him a lieutenant-colonel was a joke, said: "Haven't time, old chap. *I* have to work for my living," and went.

The Pomegranate was a night club and an odd choice for Guy. He may have thought that, as Clarence in his new glory could afford it, it would be an especial treat for Harriet.

She said: "It's expensive, I'm afraid."

"Oh well! If the food's good ..."

"There's no such thing as good food these days."

"You mean, not at any price?"

"Not at any price. But they have a singer who's very good; and it's run by a eunuch. A real one; one of the last of the old Ottoman empire."

"Oh well! That's something." Clarence got unsteadily to his feet.

The hallway of the Pomegranate was lit by an indefinite inkish glow from bulbs hidden inside paper pomegranates. The eunuch who sat there collecting the entrance fees was not fat as his kind are said to be, but marked by an appearance that resembled nothing but itself. His face was grey-white, matt, and very delicately lined, like crackle ware. It was fixed in an expression of profound melancholy. He appeared unapproachable. A walking-stick, resting between his legs, showed that he was a cripple. Harriet, who felt for him the same anguish that had been roused in her by the deliberately maimed beggar children of Rumania, had once seen him making his way like a wounded crab down University Street. People walked round him, avoiding him not because of his awkward movements but because he had been separated from human kind by an irreparable injury. He seemed to have retreated from society like someone who had been a centre of scandal and would not risk another brush with life. But he purveyed life of a sort. He had started the night club, the best in Athens, and, sitting in a basket chair at the door, watched all who came and went.

Those who entered found a vapid, colourless little hall with a dance floor. Most of the tables were taken. Any still unoccupied were marked "reserved". The "reserved" ticket was taken off for Clarence and Harriet, and Clarence said: "I hope this table wasn't intended for anyone else. I dislike being given special treatment because of my rank."

His expression was smug and Harriet said: "Don't worry. You are favoured not because you're an imitation colonel, but as a guest and an ally. The Greek army is professional: rank has nothing to do with class, only with proficiency. The Greek soldiers go wherever they can afford to go, so I hope the British command will stop all this nonsense about Other Ranks."

"I'm pretty sure they won't."

"Why not?"

"It's obvious." Clarence spoke peevishly, disliking the discussion. The Athens streets had been noisy with the newly arrived troops who, coming in from camps, wandering about, lost in the darkness, blundered in between the black-out curtains of any door that seemed to offer a refuge. They had not managed to pass the eunuch at the Pomegranate. His fee was too high.

"You don't want them in here, do you?" Clarence asked. "For one thing, there isn't room."

There certainly wasn't much room. The people present resembled those who had been at Cookson's party. The dance floor was packed with couples clinched face to face and barely able to move. Among them Harriet saw Dobson with the widow of a shipping magnate, whom he was trying to marry.

"What shall we drink?" Clarence asked, insisting on happier things. He ordered retsina and when the third bottle was opened his smile had become mild, placatory and rather mawkish: "Come on and dance," he said, but Harriet was not dressed for dancing. When she refused, he said: "If you won't, then I'll dance with that pretty girl over there."

"She'll refuse you. Greek girls don't dance with foreigners."

"Why ever not?"

"It's out of loyalty to their own men at the front."

"Loyalty?" Clarence brooded on the word then added with feeling: "Yes. Loyalty. That's the thing. That's what we need." An impassioned gloom came over him and Harriet knew he would now be willing to talk.

She asked gently: "How is it between you and Sophie?"

"How do you think? The last time I saw her she was coming

out of Sicorel's. She's just bought a thousand pounds' worth
of evening dresses."

"You're joking. Surely you're not as rich as that?"

"Rich? Me? You don't think *I* paid for them?"

"Who did, then?"

"A silly little Cherrypicker with a title and money in the
bank. He paid for them and probably paid for a lot of other
things as well."

"You mean, she's left you?"

"Yep. Not surprising, is it? What had I to offer a girl like
Sophie?"

"How long were you married?"

"Week. It took a week to get her passport, then she looked
round, sighted something better and was off like a greyhound
from a trap. I admit things were grim. I had no job – we
had only one room, in a dreadful pension. She hated me."

"Oh, come!"

"Hated me!" Clarence repeated with morose satisfaction:
"Anyway, off she went. In next to no time she'd got herself a
poor devil of a major. Not that I pity him. A bloody ordnance
officer, feathering his nest while better men rot in the desert.
She didn't stick him for long. She went on to an Egyptian
cotton king, but he was only an interlude. She didn't intend
to lose a valuable passport just to go and live in the delta. I
don't know who came next ... I lost sight of her. Cairo is the
happy hunting ground for girls like Sophie. They can pick and
choose."

"Are you divorcing her?"

"I suppose so. She said she might want to marry this last one.
She does love dressing up. As she came out of Sicorel's, her
face was glowing. It's the only time I ever saw her *really*
happy."

"But what can she do with so many evening dresses? Is Cairo
like that?"

"O *Lord*, yes!" Clarence glanced critically at Harriet's plain
suit, then stuck out his lower lip at the women with their faded
dresses on the dance floor. His eyes ceased to focus. Lost in
memory, he suddenly laughed: "Sophie had something," he
said: according a benevolent admiration. "She really was a
little trollop."

"You knew that when you married her."

"Of course I did." Clarence stretched back in his chair, relaxed and fired by wine, and smiled aloofly, having reached now the stage of philosophical titubancy which granted him insight into all things. "You just don't understand. You simplify life too much. Things are subtle ... complex ... frightening ... One does things because one does things. You're so clever, you don't know what I mean. But what a fate! Really, when you come to think of it. I don't envy her."

"Who?"

"Sophie. He won't marry her. They never do. She'll be stuck there with her British passport. In a few years' time she'll be just like all those raddled Levantine wives who got left behind in Cairo after the last war. She'll keep a pension ..."

"It's an old story."

"Yep. Life's an old story. That's what's wrong with it. Still, it interests me. I interest myself."

"I'd never have thought it."

"Hah!" Clarence turned his moist reminiscent eye and now the admiration was for Harriet. "You're a bitch. Sophie was only a trollop, but you're a bitch. A bitch is what I need."

"I don't think so. You need someone who can share your illusions ..."

"Go on talking. You do me good. You always despised me. Do you remember that night I came in drunk from the Polish party and David Boyd was there? You debagged me. The three of you. Guy and David held me down and you took my bags off."

"Did we do that? What shocking behaviour. But we were young then."

"Good heavens, it was only last winter. And before I left – do you remember? – I asked for those shirts I'd lent Guy and you were furious. Quite rightly. I didn't really want them. I was just being bloody-minded. And you were *furious*! You took them out to the balcony and threw them down into the street."

"What a stupid thing to do!"

"No, not a bit stupid. You were always doing extraordinary things – things no one else thought of doing. I loved it. I bet if I asked you, you'd get up on this table here and now, throw off your clothes, and dance the can-can."

"I bet I wouldn't."

Clarence sat up, urging her, "Go on. Do it."

"Don't be a fool." She wondered if Clarence had always held such an absurd view of her, or had she, with the passage of time, become a myth for him?

Clarence was pained and disappointed by her refusal but the waiter arrived and he forgot the can-can. Their meal was served. Clarence took a mouthful and put down his fork.

"This is pretty terrible," he said.

"It's better than you'll get anywhere else."

"Then we'll need a great deal more to drink. Let's go on to champagne."

The floor cleared and the singer came out: a stout woman, not young, not beautiful, but it was for her that people came to the Pomegranate. She sang "Anathema" and Clarence asked: "What is that song?"

"A curse on him who says that love is sweet.
I've tried it and found it poison."

"God, yes!" Clarence sighed fervently and filled his glass. He gave up any further attempt to eat.

The singer sang: " 'I've something secret to tell you: I love you, I love you, I love you.' "

The pretty girl who had attracted Clarence closed her eyes, but a tear came from under one lid. Clarence gave her a long look and, dismally bereft, turned on Harriet:

"That chap you were with today: what's he doing here?"

"He has some sort of liaison job. He won't be here much longer."

"No, he won't," Clarence maliciously agreed. He sat up, preparing an attack, but at that moment Guy arrived.

"Ah!" said Clarence, his voice rich with interest, "here he is at last."

They watched Guy as he made his way round the room greeted by people Harriet did not know, talking to people she had never seen before. Dobson, dancing with the widow, flung out an arm as Guy passed and patted him on the shoulder.

"A great man! A remarkable man!" said Clarence, deeply moved.

Behind Guy came Yakimov, the hem of his greatcoat trailing on the floor.

Clarence said: "Hell!" then added: "Never mind, never

mind," and in a mood to accept anything, shouted: "Good old Yakimov." The reprimand intended for Harriet was delayed by the new arrivals and the need to order food and more of the gritty, sweet champagne. Eventually, when they had all settled down again, Clarence looked angrily at Harriet and said: "You've the best husband in the world."

"Yes," Harriet agreed

"You're lucky – *damned* lucky – to be married to him."

"So you keep telling me."

"I'm telling you again. Apparently you need telling. What were you doing walking about holding on to that bloody little pongo?"

"I like that. You're a pongo yourself."

Guy said: 'Hey. Shut up, you two."

"I'm telling her," Clarence explained to Guy, "she's married to the finest man I've ever known ... a great man, a saint. And she's not satisfied. She picked up with a kid one pip up ..."

Guy said again: "Shut up, Clarence," but Clarence would not shut up. He continued to condemn Harriet and condemn Charles. He and Charles might have little enough in common, but both had an instinct for intrigue. To each, the very sight of the other had roused suspicion, and Clarence took Harriet's guilt for granted.

She was angry but, more than that, she was shocked. She was particularly shocked that these accusations should be made in front of Guy who seemed to her, at that moment, like some one of an older generation, who must be protected against the atrocities of sex. When Clarence at last reached an end, she said to Guy: "You know this isn't true."

"Of course it isn't. Clarence is being silly." Guy rose as he spoke, looking for a refuge, and seeing Dobson leave the floor, hurried over to his table.

"Now look what you've done!" Harriet said.

"What do I care!" mumbled Clarence. "Someone had to say it," and self-justified and self-righteous, he sank into a despondent half-sleep.

Yakimov, who had listened to none of this, was waiting for his food. When it came, the waiter was sent to summon Guy who looked round, waved, nodded and went on talking to Dobson.

Yakimov, smiling blandly, said: "I think I'll begin," and when his own plate was empty, peered at Guy's: "Do you think the dear boy doesn't want it?"

The food, some sort of lung hash, had fixed itself, cold and grey, on Guy's plate. To Harriet with her disordered stomach it looked inedible, but nothing was inedible to Yakimov. She said: "You might as well have it."

When Guy eventually returned, she told him: "I've given Yakimov your food."

"It doesn't matter."

Clarence began struggling up and calling the waiter. "I've got to go," he said frantically.

"Not yet," Guy protested. "I've only just got here."

"You got here nearly an hour ago," Harriet said crossly. "You spent all the time at another table."

"Why didn't you come over?"

"We weren't asked to come over."

"Do you need to be asked?"

Clarence persisted that he must go. "My berth's booked on the night train. I'll be in trouble if I miss it."

"Oh, all right; but I've seen nothing of you."

"Whose fault is that?"

"And I've had nothing to eat."

Harriet said: "You've only yourself to blame."

"Really, darling, need you be so disgruntled? Clarence is only here for one night."

"I must go," Clarence moaned.

"All right. Don't worry. Harriet and I are coming with you."

Yakimov was content to be left behind.

Outside in the passage, the eunuch had left his base. An Australian soldier was sitting in the basket chair weeping. Perhaps he had been excluded from the club, perhaps he could not afford to pay.

"What's the matter?" Harriet asked.

"Nobody loves poor Aussie," he wept. "Nobody loves poor Aussie."

"He's drunk," Clarence said in contempt. Stepping out to the street, he stopped a taxi in a businesslike way but, once inside it, fell across the back seat and lost consciousness.

The station was blacked out. The train, that used to be part of the Orient Express, stood darkly in the darkness. The station officials moved about carrying torches or oil lamps. One of the officials thought that Clarence must be the British officer who earlier in the day had left his suitcase in the cloak-room. Every man on the station joined in getting Clarence to his bunk. The two cases, whether they belonged to Clarence or not, were put up on the rack. Another British officer was leaning out of the window of the wagon-lit and it seemed that he and Clarence were the only passengers on the train.

Guy shook Clarence by the shoulder, trying to waken him: "We're leaving," he said: "We want to say 'good-bye'."

Clarence shrugged Guy off and turning his face to the wall, mumbled: "What do I care?"

"Isn't there anything we can do for him?"

"Nothing," said Harriet. "It's another case of 'Nobody loves poor Aussie'."

The station-master warned them that the train was about to leave and Guy, suddenly upset, said: "We may not see him again."

"Never mind. We must regard that relationship as closed."

But Guy could not regard any relationship as closed. All the way back to Monistiraki he spoke regretfully of Clarence, upset that he had seen so little of an old friend who held him in such high esteem.

"I really liked Clarence," he said as though Clarence had departed from the world.

And, indeed, it seemed to Harriet that Clarence was someone who had disappeared a long time ago and was lost somewhere in the past.

23

MARCH, AS IT MOVED INTO SPRING, was a time of marvels. The British troops were coming in force now, filling the streets with new voices, and the splendour of the new season came with them. The men were wonderful in their variety. As the lorries drove in from the Piraeus, bringing Australians, New Zealanders and Englishmen of different sorts, the Greeks shouted from the pavement: "The Wops are done for. When the snow melts, we'll drive them into the sea."

At mid-day the air was warm as summer. Every waste place had become green and the budding shoots almost at once became flowers. There were flowers everywhere. The old olive groves up the Ilissus Kifissias Road, the grey banks of the Ilissus, the stark, wet clay about the Pringles' villa – all these places dazzled with the reds of anemones and poppies, with hyacinths and wild lupins, acanthus flowers and asphodels. The wastelands of Athens had become a garden.

The flower shops, packed to the doors with flowers, threw out such a scent the streets were filled with it. If there were nothing to eat, there were carnations. Wherever they went, the British soldiers were handed posies and in the bars they received gifts of wine.

People had feared the British expedition. Some had said the British would never fire a shot, that they had only to set foot on Greek soil and the wrath of Germany would descend; but here they were and nothing had been heard from Germany yet.

The snows were melting in Macedonia. The Greek forces, taking fresh heart, would advance again. Any day now there would be new gains and new victories. The fact the Germans had occupied Bulgaria meant nothing very much. At this festival of *philoxenia*, in the midst of spring, the old hopes had returned and people pointed out that Mussolini had made a fool of himself. "Why should the Germans start another front simply to save the Duce's face?" More likely the Germans were enjoying the situation as much as the Greeks. In Athens the promise was: "Victory by Easter; by summer, peace."

The British troops went wherever they liked. The café-owners would not support regulations concerning officers and Other Ranks, and the military police could not keep the men within bounds.

The Greeks, for their part, made no complaints. They expected tumult and enjoyed it. As for the damage: that was also to be expected in a town crowded with foreign troops. They offered their losses up to the Greek cause. When the Australians were confined to barracks, the Greeks were indignant. And Mrs. Brett was indignant. At the canteen she told Harriet how she had been stimulated by contact with men who were "wild in such a natural way".

They had come into the English tea-room while she was taking tea with the padre. There were three of them, each carrying a potted plant which he had lifted from someone's window-sill. The drinking must have started early for they were all unsteady on their feet and one of them, sighting Mrs. Brett, invited her to dance with him. He swayed dangerously over the table and the padre, pointing out that there was no dance-floor and no music, suggested he should sit down. The Australian replied: "Shut up, you pommie bastard."

"Of course I know how to deal with men in that state," Mrs. Brett said. "I've had experience of all sorts, and it pays to be agreeable. Talk to them, get them interested; so I said: 'Sit down, there's a good fellow, and I'll you order you some tea.'"

The Australian had seated himself "like a lamb" but unfortunately knocked over a chair. "That's a crook chair," he said in a threatening way and he began blaming the waiters for the chair's defect. Mrs. Brett, afraid he might start trouble, tried to draw him into conversation: "How are you enjoying Athens?" "What's Athens?" he asked. "Why this is Athens. Where you are now. Isn't it a beautiful city?" "I wouldn't know, mem," he said. "I ain't never seed a city till they brought the draft through Sydney and we was all drunk when we got there." "What do you think of that! That shows judgment –

and honesty! He didn't want any tea but I persuaded him to take a cup. 'To oblige you, mem,' he said, 'I'll even drink the stuff.' We had a nice long chat and he showed me all the photographs in his wallet – Mum and Dad and Sis and so on. D'you know, he became quite attached to me. It was my evening at the canteen – but *could* I get away! No, I could *not*. Every time I stood up, he pulled me down again. 'Don't you go, mem,' he said. 'You stay here and talk to me.' Really, you know, it was quite heart-warming, but the padre got restive. I said: 'Don't be alarmed, padre. I understand men; this poor boy's missing his mother.' 'You're right, mem,' said my Australian: 'I never had a mom like the other fellas.' 'Now, now,' I said: 'What about that snapshot you just showed me?' 'That's the old man's second wife,' he said. 'And a right cow she is!' *What* a fascinating language! At last I said, nicely but firmly: 'I have to go now. You come tomorrow and have tea at my flat and you can tell me all your troubles.' 'Anything you say, mem,' he said, and I wrote down the address. I can't tell you how much I'm looking forward to seeing him again."

But the next day there were no Australians in Athens and Mrs. Brett's new friend did not arrive for tea. When it was discovered later that the whole battalion had been condemned as a menace to the peace of Athens and hurried to camps up north, the Greeks protested: "We liked them like that. They're human. They behaved as they wanted to behave. Not like you English."

Still the fun went on. The English soldiers, their first awkwardness overcome, were found to be human enough. The homage due to the men-at-arms passed over on to the civilians, and in bars and restaurants the English, simply because they were English, received tribute of wine ceremonially laced with slices of apple or sections of orange. Harriet when out with Charles was accorded a special recognition for not only was she English but the companion of an English officer who, according to the Greeks, "had the face of a young Byron".

One day the Athenians were amazed to see Highlanders in the street: men skirted like evzones and carrying bagpipes like the shepherds of Epirus. At the cellar café of Elatos two of them took the floor, placed their knives on the ground and danced, grave-faced, without music, the rhythm marked by the pleats of their kilts that closed and opened about them like fans. As the Scotsmen toed and heeled and turned in unison, the Greeks, intent and silent, understood that this was a ritual dance against the common enemy.

Harriet asked Charles: "Is there a Highland regiment here?"

"God knows," he replied. "Anyone or anything might turn up. The C.O. said: 'Just for the record; don't call this a campaign. Put it down as a skimble-skamble.' "

Harriet never saw the Highlanders again. No one knew where they came from, or where they went. Many of the men appeared in Athens one day and were gone the next. Others remained so long in the suburban camps that their faces became familiar in this bar or that as though they were on native ground; but everyone knew that sooner or later they would be gone. Expectations and preparations were in the air. The rumour that the Italians were asking for terms was not a popular rumour. No one these days wanted the Italians to ask for terms. Imagination was set on a great offensive that would finish the Italians for good and all.

Guy had postponed his production in aid of the Greek war effort. The demand was for entertainment in the camps, where entertainments were few. Immediately after the first landings, he offered the show to the tank corps at Clyfada. The offer was immediately accepted.

While Guy was absorbed into the business of entrepreneur, Charles had nothing to do at all. Like the other men, he awaited a summons, never knowing the day nor the hour when he must pack and go. He belonged to a Northumberland cavalry regiment that was sending units to Greece but had as yet heard nothing of where they would land or when.

"Do you come from Northumberland?" Harriet asked.

"Yes."

"What a long way away!"

"Do you mean from Greece? Surely not much farther than London?"

"Oh, much. Much farther."

They were walking by the sea at Phaleron, covering the same stretch of shore that Harriet and the others had covered on the Christmas walk. Now, in the light of spring air, it was a different shore. The sea was tender, the waves creeping in over sand that sparkled in the crystal light. Here, by the Mediterranean, looking across the blue of the water towards the blue-blacks and harebell colours of the Peleponnese, Northumberland seemed as remote as the Arctic.

"A distant country," she sang. "The edge of the world. Dark, silent, mysterious and far away."

He laughed: "You're thinking of Siberia."

"Perhaps. Will it soon be warm enough to bathe?"

She had taken off her shoes and stockings but the water was glacial.

Charles had hoped they might find a restaurant open even though Harriet said on Christmas Day they had been all boarded up. Christmas was winter, he said. Now it was spring and the restaurants would be re-opening. He was wrong. They were still boarded up.

Barefoot in the white, powdery sand, feeling the edges of the shells, and the black, dry scratch of seaweed, Harriet was drawn on by a dream that the restaurant keeper who had fed them at Christmas might be there again; and she imagined Charles delighted as she had been delighted. When they came to the wooden hut on stilts, she ran up the steps and looked in through the window, but the place was deserted. She remained on the balcony with her hands on the boarding, feeling the warmth of the wood, while Charles watched her from the shore, puzzled by her behaviour.

She said: "There's no one here."

"I should have thought that was obvious. If we don't get back, we'll get nothing at all."

Walking back she told him about the man who had fed them with fish bought for his own family. Charles said nothing, not wanting to hear of any part of her past in which he had no part.

Before they left the beach, she found a branch that had been washed a long time in the sea and now, thrown clear during the winter, was dried, bleached and so glossy it seemed to be some substance other than wood. She still had it in her hand when they came opposite the bus stop. The bus was coming. As he made towards the esplanade, saying: "If we can't get anything else, we can get tea at the Corinthian," she wandered down to the water's edge, unwilling to leave the dazzle of the shore.

Finding she had not followed him, he ran back to her.

"How fortunate we are! It will be wonderful here in the

summer," she said, as though their friendship would go on for ever.

"The bus is coming." He took the branch from her hand and flung it a long way out to sea. His single, accomplished movement, like that of a cricketer pitching a ball into a field, startled her and she said: "You're only a schoolboy. You remind me of Sasha," suddenly seeing his contrarieties as no more than the defences of youth.

He appeared not to hear her. Telling her to put on her stockings and shoes, he went to the bus-stop and asked the driver to wait. On the journey back he seemed in an even humour but, while they sat talking happily at the Corinthian, he broke in on their contentment, accusing her: "I suppose you've always had someone like me to trail round after you?"

"Why do you say that?"

"It is true, isn't it?"

"No, it's not. It's simply stupid."

"Then who was Sasha?"

When she saw him again after the meeting with Clarence, Charles had asked: Who was Clarence? What was he doing there? Harriet said: "He's gone to Salonika. He's in Greece to protect business interests."

"Oh, that lot!" Charles's scorn had extingushed Clarence and she had heard no more about him. Sasha would be less easy to explain away. She had been unwise in mentioning him but, having mentioned him, she had to explain. "He was a boy we knew in Rumania. His father was a banker. The father was arrested on a faked-up charge, and the son was forced into the army. He had a wretched time but, worse than that, he was in danger of being murdered because he was a Jew; so he deserted and came to Guy for help. He had been one of Guy's students. We hid him for a few months. That is all."

But not enough for Charles. That she had related Sasha to him, that she had spoken Sasha's name in a special tone: these things roused Charles's suspicions and only the most complete vindication of them could satisfy him.

She said: "If you like, I will tell you the whole story."

His voice cold with mistrust, he said: "All right. Go ahead."

As she described Sasha's innocent gentleness, the affection he had roused in her and the plan to smuggle him from Rumania that was frustrated by his disappearance, Charles was reassured. How strange, she thought, that someone who had so many advantages in life needed to be reassured!

He said: "You will never know what became of him?"

"I suppose not. The Legation was our last hope; but now we've broken off relations with Rumania. It's an enemy country."

Sasha was finished and done with: and Charles, free to sympathize, touched her hand with a contrite movement and said: "That day, when you ran after me into the shop, I knew . . ."

"What?"

"That you needed me."

"But surely you must have known from the beginning . . ."

"Why? How could I know? Why should you need me? You're married. You seem quite happily married. You have a husband whom everyone likes and admires. There was no reason why you should need me."

"What did you think, then?"

"I . . . well, I thought you were simply playing a game with me; amusing yourself while Guy was at work."

She smiled and shook her head.

"There are girls who want to bowl over every man they meet, just to prove they can do it. You might have been like that."

"But I'm not. You're important to me; you know that."

"Yes; but why? I really don't know why."

"You're a friend."

"Is that all?"

"A particular friend. You are what I need most: a companion."

"But only that? Nothing more?" He leant towards her and, moved by his looks, his ardent expectations, she felt the air charged between them. Her lips parted; she turned her head away and said: "If it were possible . . ."

"You mean it is impossible?"

"You know it is. I have to think of Guy."

He took that to be no more than conventional resistance Catching her hand, he glanced towards the wide carpeted stair-way that led from the foyer to the upper floors, and said: "We can't talk here. Come up to my room."

The impulse to please him almost drew her from her seat, but as she turned towards the stairs she saw faces that were familiar to her: Dobson's woman friend was present; there were girls who went to the School or used the School library. Knowing how easily she could become a centre of gossip, she was chilled and drew her hand away. Laughing uneasily, she said: "What would these people think if they saw me going upstairs with you?"

"Does it matter what they think?"

"That's a stupid question. I live here. Guy works here." While she spoke the waiter brought their tea-tray and she hid her confusion by pouring the tea. She imagined he would be sulking, probably blaming her for an ungenerous caution, but when she turned to hand him his cup, she found his gaze fixed on her with an expression of hurt entreaty that was more compelling than ardour. She was surprised and moved, but everything that came into her head seemed to her trite, heartless and flirtatious, so she said nothing. They took their tea in silence.

Several days passed before he made any reference to this incident. They were walking in the gardens and coming on the pergola where the wisteria was putting out a lace of leaves, he said.

"Tà kaïména tà neiáto
Ti grígorá pou pernoun ..."

She looked inquiringly at him.

"You must have heard that song," he said. " 'Poor youth, how quickly it passes: like a love song, like a shooting-star, and when it is gone, it never comes again.' "

Knowing he was blaming her for a waste of passion and misuse of time, she said: "It would be better if we did not meet again."

"Do you mean that?"

"I don't know."

"You must know."

"I only know this is an impossible situation."

"If you want me to go, I won't trouble you again."

"If you want to go, I can't stop you."

"But I don't want to go."

It was an argument carried on in the fatuity of emotional intoxication and they both knew that it would lead to nothing.

24

Guy had stopped singing the 'fun and frolic' chorus about the house. In the mornings, while bathing, shaving, dressing and preparing for the imponderables of the day, he sang in an energetic, swinging tune that stood up to his lack of tone:

"Oh, what a surprise for the Duce, the Duce!
He can't put it over the Greeks."

The words amused her at first but they soon reached a point of unendurable familiarity.

"Is that the *only* song in the revue now?" Harriet asked, speaking grudgingly, for she resented the revue and hardly ever mentioned it. Guy always had had, and always would have, some preoccupation or other, but she had persuaded herself that were it not for the revue she would not have turned to other company. Delighted by her interest, Guy did not give her the chance to add that if there were another song, she would prefer it, but rushed in to say how much the revue had improved since she had seen it in the Tatoi hangar. Then it had been no more than a parish hall show; but since the arrival of the troops the British residents, seeing the war in Greece as their own war, had taken up the revue in a remarkable way. The chorus was twice the size and made twice as much noise and the troops joining in singing the songs. Greek songs like "Oh what a surprise for the Duce" had been translated into English, and special songs had been composed by an English businessman in honour of Greco-British unity. All the camps were clamouring for the revue. Everyone wanted to see it. It was a stupendous success.

"What about Pinkrose?"

"Not a squeak out of him. He knows he's defeated."

"I can see you're having the time of your life."

"You'd enjoy it. Come and see it tonight. We're going to

Kifissia for a special show and the Naafi are supplying refreshments for the cast. Do come."

Harriet had her own plans for that evening. "I don't think I can," she said, but Guy bent over her and, catching her by the shoulders, looked down on her with an urgent and questioning intentness, saying: "I would like you to come."

"Then of course I will."

"Fine." He was away at once, hurrying round, looking for this and that. The military lorries were picking up the cast and visitors in Kolonaki Square. "I suppose you can get out of the office early?"

"I suppose so. I was seeing Charles. Do you mind if I bring him?"

"Bring anyone you like, but make sure you come yourself."

He was gone. Harriet watched him through the large window as he slammed the front door behind him and sped up the lane past the villa, impelled by all the activities he had planned for the day.

Yakimov said of Guy: "He's a dear, sweet fellow, but he doesn't understand how you feel." She had thought Yakimov was right. Now she thought Guy saw more than he would admit to seeing, understood more than he appeared to understand; but he would not let observation or understanding impede him. He was a generous man, anyway in material matters. He loved her, but his love must be taken for granted. If she put it to the proof according to her needs, she found herself sacrificed to what he saw as a more important need: his need to be free to do what he wanted to do. Challenged, he never lacked justification. He did not recognize emotional responsibility and, unlike emotional people, he was not governed by it. She suffered compunction; he did not. It was compunction – a quite uncalled-for compunction – that caused her to disappoint Charles, who had booked a table at Babayannis', and demanded that he go to Kifissia instead. She knew that he enjoyed being fêted at Babayannis', but they could go there any night. She was surprised, shocked, even, when he refused to go to Kifissia.

The office had been stirred by the news that Yugoslavia had been presented with a German ultimatum. The fate of Yugoslavia presaged the fate of Greece; yet, in the face of this new crisis, Charles and Harriet could do no more than bicker over their evening's entertainment.

They went into the Zappion Gardens where everything was bright with spring, but nothing was bright for them. Each looked inward on a private injury, determined not to yield a point to the other.

Charles kept his face turned from her but he spoke in an agreeable tone that was as cruel as a threat: "Don't worry about me. There are other things I can do. I've been neglecting my friends lately. I ought to write some letters. In fact, I shall be glad to have a free evening."

"We have to think of Guy," Harriet said. "I promised him ..."

"And you promised me; you promised me first. Still, it doesn't matter. Please don't worry. I shall be quite happy on my own."

"Guy does not object to my seeing you. He's not mean or demanding; we owe him one evening. I think we ought to go ..."

"*You* ought to go, certainly."

"We will have other evenings ..."

"Perhaps; and perhaps not."

"What do you mean by that?"

Pale and inflexible, he stared down at the path and shrugged his shoulders. "This Yugoslavia business. If they reject the ultimatum, every available man will be rushed to the frontier."

The argument was not resolved but it came to a stop. They passed under the trees and came to the pond where children were playing in the water. Everything was in leaf and flower, but all without meaning. At the pond they turned and walked back to Constitution Square.

Though it was too early for the office, Harriet paused at the side entrance of the hotel and Charles walked on without a word. She called: "Charles." He looked round and she ran to him and took both his hands: "*Please* come to Kifissia," she said.

He frowned and reflected, then said: "Very well," but he said it with a poor grace.

"Call for me here. Come early, won't you?"

"Yes." He walked off, his face still sullen, but she did not doubt he would come as agreed. As she had expected, he was waiting outside when she left the office. He refused to speak as they went to Kolonaki where the lorries waited, surrounded by Guy's company, a few people known to her and a great many unknown.

Driving out of Athens, they passed the Yugoslav legation where the Greeks had gathered to sympathize with a country threatened like their own. So far as they knew, Yugoslavia was still considering the German ultimatum. Ben Phipps said he had faith in the ability of Prince Paul who would "box clever", but Guy thought the Yugoslavs would fight.

He asked the driver to stop and jumped down from the lorry in order to add his condolence and encouragement to the demonstration. Whenever an official could be seen at one of the legation windows, the Greeks applauded but the Yugoslavs looked glum.

Ben, leaning over the lorry side, called to Guy: "Come on. We're going to be late," and, when Guy returned, said: "Oh, dry the silent tear for *they* – are going to cave in."

Guy nodded sadly and said: "You may be right."

Kifissia was fragrant with the spring. The houses and gardens that rose towards Pendeli were still caught in the honey gold of the evening sun while the shadowed area of the main road held a counter glow that was an intimation of summer. The lorry drew up beneath the pepper trees and as the passengers jumped down, the trees trembled in the first breeze of sunset.

The Naafi had hired a hall that had been unused since war began. Boxes of sandwiches and cakes, sent for the performers, were being carried into the back entrance. The lorry passengers followed, filing through a narrow, neglected orchard that was full of the scent of citrus blossom. The dark hall, when they reached it, smelt of nothing but dust. Charles touched Harriet's arm to detain her, saying: "Need we go in?"

"I must see some of it."

"Let's wait till it begins."

Left behind by the others in the sweet outdoor air, Harriet smiled at Charles, coaxing him to smile back. From a camp somewhere in the distance came the Call which Harriet had heard in Bucharest coming from the palace yard. Feeling a nostalgia for lost time, she said: "Do you know what that says? 'Come, water your horses, all you that are able. Come, water your horses and give them some corn. And he that won't do it, the sergeant shall know it; he will be whipped and put in a dark hole.' "

"Who told you that?" Charles jealously asked.

"I don't know. I think Guy told me. There's another Call that says: 'Officers be damned; officers be damned.' "

"The Officers' Call." Charles still looked sullen.

They could hear Miss Jay striking chords on the piano and Harriet took his arm and led him inside. They sat in the back row beside Alan Frewen, Yakimov and Ben Phipps, who would not be required until after the interval.

Soldiers were filling the front rows. There were not many British troops left in Attika. There were New Zealanders, tall, sun-burnt men who seemed to maintain their seriousness like a reserve of power.

The airmen, Surprise and the others, had adapted themselves to their precarious, volatile life by treating it as a joke; the infantrymen, with feet on the ground, might find life funny but knew it was no joke.

Imagining their remote, peaceful islands, Harriet wondered what had brought the New Zealanders to Europe? What quarrel had they here? They seemed to her the most inoffensive of men. Why had they come all this way to die? She felt, as a civilian, her own liability in the presence of the fighting men who were kept in camps, like hounds trained for the kill. However close one came to them, they must remain separate. Charles had warned her that, sooner or later, he would have to go. And soon they would all be gone.

When the soldiers had occupied the first dozen rows, the civilians waiting at the front entrance were admitted to any seats that remained. A great many people, Greek and English, had heard of the revue and had driven out to Kifissia in hope of seeing it. The hall was filled in a few minutes, then the curtain jerked open and the chorus, ordered to make immediate impact, rushed on, breathless before they had even begun to sing. Miss Jay struck a blow at the piano and the men in mess jackets, the women in blue and white ballet skirts began "Koroido Mussolini", the song that described the Italians at war:

"They stay inside because it's raining
And send communiqués to Rome,
In which for ever they're complaining:
'It's wet, so can we please go home?' "

The whole song sung, Guy, wearing a borrowed white mess jacket that would not button across his middle, came out as conductor of the revels. He demanded a repeat performance from the audience which, willing enough to participate and enjoy, sang louder and louder as Guy sang and waved his hands, exhorting those in front to give as much as he gave himself. He brought the hall to a state of uproar.

Ben Phipps, sitting hands in pockets, with chair tilted back and heels latched on to the seat before him, gave a guff of laughter and said: "Look at him!" It was a jeer yet, unwillingly, as he repeated "*Look at him!*" admiration came into his voice:

"What can you do with a man like that? What's it all about, anyway? Where's it going to get him?"

Where indeed! Harriet, scarcely able to bear the sight of Guy cavorting on the stage, felt a contraction in her chest. She remembered how she had watched him haranguing the stage-hands in Bucharest, expending himself like radium in order to give two performances of an amateur production that would be forgotten in a week. She had thought then that if she could she would seize on Guy and canalize his zeal to make a mark on eternity. She felt now she had expected too much from him. He was a profligate of life. The physical energy and intelligence that had seemed to her a fortune to be conserved and invested, would be frittered away. And there was no restraining him. She might as well try to restrain a whirlwind. Watching him now, she felt despair.

The first half of the revue ended, the cast of *Maria Marten* went behind to dress.

Charles said: "You don't want to see that play again, do you? Let's go for a walk."

She had, in fact, been looking forward to the play, but she followed him out into the twilight of the orchard where moths moved through the damp, night-chilly air. The pepper trees were disappearing into a fog of turquoise and violet. A single light showed between the looped curtains of a taverna. Some men were gathered outside on the pavement, the only life in the suburban street.

It would soon be dark. Charles suggested they follow a lane that went uphill between the gardens in a scent of orange and lemon flower. Here there was no noise but the croak of frogs. Above the gardens, they came into an olive grove where the undergrowth, dotted over with a white confetti of flowers, reached higher than their knees. Walking through it, they trod out the sharp, bitter scent of daisies and startled the grasshoppers into a see-saw of sound.

Though he had managed to take her away from any company but his own, Charles was not prepared to talk. She commented on things and asked questions but could not get an answer from him. His unrelenting ill-humour filled her with a sense of failure. Why need time be wasted in this way? She felt him to be intolerably demanding and ungenerous, yet she was despondent because, in a few days, he would be gone and they might never meet again.

War meant a perpetual postponement of life, yet one did not cease to grow old. She had been twenty-one when it started. At the end, if there ever was an end, what age would she be? How could she blame Guy for dissipating his energies when all the resources of life were being dissipated? What else could he do? War was a time when mediocrities came to the top and better men must rot or die in the conflict.

As for Charles, whose prospects had been so much more promising than theirs, how must he feel at seeing his youth wasted on his present futile employment? He was uncomplaining, of course. His education and upbringing required him to be uncomplaining, but what secret misery did he express in his petulance and silences and sudden shows of temper?

She stopped speaking herself until Charles said: "There's a walk along the top of Pendeli. It's rather fine. We might go up there one day."

She looked up to the spine of the hill that showed black against the stars. "Would we be allowed to go as far as that?"

"I think so. Anyway, I could get permits."

"When could we go?"

"We'll have to wait until the weather is settled. It can be cold on the top, and there's no shelter if it rains."

The quarrel, it seemed, was forgotten. Despite their uncertain future, they planned the walk as a possible, even probable, event in the time ahead. Harriet thought Guy would come and they wondered who else might join the excursion.

Talking, they made their way back between the gardens. By the time they reached the hall, they had decided to arrange the walk early in April.

Charles said: "The first Sunday in April would be a good day."

"Will you still be here?"

Charles walked up the length of the orchard path before he muttered: "How do I know?"

Inside the hall the chorus, giving encore after encore, sang:

> "Oh, what a surprise for the Duce, the Duce,
> He can't put it over the Greeks."

Harriet and Charles went behind the stage where the refreshments would be served. The wooden trays covered with tissue paper were stacked one on top of the other. The cast of *Maria Marten,* back into everyday dress, were waiting for food and as the chorus waved the audience away and the hall emptied at last, Ben Phipps slapped his hands together and said: "Now for the grub; and, *mein Gott, ich habe Hunger."*

"Haven't we all, dear boy," said Yakimov giving a whinny of gleeful anticipation. As he moved towards the trays, Mrs. Brett pushed him aside and said: "All right, Prince Yaki, I'm in charge of this department. I'll do the honours." She lifted down the top tray and removed the paper. The tray was empty. The tray beneath it was empty. All the trays were empty. A crust or two, a single cherry, some fluted paper cups, proved that food had been there once.

Some local men, hired to put out the chairs and act as stage-hands, were gathered with their women at the back door, watching, blank-faced and silent. Mrs. Brett turned and raged at them in a mixture of Greek and English.

Smirking in embarrassment, they shook their heads and held out their hands, palms up; they had nothing, they knew nothing.

Guy said: "They were hungry. Say nothing more about it."

"We're all hungry. They'd've got their share," Mrs. Brett faced the employed men again, saying: "If you didn't eat it all, where is it?" They looked at one another in wonder. Who could tell?

Their perplexity was so convincing, several people glanced suspiciously at Yakimov, but Yakimov's disappointment was plain. He picked up the crusts and ate them one by one, leaving the cherry for the last. Wetting a forefinger and pressing it down on the crumbs, he murmured: "Sponge-cake."

Mrs. Brett said: "We should have placed a guard on the food. But, there you are! One thinks of these things too late."

The weary players went for their coats. Ben Phipps, seeing a telephone on a table, lifted it and, finding it connected, shouted to Guy: "Half a mo': let's see if anything's happened." He rang the Stefani Agency. The others stood around while Ben, his eyes shifting from side to side, shouted: "They've signed, eh? They've signed . . ." He nodded knowingly to Guy: "What did I say? While you were demonstrating your solidarity, it was all over. Paul's made a clever deal. The Germans will respect Yugoslav territory."

They climbed into the lorry and sat close together in the cold night air while Guy affirmed his faith in the Yugoslavs: "They'll never stand for an alliance with Hitler."

"Be your age," Ben said. "If they can keep the Germans out, they'll save their bacon and probably save ours as well. If Hitler can't move through Yugoslavia, he'll be left sitting on the Bulgarian frontier. It's less than 300 kilometres, all mountain country. Olympus is our strong-point. We could trap the bastards behind the Aliakmon and keep them trapped for months."

In spite of their hunger, in spite of the cold, in spite of themselves, the passengers in the lorry felt a lift of hope. Their new enemy might in the end be the saviour of them all.

PART FOUR

The Funeral

25

ON THE MORNING FOLLOWING the submission of Yugoslavia, the office boy, summoned by Lord Pinkrose, returned to the Billiard Room with a foolscap draft of material to be typed.

All such material went first to Miss Gladys who would look through it, then, with explanation and encouraging noises, set her sister to work. If anything of particular interest came to hand, she would keep it for herself.

The foolscap sheet caused her to squeak with excitement and she ordered the boy to bring her typewriter to her desk. Her preparations for work were always protracted. This morning there seemed no end to them. As she fidgeted with the typing paper, her grunts and gasps and heavy breathing told Harriet that the foolscap sheet contained matter of unusual import. She supposed it must relate to the Yugoslav situation. The Legation had telephoned Alan warning him that refugees from Belgrade were moving towards Greece, the direction left to them.

Harriet had been in the News Room that morning when the call came. While she waited to speak to Alan, Pinkrose entered and signalled that he had something to say more important than anything that might be said by the Legation. His chameleon face was grey with the sweat of panic. He drummed on the desk, too agitated to know or care that Harriet and Yakimov were watching him.

Imagining that Pinkrose's needs were more pressing than those of the refugees, Alan apologized to his caller, put down the receiver and turned his long-suffering gaze upon the Director of Propaganda.

Pinkrose shot a finger at the map on the News Room wall: "You see what's happened, Frewen? You see ... you see ...!"

Alan moved round slowly in his chair. Harriet and Yakimov

lifted their heads. They all looked up at the Greek peninsula that flew like a tattered banner towards Africa.

"They've got everything," Pinkrose panted. "The Italians are in Albania. The Germans have got Bulgaria and Yugoslavia. They've got the whole frontier."

Yakimov murmured in admiring awe: "So they have, dear boy!"

"What's going to happen here, I'd like to know? Something's got to be done. I was sent here in error. I came to the Balkans in all innocence. All innocence. Yes, all innocence. No one knew the dangers; they don't know now. If they did, they would order me back. But the Organization is bound to repatriate me; it is in my agreement. And now's the time. Yes, now's the time. I want it fixed up without delay."

"I have nothing to do with the Organization," Alan said with even patience. "You are the Organization head. Surely it's up to you to fix your repatriation?"

"I *am* fixing it. I'm fixing it now. Here and now. Yes, yes, here and now, I'm putting it into your hands, Frewen. I look to you."

"Oh? Well! I don't know what I can do, but I'll make inquiries. There's no regular transport; you know that. I've heard it suggested that a civilian – one of the top brass, of course – might, if the need arose, be given a lift to Egypt by the R.A.F."

"I came on a service plane," Pinkrose said eagerly. "I travelled in a bomb bay."

"Did you indeed! Well, I'll see what I can do."

"Yes, yes, see what you can do. Give it top priority. Treat it as an emergency. Let me know within the next hour."

"Good heavens, the next hour! I won't hear anything within the next week. There may be nothing for six weeks."

"Six weeks? *Six weeks!* You speak in jest, Frewen."

"I do not speak in jest. These things take time."

Pinkrose's face quivered. Drawing in his breath, he cried in agony: "Then I'm trapped?"

"We're all trapped, if it comes to that. But I see no immediate cause for alarm. The situation's no worse. If anything, it looks a bit brighter. The Germans have agreed to respect Yugoslav sovereignty; they say they won't send troops through

Yugoslavia. I know you can't trust them, but they'll be tied up for a bit."

Pinkrose stared at Alan, then asked in a small voice: "Where did you get this?"

"It's official. And what about the lecture? Are we to call that off?"

Pinkrose swallowed in his throat and looked down at the floor. "No," he said after a long pause, "I was precipitous, Frewen, I was precipitous. Hold your hand a while."

"You don't want me to try to arrange a flight?"

"No. My duty is here. The lecture is of paramount importance. It must be given. Yes, it must be given. And there are other matters ..." Turning abruptly, he hurried off to attend to them.

One of the other matters was no doubt now on Miss Gladys's desk. She had just begun to type it when Pinkrose flustered in with another foolscap sheet. "Here's the rest," he said and, speaking in a low, intimate and conspiratorial tone, he called Miss Gladys over to a table by the wall. Pushing the maps away and spreading the sheet out, he whispered: "Read it through. Tell me if there's anything you don't understand."

A long interval followed, during which Pinkrose, running his pencil along the lines, muttered under his breath and Miss Gladys whispered: "I understand, Lord Pinkrose, I understand."

Feeling that her presence was intrusive, Harriet decided to go to the News Room. As she rose, the others were alerted. The muttering ceased. They turned to watch where she might go. She passed Miss Gladys's desk and stopped. Miss Gladys had typed: *REPORT ON GUY PRINGLE. In my opinion Guy Pringle is unsuited for Organization work . . .* Harriet picked up the draft.

In a stern tone, Miss Gladys said: "How dare you touch that! That's a confidential report."

Harriet read on. In the opinion of Pinkrose Guy had dangerous left-wing tendencies. He was a trouble-maker who mixed with notorious Greeks. He had become a centre of sedition and was disapproved by all responsible persons in Athens.

"What a pack of lies!" she said.

Further, he had staged an obscene production and complaints had been received from prominent members of the British colony. The Director had banned the production. In spite of that, Pringle was visiting army camps with a play liable to demoralize all who saw it ...

"*Lord* Pinkrose!" Miss Gladys turned on her superior, indignant that he should give her no support, and Pinkrose began obediently to chatter:

"Put it down. Put it down, I tell you. Put it down."

Harriet put it down and asked: "What else have you written?"

"It's nothing to do with you." As she approached, Pinkrose snatched up the paper: "You have no right ..." he shouted. The paper shook in his hand.

"Oh, yes, I have a right. The Organization does not permit confidential reports. If you write a report on Guy's work, you're required to show it to him. He's supposed to sign it."

"Sauce!" said Miss Gladys.

"Required! Required, indeed! I'm the Director; I'm not *required* to do anything ..." Beside himself with indignation, Pinkrose let his voice rise and at once Miss Mabel began to moan and give little cries of terror.

Miss Gladys spat at Harriet: "Go away. You're upsetting my sister."

"Yes, go away," Pinkrose screamed. "Leave this office. At once. You hear me, at once."

Harriet went to her desk and gathered up her belongings. "Before I go," she said, grandiloquent with rage, "I must say: I am surprised that at a time like this, anyone – even *you* Lord Pinkrose – could stoop to intrigue with Cookson, Dubedat and Lush in order to injure a man who is worth more than the whole lot of you put together."

She went out. Alan and Yakimov were peacefully drinking the first ouzo of the day when she burst in on them to say:

"I'm going."

"Where?" Alan asked.

"Pinkrose has sacked me; but if he hadn't, I'd go anyway."

"Have a drink first."

"No."

Near hysteria, she ran to the church hall. It was shut. She took a taxi to the School. No one there had seen Guy since early morning. She went to Aleko's. The café was empty. She walked back down Stadium Street looking into every café and bar she passed, and came to Zonar's. Guy was not to be found.

Harriet was meeting Charles at the Corinthian. As she walked towards the hotel, Guy's voice, loud and cheerful, came to her from the distance.

She saw him helping the driver to take luggage from a taxi. The luggage was being heaped up beside a man who, impressive and large in a fur hat, fur-lined overcoat and fur-topped boots, had the familiarity of a figure in a fairy-tale. Harriet at that moment had no eyes for him but seized on Guy, furiously asking: "Where have you been?"

"To the station, to meet the Belgrade Express."

"Why?"

Guy stared at Harriet as though only she would not know why. "I thought David Boyd would be on it."

"Oh!" Harriet subsided. "And was he?"

"No. He hasn't turned up yet. But . . ." Guy indicated that he had not returned empty-handed. Indeed, he seemed to think he had brought back a prize. Presenting the large, be-furred man: "This is Roger Tandy," he said.

Harriet had heard of Tandy. When he passed through Bucharest, he had been described in the papers as "the famous traveller". That had been before Harriet's time but Guy had met him briefly, and Tandy, famous traveller or not, had been grateful to see a familiar face when he turned up in Athens among the refugees from Belgrade. He and Guy had fallen on each other like old friends. Now Guy, playing the host, unloading and counting his luggage, wanted to know: "How many cases should there be?"

Tandy replied: "Only seven. I travel light."

Other taxis were off-loading other refugees – political refugees, religious refugees, racial refugees, and English wives with small children. The hotel would be crowded, but Roger Tandy did not seem concerned. He seated himself beside an outdoor table and said pleasantly to Harriet: "Come, my dear. Before we go in, we'll have a little snifter."

"Hadn't you better make sure of your room?"

"No need. I booked well in advance. At my age one knows which way the wind is blowing."

"Better make sure," Guy said, and he sped into the hotel to confirm Tandy's booking.

Tandy patted the chair beside him.

Harriet, overwhelmed both by his looks and his foresight, sat down. His face was plum-red and his moustache was the colour of fire. The two reds were so remarkable, it was some minutes before she noticed that the little snub nose, the little pink mouth and the small, wet, yellow-brown eyes were altogether commonplace.

The midday sun was hot. Tandy's face broke out in globules of sweat. He threw open his greatcoat and unbuttoned the jacket of his cinnamon twill suit, and the sun gleamed on his waistcoat of emerald and gold brocade. His waistcoat buttons were balls of gold filigree. The eyes of passers-by, lighting first on Tandy's waistcoat, became fixed when they saw that his greatcoat was lined to the hem with resplendent honey-golden fur. One of the passers-by was Yakimov. He was on his bicycle, his own greatcoat, looped up for safety, also displaying a fur lining, but the fur had been old when Yakimov was young.

Yakimov wobbled into the pavement, put out a foot and somehow managed to get down. "Dear girl," he called to Harriet, "is everything all right?"

She was reminded of her anxiety of the morning but felt this was no time to discuss it. In any case, she saw that Yakimov had stopped for one reason and one reason only. He meant to meet Tandy.

Introducing the two men, Harriet stressed Yakimov's title. Tandy's eyes grew sharp with interest.

"Sit down, *mon prince*," he said, "and join us in a snifter."

Yakimov sat down at once. His own eyes, large and tender, examined, with no hint of envy, the immense, well-fed figure of Tandy who was dressed as, in better days, he would have dressed himself. The waiter was recalled and Yakimov asked for a brandy. It came at once and as he put it to his lips his excitement was evident. It seemed a destined meeting and saying: "I must go and speak to Guy," Harriet left them to find each other.

Guy was among the crowd at the desk. "I want to tell you something," she said.

Giving one ear to her and the other to the cross-currents about him, Guy said: "Go ahead."

"No. Come over here." Exasperated by the fact he was worrying over Tandy's welfare as he would never worry over his own, she pulled him out of the press and said: "I've something important to tell you."

As Harriet told her story Guy's attention was on the bright out-of-doors and the enticing prospect of Tandy and Yakimov who at that moment were joined by Alan Frewen. She held on to him, and speaking quickly, gave the substance of Pinkrose's report.

Guy, frowning, said: "It's not important, surely. No one's going to take any notice of Pinkrose."

"Why not? He was appointed Director. They didn't appoint him in order to ignore him."

"Perhaps not; but they must know the sort of man he is. I've seen reports that Inchcape sent on my work. They were excellent. First-class. If Pinkrose sends in this report – and, after what you said, he may realize he's doing the wrong thing – it will be compared with the others. They don't relate. Someone's talking nonsense and it isn't Inchcape."

"How are they to know it isn't Inchcape?"

"He'll be called in. He'll be consulted."

"He may be dead by then."

"I don't think so. Inch always took good care of himself. He'll be flourishing; and I know he'll stand by me."

"Will he? I wonder!"

"You're making too much out of this." Impatient of her fears, he patted her shoulder and was ready to depart. "Come and talk to Tandy. I've always wanted to meet him."

"You go. I'll come in a minute."

Without waiting to wonder what there could be to detain her inside the hotel, Guy sped off like a child allowed out to play. When he was through the door, Harriet took herself to the dining-room where she had arranged to meet Charles. She was very late.

Charles, at luncheon, got to his feet and waited for her to defend herself. She cut at once through any likely accusations by saying: "I've lost my job."

"I didn't know anyone could lose a job these days."

"It wasn't incompetence. I had a row with Pinkrose."

Charles, forced to laugh, motioned her to join him at the table.

She said: "I can't stay. Guy is expecting me."

"Oh!" His laughter came to a stop.

He sat blank-faced, while she told the story of the report and concluded: "You know, this could wreck Guy's career with the Organization."

"I'm sure it couldn't. There are more jobs than men ..."

"I'm thinking of the future when there'll be more men than jobs."

"The future?" Charles looked puzzled as though the future were some unlikely concept he had not studied before, then he glanced aside: "Yes, you must consider the future. You complain of Guy but you don't intend to leave him."

"Do I complain of Guy?"

"If you don't, why are you wasting your time with me? You can't pretend to love me?"

"I don't pretend anything. But perhaps I do love you. I would like to feel we were friends for the rest of our lives."

"Yes, indeed! You want me hanging around. You have a husband, but you must have some sort of *cavaliere servente* as well. There are a lot of women like that." Throwing his napkin aside, he got to his feet. "I can't stand any more of this. I'm going up to my room. If you want to see me, you'll find me there. If you don't come, I'll know you never want to see me again."

"This is too silly—"

"If you don't come, you never *will* see me again."

"An ultimatum?" Harriet said.

"Yes, an ultimatum." He marched off, attracting attention as he passed through the room. He was watched, Harriet saw, not only with admiration, but something near tenderness. She could imagine that for these people he presented an ideal image of the ally who, with nothing to gain, had made this foolhardy venture to fight beside the Greeks. She herself had seen him a symbol touching and poetic of the sacrificial victims of war. Now she knew him better she scarcely knew how she saw him. He passed through the door, angered and injured, and made off to nurse his injury somewhere out of sight.

One thing was certain: she would not go after him. She would make sure of that by joining Guy and the other men outside, but not at once. Lingering in the dining-room, she saw again his swift, exact movement out of the room and felt drawn to follow him. Not knowing what to do, she sat on as though expecting something or someone to make the decision for her. Or perhaps Charles would come back, rather shame-faced, and treat his ultimatum as a joke.

Instead, Alan Frewen came to look for her. He said they were all going round to Zonar's. He did not ask what she was doing there, alone in the dining-room, sitting opposite some-one's uneaten meal, and she realized he did not need to be told. He asked nothing, and said nothing. He did not criticize his fellow men; nor did he wish to become involved in their prob-lems.

"Guy thought you would like to come with us?"

"Yes. I'll come with you."

As they passed through the foyer, she glanced up the stair-case with a vision in mind of Charles hurrying down to her. But there was no one on the stair and no sign of Charles.

Alan said: "Surely you haven't left the office for good? I need someone to edit my notes on the German broadcasts to Greece."

Harriet was beginning to regret her lost employment, but said: "I can't work in the Billiard Room with the Twocurrys."

"I thought you'd have more space there; but if you like, you can join Yaki and me in the News Room."

"I'd like that," she said.

26

PRINCE PAUL CLAIMED THAT HE and his faction had saved Yugoslavia. Perhaps they had unintentionally saved Greece. No one had time to find out. The Regent was gone in a night and next morning all the talk was about revolution. The Regency was terminated. Peter had displaced Paul. The quisling ministers had been arrested. The English, Americans and Russians were being cheered in the streets of Belgrade, and the whole of Yugoslavia was a ferment of rejoicings and anti-Axis demonstrations.

"Magnificent," said Ben Phipps. "But what happens next?"

"It's magnificent," Guy said, "chiefly because they didn't stop to ask what happens next. They could not accept German domination. They revolted against it without counting the cost. That was certainly magnificent. And what would have happened in any case? Would the Germans have kept the terms of the agreement?"

Called to order, Ben murmured: "Not very likely," and Harriet noted that these days Guy was more inclined to call Ben Phipps to order and Ben Phipps more ready to agree with him. As a result, although she still disliked Phipps, she was less resentful of his influence over Guy.

"Still," he said. "What *will* happen next?"

Tandy grunted once or twice and Guy and Ben looked at him. He spoke seldom. When he did speak, it was slowly, with pauses and grunts that promised some deep-set thought, not easily brought to birth. Now, at last reaching the point of speech, he said: "We must wait and see."

Waiting to see, they waited in the ambience of Tandy who spent most of his day at Zonar's, usually at an outdoor table he had adopted as 'his own. He could always be found by anyone in need of companionship. Although he had only just arrived and might soon be returning whence he had come, he was already an established figure in Athens. Large and splendid, he seemed, in a changing world, permanent and unchanging. People gathered about him as about a village oak.

Tandy came like a gift, a distraction heaven-sent, just when the fine hopes of March were changing to doubts again. Guy had discovered him but Phipps took him up with enthusiasm, and Yakimov clung to him like a lover. In spite of his fame, no one knew much about him. From occasional remarks, they gathered he had begun the war very comfortably in Trieste but, fearing to be trapped there, had moved to Belgrade shortly before the Italians entered against the Allies.

"Doesn't do to stay anywhere too long," he said.

Ben Phipps said: "You certainly left Belgrade in good time."

Tandy gave him a reproving look. He said nothing then but later conveyed, almost without words, the fact that his flight from Belgrade had not been impetuous; nor, as it might seem, premature.

"Not a private person," he mumbled. "Under orders."

"Really?" said Harriet. "Whose orders?"

Tandy silenced her with the same reproving look and Guy and Ben Phipps, when they later had her alone, told her one did not ask questions like that. The two men, conferring together, decided that Tandy must be an exile who had been placed in jeopardy by his extreme left-wing activities and would, when he received the word, rejoin the Yugoslav revolutionaries as a sort of classical demagogue.

They were displeased when Harriet said: "He seems just another Yakimov to me."

"That's only the get-up," Ben Phipps said.

Yakimov was a joke: Tandy was not. He certainly managed, while speaking seldom, to extrude a sense of gravity and intellectual weight beside which Yakimov seemed a shadow. When anyone expressed an opinion or expounded a theory, he gave the impression that he knew what was about to be said but wouldn't spoil the fun by saying it first. He could also disconcert the speaker by dropping his eyelids so there was no knowing whether he agreed or disagreed.

When news of the Yugoslav revolution went round, he had seemed to share Guy's enthusiasm while, at the same time, reflecting Ben Phipps's qualms. They waited to see what he would do now. Forty-eight hours later he was still in Athens, still sitting at his table outside Zonar's, and Harriet said: "Doesn't look as though he's going back, does it?"

Ben Phipps snorted: "I don't know what he's up to, but I'm beginning to think it's nothing very much."

Guy laughed, agreed and said: "Never mind. I like the old buffer. He may be another Yakimov, but he pays his round."

Finding he said little when drunk and nothing much when sober, Guy and Ben ceased to consult Tandy on political matters and, talking across him, did not even look to see whether he dropped his eyelids or not. Even though curiosity about him had gone down in disappointment and boredom, they liked him to be there. He was a centre of companionship, and was, as Guy said, scrupulous in paying his round. He was equally scrupulous in seeing himself repaid. He was the only person with whom Yakimov drank on equal terms. Though he paid from a bulky crocodile wallet with gold clasps and Yakimov, when his turn came, had to search his torn pockets for a coin, Tandy, compassionless, let Yakimov search. He was tolerant of Yakimov, no more. He made no concessions and this fact seemed to heighten Yakimov's regard for his new friend. Charmed and challenged by the first sight of Tandy, Yakimov, in the News Room, would murmur to himself: "Remarkable chap!" and bring Tandy's name into conversation as though he had him constantly in mind.

"We're fortunate in having him here," Yakimov said.

"Why?" Harriet asked.

Yakimov shook his head slowly and drew in an appreciative breath, marvelling at Tandy's quality. "He's travelled, dear girl. Your own Yak got around in his day but that one – *That One* has trotted the globe."

"But would you say that travel, in itself, is an achievement. It only calls for money and energy. Has he travelled to any purpose? Has he, for instance, written anything about his travels? I don't think so."

"Scarcely surprising," Yakimov smiled at her ingenuousness. "The dear boy's tied down by the Official Secrets Act."

"You meant he was sent abroad? He's a secret agent?"

"Indubitably, dear girl."

"I can't believe it. No secret agent would dress like that."

"I think I ought to know, dear girl."

"How did you know?"

Yakimov shook his head again, wordless with admiration of the man. He had told Ben Phipps: "At first sighting, I recognized Roger as a Master Spy."

"How did you do that?" Phipps asked.

"There are signs. That wallet stuffed with the Ready – the money comes from *somewhere*. But there's more to it than that. He recognized your Yak. Nothing said, of course; but we made contact."

"You tipped each other the wink, eh? How'd you do it? Tell me. A handshake, like the Freemasons?"

"Not at liberty to say, dear boy."

Guy and Phipps were now inclined to laugh at Tandy, but Yakimov refused to join in.

"Remarkable man," he insisted. "Most remarkable man! In disguise of course."

"Odd sort of disguise," Phipps said.

"All disguises are odd," Yakimov said in a tone of reprimand, gentle but dignified.

Harriet, who had not expected much of Tandy, did not share Guy's disappointment. She had liked him well enough at first and still liked him after the brief myth died. He made no demands, but he was there: his table was a meeting place, a lodgement during stress and a centre for the exchange of news.

Charles intended, apparently, to keep his word. She had rejected his ultimatum and would not see him again: and so was drawn like an orphan to Tandy's large, comfortable, undemanding presence.

"May I adopt you as a father figure?" she said, approaching his table. For answer, he rose and bowed.

His size helped him to an appearance of good nature. But would his good nature stand up to the test? It might be nothing more than the *bonhomie* of an experienced man who knew what would serve him best. She did not hope to uncover the truth about Tandy. Time was too short. He had arrived in a hurry, was hurriedly adopted as a prodigy and as hurriedly dropped. Whatever the truth might be, she suspected he had adapted himself so often to so many different situations, he had lost touch with his real self. But what did it matter? With Tandy as her chaperon, she could sit and watch the world go by.

As she expected, Charles walked past. He had said she would never see him again, but while they remained in one community, they must meet; and, meeting, she knew they would be drawn together.

He noticed Tandy first, then saw that Harriet was with Tandy. He looked away and did not look back.

Next day, he reappeared. This time, he eyed her obliquely and smiled to himself, amused at the company she was keeping.

The third time she saw him, Yakimov and Alan were present.

Alan called: "Hey!" and held out his stick. Charles stopped, growing slightly pink, and talked to Alan while Harriet devoted herself to Tandy and Yakimov. The discussion at an end, Charles went off without giving her a glance.

"I was having a word about the Pendeli walk," said Alan.

"The Pendeli walk?" Harriet asked in a light, high voice.

"You are coming, aren't you?"

"Of course. But is Charles coming?"

"He'll come if he can."

The rest of the party would be Alan, Ben Phipps and the Pringles. Alan now suggested that Yakimov and Tandy should join them. Yakimov looked at Tandy, the globe-trotter, and Tandy shook his head. Yakimov echoed this refusal: "Your old Yak's not up to it."

As the sun grew warmer, Tandy threw off his coat, but kept it safely anchored by the weight on his backside. With an identical gesture, Yakimov threw off his own coat, saying to Tandy: "Did I ever tell you, dear boy, the Czar gave this greatcoat to m'poor old dad?"

"You've mentioned it ..." Tandy paused, grunted and added: "... repeatedly. Um, um. Right royal wrap-rascal, eh?"

Yakimov smiled.

His coat-lining, moulting, brittle and parting at the seams, had been described by Ben Phipps as: "Less like sable than a lot of down-at-heel dock rats wiped out by cholera," but Yakimov saw no fault in it. He had a coat like Tandy's coat. Tandy, globe-trotter and secret agent, owning a crocodile wallet stuffed with 100-drachma notes, was Yakimov's secret Yakimov. Tandy, too, had a coat lined with – whatever was it?

"Wanted to ask you, dear boy," Yakimov asked: "What kind of fur is that you've got inside?"

"Pine marten."

Yakimov nodded his approval. "Very nice."

He would have spent the day at Tandy's elbow had he not had to earn a living elsewhere. Gathering himself together, he would say: "Have to go, dear boy. Must tear myself away. Must do m'bit." Departing, he would sigh, but he was proud of his employment. He liked Tandy to know that he was in demand.

As the British troops went, sent away with flowers and cheers, the camps closed down and Yakimov was no longer neded to play Maria. There was still talk of a "Gala Performance" to aid the Greek fighting men, but Pinkrose had complained to the Legation. Dobson telephoned Guy with the advice: "Better let the show rest for a bit." Yakimov, resting, still talked of his Maria that had been *un succès fou* and his Pandarus which he had played to "all the quailty and gentry of Bucharest".

But these triumphs were in the past; his job at the Information Office lived on. "Lord Pinkrose needs me," he would say. "Feel I should give the dear boy a helping hand."

When he saw Harriet installed in the News Room, Pinkrose said "Monstrous!" but he said it under his breath. After that he always seemed too busy to notice she was there.

He had said no more about leaving Greece. He had accepted Alan's reassurances and was apparently unaware that the revolution had cancelled them out. He may not have known there had been a revolution. The news did not interest him. He had time now for nothing but his lecture that would, he told Alan, be given early in April. The exact date could not be announced until a suitable hall was found. Alan was required to find a hall and Pinkrose came hourly into the News Room to ask: "Well, Frewen, what luck?"

Alan's task was not an easy one. Most of the halls in Athens had been requisitioned by the services. The hall attached to the English church was much too small. Alan recommended the University but Pinkrose said he wanted the lecture to be a social rather than a pedagogical occasion.

He said: "I cannot see the beautiful ladies of Athens turning up in the company of students. It would be too ... too 'un-smart'."

"If you want that sort of occasion," Alan said, "I'm afraid I can't help you. I haven't the right connections. You'd do better on your own."

"Now, now, no heel-taps, Frewen! Soldier on. Myself, as you well know, have other things to do."

When Pinkrose came in again, he found Alan had no more suggestions to make. He said crossly: "You're being unhelpful, Frewen. Yes, yes, unhelpful. I'll go to Phaleron. I'll appeal to the Major."

"An excellent idea!"

Pinkrose stared at Alan's large, sunken, expressionless face, then went angrily to the Billiard Room. A little later a taxi called for him. He set out, fully wrapped, for Phaleron.

All the Major could offer was his own garden, but it was, Pinkrose said, "glorious with spring", and in the end he accepted it. He announced the arrangements to Alan, saying: "The lecture will be combined with a garden party. There will be a buffet luncheon for the guests. I think I can safely say, knowing the Major, that it will be a sumptuous affair. Yes, yes, a sumptuous affair. I am an experienced speaker, not daunted by the open air; and it's in the Greek tradition, Frewen; the tradition of the Areopagus and the Pnyx. Oh yes! the Major has been very kind. As I expected, of course. As I expected." Pinkrose sped away, to return fifteen minutes later, his voice hoarse with excitement: "I have decided, Frewen; yes, I have decided. I will give my lecture on the first Sunday in April."

Alan gave a sombre nod. When Pinkrose went, he returned to his work, not meeting the eyes of Harriet or Yakimov. In a minute Pinkrose was back again. "I think the list should be left to the Major. The Major must compile it with my help, needless to say."

The list took so long to compile there was no time to have the invitation cards engraved and Pinkrose refused to have them printed. They had to be written out. Pinkrose suggested that those for persons of importance should be written by Alan. The cards were placed on Alan's desk but remained untouched until Pinkrose took them away and wrote them himself. Invitations for persons of less importance were written by Miss Gladys. The rest were typed by Miss Mabel after attempts proved that neither Yakimov nor Miss Mabel could write a legible hand.

"Frewen," said Pinkrose, when at last the piles of envelopes were complete, "I want them delivered on the bicycle. One can't trust these Athens post-boxes. Anyway, hand delivery is more fitting. It gives a better impression; and they will arrive in time.'

"How many are there?"

"About two hundred. Not more. Well, not *many* more."

"They could go with a News Sheet."

"Oh, no. No, Frewen, *no*. A letter handed in with a News Sheet could be overlooked. Besides, it is quite a different list. There will be English guests, but it is essentially a Greek occasion. Some of the names are very distinguished indeed. It calls for a special delivery."

"Very well."

Yakimov, half asleep during this conversation, did not grasp its import until the office boy handed him the envelopes and the list. He accepted the task without complaint but looking through the list, cried in dismay: "He hasn't invited me."

Yakimov had always treated Pinkrose with deference. When a detractor mentioned him derisively, Yakimov might smile but it was an uneasy smile and if there was laughter he would glance round fearful that Pinkrose might be in their midst. "Distinguished man, though," he would say. "Must admit it. Scholar and gent, y'know. Aren't many of them." He went through the list again, finding the names of Alan Frewen and both Twocurrys, but still no mention of his own. So there was no reward for deference and defence! He brooded over his omission until Alan looked at the clock and said: "You'd better get under way."

Yakimov pulled himself together. He began sorting the cards into batches, then suddenly wailed: "There's one for Roger Tandy! Suppose he sees me delivering it! What will he think?"

"I'm going to the Corinthian," Alan said. "I'll leave it in."

"And ... Oh dear, it isn't fair! I've got to go all the way to Phaleron to leave cards on Lush and Dubedat."

"Get on with it. There's a rumour that Dubedat's appearing as Lord Byron. You might get a look in at the dress rehearsal."

But Yakimov was not to be amused. He put the batches for delivery into his satchel and went without a word.

The Sunday of the lecture was the day of the Pendeli walk. Harriet said to Alan: "So you won't be coming?"

"Oh yes, I will. We're going to Pendeli to welcome the

spring. I'd rather take Diocletian for a walk than listen to Pinkrose."

Charles was also invited to the lecture. Harriet hoped he, too, would choose to come to Pendeli – if he were still in Athens to make the choice.

Yakimov, on his old upright bicycle, laboured three days to deliver the invitations. He could not avoid being seen as he went round the town with his brim-broken panama pulled down like a disguise about his eyes. Tandy watched him unmoved. When Yakimov returned to the office, tear-stained from grief and exhaustion, he threw the list on to Alan's desk.

"What a way to treat poor Yaki!" he said.

27

SUNDAY WAS FINE. Stepping out into early morning, the Pringles heard the sirens. They stood on the doorstep, listening for the raid. The sky was clear. The sun warm. A bee came down the lane, blundering from side to side as though making the first excursion of its life. Its little burr filled the Sunday quiet a while, then faded into the distance. There was no other noise. The silence held for a couple of minutes, then the all-clear rose.

It was not until they reached the centre of Athens that they realized there was something wrong. It was a brilliant day, a feast day of the church, yet people, standing about in their Sunday clothes, had mourning faces or made gestures of anger or agitated inquiry. They were gathered outside the Kapni-karea, the men in dark suits, the women with black veils over their hair, as though distracted from worship by news of some cataclysmic act of nature.

The Pendeli party was meeting outside the Corinthian where Roger Tandy sat eating his breakfast in the morning sunlight. Yakimov had already joined him. Ben Phipps and Alan, standing by, moved to meet the new arrivals as though they could not wait to deliver their dire news.

Germany had declared war on Greece. The night before, a German broadcast in Greek had spoken of a raid, the like of which the world had never seen before: a gigantic, decisive raid that would wipe out the central authority of the victim country and permit the invading army to advance unhindered through confusion. They had not mentioned the name of the threatened city. Everyone believed it would be Athens, yet the blue, empty sky remained empty. The sirens had announced not a raid but the fact that Greece was at war with Germany.

The Pendeli party joined Roger Tandy and watched him

as he spread quince jelly on a little, hard, grey piece of bread.

What should they do? Could they go to Pendeli at such a time? It might look as though they were fleeing Athens in alarm. Yet, if they remained, what was there for them? There was no point in sitting about all day waiting for destruction. They decided to delay their decision until Charles Warden turned up.

In a quavering, suffering voice, Yakimov asked: "Do you think they'll hold that garden party at Phaleron?"

"Why not?" said Phipps. "The world hasn't come to an end."

No one agreed with him. They sat waiting round the table in the delicate spring sunlight, in the midst of a city that seemed to be holding its breath, poised for the end.

Yakimov, looking thoughtful and melancholy, said nothing more until, suddenly, he leant towards Harriet and said: "Dear girl! Saw rather a remarkable sight. Quite remarkable, in fact. Haven't seen anything like it for years."

"Oh, what?"

"Just round the corner. Come and see. I'd like to take another look."

Though her curiosity was roused by his unusual fervour, Harriet did not move until Guy said: "Go and see. You can tell us about it when you get back."

Yakimov led her into Stadium Street and came to a stop at Kolokotroni where a man sat on his heels in the gutter with some objects arranged on the kerb before him.

"What are they? Beans?"

"Bananas," Yakimov said eagerly.

The bananas, very green and marked with black, were about two inches in length – but they were bananas. Harriet wondered how the vendor came to have a banana palm and how far he had walked to bring his rare and valuable fruit into Athens for the feast-day. Seeing the two foreigners, he shifted on his hunkers and prepared to speak, but was afraid of speaking too soon.

"Haven't tasted one for years," Yakimov said. "Never seemed to see them in the Balkans. They're a luxury here. Was wondering if you'd care to possess yourself of them."

When living with the Pringles in Bucharest, Yakimov often suggested that Harriet should buy something he had seen and envied in the shops. His penury there had been an established fact, but now she said: "Why don't you buy them yourself?"

Nonplussed, Yakimov murmured: "I suppose I *could*. Don't think I want to." He bent closer and peered at the bananas in an agony of greed and caution, then came to a decision. "Rather have an ouzo." He turned away.

The vendor sighed and sank back on his heels and Harriet, pitying him, offered him a small coin. The man, surprised, jerked up his chin in refusal. He was not a beggar.

When they returned to the square, Charles had joined the group. He swung round as he heard Harriet's voice, and seeing him, she joyfully asked: "Well, are you coming with us?"

"I'm afraid not. I'll have to stand by."

"Let's get going, then," Ben Phipps jumped up cheerfully, saying: "We've wasted enough time." When the others made no move, he began urging them to their feet.

Charles watched disconsolately. He had been up to the Military Attaché's office and Alan, tugging Diocletian out from under the table, asked: "What do they think? Have we a chance?"

"Of course." Charles assumed his air of professional optimism. "The Greeks are determined to fight it out. This isn't easy country for armour. It defeated the Italians; it may defeat the Germans."

"It may; but the Greeks have had a hard winter."

"They survived it. That counts for a lot."

"I agree."

Guy and Ben strolled on. Harriet, waiting while Alan put the dog on to a lead, glanced at Charles and found his gaze fixed on her; he raised his brows as though to ask: "Must you go?" What else could she do?

"Come on, then," Alan said, moving off.

Charles made a gesture of appeal and when Harriet lingered, whispered: "Tomorrow. Tea-time."

She nodded and went. Following Alan into the null and pointless day ahead, she felt she was leaving her consciousness behind her.

At Kolonaki, she was jolted out of her dejection by the sound of spoliation ahead. Diocletian growled. Alan gripped him by the collar. They turned a corner and found the enraged Greeks breaking up the German Propaganda Bureau. The bureau was a small shop and already almost wrecked. A young man dangling a portrait of Hitler from an upper window had roused an uproar and as the portrait crashed down, the Greeks rushed forward to dig their heels into the hated face. The road and pavements were a litter of broken glass and woodwork. Books had been ripped up and heaped for a bonfire. "A bonfire of anti-culture," said Ben Phipps. Almost the only spectators were some New Zealanders who watched with unsmiling detachment.

One of the books, its covers gone, fell at Harriet's feet. She picked it up and at once a young Greek, afire and abristle like a battling dog, held her as though he had the enemy in his hands. She appealed to the New Zealanders who said: "Let her go. She's English." "English?" the Greek shouted in disgust, but he let her go and Harriet was left with a book she could not read and did not want.

"Let me see!" Alan looked at it and laughed: " '*Herrenmoral und Sklavenmoral.*' Poor old Nietzsche! I wonder if he knew which was which?" He put the book into his hip pocket: "A souvenir," he said.

"Of what?"

"Man's hatred of himself."

The bus took them to the lower slopes of Pendeli and they climbed up among the umbrella pines, following a path fringed with wild cyclamen. Guy and Ben Phipps, stimulated by some lately uncovered piece of political chicanery, kept well ahead of the other two.

Alan began to limp on the rough ground but would not slacken his pace. Here, in the bright mountain air, away from other claims on her attention, Harriet could see how greatly he had changed. He had been a heavy man. The hungry months of winter had caused his muscles to shrink. He had belted in the waist of his trousers but the slack hung ludicrously over his hind-quarters and his coat slipped from his shoulders. His shoes had become too big for him but by balancing on his better foot and persuading the other after it, he kept going as though the walk were a challenge he felt bound to meet.

Diocletian, darting about under the pines, was a phantom dog. He was worried by the tortoises that crawled in hundreds over the dry, stony, sun-freckled earth. Tortoises were the only creatures that thrived these days and Harriet wondered if anyone had ever tried to eat them. Diocletian, sniffing, wagging his tail, was turning to Alan in inquiry, seemed to have the same idea. It was painful to watch his bones slide against his skin as he trotted to and fro, possessed by his inquisitive energy, and hungry, too. He kept coming back to the path with a tortoise in his mouth – but what could he do but drop it? When it felt safe, it crawled away, unharmed and unconcerned.

Diocletian, perplexed, looked at Alan, then looked down at the tortoise. What had they here? A moving stone?

Alan, his face crumpled with love, waved his stick at the dog. "Beaten by a tortoise! Go on, you ridiculous dog!"

They paused to rest at a hut that sold retsina. Sitting on the outdoor bench, they saw the whole of Athens at their feet, with the Parthenon set against the distant rust-pink haze like a little cage of pearly bone. There had been no raid. Ben Phipps, expecting a spectacle of fire and devastation, had brought a pair of field-glasses which he offered to Guy, and the two short-sighted men passed the binoculars back and forth until the retsina came.

Diocletian lay belly up, the pennant of his tongue lolling red between his teeth. Alan asked the proprietor for a pan and filled it with retsina.

"Good heavens, will he drink that?" the others asked.

"You wait and see."

They watched, delighted, as Diocletian emptied the pan.

Ben Phipps, the binoculars up, shouted excitedly: "Look, look!" Half a dozen aircraft were coming in from the south, but there was no warning, no gunfire, no bombs, and the aircraft, turning over the city, began to play like dolphins in the sea of air.

They were unlike anything Alan or Phipps had seen before. Drowsy with wine, the four sat for a long time, backs to the warm wall of the hut, breathing the scent of pines, hearing a twittering of cicadas so constant it was like silence, and watching the planes dip and circle and loop in the hyacinth sky. At this distance, the display was silent; if the aircraft were a part of conflict, it seemed a conflict too distant to have meaning.

Harriet said: "Perhaps they belong to the future. Without knowing it, we may have been here a hundred years and the war is over and forgotten."

Alan grunted and sat up. Diocletian, who had his eye on his

master, was on his feet at once. The walk now took them above the pines where the shale began and the going was difficult. Guy offered Alan an arm but he insisted on making his way alone, balancing and sliding on the grey, sharp, treacherous stone until they reached the top where the wind struck them violently and they knew it was time to go home.

Athens, in the light of evening had passed out of shock. It had been a resplendent day. There was no doubt now that the winter was over and the freedom of summer was at hand. Everyone was out in the rose-violet glow, crowding the pavements, their faces washed over with the sunset, carrying flowers and flags; Greek flags and English flags.

The four from Pendeli, as though they had been in some elysium outside the range of war, wandered about together, seeing the city anew. The Athenians had taken heart again. When Alan stopped a friend and asked about the strange aircraft, he was told they were British fighter planes flown from Egypt for the protection of Athens. There had been no raid but now, if the Luftwaffe came, it would not get far. The people seemed almost to be rejoicing that the worst had happened. They had a new and stronger enemy, but he would be vanquished like the other.

In University Street, where people swept to and fro across the road, an English sailor was hoisted up and with his cap on the back of his head, a carnation behind his ear, he sat on the shoulders of two men and waved happily to everyone around him. He was handed a bottle. As he tilted back his head to drink, his cap fell off and the audience applauded and shouted with joy.

Guy said: "Where has Surprise gone?" but no one knew. Surprise had gone without a word to anyone. Now another man, bearded like Ajax or Achilles, was being held aloft and, swinging the bottle round his head, he was swept away just as Surprise had been swept away. Heroes came and went these days. When they were gone, it seemed they were gone for ever.

Ben Phipps went off to his office and the others decided that Babayannis' would be the place that night; all the fun would be there. But there was no fun. A terrible sobriety had come down with the rumour that there had been a raid, just such a raid as the German radio had described. It was Belgrade that had suffered. Now the word was: "Belgrade today;

Athens tomorrow." At Babayannis' there was no dancing; the songs again were sad. When Ben Phipps arrived, he said: "Those were Spitfires we saw today; a new kind of fighter aircraft. They only came to cheer us up. When it was dark, they flew back home again."

The sirens sounded. People said from table to table: "Here it comes!" but the raid was the usual raid on the Piraeus. It lasted a long time. When Guy and Harriet reached home, a rosy smoke was welling up out of the harbour. A little crowd of local people were gathered, dark and coagulate, on the hill behind the villa. Dazed after the long day of sun and air, too tired to feel curiosity about anything, the Pringles went unsuspecting to bed. In the small hours, an explosion flung them out of bed.

Guy felt his way up from the floor but Harriet lay under the repeated roaring reverberations, imagining herself flattened beneath the water of a broken dam. Guy tried to pull her up but she clung to the floor, the only security in a disintegrating world. The house quivered. A second explosion overlay the echoes of the first and, as the stupendous clamour rose to a climax, there came from some other dimensions of time the clear, fine tinkle of breaking glass.

Guy managed to lift Harriet and seat her on the edge of the bed. Her chief emotion was indignation. "This really is too much," she said and Guy laughed helplessly. She dropped back on the bed, hearing above the final sibilations of sound, the howls of dogs; and then, when quiet eventually came, a scandalized chattering.

There were still people watching on the hill. Guy said he would go out and see what had happened. "Do you want to come?" he asked.

"Too tired," she whispered and, putting her face into a pillow, went at once to sleep.

Anastea arrived at breakfast-time garrulous with the horrors she had seen. Guy had been told that a ship, set on fire during the raid, had exploded. Anastea said the explosion had wiped out the Piraeus. The harbour was in ruins. Everyone was dead. Yes, everyone; everyone. Not a soul moved in the town. If she and her husband had not gone last year to Tavros, they would be dead, too. But they had gone. They had had to go because their house was pulled down over their heads.

They had been martyred by the authorities, but now they knew that God was planning to preserve them. It was a great miracle and Anastea, crossing herself, declared that her faith had been renewed. Then she went all over the story again.

Guy could make nothing of it. What sort of ship was it that, exploding, convulsed the city like the explosion of a planet?

Harriet shook her head, feeling detached from the problem. She said: "I think the blast blew me out of my body; I haven't come back yet."

On the Piraeus road the homeless were wandering along, carrying bundles or pushing anything that could be pushed. Those that had given up were seated round the bus stop and Guy tried to question them but, too dazed to answer, they merely shook their heads. The Pringles joined the refugees walking through the glass from street lights, windows and motor cars. It was an opalescent day that seemed, like the people about them, tremulous with shock.

At Monastiraki, they parted. Harriet went on to the office while Guy turned off to the School. Each learnt something about the events of the night.

The exploded ship had been carrying a cargo of TNT. It was to be unloaded on Sunday but, for no known reason, the unloading had been delayed. Left by the dockside, it had been set on fire during the raid and a British destroyer tried to tow it out to sea. The tow rope broke.

The two ships were still in the harbour when the explosions came. The destroyer and all aboard her had been annihilated.

"It was sabotage," shouted Ben Phipps when he came into the News Room.

Alan shook his head unhappily but did not deny it.

Harriet thought of the sailor they had seen seated on high with a bottle in his hand and a carnation behind his ear. Likely enough, he had been one of the crew of the lost destroyer. "A doomed man," she thought, a man upon the brink of death. And Surprise, too. She remembered them as valiant but insubstantial, as though already retreated a degree or two from life. But they were all upon the brink of death. In her shocked state, she felt she had gone too far and might never return to reality.

"The rope broke three times," said Phipps. "Three times! Think of it. A rope intended for just such an emergency. It broke three times."

Yakimov, exhausted by fear and lack of sleep, asked in a faint voice: "But who would do it, dear boy?"

"Who do you think? Pro-Germans, of course. Fifth columnists. The town's full of them. Just now they're ringing round all the offices to say more explosions are coming. Worse explosions. They say: 'You wait until tonight.' People are so unnerved they'll believe anything. Work's at a standstill. There's a real danger of panic."

Yakimov was amazed at what he heard. "But where do they come from, these pro-Germans?"

"They've been here all the time."

"All the time," murmured Yakimov and the others, abashed, felt that Greece was a stranger country than they knew. Living here among allies, smiled on, they had imagined themselves loved. But not all the friends were friends; nor the allies, allies. Some who had smiled just as warmly as the rest had been following a different banner and applauding, in secret, the exploits of the other side.

"How about the Phaleron do?" Ben asked. "Was it cancelled?"

"On the contrary," Alan told him. "It was a great success. And why not? I imagine quite a few of the Major's guests are hoping to shake Hitler by the hand."

"And how did the lecture go?"

"I only know that Miss Gladys looks as though she's passed through a mystical experience. She did not mention the explosion. It was nothing compared with Pinkrose's performance. I said: 'What was the lecture like?' She replied in a muted voice: 'Awe-inspiring.' Anyway, it's flattened Pinkrose. She came in to tell me that he'd be staying for a few days at Phaleron to recoup."

Harriet was to meet Charles at tea-time. During the morning she held to this fact as a sleep-walker might hold to a banister. She would not go out into the troubled streets. She sent the boy to buy her a sandwich and remained in the News Room until four o'clock. She arrived early at the Corinthian, not expecting to find Charles. He was already there.

She said: "I'm early."

"I thought you might come early."

She sat down and asked: "What is the news?"

"I don't need to tell you about the explosion."

"I've heard the whole story. What else? Any rumours?"

"Nothing good."

He was holding a book. She put out her hand to take it from him, but he shut it and placed it on the sofa out of her reach. He was frowning slightly as though trying to recall something, examining her face as though whatever it was, was there.

Gazing at each other, they seemed on the brink of revelation but there was nothing to be said. If they began to converse now, it would take a life-time, and they had no time in which to begin.

Suddenly, like someone forced to confess under duress, he said: "I love you."

When she did not reply, he said: "I suppose you knew that?" He insisted against her silence: "Didn't you? ... Didn't you?"

Unable to speak, she nodded and his face cleared. Now, his expression implied, he had given her everything; there were no grounds for any sort of excuses or delays.

He took her hand and, gently pulling her, brought her to her feet and led her towards the stair.

There may have been people watching them, but she had no consciousness of other people in the foyer and later, when she tried to remember how they had reached the floor above, it seemed to her she had been levitated, as though in a dream. They went down a passage with numbered doors. There was no noise. She thought there was no one else in the hotel – at least, no one who mattered: yet when a door opened in the passage, she had an immediate prevision of encounter. She stopped, alarmed. Charles, with no such feelings, tried to pull her on.

The door, opening at the end of the passage, showed a lighted window. When, for a moment, a tall young man was outlined against it, Harriet recognized him at once. She jerked her hand from Charles's hold. The young man, closing the door behind him, moved towards them with an apologetic smile and, reaching them, stood aside.

Harriet said: "Sasha."

The young man, slight, with drooping shoulders, his smile unchanged, lowered his head and tried to sidle past her.

"It's Harriet," she said.

He said: "I know."

"You seem to have forgotten me."

"No."

"Then what's the matter?"

Still smiling, he shook his head. Nothing; nothing was the matter. He only wanted to pass and get away. Puzzled and hurt, she said: "They must have done something to you."

"No. They didn't do anything. I'm all right."

He certainly looked well enough. He was wearing a suit of fine English cloth – an expensive suit in this part of the world. His face, with its prominent nose and dark, close-set eyes, showed no sign of ill-treatment or spiritual damage, yet it had changed. It was no longer the face of a gentle domestic animal, unconscious of its enemies, but an aware face, cautious and evasive. The meeting, that should have been a delight for both of them, had merely embarrassed him.

At a loss, she looked at Charles and said: "This is Sasha."

"Is it?" Charles smiled, a slight, sardonic smile. At one time she might have thought he was amused by the incident; now she knew better. He could hide his anger, but not his pallor. Cheated and humiliated, or so he imagined, his desire had changed to rage. He was, she realized, transported by rage and she thought how quickly she had come to know him. If she had lived with him half a century, she could not know him better.

She did not try to speak to him but turned to Sasha and asked where he was going. Sheepish and miserable, the boy replied: "Just downstairs. I'm here with my uncle. He'll be back soon."

"Let's all go and have tea." She gave Charles an appealing look that said: Let me solve this mystery, then we can talk.

He laughed and moved down the passage. "Not me, I'm afraid. I have too much to do." He entered his room and shut the door sharply and firmly. And that, she was made to understand, was that. She went downstairs and Sasha followed, meekly enough. She talked about the explosion. He said it had broken windows at the top of the hotel but he spoke as though it meant nothing. It was not his concern.

She led him to the sofa where Charles's book still lay. As

soon as they sat down, she began to interrogate him with a vigour that resulted from her own painful confusion.

He said he had come from Belgrade with an uncle, his mother's brother. How did he get to Belgrade? The Rumanian authorities had given him a ticket and put him on to the train. He was more interested in the future than in the past and, as soon as he could break in on her questions, he told her that his uncle was trying to arrange their departure from Greece. They did not care how they got away: all they wanted was to leave Europe and as soon as possible. His uncle kept going to the Yugoslav legation. He had been there that afternoon. The official said the British would arrange for the evacuation of the Yugoslavs who were either here or on their way here. He supposed they would be sent to Egypt, but his uncle was in touch with Sasha's sisters and aunts who were now in South Africa. His uncle had said: "It'll be a long time before the Germans get to Cape Town," so that was where they would go. They intended to fly there at the first opportunity.

This finished, Harriet said: "Guy went once or twice to meet the Belgrade train. I suppose you didn't see him?"

"Yes, I did. He didn't see me. He was talking to a man."

"And you made no attempt to speak to him?"

Sasha did not reply.

"Why? I don't understand, really I don't. What is it all about? Why didn't you speak to Guy?"

He looked blank, having, apparently, no explanation to offer. When their tea had been set out, she pinned him down in a more decided manner. "Now! That night our flat was raided – the night you disappeared – what happened? The men who came in were Guardists, weren't they?"

"Yes."

"Did they do anything to you? Were they brutal? Did they try to bully you?"

"No. They knew who I was. They had my picture at headquarters: they said they'd been looking for me. They made me sign a paper . . . It was for the Swiss Bank. They said if I signed, they'd let me go."

"So you signed your money away?"

He gave a shrug, slight, expressive, his head hanging down in a shamefaced way. Something about his manner suggested that he was reassuring her. He had not been physically ill-treated, so she need not reproach herself.

"And did they let you go?"

"Not then. When I'd signed the paper they locked me up. I said: 'When can I go?' and they said: 'This has to be arranged.' They kept me so long I thought they wouldn't let me go. I thought, 'Now, they'll put me in prison, like my father', but one night they took me in a car to Jimbolia. My uncle was waiting on the other side. One of the men had a permit to cross and my uncle gave him a lot of money – three million *lei*, I think it was: so I was allowed to go. They gave me papers. Everything was in order and I was able to walk across the frontier. It was terribly exciting. And the Guardists were quite decent, really. As soon as the man came back with the money, they were all jolly and laughing and we all shook hands. Then I found my uncle at the Rakek Customs and he took me to Belgrade."

"I didn't know you had an uncle in Belgrade."

"I didn't know where he was, but they knew. They knew where all my relatives were."

"So they held you to ransom! I never thought of that. And what of your father? Did you learn anything about him?"

Sasha, his voice more defined, said: "They said he was dead."

"I'm afraid that could be true."

"I hope it's true."

She paused in her interrogation while she poured the tea. After she had handed him a cup, she asked: "When the Guardists took you to headquarters, what did they tell you?"

He gave her a sudden side glance but did not reply.

"Did they say anything about Guy and me?"

He shrugged, head hanging again.

"You didn't think it was our fault that they came to the flat and found you?"

"How could I tell?"

"You thought we'd informed on you?"

His head jerked up and he gave her a swift smile, placatory, suspicious and wretched.

"What did they tell you?"

"They said: 'See what your English friends have done to you.'"

"Meaning, we'd given you away?"

"Yes, they did mean that."

"But you didn't believe them?"

"I didn't know. How could I know."

She saw he had not only believed them: it had never entered his head not to believe them. She was shocked into silence. In any case, there was nothing to be said.

When he had lived with them, a sort of domestic pet, he had seemed too innocent and unsuspecting to be allowed out into the world alone. He had been brought up in the shelter of a wealthy and powerful family, and though he must have heard the family stories of persecution, he had been insulated against mistrust by his own artlessness. Yet one lie – less than a lie, a hint that he had been betrayed by friends – had precipitated the settled doubts of his race. She was certain that however she argued, she would never convince him that they had had no hand in his arrest. One lesson had been enough. He now accepted the perfidy of the world and acceptance was born in him, an inheritance not to be changed.

She said: "If you thought we informed on you, weren't you surprised when they broke up our flat?"

"Did they break up your flat?"

"Surely you saw it happen?"

"No. Despina opened the door. They came straight in and put on all the lights. I was in bed and they said: 'Get up and get dressed', and they took me away."

"So you didn't see them turning out the drawers and pulling down the books?"

"No, I didn't. They did nothing like that while I was there."

"They did it after you went. When we came back, the flat was in chaos. We didn't sleep there. We went to the Athenée Palace."

He gave an "Oh!" of polite concern, and she knew he would never be convinced. Although his manner was still gentle, his attitude still meek, he saw the truth as he saw it, and no one would change him now.

Looking at his face, the same face she had known in Bucharest and yet a different face, she could see him turning into a wily young financier like the Jewish financiers of Chernowitz who still proudly wore on their hats the red fox fur that had been imposed on them long ago, as a symbol of cunning. No doubt he would remake the fortune that he had signed away. That would be his answer to life. She did not blame herself, but she felt someone was to blame.

She had mourned Sasha – and with reason. She had lost him indeed and the person she had now found was not only a stranger, but a stranger whom she could not like.

She said: "Guy will want to see you."

When he did not reply, she asked: "You do want to see him? Don't you?"

"We're leaving here."

"Yes, but not at once. There are no regular services . . ."

"I mean, we're leaving the hotel." There was an anxious impatience in his interruption: "We're going to stay with some people . . . friends of my uncle."

"I suppose Guy could visit you there?"

"I don't know where they live."

"If I gave you our address, you could get into touch with Guy yourself?"

He answered: "Yes," dutifully, and took the address which she wrote down for him. She watched him put it into his breast pocket and thought: now it rests with him.

People were coming and going through the hotel door and Sasha was watching for his uncle's return. She felt his eagerness to be gone and she knew he did not want to see Guy. Even if she could convince him that they were guiltless, he had left them and did not want to be drawn back to them. And she had no wish to draw him back. Why, after all, should they draw him back? He was not the person they had known.

A man entered the hotel.

"There's my uncle," Sasha said, his voice rising in relief. "I must go."

"Of course."

He leapt away, forgetting to say good-bye. She watched the men meet. The uncle, his shoulders hunched, his head shrunken into the astrakhan collar of his coat, was half a century older than the nephew, yet, seen together, the two looked alike. Their likeness was increased by the sense of understanding that united them. They belonged not to a country but to an international sodality, the members of which had more in common with each other than they had with the inhabitants of any country in which they chanced to be born.

"Jews are always strangers," Harriet thought, yet when Sasha followed his uncle upstairs, she felt a sense of loss.

While taking tea, she had seen Charles leave the hotel. He

had run down the stairs, not looking to right or left. He was still pale, still angry. She knew the situation might never be redeemed – and it had all been for nothing. Sasha, knowing she and Guy were in Athens, had made no attempt to contact them. He could have come and gone without their knowing he had even been here. Yet, out of all the seconds in a day, he had chosen that second to appear and estrange her from her friend.

She picked up the book which Charles had left on the sofa and saw it was in Greek. The fact he read this language not as an exercise but as a pleasure seemed to emphasize their division.

An acute sadness of parting and finality came down on her. Her friends were dispersing and she felt that life was reaching towards an end. She thought of Guy and knew that whatever his faults, he possessed the virtue of permanence.

She decided she would not tell him about her meeting with Sasha. She could imagine him trying to override Sasha's recoil and forcing an understanding; or an appearance of understanding, a pretence that all was well. She could not bear that. Now it would rest with Sasha and if he made no effort to see them, Guy, knowing nothing, would not be hurt.

But, the days passing, she found it impossible to keep from Guy the fact the Sasha was alive.

She said suddenly: "Who do you think I've seen?"

Guy replied at once: "Sasha Drucker."

"*You've* seen him? Where?"

"In the street."

"You didn't tell me."

"He told me he was just leaving. His uncle had managed to charter a private plane that would take them to Lydda. I meant to tell you. I forgot."

"Did you find him changed?"

"Yes. Of course, he's been through the sort of experience that would change anyone. I was glad to know he was safe and well."

"Yes. Yes, so was I."

And by an unspoken consent neither mentioned Sasha again.

It took the Germans forty-eight hours to break through the Greek defences and occupy Salonika.

Vourakis, a journalist who sometimes came to see Alan, told them in the News Room that the Yugoslav southern army had withdrawn, leaving the Greek flank exposed.

"But the advance was halted. It was halted by Greek cavalry. Real cavalry, you understand! Men on horseback."

"For how long?" Alan asked.

Vourakis shook his head sadly. "Why ask for how long? It would be like blocking a howitzer with a naked hand. And there were two forts that held the pass till the area could be evacuated. A hundred men stayed in the forts. They knew no one could rescue them, no help could come to them: they knew they must die. And they died. The forts were destroyed and the men died. It was a Thermopylae. Another Thermopylae."

Everyone was moved by the sacrifice of the men in the Rupel Pass forts, but the Germans had no time for Greek heroics. Riding over the defenders who had become the wonder of the war, they came with an armoured force which was described by refugees as "more powerful than anything the world has ever seen".

Nothing was known for sure. The news was blocked. As a precaution against panic, the authorities had decided that no one should know anything. The fall of Salonika had been expected, they said. It was inevitable from the first. They might even have planned it themselves. Whether expected or not, no one had been warned and the English who managed to get away left the town as the German tanks came in.

Harriet said to Alan: "A friend of ours went up to Salonika. An army officer. What do you think would happen to him?"

"Oh, he'd have his wits about him: he'd get away."

Which was exactly what Harriet did not think. She could imagine Clarence, with his self-punishing indifference, remaining till it was too late. But there may have been someone to harry him into a car and drive him to the Olympus line. An imitation officer, he would then be returned to Athens, so they perhaps would see him again one day – a man saved in spite of himself.

The refugees brought all sorts of stories. Now that everyone was dependent upon rumour, there was no telling truth from lies. Some people said the German tanks would reach Athens in a week and some said in a couple of days. They all said that Yugoslavia would not last the night.

Guy, meeting train after train, all packed with refugees, saw the Yugoslav officers arrive, brilliant in their gold braid. He was always picking up someone whom he had seen somewhere before, but he could get no news of his friend David Boyd.

Pinkrose returned to the office in high spirits. He came into the News Room smiling and his parted lips revealed what few had seen before – his small, neat, grey-brown teeth. No one smiled back. It was not much of a day for high spirits.

Beaming, excited, he said to Alan: "I was surprised, most surprised ... Yes, I was *most* surprised not to see you at the lecture." When Alan neither explained nor excused his absence, Pinkrose went on: "Ah, well! You were the loser, Frewen. You were the loser. You missed an excellent party. Yes, yes, an excellent party. The buffet was a splendid sight. The Major certainly lays things on. And it was a glittering party. I must say it was, indeed, glittering. The Major said to me: 'Congratulations, my dear Pinkrose, you've collected the cream.' Dear me, yes! Indeed I had. I can't pretend I knew everyone, but my eye lit on some very handsome ladies, and their praises were such that I blushed; I positively blushed. Even if my little talk did not interest you, Frewen, you would have enjoyed the food. It was delicious. I haven't eaten such food for many a long day."

Yakimov gave a sigh, his expression almost vindictive with hunger.

Pinkrose, tittering and wriggling gratified shoulders, said: "I think I gave a fillip – yes, definitely a fillip – to Greek morale."

"Badly needed," Alan said.

"No doubt."

"Last night the Germans occupied Salonika."

"Surely not? Is this official?"

"Not yet, but ..."

"Ah, a *canard* merely."

"I think not. The Legation said someone rang at day-break and told them German tanks were coming down the street. After that, the line went dead."

"Dear me!" Pinkrose lost his smile. "Grave news, indeed!"

Yakimov, glooming over the Major's hospitality, noticed nothing, but Harriet and Alan observed that Pinkrose was taking the news extraordinarily well. They waited for him to absorb it, then clamour, as he had done in the past, for immediate repatriation. Instead, he said firmly: "We can do nothing, so we must keep calm. Yes, yes, it behoves us to keep calm. Our Australian friends are holding the coast road and, by all accounts, they're the fellows for the job. The Germans won't get past *them* in a hurry." He smiled again but, noting the bleak faces of Alan, Yakimov and Harriet, lost patience with them all: "I've made my contribution," he said: "Now I must leave it to others. Several ladies said my lecture was an inspiration. They said it would spur the men to greater efforts. I must say, I don't see what else I can do."

"Why not go to Missolonghi and die, dear boy!"

Pinkrose had moved off before the words were spoken, yet they reached him. He stopped, looked round and fixed Yakimov in amazement.

Immediately Yakimov's spirit fell. He said in terror: "Only a little joke," he pleaded.

Pinkrose went without a word.

Eyes moist, lips trembling, Yakimov said: "D'you think the dear boy's piqued?"

"He didn't look too pleased, did he?" said Alan.

"It was only a little joke."

"I know."

"What d'you think he'll do?"

"Nothing. What can he do? Don't worry."

But Yakimov did worry. Throughout the morning, pondering his folly, he repeated: "Didn't mean any harm. Little joke, Look how he treated your poor old Yak! Telling me about food when I haven't had a meal for months!"

"Don't take it to heart. Worse things are happening at the front. I keep thinking of that proverb: 'Better a ship at sea or an Irish wife than a house in Macedonia.' "

Yakimov looked pained. "Not a nice thing to say, dear boy. M'old mum was Irish."

"You're right. It wasn't 'Irish'. I've forgotten what it was. Probably 'Albanian'."

Nothing would amuse Yakimov. He refused to be comforted. Something in Pinkrose's face had aroused his apprehensions and, it proved, with reason. At mid-day the office boy entered and said that Lord Pinkrose wished to see Mr. Frewen in his office. Surprised by this summons, Alan pulled himself out of his chair and went without a word. Yakimov gazed after him in fear. When he returned, his sombre face was more sombre, but he did not look towards Yakimov and he seemed to have nothing to say. After a while, when marking on a hand map the disposition of the British troops in Greece. he said casually: "Yaki, I have to tell you: the job's at an end. Pinkrose wants you to leave at once."

"But he can't do it," Yakimov wailed, his tears brimming over.

"I'm afraid he's done it. He telephoned the Legation and told them that there was nothing for you to do. We have to stop the News Sheet, so there'll be nothing to deliver. And ..." Alan lifted his head and looked at Harriet: "I'm afraid he also said that you must go. The work is minimal now. That's a fact There wasn't much I could say to the contrary."

Yakimov sobbed aloud: "Yaki will starve."

"Come on," Alan said. "Pull yourself together. You know we won't let you starve."

"And what about Tandy? I've told him I'm indispensable. What will he think?"

Alan took out a five-drachma piece. "Go and buy a drink," he said.

Harriet and Yakimov left together. Harriet had seen her work coming to an end and accepted dismissal with the indifference of one who has worse to worry about, but Yakimov bewailed his lot so loudly people turned and looked after them in the street.

"It's too bad, dear girl; it really is. Thrown out on m'ear just as I was making such a success of things. How could anyone do it, dear girl? How *could* they?"

This went on till Zonar's came in sight, then, glimpsing Tandy in his usual seat, Yakimov's complaints tailed away. His resilience, that had carried him through the shifts and disappointments of the last ten years, reasserted itself and he began to replan his life. "Have a friend in India; dear old friend, 'n fact. A Maharajah. Very tender to your Yak. Always was. When the war started he wrote and invited me to his palace. Said: 'If there's a spot of bother in your part of the world, you'll always be welcome at Mukibalore.' Charming fellow. Fond of me. Suggested I go and look after his elephants."

"Would you like that?"

"It's a career Interesting animals, I'm told. Got to think of the future. Your Yak's becoming too old to rough it. But I don't know," he sighed. "They're large, you know, elephants. Lot of work, washing'm down."

"You'd have boys to do that."

"Think so? You may be right. I would, as it were, administrate. I'd do *that* well enough. Got to get there, of course. D'you think they'd fly me as a V.I.P.? No, probably not. Must have a word with Tandy. Now, there's one that knows his way around!" They had stopped on the corner and in his enthusiasm Yakimov become hospitable. "Come and have a snifter, dear girl."

"Not just now." Leaving Yakimov in jaunty mood, she wandered on with nothing to do and nowhere to go, but restless with the anxious susceptiveness of someone who has lost something and still hopes to find it. She had heard nothing from Charles and this time she had no hope that, meeting, they would be drawn together again. He would not forgive her. She had nothing to gain by meeting him. Their relationship, without reason, had destroyed itself, yet she longed to come face to face with him. Although she looked for him among the mid-day crowds she was startled, when she saw him, into a state of nausea.

He was standing beside a military lorry in Stadium Street. The lorry was one of a convoy preparing to move off. Harriet, on the opposite pavement, watching him examining a map of some sort, expected him to feel her presence and cross over to her, but she soon saw there was no time for subtleties of that sort. One of the drivers spoke to him. There was a movement among the men. In a moment he would be gone. She ran across the road. Perturbed and breathless, she managed to call his name. He swung round.

"You're going?" she asked.

"Yes. We're off, any minute now."

"Where will you go? Have you been told? Alan says the English forces are at Monastir."

"They were, but things are happening up there. We won't know anything till we get to Yannina." Speaking with even detachment, he smiled formally, a guarded, defensive smile, and moved a little away as though on the very point of taking his departure; but she knew he would not go. This was the last moment they would have here, perhaps the last they would ever have. He could not leave until something conclusive had been said.

"Is there any chance of your coming back to Athens?"

"Who knows?" He gave his brief ironical laugh. "If things go well, we'll drive right through to Berlin." He moved towards her, then edged away, suspicious of the attraction that even here gilded the air about them. He wanted to turn his back upon the deceptive magic.

"I may not see you again, then?" she said.

"Do you care? You have so many friends."

"They aren't important."

"They only seem to be?"

The argument was ridiculous. She could not carry it on, but said: "It was difficult. Among all these alarms and threats, coming and goings, no one has a private existence. When it is all over ..." She stopped, having no idea when it would be over and knowing time was against her. To interrupt a spell was to break it. Whether they met again or not, they had probably come to an end.

The convoy was ready to start. The driver of the first lorry climbed to his seat and slammed his door shut. The noise was a hint to Charles: he must get his farewells over and return to duty.

"Good-bye, and good luck," Harriet said. She put her hand on his arm and for a second his composure failed. He stared into her face, anguished, and she was appalled to realize he was so vulnerable.

There was no time to waste now. He said: "Good-bye" and, crossing the pavement, swung up beside the driver and shut himself in. He could now look down on her from a safe distance, apparently unmoved, smiling again.

Some Greeks had gathered on the pavement to watch the convoy set out. As the first lorry started up, a woman threw a flower into the cabin, the valediction to valour. Charles caught it as it came to him and held it up like a trophy. The lorry moved. The last thing Harriet saw was his hand holding the flower. The second lorry obscured the first. The other lorries followed, driving eastwards, making for the main road to the north.

She went after them, returning the way she had come, and

watched them as they went into the distance. With the last of them out of sight, she no longer had any reason for going in that direction, but she had no reason for going in any other. She had been left alone with nothing to do and no reason for doing anything.

Her sense of vacancy extended itself to the streets about her. It was a grey, amorphous day in which people and buildings had lost identity, dissolving with every other circumstance, into insipidity. The town had the wan air of a place in which human life had become extinct. The streets seemed empty: left there without object or purpose, she felt as empty as the streets.

When she found herself back at Constitution Square, she stopped out of a sense of futility. Why go anywhere? She simply stood until she saw Guy coming towards her. Her impulse was to avoid him, but he had already seen her and as he came towards her, he asked: "What's the matter?"

"Charles has gone."

"I'm sorry." He took her fingers and squeezed them, looking at her with a quizzical sympathy as though her unhappiness were something in which he had no part. He was sorry for her. Feeling she did not want this sort of commiseration, she detached her fingers from his hold.

He asked where she was going? She did not know but said: "We could see if the Judas trees are coming out."

Guy considered this, but of course it was not possible: "I've a date with Ben," he said. "He's trying to get a call through to Belgrade. If he can't reach Belgrade, he'll try Zagreb. He may be able to find what's happened to the Legation people."

"No sign of David yet?"

"None; no news of any sort. I've met most of the trains. The road beside the School runs straight through to the station, so I can get there quickly. The trains are packed to the doors. I've spoken to a lot of people, but there's such a flap, it's hard to discover what's happening inside Yugoslavia. I suppose the Legation will see it out to the end."

"But David has no diplomatic protection?"

"No. Well, I must get on." Before leaving, Guy wanted to see her comfortably disposed and said: "Tandy and Yakimov are at Zonar's. Why don't you go and have tea with them?"

"No. I won't be in the office this evening. In fact, I won't be

going back there. My job's packed up. I think I'll take the
metro home."

"Yes, do that. I can't get back for supper, but I won't be
late."

Guy sped happily on his way, seeing her problems as settled.

The climbing plant on the villa roof had come into leaf and,
spreading over the pergola, was forming a thatch against the
sun. It had budded and now the buds were starting to open.
The little white waxen flowers had a scent like perfumed
chocolate. Anastea had told Harriet that in summer the Kyrios
and Kyria would take their breakfast and supper under the
pergola at the marble table, and soon the Pringles would be
able to do the same thing.

Since the district had taken on the verdancy of spring, its
atmosphere had changed. Harriet sometimes walked beside
the little trickle that was the Ilissus, or up among the pines
that overhung the river-bed. The villa was at last beginning
to seem a home, but a disturbed, precarious home. Though
it was not within the target area, it was near enough to the
harbour to be shaken by gun-fire, and when there were night
raids, the Pringles would sit up reading, having no hope of
sleep till the "all clear" sounded.

Up among the pine trees she had met a cat which followed
her to the edge of the wood but would not come into the open.
It was a thin, little, black female, its dugs swelling out pink
from the sparse black fur, so she knew it had kittens somewhere. She thought it must have a home in one of the shacks
beyond the trees. It was obviously a home where there was
not much to eat, but there was not much to eat anywhere
these days. Harriet knew the cat's eager attentiveness was an
appeal for food. There was nothing at the villa except the grey,
dry tasteless bread they had for breakfast. She took some
to the wood and the cat devoured it with savage exultation.

She asked Anastea to whom the cat might belong, but
Anastea treated the question with contempt. Seeing Harriet
put the bread into her pocket, she grumbled to herself. Harriet
did not understand what she said but could guess: if there was
bread to spare, there were human beings in need of it.

One day Harriet saw the kittens. She had crossed the waste-
land as far as the first of the shacks and when she reached it,

she found it derelict. The cat was a wild cat. The kittens were plain, starved creatures, tabby and white, and Harriet wondered how the mother had managed to bring them up; but they played happily in the sunlight, not knowing they were among the underprivileged of the world. One day when Harriet went to feed them, they had gone. The cat was there, perplexed and anxious, but the kittens had disappeared.

When she returned home on the afternoon of Charles's departure, Harriet had the cat in mind. It gave her some sort of attachment to life. She had fed it before out of a sense of duty to a creature in need; now, suddenly, she felt love for it, and began to fear that in her absence some harm could have come to it. She went first to the large grocery shop in University Street and queued for bread. It was a shop that in peace-time sold only the finest European foods. Now the shelves were empty. Behind the counter there were some boxes of dried figs and a sack of butter-beans. Harriet was allowed a few grammes of each, and because she was English the assistant opened a drawer and took out a strip of salted cod. He cut off a small piece and she accepted it as a sign of favour, although she felt she had no right to it.

Back at the villa, she found Anastea in the kitchen. A little skeleton of a woman in a black cotton dress and head-scarf, she was sitting on a stool, her hands lying in her lap, upwards, so Harriet could see the hard, pinkish skin of the palms scored over with lines, like the top of an old school desk. Her work was finished; she was free to go home, but she preferred to remain amid the splendours of the rich people's home.

Harriet kept the food in her bag and took it to the bathroom where she cut the fish with scissors and soaked it in the wash-hand basin. When she had got some of the salt from it, she took it to the wood and fed the cat.

28

Some time during the night an anti-aircraft gun was placed on the hill behind the villa.

Guy had almost reached the bus-stop next morning when the sirens sounded. At once the new gun opened up, so close that the noise was shattering. He hurried to the villa where he found Harriet, who had been in the bath, crouching naked under the stairs while Anastea, on her knees near by, was swinging backwards and forwards, hitting the floor with her brow and crossing herself, while she muttered prayers in an ecstasy of terror. The two women were completely unhinged by the uproar overhead.

As Guy stared at them in wonder and compassion, Harriet flung herself upon him crying: "What is it? What is it?"

"Good heavens, it's only an anti-aircraft gun." His own nerves were untouched by the racket but after two hours of it – the raid was the longest of the war – Harriet had become used to it while he, trapped inactive in the villa, felt he could bear no more.

"We can't live here with this banging away at all hours. The house has become unlivable-in," he said. "We'll have to find somewhere else."

Harriet, who could scarcely face another move, felt the responsiblity of the cat and said: "It's scarcely worth leaving now. We've stuck it so long, we might just as well stick it to the end. Besides, where can we go?" Many hotels had been requisitioned by the British military and those that remained had been packed by repeated waves of refugees. She said: "We can't afford the Corinthian or the King George; even if we got into a small hotel, heaven knows what we'd have to pay now."

The raid over, they went up to the roof and watched smoke rising in black, slow, greasy clouds from somewhere

along the coast. Anastea, who had followed them, said the
smoke came from Eleusis where there was a munitions factory. The sight seemed to inspire her and she began to talk
very quickly, making gestures of appeal at Guy. Apparently
she was urging him to do something, but it was some time
before he understood that men of the district were cutting
an air-raid shelter in the rock by the Ilissus. The shelter was to
contain seats which would be reserved for those who could
pay for them. Anastea had learnt this from the men that morning. When she said she could not afford a seat, they told her to
ask Guy to buy her one. How much were the seats? Guy
asked and she replied, "Thirty thousand drachma." Guy and
Harriet looked at one another and laughed. The sum seemed
fantastic to them, but it had no reality for Anastea. Foreigners
who could afford a villa with bathroom and kitchen could
afford anything.

"Do you think the men were pulling her leg?" Harriet asked.
"It's probably thirty drachma."

But Anastea insisted that the sum needed was thirty thousand. When Guy explained that it was far beyond anything he
could afford, Anastea's face fell dolefully.

"How old do you think she is?" Guy asked when she had
gone downstairs.

"She looks eighty but perhaps she's not much more than
seventy." Whatever she was, she had been aged out of cal-
culable time by work, hardship and near-starvation. Harriet
wondered would she herself, when half a century or more had
passed, be so eager to preserve her life. Not long ago, she
had spoken of life as a fortune that must be preserved, yet
already its riches seemed lost – not squandered or misapplied,
but somehow forfeit as a result of misunderstanding. She did
not think that any explanation could bring them back and
did not, in fact, know what explanation to give.

When Guy set out again, he asked her if she were coming
into Athens, too. She could think of no reason for going: she
had no job, nothing to do and would have to spend her time
walking about in streets that could hold nothing for her. At
least, if she remained, she had the cat.

Guy said, as he had said often before: "I'll get back early."

She laughed unbelievingly, having no faith in these promises, and found him watching her with the same quizzical

but detached concern that he had accorded her when she told him Charles had gone.

"Of course I will," he assured her. "Tell Anastea to try and find something for supper. We'll eat at home, shall we?"

"All right." She was pleased, but his insistence that he would indeed return disconcerted her like a solution of a problem that had come too late. The problem did not affect her any longer: it had not been solved but it had, she felt, been by-passed. Much more to the point these days was the question of what to give the cat. She sent Anastea to the shops and when the old woman was safely out of the way, she went to the kitchen and collected some scraps of food, but the cat was not in the wood. She walked to the hut where the kittens had lived. The cat was not there. She stood for a long time calling it, but in the end gave up the search, supposing it had gone off on a food-hunt of its own.

The evening was one of the few that they had spent in their living-room with its comfortless, functional furniture. The electric light was dim. Shut inside by the black-out curtains, Harriet mended clothes while Guy sat over his books, contemplating a lecture on the thesis: "A work of art must contain in itself the reason why it is so, and not otherwise."

"Who said that?" Harriet asked.

"Coleridge."

"Does life contain in itself the reason why it is so, and not otherwise?"

"If it doesn't, nothing does."

"But you think it does?"

"It must do."

"You're becoming a mystic," she said and after a long pause. added: "There are so many dead bodies in the ruins of Belgrade, people have stopped trying to bury them. They just cover them with flowers."

"Where did you hear that?"

"I heard it before I left the office. It was the last piece of news to come out of Yugoslavia."

Guy shook his head, but did not try to comment. There was a period of quiet, then a sound of rough and tuneless singing came from the top of the lane where some men had gathered in one of the half-built houses to raise their voices against the darkness.

As the singing went on and on, Harriet began to feel it unbearable and suddenly cried out: "Make them stop." Before Guy could say anything, she ran to the kitchen and told Anastea to go out and deal with the singers. Anastea shouted a command up the lane and the song came abruptly to a stop.

Shocked, Guy asked: "How could you do that?"

Harriet did not look at him: she was nearly weeping.

"They may be men on leave, or invalided from the front. Really, how *could* you?"

He was so seldom angry that she felt stunned by his reprimand. She shook her head. She did not know, she really did not know how she could do it, or even why she did do it. She wanted Guy to forget the incident but as he returned to his books, his face was creased with concern for the men slighted in that way. It did not relax, and suddenly she collapsed and began to cry helplessly, unable to swallow back her own guilt and remorse and the personal grief shut up inside her.

Guy watched her for a while, too upset to try to comfort her, then said as though it were only now he could bring himself to say what he had to say: "We're leaving here. Alan Frewen thinks he can arrange for us to have a room at the Academy."

"But I can't go. I can't leave the cat."

"We have to go. It's not just the raids and the lack of sleep. He says we must be somewhere where we can be reached by telephone."

She sat up, jolted by the alarm that in Rumania had become a chronic condition. "Are things worse? What is happening?"

"I don't know. Nobody knows. There's a complete ban on news."

"But surely there are rumours?"

"Yes, but you can't rely on rumours. The thing is: we have to move from here, simply as a precaution. Nothing more than that. Alan will let me know tomorrow."

They had only clothing and books, yet in her exhausted state it seemed almost beyond her power to cope with them. She begged him: "Couldn't you help me move?"

"But, of course," he said, surprised by her tone. "Why not?"

"You're usually too busy."

"Well, I'm not busy now. The revue's at an end and there's hardly anyone at the School." He sounded exhausted, too, and spoke as though he had been defeated at last. She was about to ask him what he did with himself in Athens now but at that moment Anastea came in to take her leave and Harriet said instead: "I think I'll go to bed."

The raid went on all night. There was no respite for the men at the guns, and no rest for anyone withing hearing. By morning Harriet was quite ready to move anywhere, it did not matter where, so long as she could sleep.

Guy was seeing Alan at luncheon and said he would be back as soon as he knew what arrangement had been made for them. He got out his rucksack and began taking his books from the shelves. Anastea, who had been expecting something like this, noted what he was doing, went to the kitchen and returned with a tea-pot which Harriet had bought a couple of months before. The villa did not contain much kitchen equipment, and this was the only piece that belonged to the Pringles. Nursing it in the crook of her arm, smoothing the china with her ancient, wrinkled hand, Anastea pointed out that there had been no tea in the shops for weeks. Harriet nodded and told her to leave the pot on the table, but Anastea clung to it, stroking it and patting it as though it were something of unusual value and beauty. She began to beg for it, pointing to the pot and pointing to her own bosom, and Harriet, surprised, said: "She doesn't drink tea. She doesn't even know how to make it. We ought to give it to someone who'll have a use for it."

Guy said: "There won't be any more tea, so let her have it."

Harriet waved her away with the pot and she was so eager to take it home, she forgot the money owing to her and had to be called back.

It was late afternoon when Guy returned. By that time Harriet had completed the packing and had made repeated journeys across the river-bed to try to find the cat. It had been a rather dirty little cat with scurfy patches in its fur, but its response to her had touched her out of all reason. A sort of obsessional frenzy kept her searching for it. She told herself that animals were the only creatures that could be loved without any reservations at all, and this was the only creature she wanted to love. She knew it would not be welcome at the Academy but she would take it with her. She was determined to find it.

She kept going back to the wood, expecting to find the cat at her heels, but each time met with nothing but silence. She was in the wood when Guy came back. He found her walking frantically backwards and forwards over the same ground, calling to the cat and pleading with it to appear. He did not like the gloom under the trees and, unwilling to enter, shouted to her from the river-bank. He had brought a taxi which was waiting for them.

She came to the edge of the wood and said: "I can't go without the cat," then walked back into the shadows, feeling he was a hindrance to her purpose which was more important than anything he could offer. He climbed up the bank and stood watching her, baffled. He wondered if she were becoming unbalanced. As for the cat, he decided someone had probably killed it for food, but said: "The gun-fire's frightened it. It's gone to a safer place."

"Quite likely," she agreed, still wandering round.

He said firmly: "Come on, now. The taxi's waiting and it's getting dark. You've got to give up."

"I can't," she said. "You see, this cat is all I have."

"*Darling!*"

His cry of hurt surprise stopped her in her tracks. She saw no justification for his protest. He had chosen to put other people before her and this was the result. Each time he had over-ridden her feelings to indulge some sense of liability towards strangers, a thread had broken between them. She did not feel there was anything left that might hold them together.

He called her again, but she did not move. He stood there obstinately, a shadow on the edge of the wood, and she resented his interference. She had supposed this large, comfortable man would defend her against the world, and had found that he was on the other side. He made no concessions to her. The responsibilities of marriage, if he admitted they existed at all, were for him indistinguishable from all the other responsibilities to which he dedicated his time. Real or imaginary, he treated them much alike, but she suspected the imaginary responsibilities had the more dramatic appeal.

"Darling, come here!"

Reluctantly she moved over to him. During the last weeks she had almost forgotten his appearance: his image had been overlaid by another image. Now, seeing him afresh, she

could see he was suffering as they all suffered. He had become
thin and the skin of his face, taut over his skull, looked grey.
He had at last come to a predicament he could not escape. He
would have to share the stress of existence with her, but it did
not matter now. She had learnt to face it alone. Still, she pitied
him. He had nothing to do. His last activity had deserted
him: but no activity, however feverishly pursued, could hide
reality from him. They were caught here together.

His troubled face pained her. She put her hands on to his
hands and he held her in his warm, familiar grasp.

She said: "I'm sorry. I did not mean to desert you."

"I did not think you did."

"You see, Charles loved me."

"Do you think I don't love you?"

"You love everyone."

"That doesn't make me love you less."

"I think it does."

It was not his nature to argue. He always expected understanding, and perhaps expected too much. He said simply:
"We must go. They're expecting us for supper at the Academy.
If there's a raid, we could get caught here again for a couple
of hours."

She went back with him to collect their possessions and lock
up the villa. She had lost hope of finding the cat, but she did
not feel that their talk had changed anything.

29

THE PRINGLES WERE GIVEN the room which had belonged to Gracey. There was no sign that anyone else had lived in it since he left.

Harriet looked out on the twilit garden where, from the dead tangle of old leaves, the new acanthus was rising and un-curling, and the lucca throwing up a spike of buds. The garden smell, dry and resinous, that she had described as the smell of Greece, was overhung with the fresh, sweet scent of the lemon trees.

The room was bare but here, in touch with their protectors, the Pringles felt they were safe. Her despondency lifting, Harriet said: "I like this, don't you?"

"I certainly do." Guy began to unpack and arrange his books on top of the chest-of-drawers, taking trouble as though they might be here for a long time.

The house, secluded in its garden, seemed a place safe from the racket of war, but this impression was dispelled when they reached the dining-room. Alan had not come in to supper. Pinkrose, though he had kept on his room at the Academy, spent most of his time at Phaleron. The other in-mates were talking in a subdued way but came to a stop at the entry of the outsiders. Harriet felt their retreat into dis-cretion, but the atmosphere carried an imprint of consternation.

Guy, who wanted to associate himself with the life of the place, reminded Miss Dunne that he would like to join her at tennis.

She said: "I'll give it thought," making it evident that she had more important things on her mind.

When Guy began suggesting days and times, she twitched her shoulders impatiently but could not keep from blushing.

They were served with goat's cheese and a salad of some

sort of green-stuff that roused a mild interest. Tennant went so far as to say: "This is a new one on me!"

Guy suggested that it might be samphire and quoted: "Halfe way down Hangs one that gathers Samphire; dreadful Trade." Tennant smiled, but it was clear to Guy that this was no place for badinage.

Supper over, he was eager to get down to the centre of the town and find his companions. In the Academy garden the evening was milky with the rising moon. Harriet wanted to stay out of doors and Guy followed her reluctantly into the Plaka where she walked quickly, driven still by a sense of search and conscious of having nothing she might find. She led the way towards the Acropolis.

The sky was brilliantly clear. As they climbed upwards, the Parthenon became visible, one side still caught in the pink of sunset, the other silvered by the full moon. As the sunset faded, the marble became luminous like alabaster lit from within and the Plaka shone with a supernatural pallor.

The Athenians remembered the threatened raid, knowing that some such shimmering, verdant night as this would be the night for destruction. Moving darkly in dark doorways, watching out at the passing strangers, people seemed expectant and distrustful.

Guy, who did not know the area, was afraid they would get lost in the dark. Harriet, beginning to tire, was willing to go back.

Tandy had left Zonar's. It was warm enough to sit out after dark and they found him with the others on the upper terrace of the Corinthian. They were seated round a table by the balustrade, uneasy like everyone else in a city that, salt-white and ebony, was defined for slaughter. And they were uneasy for another reason.

Ben Phipps, who had his own sources, said the British troops were already in retreat.

"If the Florina Gap's evacuated, then Greece is wide open."

"You think the Germans are on their way down here?" asked Tandy.

"It's likely. Almost certain, though there's nothing definite. I'm inclined to blame the Greek command. Papagos agreed to bring the Greek troops out of Albania and reinforce the frontier. He didn't do it. He said if they had to renounce their gains, the morale of the men would collapse. I don't believe that. I know the Greeks. Whatever happened, they would defend their own country. And now what's the result? The Greek army's probably done for. One half's cut off in Albania, and the other half's lost in Thrace."

They sat for a long time in silence, contemplating the possibility of defeat.

"Still," said Guy, trying to dispel the gloom, "we're not beaten yet."

Phipps gave a snort of derisive laughter, but after a pause said: "Well, perhaps not. The British aren't easily beaten, after all. And we're bound to hold on to Greece. It gives us a foothold in Europe. We just can't afford to lose it. We're an incompetent lot, but if we have to do a thing, we usually do it."

"If we hold," Alan said, "we could regain everything."

Ben agreed: "There have been miracles before."

Miracles offered more hope than reason and Yakimov, his eyes wide and lustrous in the moonlight, nodded earnestly. "We must have faith," he said.

"Good God!" Tandy stirred with disgust. "Surely things aren't as bad as that!"

"Of course not," Alan Frewen said.

There was silence, then Guy asked: "What news of Belgrade?"

"It's off the air," Ben told him. "Not a good sign. Rumour says the Germans reached the suburbs two days ago."

"Is that fact?"

"It's rumour, and rumours these days have a nasty habit of becoming fact."

"Then David Boyd must have left. He's sure to come tonight. The train's almost due." Guy looked at his watch, preparing to start for the station, and Ben Phipps held his arm.

"You don't imagine there'll be another train, do you? The Germans will have cut the line south of Belgrade. If your friend's stuck, he'll make for the coast. He might get a boat down from Split or Dubrovnik."

"Is it likely?"

"It's possible."

Ben Phipps, bored with Guy's anxiety for his missing friend, threw his head back and stared at the moon. His face blank, his glasses white in the moonlight, he said mockingly: "Don't worry. Even if Boyd isn't a diplomat, he'll be covered with angels' wings. If he's caught, the F.O.'ll bail him out. There's always something prepared for those chaps. Here they've got a yacht standing by. That'll take everyone of importance."

"And the rest of us?" Tandy asked.

Ben Phipps looked him up and down with a critical and caustic smile. "What have you got to worry about? You can walk on the water, can't you?"

Tandy though he laughed with the others, had a remote and calculating expression in his little eyes. He had declared his policy for survival. He did not stay anywhere too long, but here he was in a cul-de-sac. What would he do now?

As no one could answer this question, they turned their backs on a situation that was likely to defeat even Tandy, and began to talk of other things. Ben Phipps said Dubedat and Toby Lush spent their time standing in food queues. He had seen them in different shopping districts, buying up tinned foods that were too expensive for most people.

"They'll pay anything for anything," he said. "A bad sign if the Major's running short. How about Pinkers? How's he facing up to the emergency?"

"Splendidly," said Alan. "He's got only one worry: who should he get to translate his lecture into Greek? He wants it published in both languages. He keeps saying: 'I must have a scholar. Only a scholar will do,' and every day he trots in with a new suggestion. When this problem is settled (if it ever is!) we will have to decide who should print the work, then a distributor must be found ..."

"Are you serious?"

"My dear Ben, you think the question of the moment is: Will the Germans get here? If you worked in the News Room you would be required to ponder a question of infinitely greater import: how soon can we get Pinkrose's lecture into the bookshops?"

"So he's no longer concerned about his safety?"

"Never speaks of it."

"Think he's got an escape route up his sleeve?"

"If he has, I'd like to know what it is. A lot of people have to be got out of Grece: British subjects, committed Greeks, refugee Jews; four or five hundred, and quite a few children."

"I thought the children went on the evacuation boat?"

"Not all. Several women wouldn't leave their husbands. And life goes on. English babies have been born since the boat went."

"What has the Legation got in mind?"

"We must wait and see."

There were two narrow beds in the Pringles' room. Guy and Harriet had not slept apart since their marriage but now they would have the width of the room between them. Each felt cold alone, the covers were thin; and sandflies came in through the broken mesh of the window screens.

In the middle of the night Harriet woke and heard Guy moaning. He had been reading, propped up with a pillow, and had fallen asleep with the light on. She could see him struggling in sleep as against a tormentor. She crossed the room to where his bed stood under one of the windows and saw the sandflies shifting, as he struck out at them, in a flight leisurely but elusive. A moment later they attacked him again. He did not wake up but was conscious of her, and whimpered: "Make them go away."

She had bought a new box of pastilles and, after placing them on the table, the bed-head and the window-sill, lit them so the smoke encircled him like a *cheval-de-frise*. The pillow had dropped to the floor. She put it under his head, then stood at the end of the bed and watched while the flies dispersed. He sank back into sleep, murmuring: "David has not come."

She said: "He may come tomorrow."

From some outpost of sleep, so distant it was beyond the restrictions of time, he answered with extreme sadness: "He won't come now. He's lost."

"Aren't we all lost?" she asked, but he had gone too far to hear her.

Back in bed, she thought of the early days of their marriage when she had believed she knew him completely. She still believed she knew him completely, but the person she knew now was not the person she had married. She saw that in the beginning she had engaged herself to someone she did not know. There were times when he seemed to her so changed, she could not suppose he had any hold on her. Imagining all the threads broken between them, she thought she had only to walk away. Now she was not sure. At the idea of flight, she felt the tug of loyalties, emotions and dependencies. For each thread broken, another had been thrown out to claim her. If she tried to escape, she might find herself held by a complex, an imprisoning web, she did not even know was there.

Rumours, that the authorities did not deny, grew more coherent. By Sunday they had taken on the substance of truth. It was Palm Sunday and the beginning of Easter week, but no one gave much thought to Easter this year. It was a dull, chilly day with a gritty wind that seemed to carry anxiety like an infection. Everyone was out of doors, moving about the main streets, restless, aimless and asking what was happening.

Alan Frewen, walking from the Academy with the Pringles, was several times stopped by English people who lived at Psychico or Kifissia and usually spent their Sundays at home.

This Sunday, like everyone else, they had caught suddenly and for no reason they could name, the *frisson* of alarm. They had felt themselves drawn to the city's centre, imagining that someone there might tell them something. Alan, as Information Officer, would know what was going on. Again and again he was asked to deny the rumour that German mechanized forces were driving almost unopposed through the centre of Greece. It could not be true. Everyone knew the fall of Salonika had been inevitable. The northern port was too near the frontier. It could not be held. But this talk of the British being in retreat! British resistance was not so easily broken. The stories must be the work of fifth columnists?

Alan, listening with sombre sympathy, agreed that the fifth columnists were doing their worst. It was true the British had withdrawn from the Florina Gap, but that, likely enough, was part of a plan. He did not think anyone need feel unduly anxious. The British were not beaten yet.

People accepted his comfort, realizing that he was doing his best but knew no more than they did themselves. They thanked him, looked cheerful, and went off in search of other informants.

One man, Plugget, with a mottled face, wiry moustache and the brisk yap of a terrier dog, did not play his part so well. The Pringles had never seen him before. He worked for an English firm but had married a Greek and associated chiefly with Greeks, but now, like everyone else, had come out in search of news. He rejected Alan's consolation out of hand.

"Don't believe it," he said. "Things look bad, and I think they're worse than bad. I don't like it at all. What's going to happen to us? And what did our chaps come here for? Retreating without a shot fired! What's the idea? They just caused trouble, and now they'll be getting out and leaving us to face the music. Not a shot fired! It's the talk of the town," he insisted, while his wife stood on one side looking ashamed for him.

"If that's the talk of the town, it's being put round by fifth columnists," said Alan.

"You're deceiving yourself, Frewen. There aren't all that number of fifth columnists. It's a terrible business. We went to see a lad in hospital, relation of the wife. He'd just been sent down from a field depot. He said it's chaos up there."

At last, in need of comfort themselves, Alan and the Pringles were able to move on to Zonar's. Tandy, who had gone inside out of the wind, was seated with Yakimov and Ben Phipps at a short distance from a party of English women which included Mrs. Brett and Miss Jay. At the sight of Alan, Mrs. Brett jumped to her feet and hurried to him, calling out: "What's the news? They say our lads are on the run. You can tell me the truth. I'm English. I shall keep my head."

Standing over her with his mountainous air of pity, Alan let her repeat over and over again: "I'm not alarmed. No, I'm not alarmed. If we're in a fix, don't hesitate to let me know."

When his chance came, Alan said slowly and firmly: "It's a perfectly orderly withdrawal: a piece of strategy. They've decided to reinforce the Olympus Line."

Mrs. Brett gave a cry of rapture: "I knew it was something like that. I've been telling everyone it was something like that. And we can rely on the Olympus Line, can't we? That's where the Australians are." She returned to her friends shouting: "I told you so ... nothing to worry about ..." but her manner was too confident, too much what might be expected from an Englishwoman who sees calamity ahead.

Ben Phipps watched her with a sour approval and when Alan sat down, asked: "Have you any reason for making that statement?"

"We must hope while we can."

"Nothing definite, then?"

"Nothing. And you?"

"Nothing at all. And probably won't be. They could keep us in the dark till the Jerries walk in. That's what happened in Salonika. There was a camp full of Poles: no one told them, no one did anything about them. Some of the English did a last-minute bolt, but they got no warning. It could happen here."

"I doubt it," Alan said, but there was over all of them the fear of being overtaken unawares. Their instinct was to keep together. If one knew something, then the rest would know. If they were overtaken, they would not be alone. Even Guy was distracted from the urge to find distraction and stayed with the others, knowing there was nothing to be done but wait.

Though nobody except Yakimov preserved any extravagant ideas about Tandy, he acted as a nucleus for the group. He was, if nothing else, experienced in flight. Even Phipps agreed that Tandy knew his way around. If anyone escaped, he would escape; and the rest of them might escape with him.

Less than a week after Charles left, Harriet saw the first English soldiers returning to Athens. There were two lorry-loads. The lorries stopped outside a requisitioned hotel but the men made no attempt to move.

She went over to them thinking if there was news, they would have it. The tail-board of the first lorry was down and she could see the men lying, some on the floor, some propped against baggage, one with his head drooping forward, his hands dangling between his knees. They seemed dazed. When she asked: "Where do you come from? Is there any news?" no one answered her.

Two of the men wore muddy bandages on their heads. Several moments after she had spoken, one of them lifted his eyes and looked through her, and she took a step back, feeling rebuffed. They were exhausted, but it was not only that. A smell of defeat came from them like a smell of gangrene. Their hopelessness brought her to the point of tears.

People on the pavement stopped and stared in dismay. It had been no time at all since the British troops drove out of Athens singing and laughing and catching flowers thrown by the girls. Now here they were, back, so chilled by despair that a sense of death was about them like frozen mist about an iceberg.

It had been raining and the sky, bagged with wet, hung in dark boas of cloud over the hills. The wind was tearing up the blossom and the pink and white petals circled on the ground among the dust and paper scraps.

An officer came out of the hotel and an elderly businessman on the pavement said in English: "We've been told nothing. We want to know what's happening."

"You're not the only one," the officer said, and, going to the lorry, he shouted at the men: "Get a move on there."

Somehow the men roused themselves and slid down from the lorry like old men. As they crossed the pavement, someone put a hand on the arm of one of the wounded. He shook it off, not impatiently, but as though the weight of a hand were more than he could bear.

When they had all gone inside, Harriet remained standing, uncertain which way she had been going. She had left Guy in the bookshop in Constitution Square to go round the chemist shops in search of aspirin, but the aspirin was forgotten and she hurried back to the square. She had had proof of disaster. Guy, seeing her, was startled. At first she could not speak, then she tried to describe what she had seen but, strangled by her own description, sobbed instead. He opened his arms and caught her into them. His physical warmth, the memory of his courage when the villa was shaken by gun-fire, her own need and the knowledge he needed her: all those things overwhelmed her and she held to him, saying: "I love you."

"I know," he answered as lightly as he had answered when she first said the same thing on the train to Bucharest. Suddenly angry, she broke away from him, saying: "No, you don't. You don't know; you don't know anything."

He had hold of her hand and now shook it in reproof. "I know more than you think," he said.

"Well, perhaps." She wiped her eyes like a child that is promised another doll for the doll that is broken, and scarcely knew which meant more, her loss, or her hope of recompense.

"Come on, you need a drink," Guy said and, pulling her hand through his arm, led her from the shop.

During the day more lorries arrived, small convoys bringing in soldiers stupid with fatigue. At first people stood amazed in the streets, then they knew the rumours were right. These stricken men meant only one thing. The battle was lost. The

English were in retreat. Yet people remained standing about, expecting some sort of explanation. There would surely be an announcement. Their fears would be denied. The day passed, and no announcement was made. The Athenians could be kept in ignorance no longer. Disaster was upon them. They had seen it for themselves.

In the early evening, impelled to get away from a town benumbed by reality, Alan Frewen said he must give his dog a run. He suggested that they all take the bus down to the sea front and walk to Tourkolimano.

Unlike the rest of them, Ben Phipps was in an excited state for he had narrowly escaped death. While driving in from Psychico, he had been caught in a raid and had joined some men sheltering in a doorway. Two Heinkels had swooped down like bats, one behind the other, and opened fire, pitting the road with bullets. No one had been hurt and when the aircraft were gone, Ben had run out and picked up in his handkerchief a bullet too hot to hold. He could talk of nothing but his adventure and on the esplanade he brought on the bruised bullet and threw it into the air, saying: "I've been personally machine-gunned."

His delight amused Alan, who watched him much as he watched the gambols of Diocletian. "You have not gone to the war," Alan said. "But the war has come to you. Could any journalist ask for more?"

The clouds had broken with evening, revealing the vast red and purple panorama of sunset. When the colours had faded, a mist rose over the sea, jade-grey yet luminous, reminding them of the long twilights of summer. Alan began to talk of the islands and the seaside days that lay ahead.

Melancholy and nostalgic, they reached the little harbour of Tourkolimano as darkness fell. "We have been deprived of heaven," Harriet said.

"It will come again," said Alan. "Even the war can't last for ever."

They made their way through streets devastated by the explosion, climbing among broken bricks and wood, intending to catch a bus on the Piraeus road. When they saw a thread of light between black-out curtains, they stopped, glad to get under cover. They crowded into the narrow café where there were a few rough tables lit by candle-ends. The proprietor, who sat alone at the back of the room, welcomed them with a mournful courtesy so it seemed, in the silence and solitude, that they had come to a region of the dead.

During the last few days the men had taken to telling limericks and stories and talking about life in a large general way while they all drank themselves into a state of genial intoxication. In such close companionship, the sense of danger receded and was sometimes forgotten. Sitting knee to knee in the little café served with glasses of Greek brandy, they tried to remember some comic verse or anecdote that had not yet been told. Harriet said to Yakimov: "Tell us that story you told the first time we met you. The story about a croquet match."

Yakimov smiled to himself, gratified by the request, but not quick to comply. He was penniless again and dependent for his drinks on anyone who would buy them, but had no wish to return to his old arduous profession of raconteur. His pale, heavy eyelids drooped and he gazed into his glass. Finding it empty, he slid it on to the table and said: "How about a drop more brandy?"

Guy called to the proprietor and the brandy bottle was placed beside Yakimov, who sighed his content and said: "Dear me, yes; the croquet match!"

The story that had been funny in Bucharest was here, at the dark end of the lost world, almost too funny to bear. Every time Yakimov, in his small, epicene voice, said the word "balls", his listeners became more helplessly convulsed until at last they were lying about in their chairs, sobbing with laughter. The proprietor watched them in astonishment, never having seen the English behave in this way before.

When no one could think of a story that had not been told, they sat abstracted, conscious of the quiet of the ruined sea-front and the streets about them.

After long silence, Alan said: "When I camped out on the battlefield of Marathon, I was awakened by the sound of swords striking against shields." He seemed to be confessing to an experience which in normal times he would not care to mention, and the others, impressed against reason, knew he spoke the truth. Ben Phipps said that he came from Kineton and had often been told that local farmers would not cross Edgehill at night.

Roger Tandy grunted several times and at last brought out:

"Everyone's heard something like that. In Ireland there's a field where a battle was fought in the fourth century of the world -- and the peasants say they can still hear them banging away."

The others laughed but even Guy, the unpersuadable materialist, was caught into the credulous atmosphere and discussed with the others the theory that anguish, anger, terror and similar violent emotions impressed themselves upon the ether so that for centuries after they could be perceived by others.

Harriet imagined their own emotions impinging upon the atmosphere of earth and wondered how long her own shade would walk through the Zappion Gardens, not alone.

Ben took his bullet out of his pocket and rolled it across the table. Did they suppose, he asked, that his emotions had become fixed in the doorway where he had been a target for the German air-gunners?

Yakimov tittered and said: "Must have been harrowing, dear boy. Did you change colour?"

"Change colour? I bloody near changed sex."

Alan gave a howl of glee and, leaning back against the wall, wiped his large hands over his face and gasped: "Oh dear!" In this exigency, fear was the final absurdity. They could do nothing but laugh. They were still laughing when the proprietor told them apologetically that he had to close the café. In happier days he would be glad to have them drink all night; but now – he made a gesture – the explosion had destroyed his living quarters and he had to walk to his brother's room at Amfiali.

No one had come into the café except the English party and Alan asked the proprietor why he troubled to stay open. He replied that during the day the café was used by longshoremen and dock workers, and sometimes a few came in after dark. Apart from them, the district was deserted.

"Where has everyone gone?"

The man made an expressive gesture. Many were dead, that went without saying; so many that no one yet knew the number. Others were camping in the woods round Athens.

"God save us," muttered Tandy. "We've had war and famine; the next thing'll be plague. We've all got dysentry, and if we don't get typhoid, it'll be a miracle."

Sobered, they went out in the cold night air and made their way to the bus stop by the light of the waning moon.

There were English soldiers again in the cafés but they had lost their old sociability. They knew they would not be in Greece much longer and, conscious of the havoc they had brought, were inclined to avoid those who had most to lose by it.

One of Guy's students shouted at him in the street: "Why did they come here? We didn't want them," but there were few complaints. The men were also victims of defeat. Seeing them arriving back in torn and dirty battle-dress, jaded by the long retreat under fire, the girls again threw them flowers: the flowers of consolation.

On Wednesday evening Guy went to the School and found it deserted. Harriet had walked there with him and on the way back they looked into several bars, hoping to see someone who could give them news. In one they saw a British corporal sprawled alone against the counter and singing to a dismal hymn tune:

> "When this flippin' war is over,
> Oh, how happy I shall be!
> Once I get m'civvy clothes on
> No more soldiering for me.
> No more asking for a favour;
> No more pleading for a pass . . ."

He broke off at the sight of the Pringles and when Guy invited him to a drink he straightened himself up, and assumed the manners of normal life.

"English are you?" he said and, too polite to express his bewilderment at their presence in this beleaguered place, eyed them cautiously from head to foot.

They began at once to ask him about events. He shook his head and said: "Funny do. They say there were millions of them."

"Really? Millions of what?"

"Jerries on flippin' motor-bikes. The Aussies picked them off so fast, there was this pile-up and they had to dynamite a road through them. And all the time Stukas and things buzzing

round like flippin' hornets. Never saw anything like it. Didn't
stand a chance. Right from the start; not a chance."

"Where are the Germans now?" Harriet asked.

"Up the road somewhere."

"Not far, you think?"

"Not unless someone's stopped them."

Guy said: "They say the New Zealanders are still holding at
the Aliakmon."

"When did y'hear that, then?"

"Yesterday."

"Ho, yesterday!" the Corporal grunted; yesterday was not
today. When Guy ordered him another drink, he looked the
Pringles over again and felt forced to speak: "What are you
two doing here, then? You're not hanging on, are you?"

"We're hoping something will happen. The situation could be
reversed?"

"Don't know about that. Can't say."

"And you? What are going to do?"

"We're told to make for the bridge."

"Which bridge?"

"Souf," said the Corporal. "Our lot's going souf," then as it
occurred to him that he was saying too much, he downed his
drink at a gulp, picked up his cap and said: "Be seeing you,'
and went.

From this information, such as it was, the Pringles surmised
that the British forces intended to hold the Morea. They set
off to take their news to Tandy's table; but Ben Phipps was
there before them and his agitated indignation put the Corporal right out of mind.

"What do you think?" Phipps demanded of them. "You'd
never believe it I've just come from the Legation. There's
nothing laid on. Not a thing. Not a ghost of a plan. Not a smell
of a boat. We're done for. Do you realize it? We're done for.'

"Who told you this?" Tandy asked.

"They told me themselves. I said: 'What are the arrangements for evacuating the English refugees?' and they just said,
they just *calmly* said: 'There aren't any arrangements.' The
excuse is they didn't know what was going to happen. 'Well,
you know now,' I said. 'And people are getting anxious. No
one's making a fuss, but they want to know what's being done
for them. They can't just sit here waiting for the Germans to

come. What's laid on?' I asked. Nothing they said: just nothing. There aren't any ships."

Yakimov said, shocked: "Dear boy, there must be ships."

"No," Ben Phipps shook his head in violent denial. "There are no ships."

"The Yugoslavs say they're going," Tandy said.

"Oh, yes. The Yugoslavs are being looked after. The Poles, too. Someone's fixed them up – don't ask me who – but there's nothing for the poor bloody British. I said: 'Can't you pack us in with the Jugs and Poles?' And they said: 'Their boats are already overcrowded'."

Tandy stared at the street with a reflective blankness. Only Ben Phipps had anything to say: "The usual good old British cock-up, eh? Isn't it? I said: 'Don't you realize the Germans could be here in twenty-four hours?' and what d'you think they said? They said: 'It all happened so suddenly.' *Suddenly!* Yes, it did happen suddenly, but that doesn't mean it wasn't obvious from the start. We ought to have kept out of this shindig. It's not only that we've done no good. If we hadn't stuck in our two-pennyworth, they might have got away with it. We send a handful of men up with a few worn-out tanks, then say: 'We didn't know.' I ask you! What did they think?"

"They thought we'd get through to Berlin," Harriet said.

Phipps gave a snort of bitter laughter: "No foresight. No preparations. No plans. And now no ships." Biting his thumb, he muttered through his teeth with the morose rage of one who realizes that his blackest criticism of authority was never black enough.

There was a long silence at the end of which Guy mildly asked: "Meanwhile, what news, if any?"

"We've admitted a strategic withdrawal along the Aliakmon Line."

"What do you think that means?"

"Only that the Jerries are coming hell for leather down the coast road."

Tandy grunted and pulled out his splendid wallet. He put a note on the table to pay his share of the drinks and said: "Not much point in saving drachma now. If things fold up here, it won't be much use anywhere else. How about coming to my hotel for a valedictory dinner?"

"How about it, dear boy!" said Yakimov, joyfully taking up

the invitation. He and Tandy began at once to rise, but Alan Frewen had not arrived and the others were unwilling to go without him.

Eager to be off, Yakimov persuaded them: "He'll be at the office. We'll pick him up on the way." They went to the side entrance of the Grande Bretagne and, finding it shut, walked on to the Corinthian, where the refugees were ordering their departure. Although the passengers for the Polish and Yugo-slav ships – among them the gold-braided Yugoslav officers – were not due to embark until next morning, they were having their heavy luggage brought down and heaped ready at the hotel entrance. The English party, making a way through the hubbub, saw Alan Frewen sitting in a corner, alone except for the dog at his feet.

Ben Phipps, carrying his anger over on to Alan, said: "Look at him, the bastard! He's avoiding us." He caught hold of Guy to prevent him from approaching the lonely man, but Guy was already away, dodging between chairs and tables in his eagerness to rescue Alan from solitude.

Alan looked discomforted when he saw the friends to whom he could offer so little hope, but assumed a confident attitude when Ben Phipps at once accused him: "Don't you realize we're stranded? Don't you realize that nothing's been done?"

Alan said soothingly: "There'll be something tomorrow."

"Nothing today, but something tomorrow! What, for in-stance? Where are they going to find it?"

Alan checked him, speaking with the quiet of reason: "You know the problem as well as I do. The explosions wrecked everything in the harbour. Thousands of tons of shipping went to the bottom, so there's a shortage of ships. You can't blame the Legation for that. The water-front was wiped out. Dobson tells me it's absolute desolation down there."

"Is Dobson in charge of the evacuation, supposing there is evacuation?"

"No, but he's been down to the Piraeus to look around. He's doing his best for you all."

"A last-minute effort, I must say. This situation should have been foreseen weeks ago."

"If it had been, we'd have chartered ships; and they'd've gone to the bottom with the rest."

"So nothing has been done, and nothing will be done? Is that it?"

"Plenty's being done." Glancing at Harriet's pale face, then back to Phipps, Alan said: "For God's sake, have some sense!"

Tandy had not stopped to listen to this discussion. As though unconcerned in it, he strolled on to the dining-room and Yakimov, who could not bear to let him out of sight, said to Alan: "Do come, dear boy. We're all invited. Friend Tandy is standing treat."

Alan nodded and Yakimov hurried ahead. Though not the bravest of men, he still had more appetite than the rest of them, and apparently felt that while he remained in the lee of Tandy's large, sumptuous figure, he had nothing to fear.

They were served with some sort of stewed offal which tasted of nothing at all. Alan gazed at his plate, then put it down in front of the dog.

"Dear boy!" Yakimov murmured in protest, but the plate had already been licked clean.

The second course comprised a few squares of cheese and dry bread and Alan left his share for Yakimov.

Jovially chewing cheese, Yakimov added: "How is the noble lord these days?"

"No idea," Alan said. "He hasn't been in for a week. The office is empty except for the Twocurrys. Mabel of course, doesn't know what's going on, and Gladys isn't telling her."

"So you're in charge? Then how about getting your Yak back on the payroll?"

Alan's face collapsed in its odd, pained smile: "I'll see what can be done," he promised.

The air-raid sirens sounded and the dining-room became silent as the diners sat tense, awaiting the raid that would reduce Athens to dust. The minutes passed and all that could be heard was the distant thud of the Piraeus guns.

Alan sighed and said: "Just a reconnaissance buzzing around."

"What do they hope to find?" Tandy asked.

"They think we might send reinforcements. They don't know how little we've got."

"Perhaps we will send something."

"We've nothing to send."

They went up to the terrace and waited for the All Clear. A

waning moon edged above the house tops, casting an uneasy, shaded light that accentuated the clotted darkness of the gardens. The raid had brought the city to a standstill. No one moved in the square and there was nothing to be seen but a group of civic police standing, shadowy, among the shadows.

Tandy was exercising himself. Marching with a military strut, he went from one end of the terrace to the other, and Yakimov trotted at his side. Tandy lit one of his Turkish cigarettes. Yakimov, though he hated Turkish cigarettes, felt bound to imitate his companion. So they walked backwards and forwards, filling the air with a rich Turkish aroma.

Harriet, seated by the rail, watching them as they reached the end of the terrace, turned in unison and came towards her with their long coats sweeping out behind them, was reminded of other wars, remote if not distant, when aristocratic generals conferred on fronts that were not demolished in a day.

Both men were tall but Tandy, topped by the big fur hat that in battle would be an object of terror, looked too large for life. Harriet felt sorry for Yakimov, the fragile ghost, bowed with the effort of keeping up with his monstrous companion. When they came near her, she called him to her. He paused. She lifted the edge of his coat, admiring the lining: "A wonderful coat," she said. "It will last a lifetime."

"Two lifetimes, dear girl, if not three. M'poor old dad wore it, you know, and the Czar gave it a bit of wear before it was passed on. I wonder, *did* I tell you the Czar gave it to m'poor old dad?"

"I think you did."

"Magnificent coat." Yakimov stroked the fur then turned to Tandy, who was stopped beside him, and happy to share this admiration, said: "Yours is a fine coat, too, dear boy. Where did y'get it? Budapest?"

"Azerbaijan," said Tandy.

"Azerbaijan," breathed Yakimov and, putting his cigarette to his lips, he caught his breath in awe.

Their voices had carried on the noiseless air and the police were looking up. As Yakimov drew on his cigarette, they shouted a command which no one but Alan Frewen understood. Yakimov drew again and the command was repeated.

Alan raised himself in his chair, saying urgently: "They're telling you to put out that cigarette," but he spoke too late.

The police were armed. One drew his revolver and fired. Tandy ducked and Yakimov folded slowly. He said in a whisper of puzzled protest: "Dear boy!" and collapsed to the ground. His face retained the expression of his words. He seemed about to speak again but, when Harriet knelt beside him, his breathing had stopped. She pulled his coat open and put her hand on his heart: "I think he's dead," she said.

As she spoke, Guy, who had been watching, dazed by what had happened, was suddenly possessed by rage and went to the rail and shouted down: "You murderous swine! Do you know what you've done? Do you care? You bloody-minded maniacs!"

The police stared up, blank-faced, understanding him no more than Yakimov had understood them.

The shot had brought people to the terrace, among them the hotel manager. Harassed by all the bustle inside the hotel, he had neither time nor sympathy for what had happened outside. He looked at the body and ordered those around it: "Take him away," but as no one could leave during a raid, he turned in exasperation and went in again.

Harriet pulled Yakimov's coat about his body and a waiter covered his face with a napkin. When she stood up, she felt dizzy. Spent by the accumulation of events, she collapsed into a chair. Midnight chimed on some distant clock.

Ben Phipps asked Alan where Yakimov lived. No one knew, but Alan thought it was one of the small hotels in Omonia Square. He said with the practicality of shock: "No point in taking him there; no point in taking him anywhere. If they'll let us, the thing would be to leave him here. He'll have to be buried first thing tomorrow. We may all be gone in twenty-four hours. Where's Tandy? Tandy lives in the hotel: he's the one to talk to the manager."

But Tandy, unnoticed by any of them, had gone to bed.

"Trust him," Ben said bitterly. "Not much bed for the rest of us. It'll take all night to sort things out. When's this damned raid going to end?"

The manager, his fury forgotten, returned with the police. They talked to Alan, making gestures of compunction and inculpability, and explained that the man who fired had intended only to frighten his victim. Yakimov's death had been an error. The fact that he was an Englishman made the incident particularly regrettable, but he had disobeyed an order twice repeated; and in these times there were so many deaths!

They looked at the body. They wanted to see Yakimov's *carte d'identité*, his *permis de séjour*, his *permis de travailler*, and his passport. When all the papers had been found in different pockets of Yakimov's clothing, his long, narrow corpse was rewrapped in its greatcoat as in a shroud, and the napkin rearranged over his face.

One of the police handed back Yakimov's passport and gave a salute and a little bow. The English would be troubled no further. The victim was free to go to his grave.

The manager agreed to let the body rest for the night in one of the hotel bathrooms. The four friends followed as it was carried away from the terrace and placed on a bathroom floor. As the door was locked upon it, the all clear sounded. The manager, offering his commiserations, shook hands all round and the English party left the hotel. Alan, hourly expecting an evacuation order, had decided to spend the night in his office. Ben Phipps, on his way to Psychico, dropped the Pringles off at the Academy.

A message was waiting for Guy on the pad in the hall. He was to ring Lord Pinkrose at Phaleron no matter how late his return. Harriet stood beside him as he dialled the number. The Phaleron receiver was removed at once and Pinkrose asked in an agitated scream: "Is that you, Pringle? The Germans are less than six hours from Athens. They'll be here by morning. If you're wise, you'll go at once."

"But how can we go?" Guy asked. "There are no ships."

"Get down to the Piraeus. Board anything you can see. *Make* them take you.'

"We've been ordered to stand by ..." Guy protested, but Pinkrose was not listening. His receiver was replaced.

"Is that what he intends doing himself?" Harriet asked. "Do you think he's going to the Piraeus to get on to any ship he can see?"

"God knows. Let's pack our things and think about it."

The upper corridor was in darkness. No light was showing under any of the bedroom doors. They met no one whom they could ask for guidance. The silence was such, the building might, for all they knew, have emptied in their absence.

As they got their belongings together, Harriet asked: "Why do you think he warned us like that?".

"I suppose he feels some responsibility for us. He's still my boss, you know."

"I wish he hadn't bothered."

Their indecision was painful. Guy hung over his books, sorting out those that could be left behind and collected one day, when the war was over. Harriet threw her things pell-mell into a suitcase, then fell on to her bed and, lying there, eyes closed, felt herself sinking down into the darkness of the earth.

"Well, what do we do now?" Guy asked.

Rousing herself, she saw him standing in the middle of the wide, bare floor, his shirt-collar open, his shirt-sleeves rolled up. He was holding a book she knew well; the book that six months before he had picked out of the wreckage of their Bucharest flat. He was trying to look undaunted by events, but the droop of his face told her that he was as tired as she was and had no more answer than she to the problems that beset them. He presented an unruffled front to life, but she saw he was as much at sea as she was.

They had learnt each others' faults and weaknesses: they had passed both illusion and disillusion. It was no use asking for more than anyone could give.

War had forced their understanding. Though it was, as Guy said, a pre-war marriage, it had been a marriage in war, and the war had not ended yet. For all they knew it would not end in their lifetime. Meanwhile, they were still alive and still together; and they must face their commitments. She had chosen to make her life with Guy and would stand by her choice. The important thing, she thought, was that in a final contingency, they should not fail each other.

She asked: "What do you want to do?" He sighed. She held out her arms to him and he crossed the room and sat on the edge of the bed, saying: "Do you want to go down to the Piraeus now? Do you want to force your way on to some boat that is not meant for us? There are hundreds of English people here, some with children – they have as much right to go as we have. If everyone scrambled down to the docks and fought their way on to boats reserved for Yugoslavs and Poles, there'd be chaos. We don't want to make things worse for others. I feel we should take our chance with the rest. I don't believe they'll abandon us."

"Neither do I."

She put her arms round him and he lay down beside her. Too tired to undress, they slept, each holding the other secure upon the narrow bed.

Next morning, all the inmates of the hotel were sitting round the breakfast table, subdued, but scarcely more subdued than usual. Guy said: "Someone told us last night that the Germans were only six hours from Athens. He seemed to think they'd be here by morning."

"They're not here yet," Tennant said. He smiled and, knowing things were too far gone for rebuttal, said slowly: "But your informant was partly right. We heard that German parachute troops had dropped on Larissa, but that didn't mean they were coming straight here. They've still got to negotiate the pass at Thermopylae, the old invaders' bottleneck. Of course, it's not as narrow as it was. When the Spartans held it against Xerxes it was only twenty-five feet at the narrowest point. Now . . . how wide is it, would you say?" Tennant turned to consult his colleagues.

"Still, they are at Larissa?" Harriet asked.

"They may well be." Tennant bent towards Harriet, giving her a smile of surprising sweetness: "Please do not think I am withholding the truth from you. No one really knows anything. The train lines are cut in Macedonia. Telephone communication with the front has broken down. We are as much in the dark as you are."

The mourners had arranged to meet in Alan's office. At the bottom of Vasilissis Sofias the Pringles were passed by Toby Lush and Dubedat in the Major's Delahaye. Toby gave them a cheerful wave and Harriet said: "Don't you think that those two are putting a surprisingly brave face on things?"

"What else can they do?" Guy said.

"Well, Pinkrose wanted us to bolt last night. Why didn't they bolt?"

"I don't know, but they evidently didn't. Perhaps they felt as we did about it."

"Perhaps."

"They aren't such bad fellows, really."

Harriet did not argue. She saw that having grown up without faith, in an inauspicious era, Guy had to believe in something and so, against all reason, maintained a faith in friendship. If he chose to forget his betrayal, then let him forget it.

Ben Phipps was already in the News Room. He sat in Yakimov's old corner while Alan, behind his desk, talked into the telephone. He was saying as though he had said it a hundred times before: "Don't worry. You'll be rung up just as soon as transport is available. Yes, yes, something is being done all right," and putting down the receiver, said: "Can they take horses, dogs, cats, fishes? I don't know! What does one do when one has to give up one's home and all the dependent creatures in it?" He rubbed his hands over his face and, eyes watering from lack of sleep, looked about him as though he scarcely knew where he was.

"So nothing's been arranged yet?" Guy said.

"No. Not yet."

Ben got to his feet: "What about the poor old bastard in the bathroom."

"Yes, let's get that over," Alan agreed. He edged himself out of his chair and waited while Diocletian came from under the desk with a scratch and a snuffle. As they left the office, the Pringles told the story of Pinkrose's panic order the previous night. Had Pinkrose gone himself?

Alan said: "No, he rang this morning. He didn't seem unduly alarmed."

"It's odd," said Harriet, "that he's not more alarmed. And it's even more odd that Lush and Dubedat are taking things so calmly."

Guy and Alan said nothing, but Ben Phipps stopped on the pavement, screwing up his face against the sunlight, and stared at his car, then swung round and blinked at Harriet: "It *is* odd," he said. "If you ask me, it's damned odd," and, crossing to the car, he got in and drove away.

Alan looked after him in astonishment. "Where's he off to?"

Guy said: "To his office, most likely. He'll be back."

"He'll have to hurry. Dobson has ordered the hearse for ten o'clock."

They strolled to the Corinthian that was in ferment with the departing Poles and Yugoslavs. Though the ships were not due to sail before noon, the voyagers were shouting at porters,

harrying taxi-drivers and generally urging their own de-
liverance with a great deal more flurry than was shown by the
English who might not be delivered at all.

Six Yugoslav officers, their gold aflash, came at a run down
the front steps, threw their greatcoats into a taxi and crying:
"Hurry, hurry," threw themselves in after and were gone.

Some Greeks stood on the pavement, watching, silent, their
black eyes fixed in an intent dejection.

Tandy, who usually took his breakfast out of doors, was not
among those sitting round the café tables. Guy offered
to find him, and Alan said: "Tell him to hurry. It's nearly ten
o'clock."

Alan and Harriet felt it was scarcely worth sitting down and
were still standing among the café tables when Guy returned.
He was alone.

"Well, is he coming?" Alan asked.

Guy motioned to the nearest table. Harriet and Alan sat
down, puzzled by Guy's expression. It was some moments
before he could bring himself to tell them what he knew. He
said at last: "Tandy's gone."

"Gone where?"

"To the Piraeus. He left early. Apparently he came down
about seven a.m., asked for his bill and told them to fetch down
his luggage and call a taxi. He mentioned to one of the porters
that he was going on the *Varsavia.*"

Harriet looked at Alan: "Would he be allowed on?"

"He might: one man alone. And he took the precaution of
going early, did he?" Alan laughed: "Didn't want to be saddled
with the rest of us."

"He forgot this." Guy opened his hand and showing the bill
for Tandy's valedictory dinner, said apologetically: "I'm afraid
I hadn't enough to settle it all, so I gave them half and
thought ..."

Alan nodded and took the bill: "I'll pay the rest."

Tandy's flight silenced them. They not only missed his company, but were absurdly downcast by a superstitious fear that
without him they were lost. They waited without speaking for
the hearse to arrive and Ben Phipps to return.

An hour passed without a sign from either and Harriet said:
"Perhaps Ben Phipps has got on the *Varsavia.*"

Guy and Alan were shocked by her distrust of a friend.

When Guy said: "I'm perfectly sure he hasn't," Alan grunted agreement and Harriet kept quiet for a long time afterwards.

They were joined by persons known to them who, stopping as they passed, gave different opinions: one that the Germans would be held at Thermopylae; another that they could not be held, but would drive straight through to Athens. As usual, no one knew anything.

Vourakis, with a shopping basket in his hand, stopped and said: "Of allied resistance there is nothing but a little line from Thermopylae to Amphissia."

"An important line, nevertheless," Alan said. "We could hold on there for weeks."

"You could, but you will not. They will say to you: 'Withdraw. Save yourselves, if you can. We want you here no more.' That is all we can say to our allies now." Vourakis spread his hands and contracted his shoulders in a gesture of despair. "This is the end," he said.

The others kept silent, not knowing what to reply.

"I have heard – I do not know how true – that some members of the Government want an immediate capitulation. Only that, they say, can save our city from the fate of Belgrade."

"Royalists, I suppose?" said Guy.

"No. Not at all. The King himself is against capitulation and he has refused to leave Athens, though many say to him: 'Fly, fly.' Believe me, Kyrios Pringle, there are brave men in all parties."

Guy was quick to agree, and Vourakis stood up, saying his wife had sent him out to buy anything he could find. The Germans, people knew, would take not only the food but medicines, clothing, household goods, anything and everything. So they were all out buying what they could find.

He passed on. It was now midday and still no hearse and no Ben Phipps.

Alan went to telephone the undertaker's office. He was told the hearse had gone to the funeral of an air-raid victim. The need these days was great, the servitors few. He returned to say: "The hearse, like death, will come when it will come."

"An apt simile," said Guy, and Harriet, growing restless, decided to go and buy some flowers.

In case they came to look for her, she said she would go to the flower shop beside the Old Palace, but when she reached

the corner she hurried into the gardens through the side
entrance and went to the Judas grove. As Alan had promised,
the trees had blossomed for Easter. She stood for a full minute
taking in the rosettes of wine-mauve flowers that covered
the leafless wood, devouring them in mind like someone who
gazes into a lighted window at a feast, then she hurried to the
shop and bought carnations for Yakimov.

With nothing else to do in a city where life was ebbing to a
stop, the three sat on and watched the sun move off the square.
It was late in the afternoon when the hearse and carriage drew
up before the hotel.

"They've done him proud," Guy said.

Four black horses, with silver trappings and tails to the
ground, drew a black hearse of ornamental wood and engraved
glass, surmounted by woeful black cherubs who held aloft
black candles and black ostrich plumes. These splendours
pleased the mourners but they did not please the hotel management. As soon as sighted, a porter came pelting down the
steps to order them round to the back entrance.

While Alan and the Pringles stood in the kitchen doorway
Dobson arrived in a taxi and joined them. The undertakers had
taken the flimsy coffin up to the bathroom and the living
listened to the arguments and the scraping of wood as it was
manoeuvred down the grey and grimy cement stairway.

Dobson, sniffing the smell of cooking-fat, rubbed his head-
fluff ruefully and said: "This is really too bad!"

"It could be worse," Guy said. "Chekov died in an hotel and
they smuggled him out in a laundry basket."

The coffin edged round into view and reached the hall where
the bearers, placing it on the ground, lifted the lid so all might
see that Yakimov and his possessions were intact.

"We forgot to close his eyes," Harriet said in distress and,
looking into them for the last time, saw they had lost their
lustre. Despite his greed, his ingratitude, his long history of
unpaid debts, he had a blameless look and she found herself
moved by his corpse, wrapped there in the Czar's old coat, as
she had never been moved by him in life. He had died demur-
ring, but it had been a gentle demur and the gaze that met
hers was mild, a little bewildered but resigned to the mis-
chance that had finished him off. Her own eyes filled with
tears. She turned away to hide them; the coffin lid was re-

placed, the carnations placed upon it, and the cortège set out.

Dobson had asked the English *popa* Father Harvey to conduct the service: "After all," he said, "Yaki must have been Orthodox."

"But Russian Orthodox, surely?" said Alan.

"His mother was Irish," Harriet said. "So he may have been a Catholic."

"Oh, well," said Dobson. "Harvey's a dear fellow and won't hold it against him."

They drove at a solemn pace past the Zappion and the Temple of Zeus and came to a district that no one except Alan had visited before. Above the cemetery wall, tall cypresses rose into the evening blue of the sky. Father Harvey had already arrived. In his *popa*'s robes, with his blond beard, his blond hair knotted behind the veil that fell from his *popa*'s hat, he led the funeral procession through the gate into the graveyard quiet.

There had been no one to buy a plot for Yakimov. The Legation was paying for the funeral, but the coffin would have only temporary lodging in the ground. Alan mentioned that he had had to identify the remains of a friend who had died while on holiday in Athens.

"What was there to identify?" Dobson asked.

"Precious little. Bodies disintegrate quickly in the dry summer heat; soon there's nothing but dust and a few powdery bones and bits of cloth. They put it all into a box and place it in the ossuary. I prefer that. I don't want to lie mouldering for years. And think of the saving of space!"

"There'll be no one to identify Yakimov," Harriet said.

Alan sadly agreed.

There would be no one left who had known him in life or remembered that the scraps of cloth lying among his long, fragile bones, had been a sable-lined greatcoat, once worn by the doomed, unhappy Czar of all the Russias.

Passing among the trees and shrubs, they came on small communities of graves that seemed like gatherings of friends, silent a moment till the intruders went by. When the ceremony was over, Harriet fell behind the party of mourners and, walking soundlessly on the grass verges, lingered to look at the statues and photographs of the dead. She did not want to leave this sequestered safety, where the ochre-golden light of the late sun rayed through the cypresses and gilded the leaves.

The richness of the enclosing greenery secluded her and gave her a sense of safety. When the men's voices passed out of hearing, a velvet quiet came down so she could imagine herself dead and immaterial in a region where the alarms of the present could affect her no more than those of the past. She wandered away from the direction of the gate, unwilling to leave.

Guy called her. She came to a stop beside a stone boy seated on a chair. Guy called again, breaking the air's intimate peace, and she felt her awareness contract and concentrate upon the destructive and futile hazards outside.

Guy came through the trees, reproving her: "Darling, do come along. Dobson has to get back to the Legation. There's a lot to be done there."

On the return journey, Harriet asked what they were doing up at the Legation.

"Oh!" Dobson gave a gasp of amusement at the ridiculous ploys of life. "We're burning papers. We're sorting out the accumulation of centuries. All the important, top-secret documents written by all the important top-secret characters in history are being dumped on a bonfire in the Legation garden."

Alan was returning with him to help in this task so the Pringles, dropped in the centre of Athens, found themselves alone.

Guy was certain that Ben Phipps would be waiting for them at the Corinthian, but there was no sign of him.

"Let's try Zonar's."

They walked quickly in the outlandish hope that Tandy might, after all, be there. But he was not there. And Ben Phipps was not there. The table was unoccupied. Disconcerted, disconsolate, they stood and looked at it. What they missed most was Tandy's welcome. He had liked them; but he had liked everyone, in a general way, as some people like dogs, and might have excused himself by saying: "They are company." He had been in Athens only ten days and in that time had become a habit. Now he had gone, it was as though a familiar tree had been cut down, a landmark lost.

They felt no impulse to sit down without him. While they stood on the corner of University Street, some English soldiers came and began to set up a machine-gun.

"What on earth's happening?" Guy asked.

"Martial law," said the sergeant. "I'd go in if I were you. There's a report that the fifth column mean to bump off all the British."

"I don't believe it."

The sergeant laughed: "Tell you the truth, I don't, neither."

The Greeks seated in the café chairs watched apathetic, as the gun was placed in position, resigned to anything that might happen in a city passing out of control.

Standing there with nothing to do, nowhere to go, Harriet could see from his ruminative expression that Guy was trying to think of some duty or obligation that might protect him from the desolation in the air. Fearful of being left alone, she caught his arm and said: "Please don't leave me."

"I ought to go to the School," he said. "I've left some books there; and the students might come to say good-bye."

"All right. We'll go together."

The sun had dropped behind the houses and long, azure shadows lay over the roads. With time to waste, the Pringles strolled back to Stadium Street where other machine-guns stood on corners. Soldiers were patrolling the pavements with rifles at the ready. Most of the shops had shut and some were boarded and battened as a precaution against riots or street-fighting. Yet, apart from the guns, the soldiers and the boarded shops, there was no visible derangement of life. There was no violence; there were no demonstrations; simply, the everyday world was running down.

A sense of dream pervaded the town. Even at this time, human beings were entering the world, or leaving it. Yakimov had died and had to be buried, but his death had been an event in another dimension of time. Now, it was amazing to see the tram-cars running. When one of them clanked past, people stared, bewildered by men who had still the heart to go on working. The rest of them seemed to be without occupation, employment or interest. They had nothing to do. There was nothing to be done. They had wandered out of doors and now stood about, blank and silent in the nullity of grief.

Before they reached Omonia Square, Harriet was stopped by the sight of a shoe standing in an empty window: a single shoe of emerald silk with a high, brilliant-studded heel. Peering into the gloom of the shop, she saw there was nothing else.

Cupboards stood open; drawers had been pulled out; paper and cardboard boxes had been kicked into corners. The only thing that remained was the shoe with its glittering heel.

In the square they saw Vourakis again, still carrying his shopping-basket, though there was nothing left to buy. A few shops had remained open but the owners gazed out vacantly, knowing the routine of buying and selling had come to an end like everything else.

Vourakis was tired. His eyelids were red and his dark, narrow face had sunk in as though in the last few hours old age had overtaken him. He had spoken to Guy only once or twice but caught his arm and held to him, saying: "You should go, you know. You should save yourselves while there is time."

"They can't find a ship for us," Guy said.

Vourakis shook his head in compassion. "Let us sit down a while," he said, and led them to a café that smelt strongly of aniseed. The only thing kept there was ouzo and while they drank a couple of glasses, Vourakis told them stories of heroism and defiance that he had heard from the wounded who were now coming in in thousands from the field hospitals. Even now, he said, when all was lost, there were Greeks resisting and determined to resist to the death.

These stories of gallantry in the midst of defeat filled Guy and Harriet with profound sadness; and they felt the same sadness about them everywhere in the hushed city.

Vourakis suddenly remembered that his wife was waiting for him: "If you cannot escape," he said, "come to us," and he parted from them as though they had been lifetime friends.

When they went on towards Omonia Square, an ashen twilight lay on the streets. As the evening deepened, the atmosphere seemed to shift from despair to dread. There had been no announcement. Vourakis had said that telephone communication with the front had broken down. So far as anyone in Athens could know, there had been no change of any kind, yet as though the enemy were expected that night, there was a sense of incipient panic, impossible to explain, or explain away.

The School building had been shut for Easter week. Guy expected to find it empty but the front door lay open and inside half a dozen male students were moving furniture, despite the protests of the porter, George. Flushed by their activity, they gathered round Guy shouting: "Sir, sir, we thought you had gone, sir."

"I haven't gone yet," Guy said, putting on an appearance of severity.

"Sir, sir, you should be gone, sir. The Germans will be here tomorrow. They might even come sooner, sir."

"We'll go when we can. We can't go before. Meanwhile, what are you up to?"

The boys explained that they intended taking the School furniture into their homes to prevent its seizure by the enemy. "It will be safe. It will be yours, sir, when you come back. We'll return it all to you."

Three more students appeared at the top of the stairs carrying a filing-cabinet between them. Those at the bottom, shrill with excitement, began shouting up instructions and a small, dark youth with wide eyes and tough black hair, came panting to Guy, his teeth a-flash, crying: "To me, this very day, an admiring fellow said: 'Kosta, you are to make suggestions *born.*'"

Guy insisted that operations should cease for that evening. "Tomorrow," he said, "you can take what you like, but just at the moment I want to sort out my belongings."

The departing students shook him by the hand, exclaiming regretfully because he must go, but for the young there was piquancy in change, and they went off laughing. It was the only Greek laughter the Pringles heard that day.

George, the porter, his grey hair curling about his dark, ravaged cheeks, gripped Guy's hand and stared into his face with tear-filled eyes. Guy was deeply moved until he discovered that this emotion had nothing to do with his own departure.

George had replaced a younger man who would now be returning from the war. "What is to become of me?" he wanted to know. "He will turn me into the street." George had his wife, daughter and daughter's two children in the basement with him. The School was their home; they had nowhere else to go. *Kyrios Diefthyntis* must write a letter to say that George was the rightful possessor of the basement room.

Guy was disconcerted by this appeal because the old porter knew his appointment had been temporary. "What of the young man who has been fighting so bravely at the front?" he said.

The porter answered: "I, too, fought bravely long ago."

Guy suggested that the problem be referred to Lord Pink-rose, and the old man gave a howl. Everyone knew that the Lord Pinkrose, a mysterious and unapproachable aristo-crat, never came near the School. No, *Kyrios Diefthyntis*, with his tender heart, must be the one to act.

In distress Guy looked to Harriet for aid but she refused to be involved. Guy wanted only to give, leaving to others the much less pleasant task of refusing. In this present quandary, she decided, he must do the refusing himself.

She said she would wait for him in the sanded courtyard. When she left the building, she saw Greek soldiers walking along the side road and went to the wall to watch them. They were coming from the station. She had some thought of wel-coming them back, but saw at once that they were not looking for welcome. Like the British soldiers she had seen on the first lorries into Athens, these men, shadowy in the twilight, were haggard with defeat. Some were the "walking wounded", ex-pected to find their own way to hospital; others had their feet wrapped up in rags; all, whether wounded or not, had the livid faces of sick men. They gave an impression of weightlessness. Their flesh had shrunk from want of food, but that had happened to everyone in Greece. With these men, it was as though their bones had become hollow like the bones of birds. Their uniforms, that shredded like worn-out paper, were dented by their gaunt, bone-sharp shoulders and arms.

One man seeing her watching so closely, crossed to her and said: "*Dhos mou psomi*," and as he came near, she could smell the disinfectant on his clothing. She could only guess what he wanted. She opened her hands to show she could give him nothing. He went on without a word.

When they reached the main road, most of them stopped and looked about them in the last forlorn glimmer of the light. Some of them stood bewildered, then one after the other they wandered off as though to them one direction was very like another.

After they had all gone, Harriet still leant against the wall staring into the empty street.

The civilian image of the fighting man was much like that of the war posters that showed the Greeks in fierce, defiant attitudes, exhorting each other up snowbound crags in pursuit of the enemy. Now, she thought, she had seen them for herself, the heroes of Epirus.

She had been told that many of the men had no weapons, yet, like riderless horses in a race, they had gone instinctively into the fight. Starving, frost-bitten, infested with lice, stupefied by cold, they had endured and suffered simply because their comrades endured and suffered. The enemy had not had much hand in killing them. The dead had died mostly from frost-bite and cold.

The men she had seen, the survivors, had undergone more than any man should be asked to undergo. They had triumphed and at the last, unjustly defeated, here they were wandering back, lost in their own city, begging for bread.

University Street, when the Pringles walked back, was unusually bright. The raids had stopped – an ominous sign – and the café owners, knowing the end was near, had not troubled to put up their black-out curtains.

With faces lit by the café lights people could recognize one another, and Guy and Harriet, stopping or being stopped by acquaintances, were told that the Thermopylae defence was breaking. The Germans could arrive that very night. What was there to stop them? And the retreat went on. The main roads were noisy with the returning lorries. At times, passing through patches of light, they could be seen muddy as farm carts, with the men heaped together, asleep or staring listlessly at the crowds. Stories were going about the retreat itself. The returning soldiers said it had been carried out amidst the havoc of total collapse. Driven from Albania, the Greeks had found only one road open to them. The others were held by the Germans. The remaining road, which ran west of the Pindus, was choked with retreating men, refugees, every sort of transport – broken-down cars and lorries, tanks that had lost their treads, the ox waggons which had carried Greek supplies to the front, mule trains, and the hand carts and perambulators of the civilians. The whole densely packed, chaotic and despairing multitude was constantly bombed and machine-gunned by German aircraft.

Some Greeks had been cut off in Albania; some British were cut off in Thessaly. For the British now passing through Athens the important thing was to cross the Corinth canal before the bridge was blown up or taken by enemy parachutists. The English residents, beginning to lose faith in authority, told one another that if next morning there was still no sign of an evacuation ship, then they had better jump the lorries and go south with the soldiers who hoped to be taken off by the British navy at ports like Neapolis or Monemvasia. This was a rakehell season that called for enterprise. If authority could not save them, then they must save themselves.

In the upper corridor of the Academy, the wash-room door opened and Pinkrose came out, wearing his kimono with the orange and yellow sunflowers. Guy hurried after him, trying to speak to him, but Pinkrose went faster. Guy called: "Lord Pinkrose," but Pinkrose, shaking the door-handle in his haste, pulled his door open, entered and shut it sharply behind him.

Alan Frewen had remained at the office for a second night. Ben Phipps had not been seen or heard of. There was still no news of a ship for the English, and no news of anything else.

Something woke Harriet at daybreak. She jumped up and went to the window: the Major's Delahaye was standing in the drive and Toby Lush was rearranging the luggage in the back seat.

Guy was asleep, his face pressed into the pillow, his shoulder lifted like a wing over his ear. He might have been defending himself against attack, but in this icy light he looked exposed and defenceless.

Knowing she would not sleep again, Harriet put on her dressing-gown and returned to the window to see what was happening outside. Toby had gone inside and was now carrying out the canvas bag in which Pinkrose transported his books. Pinkrose followed with the blankets from his bed. Neither of the men spoke. Though he appeared agitated, Pinkrose maintained silence, moving with a purposeful caution that reminded Harriet of Ben Phipps about to bury his victim in *Maria Marten*. The manner of both men suggested that they were engaged on a secret operation. She would have said they were making a get-away, if there were anywhere to go and anything to go on. As it was, she rejected her suspicions as a sign of strain. Pinkrose and Toby had no more chance of getting away than the Pringles, yet when the car drove off, she felt deserted. The plans that had sustained them the previous night had lost their allure. It might already be too late.

A mist was rising over the garden. Less than two months had passed since she had watched Charles walk away between the lemon trees and it had seemed then that life was just beginning. For a long time she had seen herself passing unscathed through experience, but experience had caught up with her at last. In the comfortless chill of early morning, she could believe that life was coming to an end.

The telephone rang in the passage. Guy seemed heavily asleep but at the first lift of the bell he sprang up as though he had been on guard.

"This'll be it," he said and he pulled on a cardigan without undoing the buttons.

The telephone was answered. A knock came on the door and Harriet opened it. Miss Dunne stood outside in a pink dressing-gown and pink fur slippers, hands stowed away in pockets. As the door opened, her gaze lit inadvertently upon Harriet, then sped to the safety of the cornice. Her whole stance conveyed the importance of her message: "You're to go at once to the Information Office."

"Is there a ship, then?"

"It looks like it. Each person is allowed one suitcase. Not more." Miss Dunne's own personal importance had a tinge of magnanimity that made Harriet wonder if the Legation had felt some guilt about its stranded nationals.

"Are you coming with us?" Harriet asked.

"Oh, no!" Miss Dunne took a step away at the suggestion and explained that some of the Legation staff would have to go on the ship, but for persons like Miss Dunne there were other arrangements.

The Pringles set out with one suitcase and the rucksack full of books. Their other possessions and books were put into a wardrobe. "We'll get them again when the war's over," Guy said. They went to the main road hoping to find a taxi, but in the end walked all the way to Constitution Square where the uncomplaining English had formed an orderly queue to await transport to the Piraeus. Those who had found taxis had gone on ahead. The others would be taken by lorry.

Mrs. Brett at the front of the queue called down to Guy and Harriet: "This is exciting, isn't it? We're going to be evacuated."

"Surely you don't *want* to go?" Harriet said.

"Of course not. Percy's grave is here; naturally I want to stay; but, still, it's exciting to see the world. And we're going to Egypt where the news is good. We keep capturing places in Egypt."

An old coal lorry swept into the square with Ben Phipps standing up in the back. "Who's next?" he called as he jumped down, and Miss Gladys Twocurry in her green coat and Miss Mabel in her plum came out from the Information Office and closed the door behind them. Miss Gladys, guiding her sister across the pavement, looked flustered as though she felt herself at a disadvantage. Maybe she had expected to receive some sort of preferential treatment as a result of her attendance upon Pinkrose. Instead, here she was getting into the lorry like everyone else. Miss Mabel, hauled and pushed, was hoisted up and seated on a piece of luggage where she sat mumbling bitterly about the coal-dust on the floor.

When the lorry went off, only seven people remained to await its return. Ben Phipps joined the Pringles, his eyes jumping about with joy at his authoritative position. He slapped his hands together but gave no explanation of himself until Guy asked where he had gone the previous day.

"I can a tale unfold," he said. "Where do you think I went? Where did little Benny go, eh? Little Benny went to the Piraeus to have a looksee-see, and what did he see-see? He saw two ships astanding by, waiting to take Major Cookson and all Major Cookson's friends and valuables to some nice safe place. And Benny wasn't alone. Who did I meet down there but the old padre nosing around. He'd had the same idea. So we joined forces. We explored every avenue, we left no stone, we bloody well pushed our way into everything and everywhere. And there were these two old vessels tucked away in a corner: about the only things down there intact. We managed to find one of the stokers who said they'd been chartered by an English gentleman. He didn't want to say more but we put the screws on him, the padre and me. And who was this English gentleman? None other than the bloody Major. A lot of his stuff was already on board. He'd been preparing for weeks. He and his friends were going to travel in comfort, with all their possessions. 'Right!' said the padre, 'we'll see about this,' and back we went to the Legation. The padre, I'll say it for him, was magnificent. He said: 'I demand that every British subject and every Greek who is at risk as a result of working for the British, shall be given passage on those ships.' Our diplomatic friends were not at all happy about it. The Major had chartered the ships. What about his rights? – the rights of the moneyed man?"

"Private property, eh?" said Guy.

"Private property – you've said it. But the padre, dyed in the wool old Tory though he is, was having none of it. He said human beings came first. He refused to move until our F.O. friends agreed that the ships would be held until every British subject was on board. As soon as the Major heard what was going on, he tried to speed up his departure. He meant to sail at daybreak, but when he got down to the Piraeus he found the ships were being held by the military."

"Is he coming with us?"

"Oh, yes, he won't be left behind; he'll travel with the hoi-polloi, but I'm told he's hiding in his cabin. In fact the gallant Major's already feeling sick."

Guy shook hands with Ben, delighted by the Major's defeat. "A victory for human decency, a victory for human rights," he said. Ben was eager in agreement but watching him dancing in vindictive triumph, Harriet wondered what would have happened had Ben Phipps not quarrelled with the Major. Supposing he had been among the privileged few invited to save themselves on the Major's ship! Hatred, she saw, was a considerable force; and Ben was likely to go far.

She had once been ambitious for Guy, but saw now the truth of the proverb that the children of darkness were wiser than the children of light. Guy, with all his charity, would probably remain more or less where he had started.

The lorry returned and the last half-dozen fugitives climbed on board.

It was Good Friday. The town was in abeyance but already the inhabitants were abroad, wakeful and restless in their apprehension.

Ben Phipps said: "The pro-German elements are out in force," but the Greeks who waved to the lorry as it passed looked the same as the Greeks who had wandered about last evening in the despairing twilight. And there were soldiers among them.

Ben Phipps nodded at them furiously. "The whole Greek army's been sent back on leave. It's another act of sabotage. Papademas says it's been done to save them from the futile slaughter of a last stand; but if they'd joined our troops at Marathon, they could have accounted for a good few Germans. Now, the bloody Hun'll walk in."

As they came on to the long straight Piraeus road which shone empty, in the morning sun, Harriet said: "I suppose Alan Frewen's already on board?"

Ben Phipps shook his head: "Nope."

"No? Then where is he?"

"On the way to Corinth, I imagine. He wanted a car, so I sold him mine. When he saw the evacuation all set, all tickety-boo, he shoved his dog into the back and drove off."

"But where is he going?"

"Don't ask me. He was in a hurry to get over the bridge before someone blew it up. That's all I can tell you."

"So he intends to stay in Greece? Can he survive down there?"

"Can he survive anywhere? He's the sort that starts heading for the high jump the day they're born."

"And the dog will starve," said Harriet.

"Good God!" Ben Phipps gave a yelp of laughter at her absurdity and she, turning on him angrily, said: "And you let him go! You even sold him a car ..."

"I suppose he can do what he likes?" Ben Phipps blinked at her in injured astonishment. "If he wants to go, it's not my job to stop him."

"No, you're not your brother's keeper, are you?"

Ben Phipps laughed, too angry to speak.

Harriet, thinking disconsolately of Alan, the lonely man who had loved Greece and the Greeks, and could not leave them, stood up to take a last look as they passed the villa and the Ilissus and the little wood, whispering: "My poor cat."

A woman sitting behind her in the lorry said: "We left our dogs. We hadn't time to do anything but turn the key in the lock. We took the dogs to a neighbour who promised to look after them. 'They'll be here when you come back,' he said."

Her husband said: "Better to have shot them. At least we'd know what became of them."

She said: "Oh, Denis!" and her husband turned on her: "Don't you realize what's going to happen here?" he said. "Can't you see what's in store for these people?"

No one said anything more till they stopped at the docks.

In the whole of the great basin there were no objects standing upright except the cargo boats *Erebus* and *Nox*.

The sky was a limpid blue; the water beneath it black with wood scraps. Out of this dense, black, viscous surface poked the masts and funnels of sunken ships, a tangle of wreck and wreckage, lying at all angles.

The harbour buildings, burnt or blasted, lay in fragments. Among the smoked rubble, broken glass and charred ravelment of wood, green things had taken root. The Piraeus already seemed an ancient ruin, reaching again towards the desolation that covered it for eighteen hundred years after the Peloponnesian Wars.

The *Erebus* and *Nox* alone had colour: they were red with rust. They had been used for the transport of Italian prisoners and, according to Ben Phipps, were "not only derelict, but filthy".

Guy said in a cheerful voice: "Thalassa! You said you felt safe because the sea was near. Well, here we are!" but Harriet could not even remember now why the sea had seemed a refuge.

English soldiers had been detailed to help the passengers on board. They had already hoisted the Major's Delahaye and packing cases on to the deck, and carried up the baggage belonging to the Major's guests. The single suitcases of the uninvited were treated as a joke.

"That all you got?" they said when the small pile of luggage came off the lorry. "Didn't let you bring much, did they?"

Some of the recent arrivals were still on the quay. The Pluggets were getting out of a taxi. Mrs. Brett and Miss Jay were watching for the Pringles and, catching sight of them, Mrs. Brett came striding towards them in a fury of indignation, shouting: "What do you think! That Archie Callard is up there insulting everyone that comes on board!"

The Pringles had forgotten Archie Callard who, surprisingly enough, had not been flown off to join some daring desert group but had been loitering all the time, unoccupied, at Phaleron.

"What do you think he said to Miss Jay?" said Mrs. Brett.

Miss Jay, whose vast bulk had shrunk until her flesh hung like flannel over her bones, said crossly: "You've said enough about it, Bretty," but Mrs. Brett was determined to say more: "He said: 'Women should be painlessly put down when they look like Miss Jay.' "

Ben Phipps laughed in delight: "Did he, really! Come on. If we get a squeak out of him, we'll deal with him."

They went forward prepared for Callard who was leaning over the gunwale with Dubedat beside him, but he let the Pringles and Phipps pass without a word. His eye was on Plugget, who came behind them. "They're all coming out of their holes," he said. "Here's that drip Plugget. His wife's family put him up for twenty years. Now he's saving his own skin and leaving them to starve."

Plugget, pushing his wife importantly ahead of him, gasped, but said nothing. A little later, when she stood at the rail overlooking the quay, Harriet found him at her elbow. His wife's parents stood below with their unmarried daughter, an elderly girl who held herself taut with a look of controlled desperation, a suitcase at her side.

"Isn't she coming with us?" Harriet asked.

"No," said Plugget with decision. "She wanted to come but when she saw the old folk in tears, she didn't know what to do. My wife thought she ought to stay. I thought she ought to stay. Her duty, I told her."

"Poor thing! What will become of her?"

Impatient of Harriet's pity, Plugget said: "She'll be all right. You can't take everyone. Think of me landed with two women!" Turning his back on the forlorn spectacle of his relations-in-law, he said: "You people found anywhere to sleep?"

The main cabins had been taken by the Major's party and most of the deck was covered by his possessions. Any space left had been occupied by earlier arrivals. Guy and Phipps had gone off in different directions to see what they could find. Guy had at once been caught up in conversation by his many acquaintances, and it was Phipps, with his indeflectable, inquiring energy, who came back to say there was a cabin empty on the lowest deck.

Guy, Mrs. Brett and Miss Jay were called together, and the party went down into a darkness heavy with the reek of oil and human excretions. Every outlet from the lower passages had been boarded up to prevent the escape of prisoners and Plugget, who had come after them, put up a complaint: "If we're torpedoed, we'd never get out of here," but he kept at their heels until they came to the narrow three-birth cabin next to the engine-room. Inside he at once took command:

"You two ladies here," he said, slapping the middle bunk. "Pringles on top. You're young and agile. Me and the wife down here. The wife's not strong. Right?"

No one contested this arrangement, but Guy asked: "What about Ben?"

"The floor suits me," Phipps said. "It's cleaner."

The bunks, without mattresses or covers, were wooden shelves, sticky to the touch and spattered with the bloody remains of bugs.

"Like coffins," said Mrs. Brett. "Still, it's an adventure."

Peering about in the glimmer that fell from a grimy, greasy, ochre-coloured electric bulb, she said: "We might try to get the dirt off this basin."

Miss Jay pulled out three chamber-pots caked with the yellow detritus of the years. " 'Perfum'd chambers of the great,' " she said. "We'll send these up to Cookson."

While these activities went on, Toby Lush appeared in the doorway with a commanding frown. When he saw who was inside, his manner faltered: "I was keeping this cabin," he weakly said.

"What for?" Phipps asked.

"The Major might need a bit extra storage space. Or he might, f'instance, want something unpacked, and I thought . . ."

"If the Major has any request to make," said Phipps, "send him to me."

Toby Lush put his pipe into his mouth and sucked. After an interval of indecision, he said mildly: "Glad you got on board all right."

"Were you expecting us?" Harriet asked.

"Hey, there! Crumbs!" Toby shielded his face in mock alarm. "You aren't blaming me, are you? Not my fault; nor the old soul's, neither. The Major made his arrangements. He didn't consult us."

"You knew nothing about it?"

"Well, not much. Anyway, here you are. Nothing to grumble

about. I suppose you were told to bring food for three days?"

"We had no food to bring."

The air-raid warning sounded. "More magnetic mines," said Toby and, giving an exasperated tut, he made off as though he meant to deal with them himself.

"Don't want to be trapped down here," said Plugget. He hurried after Toby and the others went with him. They reached the main deck as the guns, upturned on the quay, started up like hysterical dogs. In the uproar women seized their children and asked what they should do. There was a shelter on the quay but as the passengers ran to the companionway, Dubedat shouted from the boat-deck: "We're leaving any minute now. If you get off the ship, you'll be left behind."

Bombs fell into the harbour, sending up columns of water that brought a rain of wreckage down on the ship. The passengers crowded into the corridors of the main deck where the nervous chatter and the cries of children caused Toby Lush to put his head out of his cabin: "Less noise there," he commanded. "You're disturbing the Major," and withdrew before comment could reach him.

At noon, in the midst of another raid, Dobson drove on to the quay, bringing the Legation servants to the ship. In his light, midge-like voice, he shouted to Guy: "We'll meet in the land of the Pharaohs."

"Good old Dobson," Guy said emotionally as the car turned on the quayside and started back to Athens.

"Perhaps now we've had his blessing," Phipps said, "we'll be allowed to embark." but the sun rose hotly in the sky, the reconnaissance planes came and went, and the *Erebus* and *Nox* remained motionless at their berths.

A taxi-load of students came to say farewell to Guy. They shouted up to the boat that the Prime Minister, Koryzis, was dead.

"How did he die?" the passengers asked, feeling no surprise because there was nothing left surprising in the world.

The students said: "The German radio says the British murdered him."

"You don't believe that, do you?"

They shook their heads, believing nothing, knowing nothing, buffeted and confused by the drama of existence. Other Greeks drove down to the Piraeus, their eyes bleared with sleeplessness and tears, bringing with them the tormented nervousness of the city. The English asked again about Koryzis. The Greeks on the quay, doomed themselves, shook their heads, mystified by a death that was too apt an ingredient of the whole tragedy.

To those on board, not knowing when they would sail or whether the ship would survive to sail at all, the afternoon shifted about like a disordered vision. They could only wait for time to pass. The only event was the appearance of a man selling oranges. Despite Dubedat's warning the women hurried ashore to buy, for there was no drinking water on the ship.

The Acropolis could be seen from the boat-deck. Harriet went up several times to look at it. Seeing it glowing in the sunset, she thought of Charles, scarcely able in memory to distinguish between his reality and her private image. She had condemned Guy's attachment to fantasy but wondered now if fantasy were a part of life, a component without which one could not survive. She saw Charles catching the flower and thought of the girls who had given flowers, not only as a recognition of valour but a consolation in defeat.

The hills of the Peloponnesus, glowing in the sunset light, changed to rose-violet and darkened to madder rose, grew sombre and faded into the twilight. The Parthenon, catching the late light, glimmered for a long time, a spectre on the evening, then disappeared into darkness. That was the last they saw of Athens.

Some time after midnight the engines of the *Erebus* began to throb and shake. Ben Phipps, on the shaking floor of the cabin, said: "We're about to slip silently into the night." The ship groaned and shuddered and seemed about to shatter with its own effort. Somehow it was wrenched into motion.

Next morning, when they went on deck, they saw above the southern cloud banks the silver cone of Mount Ida. On one side of the *Erebus* was the *Nox*; on the other there was a tanker that no one had seen before. The tanker, its plates mouldering with rust, was as decrepit as its companions, yet the three old ships had their dignity, moving steadily forward, unhurried and at home in their own element.

Most of the passengers took the pace as fixed and immutable, but Ben Phipps and Plugget, having conferred together, went to the First Officer with the demand that it be increased. They were told that the convoy must conserve its power for the dangerous passage past the coast of Cyrenaica.

Phipps, who had now established his authority over Plugget, went round the ship, his energy unimpaired by a night made sleepless by the thumping engine, the bugs, and the jog-trots of cockroaches and blackbeetles. Plugget felt bound to keep beside him, but Guy sat on the boat-deck, his back against a rail, and read for a lecture on Coleridge. The women, in a stupor, sat round him.

Ben kept returning to the group, trying to rouse in Guy a spirit of inquiring indignation, but Guy, refusing to acknowledge the changes and perils through which they were passing, would not be moved.

Ben Phipps had discovered that the lifeboats were rusted to the davits so there would be little hope of launching them. "Those two boy scouts, Lush and Dubedat, are trying to organize life-boat drill. If they come up here, tell them from me the boats are a dead loss." He went again and returned to report that there was no wireless operator on board, but he could work the transmitter himself and had talked to the Signal Station at Suda Bay.

"Nice to know we're not cut off," said Phipps, looking to Guy for agreement and admiration. Guy, as was expected, smiled admiringly, but it was a rather ironical admiration. Harriet began to suspect that Phipps was losing his hold on Guy. When he said persuasively: "Come and see," Guy merely stretched and smiled and shook his head. When Phipps took himself off, Guy returned to his books. He spent the day absorbed, like a student in a library. The only difference was that he sang to himself, the words so low that only Harriet knew what they were:

"If your engine cuts out over Hellfire Pass,
You can stick your twin Browning guns right up your arse."

sometimes changing to the chorus:

"No balls, no balls at all;
If your engine cuts out, you'll have no balls at all."

Drowsy in the mild, spring wind, Harriet watched Crete take form out of the cloud. The sun broke through. Two corvettes from Suda Bay circled the convoy and let it pass. A reconnaissance plane came back again and again to look at the ships, flying so low that the black crosses were clear on the wings and some people claimed they had seen the face of the enemy. Nothing more happened. The civilian ships did not look worth a raid.

They turned the western prow of Crete, a route not much used by shipping, where the island rose, a sheer wall of stone, offering no foothold for life. Grey and barren in the brilliant light, it seemed an uninhabited island in an unfrequented sea, but during the afternoon a ship came into view: a hospital ship. It slid past slowly, like a cruising gull, and remained a long time in sight, catching the sun upon its silver flank.

As the afternoon passed, people began to rise out of their torpor and appear on deck. Among them was Pinkrose in all his heavy clothing. Feeling the heat, he began to unwrap, then, in a sudden nervous spasm, he hurried away and returned without his trilby. He was wearing instead a large hat of straw. This contented him for a time, then he felt the top of the hat and was again galvanized into action. He went off and, when he made a third appearance, had placed the trilby on top of the straw.

"Good God," whispered Miss Jay, "why's he wearing two hats?"

"Because," said Phipps, temporarily back at base, "he's as mad as two hatters."

A very old man came on to the boat-deck trailing a toy dog among the hazards of bodies, baggage and packing-cases. Harriet sat up in surprise. It was Mr. Liversage who had been her companion on the Lufthansa from Sofia to Athens. She had scarcely thought of him since and supposed he had gone on the autumn evacuation boat. Instead, here he was, jaunty as ever, with his old snub face, grey-yellow hair and moist yellow-blue eyes. The dog was an old dog, the hair gone from its worn, cracked hide, but it was as jaunty as its master.

Mr. Liversage recognized her at once. "Chucked out again," he shouted. "Bit of a lark, eh?"

He squatted down with the group and Harriet asked where he had been all winter. He told her:

"Cooped up indoors. Had a nasty turn; bronchitis, y'know." He had been staying with friends at Kifissia, an elderly English couple who had looked after him well. "Bully of them to take an old codger in. Lucky old codger, that's me. They'd a lovely home." He described how his hostess had waked him early the previous morning, saying: "Come on, Victor. We've got to go. The Germans are nearly here." "The poor girl was very brave: had to leave everything; made no complaints. 'Fortune of war, Victor,' she said. So we all came on the Major's boat. Very kind of the Major, very kind indeed." Becoming aware of Phipps standing above him, Mr. Liversage said: "See this dog! Best dog in the world."

"Oh, is it?" Phipps bent slightly towards the old man but his eyes were dodging about in search of better entertainment.

"Collected thousands of pounds, this dog."

"Oh, really! Who's the money for? Yourself?"

"Myself!" Mr. Liversage got to his feet. "My dog collects for hospitals," he said.

He was deeply offended. Guy and the women attempted to assuage him but he would not be assuaged. He lifted his dog and went. Before anyone had time to reprove him, Phipps, too, was off, in the other direction.

An hour or so later the ships slowed and stopped. Word went round that they were being circled by an enemy submarine and the *Nox* was preparing to drop depth charges. As this was happening, Ben Phipps returned with Plugget in tow. He was in an agitated state and the news of the submarine was as nothing compared with what he had to tell.

"I've found a locked cabin," he said. "When I asked Lush for the key, he got into a tizzy. He refused to hand over. I said we'd a right to know what's inside. I told him if he didn't open up, I'd report the Major's behaviour to the Cairo Embassy and demand an inquiry. That made him puff his pipe, I can tell you. I'm collecting witnesses. Come on, Guy, now, get to your feet."

Guy stretched himself but stayed where he was. "I bet there's nothing inside but luggage."

"I bet you're wrong. Come along."

Guy smiled, shook his head and said to Harriet: "You go."

Bored now and ready for distraction, she rose and followed Phipps, who gathered more witnesses as he went.

When they reached the main corridor, Phipps strode past the Major's cabin and shook the next door. Finding it still locked, he gave it a masterful kick, shouting: "Open up."

From inside the Major's cabin, Archie Callard's voice rose in anguish. "This is too tedious! Do let little Phipps 'open up'."

The Major answered: "I don't care what he does. All I want is to get off this damned ship."

Toby, snuffling with defeat, came out and unlocked the door. The interior was dark. Ben strode in, plucked aside the black-out curtains and revealed a store-house of tinned foods.

"Just as I thought." he said. He swung on Toby. "The rest of us have eaten nothing for two days. There are children on board and pregnant women. This stuff will be distributed: a tin for everyone on the ship."

Toby ran back to the Major's cabin. His voice high with obsequious horror, he cried: "Major, Major, they're taking the stores."

"God save us," said Phipps. "Listen to old Lush sucking up to the head girl!"

Harriet returned to the boat-deck with a tin of bully beef. The tins distributed, Ben Phipps came round in a comic coda, sharing out the Major's toilet rolls.

"Here you are, ladies," he said as he gave three squares of paper to each. "One up, one down and a polisher."

"What about tomorrow?" Miss Jay asked.

"Tomorrow may never come," he cheerfully replied.

The sun was low. With her head against the rail, watching the lustrous swell of the sea that held in its depths the hues of emeralds and amethysts, Harriet thought of Charles left behind with the retreating army, of David taken by the enemy, of Sasha become a stranger, of Clarence lost in Salonika, of Alan who would share the fate of the Greeks, and of Yakimov in his grave.

Not one of their friends remained except Ben Phipps; "the vainest and the emptiest", she thought.

It seemed to her there would always be a Phipps, one Phipps or another Phipps, to entice Guy from her into the realms of folly, but Ben Phipps had almost had his day. Guy's infatuation was waning; and, when he had seen through Ben's last conceit, Ben would go elsewhere for attention.

If Guy had for her the virtue of permanence, she might have the same virtue for him. To have one thing permanent in life as they knew it was as much as they could expect.

Crete was still visible, shadowy in the last of the twilight, a land without lights. That night the race began. The ship's old engines pummelled into speed, her timbers cracked and rattled, and the passengers, clinging to anything that gave handhold, lay awake and listened. At daybreak the uproar slackened: the danger was past.

Their first thought was for the companion ships. They went up on deck to see the *Nox* and the tanker moving quietly on either side. The three old ships had survived the night and their journey was almost over.

The passengers had awakened in Egyptian waters and were struck by the whiteness of the light. It was too white. It lay like a white dust over everything. Disturbed by its strangeness, Harriet felt their lives now would be strange and difficult.

Someone shouted that land was in sight. She put her hand into Guy's hand and he pressed her fingers to reassure her.

She said: "We must go and see." Leaving Greece, they had left like exiles. They had crossed the Mediterranean and now, on the other side, they knew they were refugees. Still, they had life – a depleted fortune, but a fortune. They were together and would remain together, and that was the only certainty left to them.

They moved forward to look at the new land, reached thankfully if unwillingly. They saw, flat and white on the southern horizon, the coast of Africa.

TITLES IN SERIES

For a complete list of titles, visit www.nyrb.com or write to:
Catalog Requests, NYRB, 435 Hudson Street, New York, NY 10014